TARGET 5
&
COVER STORY

Colin Forbes writes a novel every year. For the past twenty-seven years he has earned his living solely as a full-time writer.

He visits all the locations which will appear in a new novel. Forbes says, 'It is essential for me to see for myself where the book will take place. Only in this way can I conjure up the unique atmosphere of the chosen locales.'

He has explored most of Western Europe, the East and West coasts of America, and has made excursions to Africa and Asia. Each new book appears on all major bestseller lists. He is translated into thirty languages.

Surveys have shown that his readership is divided equally between men and women.

COLIN FORBES

'Has no equal '
SUNDAY MIRROR

TARGET 5
&
COVER STORY

COLIN FORBES

PAN BOOKS
IN ASSOCIATION WITH COLLINS

Target 5 first published 1973 by William Collins & Co. Ltd.
First published in paperback by Pan Books 1974
Cover Story first published 1985 by William Collins & Co. Ltd.
First published in paperback by Pan Books 1986

This omnibus edition published 2004 by Pan Books
an imprint of Pan Macmillan Ltd
Pan Macmillan, 20 New Wharf Road, London N1 9RR
Basingstoke and Oxford
Associated companies throughout the world
www.panmacmillan.com

ISBN 0 330 43257 5

1 3 5 7 9 8 6 4 2

A CIP catalogue record for this book is available from
the British Library.

Typeset by SetSystems Ltd, Saffron Walden, Essex
Printed and bound in Great Britain by
Mackays of Chatham plc, Chatham, Kent

TARGET 5

For Jane

Contents

'A crippled Soviet submarine wallowing in a North Atlantic Gale . . . dashed by 50-foot waves in a 55-knot gale . . . was first spotted by reconnaissance aircraft from the American base at Keflavik . . .'

The Times, Wednesday, 1 March 1972

Opening Gambit

The Locomotive

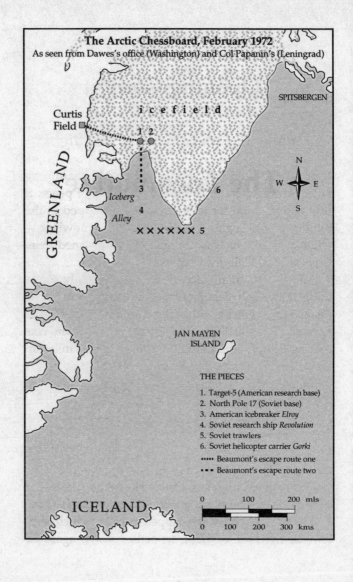

The Arctic Chessboard, February 1972
As seen from Dawes's office (Washington) and Col Papanin's (Leningrad)

SPITSBERGEN

Curtis
Field

i c e f i e l d

1 2

GREENLAND

Iceberg

Alley

3

4

× × × × × × 5

6

N
W   E
S

JAN MAYEN
ISLAND

THE PIECES

1. Target-5 (American research base)
2. North Pole 17 (Soviet base)
3. American icebreaker *Elroy*
4. Soviet research ship *Revolution*
5. Soviet trawlers
6. Soviet helicopter carrier *Gorki*

•••• Beaumont's escape route one
--- Beaumont's escape route two

ICELAND

0   100   200 mls

0   100   200   300 kms

Chapter One

Friday, 18 February 1972: Midnight

Even in the year 1972, a year which will hardly be noted in the calendar of history as a year of peace, it was not common for an express to be stopped in the middle of the night – in the middle of nowhere – while a passenger was dragged off it by armed men. Especially an American express.

And this traumatic experience was certainly something that Keith Beaumont had no inkling of as he relaxed in bed inside a sleeping-car aboard the Florida Express; for one thing, the thirty-two-car train was roaring through the Carolinas at over ninety miles an hour, while outside the February storm beat at the curtained windows; for another thing, the next scheduled stop was over two hours away.

With the windows sealed tight against the rising storm, with the central heating turned up to God knew how many degrees, it was hot and steamy and airless inside the sleeping-car, so hot that the large Englishman was having trouble sleeping as he eased himself up on one elbow and checked his watch. Close to midnight. Behind the zipped curtain which shut him off from the corridor, he settled down again on his pillow and wrapped his hands behind his broad neck, dreaming with his eyes open.

By morning he'd be in Miami, thousands of miles away from Greenland – away from guiding frightened dogs through screaming blizzards, away from hauling bucking sleds over tumbled ice, above all away from endless darkness and cold that paralysed the brain. It was also wonderful to be dry again; Beaumont pressed his stockinged feet hard against the end of the bed and revelled in the warmth.

Twenty miles ahead of the express thundering through the storm-swept night three armed men were not so dry as they huddled in the pouring rain. Standing under the canopy of a whistle-stop station in the middle of nowhere, they waited for the oncoming express which wasn't scheduled to stop for another two hours. The signals were already changing against it, the driver of the huge diesel motor hauling the long, long train was already applying his massive brakes. The emergency was imminent.

'I hope to God he's on board,' one of the raincoated men mumbled as he clenched a sodden cigarette between his teeth.

'He's on board,' the forty-year-old leader of the group assured his companion. 'And we're taking him off it.'

'It could be tricky . . .'

'This says it won't be tricky.' The older man extracted a .45 Colt revolver from his pocket, checked the cylinder, put it away again. 'And don't forget, Jo, we have to make it look good – real good.'

Less than twenty miles up the track the driver of the Florida Express was staring anxiously into the night. The signal he had just passed had ordered a reduction of speed but the next stop was two hours away, so what the hell was happening? He went on cutting the speed, applying the great brakes slowly. Rain hammered his steel cab roof, trails of spume whipped off the roof and vanished in the dark. The next signal flashed by. Red for danger, for stop. What the devil was going on? He applied the brakes more strongly. They were close to Cedar Falls, an unscheduled stop.

Two minutes later the train ground to a halt as a thunderclap burst and rain lashed the sides of the cars. Inside his roomette Beaumont settled down to sleep while the train was still, his large hands clasped outside the sheet. His eyes were closed when the curtains were torn open and a man with a sodden hat brim looked down at him while he checked a photograph in his left hand. 'It's him, Jo,' a quiet voice said.

Beaumont opened his eyes and stared into the muzzle of a Colt .45 revolver.

'Move that thing,' he murmured. 'It might go off – your hand's sticky.'

When he opened his eyes Beaumont registered several swift impressions – the sodden raincoat the man holding the gun wore, the steam rising off the man's sleeves, the scared look on the face of the passenger in the roomette across the corridor, the second raincoated man standing in the background with one hand inside his pocket. The older American, who was feeling the heat – there were sweat beads on his forehead – replied in a flat tone.

'Get dressed – you're getting off the train . . .'

'And who the hell might you be?' Beaumont demanded.

Exhausted, tired out by his long trip from Greenland to Washington, he estimated his chances carefully. A hard chopping blow to knock the Colt out of the gunman's hand, a knee in the groin . . . No, it was too dangerous – with other passengers in the sleeping-car.

'Dixon, FBI,' the man with the sweaty forehead snapped. 'And hurry it up – this train can't wait all night . . .'

'It doesn't have to – it can get moving now as far as I'm concerned. With me on board. And you've made a very bad mistake – I'm British . . .' Beaumont reached towards his jacket hanging from a hook.

'Watch it . . .' Dixon warned.

The Englishman stared at him over the width of his very broad shoulders and Dixon felt uncomfortable. 'I'm showing you my passport, for God's sake,' Beaumont rumbled. He took it from the inner jacket pocket carefully, extracted it with his fingertips and handed it to Dixon. The American opened the passport expertly with one hand, studied it for a moment, then showed it to the man behind him. 'It's as phoney as hell, Jo.'

Beaumont made no comment as he pushed back the bedclothes and showed that he was fully dressed except for tie, jacket and shoes. As the Englishman climbed out of bed and stood up Dixon backed away and stared. Keith Beaumont, thirty-two years old, was six foot two tall, broad-shouldered and weighed over fourteen stone. Not that Dixon was too impressed as he watched the Englishman quietly getting dressed; a big ox was slow-moving. After a minute he checked his watch.

'Hurry it up,' Dixon repeated. He had been right: this man was slow in the reflexes.

'Get stuffed.'

The passenger in the roomette opposite was getting over his shock. 'I'm Andrew Phillipson from Minneapolis,' he informed Dixon in a glib voice. 'This guy said he was from Greenland – Greenland where all that ice is. I thought it was funny . . .'

'He'll be off the train in a minute,' Dixon broke in, 'then you can get back to sleep.' He looked at Beaumont who had finished dressing. 'That your bag? Good. Now, place both hands on the bed – close together.' There was a faint clink of metal as Dixon's companion took his hand out of his pocket. Beaumont shook his large head which was covered with thick dark hair and smiled grimly.

'So your friend can slip handcuffs on me? I'm not playing, Dixon, so you'd better make up your mind – do I come as I am or do you shoot me?'

They went down the corridor with Beaumont's hands still free, preceded by the man called Jo who carried the Englishman's suitcase while Dixon brought up the rear. Curtains screening the roomettes were pulled aside as passengers peered out at the little procession. Behind Dixon bare feet padded down the corridor as Phillipson hurried to catch him up. 'Who is the guy?' he called out excitedly. 'He talked to me so maybe I can help . . .'

'Break-out from Folsom,' Dixon told him tersely.

Beaumont stumbled as he went down the steep steps at the end of the car, his shoulders sagging. Big, sleepy and clumsy, Dixon noted. At the bottom of the steps Beaumont paused on the track to button up his coat and pull his hat down over his ears. Cedar Falls was a small, single-storey building at the edge of a forest with a side exit leading out into a road beyond. Beaumont saw this as lightning flashed, showing a brief, stark view of wind bending trees to the south, then a curtain of rain whooshed down the track and soaked him. A few yards away one of the train crew was watching with a mixture of nervousness and curiosity. A second railroad official stood under the station canopy. Dixon came down the steps behind him, nudged him with the Colt.

'Get moving – through that exit.'

They started walking with the other American still

in front, carrying Beaumont's case. Then there was another flash which wasn't lightning at all: the rail-road man under the canopy had just taken a picture of Beaumont with his Polaroid camera. 'Jo,' Dixon called out, 'get that picture.'

Jo cut away from them, heading for the station building as Beaumont plodded towards the exit. A second flash of lightning showed him the car beyond the exit they were moving towards, a big, red, expen-sive-looking car. Rain was bouncing off its roof. His shoulders sagged a little lower, he was careful not to alter pace, to show any reaction. But he was sure now – these men weren't FBI agents.

They went through the exit into the dark, away from the blurred lights of the train, away from people, their feet tramping through pools of muddy water. Seen at close quarters the car was very big, very expensive-looking, and behind the wheel a third man had his head twisted round to watch them coming. Dixon opened the rear door for the Englishman as Beaumont fumbled inside his coat pocket, a coat Dixon had already checked before letting him put it on. Taking out a pack of cigarettes, Beaumont nodded towards the interior of the car.

'It's all right, Dixon,' he said amiably. 'I've got the message – I'm coming with you.' He cupped a hand to shield the match he had struck, still standing on the far side of the half-open door. The American hesit-ated, caught off guard by the sudden change of mood. A moment later he revised all his ideas about

Beaumont's size and clumsiness, a moment too late. The Englishman rammed his large body hard and brutally against the car door which closed – closed on Dixon's hand and arm.

It was a reasonable risk, Beaumont had calculated – at the worst the gun would be fired harmlessly inside the car, at the best the Colt would drop into the mud in the gap between almost closed door and frame. He stooped so quickly Dixon saw the movement only as a blur, then he came up with the Colt in his hand, pulled the door open and hurled the injured man face down on the back seat. The muzzle of the Colt pointed at the man in the front seat who had had no time to move. 'Take it easy, sonny,' Beaumont warned. 'These things have been known to go bang.'

In the mirror he saw Jo coming through the exit, holding the suitcase. Still watching the man behind the wheel, he roared out a command which easily reached Jo. 'Stand perfectly still – if you want your partners to live . . .'

'We're FBI, for God's sake,' the man behind the wheel said in a strained voice.

'That's right, Beaumont . . .' Dixon choked out the words as he stayed sprawled on the back seat and hugged his right wrist with the other hand.

'Prove it!' the Englishman snapped. 'And keep holding that bag – with both hands,' he shouted to Jo as he watched the third American in the rear-view mirror. Dixon repeated Beaumont's earlier performance, using his left hand to extract a card with his fingertips. 'Give me some light so I can see this thing,' Beaumont rasped. He watched the man behind the wheel press a switch and glanced quickly at the card. 'As phoney as hell,' he said cynically.

'For this you could go behind bars,' the thirty-year-old man behind the wheel informed him tightly.

'On what charge?' Beaumont inquired.

'Resisting Federal officers . . .'

'Federal codswallop!' Beaumont stared bleakly at the man lying on the back seat. 'You come aboard a train and point a gun in my face when I'm asleep. You don't show me a shred of damned identification . . .'

'It had to be like that, Beaumont,' Dixon said wearily. 'It had to look good . . .'

'I haven't finished yet and I'm not satisfied yet. Since when did the FBI sport Lincoln Continentals – or have you all become millionaires suddenly?'

'Does the name of General Lemuel Quincey Dawes mean something to you?' Dixon asked. 'And can I show you something else?'

'I think I read the name in the paper once,' Beaumont informed him coldly, still holding the Colt pointed at the man behind the wheel, still keeping Jo standing with both hands clutching his suitcase. 'And you can show me something – if you're careful.'

The something was a folded sheet of paper which, unfolded and held by Dixon under the light, showed a brief letter written in a weird scrawl he recognized.

Keith — an emergency has come up, a real bad one. I need you back in Washington fast. As a personal favour. Yours. Lemuel.

'Bugger,' Beaumont said simply. 'I'm not coming – except in here out of the rain.' He climbed inside the car and settled back cautiously against the soft leather as Dixon moved over and seated himself, still holding on to his right hand. 'Is that busted?' the Englishman inquired. He looked at the American behind the wheel, who was still twisted round in his seat, studying Beaumont like a butcher about to carve up a slaughtered animal.

'You're going to get a crick in your neck,' Beaumont remarked.

'I'd like to break yours,' the man behind the wheel replied calmly.

'OK, OK, Fred,' Dixon said irritably. 'But you know, Beaumont, you did a risky thing there . . .'

'Risky?' the Englishman exploded 'You wake me up with a gun in my teeth when my reflexes aren't functioning . . .'

'Then I just hope I'm not around when they are functioning,' Dixon said ruefully as he rubbed at his wrist. 'And I can see your point about the Lincoln Continental – my car broke down on the way from the airfield and this was the nearest one we could grab.' In the front seat Fred, who had turned his back on Beaumont, started the motor.

'He can switch that off,' Beaumont snapped. 'We're not going anywhere.'

'Switch her off, Fred.' Dixon sounded harassed. 'We're not going anywhere. Yet,' he added. 'Look, Mr Beaumont,' he said very politely, 'this was a bad night for us – even before we met you. We had to fly down from Washington through an electrical storm – no planes are flying tonight . . .'

'I know,' Beaumont said crisply as he lit a fresh cigarette, 'I was all set to fly down to Miami when they told me everything was grounded – so I had to take the train.'

'We had one hell of a trip to get to an airfield ahead of the train,' Dixon went on. 'Then we had to find a car to get us here in time to stop the express. That's how urgently they want you back in Washington. And another thing – in five years the Florida Express has never made an unscheduled stop before tonight . . .'

'We all make an unscheduled stop sometime,' Beaumont replied. 'I'm making one now. And what was that business about a break-out from Folsom?'

'It was cover,' Dixon sighed. 'The security on this thing is tighter than a steel trap. The other passengers will think we took a criminal off the train – just in case someone like that gabby Phillipson decides to contact the press. And I'm still holding that train,' Dixon added.

'That's your problem. The security on what is tighter than a steel trap? Dawes tells me less than nothing in his note.'

'I don't know anything about it . . .'

'Good night!' Beaumont opened the door, then slammed it shut again as Dixon said something else. 'We know you've spent two years non-stop in the Arctic, that you were going on holiday, but I was told to tell you as a last resort that Sam Grayson and Horst Langer have agreed to help. I gather you know these men?'

Beaumont sat upright in his seat and stared ahead at the rain slashing across the windscreen. Dixon watched him curiously, noting the short nose, the firm mouth, the jawline which expressed energy and great determination. It was the eyes which disturbed him most, he thought, the large brown eyes which looked at a man with an unblinking stare and seemed to look inside him. The Englishman took off his dripping hat, turned his large head and smiled grimly at Dixon. 'You had a rough trip flying down here?' he inquired.

'We were all air-sick.'

'Pity. I'm afraid you're going to be air-sick again. I went through a lot with Grayson and Langer, so I suppose I'll have to go back to Washington. Let the train go – then get me to the airfield fast. It sounds as though Dawes has a little trouble on his hands.' As an afterthought he handed back the Colt.

At three o'clock in the morning of Saturday, 19 February, lights were still burning on the top floor of the National Security Agency building in Washington. The NSA, which is far less well known to the public than the CIA, is one of the most effective intelligence-gathering organizations in the world, partly because it doesn't capture the limelight like its more notorious counterpart. But it spends more money more effectively.

General Dawes is a short, heavily built man of fifty-three who looks like a company executive. He wears sober, grey business suits, has a fondness for tropical plants, and he hates cold weather. Which was probably why he was appointed to oversee operations in the Arctic zone. At three in the morning on 19 February he was pacing round his office in his shirt-sleeves, sweating a little from the temperature of eighty-three degrees which was kept constant by a sophisticated system of temperature control. Eighty-three degrees was obligatory to keep the tropical plants which festooned his office alive. It was also why less reverent members of his staff referred to the room as the Jungle Box.

'Beaumont just came in – they're driving him from the airport now, General . . .'

Jerry Adams, Dawes's assistant, held a lean hand over the mouthpiece of the phone as he went on talking. 'The plane nearly flipped when it landed, but he's OK. Any special instructions? The car bringing him in is on radio . . .'

'Just get him here – fast!'

'He could go to a hotel first, get freshened up,' Adams pressed. 'It would give us time to chew this around . . .'

'We snatched him off that express,' Dawes growled. 'I know him – he'll be climbing walls already. It won't be easy to persuade him, and it will be a damned sight less easy if we park him – give him time to think. This one I'm rushing him into – so get him here!'

Adams, a thin, studious-looking man of thirty-five, raised his dark eyebrows in silent disapproval and gave the instruction. He put down the phone and adjusted his rimless glasses. 'I still don't see why we need this Englishman. The way I see this thing developing it's a simple operation and we can do it with our own boys. When we know Gorov is heading for Target-5 we send in a plane, it takes him aboard, it flies him out . . .'

'Simple?' Dawes completed one more circuit round the room with his bouncy walk and sat down behind his large bare desk. 'Simple?' he repeated softly. 'As simple as falling off the Pan-Am building – and you break your neck that way, too.'

'Given a little luck it could be a smooth run . . .'

'A little luck?' Dawes's tone was deceptively quiet. 'You could be right there, Adams,' he went on genially. 'We have an important Russian coming over to us – maybe the most important Russian who ever left the Soviet Union. Agreed?'

'That's true,' Adams said innocently.

'He's going to make a run for it,' Dawes continued in the same even tone. 'He's starting from the Soviet ice island North Pole 17,* and he'll run for our nearest research base, Target-5, which at this moment in time happens to be twenty-five miles west of the Soviet island. As of now there are only three professors on Target-5 waiting to be evacuated before the island breaks up. Are you with me?' he inquired.

'All the way, sir . . .'

'None of those three professors on Target-5 has any idea of what's going to happen – that Gorov will soon be on his way there over the polar pack.' Dawes was speaking faster now, holding Adams's gaze with his cold blue eyes. 'We can't tell them because they haven't got top security clearance . . .'

'Maybe after all we should radio them,' Adams suggested, 'give them a hint . . .'

'Hint hell! It's only recently we knew Gorov was coming. I can't send in a planeload of men too soon because that might alert the Russians. They might seal off their base which would seal in Gorov. The whole guts of the thing at this stage is that conditions at Target-5 must appear totally normal and damned quiet.'

'I still don't see where Beaumont comes in.'

Dawes studied Adams before replying. At thirty-

* All minor Soviet floating bases in the Arctic are prefixed by the words 'North Pole', followed by a number. The base so named may, in fact, be drifting hundreds of miles from the Pole itself.

five Jerry Adams had more academic qualifications for his job than Dawes could remember. He was fluent in six languages, including Russian and Serbo-Croat. He was an expert cryptographer, a specialist in radio-communications, and he was reputed to be one of the six best interrogators inside the United States. There was only one Arctic qualification he lacked – the only ice he'd seen had been inside a cocktail shaker.

'Fog,' Dawes said.

'Fog?'

'Supposing Target-5* gets fogbound,' Dawes suggested with a grim note in his voice. 'How do we get in then to take out Gorov? We can't fly in – we can't sail in across solid polar pack – so we'll have to walk in, sled across the ice. That's why we could need Beaumont.'

'He's a piece of insurance?'

'Yes.' Dawes looked at the closed door to his office as though Beaumont might fill the doorway at any moment. 'The only trouble is he doesn't know he's just a piece of insurance – and I'm not telling him. Just to put your anxious brain at rest, Adams, I'll list his qualifications . . .'

'We have no one else who could take a sled across the pack?' Adams asked with a note of incredulity. 'Surely that's a simple enough operation?'

---

* Very large ice islands in the Arctic are called Targets by the Americans. T-1 (Target-1), the earliest known ice island, was first seen by the radar office of a Superfortress off the Canadian Arctic coast on 14 August 1946.

'Sometimes I wonder why I employ you,' Dawes said with a genuine tone of wonderment. 'Sledding is the roughest, toughest job on the face of God's earth.' He stood up and walked quickly over to a huge wall map. 'Come here and I'll teach you something they forgot to tell you at Harvard.'

He stared up at the map of the Arctic zone. At the top hovered the coast of Russia with Murmansk and Leningrad to the right. The centre point of the map was the North Pole with Spitsbergen, Greenland and the Canadian and Alaskan coasts below. The marker showing the present position of Target-5 was very low down, pinned just above Iceberg Alley, the dangerous funnel of moving ice between Greenland and Spitsbergen.

'Target-5 is now drifting a hundred and twenty miles off the Greenland coast,' Dawes said quietly. 'Twenty-five miles further east is the Soviet base, North Pole 17, where Gorov will make his run from. Every day those two slabs of ice supporting those bases are drifting with the pack closer to Iceberg Alley. Beaumont calls it the most dangerous place on earth – and I agree with him.'

'His qualifications?' Adams pressed.

'Unusual. His mother was Canadian, his father British – he was killed during the war. They're both dead now. Beaumont was brought to Canada as a child in 1943 and taken to Coppermine at the edge of the Arctic. He grew up among the ice – close to where the ice islands are born when they crack off the

Canadian ice shelf. In 1952 he was sent back to Britain to complete his education and he became interested in aviation. He married in 1965 – when he was twenty-five and three weeks after the marriage a hit-and-run drunk killed his wife.'

'Traumatic,' Adams murmured.

'For the hit-and-run killer, yes. They found him, charged him, and Beaumont was in court when he was sentenced in London. Before they got him out of the witness box Beaumont got to him and half-killed him. He was let off with a suspended sentence and came straight back to Canada.'

'That would be seven years ago?' Adams estimated.

'Nice to know you can add up,' Dawes commented. 'Since then he's spent most of his life in the Arctic – working part of the time for the Arctic Research Laboratory people at Point Barrow, part of the time for us. He's the man who brought us all that data on the Soviet submarine killer chopper when it first showed in the Arctic.' Dawes grunted at the memory. 'He's got top security classification and he speaks fluent Russian. If that isn't enough there was the Spitsbergen trip.'

'What was that, sir?'

'Our security must be better than I thought,' Dawes observed with a wintry smile. 'But you were in Saigon at the time. Last year three men set out across the pack to prove something we thought was impossible could be done – they crossed all the way from Greenland to Spitsbergen by sled. It didn't get into the papers because that trip has military implications. The three men were Sam Grayson and Horst Langer – now waiting up at Thule – and their leader, Beaumont.'

'He sounds – promising,' Adams conceded. 'But we only use him if Target-5 becomes fogged in?'

'Correct! The trouble is Beaumont will only go straight back to Greenland if I tell him he's going there to bring out Michael Gorov . . .'

'But you don't know that,' Adams protested. 'The latest met report shows clear weather over the whole area . . .'

'So I show him my latest met report.' Dawes went back to his desk and extracted a typed form which he handed to Adams. 'He's just spent two bad years in the Arctic so it's going to be hell's teeth to persuade him to go back. That bit of forgery should help.'

Adams stared at the sheet of paper. It was an official met report, dated and timed eight hours earlier. *Weather conditions vicinity Target-5 deteriorating rapidly. Dense fog. Visibility nil. Temperature forty-five below. Conditions expected to worsen.* Adams looked up from the report. 'What happens when he finds out you've fooled him?'

'He'll blow his top – but by then he'll be at Thule, Greenland, I hope.' Dawes took a short fat cigar out of a box and put it in his mouth without lighting it. He was trying to give up smoking for thirty days and so far he'd lasted out a fortnight. 'You've heard about the security leak at Thule?' he asked casually.

'No.' Adams straightened up in his chair. 'What leak?'

'Callard of the FBI warned me two hours ago.' Dawes blew out the match he had absent-mindedly lit and his expression was grim. 'It appears a top Soviet agent has been sending out a stream of information for over two years. They know his code-name – Crocodile – and they expect to come up with his real identity soon.'

'That could jeopardize this whole operation,' Adams said slowly.

'I don't think so – I'm going to warn Beaumont to deal only with the security chief up there, Tillotson.' Dawes checked his watch. 'And Beaumont should be here soon, so brace yourself, Adams.'

The moon was high, the night was clear, and the sky glittered with the spread of the Great Bear constellation hovering above the polar pack. In the bitter cold of the long night Target-5 was besieged.

One hundred and twenty miles east of the Greenland coast, only twenty-five miles west of the Soviet ice island, North Pole 17, Target-5 was besieged by the pack grinding up against it, pressing against its cliff-like fringes, a constantly moving pack of billions of tons of ice which squeaked and gibbered as it tried to smash the island trapped inside its pressure.

It had been trying to smash the island for thirty

years – ever since Target-5 had broken away from the Canadian ice shelf in 1942 when it started its spectacular orbits round the North Pole. But so far the pack had made no impression on the twenty-foot-high cliffs which reared above it because it was salt-water ice – ice formed out of the sea. The massive island, a mile in diameter, was tougher.

Target-5 was made of freshwater ice, which is harder than its salt-water counterpart. And it had a long pedigree. For hundreds of years the ice shelf at the edge of the Canadian coast had been built up by the slow-moving flow of glaciers debouching into the frozen sea. Layer by layer the shelf had been formed until it was two hundred feet deep. Target-5 was a fragment of this shelf – a mile-wide fragment which had broken loose and drifted with the pack for thirty years.

It was starting its fourth ten-year orbit round the Pole, was heading once more for the Canadian Arctic coast, when the Greenland Current caught it. The huge slab of ice was dragged further south than it had ever moved before. Soon it was close to the funnel between Greenland and Spitsbergen, and then it reached the point of no return and continued heading south instead of west, south towards Iceberg Alley.

In faraway Washington Dawes was still waiting for Beaumont when Dr Matthew Conway, the fifty-year-old station leader on Target-5, came out of the headquarters hut to take another star-fix with his sextant. A normally placid man, Conway was edgy as he fiddled with the instrument, and his irritation wasn't helped by the fact that a second man joined him almost as soon as he was outside. Jeff Rickard, the thirty-two-year-old wireless operator, shut the door behind him quickly to keep in the warmth. 'Any sign of activity, Matt?' he inquired.

'Lots of it,' Conway replied with forced humour. 'A Greyhound bus for Omaha just went by.'

'Jesus, if that were only true! Any sign of the Russians, I meant.'

'I know what you meant.'

They stood in the middle of the twelve flat-roofed huts which formed the research base in the centre of the island. Across a narrow avenue of beaten snow six huts faced six more, and from a hut further down the avenue a wireless mast speared up into the moonlit night. In the distance all around them, at no point more than half a mile away, the enemy – the polar pack – was squeaking and gibbering like some huge beast in pain. It reminded them that the pack was alive, was moving and grinding up against the small cliffs which still held it back. A fresh sound came, a sharp report like a rifle crack.

'What the hell was that?' Rickard whispered.

'A piece of ice breaking off,' Conway said wearily. 'Get back inside with Sondeborg, would you, Jeff. I want to finish this job.'

'He's in one of his moods. I think he's getting worse, Matt.'

Conway, his face turned away from Rickard, tightened his mouth as he tried to concentrate on the
star-fix. Sondeborg, twenty-six years old and the
youngest of the three men, was on the verge of a
nervous breakdown, whatever that might be. It was
the isolation, of course, and it was near the end of
their time on the island. In twelve days the plane
would come to evacuate them from the doomed island
and now the hours – even the minutes – were like
years.

The research base was surrounded on all sides by a
smooth snowbound plateau running away to the cliffs
– on all sides except to the south where a small hill
rose, its summit forty feet above the plateau. Here,
over a hundred miles from the nearest coast, was a
hill littered with giant, snow-covered boulders, real
rocks, some of them the size of small bungalows. Ages
ago they had been carried down inside a glacier and
deposited on the Canadian ice shelf – and when the
huge slab of ice had torn itself loose it had carried the
hill with it.

The door behind Conway opened again and he felt
his self-control going. Sondeborg was joining them. It
was getting very difficult: no man wanted to be left
on his own in this terrible solitude, even inside a
warm hut, but when they were together they ground
up against each other like the ice grinding against the
nearby cliffs. 'Shut that door, Harvey,' Conway said
as he pressed his eye to the instrument. The door
slammed behind him.

'Those Russians have gone!' Sondeborg's voice was unsteady, close to hysteria. 'They've got more sense than we have – they've evacuated their bloody base while there was still time. Why the hell don't we wireless for our plane? Everything's packed . . .'

'That's enough!' Conway lowered his sextant and swung round to face Sondeborg. 'Everything isn't packed yet – and you still have experiments to complete . . .'

'Damn the experiments!' Sondeborg blazed. 'There's a queer feeling about this place . . .'

'You've been on Target-5 eleven months,' Conway interjected. 'It's still the same place.'

'It isn't *in* the same place,' Sondeborg rapped back. 'We're on the edge of Iceberg Alley . . .'

'Get back inside and make some coffee,' Conway snapped. 'We could all do with something hot to drink.' The door slammed again as Sondeborg stormed back inside the hut. 'Better go with him, Jeff,' Conway advised, 'you know what he's like on his own. Then you can try and get through to Thule again – I want them to know our new position.'

'I'll try.' Rickard sounded doubtful. 'There's very bad static building up. I think we're cut off. It could be a weather change coming.'

Conway was frowning as he finished taking his star-fix. The reference to bad radio communication – or no communication at all – worried him more than he cared to show. He finished taking his star-fix and paused before going inside while he scanned the familiar wilderness of frozen sea and endless ice. For a reason he couldn't fathom Conway felt afraid.

There was sub-tropical heat and tension inside Dawes's office, a heat and a tension which made the three men sweat. It was Beaumont who had introduced the tension. He sat in his shirt-sleeves, his hands clasped over his large knees as he stared up at Dawes. 'All right, you've given me the picture. Now – what makes this Russian, Michael Gorov, so damned important?'

'All you need to know is that he's important,' Adams intervened. 'The specifics are top secret.'

Beaumont swivelled his head briefly to give the assistant a hard bleak look, then he turned back to Dawes who answered quickly. 'Michael Gorov is the Soviet Union's number one oceanographer. He personally supervised the laying of their entire Sosus and Caesar* system along the Arctic seabed. And he's bringing with him the Catherine charts – the complete blueprint of that system which guides their subs under the Arctic ice to our shores. Does that tell you anything?'

'It suggests that Gorov is – important.'

'With those charts in our hands we could set about

* Sosus and Caesar: American term for the cable and sonar buoy underwater network which guides submarines along a predetermined course at great depth below the polar pack.

ripping up their whole offensive system – it could put them back ten years,' Dawes went on vehemently. 'It means even more than that – if the President goes to Moscow in May with the Catherine charts in his pocket he would be talking from a position of real strength. It's as big as that, Keith. So I need you in Greenland . . .'

'You're going too fast – I haven't agreed to go anywhere yet.' Beaumont stood up and walked across the room to stare at the wall map. For a large man he walked with great economy of movement. 'This ship, the *Elroy* . . . ' He pointed to a marker at the bottom of the map. 'Is she the icebreaker, the twin of the *Exodus*?'

'Yes. She's heading back for Milwaukee after a year in the Arctic.'

'I may want you to turn her round and send her straight back up to the icefield . . .'

Adams's voice rippled with indignation. 'You seem to have forgotten that we're planning this operation, Beaumont.'

The Englishman turned round slowly and stared. Adams found the stare uncomfortable as Beaumont took his time about replying. 'Maybe you'd like to come with me – across the rough ice?' He turned back to Dawes. 'This thing is a mess – and I don't like the sound of that security leak up at Thule. I have to go there first to pick up Grayson and Langer and get equipment before we fly on to Curtis Field.' He stabbed a finger at the nearest airfield to Target-5. 'So that leak is dangerous.'

'The FBI man, Callard, says they may have located Crocodile within hours. Any advance instructions we can radio direct to Tillotson – he's the security chief up there.'

'I still don't like it. Let me see that met report again.' Dawes handed him the faked weather report with a wooden face while Adams studied his finger-nails. Beaumont read the report and shook his head. 'It means the three of us have to fly in to the edge of the fog bank from Curtis Field. Then we sled our way to Target-5 – if we can ever find it. We pick up Gorov – assuming he ever makes it across twenty-five miles of broken ice – then we have to sled our way back across one hundred and twenty miles of moving ice, probably with the Russian security people on our tails . . .'

'We could pick you up off the ice once you get clear of the fog and fly you back,' Adams suggested.

'You could,' Beaumont agreed, 'if you ever found us, which you wouldn't. Have you any idea what it's like trying to find four men and two sled-teams from the air at this time of year? No, obviously you haven't . . .'

'People do get rescued by air,' Adams persisted.

'That's right,' Beaumont growled, 'they do. Something else you obviously don't know is that usually it's by accident – a plane that wasn't looking for them just happens to see them. Another thing I don't like,' he continued, 'is that we don't yet know when he's coming.' He waved the met report in Dawes's direction. 'Send an urgent signal to the *Elroy* – she's to turn

29

round at once and head back due north for the icefield. This may be a rendezvous point . . .' Beaumont took out a pencil and marked a thick cross on the wall map.

'That's deep inside the ice,' Adams protested.

'So she has to ram her way in. I want to be on a plane for Greenland within two hours,' he told Dawes, 'a fast machine that can get me there non-stop.'

'There's a Boeing waiting for you now,' Dawes said.

Beaumont raised an eyebrow. 'You were confident, weren't you? American organization – sometimes it frightens me. Now, let's go quickly over this dangerous business of when we'll know Michael Gorov is coming.'

Adams began talking in a quick competent voice. 'We're waiting for a man to come back from Leningrad – to Helsinki. He's contacting a relative of Michael Gorov's and he'll bring out the date when Michael Gorov is leaving North Pole 17. We do know that it will be within the next few days – and when our man gets out we'll know the exact day.'

'Supposing he never leaves Leningrad alive?' Beaumont demanded.

'He should make it,' Adams said confidently. 'He's never been behind the Iron Curtain before – that's why he was chosen. But he's a very experienced man. When he reaches Helsinki he goes straight to our embassy and they'll signal us.'

'The whole thing depends on one man inside Russia,' Beaumont said grimly.

'A first-class man,' Adams assured him. 'We'll know at the latest by one o'clock Sunday morning, our time. As soon as we hear we'll signal you at Curtis Field.' Adams's optimism was carrying him along on a cloud. 'You don't have to worry. You'll see – it will be a very simple operation.'

'It won't,' Beaumont rumbled. 'That's the one and only thing I can predict – it won't be a simple operation.'

Chapter Two

Friday, 18 February

A man was killed on Nevsky Prospekt in Leningrad at exactly five minutes past three in the afternoon of Friday, 18 February.

At three in the afternoon in Leningrad it is still only 7 AM in Washington. Beaumont had not yet even boarded the Florida Express he was to be taken off so unceremoniously seventeen hours later. But it was almost three in the afternoon when an American tourist, Harvey Winthrop, walked carefully down the five icy steps which led from the Hotel Europa to street level.

A tall, serious-faced man of thirty-eight, Winthrop was described in his passport as a writer, but writing can hardly have been on his mind as he checked his watch and walked out of the Hotel Europa. 2.55 PM. Reaching street level, he turned left and began trudging through the snow towards Nevsky Prospekt.

Overhead the sky was swollen with the threat of more snow to come and there were very few people about; in this northern latitude it would be dark within thirty minutes. In fact, the street lamps were already glowing, their light reflecting weirdly off the snow as Winthrop arrived on Nevsky Prospekt and glanced cautiously along the broad avenue in both directions. He gave the impression of a man unsure whether it was safe to cross, but really he was checking three cars parked on the far side of the avenue.

The Intourist guide, Madame Vollin, who had accompanied him on each trip to the Hermitage since he had arrived from Helsinki five days ago was nowhere to be seen – not inside one of the parked cars, not gazing into any of the dimly lit shop windows behind the vehicles, so she must have accepted his word that he wouldn't be going back to the Hermitage today, that he was too tired to look at any more Rubens. He hesitated, waited until a trolley-bus was close, which gave him another excuse to wait a little longer, to double check.

On the far side of the almost-deserted avenue a youth in a black leather jacket rushed round a corner, rammed a key into a car door, opened it and then waited as a girl followed him round the corner. A red-haired girl, she wore a tight-fitting mini coat, and she began punching the youth as soon as she got close to him. Winthrop smiled dryly as the trolley-bus rumbled past, the traction flashing blue sparks off the ice-coated wire: even the Russians had a juvenile problem, especially when the juveniles were offspring of high-up Party officials. He began to cross the wide street.

Not by chance, Winthrop could easily have been mistaken for a Russian: he was wearing a fur coat, a fur hat and knee-length boots purchased from the GUM store three days after his arrival. 'I didn't realize it would be as cold as this,' he explained to Madame Vollin. As he reached the far side and walked past the young couple who were still arguing, he checked his watch.

2.58 PM. Two minutes to the meeting-place he could see as he walked, the little tree-lined park further down the Nevsky. He trudged along the avenue with his gloved hands thrust deep inside his coat pockets, the art catalogue tucked under his arm, taking the same route to the Hermitage Museum at the Winter Palace he had followed for five days with Madame Vollin at his side. The little tree-lined park came closer. He could see the statue of Lenin by the path and in the distance a short, stocky figure had turned off the Nevsky, was already inside the park. Was this the seaman? Winthrop entered the park.

Winthrop had never met Peter Gorov, the brother of Michael Gorov, the oceanographer, and he strained his eyes to check three details before the man reached him. The duffle bag – carried under the arm instead of over the shoulder, the normal way Soviet seamen carried it. Check. A red scarf wrapped round his neck. Check. But there was one further detail and the light was fading badly. Winthrop kept his slow, casual pace. The third detail was a button, a single white button at the top of the coat while the other buttons would be dark-coloured. Jesus, he couldn't see that at all. A militiaman – a policeman – trudged into the park from the far end and started walking up behind the seaman.

Winthrop's heart skipped a beat but he maintained the same pace. It had happened – the unforeseen factor which could ruin everything, make the contact impossible. A fresh fear tingled Winthrop's nerves – was the policeman following Gorov? It didn't seem likely: it was too open a tag. Get a grip on yourself, man! Helsinki, Finland – safety – is only a hundred miles away. It wasn't a thought that gave Harvey Winthrop any comfort as he walked steadily towards the seaman approaching him: he might just as well be in Kiev, in the heart of the Ukraine where Gorov had just come from after meeting his brother, Michael.

It was getting darker every minute. The seaman came closer, trailed by the policeman who wore a dark blue greatcoat and kept an even distance of fifty yards behind the seaman. Was this another coincidence – that the policeman was maintaining exactly the same walking pace as Peter Gorov? If this was Gorov – Winthrop still couldn't see the button. He could see the red band on the policeman's peaked cap but he couldn't see Gorov's goddamned button. The seaman, less than thirty years old, was staring straight ahead and Winthrop fancied he saw strain in the stiffened jaw muscles. The poor devil must be close to screaming point: he hadn't been trained for this kind of tension. Then Winthrop saw the lighter-coloured button at the top of the coat.

Winthrop slipped on the ice in front of the Lenin

statue, slipped while the seaman was only feet away with the policeman still fifty yards to his rear. As the American fell the coloured catalogue dropped to the ground and an illustration of a Rubens painting stood out on the darkened snow like a bloodstain. The catalogue was his positive identification. In the most natural way the seaman paused while Winthrop was trying to get back on his feet and spoke swiftly and softly in Russian.

'He is coming out on 20 February ... to the American research base Target Number Five ... 20 February ...' He repeated the date in an even lower tone and Winthrop knew he was terrified about two things – that the American might not have heard the vital date, that the policeman might overhear him.

Winthrop was on his feet now, brushing snow from his coat. The seaman shrugged his shoulders as though people were always slipping in this weather and continued through the park towards the Nevsky Prospekt and the docks beyond. Winthrop picked up his catalogue, tried to walk, limped badly, then leaned against the railings round the statue. The policeman reached Winthrop and asked his question in Russian. 'Can you walk? Have you far to go?'

'I'm OK. I reckon I twisted my ankle a bit – but I'm OK.' Winthrop had carefully replied in English – no one knew that he understood any Russian, no one except Gorov who was already outside the park. The policeman stared at him without understanding as Winthrop smiled painfully – he really had twisted his ankle. 'I'm from the Europa Hotel,' Winthrop went on, anxious to get rid of the man. He waved a hand. 'Not far to go.' He smiled again and began walking slowly back the way he had come.

Winthrop limped painfully through the park, really worried now about slipping. He simply had to make it back to the hotel, and even in his pain the American's brain was working. Maybe this twisted ankle could be used to get him out of Russia.

Winthrop was due to leave for Helsinki the day after tomorrow – on the early Sunday morning flight. But that was the day Michael Gorov was starting his run for Target-5. The Soviet authorities knew his exit date, knew that he was in Leningrad to view the wonderful collection of Rubens paintings in the Hermitage in his capacity as a writer on art, so normally they might think his early departure strange. The genuinely sprained ankle gave him his reason for catching Saturday's Finnair flight to Helsinki – then the signal could be sent to Dawes in Washington a day before Gorov fled from North Pole 17.

As Winthrop limped out on to the Nevsky Prospekt it began to snow. He observed the situation along the street automatically, noticed that the leather-jacketed youth was still arguing with his red-haired girl. They must be in love, he thought ironically. No traffic was coming. He still hadn't glanced back to see if the policeman was following. He stepped off the kerb.

It was probably the fresh fall of snow which caused it to happen. The leather-jacketed youth must have been frozen and the snow broke up the argument. He climbed in behind the wheel of his car and the red-haired girl got into the front passenger seat beside him. The youth switched on the ignition, gunned the motor, pulled away from the kerb with an exhaust burst like a bomb detonating, accelerated, then remembered to switch on his lights.

Even then Winthrop might have jumped clear had he been faking the limp, but the car was screaming towards him as the lights flashed on, blinding him. In the headlight glare Winthrop's limping figure hurtled towards the car, filled the windscreen, then the radiator lifted him and hurled him a dozen yards. He crashed down on the kerb with the impact of a man falling from a great height. He was dead before the car swept away round a corner as a woman on the sidewalk began screaming.

A hundred yards further down Nevsky Prospekt the seaman, Gorov, had stopped to cross the avenue. He saw Winthrop limping over the highway, saw the car strike him, saw the body curving through the air before it dropped and he knew that the American was dead. He crossed the avenue and went on towards the docks where the trawler *Girolog* was waiting to depart in three hours.

Gorov walked like a man in a dream, hardly able to grasp what had just happened. It was a total disaster: the message would never get through to Washington and now there was no way of warning his brother. Michael would start out across the ice and the Americans wouldn't know he was coming. Crushed, Gorov walked on through the snow, his feet leading him along the familiar route. God, what could he do?

Chapter Three

Saturday, 19 February

It was eight o'clock on Saturday morning inside the Leningrad headquarters of the Special Security Service.

'This American, Winthrop, who was killed on the Nevsky yesterday – I smell something funny about him . . .'

The Locomotive – this was the nickname they used in Leningrad for Colonel Igor Papanin, chief of Special Security for the Arctic Military Zone. The dictionary definition of the word is '. . . having power . . . not stationary . . . constantly travelling . . .' It is as good a description as any of Col. Papanin. For many the word suggests a huge engine dragging hundreds of people behind it at speed – and this also is a good description of the Siberian.

'Get me a full report, Kramer! Bring in that damned Intourist nursemaid, Vollin, or whatever her name is! Bring in the policeman who saw it happen. Find any other witnesses and parade them here by noon. I'll question them myself!'

Strictly speaking, the headquarters of the Special Security Service for the Arctic should have been at the

41

port of Murmansk, but when Leonid Brezhnev, First Secretary, appointed Papanin to the post he ordered that the headquarters must be in Leningrad. And this was a matter of power, too.

Like Hamburg in Germany, like Quebec in Canada, Leningrad is a maverick city. It was in Leningrad that Communism was born when the cruiser *Aurora* fired the gun which signalled revolution. It was to Leningrad that Stalin, fearing the city's independence, sent his most trusted oppressor, Kirov – and Kirov died from an assassin's bullet. So Brezhnev sent Papanin to Leningrad.

'And, Kramer, contact the airport where Winthrop came in. They will have made a note of this man's arrival. Did he come in alone – that's what I want to know. By noon!'

Unlike Kirov, the bloody-minded citizens of Leningrad didn't try to shoot Papanin – they nicknamed him the Locomotive instead. A familiar figure striding down the Nevsky Prospekt, no Russian could miss him in the densest crowd – Papanin towered above the crowd. Six foot four tall, wide-shouldered, heavily built, his large Siberian head was shaved almost bald and he had a mouth as wide as a carp's. And when he raised his drill-sergeant's voice they swore you could hear him in Murmansk.

'Get down to police headquarters and fetch me Winthrop's personal possessions, Kramer. Go yourself! An American tourist in Leningrad in February? I tell you, Kramer, I smell stinking fish . . .'

Walther Kramer, forty-five years old, a short, stout Communist Balt from Lithuania who moved with the agility and silence of a cat, didn't believe a word of it. As Papanin's assistant he had a certain latitude in talking to his chief, a latitude about as wide as the edge of a razor blade. He voiced his disbelief cautiously.

'There's no evidence that this American was anything but what his passport says . . .'

'Haven't you gone yet?'

As the Balt left the second-floor room Papanin stood up and went over to the window, then he took out a pocket chess set from his jacket and stared at it. The window a foot from his smooth-skinned, hard-boned face was rimed with frost as he studied the tiny board. At eight in the morning it was still dark outside and he could hear below the shuffle of footsteps on the cobbled street as people hurried to work. An ancient green-tiled stove he had recently lit stood in a corner behind him and its warmth hadn't yet penetrated the chilled room. Only one wall away the most modern American teleprinter was chattering non-stop, but Papanin warmed himself with a stove as old as the revolution itself.

It was the Jewish problem which had aroused Papanin's suspicion of Winthrop, and the Jewish problem was another reason why Leonid Brezhnev was glad he had put Papanin inside Leningrad. On top of all his other duties it was now Papanin's responsibility to find out how finance was being smuggled in to help Jews emigrate to Israel.

As he stared at the chess board Papanin grunted to punctuate his thoughts. Winthrop could have been a courier, a contact man with the Jewish underground, so Winthrop – even though he was dead – was going to be investigated up to his eyeteeth. Literally. The Siberian had already ordered an intimate examination of the naked corpse. He frowned, decided on his move, shifted a pawn. He was sure he was right: there was something very odd indeed about Mr Harvey J. Winthrop.

At eight o'clock on Saturday morning Papanin still had no idea that he was engaged in a race against time – to solve the Winthrop mystery before Michael Gorov fled from North Pole 17 at midnight on Sunday.

In Washington it was still only midnight, Friday. Beaumont was still inside the sleeping-car aboard the Florida Express. At the Soviet base North Pole 17 it was four in the morning and Michael Gorov had only recently arrived from Murmansk.

Michael Gorov, forty years old, a member of the Soviet Academy of Science and the Soviet Union's most distinguished oceanographer, was almost ill with the strain, sick with the tension of waiting, of counting away the hours to Sunday.

At four in the morning he stood in the moonlight at the edge of the recently swept airstrip which bisected the ice island, North Pole 17. He was very carefully gazing towards the east, not to the west

44

where the American research base, Target-5, lay twenty-five miles away. Beyond the island the tumbled pack glittered in the moonlight like a vast endless heap of frosted glass, smashed frosted glass. Behind him lay the huts which formed the base, their flat roofs deep with snow. It was from that direction that he heard the footsteps coming, the steps of Nikolai Marov, the security man. Marov came close, stopped and watched the stooped back of the oceanographer. 'Are you feeling all right, Academician Gorov?' he inquired.

'Never felt better.'

'You're up early,' the security man persisted.

'I'm always up early – you should know that by now.'

Gorov deliberately let his irritation show and the stratagem worked. Marov mumbled something and padded back towards the base. Inside his coat pocket Gorov's gloved hands clenched: Marov was going to be a problem – because Marov always came with him when he ventured out on the pack. And there was another reason why Gorov had allowed his irritation to show: he had reached the stage where he couldn't stand the sight of a security man. It was Col. Papanin's Security Service which had killed Rachel Levitzer six months ago.

Gorov's eyes filled with tears as he thought of her. They had been unofficially engaged, but because she was Jewish, because he was an eminent Academician, they had kept their relationship secret. Then the news had come through in August 1971: Rachel had died in Leningrad.

The Security Service had come to her flat to arrest her: something to do with the Jewish underground – Gorov had never been clear on the details – but Rachel had attempted to escape, fleeing down a long staircase. A security man had tripped her and Rachel had gone down – down a flight of thirty stone steps. When they had reached her she was dead, her neck broken.

Gorov checked his watch. 4.10 AM, local time. Twenty more hours to wait before he started out across the polar pack in his desperate bid to reach Target-5. Timing was everything: he had been warned by the Americans that he must fix his own departure date – and then stick to it. Gorov's plan was to leave North Pole 17 at exactly midnight and he wondered how he was going to get through the next twenty hours while he pretended to be absorbed in his depth-sounding experiments. But at least there was one consolation: his brother, Peter, would by now have passed on the message. The Americans knew already when he was coming.

The Locomotive was building up a head of steam. By eleven o'clock on Saturday morning all witnesses had been interrogated at security headquarters – interrogated by Papanin himself. He had seen the Intourist guide, Madame Vollin – 'a cow of a woman, Kramer.

And she has bad breath. I don't know how Winthrop stood it . . .' He had spent far longer with the policeman who had seen Winthrop die. He had interviewed staff from the Hotel Europa and the airport official who had noted down Winthrop's arrival five days earlier from Helsinki. And he had found nothing remotely suspicious.

'I think we are looking down a large hole with nothing in it,' Kramer remarked as the airport official left. 'There is not one piece of evidence to connect this man Winthrop with the Jews.'

'Someone is bringing in money to them – we know that. And Winthrop still smells.' The Siberian bounded up from behind his desk and started striding round the room. 'For five days he behaves himself – he goes to the Hermitage and stares at the Rubens, always with his nursemaid, the Vollin woman. Then, what happens yesterday?' Papanin bent down, picked up a poker and began to attack the interior of the stove, stirring up the glowing coals the way he stirred up people.

'He dies in a street accident . . .'

'Before that! He breaks routine, Kramer – he tells the guide he is tired and will not be going out.' He rammed the poker in deep. 'The moment her back is turned he slips out again on his own – when it is nearly dark. Why, Kramer, why?'

'He is feeling better. He is going back to the Hermitage . . .'

'When the museum closes at four? He'd get there

47

just in time to come back. Why did he go out on his own?'

'To meet someone . . .' Kramer made the reply casually, for something to say. The Siberian's grip tightened on the poker. He withdrew the weapon from the stove, straightened up slowly and stared at his assistant. 'I don't really believe that,' Kramer said quickly.

'To meet someone?' Papanin repeated. 'You know, you could be right. But who? He didn't meet anyone – he didn't have time before he was killed.' Papanin prodded the poker in Kramer's direction. 'Let's use our heads – by which I mean let's use my head. The American goes out, walks to the park . . .'

'Twists his ankle . . .'

'Appears to twist his ankle, Kramer.' Papanin had his eyes closed as he tried to visualize the scene the policeman had described. 'He slips close to the seaman, then he starts back again. I wonder who that seaman was, Kramer?'

'Could have been anyone.'

'No – we can narrow it down! The seaman was carrying his duffle bag and was walking towards the docks . . .' Papanin put the poker back on the stove and took a file out of a drawer. Each day he received a report on events in the city, including a police report, but he was looking for the docks report. 'The only ship which sailed yesterday was the *Girolog*, a trawler, and the icebreaker which took it out. He must have been going to embark on the *Girolog*.'

'With a crew of about thirty . . .'

'True. So now I want you to drive immediately to the docks to get me the list of all personnel who sailed on the *Girolog* last night. I want it by noon.'

'There isn't time . . .' Kramer protested.

'That's your problem!' Papanin sat down behind his desk and waited until Kramer had reached the door. 'Incidentally, while I was away in Moscow this week I see you signed a movement order for Michael Gorov to go back to North Pole 17. I thought he'd finished his work there.'

'That is correct.' Kramer paused near the door, vaguely worried by this sudden change of topic. 'He wanted to take some final depth-soundings before we evacuate the base. He gave me the impression that you knew about it.'

'That's all right, Kramer. It just struck me that he hadn't planned to go there again. And get me the *Girolog* list by noon!'

Alone in his room, Papanin put one booted leg on top of his desk and stared moodily at the green-tiled stove which was now emanating great waves of heat. Without knowing it, he now had exactly seventeen hours to find out why Winthrop had come to Leningrad before Michael Gorov started his run to Target-5.

It was a six-hour flight at forty thousand feet from Washington to Thule, Greenland, and it was eleven o'clock on Saturday morning when Beaumont woke up and saw the huge runway coming up to meet the Boeing 707. It didn't feel like Saturday – by now Beaumont was so bemused that he had to think to remember the day of the week. And it didn't look like eleven o'clock in the morning as the Boeing dropped out of a moonlit night towards the wilderness of snow and ice below.

'Seems like only five minutes since we left Washington,' he called out to Callard, the FBI man who sat across the gangway from him.

The man in the neat blue suit, freshly shaven, looked back at the big Englishman as though wondering whether to reply. 'Seems more like five years to me,' he said eventually. He turned away and looked out of the window on his side.

Beaumont smiled to himself. At five in the morning Callard had jumped aboard the plane at Washington minutes before its departure for Greenland; obviously he had been flying the plane every mile of the way while Beaumont had slept. He looked out of his own window, staring down at the desolate snowbound plain of the Greenland icecap. In the distance the thousand-foot-high radar mast sheered up into the moonlit sky, the warning light at the summit flashing red. The tallest mast in the world, it had a range of three thousand miles over the roof of the world. It was the key station in the Distant Early Warning system.

'I'll see you in Vandenberg's office,' Callard suddenly called out. 'Sometime this evening, maybe.'

Beaumont nodded and he thought the suggestion significant. As the Boeing continued its descent he was certain that Callard had cracked the case, that he now knew the identity of Crocodile, that he was on his way to arrest the Soviet agent. They went down below the level of the radar mast tip and the grim panorama of the icecap slid up closer. Beaumont had a tilted view of flat-topped buildings on either side of Main Street, the snow-covered road which ran down the middle of the camp, then they were landing.

Tillotson was waiting for Beaumont when he disembarked from the plane, wrapped in a fur parka they had supplied before he left Washington. It was forty below and the still air hit him like a physical blow, taking his breath away as he stood at the foot of the steps. Tillotson, a tall, tough-looking man with a face like one of the heads carved out of Mount Rushmore, shook Beaumont's gloved hand with his own. 'I have everything ready for this trip of yours ...'

He stopped speaking and stared at Callard who had come down the steps behind Beaumont, brushed past the two men and walked quickly across to Colonel Vandenberg, the camp commander. 'Who was that?' he asked.

'No idea,' Beaumont said instantly. 'He wasn't very talkative and I slept most of the way. Maybe there's been a complaint about the hamburgers.'

Tillotson looked back at the plane where the chief pilot was coming down the steps. 'Excuse me,' he said and intercepted the pilot. 'That second passenger – who is he? Only Beaumont was reported as coming on this flight.'

The pilot, carrying his flying helmet, pulled the hood of his parka over his head. 'Every time I make this trip it gets colder up here. The guy jumped aboard at the last minute just before we left Washington. He came in a government car . . .'

'I'll check him later.' Tillotson led Beaumont to a covered jeep and started talking as he turned on the ignition. 'As I said, everything is ready for your trip. Two Sikorskys have been sent to Curtis Field on the east Greenland coast. Grayson and Langer are waiting for you at headquarters – Grayson was here but we had to scoop up Langer from Ellesmere Island.' He drove the jeep slowly along a track towards the camp, keeping well behind the car which was taking Col. Vandenberg and Callard ahead of them. 'Two Norwegian-type sleds are being sent on to Curtis . . .'

'They're useless,' Beaumont interjected. 'I specified Eskimo sleds – they're heavier and won't break up on rough ice. Your sleds will.'

Tillotson looked surprised. 'We use Norwegian-type sleds ourselves. We haven't any Eskimo sleds . . .'

'I think you have. When I was last here you had two of them stowed away at the back of the big helicopter hangar.'

'Like to check now? I could turn off and we could go straight over.'

'Now?'

'No time like the present. And I gather that for you everything is hurry-hurry.'

Tillotson changed direction as they came to a fork in the beaten snow-track, heading away from the encampment of huts as he drove towards a large hangar in the distance. A quarter of a mile ahead the wire surrounding the military airfield glittered in the moonlight – it was sheathed in solid ice. Beyond the wire a stationary orange snow-plough stood close to the hangar. Tillotson pulled a folded sheet of paper from his pocket and handed it to Beaumont. 'Met reports on the whole area – I don't know which area you're interested in. Rough ice, you said?'

'Rough ice, I said.'

Beaumont hadn't yet acclimatized to the bitter Arctic air which was streaming inside the jeep, freezing his face and making him feel short of breath. The car carrying Vandenberg and Callard was disappearing along the main track, its red light growing smaller as another jeep came tearing in the opposite direction, driving towards the Boeing 707.

'Any fog about?' Beaumont asked casually as he began reading the report.

'No fog anywhere, thank God. According to the latest report – and that's what you're reading – there's clear weather all the way from here to Norway.'

'You mean you've had it and it's cleared recently?'

Beaumont pressed. He was thinking of the report Dawes had shown him in Washington concerning weather conditions round Target-5. *Dense fog . . . visibility nil.*

'We just haven't had any fog, period. Not for the past three weeks.'

Tillotson slowed down, glanced at Beaumont who was still reading the report while the anger grew inside him. Dawes had fooled him, had shown him a faked weather report to get him to Greenland. Tillotson pulled up, left the engine ticking over. 'Mitten's slipped inside my glove,' he explained. 'I'll just fix it.' He fiddled with the glove, took it off, put it inside his coat pocket. When he withdrew his hand it was holding a .38 Smith & Wesson. He turned sideways and with one swift movement smashed the barrel against Beaumont's temple. Instinctively Beaumont shifted a second before the gun hit him and the barrel grazed rather than clubbed him, but he was hurt. He grabbed at the ignition key, tore it loose, threw it sideways out of the window into the snow. Tillotson smashed the revolver down a second time. A flash of light exploded inside Beaumont's head, a blinding flash, then a horrible wave of blackness engulfed him.

Chapter Four

Saturday, 19 February

Beaumont lay half-conscious in the snow, fighting to get a grip on himself as Sam Grayson's cheerful face bent over him, but there was anxiety in the American's expression as he eased the brandy flask close to Beaumont's lips. 'Take it easy, Keith : . .'

Beaumont forced himself up on his elbows, took the flask in one hand, helped himself to a drink. His head was pounding, his vision was blurred, then the strong spirit reached his stomach and he could see clearly. He took a slow, deep breath of the bitter night air. That seemed more potent than the brandy. 'Get me on my feet,' he said between his teeth.

'Better wait a bit . . .'

Beaumont swore, clambered unsteadily to his feet, swayed, nearly fell over as Grayson grabbed for his arm. Tillotson's jeep stood a few yards away and Beaumont remembered he had thrown the ignition key into the snow. Another jeep stood a few yards away, its windscreen shattered, the front right tyre flat. 'Tillotson shot at you?'

'Tillotson . . .?'

'Yes, Tillotson,' Beaumont rasped impatiently.

'He's Crocodile – the security leak. But you wouldn't know about that. We've got to get after him – where's he gone?' Beaumont looked towards the airfield and there was nothing in sight – only the guard-post by the gate in the wire, the orange snow-plough in the distance and the hangar beyond. Where the hell had Tillotson vanished to? 'Which way did he go?' Beaumont snapped.

Grayson, a short, wiry man of thirty-five with sand-coloured hair, was still recovering from the shock: he had thought Beaumont was dead. 'We've heard rumours about a security leak. I was late coming out to meet you off the plane and the pilot said you'd driven off in a jeep. I couldn't believe it was Tillotson when he started shooting. He ran off towards the airfield . . .' Grayson was talking to himself – Beaumont had started running towards the guard-post.

'He can't get away,' Grayson shouted as he followed Beaumont. 'Vandenberg declared a state of alert just before your plane came in. The base is sealed off . . .'

'I think Tillotson can fly a helicopter,' Beaumont shouted back. He was getting into his stride now, his legs carrying him over the snow with surprising speed for so large a man. It was willpower which kept him going; his head was aching horribly, the blood at the side of his face had congealed in the bitter cold, his stomach was on the verge of nausea. The bitter air helped his recovery as he ran and took in great gulps of it. Close to the strangely deserted guard-post he stopped and waited for Grayson to catch him up.

'Sam, have you a gun? Good – give it to me and keep back.'

He took the Colt .45 from the American and approached the guard-post. Something was lying in the snow just outside the concrete blockhouse. An American soldier still clutching his carbine, swathed in his parka, lay on his back staring up at the Arctic sky. Beaumont bent down, checked the man's pulse, then heaved him over on his stomach. He was dead and the blood patch which surrounded a rip high up in the back of the parka was already frozen. It couldn't have been difficult; after all, Tillotson was the security chief. The alert meant that no one could get on to the airfield, so Tillotson had removed the obstacle in his escape route. 'He's already on the airfield,' he told Grayson grimly as the American reached him.

'I've never heard that Tillotson can fly,' Grayson objected.

'I think he can fly a helicopter – and there are helicopters inside that hangar.' Beaumont stared beyond the wire where there was no sign of movement. 'I once saw him inside a machine. That's how he's going to try and get out – by helicopter. Come on!'

'There are two guards inside that hangar,' Grayson said quickly. 'There's a phone inside the guard-post – we must warn the men inside the hangar . . .'

Beaumont was halfway inside the guard-post doorway when he saw the phone-cord slashed and dangling. 'It's no use, Sam – he thought of that. But where the hell is he?' Beaumont ran to the open gateway and stared across the white desert of the airfield. The snow-plough.

It was smaller now, like an orange bug as it crept up to the hangar where the helicopters were housed. Tillotson had grabbed the nearest available transport to get him inside the hangar fast. Beaumont would have shouted – anything to warn the men guarding the machines – but he was too far away. He took a deep breath and began running again while Grayson followed. Unlike the American, who wore boots, Beaumont was still wearing the rubber-soled shoes he had come in from Washington, but the snow was a hard crust and again he was covering the ground with astonishing speed. He had run for several minutes, was near the hangar when he stumbled and sprawled head first in the snow. He clambered to his feet, his head aching, his face stinging, and had to search for the revolver which had jumped out of his hand. He found it half-buried in the snow and at that moment heard a sound which chilled his mind: the throbbing beat of a helicopter's motor. With the gun in his hand he ran the last two hundred yards.

'Keep back!' he shouted to Grayson.

The orange plough was parked close to the hangar entrance and the huge, power-operated doors were open now. The mouth of the hangar was a dark cave

as his tired legs carried him forward on sheer willpower, and he was within ten yards of the entrance
when the machine appeared, an H-19 Sikorsky, its
blades whirling at speed as it emerged from the dark
shadow. Snow was whipped from the ground, thrown
across the airfield, and the machine came forward
through the disturbed snow, advancing towards
Beaumont, its size enormous in the moonlight.

Beaumont stood quite still, braced himself, hoisted
the revolver, gripping the butt with both hands to
steady his aim as the machine came on. In ten seconds
it would grind over him. The gunsight was aimed
for the cockpit, for the blurred helmeted head-and-
shoulders behind the ice-rimed perspex. He took a
deep breath, aimed carefully, squeezed. The hammer
clicked. He felt rather than heard the click as the
helicopter roar hammered at his eardrums. The firing
mechanism was choked. The gun wouldn't fire.

'Look out!' Grayson shouted, his warning lost in
the roar.

Tillotson drove the machine straight at him and
Beaumont dived sideways and downwards. As he hit
the snow he rolled, took the impact on his shoulders,
kept rolling over and over while the hideous roar
enveloped him. The motor coughed, changed, the roar
became a steady, purposeful beat, and when Beaumont looked up the machine was ascending, was
already the height of the hangar roof. He climbed to
his knees, wiped snow scuffed up by the rotating
blades off his face as Grayson reached him.

'We've got to get after him,' Beaumont snapped. 'He mustn't get clear – our lives depend on it . . .'

He hardly glanced at the crumpled form lying half under the terrible blades of the snow-plough. One of the guards. It had been so easy, so coldly brutal. The snow-plough was a familiar sight on the airfield – the soldier had come out to meet it – Tillotson had driven straight over him. Inside the hangar entrance Beaumont stumbled again, nearly fell over the body of the second guard. He grasped instantly how this had happened. Tillotson had simply shouted for his victim. 'There's been a horrible accident . . .' The knife had gone in before the youngster recovered from the shock, the knife showing in Beaumont's torch beam where a handle protruded from the dead man's back.

Beaumont dropped the useless Colt, picked up the carbine the soldier had never had a chance to use and ran inside the hangar. A second Sikorsky was standing at the rear of the hangar under a hooded lamp. An electric cable plugged in to keep the motor from freezing ran from the machine to the wall. Beaumont unplugged the cable, climbed up to the machine, opened the door and went inside the cabin as Grayson came up behind him. 'He's gone,' the American warned. 'We'll never find him . . .'

'We'll find him . . .' Beaumont was fixing on the pilot's helmet and headset which was always left in the pilot's seat. Stripping off his parka, he settled himself behind the controls. 'Shut the door, Sam – we're going up.' The instrument panel faced him –

radar-altimeter, fuel gauge, rev counter, other instru-
ments. The collective stick – controlling ascent – was
on his left. The cyclic control stick – which changed
flight direction – was on his right. A twist-grip throttle, rather like a motorcycle's throttle, was ringed
round the collective stick. Beaumont started the
motor.

The whole cabin shuddered. Sound blasted across
the inside of the hangar. The rotor blades above
swivelled sluggishly, start-stop-start. Then the
machine burst into power. In the ghostly light from
the instrument panel Beaumont's expression was grim
as he built up more power. The helicopter edged
forward, drummed across the concrete, emerged from
the hangar. The radar mast which reached almost to
the stars came into view and Beaumont used the
throttle. The fifty-foot rotor blades tore through their
ellipse, whipped through the Arctic air, sounded as
though at any second they would rip loose from the
machine. The rev counter climbed on the dial. The
machine quivered like a great bird, tethered and
desperate to leave the ground, then they were going
up.

Beyond the perspex dome which vaulted above
them they saw the hangar wall descending like a lift.
The snow-covered roof appeared, disappeared as a
glow-worm of vehicle lights drove close to the guard-
post at the airfield entrance. 'They've tumbled to it!'
Beaumont spoke the words into the mike hanging
from the headset under his chin. Grayson heard him

through the earphones of his own headset as he sat alongside Beaumont in the observer's seat. The helicopter gained altitude as the vehicles rushed across the snow below and Beaumont swore as he heard reports above the muffled roar of the motor. 'They're shooting at us,' he said.

'For God's sake, why?'

'Because Vandenberg and Callard think Tillotson's aboard this machine . . .'

To escape the gunfire Beaumont was ascending vertically as the altimeter needle climbed. In the pale glowing night there was no sign of another helicopter: Tillotson had vanished again. Beaumont turned east, the direction he assumed Crocodile would take. 'And who is Callard?' Grayson asked.

'The FBI man who came up here to arrest Tillotson. Everything was beautifully laid on – the alert you mentioned put into operation just before the Boeing landed – which sealed off the base. Callard gets off the plane, drives to the camp with Col. Vandenberg, then when Tillotson arrives they confront him.' Beaumont was maintaining an easterly course as he peered ahead: nothing but the flattened-out icecap in view. 'Nice and neat, Mr Callard's plan,' Beaumont went on. 'It merely failed to take account of Crocodile.'

'What happened?'

'I imagine Tillotson had a vague notion they might be on to him – he was the security chief, remember. Then he'd wonder about the alert. Next thing he finds out from the pilot that Callard came aboard at Washington at the last minute – without anyone telling Tillotson. So he decides it's time to catch the first plane out – I don't think anyone else suspected he knew how to pilot a Sikorsky . . .'

'Over there! To the north . . .' Grayson pointed and Beaumont looked to his left. More icecap, desolate, cold, hideously barren. Then he saw it. Tillotson's machine was, at a guess, ten miles away. A shadow, a swift-moving blip of darkness scudding over the snow. Seconds later he saw the machine which was casting the shadow. He began to change direction.

'Why may our lives depend on stopping Tillotson?' Grayson asked quietly.

Beaumont grunted as he aimed his machine along the same course Tillotson was following. 'This could be a savage one, Sam, so you don't have to come. We have to lift a Soviet scientist out of Target-5. He's coming across the ice from North Pole 17 – that's about twenty-five miles east across the pack from Target-5 at the moment. We go in if fog closes Target-5 and they can't send a plane in. It means going by chopper with sleds aboard to the edge of the fog, then it's sledding the rest of the way.'

'And sledding back – all the way to Greenland?'

'I think so. Dawes doesn't – he hopes to pick us up again when we come out of the fog. I don't think they'll find us – so we'll have to sled all the way back to the coast. At least that's the official version – I've got another idea. And the Russian security forces will be on our tails. A very savage one, Sam.'

'But there's no fog.'

'So we just sit around eating American Army rations. The key date could be Sunday – tomorrow. I've arranged for two Sikorskys to be ready for us at Curtis Field on the Greenland coast.'

'Tillotson's heading due north,' Grayson commented.

The American was using a pair of night-glasses he had found in the cabin and the shadow of the Soviet agent's machine was still more visible than the machine itself. Without that shadow, Grayson reckoned they would have lost him. Beaumont glanced at the compass. Due north as Sam had said.

'I think he's heading for the Humboldt Glacier,' Beaumont replied. 'I wonder why? If he'd gone due east he'd have made the coast – they keep these machines tanked up when they're on the ground so there'd be enough fuel. What the devil can there be for him on the Humboldt Glacier?'

'Why is he so important?' Grayson asked again.

'Because he knows too much about us,' Beaumont said tersely. 'He doesn't know about Gorov – the man we have to lift out. No one up here knew about him until I arrived. But he does know about the preparations for a trip. He knows Curtis Field is involved – the nearest airfield to Target-5. He had to know that because we needed those machines sending there. I'm just hoping to God he hasn't got a transmitter hidden away up here – that if we don't get to him in time he'll transmit to Leningrad. If that happens,

Sam, none of us will qualify as very good insurance risks.'

The awesome sight of the Humboldt Glacier unfolded itself as they flew closer. From high up on the icecap a massive river of ice stretched down to a fiord far below, a half-mile-wide river of ice glistening like a sheet of fractured crystal in the moonlight. It sheered down from the icecap until it reached an icefall where it plunged over a monstrous cliff down to the fiord hundreds of feet below. As they came closer they could see, at the bottom of the steep-sided fiord, great icebergs marooned on the snowbound foreshore. Tillotson's Sikorsky had already landed, was perched on a knoll at the side of the glacier. For the third time Tillotson had vanished.

'He's the bloody invisible man,' Beaumont grumbled as he circled above the stationary helicopter.

'Maybe he's still inside his machine – he waits for us to land and then starts shooting before we can get out,' Grayson suggested shrewdly.

'Maybe . . .' Beaumont continued circling at about two hundred feet. It made him almost dizzy to look down the sheer side of the glacier, and then he banked the machine slightly. 'He's down there! See that smaller knoll further down the glacier – look, you can see him moving now.'

'Land on that knoll.'

'Too small – we could go over the edge. I'm

bringing us down alongside Tillotson's machine, then he can't get away. You stay with it in case he gives me the slip – and keep trying to raise Thule.'

Five times Grayson had used the radio to try and get through and five times he had failed. 'Damned thing never works when you need it,' Beaumont had commented. He hovered the machine, dropped it slowly and landed on the knoll fifty yards away from the stationary machine. It had a dead look, as though Tillotson never expected to return to it. He switched off his motor. 'I should be back in an hour, Sam,' he said casually as he put on his parka with difficulty.

Grayson nodded, knowing that if Tillotson was armed with a rifle the Englishman could be dead in a good deal less than an hour. But in the long dangerous trip to Spitsbergen the three men – Beaumont, Grayson and Horst Langer – had learned never to waste words or energy. You just got on with the next job. And Beaumont's next job was capturing or eliminating Tillotson.

The atmosphere inside the cabin was very warm and he tensed himself as he opened the door and picked up the carbine. The temperature dropped – from forty above to forty below. 'Get on with it,' Beaumont muttered to himself. He dropped out of the machine and the iron-hard ground hit his feet like a blow from a hammer. The paralysing cold choked him. He fastened the parka up to his neck, pulled the hood over his head. Behind him Grayson slammed the door shut quickly without so much as a word of farewell. Again no wasted words. Above him the blades had stopped whirling and an incredible silence descended, the silence of the Arctic night.

He tried to take short breaths as he trudged past Tillotson's Sikorsky to the edge of the knoll, then he stood looking down the vast sweep of the glacier slope. The second knoll further down the glacier was clearly visible in the moonlight, a small cap of rock surmounted by a crude wooden cross. Tillotson was stooping over something perched on an Eskimo grave, a sacred place in Greenland which couldn't be disturbed under any circumstances by edict of the Danish authorities. The something was a box-like object with a small mast protruding above it. Beaumont's face tightened: Tillotson did have a transmitter.

The rock side above the glacier was too steep to make his way down, so he was forced on to the glacier itself. Tentatively, he began moving down the ice with the carbine trailed in his hand: the light was too difficult to try a shot at this range. He found the surface horribly treacherous and it was rather like climbing down the side of a skating rink inclined at an angle, a skating rink corrugated with ridges and gullies. His rubber-soled shoes were not ideal footwear and he was worried that if he started to slide he might never stop before he reached the brink of the icefall. Grimly, he kept moving as fast as he dared because Tillotson might already be transmitting. And the Soviet agent, hidden behind the knoll, was completely out of sight now.

Lower down it became much more dangerous because frequently the glacier was split open, exposing crevasses of unknown depth, dark gashes which disappeared in the shadows. He had to move more slowly, using the carbine as an improvised support, treading from one rib of ice to another, crossing the narrow crevasses between. And all the time he was waiting for the first slither. The intense cold didn't help: Beaumont, whose resistance to low temperatures was phenomenal, probably because of his boyhood spent at Coppermine, wasn't properly clothed for Arctic work. The cold was penetrating his gloves, infiltrating his parka, creeping up his legs.

He was very close to the knoll, no longer using the carbine as a support, holding the weapon ready for instant use, when he looked up for the third time in a minute. Tillotson had appeared from the far side of the knoll, a tall fur-clad figure holding something in his right hand. Perched about twenty feet above the Englishman, Tillotson whipped back his hand in a throwing position. For one terrible, drawn-out moment Beaumont thought he was hurling a grenade. He jerked up the carbine and then the missile was hurtling towards him. It hit the ice, bounced, ricocheted. A rock. The realization flashed through Beaumont's mind that Tillotson no longer had a gun.

The aim was astonishingly good – or damned lucky. The rock ricocheted off the ice, flew towards Beaumont's right leg. He jumped sideways, the rock missed him, then he was off-balance, falling, sliding down the glacier like a toboggan, rushing towards the icefall brink.

The carbine was gone, slithering away under its own momentum, preceding him over the icefall brink as Beaumont, tobogganning on his stomach, desperately tried to halt the slide, to grab for any projection, to ram his foot in a gully. And all the time as the bitter air hit his face and the glacier whipped past under him he was expecting to halt, to go down instead of forward, to drop inside a crevasse. The slide went on, he was shooting over the ice down a smooth slope of polished surface tilted at an angle of thirty degrees. The parka saved his body from the friction and the grazing, but he was still plunging downwards at increasing speed. His gloves hammered at the ice, the toes of his shoes pressed in hard, but he couldn't stop the diabolical momentum.

The brink of the icefall, a hard line with nothing beyond it – nothing but a sheer drop of hundreds of feet – rushed towards him, and he still couldn't slow down, let alone stop. He was in a perfect position to swallow-dive over the abyss. He rammed his forearms down hard, reached the brink, was going over. Endless space, depth, yawned below him – and something spiky. His left arm felt the boulder, a rock embedded in the glacier.

It was pure reflex – his arm crooked, got a hold on the rock. The brief anchor point merely served as a fulcrum to shoot him over the drop. His prone body swivelled to the left, went over the brink. His left hand felt a projection on the rock, his gloved fingers closed, held on. The weight of his body, the momentum, nearly tore his arm off, or so it felt. Then he was still, hanging over the drop, held by only one hand, one curved arm, his body suspended in space.

Below he caught a brief glimpse of nothing, of the sheer ice cliff going down and down, at the bottom the splay of the glacier, huge spiked ice pinnacles. He made himself look up, concentrated his remaining energy on holding on, on levering himself back up over the brink. He wrapped his right arm round the boulder, felt his exploring fingers contact his other hand. He clamped one hand over the other. Only then did he look up the glacier past the boulder. Tillotson was coming down the glacier.

It was terribly silent – except for the crunch of spiked boots driving into the ice. Beaumont's face twisted: Tillotson was wearing crampon boots, which made his descent much safer. Where the devil had he got hold of them? He must have had the boots ready in the jeep, must have planned his departure from Thule even before the Boeing 707 had landed. And it was going to take the American less than half a minute to reach him. Too late to try and clamber back over the edge. Beaumont was having trouble with his vision now – the oncoming Tillotson looked like two men. Beaumont blinked. The vision dissolved into one man, a man with a knife in his right hand. Tillotson was very close when Beaumont's head flopped, when his right hand lost its grip.

Beaumont's right arm went limp, flopped out of sight behind the boulder. The strain on his left arm was appalling, almost unbearable, and under the parka his clothes were clammy with sweat. Tillotson paused about three feet from the boulder, decided he couldn't reach with the knife. Taking two more careful paces, he lowered himself to a sitting position behind the rock, raised his right foot, aimed the crampon spikes at the Englishman's left hand. The spikes were half an inch long, rimed with ice from the glacier. He lunged to spike the gloved hand.

As he drove the boot down hard Beaumont's right hand whipped up over the boulder, locked round Tillotson's ankle, heaved savagely sideways. The spikes grazed Beaumont's other hand as Tillotson lost his balance. He started sliding. His body skidded round the far side of the boulder, his hands flailed desperately for something to grip on. His fingers clutched the boulder, gained a hold, and he thought he had saved himself. Beaumont's right hand struck again, struck this time as a clubbed fist, smashing down with brutal force on the bridge of the American's nose. Tillotson yelped, lost his grip, went over. The scream travelled back up the icefall, a long-drawn-out scream which ended abruptly. Beaumont began hauling himself back over the edge.

He collapsed when he reached the far side of the boulder, still conscious but hardly able to move as he propped himself against the rock and massaged his left arm slowly. Clambering to his knees, he peered over the boulder into the depths. Tillotson had died in a macabre way – his body was perched at the summit of one of the numerous ice pinnacles, speared through his middle.

'You can fly us back, Sam.'

Beaumont sagged in the observer's seat as Grayson watched him. 'He did have a radio transmitter,' he went on, 'a pretty powerful one. Made by Radio Corporation of America, of course, in case anyone found it. Not that it was likely – he had it hidden in an Eskimo grave and no one goes poking about in that. We'd better get started,' he added. 'Vandenberg can send someone to collect the transmitter.'

'Had he transmitted?' Grayson asked.

'He transmitted something, I'm sure. He may not have had all that much time, the message could have been garbled – he must have encoded it before he left Thule.'

'Probably we'll never know.'

Beaumont looked at Grayson. 'Probably we will know – when the Russian security people are waiting to meet us out on the ice.'

Chapter Five

Saturday, 19 February

'I know why Winthrop came to Leningrad. I can see clear down to the bottom of your large empty hole, Kramer!'

At eight o'clock on Saturday night – eight hours before Michael Gorov planned to escape from North Pole 17 – Papanin was still in his office. The room was like an inferno, the green-tiled stove was roasting the office – and its occupants. The Siberian loved extremes of temperature, had loved them since his childhood in Omsk when the terrible winter cold stimulated him while it obliterated everyone else, but then he had also luxuriated in the warmth of Siberian stoves when he came indoors. Kramer, on the other hand, was gasping for air.

'I don't see why you're suddenly interested in Michael Gorov,' he said hoarsely. 'Why should he be mixed up in this Jewish business?'

'Like the rest of them, you'll see it next year. That's why I'm sitting in this chair – because I can see things before they happen.' Papanin leaned back in the chair, put his hands behind his neck. 'It was the shipping list which tipped me off.'

'You mean the deputy mate, Peter Gorov?'

'You'll see down this hole yet.' Papanin regarded the Balt with an unblinking stare. 'If you don't fall head first into it. Do you remember the case of Rachel Levitzer, that Jewish girl who made a run for it last August and fell down a staircase?'

'She broke her neck . . .'

'She also broke Michael Gorov's heart. Did you know that?'

'I heard a rumour . . .'

'It was hushed up – their relationship – because of the position Michael Gorov occupies. We've been looking for a grubby little courier bringing in large sums from America – someone who might at any time be searched at the airport when he comes in. I think they've been cleverer than that . . .' Papanin paused to give his bombshell maximum impact. 'I think Michael Gorov, our eminent oceanographer, is bringing in the money.'

Kramer was astounded, appalled. He stared back at Papanin, trying to guess what he was up to, always an impossible task. 'You can't mean it,' he said eventually. 'Where would he get the money from?'

'That's the clever part! He spent three years in the Arctic planning and laying the Catherine system of cables and sonar buoys along the seabed. He often visited American ice islands to see what they were up to.' Papanin hammered his huge fist down on the desk. 'And that's when they gave him the money to bring in – during those visits to American bases! He's never been searched when he came back – no one would dream of it.'

'But why?' Kramer was bewildered. 'Why would he do it?'

'That damned Jewish mistress of his persuaded him. He was going with her for three years before she died – and he's still doing it, for the sake of her memory or some such lunatic sentiment!'

'It's fantastic . . .'

'It's logical!' Papanin shouted. 'He met his brother, the deputy mate, Peter, in Kiev this month while they were both on leave. Peter comes back here to board his ship – and on the way he meets this American, Winthrop, in the park. He was passing a verbal message to Winthrop – from his brother, Michael.'

'We'll have to be careful,' Kramer warned. 'Michael Gorov is a friend of Marshal Grechko.'*

'Grechko is an arrogant hog. If I'm right about Gorov you'll find that Grechko hardly knew him.'

'It's still dangerous . . .'

'Maybe, but there's someone else we can get at – Peter Gorov, a mere seaman. You found out the present position of the *Girolog*?'

'She's five hours' sailing time from Tallinn . . .'

'Send a plane immediately to Tallinn airport to wait for Gorov. Radio the ship's master to sail straight for Tallinn. Five hours to port, half an hour to and from airports at either end, one's hour's flight to here. Peter

* *Soviet Minister of Defence.*

75

Gorov should be in my office in seven hours' time – by three o'clock Sunday morning! What are you hanging about for, Kramer?'

Alone again in his overheated office, Papanin took out his little pocket chess set and stared at the board. The Siberian, a man of many talents, was a Soviet grandmaster of chess. In July he would be in Iceland for the coming Spassky–Fischer chess match. Officially he would attend as one of Spassky's advisers; unofficially he would be chief Soviet representative to keep an eye on security.

Outwardly a flamboyant and extrovert personality, Igor Papanin had a cold, detached brain which regarded the whole Arctic as a gigantic chess board. There were Soviet pieces and American pieces on the board and in any contest of wills you had to get the opening gambit right. Curiously enough, considering the role Keith Beaumont was to play in the coming battle of wills, the Siberian was studying the English Opening.

'A message has just come through from Crocodile.'

Kramer reported the news casually when he came back into the Siberian's office half an hour later, as though it were of no great importance. 'They are just decoding it,' he added. He paused as Papanin went on reading the personal file on Michael Gorov.

'Anything else?' Papanin grunted without looking up.

'Who is Crocodile?'

'A person. Identity known only to General Syrtov and myself.' Having delivered the snub, Papanin looked up. 'I want to see that message the moment it's decoded.'

It was 9 PM before Kramer returned with the message. The *Girolog* had already changed course and was heading slowly south through the ice for the port of Tallinn. The plane Kramer had sent was due to land at Tallinn airport within ten minutes.

In Washington, where they were eight hours behind Leningrad, Dawes and Adams were waiting with growing impatience for a signal from a man who was dead. In Greenland, also eight hours behind Leningrad, Beaumont and Grayson were flying back to Thule from the Humboldt Glacier. One message – from Winthrop – would never arrive. Another signal – from Tillotson – was just being handed to Papanin.

'They had trouble with it,' Kramer explained. 'It's rather garbled. The operator says it was transmitted very erratically and he's sure it isn't complete.'

Papanin read the message. 'What a brilliant deduction,' he commented. He stroked the top of his close-shaven head while he read the message a second time. *Americans preparing ... over polar pack ... general area Target-5 ... Beaumont going in over ice to meet target ... American planes Curtis Field ... Beaumont force ...*

Without a word the Siberian stood up, strode out of his room into the office next door where the American teleprinter was still chattering away, spewing out a stream of reports from Soviet bases spread out across the Arctic. Behind chromium-leg desks four men were working away on reports and answering telephones. Papanin took a small curved pipe from his tunic pocket and started filling it from an old pouch as he stared up at the wall map.

It was not unlike the huge wall map in Gen. Dawes's office, but here the Arctic was seen from a different angle: the Russian coast low down, near the floor, the distant coasts of Greenland and Canada and Alaska high up near the ceiling. 'There is Curtis Field,' he said to Kramer, pointing with his pipe-stem to the airfield on the Greenland coast nearest to Target-5. He called to one of the men behind the desks. 'Petrov, fill me in on the position of the ships in this area . . .'

'The trawler fleet k49, sir?'

'That will do for a start.'

'As you see, it's a long way north of Iceland at the moment, but it's heading south now – to watch the NATO sea exercise *Sea Lion*. There are twelve ships – all equipped with the normal electronic gear . . .'

'Including wireless-jamming apparatus?'

'Yes, sir. The helicopter carrier *Gorki* west of Spitsbergen has also turned south with the same mission . . .'

'What about the *Revolution*? It's the closest vessel to Iceberg Alley.'

'She'll be there for several weeks – she's tracking American satellites.'

'This American vessel . . .' Papanin's pipe-stem stabbed at a marker higher up.

'The American icebreaker *Elroy*, sir. We've just moved her position, less than an hour ago. She was heading south and now she's turned due north again – a helicopter from the *Gorki* saw her.'

'Thank you.' Papanin was always polite to junior members of his staff: the more senior men like Kramer could look after themselves. He marched straight back inside his office and went behind his desk. His normally explosive manner had gone and when he issued the dramatic order to the Balt his voice was quiet and calm.

'Order a state of alert throughout the entire Arctic Zone. Every coastal base, every airfield, every ice island – including those off the Alaska coast. Radio Murmansk that I want a Bison bomber standing by night and day, fully tanked up. Warn Leningrad airport to have a plane ready to fly me to Murmansk at one hour's notice . . .'

'I clear this with Moscow first, of course . . .'

'Send Vronsky and his special security detachment to Murmansk – they must be in the air in thirty minutes . . .'

'Surely we must refer this to Moscow?'

'The detachment will wear civilian clothes and will be fully armed with personal weapons. Bring me the latest met reports of the Target-5 area . . .'

'Without reference to Moscow, sir? Operations on this scale need General Syrtov's approval.'

Papanin removed the pipe he had just placed in his wide mouth. 'You don't understand any of this, do you, Comrade? You can't stand the pressure of having two large holes to look into at the same time, can you?'

'Crocodile's message doesn't make sense . . .'

'It does, if you know Crocodile. The Americans are planning some big operation near their floating base, Target-5. They are using the code-word Beaumont for the operation. We have to get in our opening gambit first.'

'You still want Peter Gorov brought here from Tallinn?'

'Of course.' Papanin relit his pipe, watching Kramer. 'That is a separate problem. And now,' he went on without any change of tone, 'get the bloody lead out of your boots.'

Curtis Field stands on top of a three-hundred-foot-high cliff rising sheer from the east Greenland coast. It is debatable whether flying in or out is the more chilling experience – but probably the latter is worse. The plane takes off along a runway which ends at the brink of a cliff; as Beaumont put it, 'When you see nothing ahead you'll go either up or down . . .'

At nine in the evening of Saturday, Washington time, Beaumont was ready to go, a feat of organization which was little short of miraculous. In the past sixteen hours he had flown from Washington to Thule;

in pursuit of Tillotson he had flown to the Humboldt Glacier and back again; since then he had flown the breadth of Greenland to Curtis Field. And by nine in the evening everything was ready – and Curtis Field knew that a whirlwind had hit them.

'I need those two Sikorskys fully serviced, fully tanked up within two hours . . .'

'Not possible,' Fuller, the airfield controller had snapped.

'Put more men on the job! Do I have to phone Dawes in Washington? It's your damned emergency . . .'

The helicopters were ready to fly by 9.05 PM. A plane had flown out to check weather conditions near Target-5 – and came back to report no sign of fog. The two Eskimo-type sleds had been brought from Camp Century, had been packed with food, a powerful radio transceiver, rifles, ammunition – and an Elliott homing beacon.

'What's that for?' Fuller had asked.

'Insurance.'

Beaumont's reply had been abrupt and totally noninformative. Restlessly, he had prowled round the hangar where icicles hung from the girders, poking his nose into everything, checking the controls of a Sikorsky, giving a hand with packing the sleds, frequently striding into the radio room to ask whether a message had come in from Washington. His energy, which seemed boundless, injected urgency into the airfield staff, made them work twice as fast as normal.

Had Col. Igor Papanin been able to witness the performance it would have made him thoughtful.

But Beaumont would never have achieved the impossible without the aid of the short, wiry, thirty-five-year-old American, Sam Grayson. It was Grayson who spent nerve-racking hours on the phone calling Thule, the huge American air base at the top of Baffin Bay. 'I want those dogs sent here now. No plane available? Only a Hercules just taking off for Point Barrow? Then drag yourself out of that armchair and stop it. Listen! If it takes off I'll get on to Dawes and have it turned round in mid-air . . .'

'Those dogs were due here one hour ago,' Beaumont rumbled behind him.

Grayson twisted round in his seat. 'Keith, do you want them now or when they arrive?' he demanded.

Beaumont grinned bleakly. 'Both – and sooner!'

Most Arctic teams function in one of two ways. A British team has a leader and the rest do what he tells them to; other nationalities work differently – Americans and Norwegians work democratically, they exchange opinions. Beaumont's three-man team was unique. As he put it with a dry smile, 'They do what I tell them because they know I'm right.' Grayson's version was different. 'In a crisis we follow Beaumont, then argue it afterwards.' Horst Langer's version was different again. 'We have three bosses – and it works. Don't ask me how!'

Sam Grayson, brilliant navigator, marine biologist, and a first-rate marksman, came from Minneapolis.

Before going with Beaumont and Langer on the epic Spitsbergen crossing he worked for the US Geological Survey and the Lamont Geological Observatory of Columbia University. An old Arctic hand, he assured his wife before each trip, 'Maybe this will be my last crack at the ice – could be I'm getting sick of it . . .' That was until the next trip came up.

'The dogs just came in,' he informed Beaumont two hours after calling Thule.

'Horst had better check them right away . . .'

Beaumont swung round as the third member of the team, Horst Langer, came into the tiny room Grayson was using as his headquarters. 'The dogs are here – and what's that sinister bit of paper you're waving about?'

'An urgent signal just came through from Dawes – we're to stand by ready for instant departure.'

Because it was unprecedented the depression caught all the met experts off balance, the vast filling depression gathering over northern Greenland in late February 1972. This was the depression which affected the whole of north America and western Europe later in the year, which turned summer into something like winter, which sent icebergs further south than they had ever reached before, which invaded transatlantic shipping lanes and caused great liners to change course. And this was the depression which brought the fog.

The Soviet met people on Novaya Zemlya didn't see it coming. The US weather plane which flies daily across the roof of the world from Mildenhall in East Anglia to Alaska missed it. The US Weather Bureau failed to foresee it. But as Beaumont prowled restlessly round the ice-cold hangar at Curtis Field a great bank of fog, half a mile high, many miles wide, a bank of freezing black fog appeared north of Target-5 and began to drift steadily south.

Chapter Six

Sunday, 20 February

You can only die once, but sometimes it seems you are dying a hundred times over.

For Peter Gorov the flight from Tallinn to Leningrad was a nightmare. No one would give him a reason for his recall, no one would tell him who he was going to see in Leningrad, but he was treated like royalty when he disembarked from the *Girolog* at one in the morning.

A black Zil limousine with chains on the wheels took him through a snowstorm to the airport. When he went aboard the waiting plane the two pilots shook hands with him. He was invited to travel in the control cabin and was given a seat behind the co-pilot. The nightmare started from the moment the plane moved off down the runway.

It almost crashed as it was taking off – they were heading direct for the airport control tower, still on the ground, when the co-pilot shouted, 'You'll never make it!' He threw up a hand as though to ward off the collision when metal struck steel, then the pilot lifted the machine and it cleared the tower by feet, or so it seemed to the petrified Gorov.

But this was only the beginning. As the plane gained altitude and turned east away from the ice-laden Baltic, a fierce, long-drawn argument broke out between the two pilots, each accusing the other. 'You fool, Serge, there was not enough power . . .'

'Idiot! There was too much power! Would you sooner take over yourself?'

The argument raged on, the technical terms beyond Gorov. The plane suddenly side-slipped, started to drop at an alarming rate. With an oath the pilot regained control, then continued arguing at the top of his voice. Gorov watched from behind fearfully: it seemed they were more intent on their quarrel than on flying the plane. His fear was intensified when the machine climbed abruptly, heading up at an acute angle. Pressed back against his seat, Gorov was terrified. It was his first experience of flying. Halfway to Leningrad they began drinking.

The quarrel subsided suddenly and the pilots made it up with each other with a bottle of vodka. But their consideration for their honoured guest stopped short of offering him a drink; instead they emptied the bottle themselves. Gorov watched with growing horror as the effect of the vodka made itself felt in their flying performance. The machine was thrown all over the sky as they fell like a lift into air pockets, then shot upwards at an almost vertical angle. 'The met report was terrible,' Serge explained in a slurred voice. 'If you hadn't been so important we wouldn't have flown.'

'Important to who?' asked the bewildered seaman.

'Maybe the First Secretary. How the hell would I know?'

Twice Gorov had to move swiftly to the small, cramped toilet where he was violently ill, but when he returned to his seat after the second visit his head was clearer for a few minutes. He calculated roughly that wherever they were taking him to in Leningrad he would arrive about three in the morning. It would then be eleven in the evening at North Pole 17, which was four hours behind Leningrad time. He was sure now that they had found out about the American, that they were going to question him. He had to hold out until after midnight, North Pole 17 time, which was four in the morning in Leningrad. He would have to hold out for over an hour.

As they came in to land at Leningrad his stomach muscles felt tighter than the strap which Serge ordered him to fasten. They were gliding down through the snow when the first motor cut out. Seconds later the second engine failed. Could they land on only two engines? Gorov had no idea. The pilot spoke to airport control with a note of hysteria. 'Emergency situation, emergency situation . . .'

Gorov closed his eyes, felt his head starting to spin, opened them and saw the glare of the landing lights coming up. The plane wobbled badly. The co-pilot cursed, waved the empty vodka bottle at Serge. 'You're coming in too fast . . . you're going to kill us . . .' Gorov sat in his seat bathed in sweat, unable to take his eyes off the incoming lights which tilted as the plane wobbled. His clothes were soaked but his mouth was parched, his throat constricted. They were drunk, both of them, the criminals. He was going to burn to death, horribly.

At the last moment the two dead motors burst into action, the wheels bumped the runway, the machine cruised between the lights, made a perfect landing. The pilots waited until Gorov had disembarked without speaking to them, then Serge burst into laughter as he waved the empty bottle. 'I don't like mineral water – next time ask them to put the real stuff in it . . .'

Gorov would never know it, but he had been flown to Leningrad by the two most experienced pilots in the Baltic Command. They were probably the only men who could have handled the plane in such an appalling manner and survived. It was Papanin himself who had phoned the airport controller at Tallinn and given him the instructions. 'I want you to play a little game with your passenger – scare the guts out of him. When he lands he must be a jelly.'

The man in the chair was sweating and the spotlight shining on his face reflected off the sweat globules. Fear – and the green-tiled stove – were responsible. Papanin sat behind his desk in the gloom. The other men were shadows behind the chair, unnerving presences Peter Gorov couldn't see. One of them coughed

– to remind Gorov he was there. The watch on Gorov's left wrist registered 3.20 AM.

Papanin, who was completely on the wrong track, who still believed he was close to identifying the money courier financing the Jewish underground – whereas Michael Gorov had never had the slightest connection with that shadowy organization – had exactly forty minutes left to break Gorov. In forty minutes it would be 4 AM in Leningrad and only midnight at North Pole 17. In forty minutes Michael Gorov would have disappeared on to the polar pack.

'We'll go over it again,' Papanin said. 'Just to make sure I've got it right. Start with when you went into the park.'

Go over it again ... Gorov's head was reeling. He had been driven from the airport in a battered old Volga. Kramer had made him travel without his coat and with the windows open, so during the drive Gorov had become steadily frozen. It was a detail which Papanin had planned: sudden violent changes of temperature reduce a man's resistance. He had visualized the overheated control cabin in the plane, had frozen Gorov during the journey from the airport, now he was roasting him again. Gorov's stomach was empty, his nerves shattered, and he could hardly think straight as Papanin repeated, 'Go over it again.'

Gorov had lost count of how many times he had explained it. He tried to repeat it as a catechism as the heat of the stove burned his back. 'I went into the park ...'

'Why?'

'I was on my way to the docks.'

'So you went straight along the Nevsky Prospekt – it's the direct route.'

'I went along the Nevsky Prospekt . . .' The voice was a monotone, like a child repeating its rote.

'You didn't – you went into the park. Why?'

They came to the part where the pedestrian had tripped on the ice, and Papanin went on asking the same questions he had asked ever since Gorov had come in. 'We want to know his name,' the Siberian repeated. 'That's what it's all about. We want to know his name.'

'I don't know the American's name . . .'

Gorov stopped speaking. He knew instantly that he had made a fatal blunder. Papanin let him sweat it out for a minute. They hadn't said anything to Gorov about Winthrop being American, and Winthrop had worn clothes which made him look like a Russian. And Winthrop hadn't spoken to the seaman: Gorov had stated this time and again. 'Take him downstairs,' Papanin said, and then waited until he was alone with Kramer. 'Find out what he knows – quickly.'

Because their suspect was a seaman, and because a seaman's nightmare is drowning, they used the water treatment.

In the basement cellar – which was as cold as

Papanin's room had been torrid – they strapped Gorov to an adjustable couch and blindfolded him. He was stretched prone on his back, strapped by his neck and his wrists and his legs to the couch. Somewhere out of sight water slopped in a container. 'What message did the American pass you?' Kramer asked.

'No message . . .'

One man gripped Gorov's jaw, another man thrust a huge rubber funnel into Gorov's mouth, the third man started pouring water down the funnel. The choking sensation began immediately, the drowning sensation came later. On a stool beside his patient, a doctor sat with a stethoscope pressed against Gorov's naked chest.

For Gorov, flat on his back, blindfolded and unable to move, the world was water – water flooding into his mouth, water pouring down his throat, water surging into his lungs. Desperately he tried to lift his arms, his chest, to hold his breath, and then he was spluttering, choking, retching painfully, and his whole body seemed to swell up, to be on the point of bursting. His eyes bulged, his neck muscles tautened, collapsed. He tried to scream and the scream was strangled and he knew he was dying, drowning. They kept on pouring in water until the doctor looked quickly at Kramer. The Balt nodded. A foot pedal under the couch was pressed and hands lifted the rear of the couch swiftly, elevating Gorov to a sitting position. The seaman choked, spewed, gasped for air.

Then he lolled, head down, panting irregularly. Kramer pulled up the blindfold, lifted Gorov's head under the chin.

'What message did the American pass to you?'

Blurred eyes stared back at Kramer, eyes full of hate. He tried to speak twice, looked down at his left wrist, and twice only a hoarse crackle emerged, a hardly human sound. They had taken away his wristwatch. For Gorov this was the worst ordeal: now he had no idea of the time, nothing to tell him how long he must hold out. The third time he managed to get the words out, glaring at Kramer. 'No message . . .' Eyes full of hate, the Balt noted, so resistance was high. It would take half an hour, he estimated, maybe less. When the hate vanished, was replaced by agony, they would be getting somewhere. He nodded and they renewed the treatment. Gorov guessed that a good twenty minutes had gone. In fact, it was less than five minutes since they had brought him to the cellar.

The Locomotive moved into action, driving people as though he had only got up an hour ago – whereas in fact he had been twenty-two hours without sleep. It was not the information which Kramer burst into his room with which generated this explosive activity, and once again he deflated the fat Balt.

'Michael Gorov is defecting to the Americans . . .'

'It took you two hours, Kramer.' Papanin looked at the clock on the wall which registered 5.30 AM. 'That deputy mate is a courageous man – and you're too late with your news – this signal has just come in from North Pole 17.' He handed the signal form to the Balt who was already sweating from the temperature change as he read it. *Michael Gorov left North Pole 17 with dog team midnight. Security man Marov found dead on the ice. Search parties have been sent out. Please advise. Minsky.*

It took Papanin less than a minute to scribble a reply in his own hand which Petrov rushed to the signals room. *Send all available helicopters further west than Gorov can have gone. Then sweep back towards North Pole 17. Report immediately any signs of American activity near Target-5. Papanin.*

He ordered Kramer to contact Murmansk, to check that the Bison bomber was ready for instant departure, to confirm with Leningrad airport that a plane was standing by, to signal trawler fleet k49 and the *Revolution*, requesting information on any American activity in the area, to signal the helicopter carrier *Gorki* asking for an immediate check on the present position of the American icebreaker *Elroy*.

He phoned General Boris Syrtov, chief of Special Security in Moscow, not caring whether he dragged him from his bed at 5.30 AM, but Syrtov had been on the verge of calling the Siberian and the conversation opened with a battle.

'Papanin!' Syrtov's tone was sharp. 'Murmansk tells me you have ordered an Arctic alert. It isn't true, of course?'

'It is true, General . . .'

'Without my authority?'

'It was a precaution . . .'

'Brezhnev has heard about it – I have to go to the Kremlin at once.'

'Good . . .'

'What did you say?' Syrtov roared.

'The precaution was justified,' Papanin snapped. He fired his big gun. 'Michael Gorov has fled across the ice . . . He's taking more than his brains to the Americans. I've just found out he spent two hours inside the security room while I was away in Moscow – I think he photographed the Catherine charts. He's taking them a blueprint of our entire underwater system.'

Syrtov's anger collapsed, was replaced by chronic anxiety. He asked what resources Papanin needed – and the answer staggered him.

'Personal control of the carrier *Gorki*, trawler fleet k49, and the research ship *Revolution* . . .'

'You know that's unprecedented.'

'It's an unprecedented situation. The First Secretary can sanction it – which is why I'm glad you're going to see him.'

'I'll come back to you,' Syrtov said tersely. 'Meantime continue your preparations.'

'I've made them – including ordering an alert nine

94

hours ago without your authority, which has gained us nine hours of invaluable time . . .' Papanin heard the click of the receiver at the Moscow end with satisfaction. He looked up as Kramer came in, eager for news. 'Pack your hot-water bottle, Kramer – we'll be in the Arctic within twenty-four hours.'

At precisely one o'clock on Sunday morning in Washington Lemuel Dawes switched on the light over the camp bed he had set up in his office and checked the time. As usual, his internal alarm clock had woken him punctually. And he had a headache, which was hardly surprising – the heat, the lack of air and the tropical plants banked up against two walls were building an atmosphere which could only be described as nauseous. Ten minutes later Adams knocked on his door and came in.

'No news from Helsinki,' he said grimly. 'But the plane might have been delayed – he may still get through.'

'So we wait?'

'We wait . . .'

'Which could be a mistake.' Dawes scratched at his rumpled hair. 'But we can't do a damned thing about it. Gorov could be on the ice already, we could fly a plane into Target-5 now, but I daren't do it – if Gorov hasn't left yet any sign of unusual activity at Target-5 could alert the Russians.'

So while Beaumont was climbing the walls at

distant Curtis Field at the edge of the Greenland icecap, while Dawes waited for a signal from a man who had died forty hours earlier, Col. Papanin's far-reaching preparations were gaining momentum and looked like winning him the game before it had even started.

Leonid Brezhnev, First Secretary of the Communist Party of the Union of Soviet Socialist Republics, walked briskly into Col. Papanin's office at noon on Sunday accompanied by General Boris Syrtov.

As always, when he removed his fur coat Brezhnev was smartly dressed in a dark business suit, his thick hair was neatly brushed, and in Detroit he could easily have been taken for a Ford executive. No one helped him to disrobe; the First Secretary intensely disliked fuss. And as always he came straight to the point.

'Papanin, you have control of six vessels of the trawler fleet, the helicopter carrier *Gorki* and the research ship *Revolution*. None of these will make it look like a military operation – they are civilian vessels, so to speak. You see the point?'

'There must be no international incident.'

'No international incident,' Brezhnev agreed. 'In May the American President is coming to Moscow for a summit meeting and I want him to come – so be careful.'

'But there could be an international accident,'

Papanin said bluntly. 'I know that area – anything can happen there. Men can fall into an open lead, they can get lost for ever in a blizzard . . .'

Brezhnev held up a well-kept hand. 'No details, please! There is, I agree, a world of difference between an incident and an accident – that is your sphere.' His thick eyebrows lifted as he spoke with great emphasis. 'But you must bring back Gorov – neither he nor the Catherine charts must ever reach Washington. I have flown here personally to stress how vital this thing is.'

'We are three moves ahead of the Americans already,' Papanin replied. 'That's what counts . . .'

'But we must keep ahead of them.' Brezhnev glanced at Syrtov, a small, lean-faced man with irritable eyes who was holding a leather folder. 'The general has the codes and wavelengths for you to communicate with these ships. They have already been ordered to proceed to the area involved.'

'I'd like to leave at once,' Papanin took the folder from Syrtov. 'I think we may just be in time . . .'

Brezhnev grasped the Siberian's arm. 'Igor, you have to be in time. You have to be.'

It was 3 PM in Murmansk when Papanin went aboard the crowded Bison bomber. At 3 PM on Sunday, 20 February, it was night at Murmansk, a clear moonlit night. The four jets were tuning up to screaming pitch as the Siberian settled into an improvised seat near the pilot's cabin while he studied a map and marked the latest position of the American icebreaker, *Elroy*. Behind him, spread out across the bare deck, a large body of fur-clad men were packed in close as they nursed their rifles. The enormous power of the jets increased, bursts of snow bounced up from the recently ploughed runway, then the control tower gave the go-ahead and the throbbing machine began to move.

From the control tower they could see the fiery glow from the rear of the jet pods as the machine taxied forward, turned, moved on to the main runway. Then the machine really came alive, the jets ejected the growl peculiar to the Bison, the wheels whipped down the runway, left the earth. As the bomber climbed steeply its jet ejection hit the runway like gunfire, scouring snow from the concrete, hurling up clouds of whiteness. Five minutes later it was only a vapour trail in the night, thirty thousand feet high. Col. Igor Papanin was on his way. Destination: North Pole 17.

'Still no word from Helsinki.' Adams handed Dawes the message form as he sat down. 'That just came in – I'm beginning to think something's happened to Winthrop . . .'

'I guessed that hours ago.' Dawes hardly glanced at the form. 'My bet is you won't have heard from your boy come Christmas.'

It was ironical that Papanin was the man who

alerted Dawes. For hours with growing alarm he had received a stream of reports coming in from ships, from weather planes, from satellites orbiting high above the Arctic – and all the reports indicated that something very big was on the move.

First Dawes heard that the Soviet carrier *Gorki* had changed course, that she was now steaming north at top speed towards the icefield. An hour later the report came through that six vessels of the trawler fleet k49, ships crammed with electronic gear, had also turned due north, abandoning their obvious spying rendezvous with the NATO naval exercise *Sea Lion*. Finally he had heard that the huge new Soviet research ship *Revolution*, on its maiden spying exercise from the Nikolayev shipyard on the Black Sea coast, had also changed course. 'She's heading into the gullet of Iceberg Alley,' he had told Adams. Then he had made his urgent phone call.

Only thirty minutes later a quietly dressed man wearing horn-rimmed glasses had arrived at Dawes's office. The President's assistant, his closest confidant, he had listened intently for a quarter of an hour before he spoke.

'Lemuel, this is the position. If the President goes to the Moscow summit with the Catherine charts in his pocket, then he'd be talking from a position of great strength – and we may get the concessions we want from the Russians . . .'

So Dawes had been given permission to take his own decisions without further reference back to

Washington, 'Provided you don't stir up an international incident,' the brilliant, German-born assistant had warned him. 'That might spoil the summit meeting . . .'

Dawes was thinking of this proviso when he took a piece of paper out of his pocket and handed it to Adams. 'I didn't show you the met report which came in at the last minute. Dense fog has come in out of nowhere and blanketed Target-5. Looks like this is going to be Operation Beaumont after all.'

Adams said nothing as he read the report and then fastened his seat-strap. The Boeing they were travelling aboard was descending and in the distance twin chains of landing lights glowed in the whiteness of the night. Dawes had taken the first of his decisions – he was flying to the edge of the chess board to see for himself. Destination: Curtis Field.

Running Game

The Frozen Sea

Chapter One

Sunday, 20 February

The meagre airstrip on North Pole 17 rushed towards the Bison, the Soviet pilot pointed its nose between the rows of lights now blurring into continuous bands, throttled back and prayed. The strip was too short for the Bison.

The ice flew up at him, sped away below, the wheels touched down, the bomber lurched. The pilot gritted his teeth, braked. Snow clouds stormed up, splashed over the windows like white fog. Fragmented ice bombarded the undercarriage, struck it like a million machine-gun bullets. The plane hurtled on, running out of airstrip . . .

'Exciting, isn't it, Kramer?' Papanin remarked.

In the seat beside him Kramer was rigid with fear, almost in a muscular spasm as his gloved hands grasped the seat arms. The Siberian watched with interest as the Balt stared straight ahead without replying; and this, Papanin thought, is a trained interrogator, the man who goes down into the cellar and screws information out of poor broken-down suspects. Sweat it out, my little Balt, sweat it out. The bomber halted fifteen metres from disaster. 'Now you can relax, Kramer,' Papanin said genially.

He glanced out of the window, stared out for a moment, then tore off his seat-strap. He was at the door before the fifty-odd security men lying on the deck behind him had stirred. He had the door open before the ground staff outside had time to perch a metal ladder against the fuselage, then he was hanging half-out of the machine as he stared up into the moonlit night.

'Has it gone? Bloody hell!'

Papanin asked the question, fired the expletive as he stood at the foot of the ladder propped against the Bison, hands thrust deep inside his parka as he stared down at the base leader, Dr Alexei Minsky. Like Kramer, the base leader was short and stocky and he wore snow-goggles which, because the moonlight reflected off them, gave him a sinister appearance. He immediately infuriated Papanin.

'Has what gone, Colonel?'

'For God's sake! That plane I saw when we were coming in.'

'It has flown off to the west . . .'

'The radar? You've checked the radar?'

'No, Colonel. One moment – I will be back . . .'

'He's shit-scared,' Papanin snapped to Kramer who had come down the ladder behind him. 'He's more dangerous than a polar bear – he's an idiot! From now on Minsky must be kept inside.'* He stood with his

---

* Soviet security jargon for 'must not be allowed outside the borders of the Soviet Union under any circumstances'. Presumably two hundred million Soviet citizens are members of this exclusive club.

hands in his parka looking round, observing every-thing. The bleakness of the Soviet base impressed him: for a quarter of a mile in every direction the ice was reasonably level, but beyond it lay the frozen mael-strom of the pack, a hellish jumble of heaped-up ice which looked to be on the verge of lapping over the island.

'This place isn't going to last long,' he remarked.

Unlike American research bases – where the air-strip is always well clear of the camp area – the prefabricated huts on North Pole 17, their flat roofs layered with snow, were barely thirty metres from the improvised runway. A radar mast dominated the little colony, spearing one hundred feet up to a wing-like ear which revolved to face any point of the compass. The Siberian gave brief instructions to Kramer and then faced Minsky who had run back over the ice.

'Hardly a pinpoint on the radar,' Minsky panted, his goggles steamed up. 'When the American plane saw you he flew straight back to Greenland!' He made it sound like a triumph. Papanin reached out a hand, pushed the goggles up over Minsky's forehead.

'You don't need these on a night like this – or did you think you were in a blizzard? Have the helicop-ters found Gorov? Have you brought him back? Have you sent out the Sno-Cats? Have you done anything worthwhile?'

'Gorov hasn't been found . . .' Minsky sounded nervous. 'They are still searching . . .'

'Disembark!'

Papanin roared the command up to the aircraft exit and strode long-legged across the airstrip towards the camp. Now there was no danger of an American aircraft observing what came out of the Bison he didn't even bother to look back at the armed men filing down the ladder. And now he was outside Russia the Siberian was feeling free again: he had full control, could take instant decisions without Syrtov peering over his shoulder and making damnfool suggestions.

The precise date when the Special Security Service was formed is not known, but sometime in 1968 Brezhnev decided that for overseas work the KGB was a broken reed. Demoralization set in with the death of Stalin – the most repressive organization in the world, the KGB found itself repressed. Physical torture was banned, was replaced by such devices as the Serbsky Institute in Moscow,* and soon top KGB officials were vying with each other to keep within the law. This change of heart fitted in beautifully with Khrushchev's new liberal policy inside Russia, but it didn't work overseas. A terrorist organization without terror is like an impotent man trying to make love. So a new organization was formed.

The Special Security Service can operate only outside Soviet Russia – it has no power within its own borders. It can use any method to attain its objectives,

---

* The Serbsky Institute specializes in certifying those who don't conform as insane. The threat of a visit to this place is enough to make many people toe the Party line.

and because it is confined to overseas operations there is no danger that it may grow into the Frankenstein monster the KGB once became. Brezhnev made only one exception to this rule – because of the Jewish problem Papanin had certain powers inside the city limits of Leningrad. But once he left Murmansk the Siberian controlled the game.

'Those machines – why aren't they in the air?' Papanin snapped. He gestured towards six helicopters standing beyond the airstrip where they had been parked to let the Bison come in. Beside him the short-legged Minsky was dogtrotting to keep up.

'They have just arrived from the *Gorki* . . .'

'They should be in the air – searching! What about the latest met report?'

'The fog over Target-5 is expected to continue. It is making the search more difficult . . .'

'That's where you're wrong again! While the fog lasts the Americans can't airlift Gorov back to the States.' They were coming close to the group of huts where metre-long icicles hung from the rooftops, icicles which wouldn't melt again until spring. 'They'll try and get him out over the ice – make for the Greenland coast,' Papanin said, half thinking aloud. 'We'll scatter a screen of men over the ice west of Target-5. We'll keep a screen of helicopters in the air above them. We'll grab him whoever is there to protect him.'

'Might that not be dangerous?'

'We have the perfect excuse. Gorov is a madman, a murderer – he killed Marov, one of our oceanographers.

Gorov has been in the Arctic so long he's gone round the bend.'

'I don't understand,' Minsky began. 'Marov was a security man . . .'

'You're so thick it's hardly credible,' Papanin barked. 'Marov has just become an oceanographer – Gorov is a criminal who killed one of his own colleagues and we have to apprehend him. That changes it from a political case into a police affair.' There was a savage, jaunty note in Papanin's voice. Here, out in the open, he was in his element. This was the Siberian who, ten years ago, had been told to speed up the removal of the Russian missiles from Cuba. His method had been characteristically direct: he had threatened to explode the missiles over the island if the Cubans didn't cooperate. Ten years older, he had not lost his quick, savage touch.

'A police affair?' Minsky said thoughtfully as they came up to the huts. 'That makes a difference?'

'Yes! It means that if we want to we are justified in shooting at Gorov and anyone with him – after all, Michael Gorov is a dangerous maniac.' Papanin smashed an icicle from the roof with his gloved hand. 'You see, Minsky, we are starting a manhunt.'

Within minutes of meeting Beaumont at Curtis Field Dawes was in the air again, this time as a passenger aboard a two-man Cessna aircraft which took off along the runway ending at the cliff brink. The pilot,

Arnold Schumacher, who hated flying top brass, wheeled the plane away from Greenland and headed out to sea. The icecap below merged with the polar pack glued to the mainland as the plane flew like a dart due east.

'You're not expected to find Target-5,' Dawes growled, 'so just pretend you're looking for it. I'm checking conditions.'

'Terrible.' The pilot paused. 'Sir,' he added, 'I can't see anyone getting to the base over the ice. When the fog clears we'll have to fly in. The usual way.' He transferred his chewing gum to the other cheek, the cheek away from Dawes.

'That's the trouble with you people up here. All you think of is engines and machines. You can't imagine anyone fighting their way in over the pack. We're getting soft, Schumacher – if Pan-Am can't take us we don't go.'

'I'm not Pan-Am . . .'

'And take that gum out of your mouth when you're talking to me.'

Screw you, chum. But the pilot preferred this type: at least they didn't try to fraternize, kidding you up they were just one of the boys – with their pay ten times your own. The plane flew on through the cold, moonlit night at two thousand feet, a wisp of metal over the Arctic. The altitude flattened out the pressure ridges, made the pack look like a sheet of opaque glass, crazed and splintered glass. Conditions were bloody terrible. Thirty minutes later Dawes was half out of his seat, peering down into the grey murk below, a solid sea of rolling fog which masked the solid ice under it. A squat globular bug with a whizz of rotor-driven air above it was cruising towards them, barely skimming the fog bank. 'See that?' Dawes rapped out.

'Chopper. Russian.' The pilot was thinking about the pad of gum stuck under his seat.

'Submarine killer?'

'Yes,' said Schumacher.

'Must be off that Soviet carrier south of the ice. I want a closer look. Dive!'

Schumacher was irked about his lost chewing gum. Screw all generals: they ought to be abolished. Like state taxes. So he dived, dropped like a bomb. But Dawes, braced in his seat, was ready. The Russian helicopter was no more than half a mile away, floating towards them on the fog sea as the Cessna went down and down and the fog swept up. Schumacher pulled out of the dive with a jerk which could have knocked out Dawes, but again he was ready for the impact. They were now about three hundred feet above the helicopter. Then it vanished, fell into the fog.

'Hell!' Dawes was annoyed. 'I wonder why she's such a shy girl? Seen any of them about here before, Schumacher?'

'Never this far west – not that model. We've passed over Target-5,' the pilot added, 'somewhere down there in the oatmeal.' The edge of the fog bank was in sight and the polar pack loomed as a mellow crystal sheen beyond. 'Coming close to the Russian base, North Pole 17, sir.'

Schumacher's access of politeness intrigued Dawes. 'I want to see what they're up to. Does it worry you?'

'They buzz us – send a machine up and fly close. I nearly collided with one somewhere about here. They don't like us playing good neighbours with them. So we still keep on, sir? There they are.'

Twinkles of green phosphorescence glowing on the ice showed the landing strip on the ice island, showed that the airstrip was in imminent use. The buildings couldn't be seen yet, but something else could be seen, was just coming into view. Dawes leaned forward, his eyes narrowed. 'Perfect timing! You almost deserve a medal . . .' A small – at that range – Satanic-looking shadow was drifting down out of the sky, trailing pencil-thin vapour as it pointed its nose down. A Bison bomber was landing at North Pole 17.

'Go back, sir?'

'Not yet!'

A Bison bomber. That was interesting. The Russians didn't use the Bison as an Arctic taxi, but they might in an emergency use it to get here fast from Murmansk, to bring in a man – or a lot of men. The Bison swept down to ground level, swept along between the lights, and Dawes could see the buildings now, a tiny cluster of dark smudges. The moving smudge between the lights came to a stop, the green pinpoints faded, vanished.

'They've hooked us on their radar,' Schumacher warned. 'Now they'll send up a plane.'

'Not with their lights doused. Look below us.'

From seven hundred feet they could see them clearly, tiny turtles crawling over the ice. Sno-Cats, six of them, and they were west of the Soviet ice island – heading direct towards Target-5. They scarcely seemed to move, but behind them their caterpillar tracks left tell-tale furrows in the snow, furrows leading from North Pole 17. That – and the Bison bomber – decided Dawes.

'Home,' he said, and Schumacher reacted instantly, turning at speed as he gained altitude. 'Get through on your radio to Curtis Field . . .'

'There's bad static . . .'

'Get through. Go on until you do get through. Send one word time and time again. Nitrogen. Got it? Nitrogen . . .' It was the code-signal Beaumont was waiting for, the signal for him to leave for Target-5.

Chapter Two

Sunday, 20 February: 4 PM– Monday, 21 February: Midnight

The two Sikorsky helicopters came down vertically as though suspended from a cable, dropping towards the ice over a hundred miles from the Greenland coast. It was a critical moment – any landing on unknown ice is critical. For one thing you can never be sure from the air that you are coming down on firm ice; it may look quite solid and then the skids land, the ice cracks and you are going down into the ocean. For another thing, if the machine doesn't settle on a flat surface it can keel over, topple, and the whirling rotors hit the ice first. One moment the men inside are preparing to disembark, the next moment steel blades are mincing them to pieces – unless the fuel tanks detonate, in which case they are incinerated.

So it was with a certain tension that Beaumont waited for the bump which would tell them they had touched down on the polar pack. Seated in the observer's position beside the pilot, he watched with professional interest the hand holding the collective pitch stick controlling their descent. The hand seemed steady enough. He glanced at the pilot's face – what he could see of it under helmet, goggles and headset. The face seemed steady, too, but the mouth was tight. Pilot Rainer was, in fact, clenching his teeth while he waited for the bump.

Behind Beaumont Sam Grayson was perched on a flap seat and there were also nine dogs aboard, nine whimpering dogs who didn't like the sudden descent. A sled completed the congestion. Horst Langer, with a second sled and more dogs, was coming down in the other machine Beaumont could see beyond the perspex dome. Beaumont checked his watch. They would hit the pack in thirty seconds Rainer had said. Twenty seconds to go.

'Would you normally risk a landing here?' Beaumont had asked a few minutes earlier.

'No!' Rainer had been uncomfortably direct in his reply. 'But I have orders to get you down if humanly possible. So we've got to risk it, haven't we?'

Beaumont adjusted his ear-pads. Everything was shuddering – the floor under his feet, the dome, the controls Rainer was handling. Beaumont rested a hand on the dog by his side and felt the vibrations through the poor beast's fur. Transport planes the dogs minded not at all: helicopters they hated. The descent went on. Rainer adjusted the twist-grip throttle on his stick. Ten seconds to go. Maybe only ten seconds left to live.

They were now low enough to see the ice beyond the dome. It was a churned-up mess, like a blurred sea which had frozen suddenly – blurred because the dome was steamed up inside the cabin. And the grim wilderness of tumbled ice was shuddering unpleasantly, dithering giddily because of the cabin's shuddering. When they opened the door the temperature would drop eighty or ninety degrees within seconds, taking their breath away. If the machine landed steady, if it didn't topple. There were skids – skis – under this Sikorsky and that should help stability. Unless one ski skidded while the other sank. Rainer glanced at Beaumont, who winked at him. The wink was not returned and Beaumont saw the blank eyes behind the goggles. Rainer was scared stiff. Then the skids touched the ice.

The machine wobbled. Beaumont felt it going down on his side. Soft ice to port, hard to starboard. Rainer's hand was welded to the stick. Bugger this trip – he should have gone sick. The dogs sensed disaster, began whimpering pathetically. The blades were still whirling, whipping the air as the sinking sensation went on. The tension inside the cabin was a physical presence as the three men sweated out their terror. Then the machine settled, the sinking stopped. Rainer switched off, lifted his goggles and his face was seamed with sweat.

'Nice landing,' Beaumont said as he pulled off his headset and reached for the door.

'Wait . . . !'

'I am waiting – for the rotors to stop.'

It wasn't necessary – if you kept your head down when you went out – but Rainer didn't know that

Beaumont had flown helicopters all over the Arctic. Beaumont opened the door and the Arctic came in like a knife. He dropped to the ice and walked away from the machine stiffly as he looked round for Langer's Sikorsky, then frowned as he saw it was coming down on to pressure ridge terrain. It was going to crash.

Behind him Grayson was sending the dogs out and they came out joyously, barking and scampering round the machine with sheer delight at being free again. A quarter of a mile away to the east the fog bank hovered in the moonlight, a grey curtain like a dirty cloud anchored to the ice. Then Langer's machine dropped out of sight behind a pressure ridge, a twisted wall of ice ten feet high. The machine hit the ice and the blur of the rotor disc steadied above the crest. 'He's OK.' Grayson's voice was husky behind the Englishman. 'For a moment I wondered . . .'

'He isn't – he's toppling!'

Beaumont started running across the ice, his boots crunching into soft crust which crumbled under him. The whole area had only recently frozen over, was dangerously unstable. Beaumont ran as fast as he could without slipping and his heart was in his mouth – the rotor disc above the crest was no longer horizontal, it was canting sideways. He ran through a gap in the pressure wall and saw that Langer's quick reflexes had already reacted to the emergency – the door was open, dogs were spilling out on to the soft ice and running towards the gap, their legs smeared with the dark ooze they had plunged into.

The Sikorsky was an extraordinary sight – with its port skid sinking, already below the surface, its strut still going down, the machine was heeling over while its rotors still whirled at speed. The situation couldn't have been more dangerous and as he ran close Beaumont wondered what the hell the pilot was doing, why the hell he hadn't switched off. Langer appeared, heaving one end of the sled close to the aperture, getting ready to push it out. 'Leave it!' Beaumont shouted and his warning was lost in the hideous roar. He jumped up, hauled himself inside the cabin where the pilot, Jacowski, was sitting behind the controls, reached across and cut the motor.

'I'm taking off,' the pilot yelled.

'Start that motor again and I'll brain you,' Beaumont rasped. 'Our lives depend on that sled – give a hand to get it out. The machine's expendable – we're not.' He went back to help Langer. 'Take it easy, Horst – the ground's like a sponge out there ...' He saw Grayson arrive below the aperture. 'Sam, watch it as it comes down – it could sink ...'

'Hurry it up – I'm sinking,' the American called out.

They wrestled with the heavily laden sled, balanced it on the brink, and then Beaumont dropped out to help Grayson take its weight. The Sikorsky seemed temporarily stable but was tilted at an acute angle as they lowered the sled carefully and rested it on the ice. It started sinking at once and then Grayson and Langer grabbed hold of the harness and began hauling it away towards firmer ground near the gap. Beaumont looked at Jacowski who was still sitting behind his controls.

'If you stay there that's going to make a nice coffin for you – it's gone in deeper.'

'I'm going to try and take her out.'

'Better have a look first – unless you want someone to collect your insurance.'

Jacowski climbed gingerly to the ground, felt his boots sinking, moved quickly to join Beaumont where the ice was firmer. The helicopter had almost righted itself, was almost horizontal again – because the starboard skid had now sunk to the depth of the port skid. It was knee-deep in black ooze. 'The next problem is how to get rid of it,' Beaumont said roughly. 'It has to go either up or down – it can't stay here as a landmark to show some Russian chopper where we went into the fog. If we start the motor I think the vibration will take it down.'

'That's government property,' the pilot said nastily. 'It belongs to the Arctic Research Laboratory at Point Barrow. We can bring a team to dig it out . . .'

'It goes up or down,' Beaumont informed him, 'so you'd better get clear before I start her up.'

'Keith, that's damned dangerous,' Grayson protested as he came back to see what was happening. 'If it goes down too quickly while you're inside it . . .'

Beaumont was already climbing up carefully into the cabin, testing it with his weight to see the effect. Nothing happened so he sat down in the pilot's seat and looked out to make sure the others were clear. Jacowski had gone all the way back to the gap but Grayson was waiting just beyond the span of the rotor blades. Starting up the motor in these circumstances wasn't a course of action Beaumont would have recommended to anyone, but the machine had to disappear – either into the sky or under the Arctic.

It was just possible that when he started the motor he'd be able to drag her free, to take her up and land the machine close to the other Sikorsky; it all depended on the strength of the drag of the ooze gripping the skids. The more likely outcome was that the vibration would shiver the skids, open up the ooze and force her down. When that happened he'd have to take rather quick evasive action to avoid being carried down with her. Beaumont started the motor.

For a moment he thought he'd managed it, that he was going to lift her out. The machine wobbled and he could feel the power trying to haul her out, then she started going down and going over to port all at once and quickly. He dived for the doorway, went out, slipped on the ice and sprawled under the toppling, dropping machine. He was caught in a kind of closing press – between the ice under him and the descending whirling blades coming down on top of him. He scrambled to his knees, felt the ooze sucking at his boots, holding him in. The beat of the descending rotors deafened him, the ooze clamped round his boots, his hands clawed at firmer ground to drag himself loose.

Other hands grabbed his own as Grayson tugged ferociously and between them they got him out. He curled his toes upwards to stop his boots sliding off and then, crouched low, they ran in a shambling trot. The racing blades were only feet above them and Beaumont felt their wind-force beating down on his neck as they ran together, still stooped low when they were yards beyond the reach of the flailing metal. At the gap they turned to look back as the motor coughed, choked and died. The fuselage was sitting on the ooze and the motor had sucked a churning mass of the filth into its innards while the rotors whirled on their own momentum. 'Get ready to get behind the ridge,' Beaumont warned. He was foreseeing the moment when the blades broke free and started flying across the ice, but the warning was unnecessary. As the fuselage sank more slowly the rotors slowed and were hardly moving when they reached the ground. They flicked great gouts of blackness across the ice and then settled. The ooze opened up, the Sikorsky went down with a dreadful sucking sound, the ooze closed over it.

'That was government property,' Jacowski repeated peevishly.

'Tell them to take another gold bar out of Fort Knox,' Beaumont suggested.

There was a reaction after the crisis, a tendency to move slowly, but Beaumont dispelled it as he urged everyone to move faster, to get the other sled out of the surviving Sikorsky, to harness up the dog teams, to get moving before a Russian plane arrived. 'I want us inside that fog bank in fifteen minutes – there we're invisible ...' And there was another confrontation with the pilots before they left.

'We'll have to report what happened to that helicopter,' Rainer called down from his machine.

'In triplicate,' Grayson shouted back at him. 'Don't forget they like it in triplicate!'

Jacowski slammed the door in his face as Rainer started his machine. Five minutes later the two sled teams were assembled, the dogs were hitched up, ready to go. The Sikorsky had vanished, fading into the night on its way home. The feeling of isolation descended on the three men the moment the machine had gone, and the terrible silence of the Arctic wilderness was overwhelming.

They were alone on the ice, a hundred miles from Greenland, a pinhead on the frozen sea – three men, eighteen dogs and two sleds. The ice under their feet was possibly twelve inches deep, except where it had no depth at all, where the weight of a single dog could fracture it, casting the living weight down into the freezing black water they were floating on. And even though the ice seemed still it was moving all the time; caught up in the powerful Greenland Current it was drifting south towards Iceberg Alley at the rate of over ten miles a day, and under the smear of ice which coated the ocean the water plunged down ten thousand feet. Beaumont took over the leading team from Grayson. 'Let's get moving,' he said. 'I shan't be happy until we're inside the fog.'

'It looks extremely inviting,' Langer said with a dry smile. The twenty-eight-year-old German had spent two years in London and Beaumont often remarked that his English was more idiomatic than his own. 'In fact, it looks very much like one of your famous pea-soupers.'

'It won't be so bad when we get inside it,' Beaumont replied and they started off. It was always the initial start which called for an effort – to get the dog teams moving, to get your own reluctant legs moving in the bitter Arctic night. And Horst was right he thought as he held the whip in one hand and gripped the sled's handlebar with the other: the fog looked damned uninviting.

The fog bank hung over the ice like a threat, a threat of grey vapour which rose high above the ice and clung to the ground. It was bitterly cold but there was no wind, so the fog was almost motionless, like a cloud hovering above an icy plateau, a cloud which could hide any number of dangers. The danger Beaumont feared most was movement – that while they were inside the fog the ice might stir afresh, opening up leads of water, bringing them together again, heaving up pressure ridges which could crush a man, even bury a whole dog team in seconds. He cracked his whip, shouted at the team, and the dogs moved faster, hauling the sled, their legs stretched, their bodies straining at the harness.

And now the deathly silence of the ice was broken by man-made sounds – by the creak of harness, the hiss of runners coursing over the ice, the crackle of snow-crust giving way, by the crack of whips and the thump of boots treading harder ice. They were under way, heading for the fog bank, heading towards Target-5 lost somewhere inside the dense pall. Beaumont drove the lead team with Langer controlling the second team behind, while a few paces ahead Grayson moved across the ice staring down at his compass. 'It's nervous already,' he called out. Which was another problem – in this part of the world compasses were notoriously unreliable.

Langer easily kept up with Beaumont's hard-driving pace – his lead dog, Bismarck, was a big, tough-minded animal who kept the other dogs moving, the Beaumont of the dog teams. Horst Langer, five foot ten inches tall, dark-haired and clean-shaven, was a Rhinelander, a cheerful, easy-going man with a sense of humour which concealed great resilience. An expert with explosives – essential knowledge for depth-sounding work – he was also a brilliant dog-handler. As Beaumont said, 'They'll fly over thin ice with Horst when other dogs would cringe.' Born in Dusseldorf, still a bachelor – 'With so many attractive women about how can you choose just one?' – he had spent four years in the Arctic working on American bases. And like the other two men he had top security clearance from Washington.

'Something wrong, Keith?' he called out.

Beaumont had halted his team, was standing with his head turned to one side. 'Thought I heard something. Keep very quiet for a minute.'

They waited. The dogs twisted in their harness to see what was happening. There seemed to be nothing but the ton-weight of the Arctic silence pressing down on them. Beaumont, in his fur parka and fur hood, was huge and still in the moonlight as he swivelled his head like a radar wing towards the east. The fog bank was close now, only a few hundred yards away, a dirty cloud like motionless smoke. Then Beaumont heard it again, the faint beat-beat of a large helicopter growing louder, coming closer by the second.

'Run for it! Inside the fog before they see us . . .'

The urgency in his shout communicated itself to the dogs as the whips cracked, the sled teams surged forward and the helicopter's motor sped towards them. They were actually racing towards it, expecting at any moment to see it come over the top of the fog bank. Bismarck exerted all his strength, his paws flying over the ice at Beaumont's heels as the sleds lurched over uneven ground and the men behind them fought to keep them upright. A spill now would be disaster, would anchor them in the open until it was too late. Grayson ran alongside Beaumont, ready to grab at the handlebar. The helicopter beat was very close. Rat-tat-tat ... Beaumont cracked his whip, urged the dogs to move faster while he struggled with the bucking sled which was taking on a life of its own.

'Thin ice!'

Beaumont was turning the sled as Grayson shouted, turning it away from a depression where something dark showed below treacherously smooth ice. The helicopter sound had become a drumbeat which meant it was coming in very low, only a few hundred feet up. The sled caught an ice rib, was heeling over to port when Grayson steadied it and behind them Langer swerved widely to avoid the obstacle. To keep them moving, Beaumont cracked his whip a third time over their heads and they went forward in a spurt. He thought he saw something above him as they plunged into the fog, then his team was swallowed up, followed by Langer's sled, and it was like diving into moonless night as the fog closed round them. It enveloped them, drifted clammily over their faces, blurred the shapes of the dogs only feet away from their drivers. Beaumont pulled at the handlebar, called out for the dogs to halt, then turned his head upwards and stared into the murk. The engine beat was muffled and sounded to be directly overhead.

'I think it's Russian,' Grayson said breathlessly.

'Could be a routine patrol,' Langer suggested. 'North Pole 17 isn't far away – for a chopper. They're always checking on what we're doing.' The engine beat was still above them and it gave them the eerie feeling it could see the men below it, which was impossible.

'It's circling,' Beaumont snapped.

'So it could still be routine,' Langer insisted. 'Or maybe it's looking for Gorov.'

'Or maybe it's looking for us,' Beaumont replied, 'if Tillotson got through to Leningrad.'

'Fifteen killers . . .'

Papanin stood outside the headquarters hut as the last helicopter landed on the moonlit airstrip, its twin rotors spinning giddily as the jet power died. They were lined up in a row – squat, bulbous silhouettes in the moonlight, like big-bellied crows; submarine killers just flown in off the Soviet carrier *Gorki*. The sonar devices under the domes looked like pus sacs, and each of them sagged on a quadruple support of two-wheel carriages. A jet pod like a bomb was slung to port and starboard of each machine.

'I want them airborne in thirty minutes,' Papanin told Kramer. 'And then they stay up – until they've found Gorov. They can come down to refuel,' he added.

'There's only one pilot per machine,' the Balt pointed out.

'Very economical,' was the Siberian's only comment.

Thirty minutes later the fleet of submarine killers started taking off from the airstrip and Papanin watched them go. It was one of these fifteen machines which Beaumont heard coming when he rushed the sled teams inside the fog bank. And it was one of these machines which photographed them just before they disappeared, photographed them with a tele-photo lens of great range and power.

The first few hours inside the fog bank were unevent-ful hell for the three men and their dog teams – if uneventful is a true description of a time when they constantly expected to lose their lives. For one thing they couldn't see where they were going; under any other circumstance Beaumont would have called a halt, would have pitched camp and waited for the fog to move. Instead they drove themselves on, stumbling through the icy dampness, often only able to see the lead dog beyond their sled, and when it disappeared Grayson went in front to test the ground, walking slowly with the dogs coming up close behind.

If their calculations were correct, if the star-fix Grayson had taken with his sextant soon after he left the Sikorsky was anything like accurate, the ice island Target-5 was only a few miles due east when they landed. But navigation in an Arctic winter is not always an exact science and privately Beaumont had his doubts.

The tension rose as they heard another helicopter coming at the moment the fog was thinning. Suddenly it was lighter, the fog above them drifted away, a faint glow which was the moon began to percolate the mistiness. The machine came closer. 'Halt!' Beaumont tugged at the sled. 'Try and keep the dogs still. Sam, take over here a minute.' Beaumont took his night glasses out of the case strapped to the handlebar and walked a few yards away from the sled teams. Above him a hole was opening up in the fog; he couldn't see the moon but its light was all around him as he raised the glasses. The helicopter drummed in, swept into view, a blurred, huge shape flying very low indeed.

It went over quickly, so quickly he couldn't catch it in his glasses but he was sure it was Russian. Then he heard another one coming. This time he was ready for it as it flew in on the same course as its predecessor. In the lenses he caught a glimpse of a jet pod, the blur of a pilot's helmet, then it swept past out of sight. 'Submarine killer,' he told Grayson when he went back to the sled teams. 'And there's another one up there in the distance. I think they're covering the fringe of the fog bank to see what goes into it.'

'Or what comes out of it.'

'It's promising in a way,' Beaumont pointed out as he took over the sled. 'I think Dawes was right – Gorov is making his run. You don't get that number of Soviet machines down here normally.'

'Promising for us, too – if they're looking for us.'

They moved on again, often with the sound of a helicopter somewhere overhead, but the fog closed in again so they were hidden. Their progress would have been difficult in clear weather – in the fog it was dangerous. The ice was broken up, pitted with gullies, so the sleds constantly lurched from side to side, always on the verge of overturning, and soon Beaumont's arm ached with the strain of holding on to the jerking handlebar. Horst Langer suffered equally and Sam Grayson suffered also, but in a different way. The strain of moving just ahead of the dogs when the fog became really dense was appalling. Every step he took he expected to be his last, to land in icy water where a lead had opened up, exposing the black Arctic ocean.

It would have been uncomfortable in summer – when the temperature hovers at freezing point or a degree or two above. In February with a temperature of forty below it was diabolical. Despite their clothing. They wore long woollen underwear, two pairs of socks apiece inside fur-lined boots, two woollen pullovers, a fur-lined jacket, and over all this a wolfskin parka made by an Alaskan fur trader Beaumont knew in Fairbanks. But they were still frozen, their hands and feet numbed beyond feeling, the small portion of their faces exposed under their fur hoods aching and damp – always damp – with the clinging fog which pressed against them as they struggled forward.

Because they had left Curtis Field so quickly they stopped after five hours for food and drink, thankful that the dogs ate only every forty-eight hours. With the fog creeping around them they sat on the sleds to eat their pemmican, a nourishing form of dried meat which tastes rather like old leather. The nerve-racking beat of a nearby helicopter stayed with them all through the meal and it put their tempers on edge.

'Why doesn't the damn thing break down, run out of fuel, get lost?' Langer demanded.

'Because it tanked up at North Pole 17,' Beaumont snapped.

'That thought had occurred to me.'

'Then why ask the question?'

The horror occurred while they were eating and they didn't know it had happened because of the row the Soviet machine was making. At the end of the meal Beaumont took the compass off Grayson and tried to get the needle to steady. The helicopter stopped circling suddenly, flew away towards the east. He was standing up, holding the compass, when he looked up and stared into the distance. It was very faint even in the sudden quiet after the helicopter's departure, and Beaumont was the only one who heard it, a sound which shouldn't have been there. The lapping of water, a gentle swishing sound.

'I'll be back in a minute,' he said casually. 'Stay exactly where you are and don't move around.'

He was back again in five minutes and the other two men obviously had no inkling that anything was wrong. Langer had interpreted his instruction as a warning not to go wandering around in the fog; he was actually standing behind his sled ready to move off. Beaumont handed the compass back to Grayson. 'You won't need that for a while,' he said quietly.

'There's nowhere to go. We're now drifting on a small floe away from the icefield . . .'

'That's impossible,' Langer burst out. 'We'd have heard the ice cracking, making a hell of a row.'

'You've forgotten the din that helicopter was kicking up – and this time when it cracked it didn't make too much row, not enough for us to hear it above the hammering of that Russian's motor.' Beaumont gestured into the fog. 'Walk in any direction and you'll fall off before you've gone thirty yards. We're marooned on a slab of ice drifting down a huge lead. We'd better get used to the idea – we're no longer on the polar pack – we're at sea.'

The worst had happened. The icefield had opened up one of its vast leads, an expanding lane of sea which could be many miles wide. Sometimes it is the wind, sometimes the current always flowing under the ice which cracks the ice open, snapping it apart – in this case they may have been close to the brink of the lead when they had stopped to eat and a fragment, the floe they were marooned on, had broken free. Sooner or later the lead comes together again – unless the lane was close to open sea, in which case they would drift on the ocean until they froze to death.

It was the coming together of the ice which worried Beaumont, which made him issue the warning to stay constantly alert. It is not a gentle process, this coming together. The ice closes like a vice, like the impact of two steel-plated vessels steaming towards each other on collision course. When two ice edges meet the sound is like the thunder of a thousand artillery salvoes, a terrifying crash which can be heard many miles away, and like the steel plates of a ship the ice buckles in collision. It buckles and it heaves up huge pressure ridges to displace the smashed ice, moving ridges which can climb as high as thirty feet above the ice while over their crests shiver massive chunks of ice which topple down, flattening everything in their path. And when the ice edges met the floating raft would be caught between them, would be cracked open like a nut. This was why they had to stay alert.

In an attempt to see the danger in time Beaumont posted both Grayson and Langer at opposite ends of the little island. A rope was attached to one of the sleds and extended to both lookout points – so that the moment they saw the icefield coming back at them they could find their way through the fog quickly. While the two men took up position, posted like lookouts aboard a ship, Beaumont fed the dogs. He cut up walrus meat at a distance from the animals and then threw the meat to them; they devoured it with their usual lack of table manners. They weren't due for a meal but he wanted to keep them quiet.

The floe continued its eerie drift into nothingness. There was no sensation of movement – the floe was large, it was a windless night – but the current was carrying it steadily further south, away from Target-

5. Perched at the edge of the ice, squatting on his haunches, Langer strained to see through the fog. It was a bloody hopeless task he was thinking: he could barely see six feet before the grey pall blocked his view. But it wasn't quite as hopeless as it seemed. The advance of the ice edge, which would come through the fog like a moving platform, a platform of hard, solid ice, might well be preceded by a disturbance, a small wave being pushed in front of it. The first warning should be when water lapped over the ice beyond his boots.

In front of the fog the black water was like oil, oil covered here and there with a dirty sheen as thin patches of ice formed on its surface. The temperature was almost fifty below and the water was trying to freeze all the time, to form a fresh layer of ice. Only the movement of the current prevented it succeeding. He was out of sight of the sleds and the dogs; when he glanced over his shoulder all he could see was dirty vapour. A terrible sense of isolation descended on him – he couldn't get rid of the feeling that he was on his own, that he was floating on a fragment which had split off from the main floe, a fragment hardly larger than a tabletop.

Fear tingled his nerve ends. He listened with all his ears. If the ice he was crouched on split off from the floe he should hear a warning crack. It might be very slight – they had no way of knowing the thickness of the raft they were floating on – but there should be a sharp crack when the ice splintered. With his hood pulled well down, crouching at the brink of the ice, Langer looked like a furry animal in the fog, and despite the layers of clothing, the two mittens under his heavy gloves, his body felt like the block of ice he floated on. His hands were numb, his feet ached with the pain, his face was cruelly frozen – but fear kept him alert. Then he heard a cracking sound.

Trembling, he forced himself upright, his leg muscles taut with tension. He was alone. His piece of ice had broken off from the floe. If he took two steps in any direction he would go down into the freezing water which would kill him inside three minutes. In a panic he swung round. The fog pall came up to his face. He was absolutely alone, he had lost his two companions, he would never see anyone again. Blind, horrible panic welled up. He shivered, clenched his teeth. Get a grip on yourself for Christ's sake! He stood quite still, shivering, forcing the panic down. Then he felt the rope he had forgotten, the rope end he was still holding in his right glove. He was still attached to the floe: he had imagined the horror. Wearily he sank down on his haunches and his ice-coated boots creaked again, made the same cracking sound he had heard before. He felt weak with relief and very foolish. The strain was already telling and they had been adrift for less than an hour. Twenty-four hours later the lead closed.

*

Beaumont's watch registered 10.30 PM. The floe was wobbling, turning slowly, caught up in a cross-current. And to the east the fog was thinning. 'It's clearing over there,' Langer said, standing up and pointing. 'Dear God, it's clearing. We may see something . . .'

'I can see something now,' Beaumont said grimly. 'It looks like land.'

He used the word land automatically, although the blurred line he was staring at could only be more ice – if he was seeing anything at all. When you stared into the fog for a long time your eyes played you tricks, showed you trees and mountains and other impossible things where you knew there was only fog. He closed his eyes, opened them again. The fog was thinning out rapidly as moonlight percolated through and globules of moisture caught its reflection. Yes, he could still see the blurred line, but was the damned thing stationary? Were they – he hoped to God they were – being carried by a change in the current gently towards static ice?

'I think it's coming this way,' Horst said tersely.

It was less than a quarter of a mile away across the water, a white platform like the edge of a continent. In front of it was a shadowed ripple as the sea was thrust back by the immense icefield moving west-ward, westward towards the fragment of ice floating in its path. 'Horst, stay here and keep an eye on it. I'll warn Sam.'

Beaumont moved across the floe, looping up the rope which was no longer needed – the fog had dispersed enough for him to see Grayson who was staring in the opposite direction. And it was continuing to thin out, so he could see across several hundred yards of calm water beyond the western brink of the ice raft. Beyond that the fog was as thick as ever. 'The icefield's coming up behind you, Sam, coming up fast from the east.'

'That means trouble.'

'It means trouble. The dogs are ready and it looks as though we'll have to jump for it. You'd better stay here – just in case something else happens. When I call you, come like a bat out of hell.'

Just in case ... There was no need to elaborate. Beaumont's great fear now was that the whole lead was closing up – with jaws of ice closing on them from both east and west. It was the fresh movement of the floe he didn't like – it was revolving slowly, which indicated more than one current was on the move. He spent a moment with the dogs and then went back to where Langer was staring fixedly to the east.

'Look at the wave,' the German said.

The ripple of black water had become a wave, only a small wave but it was a warning of the tremendous force pushing up behind it as the icefield cruised towards them with the power of millions of tons of polar pack behind it. The fog had thinned even more, although further back on the icefield it was as dense as ever, and the platform was like a whole coast advancing, a low coast of tumbled ice and frozen pressure ridges.

'Keith . . .!'

Beaumont swung round at Grayson's shout, and for seconds his mind froze with his body. A wave was almost on top of the floe, a wave from the other direction. Behind it the second jaw of the ice was sliding towards them, shooting the wave ahead of its slide. He shouted to Grayson and the American was running towards him as Beaumont swung round again to check the position to the east. It was going to be disaster – he saw this instantly. The western jaw was going to catch them just before the eastern jaw reached them – and they had to go east. 'Get to the dogs, Horst!' He heard a noise behind him and looked back. The wave was breaking against the floe, sending black water skidding over it. The water caught up with Grayson and washed over his boots. The dogs, water swirling round their legs, were going mad as they reached the animals and grabbed the harness.

'It may push us – the ice behind us . . .' Beaumont shouted.

While Horst wrestled with his team Beaumont fought for control of his own, one hand on the sled's handlebar, the other holding the whip. Water swirled round them; for seconds the floe disappeared and they seemed to be standing on the sea. The dogs were terrified, thought they were on the verge of drowning. They might all be drowning within seconds – it depended on the strength and depth of the invisible ice they were standing on. If the massive blow of the ice sheet coming up behind them caught a weak point, fractured the floe, they would be in the sea with nothing under them, struggling in icy water until the two jaws met and pulverized them to thin layers of flesh.

The eastern jaw was still a hundred yards away, its wave hadn't reached them, when the impact came, a shattering blow which quivered the ice under them. The dogs stopped going berserk, stood quite still in sheer terror. The sea had flowed off the raft, leaving pools behind in depressions, but it was still intact. And now they could feel the raft moving, being carried forward towards the advancing sheet heading towards it for collision. Beaumont glanced back, saw the ice sheet behind, a foot higher than the floe, like a giant step. 'Get to the other edge,' he shouted.

They used the whips, drove the demoralized dogs forward the short distance until they were almost at the brink. Really, they hadn't a chance in hell. Beaumont wished now that he had turned round, taken the teams back on to the jaw behind them, but it was too late. The wave from the east splashed down on the floe, threw water round their legs, and the dogs tried to go berserk a second time. Beaumont tightened his grip, held the whip ready for one sharp crack. The water was still around their feet when the gap closed. The sleds were alongside each other when the whips cracked, the men shouted, the dogs leapt forward seconds before the point of impact. Under them the sea flooded the raft, surged knee-high, submerged it totally.

The dogs leapt forward, took the sleds with them over the gap before the ice met in thunderous collision. Something reared up under Beaumont's right leg but the momentum of the sled took him forward with the boom of the ice in his ears. The icefield was smooth near its brink and the sleds scudded forward, the friction breaking off the newly formed ice on the runners where the sea had frozen. They were deafened by the boom, deafened so they hardly heard the monstrous smashing sound as both jaws of the ice sheets broke off and heaved up a pressure ridge, heaved it up twenty feet high, shot up a wall of jostling ice with great blocks wobbling on its crest. Then Grayson, dog-trotting beside Beaumont, slipped and went down. Behind him the pressure ridge came forward like a lava wall, toppling the blocks in front of it.

Beaumont saw him falling, held on to whip and sled with one hand while he grabbed. Grayson was on his knees when Beaumont grasped one arm, jerked it up savagely. The American's gloved hand locked on the handlebar and he was dragged forward on his knees some distance before he scrambled up. Behind them a massive block of ice weighing many tons thudded down where Grayson had fallen. Still shaken, still gripping the handlebar, he stumbled forward as the sled kept moving, a little way behind Langer's team. To their rear the pack, caught up in the gigantic collision, was a chaos of movement.

Fissures shivered the weak points. A dark gash knifed past Beaumont's sled and ahead of it. He swerved to avoid it and swerved again to escape a second opening. The noise was tremendous, like a bombardment as the erupting icefield roared and hammered. They kept moving, driving the dogs, running for their lives away from the chopping hell behind them, and when they had covered half a mile, when they were close to the edge of the fog, Beaumont called a halt. Panting for breath like the dogs, the clothes under their parkas clammy with sweat, they looked back. In the distance the icefield was still heaving and writhing. It could be hours before the turmoil ended, before the icefield sealed over once more, locking down the sea while an Arctic silence you could almost hear descended.

'Who the devil were they?'

The flickering image of three fur-clad figures seen from the air hovered in the smoke, then vanished and there was fog and more smoke. The projection screen inside the headquarters hut went blank. Papanin stirred in his seat beside Kramer as the projectionist removed the film reel and someone switched on the light. The smoke came from the little curved pipe he was puffing away at steadily, the smoke which filled the overheated hut, which obscured the 'No Smoking' sign hanging from a wall. The atmosphere was torrid, glowing with warmth.

'It was interesting,' Kramer ventured.

'That film doesn't tell me a damned thing,' the Siberian replied. 'Just three men and two dog teams at the edge of the fog. Where is the Beaumont force? We're looking for a large body of men – for an expedition. Those thick-skulled pilots aren't looking in the right place.'

Swivelling round in his chair, his little pipe clenched in his teeth, Papanin stared at a map of the lower Arctic spread out on a table. The latest positions of all vessels in the area were marked – the six vessels of trawler fleet k49, the carrier *Gorki*, the huge research ship *Revolution*, and the American icebreaker *Elroy* which was steaming steadily closer to the icefield.

Alongside the map was a blown-up aerial photograph of Target-5. The picture had been taken four weeks earlier, a routine act to keep up to date their file on all American Arctic bases. 'The ramp at Target-5,' Papanin said, 'that place where they take their Sno-Cats down on to the pack. The sabotage team should be there by now.'

Kramer checked his watch. 10.30 PM. He didn't know it but the lead was closing on Beaumont at this moment twenty-five miles away to the west. 'Our men arrived there an hour ago,' the Balt replied. 'With their radar they'll have found the American base even in the fog.'

'And the airstrip – that must be sabotaged as well.'

'The same team deals with both – ramp and airstrip. They'll do it the way you suggested . . .'

'No international incident, remember,' Papanin warned.

'If anything happens it will look like an accident – or a series of accidents. Within thirty minutes Target-5 will be sealed off from the outside world . . .'

'Not if their wireless hut is still in action!'

'It won't be. The same sabotage team is dealing with that, too.'

But Papanin was hardly listening as he slumped with his arms folded across the back of the chair. 'Beaumont,' he muttered. 'Beaumont,' he repeated. 'That name rings a bell somewhere. Kramer, get me a message pad. I want to send an urgent signal to Petrov at Records in Leningrad.'

'I think you're dead wrong . . .'

'We go due east,' Beaumont told Grayson for the third time, 'and sooner or later we'll hit Target-5.' He lit a cigarette and it tasted bad because of the fog which had got into everything – including their lungs. The argument had been raging for ten minutes – which was the right way to go?

'We drifted a long way south on that floe,' Grayson insisted. 'Since I'm the navigator I should have some say . . .'

'You've had your say – and I don't agree with you.

Everything is drifting south – and too quickly for my liking. The icefield, Target-5, the Russian base, the floe we nearly got killed on – it's all drifting south at the same speed, so you discount the floe drift.'

'Up to a point you're right . . .'

'I'm dead right. And this isn't the House of Commons where they talk to save themselves doing anything – so we'll get moving.'

'Due east?'

'Where else?'

They started moving through the smothering fog. Over rough ice. So once again they had to keep a tight grip on the handlebar of each sled in an endless struggle to stop them keeling over. And soon after they had moved off they came up against a static pressure ridge they couldn't get round. They had to use ice-axes to chop a gateway in the wall, and it was back-breaking work, work which delayed them and used too much energy. The only bonus on the credit side was that they hadn't recently heard a single helicopter.

'It looks as though the Russians have given up,' Langer said hopefully as they passed through the gap in the ice wall. 'Or else they've run out of fuel.'

'Maybe,' Beaumont replied noncommittally. He was wondering whether they ought to pitch camp for the night. It was 11.30 PM and everyone was moving lethargically – even the dogs. The tension of the past few hours and the bitter cold was wearing them down – especially the cold. He glanced at the man walking beside him. For a while they had travelled with their snow-goggles over their eyes, but soon the fog had smeared them and they couldn't see where they were going, so now each man wore his goggles pushed back over his hood. The goggles above Grayson's hood were lenses of solid ice. His breath had frozen on the glass.

'We'll stop soon when we find a place to bed down,' Beaumont said.

'Thank God for that!' The American decided he had been a bit too eager to accept the suggestion. 'I could try one more radio-fix,' he suggested.

Among the equipment they were carrying on the sleds was a Redifon GR 345 transceiver and direction-finder, a portable high-frequency set with a peak power of only fifteen watts. But with this set they could communicate with Thule, let alone Curtis Field. They had stopped and listened in on the set three times since the Sikorskys had dropped them on the ice, hoping to hear a transmission from Target-5. They heard nothing – the island seemed to have gone off the air.

Had they heard only one transmission they could have used the direction-finder to locate Target-5's radio hut – to take a rough bearing they could have moved along. The absence of any transmission worried Beaumont, but he kept the worry to himself. 'Probably a lot of static – they know they can't get through so they don't try,' he said airily to Langer when he had queried the air-wave silence.

Ahead of them the fog began to thin out at ground level, but not higher up. They came to a more even area of ice, the best surface for pitching camp on they had come across so far, and Beaumont decided they had better stop. The dogs were slipping on the ice frequently now, a sure sign that they were feeling the strain, and a moment earlier Langer had called out a warning. 'Bismarck's lagging. The whole lot will pack up soon if we try to keep going.'

'I don't think we'll find a motel at this hour,' Beaumont called out, 'so we'll kip down here . . .'

He broke off, still holding the handlebar, staring straight in front of him. In the thinning fog something flared redly, vanished, flared up more fiercely. He couldn't believe it. He blinked, sure that he was seeing things, stared again. The fog drifted, rolled a curtain across the sight, a transparent curtain. The red flare burst out again, penetrated the curtain, climbed higher and billowed and wavered. There was a faint stench in his nostrils, a stench of smoke, and now the dogs caught the scent and became restless, sensing fire.

'What the hell is it?' Grayson croaked.

Beaumont didn't reply. Taking the compass from the American, he bent over, staring at the luminous dial carefully as he took a bearing. When he looked up the flare had become a dull, dangerous-looking glow, the kind of glow he had once seen from four miles away across the ice when an American research base off Alaska was burning.

'What is it?' Grayson repeated. 'It looks God-awful.'

'Forget about your kip,' Beaumont said grimly. 'We're moving again – as fast as we can drive the dogs. That's Target-5 going up in flames.'

Chapter Three

Tuesday, 22 February: 12.15 AM–8 AM

'Some maniac has done this crazy thing deliberately –
it's sabotage . . .'

Matthew Conway, the fifty-year-old station leader,
was blazing, blazing almost as furiously as his radio
hut had blazed when it became a flaming beacon in the
night. Beside him in the drifting fog Beaumont studied
the wreckage as Dr Conway played a powerful lamp
over what had recently been a large hut. Charred stumps
showed where the walls had stood, a twisted hunk of
metal lay half-buried under a pile of ash, and an acrid
smell of burning was still present in the windless
night. The hut had burned down to its foundations
and smoke wisps eddied and mingled with the fog.

'Why sabotage?' Beaumont asked as he hitched up
the rifle looped over his shoulder.

'When I got here the place was well alight but it
wasn't like this,' Conway said savagely. 'Rickard, the
wireless operator you met when you arrived, found it
on fire. When I got here it was becoming an inferno –
but the door hadn't gone. I noticed fresh wood splinters round the lock – it looked as if it had been forced
open.'

'Could have been the fire,' Beaumont said casually. He was trying to calm everyone down; since they had arrived ten minutes ago he had detected an air of tension in the three men waiting to be evacuated from the doomed base, a tension which had been there before the hut went up in flames.

'It didn't look like it,' Conway protested. 'Then there was the Coleman space heater – that twisted bit of metal. I could see through the open door and it was lying on its side. It was upright when Rickard left the hut earlier.'

'Maybe the fire caused it to keel over . . .'

'For God's sake, do you think I'm going out of my mind? I may have been on this island for three years but I've still kept my sanity! Those space heaters are heavy – you'd have to kick one hard to send it on its side.'

'All right, Matt, take it easy.' Beaumont walked round the smouldering ruin. He had known Conway for three years off and on, and twice he had visited Target-5 when it was drifting many hundred miles north of its present dangerous position. But in the fog it had all seemed different. When they saw the fire they had rushed across the ice and made their way up on to the island without trying to find the Sno-Cat ramp. They had dragged the sleds up a gully in the twenty-foot-high cliffs which reared above the pack and headed for the orange glow in the fog.

'That chunk of metal you can hardly see in the

corner is our transmitter,' Conway called out. 'Was our transmitter,' he amended. 'Now there's no way of getting through to the mainland – we're cut off until our plane comes in.'

'Which is in ten days' time,' Beaumont said as he stood next to the American. 'Why did they leave it so late?'

'It was my crazy idea.' Conway sounded disgusted. 'We've never had the chance to carry out depth-sounding and salinity tests this far south so I thought it was a heaven-sent opportunity. But I didn't count on the fog coming. And now this . . .'

'Who could have sabotaged the hut anyway?' Beaumont asked.

'There are only the three of us here – so no one. I don't know, the strain must be telling on me as well.' He changed the subject. 'What about this Russian that's supposed to be coming here?'

'He's a man called Gorov, Michael Gorov.' Beaumont's tone was off-hand and vague: Conway hadn't got top security clearance for his work. 'I don't know a lot about him, but I gather Washington thinks he could tell them something about the political set-up in Russia. He's supposed to be on his way here from North Pole 17.'

'And that's why you're here?'

'I have to pick him up and take him back to Curtis Field. It's as simple as that.'

'Simple – going back across the pack?' Conway

stared at the Englishman. 'I wouldn't make that trip for sixty thousand dollars.' Conway grinned as he rubbed globules of ice off his eyebrows. 'And I could do with sixty thousand dollars. Do we get back to the others now?'

'Is there somewhere we can talk first – on our own?'

'The research hut's just across here.' Conway led the way along a beaten snow-track between the surviving huts and Beaumont was pretty sure that the fog was thickening again. He was also sure that Conway was dead right: the radio hut had been sabotaged. But there was no point in increasing the tension on the island and he had a grimmer reason for keeping quiet. If Gorov did get through and they took him out they would be leaving the three men behind on Target-5. Conway he had no doubts about, but Rickard he didn't know and Sondeborg he didn't have to know: one look at the gravity specialist had told him he was on the verge of a crack-up. If the Russians arrived after they had left with Gorov and started putting on the pressure the men staying behind couldn't tell them anything – if they didn't know anything.

'You'll thaw out in here,' Conway said as he unlocked the door of a hut at the end of the line. 'We've left the heater on.'

The hut was about the same size as the head-quarters building they had gone inside when Beaumont arrived, one large room measuring about fifteen feet by twenty. Packing crates ready for the evacuation were pushed against the walls, but at one end a huge iron tripod reared up and supported a large winch mechanism. Conway pointed at the tripod. 'That's where we sling the underwater camera we send down to take a look at the seabed. We've sent the drilling core down through the same hole. Care to take a look?'

Conway bent down and levered up a section of the floorboards under the tripod. It came up as a large trap and Beaumont stared down a square hole about four feet across. Six feet below there were more floorboards. 'That's where we could hide Gorov in an emergency,' Conway suggested. 'He'd be damn cold but it's the best I can do.'

Beaumont stared at Conway across the deep well. 'What are you talking about?'

'Look, Keith, I told you I was still holding on to my sanity. And I can still work things out for myself. You bring two men over the pack from the edge of the fog – and all of you were flown there by chopper, you said. So this Gorov character, who must be pretty important, has taken off from the Russian base to come here – which means the Russian security people will be after him now. Correct?'

'I told you that.'

'Yes, but you didn't tell me that's why my radio hut has been sabotaged! They've done that to cut us off – so we can't signal Curtis Field when your Russian arrives. I worked that out while we were walking here from that mess up the street. Correct?'

'What's under that next lot of floorboards?' Beaumont asked. 'And you're correct – but don't spill any of it to Rickard or Sondeborg.'

'Soul of discretion!' Conway bent down again, took hold of a rope attached to a hook, pulled it. The lower boards opened up as a hinged trap and below there was darkness. Conway switched on his lamp, shone the powerful beam down the hole and the beam lost itself in a blackness which didn't end. A sour tang of salt drifted up into Beaumont's nostrils. At the edge of the beam walls of ice glistened.

'That's the Arctic down there,' Conway said. 'Two hundred feet down through the ice. Make a good place to hide a body.'

'Let's hope it doesn't come to that,' Beaumont replied tersely.

'It was a joke – helps to release the tension.' Conway lowered the trap on the sinister hole. 'You've probably noticed I'm a bit jumpy – maybe you'll understand why when I tell you I've got Michael Gorov in the next hut.'

The Russian fugitive, the Soviet Union's chief ocean-ographer, the architect of the Catherine system, lay unconscious in the single bunk which stood against one wall of the hut. Blankets pulled up to his chin still showed the hideously scarred face, the thick lips which were half-open as Gorov breathed noisily, the mass of straight dark hair pushed back over his forehead. Like Leonid Brezhnev he had thick eyebrows, but his cheeks were pinched and sallow.

'He arrived half an hour before you came in,' Conway explained. 'I was alone by the burning radio hut when he came staggering through the fog. I brought him in here to start with because it was the nearest place.'

It was ironical, Beaumont thought – someone had made a very bad mistake when they set fire to the hut. Because it was the blazing beacon of the burning hut which had shown him how to locate the ice island – and Gorov had undoubtedly used the same flaming landmark to find his way to Target-5. The Russian stirred restlessly in his sleep, murmured something which could have been a girl's name – Rachel – then he subsided again.

'Is he very bad?' Beaumont asked. 'You practised medicine once, so you should know.'

'The frostbite isn't as bad as it looks. Some of it is old scars and the fresh wounds I've treated. He couldn't stop talking and he was a bit hysterical, so I gave him a mild sedative to help him rest. He talked as though I should know he was coming so I let him – I thought that was part of the hysteria.'

'How did he get here?'

'He came over the pack by sled apparently . . .'

'Don't you know, Matt?' Beaumont demanded.

'There's no need to blow your top . . .'

'It's important! If that sled is lying out in the open and the Russians find it they'll know he's here.'

'I'm sorry, I see what you mean. He told me he lost his dogs somewhere close to here – he was taking a catnap and he hadn't tethered them properly. He had to manhaul the sled the rest of the way and it nearly killed him. Then he saw the hut blazing in the distance, so he took a quick compass bearing, abandoned the sled and made it here on foot.' Conway took the cigarette Beaumont offered him and the Russian stirred again as a match was struck. 'My guess would be he left the sled maybe half a mile beyond the cliffs. Is that bad?'

'Not too bad. How do you know he's Michael Gorov?'

'He said so . . .'

'Is this his jacket?' Beaumont picked up the jacket off a table and started going through the pockets. 'I don't remember you having a bunk here when I was last on the island.'

'I didn't.' Conway smiled grimly. 'The official reason is I do a lot of calculations in here and when I'm finished I can just tumble into bed. The real reason is it gets me away from the others for a few hours.'

'From Sondeborg in particular?' Beaumont was examining the contents of a wallet carefully, laying out items on the table.

'From Sondeborg especially – he's cracking up fast. And it's going to affect Rickard soon – panic is the most infectious of all human ailments. Is it necessary to go through his personal things?' Conway inquired with an edge in his voice.

'Yes! This card says he's Michael Gorov,' Beaumont replied sceptically. 'The trouble is we've got no picture of him. Did he say the security people were after him?'

'No, he clammed up just before I put him to bed. I think he was suspicious I didn't know anything about him. There was another reason I put him in this hut – kept him here, that is.' Beaumont stared at him without speaking as he picked up the Russian's damp parka. Close to the space heater which Conway had lit, snow had melted on the fur. 'The others don't know he's here,' Conway went on. 'He said enough for me to grasp he was a fugitive and I guessed Russian security might be on his tail – I don't want more panic than I've got on my hands already.' Conway paused. 'And if I had to hide him I didn't trust Sondeborg to keep his mouth shut.'

Beaumont looked at the American with fresh respect. 'That was clever of you, Matt, very clever. And it may be helpful – if the Russians do come. We may have to hide Gorov down that nasty hole of yours yet...'

'I didn't mean a live body,' Conway protested. 'I told you – it was a joke. My God, if you put him down there he'd freeze to death.'

'Not if we wrap him up well – cocoon him – and put a small heater down there with him. It would only be for a short time – while the Russians searched the base.'

'Searched the base!' Conway was outraged. 'They can't run a search here – this place has the American flag flying over it . . .'

Beaumont fetched up a long tube out of one of the parka's deep pockets, a tube measuring about a foot in length and heavy to hold. 'Matt, you haven't quite grasped it – and this is something else not to tell the other two. We're marooned on this base, cut off. No plane can fly in because of the fog, the radio transmitter has been eliminated. If every man on the island at this moment vanished into thin air no one could ever prove what had happened.'

Conway sank down on a hard, wooden chair slowly and stared up at Beaumont. 'Who's panicking now?' he asked with a forced smile. 'You can't really believe that – they wouldn't dare . . .'

'Get this very clear,' Beaumont said coldly. 'It wouldn't involve much daring, only a touch of ruthlessness. Supposing one of your Sno-Cats was found abandoned on the pack only a few miles away from here – out of fuel. When the fog lifts and someone flies in from Curtis they'd find the base empty, the radio hut burned down, the Sno-Cat out on the ice. What conclusion would they draw? That you'd all panicked when the fog closed the place in, when you lost your only means of communicating with the mainland, that you'd tried to get out on your own.

You run out of fuel and start back towards the island – on the way something happens to you. A lead opens up, a moving pressure ridge buries all of you . . .'

'This is horrible,' Conway protested. 'You're talking about a blueprint for mass murder . . .'

'I want you to know the score, Matt,' Beaumont said quietly. 'I'm talking about the Russian Special Security Service.'

'When are we moving out?'

Langer asked the question as he settled the dogs inside the hut opposite the headquarters building. The preparations for evacuating the base were well advanced and half the huts on the ice island were now unoccupied. The walls of the hut chosen for the dogs were lined with packing crates filled with equipment and waiting for the plane due in ten days' time.

'As soon as Gorov is fit to travel – sooner if there's an emergency, which there may well be,' Beaumont replied.

Langer adjusted the space heater he had carried to the hut and looked up wryly. 'We're expecting company? The wrong sort of company?'

'They've been here once – when they fired that radio hut. I think they're still very close. Horst, when you've sorted things out here I want you to unpack the transmitter and send a message in clear to Curtis Field. This is the message – Target-5 radio hut out of action. Sabotaged. Go on repeating the word sabotaged a few times, then sign off and pack the set up again.'

Langer patted the sleeping Bismarck who opened one bleary eye and closed it again. 'You mean I don't wait for confirmation on message received?'

'The message isn't for Curtis Field – it's for the Russian monitoring set at North Pole 17.'

'You wouldn't care to explain the mystery, would you?' Langer asked humorously. 'Just so I know what I'm doing, what's going on?'

'Later. And when you've done that I want you to take turns with Sam guarding that hut where Gorov is. If you run into trouble and there's no time left, fire one shot from your rifle into the air. When you're not guarding the hut, try and get some sleep.'

'You could do with some yourself,' Langer observed. 'We had the lion's share when we were drifting on that floe. And I'll forget about sleep if it means moving out of here faster. This place gives me the creeps – you know those three characters waiting for evacuation are on the edge of cracking up?'

'So we tread gently,' Beaumont warned.

He went out of the hut into the icy night and his expression tightened as he shut the door. He could just about see the headquarters hut which was only six feet across the beaten snow-track running between the two rows of buildings. The fog had thickened again, seemed to be intensifying as he stood for a moment and listened. Nearby he heard it, the quiet chugging of the generator which provided Target-5's lighting; and a long way off he heard something else – the muffled creaking and groaning of the polar pack surrounding the island.

When Target-5 cracked under that terrible weight the catastrophe would be very sudden. Fissures would appear out of nowhere, would widen into crevasses, which in turn would open up bottomless chasms as the whole island finally gave up after thirty years' resistance to the ceaseless squeeze of the polar pack.

But it wasn't the island Beaumont was worried about at this moment – it was what might be moving on it out of sight inside the dense rolling fog drifting all around him. He looked towards the hill he couldn't see, that strange forty-foot-high eminence with its embedded boulders, floating in the sea a hundred miles from the nearest coast. His eyes prickled with the cold; Horst was right, he was damned tired. He crossed the track, opened the door in the headquarters hut and called out to Grayson to join him. Then he waited outside while the American put on his parka.

Typically, the American asked not a single question while Beaumont explained about Gorov. He only made one comment as he hoisted his rifle over his shoulder before going up the track. 'Trouble in there. I'd like to drop that Sondeborg into the nearest open lead.'

Beaumont stiffened as he went inside and shut the door. He had heard raised voices from the outside but now Sondeborg was shouting as he argued with Conway. 'We can't get through to the mainland with the transmitter busted,' Sondeborg raved. 'Supposing the island starts breaking up before that plane gets here? We're trapped . . .'

The lean-faced gravity specialist stopped shouting as Beaumont closed the door. Along the facing wall stood a couple of two-tier bunks and Jeff Rickard, the wireless operator, sat on one of the lower bunks, chewing a matchstick as he watched Sondeborg. Conway was leaning against a table in the middle of the room with his arms folded and the flush on his pale face had nothing to do with the heat of the room.

'Get some sleep, Harv, for God's sake,' Rickard snapped. 'We've got company, so stop spilling your guts out.' The wireless operator, a cheerful thirty-two-year-old with curly black hair, reached out a hand to grasp the other man's arm. Sondeborg snatched it out of reach and glared at Beaumont. 'Why have you come here?' he demanded.

'I told you before,' Beaumont explained patiently. 'Our helicopter crashed on the ice and we were lucky to make it . . .'

'I don't believe a damn word!'

'Sorry to hear that.' There was an edge in Beaumont's voice as he propped his rifle in a corner. He took off his parka and laid it on the table. 'You've been drinking, haven't you?' It wasn't a brilliant deduction: he could smell the liquor on the gravity specialist's breath six feet away from him.

'He's got a bottle stashed away somewhere,' Conway informed Beaumont. 'I haven't been able to locate it yet. And this is his last Arctic trip.'

'Brother, are you telling me!' Sondeborg sneered. 'When I get on that plane the only ice I'll want to see is in a bar.'

'Which is where you'll take up your living quarters, no doubt,' Beaumont observed nastily.

Something snapped inside Sondeborg. He bent down, grasped an ice pick from under the table, a small-handled pick, stood up again slowly, staring at Beaumont with a blank expression.

'Put that down!' Conway said sharply.

'This big Limey takes up too much room,' Sondeborg said slowly and his right foot moved forward.

'Stay where you are, Rickard,' Beaumont warned. 'It doesn't look as though I'm too popular round here,' he went on as he picked up his parka from the table. 'I don't want to cause trouble, Conway,' he added. 'I'll move to one of the other huts . . .' He held the parka as though about to put it on while Sondeborg watched him uncertainly, then with a swift throwing movement like a matador wielding a cape he brought the coat down over Sondeborg's right arm. Sondeborg flailed with his arm to get the ice pick free and then Beaumont hit him. He hit him very hard with a powerful, short-armed jab which knocked Sondeborg back against the bunks. The gravity specialist sagged, fell half inside a bunk, then collapsed unconscious on the floor.

'Check him,' Beaumont snapped. 'How long before he comes round?'

Conway bent over the man and examined him quickly, then spoke over his shoulder. 'He's out cold. With the drink inside him he could be this way for several hours . . .'

'Can we get him out of here – into another hut?'

'The one next door has two bunks . . .'

'I'd like him shifted there,' Beaumont said crisply. 'I'd like him tied up, too.'

'Tied up?' Conway sounded surprised and uneasy.

'Tied up.' Beaumont lifted the ice pick off the floor. 'Any man who would threaten someone with this thing needs restraining. Restrain him – and padlock the door.' Conway opened his mouth to say something as Rickard was lifting Sondeborg over his shoulder. 'I've got a reason,' Beaumont said firmly, 'so padlock the door.' He went over to a tall cupboard standing by the wall, reached up over the top and brought something down in his hand. Conway stared at the object Beaumont put on the table.

'So that's where he kept it.'

'I'm taller than you are,' Beaumont pointed out, 'so I saw it when I came in this time. And there are two more of them up there.'

'Where the hell did he get this?' Conway picked up the bottle from the table and gazed at it as though he could hardly believe his eyes. He was holding a large bottle of Russian vodka. 'He couldn't have got it from Minsky, he's harmless – that's the man in charge at

North Pole 17. But he has been here from time to time to see how we're getting on.'

'To get information,' Beaumont replied. 'The Russians keep a detailed file on every American base in the Arctic – that's common knowledge. Minsky got his information from Sondeborg in exchange for the liquor you wouldn't let him have. Now maybe you'll agree to lock him up.'

'That signal worries me,' Dawes said. 'I think a crisis is building up – so I'm sending a plane in to Target-5.'

'But it's still fogged in,' Adams protested. 'How can anyone land?'

'That signal said the radio hut had been burned down – sabotage is the word they used. I'm sending in the transport we have standing by in case the fog clears – I'm sending in Ridgeway.'

'But how can it land?'

'I don't know,' Dawes admitted. 'But if anyone can land it's Ridgeway. He's made five landings on Target-5 in different parts of the Arctic and he's the finest civilian pilot within a thousand miles. Give Fuller the order.'

'I don't like it,' Adams said as he picked up the phone to talk to the airfield controller.

'Ridgeway won't like it either,' Dawes replied.

*

'I sent the signal,' Langer informed Beaumont as he shut the door. He looked round the hut. 'Where is everyone?'

'Putting Sondeborg to bed – after I'd put him to sleep.' He told Langer what had happened. 'I don't think anyone spotted it, but I tempted Sondeborg into a fight. I'm clearing the decks.'

'You're worried the Russians will come?' Langer dropped his parka on top of Beaumont's on the table. 'God, it's cold out there – I'd better go and relieve Sam in a few minutes.'

'I'm not worried the Russians will come – I'm sure they're coming,' Beaumont replied emphatically. 'The big question is whether they come before or after we've left. If it's before, I don't want a weak sister like Sondeborg available for them to question.' He pointed at the vodka bottle. 'Especially when he's already given them information to get drink. He told them about the radio hut.'

'They needed telling – with the mast sticking up above it?'

Beaumont leaned across the table and poured coffee out of the flask Conway had prepared for them. 'Get some of this inside you. Yes, they needed telling – that no one slept there. In some Arctic huts the operator has a bunk so he can stay on the job. Here it isn't necessary – Rickard only visited the hut when he was using the transmitter.' Beaumont poked at two foot-long metal tubes lying on the table. 'Recognize them?'

'Twenty-five thousand years of history inside one of these.' Langer picked up a tube and examined it casually. 'Amazing the way they send one of these down at the end of a drill, drive it into the seabed ten thousand feet down, and come up with a core. And the hollow tube they drive in comes back with a sample out of the seabed. Over thousands of years the geological layers at the bottom of the ocean are enormously compressed under the sea's weight, so we end up with this. Twenty-five thousand years and you can carry it about in your coat pocket.'

'Gorov did. See any difference between them?'

Langer examined the two tubes. Both were corroded and abraded by their long vertical journey through the sea, by the frictional drive of the drill forcing them into the far-down seabed, and both were filled with core material. 'They're just cores,' Langer replied, 'like those over there.' He nodded towards a collection of tubes Conway had arranged on top of a crate.

'This one is Gorov's.' Beaumont took the core and levered at its extremity with the tip of his penknife. A solid piece of core about three inches long dropped into his hand when he up-ended the tube. The piece of core at the other end remained in place as he shook the tube, and then something shiny and tightly rolled fell into his palm. He winked at Langer as he held a section of the 35-mm film up to the light. 'And this, unless I'm very much mistaken, is a microfilm of the Catherine charts.'

'My God . . .'

'Exactly. I'm holding in my hand a record of Russia's entire underwater system in the Arctic.' Beaumont re-rolled the film, slipped it back inside the tube, replaced the piece of core. 'So if we do lose Gorov we've still got this.'

'When he wakes up he'll notice it's gone,' Langer warned. 'In his place it would be the first thing I'd check the moment I did wake up.'

'So we'll keep him happy – by putting this one back in his parka.' Beaumont held up the second core tube, then checked his watch. 1 AM, local time. 'You might do that for me when you relieve Sam. And now I'm going to get some kip before I fall asleep in this chair.'

He had just taken his boots off and climbed into one of the lower bunks when the door was thrown open and Langer came back. 'I think the Russians are here – Sam heard their engines . . .'

The Siberian came across the ice from North Pole 17 by helicopter which landed at the eastern edge of the fog bank. Here he transferred to a waiting Sno-Cat, the curious tracked vehicle used for short-distance journeys in the Arctic. It has four caterpillar tracks – two at the front which support the driver's cab, and two more at the rear which carry the truck-like part of the vehicle.

'We should reach the American base at about one

o'clock,' Kramer said as he settled himself beside Papanin who had elected to drive the Sno-Cat.

'Which is the approximate time we estimated Gorov might arrive – if he was very lucky.'

Despite the fog they had no trouble locating the ice island. The security detachment which had made its way to Target-5 earlier had planted an electronic device at the summit of the hill behind Conway's encampment, a device which the box Kramer was holding locked on to, guiding them straight to their objective. But it was a hideously cold journey and Kramer was shivering when they arrived – as were the ten armed men huddled close together in the compartment behind the cab.

They avoided the snow ramp which would have allowed them to drive up on to the island; instead they left the Sno-Cat on the pack and went the rest of the way on foot. As in a chess game played by a grandmaster, everything was foreseen. When they came to the cliffs they used climbing equipment to haul themselves up the twenty-foot-high obstacle. When they had scaled the cliffs Kramer used his little box to guide them through the fog to the top of the boulder-strewn hill. And from the summit an erratic compass bearing showed them which was north – the side where the group of huts lay.

'Something's gone wrong,' Papanin whispered when they had gone down the slope and found nothing.

Something had gone wrong; since the last aerial

shot of Target-5 had been taken, since the fog had descended, the island had turned a few degrees, so it was only by good luck that the Siberian crashed into one of the empty huts before he knew it was there. A few minutes later, stumbling round like a blind man, he found the headquarters hut which now had a light burning outside it. He hammered on the door with his gloved fist, shouted in English, then opened the door and walked inside.

The Siberian's command of English was fluent; trained in a language laboratory at Kharkov in the Ukraine; perfected during long conversations with Guy Burgess in Moscow – when the English defector was sober enough to enunciate clearly – the Siberian had spent most of 1967 attached to one of the Soviet consulates in the south-western United States, consulates which have only one purpose to justify their expense: espionage.

Coming out of the fog the light dazzled Papanin. He lifted his hand to cut down the glare and saw three men inside the hut – the number Minsky had reported as still on Target-5 waiting to be evacuated. A very large man in his thirties was sitting on a bunk while he cleaned a rifle – and the muzzle was aimed at the doorway. A shorter man, fair-haired and also in his thirties, stood nearer the door with a rifle crooked in his arm while he held an oily rag in the other hand. The oldest man, in his fifties, was leaning against a table with his arms folded and a tense look.

'Come inside and shut the damned door,' the big

man snapped. The rifle elevated. 'No! Just you – the others can stay outside.'

Behind Papanin more fur-clad figures, all of them at least a foot shorter than the huge Siberian, stirred in the fog as he stepped inside the hut and stared at the man on the bunk. 'I am from North Pole 17 . . .'

'I said shut the door,' the big man said very quietly.

'Dr Kramer should be present,' Papanin insisted stiffly, 'he has something important to warn you about.'

'All right, Kramer comes in, too – the rest of them stay outside . . .'

'It is very cold . . .'

'No one invited you here.'

Papanin's expression was grim and he felt his temper rising as Kramer pushed in behind him. The fair-haired man with the rifle slammed the door in the faces of the men outside, bolted it with a savage, grating sound. Papanin glanced quickly round the hut for any sign of Gorov's presence on the base. He saw drilling cores laid out on a crate, an ice pick beside them, more packed crates, a flask and cups on the table the oldest man was still leaning against. Papanin was tall enough to have seen the two remaining bottles of vodka on top of the cupboard – except that they had been removed. The Siberian took off his damp parka and dropped it over the back of a chair.

'My name is Vassily,' he explained, his eyes still wandering round the hut. 'I am the administrative officer for various Soviet research bases, including your neighbour, North Pole 17. Dr Kramer is the medical officer there. Is everything all right here?' he inquired.

'Shouldn't it be?' Beaumont asked.

'I smelled something when we came through the fog, something burning . . .'

'Our wireless hut burned down,' Conway burst out. 'It was burned down deliberately. Is that the sort of trouble you had in mind?'

Beaumont inwardly congratulated Conway; the American had reacted exactly as he had suggested, which gave him his opening to throw the Siberian off balance. 'It's a pretty serious business this, Vassily – we've sent a signal to Greenland reporting the sabotage and someone's going to have to answer a lot of awkward questions.'

'You sent a signal about the fire?' There was a mocking tone of disbelief in Papanin's voice. These people must be wood from the neck upwards. 'Can you tell me how it is possible to use a transmitter when it was destroyed in the fire?'

'Spare transmitter,' Beaumont informed him laconically. 'We always keep a spare – do they only let you have one on Russian bases? I suppose we'll have to put it down to the extravagances of the capitalist system. Incidentally,' he went on, 'your monitoring unit at North Pole 17 will tell you about the signal when you get back.'

Beaumont waited, wondering whether his insurance policy was going to pay a dividend. The Siberian clearly hadn't yet been told about the signal, but it was vital: so long as he grasped the fact that a signal had been sent, that it had already been reported to Greenland that something very strange was going on at Target-5, he would hesitate to take extreme action. And this was all that Beaumont hoped for – hesitation, delay to give them time to get Gorov away from the ice island.

'Monitoring unit?' Papanin asked blankly.

'Oh, come off it!' Beaumont stood up and the two men seemed to fill the hut as they faced each other. 'Monitoring unit! Everyone knows you've got monitoring units all over the Arctic checking up on our signals. It's normal procedure, Vassily, so why make a big secret of it?'

Conway quietly put both hands inside his trouser pockets to hide the fact that he was sweating profusely. Beaumont was walking a high wire he could so easily fall off; there were armed men, a lot of them, just outside the hut, and no one might ever know what had really happened on Target-5 inside the fog. He was still doubtful whether the Englishman could out-manoeuvre the Russian, still horribly conscious of the fact that Gorov was hidden only yards away from where he stood.

'This is not what I came here to talk about,' Papanin snapped. 'I am afraid that one of our people may be responsible for burning down your hut,' he went on in a tone which was hardly apologetic.

'So there'll be a big inquiry,' Beaumont said

bluntly. 'By now Washington will have heard about it – you can imagine how they're going to react to the word sabotage!'

'If you will let me continue . . .'

'It could be hitting the world's headlines tomorrow – Russians attack US base . . .'

'That's ridiculous . . .'

'Buy tomorrow's paper and see.'

For the first time in many years Papanin was rattled. In case a signal had been sent he was going to have to tread carefully here. 'No international incident . . .' He could hear Comrade Brezhnev's instructions repeating in his brain as he tried to regain command of the situation.

'I am talking about Nikolai Marov, a junior oceanographer,' he explained. 'He has gone mad and murdered another man called Gorov. Then he escaped in this direction with a sled team. Marov has taken his victim's papers and may try to pass himself off as Michael Gorov . . .'

'Why should he do that?' Beaumont demanded.

'Because he left his own papers in his hut,' Papanin said smoothly. 'He would know that you might ask to see proof of his identity . . .'

'What makes you think he's mad?' Beaumont interjected.

Papanin glared at him, his patience wearing thin with the constant interruptions. He tried a new tactic, raising his voice. 'For God's sake, he burned down your hut! He committed a brutal crime! It was not a pleasant murder . . .' He took a step closer to Beaumont, trying to break him down by the force of his personality. 'He killed poor Gorov with an ice pick and then hacked him about the face! Don't you understand? He has spent three years in the Arctic and his mind has gone – he is like a wild animal roaming round somewhere out there on the ice . . .'

'Then you'd better stop wasting time and get out there and find him.'

Papanin calmed down suddenly, gestured towards Kramer. 'This thing is a great worry to us. When you have heard what it is all about you may wish us to stay. I think Dr Kramer had better explain – then you will understand how serious it is. I may sit down?' He pulled out a chair and sat down before anyone could agree, smiling amiably round the hut. 'Get on with it, Kramer.'

'Marov is a psychopath . . .' Kramer began in careful English.

'We don't want his medical history,' Beaumont said unpleasantly, determined to get the Siberian on his feet again. 'We've got quite enough on our plate without you people settling in for the night.'

Papanin stood up slowly, flexing his fingers to release some of the tension building up inside him. He had to be very careful; somehow the whole thing had turned round – instead of frightening these Americans Papanin himself felt dangerously off-balance. 'We came here to warn you,' he began as he collected his parka off the table, 'to ask for your cooperation . . .'

'We've been warned, we cooperated, we listened. Thank you. And now we've got a lot of work to do,' Beaumont broke in crisply.

'I was going to suggest we searched your huts – one of you could accompany us – in case Marov is hiding here.'

'Not necessary – we searched them ourselves when we saw that someone had fired the hut . . .'

Conway intervened, made a magnificent job of his intervention as his voice shook with genuine fury. 'This is an outrage! You come here and suggest searching the place? This is United States territory, Mr Vassily.' He stood away from the table as he faced Papanin. 'I hope I don't have to remind you that the American flag flies over this ice island?'

Papanin paused, stooped over, half inside his parka as he looked at Conway. He was going to shake these people before he left. 'I saw the flag when we came in – hanging limp like a piece of frozen cod.' He stood upright, fastening his coat. 'It might be safer if none of you leave this ice island until your plane arrives.'

'Safer from what?' Beaumont asked.

'If we see something moving on the pack my men may assume it is Marov and shoot,' Papanin said grimly. 'I have told them he must be taken unharmed – if possible. But Gorov had many friends and some of them are outside this hut – and all of them are armed.' He pulled the fur hood over his shaven head. 'Kramer, we did ask for these people's cooperation. Since we are no longer welcome we will go.' He glanced round the hut. 'A pleasant trip back to the United States, gentlemen. Here you are living on borrowed time.'

When they had gone Beaumont sent Grayson out to make sure they had really gone, then he looked at Conway who was drying his moist palms with a handkerchief. 'It's going to be extremely tricky from now on,' he warned. 'The man who called himself Vassily is Col. Igor Papanin, head of Special Security in Leningrad – I was shown his photograph before I left Washington.' Beaumont checked his watch. 1.45 AM. 'I'm going to take Gorov out by sled at eight o'clock this morning – in six hours' time. That will give us the best chance of avoiding the Russians.'

'Why eight o'clock?'

'Because by then they'll have been up all night somewhere out on the pack – waiting to see what happens. They'll have had six hours of it – listening hard, shivering, straining to see any sign of movement. By eight o'clock they'll be bad-tempered, bone-tired and not very alert. But it would help if I had a diversion when we move off.'

'I'll drive the Sno-Cat around,' Conway suggested quickly. 'I can take it across the island, down the ramp and move round on the pack a bit.'

'Which was what I was going to suggest – up to a point anyway.' Beaumont stood up, his eyes heavy, his limbs sluggish. He started walking around to keep himself awake. 'They found their way here in Sno-Cats – God knows how – and they may be carrying some kind of mobile radar. If you take the Sno-Cat out they'll concentrate on it – while we slip off the western end of the island.'

'It should fox them . . .'

'Listen, Matt.' Beaumont spoke with deliberation to stress the risk Conway would be running. 'There's a bunch of armed Russians within a mile of this hut, so you're not to take any unnecessary chances. I think I knocked Papanin off his perch when I said a signal had been sent . . .'

'He'll find out when he checks with his monitoring unit.'

For a moment Beaumont wondered whether to tell Conway about his own transmitter, then he decided against it. It was an even chance that Papanin would be back again, and next time he might ask questions rather more forcefully. 'That won't be until he gets back to North Pole 17,' he said. 'You can drive your Sno-Cat safely round the eastern part of the island – in this fog?'

'I've lived on this island for three years – in all weathers,' Conway assured him. 'I can put on the airstrip landing lights to guide me, I've got an angled beam on the Cat which shows me the way down the ramp . . .'

'Not down the ramp!' Beaumont said sharply. 'The island has your flag flying over it – once you go down on to the pack it's no man's land. If you're going to help at all you just drive around slowly on the island for an hour or so. On the island,' he repeated.

They had a great deal to do during the next half-hour. They called Langer out of the hut where he had stayed with the dogs to keep them quiet during Papanin's visit. They released Rickard from the hut next door where he had been locked in with the unconscious Sondeborg – ostensibly to keep an eye on the unstable gravity specialist, but also to prevent his hearing about the presence of Gorov on the island. Beaumont was determined that Conway would be the only man left behind on Target-5 who would know about Michael Gorov.

They left Conway and Rickard in the headquarters hut, and then Beaumont took the others with him to 'get Gorov out of the refrigerator', as he put it. Mercifully the Russian oceanographer was still asleep, still under the influence of the sedative when they lifted the trap-door in the research hut and hauled up his cocooned body. Had he woken up inside the deep tomb alone his reaction was something the imagination preferred not to dwell on – until he discovered the scribbled note Beaumont had left beside the lamp they had lowered with the heater.

Wrapped in many blankets, Gorov was surprisingly warm when they lifted him into the single bunk Conway had installed inside the research hut. He woke up as Conway slipped inside and closed the door. 'I wanted to see if he was OK,' the American explained. 'It gave me the horrors to think of him lying down there.'

'This place is different,' Gorov said as he eased

himself up on one elbow. 'You have moved me to a new hut. Why?'

Surprisingly alert, Beaumont noted, but a man who had made his way alone across the pack from North Pole 17 had to be unusually tough. He asked Conway to examine him again and lit a cigarette while he waited impatiently for the verdict. He was convinced they only had a few hours to get away from the ice island. Papanin would soon recover from the shock of his initial reception and then he would be back – and the second visitation would be much more dangerous than the first.

'He seems in good condition,' Conway said as he stood up from his patient. 'I can't understand it – after that ordeal.'

Beaumont started his interrogation at once, firing questions at the Russian who spoke good English. Like Papanin, Gorov had learned his English at the Kharkov language laboratory, a knowledge essential to his work. Once French had been the international language of the scientific fraternity, but for a quarter of a century it had been replaced by English – and Gorov liked to read scientific works in the original language. He was obviously taken aback by Beaumont's verbal onslaught.

'When were you last in Kiev?'

'Last week.'

'Meet any relatives there?'

'My brother, Peter . . .'

'He's in the Navy?'

'No, he's on a trawler . . .'

'What was the name of your girlfriend who died?'

Gorov's thick lips tightened. He stared bleakly at Beaumont. 'She was my fiancée. We were going to be married . . .'

'I asked for her name.'

'Rachel Levitzer. Is all this really necessary?'

'Yes! Is it by God?' Conway burst out, appalled by Beaumont's brutality.

'Yes, it is by God,' Beaumont replied tersely. He watched Gorov very carefully. 'Col. Igor Papanin was standing in this very room half an hour ago.'

Fear flashed into the Russian's eyes. He stared round the hut like a trapped man, tried to say something, swallowed uncomfortably. It was the instantaneous reaction Beaumont had been hoping for; if this man had been a stooge – sent to the island by Papanin as a spy – he couldn't have pretended naked fear so spontaneously.

Beaumont explained what he had been doing and the reasons for it. No photograph was available in Washington of Michael Gorov and this was the only way to check his identity. At least now when they started out across the ice on their terrible journey they would know they were taking the right man.

Conway gave Gorov a drink from the bottle of brandy he had brought with him, a bottle he kept securely locked away in a cupboard so that Sondeborg wouldn't guzzle the lot. At Beaumont's suggestion he prepared food for the Russian on a primus in the research hut, and all the time the fugitive sat at the edge of the bunk, lacing and unlacing his strong fingers, running them nervously through his lank black hair.

Earlier, soon after the interrogation had ended, he had got up to stretch his legs and had wandered over to the chair where his parka lay draped. Casually, he had lifted the parka to sit for a moment; even more casually he had run his hand over the pocket which contained the core tube, had felt its cylindrical shape under the fur. Langer, standing near the door, smiled to himself as Gorov sat down, visibly relaxed that his precious possession was still safe.

That night it was fatal for Beaumont to think of sleep. He had just said that he was going back to the headquarters hut to lie down for a while when they all heard it. The distant drone of an aircraft coming in. The Hercules C130 transport which Dawes, worried stiff by the 'sabotage' signal, had sent, was circling overhead, waiting to land.

Col. Igor Papanin was also listening to the drone of the American transport plane. A few hundred metres away from the snow ramp leading down from Target-5 he sat in the cab of his Sno-Cat alongside Kramer, calmly puffing at his little curved pipe. The atmosphere inside the sealed cab was thick with smoke, so thick that Kramer thought he would soon expire. But he dare not open a window because that would let the Arctic flood in.

'They've switched the landing lights on,' he said nervously. The blurred glow of a single landing light wobbled beyond the top of the cliffs, then the fog masked it.

'Naturally,' Papanin said, 'they have to show their plane where to land.'

'And you still think Gorov isn't there?'

'I said I wasn't convinced that he had yet arrived – a different thing, Kramer. I was looking for fear and anxiety when we arrived but all I detected was indignation. That big man was very aggressively indignant,' he said thoughtfully.

'But if he has arrived – and the plane lands?'

'You worry too much. It's going to be all right – you'll see.'

Seven hundred feet above Target-5 the plane's pilot, Alfred Ridgeway, sat in front of his controls as he circled over what another pilot, Arnold Schumacher, had called the oatmeal, the thick bank of dirt-grey fog below him. In the cargo compartment behind him two rows of bucket seats lined the fuselage and the rear seats were occupied by twelve men in Arctic clothing who carried concealed weapons.

The twelve men belonged to the US Coastguard Service and they had been specially chosen for this job. In Leningrad the Russians had sent a Special Security detachment to the Arctic because this gave the expedition a non-military character – which neutralized the danger of an international incident building up only a few months before the summit meeting in Moscow. Washington was taking the same precaution for the same reason: there must be no danger of an international incident.

The two seats nearest the pilot's cabin were occupied by a different type of passenger, by a doctor and a nurse. Dr Maxwell Hergsheimer, forty-eight years old and grey-haired, who was equipped with a medical kit and oxygen cylinders for his Russian patient, stared out of the window as the fog rolled in great banks below. Behind him sat Nurse Anne Clyde from Brooklyn, the thirty-year-old girl who had volunteered to come with him. Hergsheimer was worried about her; not every girl would have so calmly contemplated a trip out over the polar wastes. And to emphasize the civilian character of their mission she wore her uniform. She leaned forward over his shoulder. 'Do you think Captain Ridgeway will get us down?' she inquired.

'I think so, yes. He comes from my home state, Illinois, and I've known him for years. He'll go on circling until he does see his way in.'

In the pilot's cabin Ridgeway's sentiments were rather less optimistic. In fact, Ridgeway was very worried indeed. There was no sign of a gap in the fog anywhere; if anything it was getting worse as it floated like a dark, poison-gas cloud under the pallid light of the moon. He glanced at the fuel gauge. Plenty left: he'd damned well go on circling until there was only enough gas to get them back to Curtis.

'I'm beginning to wonder whether I saw those landing lights at all,' van Beeck, his co-pilot, commented.

'Want to go home, Jim? You said you saw them – did you?'

'I saw them, Captain.'

'OK. So we keep circling.'

Beaumont was sweating with anxiety as he stood close to one of the landing lights Conway had switched on. In the fog it glowed like a small greenish fire. He was standing with Conway at the edge of the airstrip, a quarter of a mile away from the cluster of huts where five more men waited in equal anxiety. Then he heard the faint drone of the plane coming back, a drone growing steadily louder.

'Thank God,' Conway muttered. 'I thought he'd given up.'

Thank God, Beaumont agreed to himself. And the fog was thinning a little. The plane only had to land to secure their salvation; at Curtis Field Dawes had told him about the coastguard detachment standing by and Beaumont was confident it would be on board. With a detachment of a dozen armed men on the island Papanin would be checkmated.

'Do you think he can land in this stuff?' Conway whispered.

In the fog, whispering came naturally. It shifted all around them, assuming strange, menacing shapes, and the cold was intense. They shifted their boots frequently, stretched their toes inside them, anything to keep a fraction of circulation moving while they waited and the invisible plane's engines built up into a muffled roar. Soon it was dead overhead, and the fog thinned a little more. But not enough, Beaumont was thinking. 'He can't be thinking of landing yet,' he murmured. 'I wonder what visibility is like up there . . .'

Visibility from five hundred feet up had improved: instead of being impossible it was bad to awful. Ridgeway banked the plane more steeply to get a better look down and grunted. It was a habit of which he was unaware – grunting – but the noise was significant for van Beeck. It told the co-pilot that his captain had just taken a tricky decision. He waited while Ridgeway stared hard into the fog.

The pilot had seen the landing lights, he had guessed that this improved situation would be short-lived, that soon the fog would roll over again. It would have been a considerable overstatement to say that the parallel lines of lights were visible – they showed to Ridgeway in the banked plane as two vague strings of pale glows: no more, but they showed him where the airstrip was. It was between those two faint lines and that was enough for him.

'We're going in,' he said. 'Tell them.'

The co-pilot left his seat, went back into the cargo compartment and called out to his fourteen passengers. 'Time to strap yourselves in – we're going down . . .'

'You see,' Dr Hergsheimer told Nurse Clyde, 'I was right – he's from Illinois.'

In the control cabin Ridgeway was banking his machine away from the island, turning in a wide sweep to give himself a good run-in. The lights had vanished now and he was praying he would see them again when he had completed his turn. The sweep continued, swinging out over the desolate polar pack which was invisible, then he was on course, screwing up his eyes as he stared ahead.

The damned lights seemed fainter now, hardly more than a blurred phosphorescence beneath the fog. The machine went into a shallow glide, the blur came up to meet it. Gear and flaps down. The four propellers whipped through wisps of fog, the motors beat steadily, the ice island came up to meet them. It was an exercise Ridgeway had repeated many times before. He had landed five times on Target-5 in various parts of the Arctic – all of them hundreds of miles north of this latitude.

Don't overshoot! The warning flashed through his brain. There was just sufficient length of airstrip to land on – provided he touched down in time. The lights merged into glow-lines, the skids touched down, the machine wobbled as though starting to skid, so they were tearing over the ice blind except for the glow rushing past them on either side. So long as there was no obstruction in the way ... The propellers beating the air thrashed up a storm of snow, obliterating the glow on either side, and then Ridgeway completed the landing, reversing propeller pitch and braking to bring the machine to a halt.

Beaumont and Conway were at the edge of the airstrip when they heard the increase in engine sound and realized the transport was coming in to land. 'Get well back!' Beaumont shouted. They moved away from the airstrip, went back a short distance, and when they turned round the lights of the plane were visible, dropping towards them at what seemed slow-motion speed.

'God! He's going to overshoot ...' Conway stood quite still, frozen with fear as well as with cold.

'He'll make it!' Beaumont shouted the words above the roar of the engines. The fog made distance impossible to judge, visibility from above must be better than it seemed at ground level – otherwise the pilot would never have attempted the landing. Beaumont saw the wings which carried the lights, a dark silhouette plunging through fog swirls as it thundered along the airstrip. In the Arctic night the engines were deafening, a thudding roar, then the machine touched down, sent up spurts of snow as the skis sped along the ice, sent up cloudbursts of snow as the propellers churned. The plane seemed enormous bursting through the fog. Then it was past them and Beaumont thought he heard the hiss of skis above the roar. Their aerial taxi had arrived.

The plane went on through the fog. They heard the engine sound change as the pilot reversed propeller pitch. In a moment the machine would be stationary, its propellers ticking over as the pilot cut his motors. They could still see it as a blurred, retreating shape when the silhouette altered. One moment it was horizontal, the next moment it was swinging up vertically, the tail high in the air, then the tail smashed down, vanished. The vibration of the impact travelled through the ice, echoed up their legs. The petrol tanks detonated, deafened Beaumont. The flare of flame, the flash which seared right through the fog, blinded him for a moment. Then there was crackling fire, black smoke.

As the echo of the detonation died away Papanin opened the window and knocked out his pipe. 'You see, Kramer, I said it would be all right.'

There were no survivors. The heat was so intense that for a brief time it burned a hole in the fog, exposing moonlit sky before the smoke masked it again. The plane was burning itself to cinders on a carpet of ice and the inferno faded suddenly, leaving only creeping smoke and a nauseous stench which turned Beaumont's stomach, a stench compounded of petrol, plane – and people.

He had completed a careful circuit of the disaster when Conway, breathing heavily, caught up with him. 'There must be someone alive . . .'

'It's hopeless, Conway. No one could survive that – you might just as well have shoved them head first into an incinerator.'

'Beaumont – look at this . . .' The American's voice trembled and he was holding something in his hand, something crumpled and smeared with oil. He opened it out, reassembled it into a caricature of its original shape. 'Beaumont, it's a nurse's cap.'

'They must have brought her to attend to Gorov . . .'

'Why the hell had that plane to crash? It was down – it was safe, it was stopping when . . .'

'Come over here.' Beaumont walked a few paces on to the airstrip, bent down and heaved at a large object close to a skid-mark which scarred the snow. 'This is why, Conway. The plane caught this rock and somersaulted. One of the machine's skids is over there – it must have ripped away when it struck the boulder.'

'I swept the airstrip with the snow-plough – swept it two days ago.' Conway sounded bewildered, in a state of shock. 'I just couldn't have missed a thing that size . . .'

'You missed this one, too.' Beaumont moved a few feet further across the airstrip and hammered his boot against a second snow-covered boulder. 'And that one . . .' He had only just seen the third obstruction and he bent down to examine it, telling the American to focus his lamp on it. Conway stared down at the rock in silence as Beaumont heaved it over and scraped at the underside with his gloved fingers.

'You missed all three of them,' Beaumont continued, 'for the very simple reason they weren't here when you swept the airstrip. There's very little snow underneath this rock and not much more on top – what there is came from the whirling propellers.'

'You mean . . .'

'Yes! These boulders are from the hill behind the camp and boulders don't walk a quarter of a mile. They were carried here in case a plane did try to land. It's sabotage again, Conway – sabotage of the most brutal kind. God knows how many poor devils were on that plane besides the nurse.'

'The bastards!'

'Take it easy. We've got to get back to the camp.'

'I'll see this gets into every newspaper in America . . .'

'You won't, you know.' Beaumont took a grip on Conway's arm and started him moving. 'You haven't got a shred of evidence to back up that statement . . .'

'The boulders, for God's sake!'

'The Russians would say the rocks must have been there all the time, that the wind blew snow away and exposed them – maybe even that it was your fault for not sweeping the strip properly. Someone has organized a very nasty and very effective accident. I just hope it's not setting a pattern for the future.'

The Sno-Cat ground its way through the fog, the two pairs of heavy tracks kicking up the devil of a row as they revolved over the ice. One headlight beam poked at the fog beyond the cab, the second light mounted outside the cab window was angled downwards. Inside the cab Conway leaned well over to check the angled light: he was going to depend on that lamp soon, depend on it to stop him plunging twenty feet over a sheer drop down on to the polar pack.

Muffled inside his fur parka and fur hood, he checked his watch. 8 AM exactly. So he had got the timing right; in a few minutes he should see one of the airstrip landing lights he had switched on. He moved the gear lever, moved the big lever which turned the tracks, checked the milometer as he changed direction. Conway, a peaceable man, had a loaded rifle on the seat beside him as he drove on into nothing with the memory of the nurse's cap vivid in his mind. Screwing up his eyes, he frowned: the windscreen was messed up and the wipers were spreading dirt over the glass. He stopped the Cat, left the engine ticking over and climbed out with a cleaning rag.

Fog rolled over the Sno-Cat, blotted out the rear of the vehicle, and Conway looked round nervously as he rubbed at the glass. Fog everywhere, fog which could conceal an army of Russians. He cleaned the glass quickly, got back up into the cab, and the closing of the door was a relief, made him feel a little safer because he was high up and enclosed. He checked the milometer, moved the big lever and the cumbersome machine ground slowly forward. The dangerous part was coming.

Crouched over his levers, the American leaned close to the windscreen where the wipers kept a fan-shaped segment clear of moisture. He must be close to the cliff now – if he had any idea of where he was going – and now he was staring at the ground below the angled headlight. Entirely on his own, Conway was extending Beaumont's deception plan – he was going to drive the Sno-Cat to the ramp, take it down on to the pack and drive it a quarter of the way round the island. With the aid of the angled headlight he could keep the cliff in view and avoid any risk of losing himself out on the pack.

Then he was going to abandon the Sno-Cat, walk back to the ramp and return to camp. He would leave the Sno-Cat with its nose pointed north, its steering mechanism jammed. When the Russians found it they would assume that someone had escaped from the island – panicked by the plane crash – and that they were heading north instead of west.

With one hand he lit a cigarette, and that made him feel a little better. Then he changed course suddenly. The angled light had projected its beam into a vacuum, into nothing. He was moving along the edge of the cliff-top. For safety's sake he took the vehicle back a dozen yards, then he watched for the lamp on top of the wooden post which would tell him he had made it. In a few minutes he would be going down the ramp.

'East . . . east . . . east. The ramp.'

Kramer switched off the microphone which linked him with the men on the pack surrounding the island, the men equipped with the Soviet version of the American walkie-talkie transmitter. They would all now be converging, hurrying towards the Sno-Cat – and the ramp.

The Balt was sitting next to Papanin inside the Sno-Cat which was stationary in the fog. In the compartment behind them the radar operator gazed at his scanner, tracking the slow approach of Conway's vehicle across the island. Above him on the roof the radar wing revolved, turning through the fog. It was very quiet out on the pack as Papanin clenched his pipe and stared towards Target-5.

'Do you think Gorov will go with them?' Kramer asked.

'How the hell do I know? There are two possi-bilities – he is with them, or he isn't. If he is, the problem will be solved. If he isn't, we can go and take possession of an empty camp and wait for him. Can't you work out anything for yourself?'

The Siberian looked through the window to his left. When the fog drifted he could just see the outline of a second Sno-Cat, also stationary and with its engine silent. It carried eight more men, four of them armed with automatic weapons. He looked at his watch. 8.05 AM. By 8.15 another piece would have been removed from the board.

Conway was on top of the ramp. He manoeuvred the Cat with great care as he felt the front tracks dropping. Three years ago they had built up the ramp with supporting rocks taken from the hill, they had curved it to follow the cliff wall with a drop to the right so he had to turn the vehicle to the left slowly, keeping very close to the cliff wall.

He braked, kept the engine running, peered out of the window. The angled light shone on no firm surface: it dropped into the fog, gave you the feeling you were looking down a mountainside. Conway's hands were sticky inside his gloves as he went on peering down. Normally he would never have attempted the descent in conditions like these – he was wondering whether to reverse, to go back on to the island.

'To hell with that!'

He spoke the words aloud, a habit he had developed because he was so often alone, carrying out experiments on the pack. The fog obscured everything on the dangerous side; on the other side the light showed a blur of cliff wall. He'd have to concentrate on keeping close to the blur, resisting the temptation to look towards the drop.

Releasing the brake, he started the vehicle turning down the curve, a tricky operation because the huge rear tracks had to haul themselves round after the front caterpillars. He stared at the blurred wall barely a foot away and his seat tilted him forward as the Sno-Cat slanted downwards, its right-hand tracks less than a foot from the brink where the fog hid the pack below. The tracks crawled down the ramp, Conway's hand gripped the lever tightly, sweat dripped off his forehead. Thank God the Cat was responding, was going down nicely. Without warning the vehicle keeled and Conway felt it turning, dropping.

The outer edge of the ramp where supporting rocks had been levered out of the ice collapsed. The huge weight of the vehicle completed the disaster. While Conway was still fighting with the controls the Sno-Cat went over sideways, then went straight down twenty feet on to the hard pack. Conway had switched off the engine, an instinctive reflex when he was going

over, and then he was upside down. The roof struck
the ice and the terrible weight of the tracks came
down on the up-ended floor of the cab, concertinaing
the tiny compartment, crushing the man inside into
an unrecognizable shape of smashed bone, tissue,
metal and glass.

A mile away on the far side of the island, unaware
of the tragedy, Beaumont led his small party down on
to the pack the Russian security guards had just left
and headed westward.

Chapter Four

Tuesday, 22 February: 10 AM–Noon

This was how the whole world – Europe, the Americas, Australasia, Asia, Africa – might look one day; a lifeless, sterile, frozen desert when the earth moved away from the sun and became an extinct satellite. It was like a preview of the death of the human race.

Wafted by the merest of breezes, a chilling stream of ice-cold air which came direct from the North Pole, the fog had shifted south, exposing the moonlit frozen desert Beaumont and the two sled teams were moving over. They had an endless view to the west and the north, the same God-awful expanse of ice, ice and more ice. Even in the land deserts of the world something grows somewhere; there are isolated oases, pockets of green trees and burning blue water. Here there was nothing but hideous ice – going on for ever.

Pressure ridges loomed in the moonlight ahead of them, a chaos of static ridges ten to twenty feet high. Guided by Grayson's erratic compass they were heading due west, sledding towards distant Greenland over a hundred miles away, and Beaumont was still wondering whether to take out his insurance policy –

to head due south instead of west, south to the most dangerous place on earth, Iceberg Alley.

Since the fog had withdrawn its concealing curtain over an hour ago they had seen no sign of the Russians. It was possible that Papanin's men were still patrolling the fringes of Target-5, waiting for Gorov to come in. Beaumont glanced over his shoulder as he drove his sled and Grayson hurried up to him. 'How is our first-class passenger getting on, Sam?'

'Gorov is a pain in the ass,' Grayson said inelegantly. 'He's still sulking over that cross-examination you put him through, and he sits on Horst's sled as though he's some kind of emperor. I'd make the bastard hoof it.'

'Later. He'd just hold us back at the moment...' Beaumont broke off, looked quickly into the sky. A small dark blip was coming in from the north-east, heading directly towards them. Like an ugly bird it cruised across the night sky, too far off yet for the blur of its rotor disc to be seen, for the sound of its engine to be heard.

'Chopper! Get under cover...'

Beaumont cracked his whip as he shouted the warning, driving the dogs faster towards the shelter of the pressure ridges while behind him Langer shouted at Gorov to get off the bloody sled, to run. The Russian tumbled off the moving sled, fell over on the ice, swore in his own language and then stumbled after them in desperate haste. The sound of the engine beat of the oncoming machine could be heard now, a faint sound growing louder by the second. Beaumont's team plunged through a gap in the first ice wall and then they were inside a corridor, halting as Beaumont pulled at the sled. Langer followed them through the gap as Gorov tried to catch up, still out in the open as the Soviet machine drummed closer. With a curse Grayson grabbed at the Russian and threw him under the lee of the ice wall. They waited, staring up while the dogs, huddled together, also gazed at the sky.

The machine they could no longer see was flying low, no more than two hundred feet above the ice, and if it passed over them they were bound to be spotted. Crouched against the pressure wall which climbed fifteen feet above them, its crest curling over them like a breaking wave, they listened and watched for the helicopter to appear overhead. The throb-echo grew louder, vibrated down the ravine where they pressed themselves against the ice. And then Langer was in trouble with the dogs as two of them started to jump about, hating the helicopter's noise, equating it with the machine which had brought them to the edge of the fog bank. He slapped one hard and the animal turned on him, showed its teeth, let out a menacing growl. If the dogs careered out into the ravine it was certain they would be seen. Nothing shows from the air like movement.

Beaumont glanced over his shoulder anxiously, unable to leave his own team which was becoming infected by the commotion. He was astounded to see Gorov crawling along the ground on his knees, stretching out a hand and squeezing the rebellious animal's neck as he called to it in Russian. The animal relaxed, permitted itself to be stroked, and the second dog stopped struggling, staring as though it resented the special treatment its colleague was enjoying. Then something flashed over the ravine, the shadow of the machine.

Before there had been tension, anticipation, now they froze with fear, holding their breath without realizing it. And the dogs froze, too, remained absolutely still. They didn't see the helicopter – only its shadow – then it was flying westward, away from them. 'Stay here till I get back,' Beaumont ordered. Shielded by the pressure wall, he stood up and walked along it until he found a high point on its crest. He clambered up the wall carefully, jabbing his boots into crevices until he could peer over the crest.

It was a good look-out point. Beyond him more jagged ridges spread away, lower ridges he could see over, and about half a mile away the ridges ended and the ice flattened out. The belt of flat ice stretched into the distance like a sheet of plate glass, ideal terrain for them to sled across except for one thing – the Russians were in the way.

Small groups – he counted a dozen – were spaced out over the belt with long distances between them. And they were all sled-teams, moving slowly away from him, heading west towards faraway Greenland. Several miles across the ice two helicopters flew above the pack as though patrolling. The machine which had passed near them landed while he was watching, came down on the level ice close to one of the sled-teams. The rotors had hardly stopped whirling when the door opened and a stream of dogs poured out on to the ice. Men followed the animals, sleds were unloaded, and within minutes the men were harness-ing the dogs. The speed of the operation impressed Beaumont. Ten minutes after he had first looked over the crest the helicopter took off, climbed to about five hundred feet and flew off to the north-east. Beaumont slithered back into the ravine, hurried back to where the others were waiting. The argument flared up almost at once.

'Well, it missed us, thank Christ,' Grayson said.

'It wasn't looking too hard – it's just unloaded more sled-teams.'

'More?'

'Sam, not more than half a mile away to the west the ice is lousy with Russian search teams. Some of them are a long way west – and they've got choppers above them.'

'They're coming this way?'

'At the moment they're heading away from us . . .'

'OK. So we creep along behind them.'

'It won't work. Remember that wide belt of smooth ice we saw when we flew in over the pack? They're spread out across that. If we try to cross that belt they'll spot us. Papanin just slammed the door in our faces.'

Short of sleep, the memory of the air crash horror still fresh in his mind, Grayson faced Beaumont and his temper was going fast. 'You're dead wrong, Keith,' he said quietly. 'The only safe way out is westward. We have to hit the Greenland coast. Once we get there we're OK – the Russians can't invade Greenland.'

'A perfect plan,' Beaumont said sardonically, 'except the bit about hitting the Greenland coast. I keep telling you – the Russians are in the way . . .'

'We can slip through those search teams. The ice is big – too big for them to cover it all.'

'You're not getting the message. It's not only the men on the ice – they're patrolling that belt from the air . . .'

'So which way do we go?' Grayson flared. 'North towards the bloody Pole? East back to Target-5 where Papanin's waiting for us? South . . .'

'South,' Beaumont interjected. 'That's where we're going.'

Gorov, who had been listening intently, added his own contribution to the growing tension. 'South? That is madness . . .'

'You're not invited into this debate,' Grayson told him roughly. He turned back to Beaumont. 'We'd be heading straight for the edge of the icefield, straight for Iceberg Alley. I suppose when we get there we make the sleds seaworthy and float 'em all the way down to Cape Farewell?'

'Stop busting a gut,' Beaumont rapped back. 'We'll be going aboard the icebreaker *Elroy*. She's already coming hell for leather up Iceberg Alley – I fixed that with Dawes in Washington in case something like this happened.'

Grayson was astounded. 'And you really think we have a snowflake's chance in hell of rendezvousing with her?'

'We will rendezvous with her. She's coming up the tenth meridian and we go down it to meet her. You'll have to take frequent star-fixes to check our position.' The decision taken, Beaumont started forming up his own dog team, but Grayson hadn't finished yet.

'You make it sound like we'll be going down the New Jersey Turnpike. The star-fixes may not be accurate – you know that. It would be one pinpoint trying to find another pinpoint . . .'

'With the aid of a little science.' Beaumont pointed to his sled. 'Don't forget we have the Elliott homing beacon. When we get within range of where the *Elroy* should be we'll send them a signal on the Redifon set. They'll send up the helicopter they have on board and it will home in on our beacon.'

'I don't like it.' Grayson looked at Langer who had listened to the argument in silence. 'Do you like it?'

'Look, Sam . . .' Beaumont's voice hardened. 'That's the way it's going to be. We did the same thing once before when we made rendezvous with the *Edisto* near Spitsbergen.'

Grayson exploded. 'We were heading for land then! This time we'll be heading for the edge of the icefield – beyond that there's nothing but Iceberg Alley, the ocean . . .'

'Sam,' Langer intervened, 'before Keith started talking what was the last thing you'd have expected him to do?'

'Head south . . .'

'So that's the last thing Papanin will expect us to do.'

Gorov, who had been clasping and unclasping his gloved hands, burst out suddenly. 'I do not think we should do this very crazy thing.'

Grayson turned round and spoke very deliberately to the Russian. 'If it wasn't for you, we wouldn't be in this mess. If you don't like it, you'd better start hiking your way back to Leningrad – because we're going south!'

He formed up his dogs and they moved off with Beaumont in the lead. Within five minutes they were turning through an angle of ninety degrees, heading south away from the great belt of ice where the going would have been so much easier. For over two hours they travelled across ice littered with ravines and pressure walls they had to thread their way through, then Beaumont called a brief halt. It was Grayson who sent the signal on the prearranged wavelength, the signal Dawes was waiting for at Curtis Field.

'Oxygen ... Strongbow ... Oxygen ... Strongbow ...'

He repeated the signal for five minutes before
Curtis acknowledged, which was too long because it
might be long enough for the Soviet monitors at North
Pole 17 to take a radio-direction fix. But the signal had
to get through. 'Strongbow' informed Dawes that
Michael Gorov had been picked up; 'Oxygen' told
him that Beaumont was heading south. Grayson tele-
scoped the Redifon aerial back inside the set and
looked up at the sky.

'No Russian planes for two hours,' he said. 'And
no American planes either,' he added. 'Those pilots at
Curtis must have gone home for the winter. I hope to
God the icebreaker *Elroy* hasn't gone home too ...'

'... *urgent you penetrate icefield for possible rendezvous.
Maximum risk must be accepted. Repeat. Must be
accepted.*'

Commander Alfred Schmidt, USN, captain of the
6,515-ton icebreaker *Elroy*, still didn't like the signal
he had received from Washington three days earlier,
and the more he thought about it the less he liked the
last part of the signal. 'Maximum risk ...' What the hell
was a maximum risk in these waters? Did you decide
that maybe you'd had enough when the ship was going
down because it was overladen with ice, because it
had just struck an iceberg? Schmidt, forty-three years
old, five feet eight tall and very wide-shouldered, had

thick dark hair and thick dark brows. His expression was invariably bleak, not to say grim. And he only smiled in moments of extreme danger, which was the origin of the toast seamen drank to when they had their last beers in a bar in Milwaukee, the *Elroy*'s home port.

'Here's hopin' – no smilin' from the Cap'n till we hit port again.'

'Care to take a look, sir?' Vance Carlson, the mate, stood back from the radarscope and pulled up the collar of his coat. The high bridge of the *Elroy* was heated but something seemed to have gone wrong with the system. Perhaps the something was the Arctic conditions outside which were keeping a team of men permanently at work shovelling ice over the side, ice which seemed to form as rapidly as they cast it into the floe-littered sea.

Commander Schmidt didn't care to take a look, but he looked all the same. Three hours earlier when he had looked down inside the rubber hood he had seen isolated blips showing on the scope, blips which were not ships, blips to the north-west and north-east. He stared down as he watched the sweep turning remorselessly round the greenish glow inside the hood. No more isolated blips now; instead a solid unbroken pattern of echoes filled the screen, congealing into a wall-to-wall band.

'The barrier,' Carlson commented unnecessarily. 'Dead ahead.'

Schmidt remembered the end of the signal again as

he continued staring down into the hood. The barrier. A solid wall of icefield was stretched across his path and the *Elroy*, its engines beating heavily, its reinforced bow brushing aside great floes of ice like matchsticks, was heading straight for the dreaded wall which stretched from the coast of Spitsbergen to Greenland. The trouble was that Schmidt had to find a way in, a place where the icefield was barely above sea level, a point where he could use the massive bows of the ship to smash his way inside the ice. At least they had the radar to show them what lay ahead. He prayed to God there wouldn't be fog.

Two hours later the menace drifted off the icefield. Fog trails like wisps of steam floated off the ice across the *Elroy*'s path. Schmidt was standing close to the clear-vision panel at the front of the bridge, looking down at the deck and ahead alternately. Neither view enchanted him. The ice on the fore-peak was piling up faster, the new team of men was fighting a losing battle as they heaved it over the ice-coated rails where it toppled down on to more ice drifting on the sea. The temperature was fifty below.

'Polar bears . . .'

At the starboard side of the bridge Carlson was looking at the top of the ice wall which was as high as the bridge itself and no further away than a few cable-lengths. On the foredeck below men glanced up at the wall above them; it was like looking up the side of a building. In the moonlight three yellowish blurs stared down at them, three polar bears at the brink of the icefield attracted by the smell of the garbage the cook had just emptied overboard.

The engines were dead slow, a regular, powerful throb which reassured Schmidt: earlier they had been badly delayed in their dash back to the north because of engine trouble. The view ahead did not reassure him at all. 'Vance, I think you'd better take a spell in the cage. We don't want to miss our way in . . .'

There was reluctance in the voice which gave the order, a reluctance certainly shared by the mate a few minutes later as he mounted the ice-sheathed ladder up the hundred-foot mast leading to the observation cage. It wasn't the most comfortable post on the *Elroy* – not in a temperature of fifty below and not with fog coming up. The observation cage at the *Elroy*'s masthead wasn't larger than two telephone kiosks and Carlson experienced his usual sense of claustrophobia as he settled on the leather-topped stool. Thirty-two years old, the same age as Beaumont, Vance Carlson had got married only one day before his ship left Milwaukee. He had been counting the days of the voyage home when the ship had turned round and headed back to the icefield. Like the Captain, the mate did not love Beaumont.

After a quick glance through his clear-vision panel Carlson hitched the harness over his head, adjusted the mike under his chin and checked with the bridge. 'In position, sir. There's a big berg dead ahead.'

'We've seen it . . .' Schmidt's voice came up the wire. 'Any sign of an entry point?'

'None at all, sir. It's as solid as a mountain.'

'Keep looking.'

Carlson experienced a sense of claustrophobia inside the cage; perversely he also experienced a sense of being horribly exposed. The walls which surrounded him, which he could reach out and touch with his extended elbows, were armour-glass, and their transparency made him feel, if this were possible, even colder. On the bridge below the heating wasn't totally effective; inside the observation cage it seemed totally ineffective, as though it had lost itself on its way up the mast.

One hundred feet above the deck, Carlson had an all-round view. To port, to starboard, below. The vessel seemed to be hardly moving, the bow slamming into huge floes as big as houses, cube-shaped floes which looked like sugar lumps seen from the cage. The flock of cubes divided, slid past either side of the ship, and beyond them the minor monster loomed, its peak high above Carlson's head, apparently motionless as though anchored to the seabed. But the berg wasn't anchored, it was drifting south, south towards the *Elroy* while the ship steamed north.

Carlson clubbed his gloved hands together, leaned sideways off his stool as he stared one way, then another. Above where he sat the large radar wing revolved steadily, transmitting its warning echoes to the hooded scope on the bridge. To starboard the ice wall slid past, the polar bears long since vanished. Below the lozenge-shaped deck was so laden with ice that from the cage it appeared to be a fragment broken away from the main icefield. Carlson pressed the send-switch. 'Heavy fog coming up, sir. About a quarter-mile away – dead ahead . . .'

Thirty minutes later Carlson was isolated. He couldn't see a thing. He was also very cold. The numbness which had begun in his feet and hands was spreading. To keep himself alert he was standing up and the four walls of glass were frosted over, coated with a deadly white rime which was growing thicker by the minute. His only view was through the clear-vision panel, and when he peered through this he saw only fog, creeping, ice-laden fog which had blotted out the icefield. Even the deck was invisible and he might have been inside the cabin of a plane in the night.

'You'd better come down, Carlson,' Schmidt ordered.

'I'll stay up a bit longer. It may clear.'

'Fifteen minutes. Then come down . . .'

Carlson pressed his face against the clear-vision panel and the glass was freezing, like pressing into ice itself. He saw nothing. A dense mass of moisture. Nothing more. The vessel was almost stationary, moving at slow-slow speed with the aid of the radar wing above Carlson's head, the metal eye which would throw back a warning echo when an iceberg loomed dead ahead. But the mechanism wasn't fool-proof under these conditions and on the bridge below

DaSilva, deputy mate and an experienced radar man, was staring anxiously down at the scope, waiting for it to go wild, to ping-ping-ping – warning that something big was close to the bows. The engines beat with a slow monotony while Carlson, the loneliest man aboard, went on staring hypnotically at the fog rolling inches from his face.

'Anything yet, Vance?'

'Nothing yet.'

In the cage Carlson had checked every window when he saw a change in the fog ahead. He couldn't see anything specific, but there was a change, a faint motion as though the vapour was affected by the merest of air currents. He stopped banging his gloves together, stood quite still with his face again pressed into the panel. Yes, there was something, something which was disturbing the fog like a giant spoon stirring it gently.

The warning ping on the scope came too late, too suddenly, and afterwards Schmidt had to speak forcefully to convince DaSilva that there was nothing he could have done. Nothing. It was too quick. On the scope the sweep went round and abruptly there was a new image. DaSilva raised his head, started shouting . . .

Carlson probably never saw it coming. If he did it could only have been for a fraction of a second. The ice claw, the huge rampart projecting across the *Elroy*'s path was eighty feet above the deck surface. It stretched out like a gigantic arm, thrust out across the path of the *Elroy* as though trying to hold it back. The ship steamed on, slowly. The claw came over the bows, over the deck, and the masthead struck it. One shattering, shearing blow. They heard the crack on the bridge as DaSilva had his mouth open to shout a warning, a crack which sent terror into their brains. The masthead was sliced off, eighty feet above the deck. The cage, eighty-five feet up, toppled with the severed mast. Sealed inside the cage, Carlson went down with it. It hit the deck-rail, eighty-five feet below, on the starboard side, smashed away a section, went on down into the sea with Carlson inside it. The severed head weighed five tons and went straight down, taking Carlson and the radar wing with it, down into the Arctic where the depth varies between nine and ten thousand feet. It can only be hoped that the mate was dead before the sea burst in.

The roll of the dead was beginning to mount. Vance Carlson was the twentieth casualty so far – including Nikolai Marov, Gorov's security guard, Tillotson, the sixteen who died aboard the plane on Target-5, and Matthew Conway.

And the radar was gone. The *Elroy* was blind, engulfed in fog, surrounded by ice, on the verge of the icefield itself, an icefield no one could see. This was beyond maximum risk, far beyond it; if any situation justified Alfred Schmidt in turning round and making slowly for home, this was it.

*

At Curtis Field the code-signal, 'Oxygen-Strongbow', had been received and understood. 'We have Gorov, we are moving south to rendezvous with the *Elroy*.'

It was not the only information Dawes had received as he paced round the small office which had been made over to him, an office which glowed with warmth from the three heaters under the windows. The atmosphere was seventy degrees and the warmth caressed his red face as Adams perched on a chair tilted against a wall and watched him.

'The ice west of Target-5 is crawling with Russians,' he growled as he chewed at his unlit cigar. 'They've got choppers over the ice and sled-teams down on the pack – and the Cats are beginning to appear.'

'It looks tricky,' Adams said.

'In Washington you said it would be simple,' Dawes reminded him. He looked up as Fuller, the airfield controller, hurried into the room. 'Time you got here. I want intensive air surveillance over the entire area between the coast and Target-5. I want one-third of the machines you send up concentrated on the ice north of Target-5 . . .' He went over to the map he had brought with him which was pinned to the wall. 'Here – and here.'

'Nothing to the south?' Fuller queried.

'Nothing! And I want non-stop surveillance. They go out, they come back, they refuel, they go out again . . .'

'There's a limit to how much the pilots can take,' Fuller pointed out.

'Find that limit – then push them beyond it.'

'I don't get it,' Adams said when Fuller had gone. 'Beaumont's heading south, so why send the aircraft west and north?'

'If you don't get it, maybe Papanin won't. Our chances of spotting Beaumont from the air in the polar waste are nil unless we got lucky. I'm not counting on that. So I'm launching a deception operation.' Dawes paused as the blast of a helicopter's rotor went past beyond the window. 'Papanin has a whole fleet of choppers scouring the ice. In a couple of hours he'll hear of my air surveillance, so what will he assume? That I'm looking for Gorov – that I know where to look. He'll withdraw his machines from the south and that may give Beaumont a chance to get out of range.'

'It could work, I suppose . . .'

'It will work!' Dawes grinned crookedly. 'I'm sending that bastard Siberian a signal – Beaumont is coming out north or west.'

'North or west?'

Papanin muttered the words to himself as he gazed down at his pocket chess board in the headquarters hut at North Pole 17. On the table beside the board was a book open at the page recording the moves in the Fischer–Spassky game at Santa Monica in 1966. The Siberian prided himself on being able to do three things at once: play his own game, study another man's game, and take a decision on the current operation.

'All the machines are in the air,' Kramer reported from behind his chair. 'They are concentrating on the northern and western approaches to Target-5 – all except the six helicopters you told me to hold back.'

After the American Sno-Cat had crashed over the ramp they had paid a second visit to Target-5 and they had found the island deserted. No one was there – although Papanin did not realize that two men, Rickard and Sondeborg, should have still been at the camp. The Siberian had left a small detachment to wait in case Gorov arrived, and had then gone straight back to his own base. Until he received the signal from Petrov at Leningrad Records he had been puzzled.

'The Beaumont force we kept talking about doesn't exist,' he commented as he fingered a pawn.

We? The Balt said nothing. When things went right Papanin invariably referred to events in the first person singular. When trouble loomed there were references to 'we' as the Siberian included him in the mess.

Papanin pushed back his chair, placed one booted leg carefully on the table beside the little chess board, and explained. The signal had come back from Leningrad in reply to his query. The diligent Petrov had buried deep into the massive archives and the mystery was solved.

In 1971 the Americans had sent a three-man team clear across the pack from Greenland to Spitsbergen. The achievement was never reported in the press, but a Soviet agent in Spitsbergen had sent a vague report. The expedition had obvious military implications: in case of real trouble Soviet forces might attempt to occupy Norwegian Spitsbergen – as the Americans had occupied Iceland in the last war. The Americans had foreseen this; if they could send men in over the pack they had a chance of occupying Spitsbergen first. So they had quietly sent a small team to see if it could be managed.

'It doesn't seem relevant,' Kramer protested.

'Doesn't it?' Papanin grinned unpleasantly as he filled his pipe. 'Beaumont is the name of the British Arctic expert who led the team to Spitsbergen. He had two men with him – an American, Samuel Grayson, and a German, Horst Langer. I think that big swine who had so much to say for himself at Target-5 was Beaumont.'

'They wouldn't send in only three men to take out Gorov . . .'

'Wouldn't they? It could be clever, it could be enough. How easy is it to spot four men from the air in the polar wastes, Kramer?'

'So there's no large expedition?' Kramer said dubiously.

'Just Beaumont and his friends. Remember those three men we filmed slipping into the fog two days ago?' Papanin's tone changed. 'Send a coded signal to all planes in the air – they are looking for a very small group. Probably two sled-teams and four men only.'

'And the six machines still waiting?'

'They are to fly south – due south of Target-5.'

'But the Americans are looking north and west . . .'

'Carry out my orders immediately,' Papanin said quietly.

Alone in the hut, the Siberian dropped his leg to the floor and frowned as he studied the chess board. Some of his more bizarre decisions he never explained: it was part of his technique for keeping his subordinates in permanent awe of their huge chief. Like De Gaulle, Papanin believed in surrounding himself with a certain mystic aura – it also helped when some of the decisions turned out to be wrong. No one knew what you had been trying to do in the first place.

But Papanin had a definite suspicion in his head, a growing suspicion. During the flight of the Bison bomber from Murmansk he had studied a dossier on Lemuel Quincey Dawes, whose speciality was deception operations. He couldn't ignore the obvious – that the concentration of American machines north and west of Target-5 was indeed searching for the Beaumont group; if it all went wrong he would be severely criticized for not checking those areas. But the southern sector was beginning to interest him.

Kramer came back into the hut a few minutes later. 'They will be airborne within five minutes,' he informed the Siberian.

'Excellent. Now send a signal to the carrier *Gorki* that I need an immediate check on the position of the American icebreaker *Elroy*.'

Mystified again, Kramer hurried away to the wireless hut. And again Papanin carefully did not give his reasons. When the Beaumont team was approaching Spitsbergen in 1971 it had made a prearranged rendezvous with the icebreaker *Edisto*; now another icebreaker was involved, the *Elroy*. Papanin had an idea he was getting close to Beaumont as he made up his mind and moved the pawn.

Chapter Five

Tuesday, 22 February: Noon–7 PM

Beaumont wouldn't listen to reason; perhaps it would be more accurate to say Beaumont wouldn't listen to anyone as he kept men and dogs moving remorselessly, driving them on, refusing to stop for food or drink, refusing to stop for anything or anyone as they moved further and further south down the tenth meridian and closer and closer to the edge of the icefield, to Iceberg Alley.

Hemmed in by pressure ridges, huge walls of jagged ice which loomed all around them, they sledded south down the ravines in the moonlight. And Beaumont had now taken over Langer's team, had the powerful Bismarck as his lead dog as he gripped the handlebar and cracked his whip over the dogs' heads. Which was an unmistakable sign that they were going to be driven to their limits as Langer observed to Grayson – to their limits and beyond them.

This was what had happened during the last stages of their drive over the pack to Spitsbergen and their rendezvous with another icebreaker, the *Edisto*. Beaumont had taken over the Bismarck dog team and they had never let up for twelve hours – not until the *Edisto* was in sight, the Elliott homing beacon had been switched on, the radio signal had been sent and the chopper from the icebreaker had come winging towards them. This time it was Langer who started the argument, who thought that Beaumont had over-reached himself. He handed over his sled-team to Grayson, ran ahead down the ravine and caught up with Beaumont.

'I don't think we can keep this up much longer . . .' he panted.

'Keep moving!'

Beaumont, his face set inside the narrow aperture of fur hood, cracked the whip, coaxed a little more speed out of Bismarck and the other animals increased pace. They came to a bend in the ravine but Beaumont didn't slacken pace; he took the sled round on one runner and it scudded over the hard ice.

'This is crazy,' Langer blazed. 'We need some rest – the dogs need some rest. The *Elroy* is miles and miles away. We can't possibly make it tonight . . .'

'We have to keep moving, for Christ's sake! Every half-mile is a half-mile closer to the *Elroy*. It's better than that – the bloody ship is moving towards us!'

'Gorov is feeling the strain.'

Beaumont glanced quickly over his shoulder. Behind him Grayson was driving the second team, forcing them to keep up with Bismarck – and Beaumont. Behind them the Russian followed on foot, his teeth gritted as he fought to keep up with them. It was a deliberate, brutal act of policy on Beaumont's part to put him at the rear; travelling on a sled he slowed everything down, but following them on foot Gorov was constantly afraid that he would be left behind, lost in the polar waste, and his fear of being left was keeping him moving, was forcing him to summon up reserves of energy he didn't even know he had. 'He'll move if he's scared,' Beaumont had said three hours earlier, 'so keep him scared.'

'He knew it wouldn't be any picnic when he left North Pole 17,' Beaumont snapped. 'Don't talk to him – I want him running scared. And don't talk to me – I have to watch this sled.'

Langer dropped back: Beaumont was in one of his foulest moods, you couldn't reason with him any more. They'd just have to keep moving. But Beaumont's temper was under perfect control: he had simply chosen the simplest method of shutting Langer up. And his grim rush across the ice was based on cold calculation. For three hours they had seen no sign of a Russian helicopter. Why, he had no idea, nor did he care, but now the moonlit sky above the pack was clear of the enemy he was determined to make the most of it, to get as far south as possible while they didn't have to worry about hiding from Papanin's eyes in the sky.

Nor had he thought it wise to reveal to the others that if humanly possible they were going to keep moving until they sighted the *Elroy*. For some unknown reason they had been given a golden opportunity to get clear, an opportunity which might never recur. Privately he doubted whether they would sight the *Elroy* that night, but it wasn't an impossible hope and he was going to drive them until they dropped. An hour later the American plane appeared to the south-east.

'Halt!'

Beaumont jerked up his arm to warn those behind him and it felt like jerking up a heavy weight. He pulled at the sled to stop the dogs, handed the whip to Grayson, then forced himself to start climbing the pressure wall to his left. His fatigue was so enormous it felt like climbing a mountain and as he clawed his way up the ice wall the distant murmur of the machine's engine urged him to hurry, hurry. It was a different sound, not the deadly beat-beat of a Soviet helicopter. Once he slipped but his clawing gloves saved him as he grabbed at the crest of the ridge and hauled himself over it. The night-glasses slung round his neck struck his jaw but he was hardly aware of the pain as he sat astride the crest and raised the glasses.

They were almost out of the pressure ridge maze: just ahead of them the frozen sea stretched away like a level plain; very much like a frozen sea with ripples congealed on its surface. The plane, two thousand feet up, was flying south-west and would soon pass them at a distance of about half a mile. He fumbled with the focusing mechanism. Russian or American? The silhouette came up as a blur, so he thought he had the focus wrong, then he realized it was his tired eyes. His eyes cleared, the machine crisped in the lenses, a white star painted on its fuselage. American!

'Sam! Get a smoke flare off my sled. It's American . . .'

The exhausted men down in the ravine were galvanized. Grayson tore open the fastenings, Langer grabbed a flare while Gorov watched the dogs, climbed halfway up the ice wall with the flare which Beaumont took from his extended hand. His fingers were so frozen he had trouble dealing with the flare. He tried to set it off, tried again. Nothing happened. 'Give me another,' Beaumont shouted. 'This one's a dud . . .'

There was a frantic scramble as Grayson and Langer struggled to locate a second flare, and while they searched, the plane with red and green lights at its wingtips began to turn, moving in an arc which would take it on a fresh course due south. 'Hurry up, for God's sake!' Beaumont roared. He saw that Grayson had found a flare, was going to bring it up to him. 'Set it off down there in the ravine!'

The flare ignited, gushed dark smoke, climbed in the still air like an Indian signal, billowed, went higher and higher. And the plane went away, continued south, growing smaller and smaller by the second. Grayson and Langer scrambled up on to the crest beside him.

'It hasn't gone . . .'

There was anguish in Grayson's voice, crushing

anguish, and his shoulders sagged. 'Look back, you bloody fool,' Beaumont said quietly. They watched the plane to vanishing point. A silver pinhead in the moonlight, it disappeared suddenly, leaving behind only the fading sound of its engine. 'It was a routine weather flight,' Beaumont observed, 'they weren't looking for us.'

'I would like to shoot the Goddamned so-called observer in that machine,' Langer said with quiet venom. 'Maybe we should have used the radio.'

'No!' Beaumont's tone was sharp. 'We're not using that till we're within range of the *Elroy*. At this very moment there will be a Soviet monitor crouched over his set waiting for us to do just that – so he can take a radio-direction fix. We'll get moving.'

The smoke flare climbed above them as they moved off in silence. Even the dogs seemed subdued, felt to be pulling the sleds with less vigour as they emerged from the pressure ridges and went out on to the plain of ice. Afterwards Beaumont blamed himself for not thinking of the danger, for taking them out on to the exposed ice too soon, but the disappointment and the fatigue had dulled his brain. His arms and wrists were aching with the strain, felt as though they were on fire, half-pulled out of their sockets after hours of wrestling with the bucking sled. The numbing cold was weakening his grip on the handlebar, he had to make an enormous effort to keep tramping forward with an appearance of vigour, to keep the others moving.

'Look out!'

It was Langer who shouted the warning. 'Keep still!' Beaumont shouted his own warning as he brought the dogs to a sudden halt. Behind them the night was shattered with a beating roar. Rat-tat-tat throbs echoed across the ice. The nose of the shadow was bulbous with a second, smaller bulb below it. Twin rotors whipped the air, one above the other. A double-finned tail. Like an evil metal bird it swept over their heads at fifty feet, the ground shadow slicing over the ice. A twin-jet submarine killer. The latest Soviet helicopter.

'Don't move!'

Beaumont reinforced his warning as the machine flew away from them, climbing now and beginning to turn. There was a chance that the men inside the Russian machine hadn't seen them. Moving at fifty miles an hour – Beaumont's estimate of the helicopter's speed – flashing over the ice where it had suddenly burst upon them from behind the pressure ridges, a Soviet observer would need sharp eyes to spot them. Seconds later he knew that sharp eyes had looked down on them from the machine. It was coming back. It was the smoke flare which had caused the disaster: the flare the American plane had never seen had guided a nearby Russian machine to them.

'What the hell is he going to do?' Langer asked.

'Depends how many men he has aboard,' Beaumont replied tersely.

It was travelling slower – and higher – coming in

at least two hundred feet above them. So they had not only spotted the sled teams, they had also seen the rifles looped over the men's shoulders. Beaumont handed over his restless team to Grayson and stood a few yards away, his rifle in his hands. The oncoming submarine killer was a menacing shape, all bulges and rotors, and when it was almost above them it began hovering while its drumbeat hammered the ice. Beaumont hoisted his rifle.

The helicopter ceased hovering, banked and began swinging in a wide circle, trailing a gauze of vapour in the cold atmosphere. They had to swing on their heels to follow the helicopter as it went round them, its engines drumming away. Then Langer grunted, hoisted his weapon. 'They've got a telescopic sight on us . . .' Looping his rifle over his shoulder, Beaumont snatched up his night-glasses.

'Drop that rifle!' Beaumont spoke quickly as he continued watching the machine through his glasses, pivoting on his boots. A window had been lowered in the dome and the moonlight reflected off something with a cylindrical muzzle. 'It's a cine-camera,' Beaumont warned. 'They're taking pictures of us – a nice peaceful occupation. With a telephoto lens,' he added.

As he spoke the helicopter turned away, presented its double tail-fins towards them and flew off to the north-east. The beat of its twin rotors was fading rapidly as Beaumont ran back to his sled and took over from Grayson. 'I can't figure why it didn't land,' the American said.

'My guess would be they hadn't enough men aboard.' Beaumont stared across the belt of level ice into the distance where more ridges reared up like hill ranges. 'And now we really have to get moving before they catch us in the open again. Because when the Russians do come back they'll have more than enough men.'

'Hold that frame!'

The Siberian's voice roared in the silence of the smoke-filled hut, a silence broken only by the whirring of the film projector. The operator stopped the machine, the image on the screen froze, the image of four men staring up at the camera, one man with a rifle, another man aiming a pair of glasses. A bloated shadow crossed the screen as Papanin stood up and pointed, his shadow fingertip touching a man holding the handlebar of a sled.

'That's him,' Papanin rumbled. 'That's Gorov. I'll bet my pension on it.'

'You can't see his face,' Kramer objected from the darkness. 'You can't see any of the faces . . .'

'Bugger the faces! I watched the way this man moved, the way he cocks his head to one side. That's Gorov, that's our target.' The enormous fingertip shadow moved, touched the fur-clad figure with glasses. 'And I think that's Beaumont. The other two must be Samuel Grayson and Horst Langer.'

'We recall all the planes from the north and

west?' the Balt asked, anxious to anticipate the next order.

'You switch on the damned lights in this hut first,' Papanin said softly. He looked round at one of the men sitting behind him. 'Vronsky, you can find them again?'

The twenty-eight-year-old Russian who had led the security detachment brought from Murmansk stood up and went over to a wall map. Small, lean and mournful-faced, Andrei Vronsky had lost both his parents a month earlier when they had tried to drive over the frozen Volga near Stalingrad: the river had cracked and swallowed them up. 'Here, Colonel,' he pointed to the cross he had drawn. 'We took a star-fix . . .'

'So you are confident?'

'We did find them . . .' Vronsky stopped speaking when he noticed the Siberian's expression.

'You found their bloody smoke flare!' Papanin roared. 'You saw it from five miles away and changed course – you said so when I questioned you. God knows why they let off that flare – maybe it went off by accident.'

'I suppose we were lucky . . .'

'So I'll show you how to be lucky again!' Papanin took the pencil off Vronsky and stared at the map. 'They are heading for a rendezvous with the American icebreaker *Elroy* which is here. Draw a line down from Target-5 and you see they are moving down the tenth meridian.'

'So we fly down that . . .'

'You shut up and listen! They will change direction for a while to throw us off the scent – they'll go either south-south-east or south-south-west.' Papanin drew two slanting lines from the south to the point where Beaumont had been seen. 'Later they will resume their course due south. Allowing for star-fix error, for ice-drift, you will find them inside this triangle. Understand?'

'It makes sense, Colonel . . .'

'Everything I say makes sense.' He looked over his shoulder at Kramer. 'This time every machine must carry a section of armed men.'

'We haven't enough for all the machines.'

'Who the hell said we were going to withdraw all of them – and immediately warn Dawes that his deception operation has failed? I'm leaving half the pieces on the board to the north and west of Target-5. The other half come back here, refuel, and then scour my triangle.'

They left the hut quickly before the Siberian could comment on their slowness while Papanin remained staring up at the wall map and sucking at his little pipe. 'I think I've got you this time, Mr Beaumont,' he said to himself.

Chapter Six

It had become a nightmare: Russian machines were within hearing all the time. Sometimes the deadly rat-tat-tat beat was a long way off, little more than a murmur in the bitterly cold night as they dragged their weary limbs down more ravines, under the lee of more pressure ridge walls, but even when it was only a murmur you had to listen hard, to concentrate – so that you detected the moment when it started becoming louder, when it was coming in your direction.

At other times it was close, far too close for comfort, the wicked beat rising to a loud cacophony which echoed along the ravines and reverberated over the icy crests. It was, Beaumont admitted to himself, only a matter of time before they were seen – unless they were incredibly lucky. It was only a matter of time because, despite the frequent requests of Grayson and Langer, he obstinately kept them moving and movement can be seen from the air.

The constant need to listen, to stay on the alert, was now wearing them down as much as driving the sleds, driving their own legs to keep on the move. By ten in the evening the four exhausted men were moving like automatons, their limbs sluggish, their eyes half-closed with the fatigue and the cold, and Gorov had twice said he couldn't go any further, that he must travel on one of the sleds. Beaumont's reaction had been quick and to the point. 'You'll either keep up or die on the ice.'

'But this is why you are here!' Gorov had protested as he stumbled alongside Beaumont's sled. 'You came to collect me!'

'It's got beyond that now,' the Englishman had told him grimly. 'It's a question of our survival – so keep up or drop, I don't care which any more.'

When Gorov had dropped back Beaumont sneaked a look over his shoulder, and the Russian was plodding on beside Langer's sled while in the distance Grayson was completing another star-fix. Beaumont had no intention of leaving the Russian behind; if he collapsed he would have to be carried on a sled. Oddly enough, faced with the prospect of a lonely death on the ice, Gorov was able to keep going.

But the real havoc was played with their nerves and tempers, and now it was becoming dangerous for one man to speak to another because whatever was said it was always the wrong thing. It was just after ten o'clock when Grayson decided that he had had enough, that they had run out of luck, that this time they had to stop before Beaumont's madness destroyed them all. He finished packing the sextant back inside Langer's moving sled and hurried to catch up with Beaumont.

'Another plane coming up – from the east. I'm getting on top of a ridge to check . . .'

'Conserve your energy,' Beaumont snapped. 'It's a long way off . . .'

'It's coming this way! It's louder already. Do we wait till the bloody thing is on top of us?'

'Yes!'

'Why, for God's sake?'

Beaumont took a tighter grip on the handlebar, and there was barely suppressed fury in his voice as he replied. 'Because we are not playing their game – Papanin's game. Haven't you grasped what's happening? These are random flights – crisscrossing the ice.'

'One of them will spot us . . .'

'If he's lucky, yes. But he'll have to be damned lucky to spot us down inside these ravines. To do that he'll have to fly direct overhead. When that's going to happen we freeze against the wall – I've already hammered that into you.'

'It may be too late then.'

Beaumont took a deep breath, stared at Grayson, then grabbed at the sled with both hands as it nearly toppled sideways. He spoke in a cold, deliberate monotone. 'We have to get further south than Papanin thinks is possible before we rest. These planes are looking for us, yes. But they're also trying to wear us down, to make us stop every time we hear one, so that we never get a chance to reach the *Elroy* . . .' He stiffened as the rat-tat-tat he had been listening to while he talked loudened to a roar. 'Get under cover!'

They stopped the dogs, sprawled beside them to calm the animals, crashed down full length on the ice and seconds later the helicopter boomed over them, the hellish clatter of its engines deafening them. It swept over them from east to west, flashed across the ravine two hundred feet up, then it was gone. They remained perfectly still because they didn't know yet whether they had been seen. If they had, it would come back. Dropping prone on to the ice shook each man badly, muffled as they were in their layers of clothing, because prone they didn't feel like getting up again. They lay in the ravine alongside their twitching animals, calming them, their bodies frozen, their resistance very low indeed. When the machine didn't come back they clambered slowly to their feet and Grayson tried once more, croaking the words.

'Keith, we ought to stop . . . to eat . . .'

Beaumont shook his head slowly, listened, and couldn't hear the sound of any machine. Painfully, he began to climb up the nearest ice wall, slithering back several times before he got anywhere near the crest. It was time to check the view ahead. Once more. Reaching the top, he nearly fell backwards, but regained his balance. He rubbed at the lenses of his night-glasses to clear them, perched his elbows on the crest, raised them to his weary eyes. He could see a long distance, a very long distance indeed. He scanned the blurred horizon, dropped the glasses a fraction, stared through them steadily, then lowered them as he looked down into the ravine. 'I think you'd better come up here,' he said quietly.

'Well?' Papanin demanded.

'Nothing yet.' Vronsky closed the door of the hut. 'I've just come back – it looks pretty hopeless.'

'Hopeless, did you say?' Papanin stood up slowly from his chair and Kramer, who knew him, took an involuntary step away from the Siberian. 'You're gutless, Vronsky. You're not fit to lead a detachment. In this game it's the man who goes on longest who wins. I'll have to consider your position when this is over. You were going to eat? Skip the meal, Vronsky – you're aboard the next helicopter that takes off.' He waited until the Russian had left. 'It's going to be difficult if they reach the *Elroy*, Kramer,' he remarked.

The Balt was startled. It was the first time Papanin had even suggested that Beaumont might reach the ship. 'Difficult?' he queried. 'Impossible once Gorov is aboard an American ship . . .'

'Not impossible, but difficult, yes.' The Siberian's tone was deceptively quiet. 'The thing would begin to assume huge dimensions. Our people back home would start fretting – because of the American President's visit to Moscow in May.'

'We may be lucky . . .'

'I make my own luck!' Papanin's fist crashed down

on the table which was now bare: the little chess set was inside his pocket. 'We are changing our tactics,' he rumbled. 'From now on we sweep north from the *Elroy* – we'll meet them coming in over the ice. When a machine finds our target it lands as close to them as possible – I don't care how bad the ice is under them.'

'And if the men with Gorov resist?'

'This is the second order you will issue at once. Give it personally to each leader of the armed parties – the pilot must not hear you. We don't want the men with Gorov – they are an embarrassment, so lose them. Bury the bodies under the ice – if an open lead is available drop them into it. The dogs must be killed as well – poisoned meat would be best. And lose the sleds. By midnight, Kramer! Earlier if possible . . .'

It had to be a mirage, Beaumont thought when he first saw it in his night-glasses. The image blurred, went away, then came back again as he readjusted the lenses to their original fix. He called down to the men inside the ravine. Langer reached him first; caught by something in Beaumont's voice he mounted the ice wall quickly, then flopped beside the Englishman on the crest. His face was whiskered as he pulled open his hood to use the glasses, whiskered and still smeared with fog streaks many hours old.

'Over there. The thing sticking up.'

Beaumont pointed and Langer, his fingers trembling with anxiety, tried to get a fix. For another three miles ahead the terrible jumble of pressure ridges continued, like a stormy sea with massive waves coming towards them, a stormy sea frozen suddenly in mid-fury. Beyond this was level ice, very level ice indeed, a vast sheet gleaming in the moonlight. In the middle of it was the mirage, something which, if photographed, would look totally unreal. 'Good God!' Langer muttered the exclamation and fell silent.

The mirage was a high-masted ship with a high bridge, a ship made of ice and snow, almost like an unsuccessful wedding cake. In the night-glasses Langer saw that its bows pointed towards him, that it was crusted and coated and mired with ice so that in the moonlight it glittered like a ship made of glass. Icicles hung from the crosstree, from the jagged tip of the mast. Its rails dripped a curtain of ice like the edge of a counterpane flung casually over the foredeck. The bows were very high, as though mounting a huge wave, but the vessel was absolutely stationary, embedded in the pack, and the only clue that it might not have been abandoned was the lights at the tips of the crosstree. It was not a mirage. It was the American icebreaker *Elroy*, ten miles from the nearest ocean, hemmed in by the pack.

'Good God!' Langer muttered again.

'You said that before,' Beaumont reminded him. 'You must be getting old – you're repeating yourself.'

'I feel old.' Langer corrected himself. 'I felt old! Hey, Sam, it's the *Elroy*!'

Leaving Gorov to watch over the dogs, Grayson

had hauled himself up on to the crest. 'Don't kid me,' he croaked. Langer handed him the glasses. 'See for yourself.' The American opened his hood, exposed an equally haggard, grizzled face, and focused the glasses.

'How the hell did it ever get in so far?' Langer wondered.

'Guts,' Beaumont said. 'I've never met Schmidt, the captain, but he's smashed his way through that stuff inch by inch to get in close to us. The funny thing is I can't see his radar.'

'I do know him,' Grayson said quietly. 'He's a number one bastard – and that's why he's here. How close do you reckon he is?'

'Seven miles away at a guess,' Beaumont replied. 'Any objections to us pushing on?'

They pushed on for two miles at a speed they hadn't achieved for hours, threading their way through the maze of ravines until they were within one mile of the open ice. And because there were still no Russian choppers in the sky Beaumont decided that now they could send the signal and activate the Elliott homing beacon which should bring the *Elroy*'s helicopter over their heads.

It was very cold, colder than ever it seemed, but this could be their overwhelming fatigue. And it was still clear, clear except for the plume of steam-like vapour which hung over the sled-teams as they moved forward, the vapour which was breath of dogs and men condensing in the bitter atmosphere. Unlike the popular conception of the Arctic, screaming blizzards were rare in this latitude; it was simply one of the coldest places on earth.

They halted inside a ravine. Grayson had pointed out that no helicopter could land in this mess but Beaumont had told Langer to unload the transmitter. 'They can winch us up, Sam, one by one,' he explained, 'then I'll take the dogs out on to the open ice.' Langer was unfastening the canvas flaps round the transmitter when Gorov came down the ravine, moving so quickly that Beaumont watched him in surprise. The Russian was breathing heavily as he stopped and spoke almost hysterically. 'Now we are safe I demand you return my property immediately!'

'What the hell are you talking about?' Beaumont was looking down as he spoke, gently heeling his right boot into the ice. It didn't feel too hard and he suspected that the pressure ridges on either side had only recently been formed by the closing of a lead.

'My core! You stole my core! One of you stole it!' Gorov was getting excited as he pulled out the heavy tube from his parka and waved it in Beaumont's face.

'You're holding it,' Beaumont said. He frowned again as the heel of his boot suddenly sank a few inches. When he pulled it came up with an oozing plop. Soft ice. Gorov was too absorbed to notice anything wrong.

'This is not the same core . . .'

'You mean the other one had the Catherine charts

239

inside it?' Beaumont was staring directly at Gorov. 'As you said, we may be almost safe. Not a good time to start shouting the odds, is it?'

'The odds?'

'Go back and give Horst a hand with that set.'

Langer had hoisted the man-pack transceiver over his shoulder and was now a long way back down the ravine, carrying it to a more level section before he set it up. It was almost too much for him in his weakened state but he plodded on and then found a level gap in the wall. He put it down carefully as Gorov raved on in the distance.

'I must have my core! It is that core which makes me valuable to Washington . . .'

Gorov was still waving the metal tube about like a blunt instrument when Grayson took it off him. 'Valuable?' the American said. 'Until we reach that ship not one of us is worth a bent nickel. We may not have heard one of your choppers for over an hour, but we're not on board that ship yet. Now, give Horst a hand with that transmitter when he's finished.'

'Ground's sticky underfoot, Sam,' Beaumont murmured as Gorov went back up the ravine. 'We'll have to watch it.'

'I suppose it figures,' Grayson replied as he fondled Bismarck to keep him quiet, 'we're getting close to the sea . . .'

They heard the Russian shout, looked along the ravine, saw him falling. He crashed full length along the ravine, tried to get up, fell down again, 'Christ!'

Beaumont snapped. 'He's twisted his ankle.' Langer was ready to transmit, had the telescopic aerial extended, and he was just moving the set to a more level patch of ice when he heard the shout. Swearing, he left the set and went down the ravine to help the Russian.

Gorov had twisted his ankle. He tried to stand up a second time and collapsed as Langer reached him. The German grabbed him under the armpits, lowered him to a sitting position with his back to the ice wall, then noticed the boot of his right leg, the one which had brought him down. Black ooze clung to the boot, ooze which was already freezing. 'Keith! Soft ice here – and Gorov can't walk...' With Grayson to help him, he formed an arm cradle and they carried Gorov back to the sled where he settled himself, looking anywhere except in Beaumont's direction.

'Better hurry up with that signal,' Beaumont said.

Langer and Grayson went back up the ravine slowly, careful of where they placed their boots, and when Langer reached the gap in the ice wall he stared, wondering if he was going mad. Then he let out a shout which brought Grayson running. The Redifon set had sunk. The main part of the transmitter had vanished and only the disappearing aerial still showed above the surface as a froth of bubbling ooze closed over the box. Langer dropped to his knees, scrabbled desperately in the icy mess, but the box had gone below the level his gloved fingers could reach. In despair he grabbed at the aerial. A piece snapped

241

off and he was left holding it as the rest of it went down. It was gone. They had lost their only means of communicating with the *Elroy*.

'You have dealt with the caviar?' Papanin demanded.

The Siberian had a new temporary headquarters, a mobile headquarters a thousand feet above the pack as the submarine killer flew steadily south. And he was talking to Vronsky in another machine much further south, using the code-word caviar for *Elroy* because he was talking direct on the radio-telephone.

'The caviar is sandwiched,' Vronsky replied.

Papanin grunted as he switched off and stared down at the icefield below. It was getting close to some kind of climax in the game and he wanted to be there to direct the moves himself. 'By midnight we'll have them,' he said.

'They haven't been seen yet,' Kramer pointed out, ever pessimistic.

Papanin frowned ferociously to shut him up as static crackled in his ear. He listened with an expressionless face, acknowledged the new message, then glared at the pilot. 'Get this thing moving,' he said coldly, 'or are you anchored to the ice?' He turned round and stared at Kramer who was perched on a flap seat at the back of the cabin. 'By midnight, I said. They have just located the target.'

*

'Keith, the bastard's coming in to land!'

'I expected that.' Beaumont stared up from the top of the ice wall while he watched the submarine killer dropping, both rotors moving more slowly as the machine came down vertically to a point on the level ice a quarter of a mile from where he crouched.

They had been spotted. The helicopter now landing had flown over them twice, and it was landing between them and the icebound ship. He lowered his glasses. Papanin never missed a trick: a second helicopter was hovering over the ice-encrusted silhouette of the ship, poised over the launch pad so Schmidt couldn't send up his own machine.

'We were nearly there,' Grayson said bitterly as he crouched beside Beaumont. 'Another couple of hours and we'd have made it . . .'

'Might as well be a couple of hundred,' Langer said from the other side of Beaumont. He slithered back inside the ravine quickly as the dogs started jumping about. The beating roar of the descending machine echoed along the pressure ridges which crisscrossed the ice in all directions. It touched down, its rotors still whirling. A door opened and men began dropping to the ice, men with rifles. Furry and hooded in the moonlight, they spread out in a broad crescent and began advancing towards the pressure ridges. Again the speed of the operation impressed Beaumont.

'I didn't know that machine could hold so many,' Grayson said grimly.

'You know what you have to do,' Beaumont reminded him. 'Keep a close eye on Gorov – I don't want him panicking at the psychological moment.'

'You're committing suicide . . .'

'We'll die if we just wait for them. They want Gorov and we're expendable witnesses.'

Beaumont slipped down the side of the ice wall, trailed his rifle and began running down the ravine. Behind him the others watched him go until Grayson gave them a sharp order. Despite the fact that the ice walls on either side towered above him Beaumont ran in a stoop, ignoring the fact that there could be soft ice ahead, praying that the ground would stay firm. In the emergency the fatigue had temporarily left him; he was clear-headed and he had complete control over his limbs. It was hardly surprising that Grayson had called what he was trying to do suicide – Beaumont was running straight towards the Russians.

It was not quite as foolhardy an action as it seemed. He had waited to see what came out of the machine; now they were advancing towards the pressure zone, and now he was running towards the approximate centre of the crescent of men he couldn't see. They would come inside the ravines trying to keep their crescent-shaped formation – so when the right moment came the security detachment could close their crescent, encircling their target. It was the element of surprise Beaumont was counting on: the last thing the section leader would expect would be for one of the hunted men to run towards him.

He ran light-footed, making as little noise as possible as he followed the snaking ravine which twisted and turned; from his high point on the crest Beaumont had noted the course of this ravine, and so far as he could tell it eventually led out on to the open ice at a certain point. In places the ice corridor was in shadow, in other places as he went round a corner he ran into moonlight. Soon he would have to slow down because soon he would be close to the incoming Russians. As he ran he heard in the distance the faint humming beat of the helicopter muffled by the ice walls. The pilot wasn't taking any chances; he was keeping his engines going for fear they might never start again in this temperature. He stopped running, began moving very cautiously. He would meet the Russians soon.

Crouched close to the lee of the right-hand wall, he crept forward, noting alcoves he could dodge back into when he heard them coming – if he heard them coming in time. Beaumont was under no illusion that he faced amateurs: the Soviet Special Security detachments which operated in the Arctic were trained men accustomed to operating in sub-zero temperatures. But they weren't too accustomed to moving on foot over the pack. He was holding his rifle in both hands when the fur-clad Russian came round a corner very quietly.

Both men were startled, but the Russian hadn't been expecting to meet anyone so close to the helicopter. He was carrying an automatic weapon over his shoulder and he made a mistake: he tried to unsling it. Beaumont reacted without thinking, swinging the rifle round in his hands so that the heavy metal butt-plate faced the Russian. He slammed it forward at head height. At the last moment the Russian jerked his head sideways and the butt-plate only grazed his jaw, but it was enough to unbalance him, to send his boots slithering over the ice as he fell backwards and Beaumont moved forward.

The Russian hit the ice with the back of his head. The blow was cushioned by the fur hood he wore. Still sprawled on his back, his own weapon dropped and out of reach, he grasped the Englishman's right boot and the hand was large enough to encircle the ankle. The fingers locked and prepared to heave sideways. Beaumont ignored the danger, concentrating on what he had to do. The rifle came down from high up, hammered down on the Russian's forehead, and the force of the downstroke was so great that the butt rebounded. The hand locked round his ankle relaxed, the head flopped sideways and the man lay still as Beaumont bent down and heaved him over on to his stomach. The impact points – jaw and forehead – were now in contact with the ice, so when they found him – if they ever found him – it would look like an accident, an accident caused by the Russian tripping and smashing his face down on the iron-hard ground.

He took an even bigger risk now: he started running again. He had counted about twenty men coming out of the machine and they had to be spread over a rabbit warren of ravines, so probably the arrangement was that when one of them located the fugitives they would open fire to bring the others running. He was still running when he turned a corner and a sheet of light came into view. He had reached the exit – the open ice was ahead.

The roar of the waiting machine's rotors blasted his eardrums coming inside the ravine and he saw it barely a hundred yards away, its double fin facing him, the pilot's cabin looking the other way. It was a point he had noted from the ridge crest and he had been praying the pilot hadn't swung his machine round. He hadn't. And there was no guard waiting at the edge of the ice. It didn't surprise Beaumont; when you have twenty men at your disposal and you go in to capture a group of four men you'd hardly anticipate that one of them would be mad enough to head straight for the machine. Beaumont headed straight for the machine.

He looped his rifle over his shoulder and began walking at a moderate pace towards the rear of the helicopter. It seemed a crazy thing to do, to walk slowly, but Beaumont was gambling on elementary psychology in case the pilot inside the cabin did look behind him. Reflexes moved fast when jerked into action – the sight of an armed man running across the ice towards the machine would provoke one reaction in the pilot. He would pull the lever, take the machine vertically off the ice. A five-second job. Beaumont kept walking slowly, coming closer to the submarine killer.

Beaumont was fairly confident now that he was going to make it; although his fur hood and parka hardly matched the security men's outfit it was similar – similar enough when seen by moonlight through the ice-rimed dome of a helicopter. As he neared the machine, as the deafening drumbeat increased in decibels, every nerve in his body was screaming at him to run, to cover the last fifty yards before the pilot turned his head. Beaumont kept walking at the same even pace, coming up directly behind the old-fashioned-looking tail, the kind of tail biplanes had once sported. Unlooping his rifle, he walked past the tail, climbed up and hammered with his gloved fist on the misted dome.

The vibration shuddered him and nothing happened. He beat with his fist a second time and then the window slid open. The rifle went inside at the same moment as warm air wafted in his face, the muzzle pointed at a helmeted figure who had jumped back into his seat behind the controls. 'Get out! Come on! Get out – quick!' Beaumont shouted in Russian and jerked his head to show the pilot what he wanted – with the drumbeat going full blast the pilot probably couldn't hear a word. Beaumont leaned in through the window, jabbed the rifle muzzle hard into the pilot's side. The Russian had goggles down over his eyes but Beaumont had the impression he was young, maybe in his late twenties. Young enough to be a hero. The pilot's right hand moved towards a lever.

The lever, Beaumont guessed instantly, would elevate the helicopter. Suddenly the machine would be climbing and he would be suspended in mid-air, maybe jerked off to smash on the ice below. 'Don't try it . . . !' To drive the message home he rammed the muzzle harder into the pilot. The Russian stared sideways and Beaumont read the man's mind. He had guts: he was checking the weapon, wondering whether he could survive the bullet. The calibre must have scared him: his hand moved away from the lever. 'Get up! Up! Up!' Beaumont jerked his head and the pilot disconnected his headset and slid carefully out of his seat.

Something in the pilot's stance warned Beaumont. The Russian paused halfway out of his seat, crouched like a cat, the lenses of his goggles catching the light from the instrument panel so his eyes were invisible. 'Come on,' Beaumont snapped, 'hurry it up.' The Russian came closer as Beaumont withdrew the rifle, cuddling it under his arm, his finger still inside the trigger guard as he used his other hand to press down the door handle, to slide it open. The pilot spread his hands in a slow gesture of surrender.

But the heroics weren't over yet. The pilot came slowly through the doorway and then he was very close to Beaumont. He turned, as though obeying Beaumont's gesture for him to drop to the ice; then, still crouched under the whirling rotors, he grabbed

for the rifle, a reaction the Englishman had anticipated. Beaumont slammed down the butt, struck the
Russian on the shin, and the pilot grabbed for the
door frame to regain his balance. Holding on to the
frame he straightened up on one leg. He came within
range of the steel blades of the lower rotor. They
beheaded him.

Still crouched and clinging to the window frame,
Beaumont was stunned with horror. He swallowed
bile. The corpse was below him on the ice. Dark spots
flecked the ice around the huddled heap. The head
had been hurled God knew where by the whipping
blades. It was incredible – a helicopter pilot decapit-
ated by his own rotor – but the majority of accidents
happen in the home, and for the pilot the machine
had been home. Shaking – and not only from the
vibration – Beaumont went inside the cabin and
closed the door on what lay below it. Then he eased
himself into the pilot's seat and stared at the control
panel.

It was not entirely unlike the Sikorsky's control
panel. And a year earlier Beaumont had visited the
Soviet base, North Pole 15, now orbiting the Pole
somewhere off the Siberian coast, where a vodka-
filled pilot had shown him his submarine killer before
the security man had arrived to drag them both out of
the machine. Beaumont had sent a report to Washington and London about that machine and now he
desperately tried to recall its details.

The altitude readings were in metres, of course.

Most of the dials and levers he understood, but there was one dial and two switches he couldn't fathom. Cautiously he touched the lever the pilot had reached for. Nothing happened. He pushed it a shade further and the machine left the ice. He pulled it towards him and felt the bump as the skids touched down again. The spare helmet he had taken from a hook and put over his head as soon as he sat down was loose-fitting. He fastened it more tightly, clamping the ear muffs closer to cut out the hellish row. The instrument panel was juddering badly but he suspected some of this was his own fatigue. Fiddling with several other controls, he sorted out the set-up calmly, knowing that at any moment the Russians on the ice might reach the sled-teams. But he had to grasp the mechanism of this thing. He opened the throttles and the twin jets boomed. He took a deep breath, operated the ascent lever.

Chapter Seven

Tuesday, 22 February:
11.30 PM–Midnight

The machine climbed faster than he'd expected, shot up vertically with a drumming roar. When the altimeter registered one hundred metres he hovered, then flew forward. He changed direction, flew through the arc of a circle. Beyond a clear patch in the perspex dome the *Elroy* appeared like a stranded toy, then vanished. The small lever which had puzzled him banked the helicopter. It was responding to his touch now. Reluctantly. He had a feeling of enormous power locked in behind the panel, power itching to break loose, and in flight the cabin vibrated more than a Sikorsky's, vibrated like an old washing machine.

From above, the ridges looked weird in the moonlight, levelled down to ribs of ice like the burial ground of prehistoric monsters, their long-dead bones bleached a pale colour. He saw two men moving along an ice corridor. He ignored them, searching for the assembly point, the strangely shaped area they had crossed shortly before they heard the Russian machine coming. He sent the sled teams back there to

wait for him because it was the only place inside the
ridges where a helicopter could land – a tiny amphitheatre of ice, a bowl surrounded with pressure ridge
walls. He flew over more Russians who stopped and
stared upwards, flew on some distance, then realized
he had overshot the amphitheatre and turned.

Beaumont was becoming worried now. If he
couldn't find the amphitheatre first the Russians
would reach the sled-teams, might even have reached
them already. He saw other fur-clad figures moving
along the ravines, some of them running, and all of
them stopped to stare up at him, wondering why the
hell their machine had taken off from the ice. And
conditions inside the large cabin could have been
better: the heaven-sent warmth was counteracted by
a smell which kept intruding on his stomach, a stench
of petrol fumes which was nauseating. Either there was
something wrong with the machine or Russian engine
technology lagged sadly behind British and American.
Then he saw it – a white circle among the shadows.

He operated the lever and started going down.
Three men, two sleds, the dogs were in the middle of
the bowl, and one of the men was waving frantically.
Then five Russians came over a nearby ridge crest and
looked down into the bowl with rifles in their hands.
Under the helmet Beaumont's face was grim: he had
arrived too late.

Pressing himself hard against the seat back, he
banked the machine, lost altitude, increased the revs,
flew straight for the Russians. Beyond the perspex

dome he saw them standing on the crest, frozen with astonishment. The helmet and goggles he had put on helped the illusion, heightened the tension – because from the crest the five men saw their own machine, piloted by their own comrade, come screaming down towards them.

The row inside the cabin was deafening. The frame was vibrating as though soon it would shake every rivet free from the fuselage. Beaumont increased the revs again and beyond the dome the five men flew towards him. He moved the stick and the machine thundered over the crest, rotors whipping, the skids just clearing the ridge – and the men were gone, tumbling down the far side of the ridge as they took desperate evading action. Beaumont climbed again, turned, saw the Russians on their feet inside a wide ice corridor. He dived, aimed the machine point-blank along the corridor, and the security men, seeing what was coming, fled. Beaumont continued his power-dive, took the machine down dangerously low, levelled out just above the crests, continued on course along the corridor.

The skids missed the men's heads by feet – down inside the corridor it must have seemed like inches as they flung themselves to the ground and the reverberations of the engines pounded their eardrums. When Beaumont looked back they had started to run again – away from the amphitheatre, demoralized. His terror campaign was beginning to work. And it must seem terrifying to the security detachment who were bound to assume their own pilot was behind the controls, a pilot who had gone berserk. The irony was that no one would fire a single shot at him – the machine he was flying was their only transport out of the terrible polar wasteland. He made three more circuits of the amphitheatre and then went down.

His eyes were watering from the petrol fumes which had seeped under his loose-fitting goggles as he descended into the bowl. In his anxiety to get down fast he landed heavily on the ice: it was only a matter of time before the Russians pulled themselves together and then they would be swarming towards the place where they had seen the helicopter landing. Leaving the rotors running, he unfastened his seatstrap, went to the door, opened it. He was rather careful of the whirling blades above his head as he jumped down on to the ice.

'Watch those damned rotors,' were his first words. 'Get the dogs aboard first – if trouble comes we leave the sleds.'

The dogs had already been released from the traces and they scrambled them inside the machine, lifting each kicking animal and shoving it unceremoniously aboard. Beaumont waited a short distance from the machine, leaving it to Grayson and Langer to hoist dogs and Gorov inside while he stared round the circle of crests with his rifle ready. The sleds went on board last, and when Beaumont followed them there was no trace left on the ice that the Beaumont party had ever existed.

*

Beaumont went straight up to a thousand feet, taking them out of range of rifle fire before he set course for the *Elroy*. Langer stood close to the transparent dome as they climbed, hemmed in by whimpering dogs. He pointed downwards. 'We were only just in time.' Beaumont nodded. A group of six Russians was moving close to the amphitheatre as they ascended.

From their altitude of one thousand feet the *Elroy* looked like a ghost ship, one of the legendary vessels which drift round the oceans of the world without a crew, a ghost ship set in solid ice. As they came closer Beaumont saw a channel beyond its stern, a dark slash of sea where the icebreaker had battered its way through the polar pack, but beyond the slash there was continuous ice. As the ship hammered its way north the icefield had closed behind, locking it in.

'That other sub-killer is still hanging over the ship,' Langer said suddenly.

'I know,' Beaumont replied. 'We're going to have to shift it.'

He moved the stick and they started losing height, close enough to the ship to see men running to the rails and staring up as a second Russian machine homed in on them. And some of the seamen carried rifles. Aft of the high bridge, close to the stern, they could see now far below another helicopter, a Sikorsky, resting on its launching pad while the Soviet machine clung to the air above it. So long as the hovering machine held its present position it was impossible for the American plane to leave its pad – it would have ascended directly into the other machine. 'I suppose that other sub-killer thinks we're his pal,' Grayson remarked as he patted one of the dogs.

'He's in for a shock,' Beaumont said tersely.

'They may try to crash us . . .' Gorov who had sat in silence on a folding seat at the back of the cabin was now alarmed enough to speak. He stood up to get a better view, holding on to a rail to take the weight of his injured ankle.

'Sit down, Gorov!' Beaumont shouted. 'Didn't you hear what Grayson said? The pilot will think we're Russian, which gives us the edge.'

'Two pairs of rotors whirling close together, Keith,' Grayson warned. 'We could end up with both of us taking diving lessons . . .'

'I want that machine out of the way,' Beaumont insisted. 'I want it out of the way before we land . . .' He was almost over the ship now, flying slowly at an altitude of five hundred feet while four hundred feet down the other submarine killer maintained its hover, hanging over the Sikorsky like a threat. The ice-coated rails of the ship were lined with seamen now, all of them staring up at the new arrival, wondering what was going to happen. Standing close to the dome, Langer stared straight down on the machine below, saw the dizzy circle of its rotors whipping through the night, the gauze of vapour spiralling up towards him.

'Keith!' he shouted above the throbbing din. 'Could you take us down slowly alongside that bastard?'

'Yes. Why?'

Langer took down a folded toolkit bag hooked to the side of the dome, opened it, extracted a large steel monkey wrench. 'With our window open I might get his dome. Then he would . . .'

'Got it – we'll try it,' Beaumont shouted. 'You know I can't get too close to his rotors?'

'I'm ready.' Langer pushed two of the dogs away, took a firm grip on the monkey wrench and opened the window. A blast of icy air streamed inside the heated cabin as Beaumont started to go down. Langer's dark hair flew out behind him as he pushed back his hood to see clearly and leaned out of the window. No one spoke again inside the cabin; Gorov hunched nervously on his flap seat; and Beaumont was acutely conscious that he was handling a strange machine, that he was attempting a dangerous manoeuvre which could easily end in total disaster.

The drop went on as Beaumont took the helicopter down slowly. From the window Langer watched the deck of the *Elroy* coming up, the line of heads staring towards him, a peaked cap which poked out of the bridge window to look up, but above all he watched the giddy ellipse of the lethal rotors below him, slicing the air, rising up to meet him. So far as he could tell Beaumont was gauging his descent with murderous accuracy – accurate because when he came alongside the second machine his own racing blades should clear the rotors below, murderous because the margin of safety was so small.

Exposed to the bitter night air after the brief spell of warmth, Langer's face was already numb and frozen; his eyelids felt like leaden weights, desperately wanted to close, but he forced himself to keep them open, to stay hanging out of the window. Then he saw the vague shape of the top of a helmet under the dome; as he watched it the helmet tilted and something pale came into view, a pale blur seen under a clear patch in the ice-rimed dome – the pilot's face watching Beaumont coming down almost on top of him. He had had no signal to leave his post. Now it was too late.

For the Russian the position was reversed. He had successfully immobilized the American helicopter, holding it down on its pad, but now he was sandwiched, unable to go down, unable to climb, caught in a press between the other two machines, and the press was closing, coming down on top of him. Beaumont had hoped that the pilot's nerve would crack, that the slow descent would make him run, and while they had been at five hundred feet the Russian could have escaped. Now it was too late. Caught in an emergency the Russian pilot's nerve hadn't broken, it had frozen. Unsure of what to do, he did nothing. Beaumont's descent continued, the gap closed, the skids of his machine hovered close to the Russian's transparent dome.

They were so close now that the air disturbance was exerting full power, sucking air down, and Langer had the sensation that it was about to tear him out of the window down into the mincing machine of the whirling rotors. He pulled his head in, slammed the window shut, continued watching from inside. The air disturbance was now causing another danger-ous reaction – the machine was rocking from side to side. It wasn't impossible that a whirlpool reaction would start – drawing both helicopters towards each other until their rotor tips met in one brief grinding clash. Then they were alongside each other and Langer opened the window again.

There was an observer as well as a pilot in the Soviet machine and Beaumont could see him operat-ing his headset, talking non-stop as he kept glancing across at them. A signal was being sent to someone. Then Gorov did a stupid thing. Restless with anxiety, he stood up and peered towards the dome of the other helicopter. 'Sit down!' Beaumont roared. He didn't think Soviet pilots were insane enough to use suicide tactics but he didn't know what instructions they had received regarding Gorov. Beaumont held his own helicopter in a hover, ready to fly forward, much of his attention focused on the thick silhouette of the mast which had to be avoided whatever happened. 'OK, Horst,' he shouted. 'Get on with it!'

Below them the deck of the *Elroy* had cleared suddenly; either by order of the ship's commander or through instinctive self-preservation, the American seamen had disappeared, taken cover. Beaumont watched Horst, his hand on the lever which would take them forward, away from machine, ship and mast in a burst of speed. The noise inside the cabin was terrible now, shattering as the engines of the other machine added their blasting roar to the din. And the Soviet helicopter was rocking badly too, quaking as though about to split open.

Langer screwed up his eyes to see more clearly, saw the curve of the Russian's dome only yards away. For seconds they wobbled close to each other. Langer leaned well out of the window and was deafened, paralysed with the cold. He raised his right arm, paused, hurled the monkey wrench in a careful arc, slammed the window shut.

The missile struck the shatter-proof dome, a dome shuddering with vibration, hurtled away at an angle into the night. Langer stared through his own dome. It had worked. Shatter-proof, the Russian's dome hadn't shattered – it had crazed. No longer transparent, its curved surface was milky – the pilot inside was blind, couldn't see a damned thing. Beaumont shot away from the blinded Russian, banked away from the ship's mast which loomed like a gigantic flagpole, flew on out over the ice.

Every helicopter has a smaller rotor at the tail. Without a tail rotor mounted at right-angles to the pitch of the main rotor no helicopter would fly. The enormous power of the overhead rotor has a natural torque reaction – whirling through the air it would sweep the fuselage it supports round and round at ever-increasing speed

– but for the counter-force of the tail rotor. This was something the Soviet pilot and his observer were about to experience for brief killing seconds.

As Beaumont had anticipated, the Soviet pilot did the wrong thing. It was understandable; it was also fatal. At one moment, sitting behind his controls, the pilot still had a clear view of his surroundings. Then Horst's wrench struck and he was surrounded by opaqueness, by crazed windows he couldn't see through at all. The world went milky on him. He was confined to a view of his cabin. He panicked.

He had to get away from the mast, to fly clear of the ship and out above the open ice where Beaumont had gone. He moved a lever, misjudged it, went forward in a shallow curve, banking to escape the menace of the huge mast. He was only half successful, his main rotors swung clear, but he forgot his tail and curved too sharply. The tail rotor kissed the mast and the whole mechanism left the machine. The balance-force which countered the torque tendency was gone. Basic aerodynamics came into play.

Once in Sydney, Australia, Beaumont had seen a film taken from an automatic camera mounted in a helicopter which flew too close to a building in Sydney Harbour. The tail rotor kissed the building, dropped into the water, and the camera recorded what happened. Later it was dredged up from the wreckage containing two bodies and the film was re-run. It was terrifying. He recalled the film as he saw what happened to the Soviet helicopter, knew with a horrible clarity what was happening inside the doomed machine.

The cabin began to rotate, to whirl like a top, and the two men inside rotated with it ... Faster and faster they revolved on their own axis with the machine still in mid-air, spinning round and round and round at ever-increasing speed in endless gyrations. In seconds both men were disorientated, powerless, spinning, spinning, spinning. Strapped into their seats, they experienced the full force of the terror, whirling like a roundabout gone mad, at a speed no roundabout out of control would ever attain.

They would have gone mad had it lasted long enough, but it didn't last long enough. The machine lost its equilibrium, banked over sideways, fell towards the ice. The whirling rotors were still hurtling the fuselage round when the smash came. The fuselage broke in two pieces, flew across the ice three hundred yards away from the *Elroy* as the rotors disintegrated. The fuel tanks detonated, sent out a sheet of flame which melted the ice on the port rails. Black smoke rose and wavered in the breeze which came from the north.

There was another watcher who saw the Soviet helicopter's destruction. Two miles away, flying at three thousand feet, Col Igor Papanin lowered his nightglasses and sat in silence while the pilot beside him waited for instructions.

'What happened?' Kramer asked from the seat behind. 'What was that flame?'

'Shut up! Let me think.'

Papanin was in a state of shock. Only an hour earlier he had flown to where the *Elroy* was hemmed in by ice to see what was happening. On the way he had received the signal from one of his helicopters: the Beaumont party had been found, men were being landed on the ice to cut them off from the American ship. It had sounded like a triumph.

He had arrived in time to see the Soviet helicopter still hovering over the *Elroy*. He had sent a signal over the radio-telephone himself, ordering it to keep its position. Then the second machine had appeared. For a few minutes Papanin had no idea what was happening, then the helicopter over the ship had started reporting. For once the Siberian had listened without interrupting, without saying a single word as the communications became more and more tense, climaxing in a report which had chilled him as he listened to the taut words coming through the earphones.

'Machine coming down on us ... several men inside ... window opening ... Gorov! Gorov! In the machine! ... many dogs ... three other men ...'

Then the message ceased. Papanin saw why when he raised his night-glasses and aimed them with difficulty, focusing just in time to see the obscene spectacle of his own helicopter whirling crazily in mid-air before it crashed.

Sitting behind him, Kramer saw the sagging shoulders stiffen. Papanin swung round in his seat and his expression frightened the Balt. 'Send a signal to the *Revolution*! Tell them I am on my way. Tell them to start radio-jamming at full power immediately! All vessels! We will establish our headquarters on board the *Revolution* and wait for the *Elroy* to come to us.'

'Hydrogen–Strongbow . . . Hydrogen–Strongbow . . .'

The two-word signal which Beaumont asked the *Elroy*'s captain to radio immediately to Curtis Field the moment he arrived on board reached Dawes close on midnight. 'Hydrogen–Strongbow . . .' The signal told Dawes everything – or almost everything. 'We have Gorov, we are aboard the *Elroy*.' He asked for a call to be put through to Washington immediately on the hot line.

The hot line went through Curtis Field on its way to Iceland and Europe; the other way it went back through Dye Two, a remote Distant Early Warning Station perched on the icecap, before it continued its long journey to Washington. When the call came through Dawes spoke to a man in the Defense Department and Adams listened, hearing only one end of the conversation.

'Sure we've got Gorov aboard an American ship,' Dawes said at a later stage in his call, 'but for the third time I'd feel a lot happier if we could send an escort ship to take the *Elroy* home . . .'

'No, I'm not suggesting they'd board an American vessel . . .' he growled at an even later stage.

Two minutes later he slammed down the phone and absentmindedly lit his cigar, the first live smoke he'd enjoyed in seventeen days. 'They won't give her an escort,' he said. 'They say it's all over.' He began pacing the over-heated office and staring at the wall map which showed the position of all ships in the area south of Target-5. 'All they can think of is that the President is at this moment in Peking clinking glasses with the Chinese.'

'You lit your cigar,' Adams pointed out. 'You're celebrating?'

'Not yet.'

When Adams had gone to bed Dawes was still pacing slowly, still gazing at the wall map, so uneasy that he knew he wouldn't sleep even if he did go to bed. And in this foreboding Dawes showed more insight than the man in Washington who had said it was all over. It was, in fact, just beginning.

Checkmate

The Killing Ground

Chapter One

Wednesday, 23 February: 1 AM–5 AM

'Take her down! You have to land on that blasted thing one day!'

Papanin shouted the command to make himself heard above the drumming of the rotors as the helicopter hovered uncertainly, hovered over the 16,000-ton research ship *Revolution*. The aircraft canted sideways, caught by a gust of wind, and Papanin, standing up, grabbed at his seat to save himself. Bloody amateur! The so-called pilots the flying schools turned out these days were a disgrace. Behind the pilot Kramer clung nervously to the flap seat he was perched on: he hated flying and this had been a very rough ride. The pilot regained control of his machine and spoke to the Siberian without looking at him.

'It would be safer if you sat down, Colonel!'

'It would be safer if we were already aboard that ship! Take her down, I said!'

'Landing conditions are very dangerous. I have enough fuel left to stay up . . .'

Papanin sat down next to the pilot in the observer's seat, put his face close to the pilot's, enunciated the words carefully. 'I am ordering you to land on that ship. I have not got the time to hang about in mid-air because you require the sea to be as smooth as a baby's bottom! Take her down!'

He turned away from the pilot and looked down at the ocean. The view was scarcely encouraging. The huge research ship, the showpiece of the Soviet merchant marine, her vast radar dome aft of the bridge gleaming in the moonlight like some strange seaborne mosque, was heaving slowly in a considerable swell. Three hundred feet below them, she rode great sea crests trundling south, her whole structure tilting and then falling, the spike at the top of the radar dome tipping sideways, pausing, climbing again as the seas lifted the vessel. Close to the icefield, ice floes drifted in the surging waves, climbed a crest, slammed down against the bows. The helicopter began to descend.

The pilot, his facial muscles tight, leaned well forward for his first sight of the radar dome. Under these dangerous conditions the dome was his only guide to the whereabouts of the landing pad, immediately aft of the dome. He had to touch the pad at just the right moment – when it was level – otherwise they would tip over sideways. Spume, caught by the wind, came up and splashed over the perspex, obscuring his view. Feeling the Siberian's stare, he continued the descent. Something like a huge pendulum swivelled beyond the perspex. The masthead, topped by a radar wing. The mast was laden with electronic gear. The *Revolution*, launched officially as the world's greatest research vessel, was really the Soviet Union's largest spy-ship.

The machine went lower. The dome filled the view now, sliding with the massive sea swell, but the pilot hardly saw it: he was watching the masthead beyond, swinging towards the vertical. When it reached the vertical, paused there for brief seconds, the invisible landing pad would be level. The skids below the undercarriage hit the pad, slammed into it. Waiting technicians rushed forward, clamped the anchor rings tight. The Siberian opened the door while the rotors were still whirling, looked back at the pilot.

'You see! You never know what you can do until you try!'

He jumped to the deck as the pilot glared at him, crouched to avoid the rotors, splayed his huge legs to hold his balance, then he was clawing his way along the rail when the sea sent an avalanche onboard. He clung to the rail, holding his breath until the water receded, and there were frozen spits of ice on his sleeves as he hauled himself up the tilting ladder leading to the great bridge. Captain Anatoli Tuchevsky, the ship's commander, opened the door to let him in.

'Colonel Papanin!' The Siberian, dripping water, took off his sodden parka and dropped it on the floor. 'You are Tuchevsky? Good. A change of clothing, please! Something belonging to the largest rating aboard! Why are you heading north at this turtle pace?'

Tuchevsky, a lean, self-contained man with a beard, grim-faced and thoroughly alarmed about what was happening to his ship, gave an order for fresh clothing to be brought and then led Papanin to the chart-room behind the bridge. He sent away an officer working over a chart with a pair of dividers, shut the door and faced the Siberian.

'I have to protest most strongly . . .'

'Protest noted!'

'I haven't told you what I'm protesting about yet . . .'

'I'm not interested!'

'These are dangerous waters for a vessel of this size . . .'

'Now tell me something new!' Papanin stripped off his outer gloves, peeled off his mittens underneath, dropped the sodden articles on a side-table. Taking out a pair of steel-rimmed spectacles, he stared at the chart on the table, picked up a pencil, made a cross. 'The American icebreaker *Elroy* was about there when I last saw her. She will now be smashing her way out of the ice. She will sail due south . . .' He scrawled a brutal line down the chart. 'We continue sailing due north.' His pencil went straight back up the line. 'So get on this course. And make this old tub of yours move!'

Tuchevsky took off his cap, dropped it on the chart so the Siberian could make no more markings, folded his arms and stared straight at Papanin. 'I command this vessel. I have an order to receive you, to carry out your instructions – but I am still in command . . .'

'Of course!' Papanin towered over the five-foot-six Tuchevsky as he beamed down at him. 'I fashion the bullets, you fire them!' Sitting down on the floor, he tugged off one boot and then the other, still grinning at the captain.

'I wish to protest formally about this order to proceed due north,' Tuchevsky continued with an edge in his voice. 'The *Revolution* is our latest and most modern research vessel. It cost millions of roubles. And yet I am ordered to take this vessel into a sea littered with icebergs . . .'

'The *Elroy* made it – and part of the way without radar. I saw she had lost her masthead equipment. You have that damned big ear twitching at the top of your mast – use it!' Papanin stood up in his stockinged feet and began padding about the chart-room, looking at things. 'I want to speak to the radio-jamming officer,' he went on. 'There will be a short pause to send a signal to the *Gorki* – all helicopters are to search for the present position of the *Elroy*. The first one to find it flies here immediately to report . . .'

'Why?' flared Tuchevsky. 'Why are we doing this insane thing? I shall radio an immediate protest to Moscow.'

'No you won't!' Papanin looked at him over his shoulder. 'The pause in the jamming will be very brief – only sufficient to send off my signal to the *Gorki*.

The *Elroy* is sailing south into a sea crammed with icebergs. She will be sailing blind – her radar is gone. She will be lost to the outside world – the radio-jamming has isolated her. Get me some tea, please, Tuchevsky, and I will tell you what it is all about.' The Siberian paused. 'You see, we are going to inter-cept the *Elroy*.'

The murderous, shuddering impacts of steel smashing into solid ice woke Beaumont after three hours' sleep at four in the morning. Had an earthquake been erupting outside the effect would have been mild compared with the quivering, grinding sensation he woke to as the bows smashed and drove into the polar pack. And of all men aboard Beaumont was receiving the full treatment – his cabin, the only other quarters available apart from the one amidships he had given to Grayson and Langer, was under the bows.

Befuddled with sleep, he blinked, wondering why the cabin walls seemed to be oscillating, as though some tremendous force just beyond was about to burst through the plates and crash down on him. He checked his watch. 4 AM. He'd had three hours' sleep since coming aboard. The oscillation of the cabin walls was quietening down but the reverberating crash was still in his ears when the door opened and Pat DaSilva, acting mate, peered in cautiously with a mug of steaming coffee.

'I wondered if you were awake,' he said solemnly.

'And you'd better swallow this fast before the next ram.'

'Thanks.' Beaumont took the mug and sipped cautiously while he studied DaSilva. The acting mate was a short, stocky man of about forty with curly black hair and a squarish head. At first glance he looked tough and uncompromising, but there was a glint of humour in the steady grey eyes if you studied him carefully. Beaumont swallowed a lot of the scalding liquid. American coffee. Very strong.

'Here it comes again,' DaSilva warned as he grabbed hold of the door frame. The vessel was moving forward, its engines throbbing with power. Just beyond the wall of the cabin was the bow. Somewhere just beyond that was the ice as the steel bow cut through black water. Beaumont put out a hand and waited, his coffee mug three-parts empty, his hand pressed against the end of the bunk. The ship struck.

The cabin vibrated with the massive collision. DaSilva almost lost his grip and was hurled across the cabin, but he saved himself. Beaumont had the feeling that the bows were breaking, the plates buckling, that within seconds the cabin wall would crumble while an avalanche of smashed ice deluged in over them. But at the back of his mind he knew this wouldn't happen: this was an icebreaker. The ship stopped, the engines still throbbing. Beaumont looked at the coffee splashed over the opposite bulkhead. 'Are we getting anywhere?' he asked.

'No place fast. It's been going on for over an hour – God knows how you slept through it – and we're stuck solid. The trouble is we've lost not only the radar – the observation cage went down as well. With the mate inside it,' DaSilva added soberly. 'Which promoted me to acting mate. I could have done without it – Carlson was a good guy. We need someone up top,' he explained, 'to see what angle to hit the ice at. The trouble is there's no top to send anyone up to.'

Beaumont was getting dressed, putting on his boots and his parka as the vessel withdrew from the ice. The cabin shuddered again; the grinding, grating sound of steel withdrawing itself from the vice of the pack was appalling. 'I'm going up to the bridge to see what's happening,' Beaumont said as he fastened the parka. He looked directly at the mate. 'Could I have imagined it,' he inquired, 'or was there a certain lack of enthusiasm as we came aboard?'

DaSilva looked uncomfortable. 'You don't want to take any notice of it.' He hesitated. 'The fact is Schmidt wasn't too happy about bringing the ship as far north as this in February. The rumour is he received some gut order from Washington – get the hell north and damn the consequences. He kind of blames you for being alive, for bringing him up here.'

'Some of the crew too?'

'Maybe a guy here and there. We were going home to Milwaukee when the order came through. They'll get over it . . .'

278

But they hadn't got over it yet. Beaumont sensed the hostility around him as he made his way up to the bridge. He'd have had to be blind not to have sensed it. Seamen he passed didn't seem to see him coming. One burly character on his hands and knees in a companionway who was cleaning the floor moved his bucket in front of Beaumont.

'Shift that bucket fast, Borzoli,' the acting mate snapped.

The burly man looked up. 'I didn't see you, Pat . . .' He moved the bucket quickly. It wasn't just that they had been sent up Iceberg Alley, Beaumont reflected as he mounted a staircase; DaSilva hadn't told him the whole story. He was being blamed for the death of the mate, Carlson. It looked as though the voyage could be marred by the odd incident; the men who crewed an icebreaker weren't the gentlest characters who went to sea. Commander Schmidt's opening remark wasn't exactly encouraging either.

'I'd keep to your quarters if I were you, Beaumont. You need the rest.'

The high bridge gave a good view out over the ice ahead and the vessel was driving along the channel for another ram. At least the surviving channel had been wide enough for Schmidt to turn his ship round before he attacked the pack, searching for a way out south. At the end of the channel the ice was battered but still intact, and when the bows struck no crack appeared. Beaumont released his gloved hands from the rail he had gripped and looked at Schmidt. 'We're in trouble. At this time of the year the icing up will go on – if we don't get out soon we'll be stuck here till spring . . .'

'You think you're telling me something?' The dark-browed commander stared bleakly at Beaumont from under his peaked cap. 'Against my better judgement I came up here on account of you people. What I can do without is your comments.'

'You need a man high up,' Beaumont insisted, 'a man eighty feet up so he can guide the angle of the ramming, so he can detect the slightest trace of a fissure which will tell him where to ram next time . . .'

'Come with me!'

Schmidt's expression was even bleaker as he gave an order for the ship to be stopped and then left the bridge quickly. They went backwards down a slippery ladder which had recently been cleared of ice, and on deck teams of men were shovelling ice over the sides, great slabs of ice which other men were levering off the deck with crowbars. The *Elroy*'s Sikorsky was just coming in to land, hovering over the pad aft of the bridge and then dropping. 'Checking up on those Russians out on the ice,' Schmidt snapped. 'Like you suggested,' he added grudgingly. 'A Soviet chopper airlifted them out half an hour ago.' They arrived at the base of the huge mast. 'Take a good look,' Schmidt growled.

The huge structure speared up into the moonlight. Eighty feet above them, the tip of the spear was jagged and torn, looked as though it had run into the wall of a building. The crosstree below was intact, and even from their great distance below it Beaumont could see that the crosstree was sheathed in ice. A seaman levering up an enormous slab of ice tipped it over. It smashed down inches from Beaumont's right foot – because Beaumont had moved the foot just in time. 'Do that again,' Schmidt roared, 'and I'll have you in the brig. Get over to the port side!' He waited until the seaman had gone before he spoke again. 'They all liked Carlson,' he said.

'And they hold me responsible for his death?'

'I didn't say that. Now, for God's sake, look at it! And you say I ought to send a man up there!'

A metal ladder ran up the side of the ice-coated mast, its rungs encased in gleaming ice; the rigging was festooned with ice, ten-foot-long icicles hung from the tips of the crosstrees. Seen from the deck as Beaumont stared up, the mast was like some weird glass pylon. It looked totally unassailable.

'I didn't say you ought to send a man up,' Beaumont replied. 'I can get up there myself. I'll need a leather strap to hold me, canvas padding round the mast, and a telephone set to communicate with the bridge . . .'

'And a coffin to bury you in,' a voice behind him added.

'This is Quinn, the chopper pilot,' Schmidt said gruffly, so Beaumont shook hands with Quinn, the first man who had extended him this courtesy since he had come aboard. Lean and lanky, in his early thirties, Quinn reinforced his warning.

'You should have died on the ice. You didn't – so stick to your cabin till we hit Quebec. We'll get there one day.'

Schmidt was staring resignedly up at the mast. 'It's what we need – someone high up. But what damned use would you be up there?'

'I did the same job for your sister ship *Exodus*,' Beaumont replied quietly. 'Three years ago north of Baffin Bay. She was trying to head up Smith Sound and she had the same sort of problem – solid ice ahead. I knew the area so I went aloft and guided them through.'

'That's MacDonald's ship.' Schmidt stared at Beaumont and then up at the mast again. 'We have a telephone box up there already and the mast is padded – DaSilva went up to locate a way into the icefield, but I brought him down before we started hammering the pack.'

'Mac was the captain when I was on the *Exodus*.' Beaumont smiled dryly. 'He wrote out a dummy certificate for me afterwards – to show I could act as pilot in Smith Sound. And I think we ought to get out of here – that radio-jamming bothers me.'

'Standard procedure when Ivan is in a bad temper. You know what's going to happen if you're up there when I slam into the pack? It's suicide.'

Beaumont looked round the deck where seamen were continuing to heave ice overboard. Heads turned away when he caught their gaze, one man spat on the deck and then hurriedly resumed work as Schmidt glared at him. 'Suicide?' Beaumont repeated. 'Then everyone here will be happy.'

Three hours' sleep had revived Beaumont, but he was hardly his normal energetic self as he mounted the ice-coated ladder, swaddled in clothing, the leather chest-strap clamped round his body, the second snap-clip strap for fastening round the mast dangling, the telephone headset in position under his fur hood. Below him on the deck a subtle change had come over the seamen who ten minutes earlier had been so hostile. They paused in their work, staring up with some awe at the huge Englishman climbing the deadly ladder. Beaumont had noted the change when he came on deck the second time, had ignored it. To hell with them.

Twenty feet above the deck he stopped to smash his boot down hard to break the ice. His boot slipped, his gloved hand tightened on a rung, and the ice he had hammered was intact. He was mounting a ladder of pure ice. As he went on up he felt the sub-zero temperature penetrating his gloves, seeping through the mittens inside them, rasping at the raw skin of his fingers. He felt the bitter night air freezing his face, prickling his eyelids, catching his throat. His eyes watered, his vision blurred. He went higher and the sensation of relentless cold began to blot out everything else – the throb of the waiting engines, the searchlight Schmidt had projected over the bows, the endless icefield planing away to the south.

He was forty feet up when the snap-clip dangling from his chest-strap hooked on to one of the rungs; he went on up, not realizing what had happened. He had one foot on a lower rung, the other reaching for a higher perch, when his body jerked taut in mid-air. It caught him off balance and he lost his equilibrium. The foot in mid-air thrashed about in space and the boot lower down, poised on a rung of ice, had to take all his weight, the shock of the sudden halt. Then the lower boot slipped off the rung. He dropped.

Suspended forty feet above the ice-coated deck by only his hand-holds, gloves clawing at slippery ice, he fought to regain control, his boots swinging in air as he tried to find rungs he couldn't see. He felt his hand-holds losing their grip, slithering round the icy rungs, then one foot found a rung, took some of the weight, and within seconds he had his other foot back on the ladder. As he paused for breath he had a glimpse downwards of the deck, of tiny faces staring up at him. He waited for his heartbeats to slow down to something nearer normal, then he resumed his ascent.

The crosstree was a right royal bastard. The steel ladder ended just below it, so he presumed it must have led straight up through a trap into the observation cabin where Carlson had died. He now had to climb beyond that, climb up over the crosstree before he could straddle on it and attach the chest-strap to the mast above it. And he was now eighty feet above the deck. Before he attempted this tricky manoeuvre he reached up with one hand to test the canvas padding wrapped round the crosstree. He found that it revolved, gave no safe purchase at all.

It took him ten agonizing minutes to get up over the crosstree, to get seated on the unstable canvas sleeve with the mast between his groin, to get the second strap looped and fastened round the mast, to attach the telephone terminals into the box already fixed to the mast. Only then did it occur to him that under his clothes his body was covered with sweat, that sweat was running down his face. He fumbled a handkerchief out of his coat pocket and used it to wipe his face. Beads of ice came away from his forehead. Before communicating with the bridge he looked around and the view was spectacular.

He pulled back the side of his hood to listen. No, he hadn't imagined it: weird gibbering and squeaking echoes were coming across the ice, then a low rumble like a volcanic upheaval. Half a mile away he saw the turbulence starting – half a mile ahead of the *Elroy*. Walls which seemed no larger than ripples from that height and distance began to heave up, to creep over the plain of ice, moving away from the *Elroy*, moving south. As he watched, a ribbon of dark water appeared, spreading away from the icebreaker. The night was full of the sound of ice cracking, ice shattering against itself. And the lead went on expanding, creeping towards a distant belt of darkness which was the ocean. The *Elroy* had to break through to that lead.

Twisting round, held to the mast by the chest-strap, he looked beyond the stern. A half-mile of open channel lay behind the vessel, and at the end of that channel, a long way down, lay the ruins of the Soviet helicopter Beaumont had flown to the ship. He had deliberately landed the machine under the bows of the *Elroy* and later Schmidt had completed the job, reversing his vessel a short distance and then ramming into the ice, into the machine perched at the brink. When he withdrew the steel bows dragged the remnant with it, dropped it into the sea. But it wasn't the end of the channel Beaumont was staring at now; appalled, he was looking at something well beyond it.

Carried forward by a rising breeze from the north, a black pall was creeping towards the ship, a pall quite different from the fog which had blanketed Target-5, a black curtain hundreds of feet high, a curtain which glittered ominously in the moonlight. A bank of black frost was drifting towards the ship, the most dreaded phenomenon in the Arctic. What Beaumont was staring at was a bank of frozen fog, a rare weather condition so insidious that it can cause frostbite requiring instant amputation if it settles on a man. If it caught him at the masthead he could be dead within seconds. And it was already invading the pressure ridge zone. He spoke quickly into the mike dangling from his chin.

'Schmidt! Reverse her!'

He clung to the canvas-padded mast as the engine throbs increased in power, then the vessel was moving back, sliding through the dark water behind its stern. The immediate effect at the masthead was more gentle than Beaumont had feared; no more than a slight sway as the icefield drifted past below and dark water appeared on both sides, a dark stain against the pallor of the pack. Then the vessel slowed, stopped. Knowing what was coming Beaumont felt his stomach muscles tighten. It took a conscious effort of will to start the process, to give the order into the mike.

'Half speed! Forward!'

'OK, Beaumont, here we go! Hold on tight.'

Beaumont hugged the mast, his head to one side, prepared to take the impact. The power increased, quivered up the mast, the vessel moved forward. The icefield slid past in the opposite direction far below, the water stain narrowed, and Beaumont watched the narrowing stain – because when the stain vanished the icebreaker would hit, ship against ice, steel against the barrier, a moving force against an immovable force. The stain narrowed, faded to a ruler-line, vanished. The ship went on, moving faster . . . Grkkk! The steel bows struck. The impact shuddered the entire vessel, raced up the mast, and the mast shuddered, whipped, vibrated to a maximum at its tip. It hit Beaumont like a hammerblow as he clung desperately to the mast, his body pressed into the canvas. Then the vibration slowed, stopped. The icebreaker was stationary, locked into the ice.

Beaumont relaxed his grip, stared ahead. A dark crack extended beyond the bows, but no more than a few feet. He looked either side of the crack, searching for a more promising fissure, found nothing. The ice was intact. His concentration was so great that it took him a few moments to realize that Schmidt was talking to him. He took a firmer grip on the masthead, saw half a mile away that the lead was still growing wider, then he heard Schmidt again and there was a hint of anxiety in the firm voice.

'Beaumont, are you receiving me? Beaumont . . .'

'I'm OK. We didn't do much this time. Same again is the answer – and hit the ice in exactly the same place if you can.'

'Reverse?'

'Take her back, Schmidt.'

The engine power built up, the screw thrashed the dark water at the stern, and from his great height Beaumont could sense the icebreaker fighting to tear herself free. Hurling her great bulk against the ice the *Elroy* had trapped herself; the ice had parted, let the bows bite into it, then closed round them like a massive vice. The throbbing built up a second time, built up greater power, and when Beaumont was certain Schmidt had failed again the ship suddenly wrenched herself loose. The sound of rending ice came up to him above the engine throbs, then the *Elroy* slid backwards, leaving a dark smear on the port side where the remnants of her paint stained the damaged ice. As the vessel went back Beaumont looked back. The black frost curtain was advancing over the belt of smooth ice, coming closer to the ship. He waited until the ship stopped again.

'Half speed! Forward!'

Schmidt had taken the ship further back down the channel this time, so when the bows met the ice they would be moving faster. Beaumont braced himself. Eyes half-shut, staring down, he watched the narrowing stain of water, not knowing that Grayson and Langer were on deck, gripping a rail, staring up in horror. The gap closed, the ice was under the bows, the impact was far greater. The tremor shot up the mast and Beaumont was in trouble, shaking like a leaf with the mast's brutal vibration. He had his eyes still half-open and the vast icescape shuddered horribly, shuddered as though in the grip of an earthquake. Then the ship was still.

Thirty minutes it went on at half speed, thirty bruising, battering minutes. Beaumont changed the angle of attack, used the *Elroy* as his own personal battering ram, hammering into the icefield, and slowly something began to happen. The ice began to fracture, to show a pattern of dark zigzags. And something else was happening, not so slowly. Beaumont was methodically being reduced to a state where he hardly realized what he was doing. His face was horribly sore and bruised, sore with the aching cold, bruised with pressing it into the canvas at the moment of impact. And now the black frost had almost reached him – they had to break out quickly before it killed him.

'Reverse, Schmidt,' he croaked. 'Take her back to the end of the channel this time.'

They went back. They went too far back. A finger of black frost was creeping out over the point where the submarine killer had gone down. The finger curled out to the masthead and Grayson, seeing what was happening, bellowed up to the bridge in a way passengers don't normally address ships' captains. 'You stupid idiot – get her moving! Beaumont's in the frost!'

Beaumont felt the deathly freeze as darkness blotted out everything. The icefield went, the water below disappeared, the damned deck vanished. He had been looking ahead, gauging the next ram, when the black frost closed over him. Panting with exhaustion he took a deep breath and a grisly sensation passed through him. His lungs felt as though they were congealing, filling up with liquid ice. He was gasping for breath, felt a great weight descending on him, trying to drag him off the crosstree. The vessel started moving forward, took him clear of the freezing menace. He opened the eyes he had instinctively closed and saw with a shock of horror that his parka was coated with ice crystals, layered with them. He had been freezing solid.

'Are you OK, Beaumont? Beaumont, Beaumont . . .' Schmidt's voice had lost its normal detached control, was filled with urgency and anxiety.

'I'm OK. This time we do it.' Beaumont paused for breath. 'We hit the port side of the ice fifty yards before the crack. Got it?'

'Fifty yards before the crack?' Schmidt sounded incredulous.

'Yes. Port side! Fifty yards! I'm going to bounce her into a starboard crack. Full power!'

'Full power! I'll kill you . . .'

'Get this fucking ship moving, Schmidt!' Beaumont was shouting down the mike. 'When I say full power I mean full power!'

'OK. It's your decision.' Schmidt just stopped himself in time: he had been on the verge of saying it's your funeral.

The *Elroy* sheered forward, throbbing in a way it hadn't throbbed before, pushing aside the dark water, sending a bow wave coursing against the ice on both quarters, building up maximum power for its next run against the barrier. Beaumont's tactic was unusual: he was directing Schmidt to hurl the massive weight of the moving vessel against one point of the ice so that its rebound would strike a segment of ice it couldn't otherwise have reached, a segment where a wide zigzag extended a long way towards the ever-widening lead in the distance. It was a tactic he had experimented with – which had succeeded – when he had led the *Exodus* into Smith Sound three years before. But not at full power.

He talked Schmidt in this time, guided the ship's onrush, taking it towards a precise point on the port side of the ice. Below him there was a significant development: Schmidt had ordered the deck cleared of men prior to the coming impact. Grayson had gone up to the bridge, was leaning out of a window, staring up at the tiny figure he could hardly see poised on the crosstree. Full power ... If it had been possible he would have countermanded Schmidt's order.

At the masthead Beaumont was staring to port, laden down by his outer clothes which were like a steel canopy, solid with the crystals. He issued one last instruction, 'If you feel her going through, Schmidt, keep her going ...' The vessel surged forward, the engine throbs echoed in Beaumont's brain, he clasped his arms tightly round the canvas-wrapped mast, he took a deep breath, the vessel hit.

The *Elroy*'s bows slammed into the ice on the port side, hitting the barrier at an angle, a glancing blow. They bounded off the barrier, swung at an angle, rammed forward with terrible momentum into the starboard ice. Beaumont had used the icebreaker like a gigantic billiard ball, cannoning the bows off one side so they would strike the opposite side close to the zigzag. Above the throb of the beating engines came a different sound, a grinding smash which travelled through the ship, which stunned the crew below. But the effect at sea-level was nothing compared to what happened at the masthead.

The mast began to vibrate like a tuning fork, whipping back and forth as though about to rip itself out of the ship, whipping Beaumont back and forth, whipping like a flexible cane instead of an eighty-foot-high mast. The ordeal was appalling, well-nigh unendurable, and Beaumont became disorientated as the whipping went on – back and forth at incredible speed. He felt his strength, his mind, going. He felt as though his teeth were being shaken out of his head, his head loosened from his body, his whole body structure coming apart.

He opened his eyes, his hands still locked round the mast, and everything was blurred. He couldn't make out whether they were stopped or still moving forward. He looked down, saw a huge crack, a crack which was almost a lead, and flopped against the mast he felt the cold mike against his chin. He spoke without realizing it, spoke like a man repeating a rote. 'Keep her moving, Schmidt . . . keep her moving . . .' There was a salty taste in his mouth, blood, an agonizing pain across his shoulder blades. He wondered whether his back was broken. 'Keep her moving, Schmidt . . .'

Schmidt kept her moving. From the moment they struck the starboard ice, from the second he felt the penetration, Schmidt kept her moving. The scarred bows battered, heaved, forced their way forward, thrust aside huge slabs of ice, up-ended them, bulldozed them, bit deeper and deeper, went on and on and on, smashing through the barrier which was at last giving way. Below decks the chief engineer stared at his gauges, unable to drag his gaze away from the needles quivering well above danger point. If Schmidt wasn't careful the boilers would blow.

Schmidt wasn't careful, he maintained full power. And the vessel responded, wouldn't stop, was mounting its bows on top of the ice, riding up on it, breaking it down with sheer weight and power. From the masthead, barely conscious, Beaumont began to grasp what was happening, saw the ice parting, the crack widening to a lead, the lead spreading back and back, and he knew they were going through all the way. Then he lost consciousness, relaxed his hand-grip, slipped from the crosstree, and like a man hanging he hung there, suspended by the chest-strap, his body swaying like a pendulum.

It was Borzoli, the burly seaman who had shoved a bucket in Beaumont's way, who went up to get him. Grayson had one foot on the icy ladder when Borzoli pushed him aside with an oath, 'You're too small for this job, friend . . .' And probably the seaman was the only man aboard who could have attempted it; a couple of inches shorter than Beaumont, he was built like a wine cask. He clawed his way up the swaying mast, went up and up while the icebreaker continued driving through the ice.

'Christ, he must be dead . . .' Langer stood beside Grayson, holding on to the ladder to keep himself upright as they stared up in horror at the body swinging eighty feet above them in the night. Like a man hung from a yardarm two hundred years ago, Beaumont swung backwards and forwards, swung free of the mast as he pivoted in space. 'That strap won't hold his weight much longer,' Grayson murmured. Borzoli was smaller now, was moving up at an incredible pace, and Grayson had his heart in his mouth for both men – for Beaumont whom he expected to see spin off the crosstree at any second, for Borzoli who had only to make one mistake to bring himself crashing down sixty feet – or was it seventy? – he was close to the crosstree now.

Hardly daring to believe the evidence of his own eyes he saw the tiny climbing figure stop. Grayson looked away, not able to watch any more, and then the vessel lurched with a terrible violence and he lost his grip on the ladder, went hurtling across the icy deck to crash against a bulkhead. He lay there for some time, the wind knocked out of him, trying to get his breath back as Langer bent over to make sure he was all right. That terrible impact had, of course, knocked both men above them off the ship; they were now lying somewhere on the pack, dead.

'Get me up, Horst . . .'

Langer helped him to his feet and he stood there, holding on to a rail, not daring to look up. Both men stared upwards at the same moment and then went on looking, hardly breathing, scared out of their wits. Borzoli was on his way down, was on his way down with Beaumont suspended from his back by the chest-strap he had released from the mast. How the hell could the seaman stand it? Grayson wondered. He was descending a ladder of sheer ice, a ladder rocked by the continuous collisions of the bows with the pack, descending with another man's weight trying to tear him backwards off the ladder with every downward step he took.

Borzoli grew larger, Beaumont grew larger as the descending man came nearer the deck, and now, feeling his strength ebbing, the seaman was coming down as fast as he dared, his great boots hammering at the ice-coated rungs, smashing off the ice because it was the combined weight of two outsize men battering at the rungs. Splintered ice showered over Grayson and Langer. They ducked their heads to save their eyes, and when they looked up again Beaumont's swaying body was only just above them. They grabbed at it, took the weight off the exhausted Borzoli, and then both men were at deck level as the *Elroy* surged forward into the open lead, towards the ocean beyond.

Chapter Two

Thursday, 24 February: 6 AM–Midnight

'What would happen if there was a collision?'

Papanin stood on the bridge of the *Revolution* close to Tuchevsky who was watching the radar. The bridge was very large, had a great sweep of armoured glass beyond the helmsman, was fitted with every scientific device available that might help navigation. Compared to the Russian ship, the 6,500-ton *Elroy*, her radar gone, was back in the nineteenth century.

The vibration of the powerful diesel motors was gentle, barely more than a persistent humming, and a battery of searchlights poised at different angles beyond the bridge shone out into the dense mist. The helmsman was several yards away as Papanin spoke in a low tone, too low also for the officer of the watch to hear as he stood in front of an outsize clear-vision panel. 'What would happen,' Papanin continued, 'if we came out of the fog and struck the *Elroy* amidships with our bows?'

The *Elroy* was at sea, a weird and terrible sight, and she was sinking. It was dark, total darkness, although somewhere above the screen of black frost the moon still shone down. Her lights – the searchlights projected over the heaving ocean – showed glimpses of the horror.

The bridge, the mast, the rails, the deck were mantled with the deadly crystals where the atmosphere itself had frozen over the ship, coating her, polluting her, tarring her with the evil black sheen which glistened when light caught it. The temperature was −39°F – seventy-one degrees below freezing point. The air was colder than the ice-cold sea, was liquid ice which hung over the ship like a black cloud, a cloud of death. And there were over five hundred tons of ice on the deck which listed dangerously to port. It was only a matter of time before the *Elroy* capsized, went down.

It was horrible on deck – horrible and dangerous where groups of men, all the crew which could be spared, fought to heave the ice overboard in time, and as they fought the black frost hovering all round them added more layers to overwhelm them. They couldn't see – except by the glimmers of light from bulkhead lamps smeared and half-obscured by the molasses-like frost encrusted on the glass. They couldn't stand upright – because the deck was permanently canted over to port by the great weight of ice they desperately tried to shift. They could hardly breathe – because when they took in breath they took in air which had crystallized to liquid ice, air which it was no cliché to say was as heavy as lead.

Frozen with the terrible cold, their clothes weighed down by ice crystals, they used picks and axes and hammers and shovels to smash at, break up, lever up and heave overboard the tonnage which was killing them. The sound of the slow-beating engines was almost muffled by the hacking, smashing, cracking noises. And the unquiet sea heaved the vessel up and down, made their impossible task infinitely more dangerous as, caught off balance, they grabbed for lifelines sheathed in ice. It had been going on for twenty-four hours.

Beyond the plunging bows the sea hissed and rolled in the searchlight, and in the beam, looking down from the high bridge, Schmidt saw ice descending in mid-air, black ice. 'It's beating us, DaSilva,' he said grimly. 'More ice is forming than we're getting rid of.'

At the port window DaSilva peered down and he wasn't prepared to give the captain an argument: the ice on deck was nearly rail-high. He pressed his face close to the armour glass, withdrew it quickly as his nose felt the temperature. A seaman, Borzoli he thought, had pulled his hand up quickly and the glove he should have worn was gone, trapped under a slab of ice. Even though he wore mittens under it frostbite would attack him within seconds, Borzoli was running, his hand tucked under his armpit, running for the nearest stairwell, and DaSilva prayed it wouldn't mean amputation. Then he couldn't see anything as spume from a wave hurtled through the air and hit the glass with a crack, freezing as it landed.

'I hear Beaumont is OK,' Schmidt said.

'Beaumont is recovering,' DaSilva agreed. 'He must be like this glass – armoured.'

Inside Langer's cabin Beaumont was sitting up alone, listening to the thump of ice floes against the hull beyond the cabin wall. He could tell that something was wrong from the tilt of the cabin: it was almost permanently canted to port. But he was thinking about Papanin, about things Schmidt had told him three hours earlier soon after he had woken.

'They're about forty miles south of us – the six Soviet trawlers,' Schmidt had said, pointing to his chart. 'Spread out across our path like a screen. Quinn found them – before the black frost caught us he took his machine south to the limit of his fuel – and he thought he had a glimpse of a much bigger ship just about here.'

'Less than thirty miles away. The *Revolution*?'

'Could be. The fog down there closed in just as he spotted her. He thought he saw a big radar dome – the equipment she uses for tracking our satellites. We'll just have to make sure there's no collision when we're passing them . . .'

Beaumont eased himself to a more comfortable position in the bunk. McNeill, the ship's doctor, had told him in a voice of some wonderment that he was still in one piece. 'Your clothes and that canvas buffered you. The fact that you swung free from the mast without striking it helped – but you'll be here till we hit Quebec . . .'

Beaumont didn't think so: he'd be up soon now. His torso was badly bruised, felt twice its normal size, which meant it felt very large indeed, but soon now . . . As he settled himself he winced. Well, maybe in a few hours. As he stared at the opposite wall without seeing it he thought about the short time he had spent with Papanin in the hut on Target-5. He was remembering the Siberian's huge, shaven head, the very wide mouth, the almost Mongolian bone structure. A ruthless man.

And now there were at least seven Soviet vessels in front of the *Elroy* which was carrying Gorov – and the Catherine charts. Reaching behind him, he fumbled in the pocket of his parka and took out the core tube. He weighed it in his hand – the entire Soviet underwater system, and Papanin knew where it was. 'We'll just have to make sure there's no collision . . .' Schmidt had said, and Schmidt had been thinking of an accident. Beaumont was thinking of something quite different as he returned the core to his parka pocket, pulled the blankets up under his chin, and stared into the distance, trying to see the future. Then, without realizing it, he fell asleep.

The *Elroy* had increased speed dangerously, was ploughing forward at half speed, her bows plunging deep inside a trough as a wave crashed over the port rail and submerged it. When the bows lifted again half the wave crest was attached to them, frozen solid to the rail which was now six inches thick with ice.

'We'll have to take a chance,' Schmidt had decided ten minutes earlier. 'We'll have to increase speed in the hope that we take her out of the black frost.'

'She'll go over . . .' DaSilva had stopped speaking when Schmidt looked at him, understanding the glance: they were going over anyway, so what was the difference? And every possible factor was deteriorating.

The wind had increased to thirty-five-knot strength, was howling like a banshee among the ice-clogged rigging, hurling spume onboard, spume which froze in mid-air so it landed on the backs of the stooped men on deck like lead shot. They were losing the whole battle for survival on every front – and they knew it. The ice still piled up faster than they could get rid of it, was now solid to rail height on the port side. The rising wind was turning the sea they had to plough through into a churning cauldron of forty-foot waves, great green combers which came rolling above them, half as high as the remnant of the mast which was also canted to port.

The giant combers inundated the deck frequently, swirled waist-high round men clinging to the icy lifelines, submerging the ice they were struggling to shift overboard. And frequently it brought with it floating spars of ice which crashed into the bulkheads with lethal force, such force that one spar shattered into pieces before the sea retreated. They lost one man in this way – hanging on to a lifeline he was pinned to the bulkhead, the whole of his middle crushed in by a heavy spar which came at him like a torpedo. It worried the men that they hadn't saved the body, but privately DaSilva thought it a blessing – the mangled corpse would later have had to be buried ceremonially. As Schmidt had said, they had to take a chance. So they went up to half power.

'I think we ought to clear the decks,' DaSilva said fifteen minutes later.

'Why?'

Schmidt joined him at the port window and saw why. The port rail was submerged again and looking down from the bridge it was an extraordinary, terrifying spectacle. Only the top half of men waist-deep in water showed. The rail was gone, the mountain of ice had vanished, it was as though the bridge was floating by itself. Frozen spume bombarded the window and Schmidt had to move to find a still-uncovered patch he could peer down through. Schmidt went back to keep watch on the bows.

'Keep them at work,' he ordered.

'They can't work, for God's sake! How can they – waist-deep in sea?'

'Are they waist-deep now?'

'No, not at the moment, but they will be when the next wave comes.'

'Keep them at work.'

Deep down inside himself DaSilva knew that Schmidt was right. Every pound of ice they could lever overboard between inundations gave the ship a little longer to float, to live, to move forward to what might be safety, or a kind of safety. They had to get clear of the black frost or die.

So for sixteen hours they changed the work teams at even more frequent intervals, gave the men time to go below to dry out and warm up before they froze to death, and then after a short break they toiled up again, to start all over again, to get rid of a pitifully small amount of ice, to face the cold and the wind and the sea and the danger of ice spars flattening them against the bulkhead walls. Only a man like Schmidt could have subjected them to such an ordeal; only for a man like Schmidt would they have submitted to the ordeal. And Grayson and Langer took their turn with the rest while Gorov, the man who had brought them all to this, lay on his bunk sea-sick.

The break came suddenly, and DaSilva was the first to grasp what was happening. Down on deck for the fourth time, levering at a slab of ice, he looked up and stared at the others. They were still working, still hacking at the ice, still unaware of any change. He threw his crowbar down a stairwell, ran to the ladder, climbed up to the bridge. 'It's lighter!' he shouted as he burst inside. 'We're through!'

'I do believe we are.'

There was no relief, no satisfaction in Schmidt's voice as he gazed through the rear window. It was simply a statement of fact. The vessel was still tilted to port, there was still a small mountain of ice on that side, but the atmosphere was clearing and something like moonlight was bathing the deck in its pale wash. And the curtain of black frost was a distinct curtain, drifting away from them in all its horror many cable-lengths behind the stern.

It was 11 PM when Beaumont made his way slowly and painfully up the stairwell which led to the fore-deck, wondering what the hell was going on. He had just seen a seaman running up the staircase ahead of him and out on deck, and above him he heard the excited clatter of other running feet. Nobody ran about a ship layered with ice unless he was very bothered indeed.

When he entered the bridge Schmidt – in these weather conditions – had opened a window and was staring through his night-glasses. Beaumont glanced at the helmsman, at DaSilva, and decided not to ask any questions at this moment. Both men were stand-ing in attitudes suggesting more than a little anxiety. The answer came to him unasked as he moved closer to the open window and heard a reedy lookout's voice travelling up to the bridge.

'Icebergs on the port bow! Icebergs on the starboard bow! Icebergs ahead!'

'No!' Tuchevsky exploded. 'I would ask to be relieved of my command before even thinking of giving such an order. In fact, I shall take action now. I shall order the radio-jamming to be stopped – until I have sent a signal to Moscow and had a reply . . .'

'You can't!' Papanin's tone was matter of fact. 'You know we have a Special Security detachment aboard this ship – it has already taken control of the jamming section.'

It was very warm inside the large chart-room behind the bridge of the *Revolution* and the argument had been going on for ten minutes. Papanin was, in fact, wearing down this prig of a captain, a tactic he had known would be necessary the moment he set eyes on him. Tuchevsky protested again.

'When I took command of the *Revolution* it was to carry out research, oceanic research . . .'

'Hypocrite! You have been tracking American satellites. This is research, of course – military research!'

'We also do oceanic research,' Tuchevsky snapped. 'Water temperatures, salinity . . .'

'All of which vitally affects submarine operations! You make me sick, Tuchevsky! You know that all the data you collect goes to our military intelligence people – who decide what scraps they will hand on to the professors . . .'

'I will not do it!' Tuchevsky shouted. 'I will not sink the American icebreaker. You must be mad – we could never get away with it . . .'

'You are wrong again,' Papanin observed cynically. 'The *Elroy* is steaming south without radar – we know this from the helicopter which found her two hours ago. And she cannot communicate with anyone – the jamming barrage has completed her isolation.'

'She has a helicopter,' Tuchevsky said viciously. 'I suppose you'd overlooked that?'

'No.' Papanin went over to the chart table to hide his irritation. Tuchevsky had touched a tender nerve there; for hours the Siberian had tried to think of a way of immobilizing the *Elroy*'s Sikorsky. 'Gorov and the Catherine charts are on board that ship,' he explained patiently. 'If we cannot get them back we must destroy them . . .'

'I will not do it.'

'I don't remember asking you to do anything. But these waters are littered with icebergs – and accidents can happen. And you should think of your family,' Papanin added casually.

'My family? What has this to do with my family?'

'Your wife, specifically,' the Siberian said woodenly. 'She is a Jewess . . .'

'That is a lie!'

Papanin sighed. 'She is half-Jewish. Her mother was a Jew. You seem to have forgotten that one of my duties is to check on Jewish agitation in Leningrad . . .'

'She has nothing to do with that . . .'

'Tuchevsky! Please keep quiet! Have you forgotten the signal ordering you to carry out my instructions?' Papanin went on explaining patiently. 'If it was discovered that your wife is mixed up in certain anti-

Soviet activities I could easily arrange for her to be sent to Israel. You would never see her again, would you?'

'You wouldn't dare . . .'

'What would happen next? For a few years she would hope – hope you would come. Women are very strong on hope. Then she would realize it was all over, that she must live her own life. We might even arrange for a divorce if she requested it . . .'

'You bastard . . .'

'I have to be,' Papanin agreed calmly. 'It is one of the main qualifications for my job.'

'There must be some other way . . .'

'If you think of it, let me know.'

'Your Sikorsky is on the way back, Beaumont,' Schmidt said without the trace of a smile.

Beaumont didn't reply as he stood on the *Elroy*'s bridge with Grayson and Langer. 'Your helicopter . . .' It was Beaumont who had urged Schmidt to send up Quinn again to check what lay ahead of them – if Quinn was willing. The fact was that Quinn had been itching to take up his machine ever since they had emerged from the black frost. Not unnaturally, Schmidt was most concerned at the moment with the problems of navigation.

Icebergs surrounded them on all sides, icebergs only dimly visible in the heavy sea mist drifting over the suddenly calm ocean. Two hours ago the scarred and battered ship had been fighting for her life in forty-foot seas, and now she was cruising slowly forward over water like cold milk. But she was still listing heavily to port, she still carried the enormous burden of the great load of ice pressing against the port rail, and it was still diabolically cold.

One massive berg, over a hundred feet high, a jagged cliff of floating ice, drifted less than a quarter of a mile away on the port bow. Mist curled at her base, another belt of whiteness was wrapped round her waist, but her enormous peaked head loomed up clear in the moonlit night. A smaller berg, her summit fretted and turreted like a Spanish castle, floated the same distance from the ship to starboard. They seemed like mountainous islands from the bridge, appearing, vanishing, then reappearing.

Langer moved closer to Beaumont, whispered the words. 'You asked me to check with DaSilva whether there were explosives aboard. There are . . .'

'Later,' Beaumont murmured. He was worried about Quinn – he felt responsible for this latest flight and he wouldn't feel happy until the chopper was safely back on its pad. At his suggestion one of the powerful searchlights near the bows had been switched on and elevated almost vertically into the night. It was this beacon poking up through the mist which Quinn was homing back on from the south, as yet only a tiny blip in the distance where it was caught by moonlight. The mist drifted, the blip vanished. Beaumont shifted his feet restlessly.

'I wonder whether he found those ships,' Grayson ruminated aloud.

'If they're still steaming north he probably has,' Beaumont guessed. 'He had seven vessels to look for – he should have spotted one of them . . .'

'I don't give a damn where they are,' Schmidt growled as he looked to starboard. 'We're on the high seas – we'll steam straight past them.'

Behind the captain's back Beaumont caught DaSilva's glance, a very dubious glance. The acting mate did not share Schmidt's sublime confidence in the freedom of the seas, a doubt which Beaumont had detected earlier, which had encouraged him to ask Langer to talk to DaSilva about explosives. 'Find out if they have any on board,' Beaumont had suggested. 'It's likely they're carrying something to blast their way out of ice. You're an explosives expert, so he won't think the question funny.'

The ship throbbed its way slowly forward over the oily sea, a sea which was dark and shiny in the moonlight, which made it look very much like a lake of oil. The mist so far was patchy, clinging to the iceberg zone on either side, and at this time of the year the sea was often calm like this in these waters. Perhaps it was the great weight of the floating masses of ice which gave it stability. Faintly, they heard the beating of Quinn's chopper coming in, but they still couldn't see him.

Beaumont looked to starboard where a searchlight was playing on the nearest berg. Illuminated, it looked gigantic, more like a Spanish castle than ever as the light shone through windows high in the turrets, through holes which penetrated the ice to the atmosphere beyond. It was almost frightening in its proximity and vastness. 'Couldn't be a ghost berg, I suppose?' Grayson murmured.

'I hope not – they're liable to collapse if you shout a rude word at them.'

Which was literally true, Beaumont thought, incredible though it might seem to people with no knowledge of the Arctic – that an unguarded human voice could bring down a colossus weighing millions of tons. Eskimos knew this; in their kayaks they glided past a ghost berg, not even daring to whisper, so fragile were these floating giants on the verge of collapse. Beaumont watched the light playing over the castled berg, hovering at its summit, then the summit burst.

One minute the peak was there, then it had gone, vanishing in a cascade of ice bursting outwards in all directions as the echo of its detonation reverberated across the ocean, echoing from berg to berg. Fragments of ice shot down the beam of the searchlight, vanished into the floe-littered sea. At least twenty feet of the summit had disintegrated. Schmidt gave a quick order, altering course a few degrees to port, away from the monolith.

'Not a ghost berg – an exploding berg,' Grayson commented. 'I don't want to meet any more of them.'

Quinn's Sikorsky came into view, was close enough

311

now to see the rotor disc haloed by the moon, was less than a quarter of a mile away as it lost altitude and came down to two hundred feet, heading for the *Elroy* on a course which would take it over the summit of the huge berg to port. Schmidt gave a fresh order to slow the engines while Quinn landed. The mist round the berg's waist had drifted away, showing the immensity of the great cliff of ice rising sheer from the mist at its base.

'I hope he found the *Revolution*,' Langer said.

The vast berg exploded as Quinn flew over it, exploded like a gigantic bomb no longer able to contain the pressure inside. But this time it wasn't just the summit which disappeared – the whole berg blew up with a boom that thundered out across the ocean, deafening the men on deck below the bridge. The bridge itself shuddered under the shock wave. The face of the overhead compass shattered, showering glass over the helmsman. Schmidt grabbed at the wheel to keep them on course.

The roar went round and round among the bergs, and came back to the ship as a shattering echo. Foam and vapour where the berg had been shot five hundred feet up into the night, a massive geyser which rivalled Old Smoky. As the vapour column fell back to sea level it revealed nothing but boiling water. The berg had gone, the Sikorsky had gone, and Quinn had gone.

Beaumont went to Schmidt who had handed back the wheel to the helmsman and was standing close to the window, staring at the frothing lake of sea. 'He was right over the summit when it exploded . . .'

'I know,' Schmidt replied quietly. 'Dear God . . . Quinn.' He squared his shoulders and spoke without looking at the man beside him. 'If you get any more bright ideas, Beaumont, you know what you can do with them.'

It wasn't so much the words as the quiet way he said them which expressed the bitterness. Beaumont walked away, nodded to Grayson and Langer, and they followed him off the bridge. He was appalled at the death of Quinn, but if possible he was even more appalled at the loss of the helicopter. The radar was gone, the wireless-jamming made it impossible to send or receive any signal, and now their last link with the outside world had been taken away from them. With Papanin to the south of them they were isolated. One hour later the *Elroy* struck the berg.

Chapter Three

Friday, 25 February

'One hundred pounds of gelignite, timer mechanisms, and a few hundred foot of cable . . .'

'Where do they keep it, Horst?'

'You'd never guess – inside a cabin off the main deck.' Langer grinned at Beaumont. 'Strictly against the regulations, DaSilva says, but he also says that when he has to heave defective jelly overboard he doesn't want to carry it all the way up from the explosives store.'

'DaSilva has his head screwed on the right way,' Grayson said. 'Those people back in Washington who write out regulations never travel with the stuff.'

The three men were sitting inside Beaumont's cabin while they ate their lunch of clam chowder and cinnamon pie. The fact that the meal had been sent to the cabin suggested that once again their popularity had waned. 'We're in the doghouse,' Grayson observed as he put down his coffee cup. 'Anybody would think you sent Quinn out so he'd be blown up by that berg . . .'

'Schmidt's more worried than he lets on,' Beaumont replied. 'He pretends he's concentrating on his

315

navigation but I've an idea he's as worried as we are about those Russian vessels. It's the *Revolution* I'm bothered about – all sixteen thousand tons of her. The trawlers the *Elroy* could push out of the way. What's that, Horst?' The German was showing a key in the palm of his hand with a smug expression.

'Key to the explosives cabin. DaSilva doesn't see eye to eye with Schmidt on this "we're on the high seas so no one can touch us" business. And somehow that hundred pounds of gelignite has got itself tucked away inside a couple of shoulder-packs – just in case . . .'

The cabin lurched under the massive blow, shuddered as though the bulkheads were on the verge of caving in. The cabin walls tilted to port, back to starboard, then upright again. From under the ship came a terrible grinding sound as though its keel was being torn out and the grinding went on and on. 'Christ . . .' Grayson hauled open the cabin door and they heard shouting, the thud of running feet, a terrible crash beyond the port bulkhead, then the vessel was still with its engines ticking over. The lights dimmed, almost went out, came back to full power reluctantly.

'We've struck,' Horst yelled.

'Unless the *Revolution* just hit us . . .' Grayson began.

'More like an iceberg!' Beaumont was dragging on his parka. 'Make for the bridge.'

Beaumont ran along the deserted companionway,

paused at the bottom of the staircase to button his parka, to slip on mittens and gloves, and from the deck above he heard men's voices, voices with more than a hint of panic. He went up the staircase, opened the door, and the mist met him, cold clammy mist with silhouettes moving about inside. It was impossible to see what had happened, what was beyond the port rail. Beaumont couldn't even see the damned port rail as he felt his way towards the ladder leading up to the bridge. A large burly figure came out of the mist and cannoned against him. Borzoli.

'We've struck!' he gasped hoarsely.

'Going down?' Beaumont asked, feeling the core tube inside his parka pocket.

'God knows . . .'

Beaumont went up the ladder to the bridge, had almost reached the top when the mist beyond the bows shifted. Something like a mountain appeared and then vanished, a mountain only yards away. He went on to the bridge cautiously as Grayson and Langer came up the ladder behind him. Schmidt was standing at the front of the bridge with a window open and the icy air was rapidly dispersing the warmth. The helmsman was still holding the wheel although they weren't going anywhere, and the floor was canted towards the stern. DaSilva was hanging out of another open window, staring to port. And the engines had stopped. Glancing over his shoulder, Schmidt saw Beaumont.

'Come over here a minute, Beaumont,' he called

out. His tone was neutral, the mood of anger gone. 'It's the damnedest thing – we've ridden up on an iceberg.'

It took them an hour to assess the position, the extraordinary position they were now in. Steaming very slowly through thick mist, the *Elroy* had passed inside a small bay on the coast of a giant iceberg; in less than a minute it had crossed the bay and the bows had driven inside a wide, scooped-out gulley of ice eroded out of the side of the berg, a huge natural ramp tilting up out of the sea. At the first grinding scrape Schmidt had acted, but by then the bows, the forepart of the ship, were lifted out of the water like a ship in dry dock, while at the stern the screw was still in deep water.

Schmidt had stopped the engines but the 6,500-ton vessel was marooned, the bows and a third of the hull resting on the ice chute, the other two-thirds of the ship and its stern still in the bay. At the end of the trough the wall of the berg rose sheer in the mist, greenish and massive like a cliff in the searchlight's beam. To Schmidt it had seemed incredible, but to Beaumont it was only strange: a year ago a British trawler had endured a similar experience off Spitsbergen; in heavy fog she had driven her own bows deep inside a chute at the edge of the icefield. The captain had used his common sense, faced with this unique experience – he had simply reversed his engines and the screw had dragged the trawler back into the sea.

'Jesus!' DaSilva called out from the rear of the bridge. 'How the hell did we ever get inside here?'

They went to the rear window and Schmidt blinked. The mist had cleared a little for the moment and beyond the stern was a small bay with arms which curved out to flank a narrow entrance. It had been little short of a miracle that the *Elroy*, moving blind through the mist, had cleared both arms of the bay when she steamed direct inside. The mist drifted over, blotted out the arms of solid ice.

'With a little judgement, a lot of luck, we should be able to manage it,' Schmidt said thoughtfully. 'Most of the ship is still in the water so if I reverse the screw it should haul us off the ice chute.' He let out a deep breath. 'Isn't it the damnedest thing?'

'You know the ice went?' DaSilva asked Beaumont. 'It went as we hit the chute – you can see now.'

Beaumont looked down out of the port window where the mist had lifted off the chute. It wasn't surprising he hadn't been able to see the port rail when he came up on deck – the port rail hadn't been there to see. As the keel ground its way up inside the chute the mountain of ice they had tried to shift for many back-breaking hours had left them, had taken the rail with it. Beyond the ship a vast mass of heaped-up ice lay on the chute floor with here and there a fragment of rail sticking up out of the heap. Fur-clad figures, the seamen Schmidt had sent down rope ladders to explore the berg, were moving like ghosts in the mist. A head came up over the side where the rail was still intact close to the bows. Langer's. He scrambled up the ladder and joined them on the bridge.

'It's not a ghost berg, Keith, I'm sure . . .'

'You're certain?'

'Dead certain. Sam and I climbed up as far as we could and it's solid – a cliff of ice . . .'

'You can see it now,' Schmidt called out from the front of the bridge. The mist, swirling, in constant motion, had drifted away beyond the bows and for a few minutes the majesty of the berg they were marooned on was exposed. A hundred yards beyond the bows the ice sheered up vertically like the cliffs of Dover. The mist drifted further and they saw the cliff sweeping away on both sides until it disappeared inside the drifting whiteness. They were marooned on a floating island of pure ice, on a leviathan of a berg which could easily be half a mile long, maybe longer.

'Recall the men,' Schmidt said crisply to DaSilva. 'Use the loudhailers. We're getting out of here.'

'I suppose we have to leave the berg right away?' Beaumont asked quietly.

'As soon as we can make it . . .' Schmidt stopped speaking and stared at Beaumont. 'Just for a second I thought you were coming up with another of your bright ideas.'

'It might be safer to stay where we are for the moment.'

'Stuck here? Getting nowhere? You want to get home some time, don't you?'

'We are getting somewhere,' Beaumont pointed out. 'I know we don't feel to be moving but both of us know we are. This huge berg is being carried south all the time by the Greenland Current – at a rough guess the berg is moving at a rate of twenty miles a day . . .'

'Not exactly breaking nautical records, is she?' Schmidt observed dryly.

'Do we have to?' Beaumont persisted. 'A few hours ago Quinn reported that those Soviet trawlers were forty miles south of us, that the *Revolution* was only thirty miles away – they'll be much closer now. This berg is acting as a gigantic transporter for the *Elroy*. If we stay on her the berg will carry us past those vessels some time during the night.'

'We'd be stuck here – unable to manoeuvre . . .'

'Does it matter?' Beaumont rasped impatiently. 'If they don't see us? The *Revolution* carries the latest radar but what will her radar pick up when we're close to her? Only another iceberg!'

'The berg as a giant transporter!' DaSilva was excited. 'I like the idea . . .'

'I don't!' Schmidt walked over to the voice-pipe to speak to the engine-room. When he had re-stoppered the tube he looked at DaSilva. 'Chiefy reports there's no structural damage to the engine-room. The glass on the gauges shattered, one man got steam-scalds,

321

but he thinks the engines are OK. And I think, Mr DaSilva, I asked you to recall the men on the ice. I'm starting up the engines to check them . . .'

'That is inadvisable,' Beaumont said bluntly. 'The *Revolution*'s hydrophones will pick up the vibrations . . .'

'And then,' Schmidt went on, ignoring Beaumont, 'we'll steam out backwards the way we came in.' He gave Beaumont the benefit of his attention. 'You are getting to be too much of a sea lawyer for my taste. And whether you like it or not this ship is disembarking off this berg in two hours' time!'

'The *Elroy* is very close to us – we have picked up her engine beat on the hydrophones!'

Kramer had run on to the bridge of the *Revolution* with the news, had hardly recovered his breath before he gasped out the words. The Siberian, who was standing next to a silent Tuchevsky, took his pipe out of his mouth and waved it at the Balt.

'Calm yourself, Kramer – and report to me every five minutes from now on.'

Tuchevsky stiffened his shoulders as Kramer left the bridge, turned to Papanin and spoke emphatically. 'So now I can start my engines again – I have warned you repeatedly that it is terribly dangerous to drift in these waters without power . . .'

'You will do nothing of the sort! You have the most advanced radar in the world – use it! We must continue drifting to give our hydrophone operators the best possible chance – I want to locate the American icebreaker's exact position.'

Papanin put his little pipe back in his mouth and went to the bridge window, leaving Tuchevsky on his own. Beyond the clear-vision panel he saw a world of mist and sea. And somewhere out of sight were the icebergs. The radar operators were at this moment plotting the monsters' course as they drifted steadily south with the Greenland Current, their eyes constantly focused on the greenish glow inside the rubber hoods where the sweeps went round and round and the echoes never stopped, the echoes coming back from over a dozen enormous icebergs.

Everyone was aboard, the engines were ticking over steadily, the bridge was fully manned, lookouts had been posted, the *Elroy* was ready to disembark from the berg, to put to sea.

Schmidt, his hands clasped behind him, for once stood looking the wrong way – towards the stern through the rear window – as he waited to perform two dangerous manoeuvres, taking his ship out of the chute, steering her backwards between the arms of the bay. Beaumont stood beside him, ignoring the chilly expression on the captain's face as he stared into the distance beyond the bay.

The mist had returned at just the wrong moment, was rolling like fog just beyond the two white peninsulas of ice which almost enclosed the bay. Towering above them, Beaumont stood between Schmidt and DaSilva, who stood with almost as bleak a look on his face as Schmidt's. He totally disagreed with the decision Schmidt had taken, but he couldn't say anything; still only acting mate, he couldn't say as much as Carlson might have done had he been standing in his place. The engines built up more power, they would soon be moving, stern first, into the water – if the screw managed to haul them out.

Grayson, who had been standing near the lookouts at the stern, burst into the bridge without ceremony, speaking with even less ceremony to a man whose word was almost life and death aboard his ship. 'You'd better wait! There's something out there – just inside the fog!'

'What?'

Schmidt's single-word question was explosive, betraying some of the inner tension he was labouring under, and he stared at Grayson with a look the crew knew and feared.

'I don't know . . . but there's something . . .'

'I can see it myself,' Beaumont said grimly. 'You'd better not move this ship yet, Schmidt.'

'God, it's the *Revolution* . . .' DaSilva muttered.

But it wasn't the *Revolution*, it was too big, infinitely too big even for a 16,000-ton ship, the thing which was coming slowly through the mist towards the exit from the bay. It sheered up like a ten-storey building, a moving ten-storey building, its invisible summit way above the height of the *Elroy*'s masthead, lost in the mist. The stern lookouts were shouting now, shouting at the tops of their voices as Schmidt opened the window and leaned out into the night. Ice-cold air flooded in over them and they were hardly aware of it as they stared, hypnotized by the menace coming towards them. It looked like a towering headland now, a headland of ice as it brushed aside the mist and came on, drifting straight for the bay. Even across the width of the bay it seemed to hang over them, above them, a colossus of an iceberg heading straight for the leviathan they were beached on.

Schmidt reacted very quickly to give warning. He hardly seemed to move and then he was talking into the tannoy system which would reach every corner of the ship. 'Hold on tight. Hold on tight. Major collision coming!'

DaSilva grabbed Beaumont's arm. 'Look! Inside the bay!'

'Underwater spar.'

A spur of ice projecting from the giant berg, a spur which could be up to fifty feet in diameter, was spearing across the bay after slipping inside the entrance, disturbing the moonlit water, water very palely lit by a shaft percolating through the mist. Behind the leg, the body followed. The men on the bridge were gripping rails, bracing themselves for the coming impact, and below them the lookouts clung to the rails still intact. Beaumont's head moved slightly as something fell out of the sky, something huge,

325

bigger than a mansion, something from the summit of the berg which hadn't even touched the opposing ice yet. The mansion, the enormous chunk of ice, hit the water just beyond the bay and sent up a great funnel of water. 'Christ!' Langer gasped. 'This is a ghost berg . . .'

Which meant that the entire edifice, millions of tons of ice, could collapse at the moment of impact, bringing an avalanche down over the bay, over the ship, burying it. Like waxwork figures they waited for the impact. At the last moment Schmidt gave the order to stop the engines. The colossus floated out of the mist and showed them its enormity, then the spur reached the shore of the bay and the bergs met.

The impact sound was deafening, a sound like the end of the world. The shattering collision sent a tremor through the iceberg which had been struck, a tremor which shuddered the *Elroy*, shaking the hull, rattling the plates, hurling rivets on to the ice. The impact threw DaSilva clear across the bridge, shook a man off the catwalk above the engine-room and sent him to his death twenty feet below. It shattered crockery, wristwatches, fractured the still-intact glass on the engine-room gauges, made compass needles spin. Then it was suddenly quiet, frighteningly quiet.

The engines had been stopped before the impact. No one spoke. For a short time no one moved. They were gazing at the exit from the bay, an exit which was no longer there. The ice cliff filled it, locked into the opening like a cork into a bottle. The bay had become a lagoon, a lake without an exit. They were trapped inside their giant transporter, an iceberg drifting with the Greenland Current at twenty miles a day. But the ghost berg hadn't collapsed yet despite the collision. Beaumont was the first to break the silence and everyone on the bridge stared at him as though it were strange to hear a human voice.

'Now we'll have to drift with the berg, Schmidt. No option.'

'No option,' Schmidt agreed grimly. 'And all the time we'll be waiting for that thing to fall on us.'

'Their engines have stopped!'

Kramer sounded alarmed, bewildered, and Papanin left the bridge with the Balt to go down and see the hydrophone section for himself. The seaman in vest and shorts who was listening to the instrument looked up as Papanin came in. 'Kramer tells me you can't hear them any more. Is your instrument defective?'

'No. Their engines have stopped. We are getting no echoes.'

'How far away?'

'A mile, maybe even closer . . .'

'They were that distance ten minutes ago!' Papanin glared at Kramer. 'Listen to me! They were a mile away only ten minutes ago. Their engines continued beating until a few seconds ago. They are still a mile away. It's not possible! We are drifting – they are moving south under power. They must have moved closer!'

'It's true,' the seaman said.

'It cannot be true – it's technically impossible!' the Siberian stormed.

'It's been puzzling me . . .' the seaman began.

'That's a hell of a lot of use!' Papanin folded his arms and stared at the seaman. 'If they were drifting with the current like we are, then it would be true – we would remain the same distance apart. But they're not drifting! You heard the sound of their bloody engines!'

'Very distinctly – until a minute ago.'

'How do you explain it?' Papanin gestured towards the hydrophone equipment. 'It's your job to explain things!'

'I can't . . .'

The Siberian said nothing, standing with his arms folded while he mastered his frustration. When he spoke again it was in such a reasonable tone that the seaman was frightened. 'Don't worry about it – just go on listening with those earplugs of yours.' He turned to Kramer. 'There is another way of checking – since they are so close – send up that helicopter. The pilot can't come back until he's found the *Elroy*.'

Perched aboard its giant transporter, hemmed in by the two coupled bergs, the *Elroy* continued to drift south with the current. It drifted for many hours, timeless hours, because for the men imprisoned inside the ice there was no longer any way of being sure of the time.

It had seemed incredible at first, so incredible that Schmidt had ordered a check on every timepiece aboard the ship, and when the check had been made the incredible was found to be true: every single clock and watch had stopped, stopped presumably by some freak tremor which had passed through the vessel at the moment of impact when the ghost berg struck. There was a frantic search for one clock or watch which was still going, and there wasn't one.

So they had to guess at the time and from then on the ship's log carried strangely imprecise entries. 'Approximately 1900 hours . . .' 'About 2200 hours . . .' Not knowing the time gradually got on men's nerves, the proximity of the ghost berg got on their nerves, the knowledge that at any second millions of tons of ice might simply topple, come down on them, flattening the ship and everyone inside her.

And there was nothing to do, nothing they dare do. All normal work ceased: they couldn't even occupy themselves with levering up and throwing overboard the remaining ice on deck – because they were afraid that some unguarded echo from the hammering of a tool might be just enough to bring the colossus crashing down on top of them. The atmosphere became far worse after Beaumont and Langer returned from an exploratory tour of their overhanging neighbour.

'It has all the appearance of a ghost berg,' Beaumont said when he proposed the tour to Schmidt, 'that huge piece of ice which came down from the summit was pretty significant, but I think we'd better check before we all go crazy . . .'

It was a ghost berg, the biggest Beaumont had ever seen. The far side of the two hundred-foot-high cliff, the side facing away from the sea, was like something out of the Arabian Nights. To get there they crossed the great spar of ice sticking up out of the bay and made their way along a narrow ledge at the base of the cliff, and when they turned a corner they looked up in horror. Enormous alcoves and caves were hollowed out of what had seemed solid berg from the outside; great roofs of ice were precariously poised on frozen columns fifty to a hundred feet above them; and below where they had paused, a long way above sea level, was a gigantic hole at least three hundred yards in diameter, a hole which might have been gouged out by a meteorite. The hole was a lake of blackness and as they listened they heard the faint lapping of water, the splash of the Greenland Current against ice. The ghost berg, at least half a mile long, was hollow, a dangerous sham, like an enormous rock pinnacle eroded by termites. It was about as stable as sweating gelignite.

'Can't understand why it didn't come down when it hit us,' Langer whispered.

'They can take a lot of punishment and then they

go suddenly,' Beaumont replied. 'We've seen enough. Let's get back.'

'God in heaven, look up there, Keith . . .'

The mist had drifted away from a giant column of ice, exposing a good two hundred feet of ice tower, a tower whose summit was hidden. The tower was massive, at least a hundred feet wide, but there were huge windows cut out of the tower, windows which were holes in the ice, so many that Beaumont couldn't understand why it was still vertical. The mist cleared from higher up and Beaumont's expression tightened as he saw the tower was supporting a great overhang from the back of the cliff, was probably supporting the whole damned cliff.

'It won't last much longer,' he said. 'We'd better get back.'

Only a few men aboard the ship were told what they had found, but within an hour the grim report had spread through the *Elroy*'s grapevine. From then on the tension became appalling. If a man banged his elbow against a bulkhead his comrade glared at him; they found their appetites had gone, that they couldn't sleep, that they could do nothing but keep quiet and keep still, and the inactivity crucified their nerves. For seamen accustomed to the movement of the ship the lack of movement was another source of tension. The bergs were moving all the time, rotating slowly in the current, but there was no sensation of movement. Given time, just a little more time – the time they couldn't gauge – they would become a bunch of screaming neurotics.

'Why are we so interested in explosives?' Grayson asked at one stage while they were sitting in Beaumont's cabin.

'If we ever get out of here we may need some kind of weapon to defend ourselves. I don't know how or where or when – but I don't share Schmidt's optimism. I'm thinking of some kind of floating mine – I've actually talked to DaSilva about it.'

'He wasn't worried – about Schmidt?' Langer inquired.

'DaSilva is in a mutinous frame of mind,' Beaumont told him. 'Normally he wouldn't be – it's the silence and the stillness that's getting him, getting us all,' he added with a bleak grin. 'The *Elroy* doesn't even creak any more.'

'You feel we might get out one day?' Grayson asked.

'If we do, it will be when the ghost berg is on the southern side of us – with the current tugging at it. There's just a chance that it might break loose again, drift away.'

'And you still think you heard a chopper while you were on the ghost berg?' Grayson asked. 'Schmidt didn't look as though he believed you.'

'That's because Horst didn't hear it. I not only heard it – I think I saw it for a second when the mist cleared for a few seconds.'

'Which means Papanin now knows where we are?'

'I fear so. Time – whatever it is – will tell, if that ghost berg cuts loose.'

The ghost berg broke loose some time on Friday, 25 February. 'Approximately 2200 hours . . .' the log recorded. Its departure was not spectacular, there was no great rending of ice, no inundation of sea rushing in; there was simply one loud terrifying crack which stopped the pulse of every man aboard. From his post at the rear of the bridge DaSilva saw what had happened. The huge spar jammed inside the bay had snapped; the ghost berg, still intact, still not collapsing, moved away from the entrance to the bay while DaSilva watched it go. And something like a half-submerged monster, the huge severed spar, was following the mother berg into the current.

When Schmidt reached the bridge with Beaumont the view they had become used to – the land-locked lagoon with the towering cliff on the far side – was transformed. The exit was again open. Beyond it the colossus was only faintly visible in the gathering mist, disappearing even as they watched her go. Schmidt permitted himself a rare display of emotion: he let out a deep breath.

'That's it. We take off as soon as I can get the screw moving – whatever there is waiting for us out there.'

*

The developing situation in Iceberg Alley – so far as it was known – had been anxiously followed for days by Leonid Brezhnev in Moscow, still worried that something might happen which would cancel the American President's visit to the Russian capital in May. Then all communication with Col Papanin ceased: the radio-jamming which was so effectively isolating the *Elroy* also cut off the *Revolution* from the outside world.

On Friday, 25 February 1972 – while the American icebreaker was still drifting aboard its giant transporter – Brezhnev undoubtedly consulted Marshal Andrei Grechko, and the Soviet Minister of Defence decided that a diversion was necessary, something to distract certain journalists who were already checking rumours that something was happening in the Arctic. Whatever happened, there must be no reference to the crisis in the world's press, so something else happened – something close enough to Iceberg Alley to account for the rumours, but something far enough away to distract attention from the events taking place hundreds of miles further north.

The Times, published on Wednesday, 1 March, carried the first report, datelined Washington, 29 February.

A crippled Soviet submarine wallowing in a North Atlantic gale for the past four days, was taken in tow today by a Russian tug according to a United States Navy spokesman.

Rough seas ... now subsiding, enabled the tug to get a line aboard the vessel six hundred miles north-east of Newfoundland.

The submarine of the 3,700-ton H2 'hotel' class has a crew of ninety. It was first spotted on Friday by reconnaissance aircraft from the American base at Keflavik, Iceland ...

The Soviet ships, the tanker *Liepaya*, and the fish factory trawler *Ivan Chigrin* have also entered the immediate area.

The cause of the Russian vessel's trouble was not known here.

Despite the fact that the world's newspapers were full of their accounts of the American President's return from his recent visit to Peking, the report of the near 'disaster' to the Soviet submarine appeared in many newspapers, together with aerial pictures showing the supposedly stricken vessel wallowing in fifty-foot waves under the lash of a fifty-five-knot wind. And the diversion worked – not a line was written about the missing *Elroy*, which should have been well on its way to its home port of Milwaukee via the St Lawrence Seaway.

It must have been just about the time when the American aircraft from Keflavik first spotted the Soviet submarine that the *Elroy* left the iceberg and steamed out into the fogbound channel.

Chapter Four

Friday, 25 February: the last hours

The huge screw at the stern of the *Elroy* was revolving, churning water, slamming aside small floes as it whipped up a white froth. Schmidt gave the order and the icebreaker began moving backwards slowly, then it stopped and Schmidt increased the power. The screw thrashed, the engines throbbed as though they were coming up through the deck, and the *Elroy* moved again. She came down the chute very slowly, like a ship being launched the wrong way, and the noise was terrible as the keel ground over the ice under it, spitting out sparks, channelling deeper into the iron-hard ice.

The screw churned on, its dragging power greater now that more of the ship was in the water, heaving the *Elroy* back into the sea. There was an enormous splash as the bows went down, but the crew on deck behind Beaumont at the stern didn't make a sound as the vessel edged her way across the bay and out between the narrow exit. Beaumont left the stern, walked along the vibrating deck towards the bows.

They had chosen the moment for departure carefully. Above them the mist had cleared briefly and the moon shone down, reflecting off drifting floes, off the ice-coated starboard rail, but ahead of them as Schmidt turned his vessel slowly there was dense mist only half a mile away. 'I don't like it,' Grayson said as he stopped behind Beaumont close to the bows, 'I think we should have stayed on the berg. DaSilva thinks so, too. And why the hell do we have to come out like a flaming cruise liner?'

The simile was apt. On Schmidt's specific orders the *Elroy*'s lights were ablaze. Every possible light which could be lit was switched on, and her searchlights beamed out to port and starboard and over the bows. 'We'll be on the high seas,' Schmidt had repeated for the hundredth time. 'If I go down Iceberg Alley with my lights ablaze and the horn booming there's no possible excuse for a collision.'

'You think they need an excuse – with Gorov and the Catherine charts aboard?' Beaumont had demanded. 'When we're totally out of touch and can't even signal what may be happening?'

He had lost his argument – as he knew he would. And up to a point Schmidt had reason on his side: if they tried to slip south without lights and in silence Papanin could afterwards say that the collision had been the Americans' fault – how could they have seen them or heard them in the fog? As they headed south Beaumont raised his night-glasses and swept the water.

'See anything?' Langer asked anxiously in his ear.

'Just ocean. And mist.'

'See anything?'

It wasn't Langer who asked the question this time. DaSilva had come quietly down from the bridge and stood at Beaumont's left shoulder. 'With your eyes,' he added, 'you ought to be up top where you were before.'

Beaumont looked behind him, stared up at the eighty-foot mast where a seaman hung from the crosstree with a headset clamped under his fur hood. This was the lookout who would try to warn Schmidt of any obstacle in the *Elroy*'s path. 'No thanks,' he said. 'Not again. And I can't see anything out there – yet.'

'The Carley float is near the stern, starboard side,' DaSilva murmured. 'Near the cabin where the explosives are – and Langer has a key. If we need him, Borzoli will help us with the launch – he's on lookout duty near the float. Mind telling me what you have in mind – if something does happen?'

'I'll have to try and scare them off,' Beaumont replied vaguely.

'OK, so play it close to the chest.' DaSilva paused, looking back at the bridge. 'Maybe it's better that way – considering Schmidt doesn't know a thing about it yet. I could end up as a clerk in a shipping office for this.'

'Better that than a skeleton floating at the bottom of Iceberg Alley,' Beaumont replied brutally.

*

'She's coming out,' Papanin said. 'That other berg we saw in the aerial shot must have broken away.'

On the bridge of the *Revolution* the Siberian bent over the radarscope hood, his head almost inside it, and the greenish glow from the scope bathed his smooth-skinned face, his close-shaven head and his hands, making him a green man.

'How long?' Kramer asked nervously.

Papanin looked up briefly from the hood, glanced across the bridge to where Tuchevsky was standing with his back to him, his hands clasped tightly behind him. 'You can start your engines now,' he called out. 'From now on we can track her by radar.' He put his eyes close to the hood again as he replied to Kramer's questions. 'By midnight I would guess – by midnight it will all be over.'

The *Elroy* was steaming due south down Iceberg Alley, her engines ticking over at half power, the bows sliding through water like milk, her lights blazing. But now there was an added factor to pinpoint her position: her powerful foghorn was booming non-stop, a deep-throated, mournful sound which echoed back to them across the ocean – and the echoing was significant. Somewhere inside the mist there had to be walls off which the echoes were rebounding, walls of ice.

Four men stood at the bows, chilled and numbed

with the bitter cold, moving about frequently with the lookout Schmidt had posted. Beaumont moved about less than any of them, was constantly staring through his night-glasses as he swept the sea ahead. Feet crunched behind them.

'Coffee for you guys . . .'

DaSilva and Borzoli poured them mugs of steaming coffee from an insulated jug, but the coffee was still half-cold before they could swallow it. The acting mate sent Borzoli back to his post near the Carley float, sent the lookout away to check something imaginary on the port quarter before he spoke. 'Schmidt is feeling he took the right decision.'

'I'm glad somebody's happy,' Beaumont commented.

'It's looking good so far.'

Beaumont said nothing as he finished his coffee and raised his glasses again. His arms were weary with holding them, his eyes were sore with the cold, with the strain of staring into the lenses. There was a narrow channel of calm, moonlit sea ahead for almost a mile and then it was lost behind more mist. On the port side a huge berg was coming up, an ugly monster with a table-top summit. To starboard lay a great bank of mist, a dense pall rising at least two hundred feet above the ocean, and it stretched the full length of the channel they could see.

'Nothing over there,' DaSilva remarked as Beaumont swivelled his glasses on the bank. 'Just a load of mist.'

'Is the radio-jamming as strong as ever?' Beaumont inquired.

'Stronger. The worst yet.'

'Which means we're getting very close to the jamming source.'

The *Elroy* moved closer to the bottleneck formed by the monster berg to port and the mist bank to starboard, altering course a few degrees to pass down the middle. Ice crunched underfoot as Grayson moved his numbed feet. Langer banged his arms round his body to try to get some circulation back into his system. Behind them a door slammed high up as DaSilva returned to the bridge, and they were alone with the seaman on watch.

Langer watched Beaumont as the Englishman perched his elbows on the rail and stared through his glasses, sweeping them slowly to starboard. It was the huge bank of impenetrable mist which seemed to intrigue Beaumont, the bank which drifted less than a quarter of a mile away, the bank which would hem them in between itself and the iceberg once they entered the bottleneck.

'What's that? That thing in the mist well south to starboard?' Grayson called out.

Beaumont was already looking at the huge mass which had come out of the mist like a moving cliff. It was the ghost berg presenting its false face of rock-like stability. They were inside the bottleneck now with the table-topped monster coming up on the port bow. Beaumont glanced at the mist bank and stiffened. The bows of the *Revolution* broke the mist, bore down on them like a battleship.

'The American ship is heading due south – on a course at right-angles to us . . .'

'You'd better get ready,' Papanin ordered Tuchevsky.

The mist was smothering the *Revolution*, drifting just beyond the bridge window as Tuchevsky bent lower over the radarscope, watching the echoes which registered the *Elroy*'s approach. It was going to need very careful timing – he had to bring his huge ship out of the mist at exactly the right moment, otherwise he would fail. 'Maintain present course,' he ordered the helmsman.

The *Revolution* was creeping forward at her lowest speed, her engine beats muffled by the mist, moving forward on interception course. Tuchevsky stared at the echoes, his face gleaming with sweat, his beard moist. His calculations had to allow for the speed of the *Elroy*, his own speed, the distance which would separate them when they first saw each other. He sensed the presence of the Siberian behind him.

'I want you to hit her amidships . . .'

The sweep inside the hood was pinging non-stop, tracking each fresh position of the *Elroy* as she approached the bottleneck between mist bank and iceberg. Tuchevsky heard Papanin's boots stirring restlessly. 'Aren't we moving too slowly?'

'You want us to come out too soon?'

There were no lights showing aboard the *Revolution*, the ship was in complete darkness, but Papanin's eyes were accustomed to the gloom as the ship crept forward. He could just make out the bridge window frames and the faint blur beyond them, otherwise they might have been in a fogbound port, so smooth was the sea, so quiet the hum of the vessel's slow-beating engines.

'Maintain your present speed,' Tuchevsky droned.

'For how long?' the Siberian demanded.

'For as long as is necessary.'

Papanin fumed, remained silent, his nerves screaming with the tension. They had to destroy the American vessel first time. One annihilating blow out of the mist, steel smashing into steel, the bows of the *Revolution* grinding into the *Elroy*'s starboard side, cutting clean through her. He imagined what it would be like – the Russian ship astride the American, driving her under, the broken stern to his left, the wrecked bows to his right. Which section, he wondered, would go down first?

'Papanin! Get to the back of the bridge! Hold on to the rail!'

The Siberian did as he was told, went back and held on to the rail with both hands as the helmsman, one of his own men, took a tighter grip on the wheel. Papanin was watching the mist beyond the bridge. When it lightened they would be coming out, they would see the *Elroy* under their bows. Why wasn't

Tuchevsky increasing speed? The captain left the radarscope, took a firm grip of the telegraph handle, pressed it down to 'Half Speed', then ran back to the scope.

'Maintain present course!'

A flicker of pale light passed beyond the bridge window. The mist wavered as the engine beat increased enormously. It was very warm inside the bridge and Papanin wiped a hand quickly over his forehead to stop sweat dripping into his eyes. The mournful booming note of the *Elroy*'s foghorn they had heard before became very loud, dead ahead. Tuchevsky was staring into the radarscope, praying, then they were through.

Moonlight flooded the bridge. The lights of the *Elroy* were a glare. Dead ahead. The *Revolution*'s bow wave spread out to port and starboard with the increased speed. The hull of the icebreaker rushed towards them. Tuchevsky gripped both sides of the radarscope as he stared through the window. Never before had he concentrated on a scope with such intensity – and he had calculated exactly. Or had he? Increase speed! He prayed for the *Elroy*'s captain to react in time, tried to will the order into the American's brain. Increase speed! Get out of the way! I gave you one chance, one warning – please, please, please!

The *Elroy* was moving faster already. The order had been given the instant the *Revolution* appeared out of the mist. Exhausted as he was, Schmidt had reacted with all the decision Tuchevsky had prayed for. The Russian continued on course, heading point-blank for its target, so it seemed to Papanin from the back of the bridge where he couldn't see clearly. The *Revolution* swept forward, the American ship's hull slid across at right-angles to the sweep, its mast towering above the Russian ship's bridge. Tuchevsky ran to the starboard side, looked down beyond his own ship's rail. He saw the *Elroy*'s screw churning the water and his own bows cut through the turbulence.

'You missed her!' Papanin's control went. 'Next time I will take command!'

In his blind fury he strode across the bridge and began swearing at Tuchevsky, standing over him. The little captain pushed him out of the way, caught him off balance and pushed him across the bridge. 'You stupid animal – we're going to hit the berg!' Papanin stared in horror as he looked to the front. The monster berg with the table-top summit had filled the window.

Beaumont was close to the stern of the *Elroy* when the bows of the *Revolution* plunged towards them. Collision seemed inevitable, the *Elroy* was presenting her midships to the 16,000-ton Russian ship as the bow wave came forward, as the huge bows reared above the ship's rail. At the last moment Beaumont was certain the bows would smash the *Elroy*'s screw, destroying her motive power. Then the Russian ship was sweeping past beyond their stern, missing its target by yards as it sped on towards the monster berg.

'She's going to hit the berg,' Grayson said.

'I hope to God she does . . .'

Beaumont stayed near the stern, saw the frantic effort to bring the *Revolution* round in time, saw the great wake behind her which showed the extreme course she was taking to save herself, then he saw that she had saved herself. He gave very brief instructions to Grayson, Langer and Borzoli, and went straight to the bridge of the *Elroy*, his face grim, his boots thudding on the deck. When he reached the bridge Schmidt turned round from the rear window he had been gazing through.

'You were right, Beaumont,' he said tersely. 'She tried to sink us.'

'She'll try it again. You can't outrun her.'

'Outrun her? With my top speed sixteen knots?'

'So if possible she's got to be stopped. For the sake of your crew, for the sake of everyone on board . . .'

'DaSilva is cooperating with you over the explosives?'

Beaumont stared at Schmidt who was nodding his head cynically. 'You think I don't know what's going on aboard my own ship, Mr Beaumont?'

'She's got to be stopped,' Beaumont repeated.

'This is something I may forget to put in the ship's log.' The captain looked across the bridge at Beaumont and spoke two words. 'Stop her.'

*

The Carley float, a raft for throwing overboard if the ship had to be abandoned, was packed with one hundred pounds of gelignite, was wired for detonation. The timer mechanisms were in place, the clocks had been set to trigger detonation in ten minutes' time, but they hadn't been activated. The float was now a potential mine.

Schmidt had to reduce speed considerably when they winched the launch over the side near the stern, and this was a nerve-racking decision because the *Revolution* was now coming up behind them, still a distance away, but she was overhauling the ice-breaker. And the view ahead from the bridge was hardly more encouraging than the view beyond the stern. Heavy mist still drifted to starboard, half-obscuring the ghost berg which lay half a mile ahead. To port a whole column of icebergs had appeared, narrowing the channel of clear water, and in the distance dead ahead two massive bergs stood on either side of the channel, like sentries guarding a gateway. It was indeed an alley of icebergs Schmidt had to take his ship through.

'How long before she overtakes us?' Beaumont asked DaSilva.

'I'd say about ten minutes – and that's a guess.'

'Looks more like five minutes to me,' Grayson said grimly. He frowned and looked to starboard. 'Schmidt's changing course – he's moving closer to that line of icebergs.'

'I asked him to,' Beaumont snapped. 'He's going to

leave a wider channel between the *Elroy* and the ghost berg.'

'So the *Revolution* can slip through on that side? He must be crazy . . .'

'Then I'm crazy, too. We'd better get down in that launch.'

DaSilva followed him across the deck to where Borzoli and other seamen waited by the launch suspended from davit cables. 'Beaumont, I still haven't asked you what you're going to do – my guess would be you hope this blows up under the bows of the *Revolution*.'

'It wouldn't work – she's moving too fast. Now, lower us – and for Pete's sake watch that float when you send it down.'

The whole operation was diabolically tricky. The launch – with Beaumont, Langer and Grayson inside it – had to be winched down over the side of a moving vessel and then held there until the float joined them. The only thing working in their favour was the calmness of the sea. They hit the water with a heavy slap and then held on to the cables while they looked up. The float was already on its way down to them.

While still on deck Langer had given DaSilva a little warning. 'Technically, if the float hits the side of the hull on its way down nothing will happen.' He had paused and smiled without humour. 'And heaven is full of demolition experts playing harps who said the same sort of thing.'

The airborne mine came down to them with a

terrible slowness, suspended from ropes gripped by seamen high above them. Langer watched its descent with his hand gripped tightly round the winch cable. They only had to unbalance it, to let it slant downwards, and securely as the gelignite was lashed something devastating could happen. Then somebody let a rope slip. The large missile suspended above their heads canted at an angle and Langer drew in his breath with a hiss of fury and fear. 'They'll do Papanin's job for him,' he muttered.

The angled float swayed, bumped with a heavy thud against the ship's hull, a thud heavy enough to dislodge its cargo. Beaumont glanced towards the stern, suppressing his impatience; now the *Revolution* had changed course and she was heading fast for the open channel which would take her to starboard of the *Elroy*. For Christ's sake hurry it up! His prayer was answered – with unnerving speed. The float dropped and kept on dropping, coming down on their heads.

It jerked to a halt three feet above them, still canted at its dangerously unstable angle, then it was lowered more gently. Langer activated the clocks – the only clocks aboard which hadn't been put out of action because they hadn't been working when the ghost berg struck. The float was put over the stern, attached by ropes to the launch. Beaumont started the engine, took over the wheel, shouted up to DaSilva, the winch cables were released and they moved away from the *Elroy* at speed, dragging the float behind them.

'I think we're too late,' Langer shouted, looking back at the Russian ship.

Beaumont opened the throttle wide and the launch roared across the calm sea, heading direct for the ghost berg, following a course at right-angles to the receding *Elroy*, to the oncoming *Revolution*. The mist was parting now, drawing back to expose the towering wall of ice they were speeding towards. The berg reared up like the edge of some great continent, seemed even bigger than when they had moved across its treacherous surface behind the cliff wall.

As they came closer to the section of the cliff they hadn't seen earlier Beaumont saw that it was hollowed out at the base, arched into caves which disappeared inside the cliff. For the first time he realized how the ocean reached the lake they had found on the far side of the cliff; there were subterranean channels leading into the lake, channels under the arched caves. He took his decision almost without thinking.

'We're going in closer – we'll let the float go at the edge of the iceshelf,' he shouted.

'We'll never get back to the *Elroy*.' There was alarm in Grayson's shout. 'We'll never catch her up again.'

'We'll have to chance that. I'm going to get the float inside one of those channels – then it may detonate on the far side of the berg.'

Beaumont's plan was simple, a very long shot indeed. The ghost berg was on the verge of collapse, should have collapsed when it first struck the bay where the *Elroy* was marooned; even more it should have collapsed when it wrenched itself free from the other berg. But it was still intact and every hour it drifted brought it closer to final dissolution. It could be that the detonation of a large quantity of gelignite close to the ice would trigger off the catastrophe. Or it could no more than tickle the berg, blowing up a few pounds of ice.

And yet there were recorded cases where the unguarded shout of an Eskimo in his kayak had shattered one of these monsters, had brought it down into the ocean, falling like a mountain. Beaumont's plan – his faint hope – was to bring down the ghost berg ahead of the *Revolution*, filling the channel with minor bergs which would stop the Russian ship. It was a very long shot indeed.

'We are gaining on them! When the time comes I will take the wheel myself,' Papanin growled. He was staring through the clear-vision panel, watching the distant silhouette of the *Elroy* pass through a mist trail. 'You will take charge of the telegraph, control the speed,' he told Kramer.

'There will be no room for manoeuvre,' Tuchevsky protested. Unlike the Siberian he was constantly switching his gaze from port to starboard and back again. And he was impressed by the enormous size of the great berg to starboard coming up, but he had no suspicion of its fragility as he stared at the towering wall. 'A launch has left the American vessel,' he said suddenly. 'It is crossing the channel ahead of us . . .'

'Don't worry about that! Increase speed . . .'

'It is dangerous – we are going too close to that berg . . .'

'Full power!' Papanin shouted at Kramer. 'Full power . . .'

The cliff rose vertically above their heads as the launch nosed its way through ice floes close to the shelf where the ocean lapped the base of the ghost berg. Throttled back, the launch bobbed among the floes, a mere speck under the lee of the berg. Twenty yards to the south of them a great cave went inside the ice, the current flowed in under the berg. Beaumont could see the turn of the moonlit water as he shouted the order. 'Release the float!'

Grayson was ready with his knife. He slashed at the rope, holding it in one gloved hand while he sawed with the other, and it took him longer than he had anticipated to cut through the tough fibres. Behind him Beaumont and Langer suppressed their impatience with difficulty. Beaumont estimated they had about five minutes left before detonation but without a working watch he couldn't be sure.

Grayson cut savagely at the frayed rope – the last few strands still held them to the float. Langer cursed, struggled to get his own knife out of the sheath under his parka. Beaumont watched helplessly, unable to leave the wheel. The arched opening drifted closer. Langer found his knife, hauled it out, cut at the rope Grayson was holding for him. The fibres parted. The float left them. Beaumont opened the throttle and the craft surged away from the ghost berg with a burst of power. The engine beats of the *Revolution* were much louder as he headed out diagonally down the channel, speeding after the *Elroy* he could hardly see.

In the stern Grayson clung to the gunwale, twisted round as he watched the Carley float bobbing in the current, sailing past the arched entry under the berg. At the last moment the float caught on the ice, hovered, then the current sucked it inside and sent it down the ice tunnel leading to the lake on the far side.

'It went in!' Grayson shouted.

The throttle was wide open, the launch was tearing down the dangerous, ice-strewn channel as Beaumont swung the wheel, avoided a large floe by inches, straightened up. More and more ice was appearing, small floes bobbing in the moonlight, large growlers drifting with the column of icebergs to port. Speed in such waters was excessively dangerous – and speed was vital. The ghost berg still loomed to their right, stretched away beyond them to the south, went on for ever it seemed as Beaumont kept the throttle wide open and wrestled with the wheel.

A single light glowed at the *Elroy*'s distant stern, the only light showing aboard the icebreaker since Schmidt had ordered all lights turned out, the light kept on to guide the launch back to the ship. The greyish spume of her vanishing wake showed to their left, the bitter air whipped at their faces, the launch zigzagged wildly to avoid more floes. And behind them the *Revolution* came on, was now moving alongside the ghost berg – because everyone had underestimated its speed.

'That gate's closing,' Langer said in Beaumont's ear. In the distance beyond the *Elroy*'s silhouette the view was changing. It looked as though Schmidt was going to be too late. The two great bergs which flanked the exit from the channel were moving closer together, caught in a cross-current. By the time Schmidt reached them there would be no way out. As Langer had said, the gate was closing.

Beaumont swerved to avoid a large growler, an ice floe large enough to smash in the gunwale if they struck it, then he was swerving in the opposite direction to avoid a second one, using the launch like a powerboat. It was only a matter of time before they hit one of them, but the stern light of the *Elroy* was a little larger, was coming closer. When he glanced to starboard again he was surprised: they had moved past the end of the ghost berg, were speeding well beyond it.

'More power!' Papanin fumed. 'Overtake her!'

Tuchevsky said nothing. He was no longer in command of his own ship. Beyond the starboard window the huge iceberg reared up, towered over them, and for the first time Tuchevsky noticed the arched openings at her waterline.

Behind the ice cliff the Carley float had left the tunnel, had emerged into the dark lake beyond, was drifting round the edge, bumping up against the ice, covered with frost which had descended on it inside the tunnel. It caught a spur of ice and hovered. Above it the eroded ice tower sheered up, the tower which held up the overhang.

Close to exhaustion, Beaumont missed the floe, but the floe didn't miss the launch. The prow struck the ice spar floating underwater, leapt into the air, and the launch soared over it. As they went up Beaumont's heart stopped – the screw was going to catch the ice, would be buckled, maybe even torn out of the craft. The launch continued its arc, the spar cracked under the pressure, went down as the screw flew over it intact and thrashed back into the sea. Behind the ice cliff the floating mine detonated.

The ice tower holding up the overhang began to collapse. The honeycombed pillar collapsed slowly, disintegrating chunk by chunk, dropping great masses of ice into the lake below, then it sagged, settled, broke. And when it broke the enormous weight of ice above it came down, falling three hundred feet, shattering into thousands of pieces at the edge of the lake, sending an avalanche of ice over the brink. The tower was gone, the vast overhang above was gone, all support which had helped to hold up the ice cliff was gone. The ice cliff itself started to come down and one of nature's most terrifying spectacles unfolded.

The cliff fell inwards – away from the *Revolution* – and the sight from the bridge of the Russian ship stunned the men aboard. The entire cliff, which a moment earlier had climbed sheer above them, fell backwards. For a moment Papanin could hardly believe his eyes, then he saw the captain's petrified expression. 'It's a ghost berg . . .' The continuing roar of its crash was still resounding when Tuchevsky took a grip on himself, turning on the tannoy system which would relay his message throughout the ship. 'There is no cause for alarm . . . no cause for alarm . . .'

He was wrong, and Beaumont who knew Iceberg Alley as well as any man alive could have told him how terribly wrong he was. The tremendous spectacle the Russian had witnessed was a mere prelude to what was coming.

'The damned thing fell the wrong way!' Grayson shouted. 'It fell backwards . . .'

'Hang on!' Beaumont yelled.

The water was turbulent now, swelling with waves the iceberg had caused as it vibrated at the waterline. This didn't worry Beaumont: it was the tidal wave which haunted him as he desperately tried to coax more speed out of the roaring engine, the tidal wave which would come sweeping up behind them when the major catastrophe broke. If they didn't reach the ship in time they'd be overwhelmed.

The *Revolution* was still on course, moving past the wrecked berg, when the giant lost its equilibrium. The cliff which had reared up at one end of the berg was now gone, spread out over a vast area, so the immense platform which was left – half a mile long – began to turn turtle. The cliff which had stood above its surface had seemed vast, but this was nothing compared with the bulk which lurked beneath its surface, and this submerged cliff now came up out of the sea like some primeval upheaval when the very surface of the earth is transformed, dripping huge cascades of water which poured off it like a Niagara.

The sea itself began to boil, to churn as it felt what was coming up from the depths. Great dripping cliffs of ice began to tower, mounting high above the bridge of the *Revolution* where Papanin and Tuchevsky stared in horror. The Niagara of sea flooded down on the vessel. Chunks of ice larger than houses crashed down on the hull, tore away rails, left them like jagged rows of teeth. And still the berg continued to revolve, tens of millions of tons of ice on the move, mounting up as the berg continued turning its mass through a hundred and eighty degrees.

'God! It's like the earth coming up from the sea bottom!'

Grayson was staggered by the sight as the launch sped closer to the *Elroy* and Beaumont glanced back, glanced back only once and then concentrated his whole mind on reaching the *Elroy*. The tidal wave would be coming any second now. They had to reach the ship in time. Behind them the ghost berg overturned.

It swivelled, loomed above the *Revolution*, then millions of tons of ice descended, came down like the fall of an Alp. On the bridge of the Russian ship they saw it as an enormous shadow, a revolving shadow. Papanin was still on the bridge when the shadow struck, dropping a solid ice wall on top of the radar dome. The dome deflated, disappeared, the bridge was levelled to the deck, the deck was submerged. The bows went down, straight down, and the stern tilted up as though turning over an invisible fulcrum.

The stern went on climbing at an acute angle until it was vertical, with the screws still spinning like a helicopter's rotors. Two-thirds of the ship had vanished, buried under the falling cliff, but the stern paused with the screws turning more slowly as the power died. Grayson saw it hovering, like a ship about to plunge to the bottom, although the rest of the ship had already gone. Then another arm of the berg came down on it, hammered it down with one gigantic blow which drove it nine thousand feet to the bed of the Arctic. Then the wave came.

'Jump!' Beaumont shouted.

The launch had passed the *Elroy*'s stern, throttled back, had drawn amidships and bumped the hull as Beaumont tried to keep pace with the slow-moving vessel. Schmidt had seen them coming a long way off, had reduced speed even before the destruction of the *Revolution*. Men peered over the rails above them, pointing to rope ladders slung over the ship's side. 'Jump!' Beaumont shouted again.

Langer grasped a dangling ladder, started climbing it while Grayson grabbed another swaying rope. Beaumont waited by the wheel, keeping the launch alongside the moving hull, and beyond the *Elroy*'s stern the ocean was wild, turned in seconds from a milk-calm sea into a raging tumult. A fresh ladder thrown with skill by DaSilva slapped against Beaumont's chest. He let go of the wheel, grasped the ladder, felt the launch moving away under him, rammed his boots into swaying rungs. Above him by the rail DaSilva was screaming at him to hurry.

The tidal wave which was coming, about to pass the stern, was already twenty feet high and climbing every second. And it was composed not only of water – on its passage down the channel it had gathered up a collection of huge ice floes, floes which toppled at its crest, great rams of ice which could crush a man with one glancing blow. Langer was over the rail, followed by Grayson, when DaSilva shouted his last warning, knowing it was too late to do anything for the doomed man hanging from the side.

Halfway up the ladder Beaumont looked towards the stern, saw a foaming wall of green climbing above his head, saw the nose of a huge growler projecting through the froth. He was going to be mashed to a pulp, swept off the hull. The tidal wave hoisted the stern, lifted it high with an awful violence, and the bows went down. Beaumont clenched his gloved fingers round the rope, buried his elbows hard into his sides, squeezed his head between his forearms as he felt the stern going up like a lift.

An inundation of freezing water fell on him, a great weight pressing down on his shoulders, trying to rip him loose from the ladder. There was a roaring in his ears and then something slammed with immense force against the hull beside him. He shuddered with the impact, felt ice splinters shower against his face like a thousand tiny knives. The force of the water swept the ladder sideways, whipped him towards the bows where the launch had just been hurled and broken open.

Beaumont was frozen, the breath he held in his lungs bursting, petrified by the floe which had smashed so close to him, sodden with sea, scraped and swung up almost to the rail by the sway of the rope ladder. The roaring in his ears increased, he felt his strength going, his grip on the ladder weakening as the sea tugged and tore at him. Then the bows climbed and the ladder was swinging back in the other direction, banging his body brutally against the hull. Only extreme fear, a spark of self-survival, kept him conscious, aware that his numbed hands were still locked round the ladder. Then the sea dropped away and he felt himself falling, turning over and over. *It's your mind, you're still on the bloody ladder* . . .

A long way off an American voice was shouting,

shouting again and again. 'Hold on! We're hauling you up! Hold on!' Then he hit something very hard and hands were pawing him, fiddling with his hands, trying to unlock the fingers still clamped round the rope. He opened his eyes and saw a broken mast silhouetted against a moonlit sky, a mast whipping backwards and forwards. Something fell from it, came whirling down towards Beaumont's face and hit the deck with a horrible thud only two yards away. The lookout had fallen. Beaumont thought he was imagining things but there was a dead American seaman on the deck two yards away, his skull crushed in.

He was still unable to move as hands hauled his bruised and blood-stained body upright and started carrying him towards a staircase. He was muttering something as they carried him, and DaSilva had to ask him to repeat it before he understood. 'Grayson and Langer are safe,' the mate told him. 'We're OK. We're on our way home.' It was not a sentiment shared by Commander Alfred Schmidt at this moment who was asking for full power at all costs. The icebreaker was heading for almost certain destruction.

Everywhere the icebergs were coming together, caught in the cross-currents, closing in on the *Elroy* as her engines beat faster. But it was the two huge bergs dead ahead that Schmidt was watching with great anxiety. The silhouettes of the bergs rose to port and starboard, castles of ice in the moonlight, castles converging on each other across the perilously narrow channel the *Elroy* was steaming down. Another five minutes and they would know whether they had made it. Another five minutes and they would be through the gate or crushed between the closing bergs.

'Full power . . .'

DaSilva came on to the bridge as the commander repeated the order, something which he had never done before, something to drive home to the chief engineer below that this was a terrible emergency. In front of DaSilva Schmidt's head was constantly swivelling on his neck as though supported by ball-bearings. Port, ahead, starboard. The view was always the same – icebergs, moving icebergs, and every time Schmidt looked they seemed to have moved closer. The bows thrust forward, brushing aside huge floes, pointing towards the ever-narrowing gate.

The repetition of the same order had communicated its message to the engine-room, and without being told the men below guessed what was happening. The chief engineer stared at his bank of gauges but his mind was outside the ship, imagining cruel jaws of ice coming towards him. He sensed the tremendous impact when ice met steel, saw the hull coming in on him, first a spur of ice, followed instantly by an inundation of water. The engine-room crew watched him and he tried to maintain a bored look. They would never get out in time, of course. The engine-room was the ship's graveyard. As he had done on other occasions, he swore to himself that if he got out of this one he would never go to sea again.

The icebergs were on either quarter of the bows, so

close it was like entering a deep cutting, like proceeding inside the Corinth Canal with rock walls towering on either side – but these were walls of ice, moving walls. Schmidt stared in front of him, refusing to look sideways any more, knowing that DaSilva, the helmsman and the officer of the watch were glancing at him in terror. Then he took out his handkerchief, mopped his forehead, and spoke in a casual voice. 'Getting a bit warm in here.' From the bridge window he could have thrown out a bottle and hit the iceberg on the port quarter. And no moonlight shone on the foredeck which was dark with the shadows of the icebergs. DaSilva, his hands clasped tightly behind his back, could have screamed with the tension, but Schmidt's erect figure, his recent remark, his refusal to look to port or starboard, kept him under control. Like the captain, the other men on the bridge stared stonily ahead.

'Take a look through the rear window, Mr DaSilva,' Schmidt suggested.

'We're through! We're through the gate!'

'Maintain your present course.'

Ahead there was a pale cold light in the distant sky, the sun returning to the Arctic, the sun whose palest glimmer had been blotted out by a heavy cloud bank for days. DaSilva looked back through the rear window. The gateway between the bergs was so narrow that even a launch could no longer have passed through. The silhouettes merged and across the ocean rang the appalling crack of collision, a terrible rumbling crack followed by a roar as the bergs ground up against each other. Then an echoing boom which went right out across the Arctic. DaSilva jumped when he heard Schmidt speaking.

'Clear water ahead, Mr DaSilva. We're going home.'

On Wednesday, 7 March, Beaumont went ashore at Quebec, limping as he moved down the gangway with the aid of a stick, and his face was so covered with bandages that only the eyes showed, eyes which were bleak and remote. Schmidt, Grayson and Langer leaned out of a bridge window to watch him go, but he didn't look back as he hobbled on to the dockside. Seamen lined the rails in silence, ready to wave, but he didn't even glance in their direction.

It was cold on that March day long ago, and ice drifted in the St Lawrence while snow glistened on the rooftops of the Château Frontenac as the sun came out. Lemuel Dawes and Adams were waiting for him, hurried forward, and then hesitated as the tall, heavily built Englishman stared at them from between his mask of bandages. Beaumont shook hands formally and quickly. 'I have to get away,' he growled. 'Grayson can give you any details you need – and I've written you a report.'

He took the core tube out of his parka and gave it to Dawes. 'What you want is inside this core – take the top bit of rock out with a knife and you'll find it.'

He paused as Dawes took the core. 'I hope it was worth it – a lot of men died.'

He hobbled away before Dawes could reply, hobbled past the official car and got into a taxi. 'Airport,' he told the driver. He was silent for most of the drive, staring out of the window without taking in anything he was passing. As they came close to the airport he asked a question. 'Any idea when the next flight for Miami takes off?'

Chapter Five

Aftermath. May–July 1972

The ice island, Target-5, continued its drift south into Iceberg Alley – into destruction. On 7 March, the day Beaumont went ashore at Quebec, a C130 transport landed safely on the airstrip, stopping a few yards from the burnt-out wreck of its predecessor. It was in no danger of repeating the earlier aircraft's suicidal performance because the rocks had disappeared off the airstrip.

The men who came out of this plane hurried to take on board the crated equipment – nervous about the island's nearness to the sea and worried because the fog was closing in again. When they found Matthew Conway's body under the wrecked Sno-Cat they assumed he had driven off the ramp in the fog; they hurried to put the body aboard the plane and later it was flown to Cincinnatti for burial. What did puzzle these anxious men was that they could find no trace of Rickard, the wireless operator, or Sondeborg, the gravity specialist. Their disappearance became a mystery.

In May the American President visited Moscow and among the many agreements concluded was one which promised there would be no more close-shadowing – which might result in collision – of American vessels by Soviet ships and vice versa. No one outside government circles wondered why this particular moment was chosen to make this pact when near-collisions between American and Soviet vessels spying on each other – although rarely reported in the press – had been commonplace for years.

Also in May, Target-5, which had earlier broken into four pieces, further fragmented into eight separate slabs between Greenland and Iceland, and American planes from Keflavik kept a special watch on the slab supporting the huts. Then, while it was hidden from them by dense mist, they lost it for two months.

In July, a Danish liner cruising off Frederikshaab on the west coast of Greenland reported sighting an ice floe which carried buildings. Police boats were sent out from port and passengers on board the liner watched from the rails as the police entered the still-intact huts. It was an Inspector Gustaffson who went inside the research hut and examined it thoroughly. When he lifted the floorboards covering the hole where the core drill had once been lowered a four-month-old mystery was solved.

Jeff Rickard and Harvey Sondeborg were lying frozen on the lower platform of floorboards, the platform which covered the hole going down into the Arctic. An autopsy was carried out and it was concluded that Rickard had probably been murdered by Sondeborg, who was still clutching an ice pick when the bodies were found. Gustaffson then suggested – he had no proof – that Sondeborg had killed his fellow-American and had tried to hide the body inside the hole.

In Gustaffson's opinion Sondeborg had intended dropping the corpse below the second platform into the Arctic, but he slipped and fell himself, dying beside his victim from injuries received during his fall. In Washington Gustaffson's report was disbelieved and filed. Probably no one will ever know positively how these two men died.

It was in July that a shipping correspondent in London made a routine inquiry at the Soviet Embassy in Kensington Palace Gardens. Looking for copy for a projected article on modern ships, he asked for information as to the present whereabouts of the *Revolution*, nursing a faint hope that one day he might be shown over this showpiece vessel. The Soviet official he met consulted a more senior official, then told him that the *Revolution* had returned to a Black Sea port for an extensive refit. Apparently she had collided with an iceberg while undertaking research in Arctic waters.

And it was in July 1972 that the Fischer–Spassky world chess contest opened at Reykjavik in Iceland, the contest a certain Igor Papanin was to have attended, officially as one of Spassky's chess advisers, unofficially as chief of security for the duration of the contest. Another man, less qualified in both fields, quietly took his place.

COVER STORY

For Marjory

Contents

Prologue

'Haven't you had enough?' Howard enquired in the darkness of the private cinema. 'This is pretty horrible – and this is the third run-through . . .'

'Kindly shut your trap. It's my wife . . .'

Newman sat like a frozen man as the projectionist ran the reel again. His face lacked all expression. He stared at the screen as though hypnotized.

The man who had held the cine camera filming the scene had been a professional. The short film opened again showing Alexis clearly, standing on the unknown road in the moonlight. She threw up her hand as the car's headlights hit her smack in the eyes. Behind her the weird castle loomed. The car moving at speed hit her for the first time, lifted her lovely slim body like a rag doll and rolled over her.

Newman's stomach muscles tensed. He *felt* the wheels crushing her slumped body, breaking bones, crushing her skull. The car jerked to a halt. Behind it Alexis lay in the road motionless. Newman could hear the driver clashing the gear into reverse. There was no soundtrack, only the ratcheting click of the reel in the projection room. His cigarette had gone out, clenched between his fingers. His eyes switched from the crumpled form to the castle perched high up, a dark silhouette, like something out of a Hans Andersen illustration. It began again.

The car reversed at speed. The driver had not turned his wheel a fraction of an inch. He drove back over the body lying in the road. Newman heard more bones crack. Her beautiful face would be mashed to a pulp by now. The car stopped a few yards away from Alexis, drove forward once more.

The film flickered. Lights danced before Newman's eyes. A blank white screen. He stood up and moved into the aisle and walked out of the small, claustrophobic cinema. Howard hurried after him, caught his arm in the foyer. Newman shook it off as though any kind of human contact was distasteful.

'It was your wife?' Howard asked.

'I told you before. That was Alexis.'

He was already talking of her in the past tense. He walked down the bleak corridor like a robot, staring straight ahead. One foot in front of the other. Left, right, left.

'I'm so very sorry,' Howard began again. 'Was she after some story – '

'I said shut up. I've identified her. That's it.'

'The reel was posted inside a canister. From a post office very close to your flat. Postmarked SW5 – '

Newman continued walking. The dead cigarette was still between his fingers. Dead as Alexis. His expression still showed no emotion. He walked with long strides. Howard had to hurry to keep up. He tried another tack.

'There was a brief message written in crude block letters. *Tell other people to keep away from Procane.* It was a – ' Howard hesitated. Newman was beginning to frighten him. 'It was a deterrent, we think. Come and sit down for a while in my office. Have a cup of coffee. Maybe something stronger? We've had several of my staff watch it – trying to place the country. That castle – '

'I've seen it somewhere,' Newman said in the same blank tone.

'Where?'

He realized he had put the question too eagerly. Newman was going to walk out of the front door. He replied as he kept walking.

'In a picture. I don't know where. Will Tweed be in charge? And who is Procane?'

'We haven't the slightest idea.'

'All right, lie to me.'

Newman had noticed the brief pause before Howard answered. He reached the reception desk and the guard in civilian clothes rose to ask for his entry form. Howard shook his head and the guard sat down again as Newman opened the door and without a look back or a word walked down the steps into Park Crescent.

This was the first event which triggered off the huge manhunt in 1984 – because the American Presidential Election was due to take place on 7 November.

3

At seven on that coolish morning – before the temperature had started to soar in the current, two-month-old heatwave – when Newman caught a cab back to his flat, it was still Thursday, 30 August.

Part One

LONDON

Adam Procane?

Chapter One

The second event occurred twenty minutes later and was a pure chance happening. Sitting inside the cab as it approached his flat in Beresforde Road, South Kensington, Newman decided he couldn't face making his own breakfast.

He told the driver to stop alongside the garden surrounding St Mark's Church. Getting out, he paid the fare and started to walk westward towards the Forum Hotel. He didn't, therefore, see the blue Cortina which was illegally parked facing the entrance to Chasemore House where he lived. Two men sat in the front of the vehicle. Later a witness told the police they wore dark business suits but could give no further description.

Newman did, however, meet the postman standing on the pavement. The postman was checking a batch of letters he was delivering. He looked up and grinned.

'Mornin', Mr Newman. Another lovely day. Think this heatwave could last till Christmas?'

'With a bit of luck.'

Newman answered automatically in the same

monotone Howard had found so disturbing. The postman extracted three envelopes and looked at Newman again. He saw a well-built man of forty, clean-shaven with thick sandy hair, whose expression was normally droll as though he found most of life amusing. The strong face which stared back at the postman that morning was like stone. Another fact later reported to the police.

'Three for you, this mornin',' the postman commented. 'Only one from abroad. Business must be quiet.'

'Thank you.' Newman ignored this reference to his profession of foreign correspondent and walked on towards the Forum Hotel, a sixteen-storey concrete tower which dominates that part of London. Two bills in the usual brown envelopes. As he glanced at the third envelope he stopped walking and stood perched on the kerb.

He recognized her long, sprawling writing and felt very cold. Alexis's. A letter from the dead. A blue label stuck on at a hasty angle was printed with the words *Par Avion, Lentoposti, Flygpost*. French, Finnish, Swedish. The postmark was clear. Inside a red circle *Helsinki*, then *25.8.84*, then *Helsingfors*, the Swedish name for Helsinki.

It gave him an odd feeling. Today was Thursday. Alexis had been alive the previous Saturday when she had air-mailed the letter. His long experience as a foreign correspondent forced his brain to work despite the numbness.

8

The canister containing the dreadful film Howard had screened for him could only have been brought to Britain and posted locally by someone who had flown to Heathrow from Helsinki. It had all happened during the past four or five days.

He walked to the Forum on automatic pilot, the unopened letter in his pocket. He climbed the steps to the coffee shop, went inside, ordered coffee and toast and sat down at a table away from the other customers. He drank two cups of black coffee while he stared at the outside of the envelope, which also carried the name and address of a hotel printed in dark blue in the upper left-hand corner.

Hotelli Kalastajatorppa, Kalastajatorpantie 1, 00330, Helsinki 33. He had once visited Helsinki on an assignment but he'd stayed at the Marski in the centre of town. He'd never heard of this hotel which was such a mouthful. He buttered a piece of toast with great deliberation, added marmalade and forced himself to eat while he opened the envelope.

It contained one sheet of paper headed with the name of the same hotel. His blue eyes scanned the brief, bold sweep of handwriting which always reminded him of the waves of the sea and the first time he took nothing of its message in. He began a second time.

Dear Bob, In one hell of a hurry to catch the boat – it leaves at 10.30. Adam Procane has to be stopped. Archipelago is my best bet. Am leaving now. Will post this on my way to the harbour. Alexis.

Just *Alexis*. Not *Love, Alexis*. So, even at the end, nothing had changed. The break between them had been complete and permanent. This was a professional communication. But she paid him one last, bitter compliment. Whatever emergency she had been investigating for *Le Monde*, she had believed he was the man who could carry on if the worst happened. And the worst had happened.

Procane.

Howard had mentioned Procane, had then unconvincingly denied he knew anything about Procane. Newman poured more black coffee and lit a cigarette as he added up what he had. Damned little.

Adam Procane, whoever he might be. A boat leaving somewhere – presumably Helsinki Harbour – at 10.30. That meant in the morning. Alexis would have written 22.30 if it had been the evening she was referring to. A boat leaving for where? Not Leningrad, he hoped to God.

Archipelago. Which one? There was the Swedish archipelago stretching out its chain of islands from Stockholm towards the Abo archipelago – or the Turku archipelago, as the Finns called it. The latter was the second largest in the world, a labyrinth of islands and islets, many little more than rocks just protruding above the surface of the sea. Why was an archipelago important? And which one had she been referring to?

Finally, he had two more things. The name of a Helsinki hotel where Alexis must have stayed. And that weird castle in the background of the film when she had been mowed down by that swine of a driver. It would come back to him – where he had seen that very odd building perched up above the surrounding town.

He paid the bill and walked back to his flat. It was 8.30 and London was stirring for another day of toil and strife. A handful of pedestrians hurried along the pavements. His first warning of the incident was when he saw the police car with the blue light on its roof parked outside Chasemore House.

Tweed was in a rare state of cold fury. Arriving late at the headquarters of SIS – the Secret Intelligence Service – Howard had just told him about Newman's earlier visit. Plump and middle-aged, Tweed stood behind the desk in his office on the first floor overlooking Park Crescent. The two men were alone.

'I thought he had a right to see the film,' Howard told his second-in-command. 'In case you've forgotten, Alexis was his wife,' he added with a tinge of sarcasm.

Tweed took off his horn-rimmed glasses and began cleaning the lenses on a corner of his handkerchief. He stared at Howard who stood six feet tall and, as usual, was faultlessly dressed in a dark blue Chester Barrie suit. Smooth-faced and clean-shaven, Howard found the stare unnerving and rattled loose change in his trouser pocket. Tweed carefully hooked the handles of his glasses behind his ears before replying. He extracted an envelope from his rumpled jacket pocket and placed it carefully on his desk.

'I am aware Alexis was his wife,' he began, 'which is why I consider it an act of the utmost brutality to screen it for him.'

'I make the decisions here,' Howard told him stiffly.

'Not on this Procane thing,' Tweed corrected him in his normal gentle tone. 'I was summoned early this morning to meet the P.M. You had better read the letter in that envelope.'

'Not another bloody directive giving you full powers, I hope,' Howard rasped.

He snatched the folded sheet from the envelope, read it quickly and threw it back at Tweed. 'That's the second one. I shall protest.'

'You know the procedure.'

There was a hint of indifference in Tweed's tone which made Howard gaze at him closely. He ran a manicured hand through his hair which showed streaks of silver. Then he walked over to examine a map which had been attached to the wall by Tweed's assistant, Monica, earlier that morning. The map showed Scandinavia from the west coast of Denmark to the Soviet border with Finland in the east.

'What's this for?' he demanded.

'It's probably the battleground.'

'Battleground?'

Howard swung on his heel, thrust his right hand in

his jacket pocket with the thumb protruding, a characteristic pose. Once again Tweed had startled him: he
hardly ever resorted to dramatic phraseology. Tweed,
still standing, hands entwined and clasped over his
stomach, waited. Monica, a comfortable-looking
woman with dark brown hair and alert eyes, chose
this moment to slip into the room. She paused until
Tweed nodded that it was all right and then she sat
unobtrusively behind her own desk.

'From rumours beginning to come in from Europe,'
Tweed explained, 'it appears that the American, Adam
Procane, may go across through Scandinavia – '

'And who the hell is this Procane?'

'I have no idea. The rumours speak of someone
high up inside American Security who is about to
cross over to Russia. You can imagine the effect inside
the United States if they had someone much bigger
than Kim Philby arriving in Moscow – especially with
Reagan coming up for re-election on November 7.'

'Oh, my God!' Howard slumped into the only
leather armchair in the room, the chair Tweed used
when he wanted a visitor at ease and off guard. 'I
gathered it was something like this but I had no idea
it was a big fish.'

'Shark-sized.'

Again it was not Tweed's normal way of speaking.
Monica was surprised and glanced up, studying
Tweed. His face showed no particular expression and
she guessed he was hoping Howard would leave their
office.

13

'Why Scandinavia?' Howard asked eventually.

'It's the easiest way to cross into Russia. Procane is hardly likely to turn up at Checkpoint Charlie in Berlin. Now, I want to know why you really showed that poor devil, Newman, the film.'

'I casually mentioned the name, Adam Procane, after he'd seen it – '

Tweed blinked, incensed. 'You set him running, hoping because of his vast experience as a foreign correspondent that he'd lead you to Procane. That was it, wasn't it?'

'It would be a feather in our cap – ' Howard made a gesture of resignation ' – if we saved the Americans' bacon for them. God knows we need to build up credit – and credibility – in Washington.'

'And how were you going to achieve that – putting aside for the moment the callous aspect of what you've just done?'

'Leadbury followed him when he left the building – '

'Leadbury!' Tweed made no attempt to conceal the contempt and distaste he felt. 'You really think Newman won't spot him within an hour? He's probably spotted him already.' Spreading both hands on the desk-top, he leaned towards Howard. 'You know what you've just done? You've put the wrong piece on the board in the wrong place. He'll have one object – to find out who murdered his wife – '

'They weren't getting on at all well together,' Howard objected. 'Alexis was foreign correspondent for *Le Monde* – she was already clashing with Newman because they were in the same field. That marriage – after only six months – was heading for the rocks.'

'And you think that will make any difference to Newman? We have a rogue elephant on the rampage. From now on, Howard – ' Tweed tapped the directive from the P.M. ' – I operate entirely on my own. That document says so. I don't think we have any further topic to discuss.'

Half an hour later Tweed received the first reports of the incident at Chasemore House.

When he saw the police car parked outside the entrance, Newman did not immediately cross Beresforde Road. Instead he strolled past the garden of St Mark's Church. He stopped outside the church to light a cigarette and heard the sound of the urgent siren of another vehicle.

An ambulance appeared from the direction of Fulham Road and stopped, double-parked alongside the police car. Two attendants alighted, went to the back of the ambulance, opened the rear doors and went up the steps and inside Chasemore House, carrying a stretcher.

Newman remained where he was, smoking, knowing he was no longer conspicuous. Just another ghoul attracted by the signs of disaster. A few minutes later the attendants resppeared carrying a man on the stretcher. His head was bandaged but Newman recognized the postman who had earlier handed him his mail as he made his way to the Forum coffee shop. He waited until the ambulance drove off, threw away his cigarette and crossed the road.

The door to the entrance hall was open and he was stopped by a man in civilian clothes who had police-man written all over him. No more than thirty, his manner was polite but firm.

'You live here, sir?'

'I do. What's going on?'

'May I have your flat number?'

'Why?'

'That one?'

The policeman stood aside and gestured along the hall. One door hung at a drunken angle from the top hinge. Near the end of the wall-to-wall carpet cover-ing the hall floor was a dark stain which could have been blood.

'Christ! That's all I need. A break-in – '

'Could you furnish any identification, sir?'

Newman gave him his press card and glanced out into the street. Standing in the exact position outside the church where he had paused, was a man in a soiled raincoat and a crumpled trilby, staring upwards with interest. Leadbury. But no jumbo was passing overhead in the clear blue sky.

'Thank you, sir. I'm Sergeant Peacock.'

'Show me your warrant card.'

'Very wise, sir. Not many people think to ask.

Would you be Robert Newman, the foreign correspondent who – '

'Yes! Now can I look at the mess? And is that blood on the carpet?'

'I'm afraid so, sir. The postman was attacked. We think they followed him in, probably pretended to be residents. May I come inside with you? Thank you. Were you expecting something important or valuable in the mail?'

Newman was walking along his lobby to the large sitting room with bay windows overlooking Beresforde Road. He answered over his shoulder.

'No. Why do you ask?'

All the drawers in the Regency sideboard at the end of the room furthest from the window had been pulled out, their contents strewn over the floor. Newman went up the two steps which led to his compact kitchen open to the living room. He filled the electric jug with water and pressed the switch. He turned on the overhead spotlights and faced the room, looking at the large silver-framed photograph of Alexis still perched on the sideboard.

A half-length portrait, her long black hair falling to below her shoulders, her pointed chin was tilted in that defiant, challenging stance he knew so well. His throat was dry as a desert. Peacock, a thin-faced man with sharp eyes, followed his gaze.

'You've just lost all your colour, sir. A good job the lady was away when this happened.'

'Yes. That mail-satchel over there, the letters. I think you asked me a question when we came in?'

'Were you expecting something important or valuable in the mail?' Peacock repeated in the level tone policemen adopt when they are interrogating a reputable citizen. 'You said "No" and then you wanted to know why I asked that question.'

'Well, why the hell did you?'

Newman turned his back on Peacock and spooned instant coffee into a brown mug ready for the boiling water. The main problem at the moment was to get rid of Peacock. He had very little time to make a lot of arrangements.

'Because, sir, we reconstruct what happened like this. First, the postman is hit over the head in the hall – probably with a leather cosh. They check the mail he's carrying quickly. They don't find what they're looking for. They then break into your place and search it – I'm afraid the main bedroom at the back is a bigger mess. Sheets ripped off the beds, and so on.'

'How is the postman?'

'He'll be all right, sir. Luckily when we phoned from here we caught an ambulance on its way back to St Thomas'. I'd say a night in there and a bad headache will be his worst worry. But I was explaining – '

'And I answered you. Now, Sergeant Peacock, I don't want to seem rude but I have an urgent appointment in the North of England, a train to catch, a bag to pack . . .'

Newman understood the unnerving power of silence. He made his coffee and started sipping. He had to get this bloody copper out of the room so he could use the phone. He looked everywhere now – except at the photo of Alexis. It looked so *alive*.

'We'll have the fingerprint boys here soon, sir.'

'I'd like a few minutes on my own. *If you don't mind*, Sergeant Peacock – '

'Of course, sir. This kind of thing is always a shock.'

As soon as Peacock left the room Newman moved the wooden wedge which held the heavy door open, and closed it. He had been going to buy metal drop-leg wedges for the doors ever since he had bought the flat. He lit a cigarette, and walked to the phone resting on a small table next to the huge couch stretching across the window.

Taking out the Telecom Dialling Codes book, he checked the code for Finland. 010 358. For Helsinki you added 0. He noted also Directory enquiries for Helsinki. 155. He next looked up in the London directory the number of the British Airways office in the Cromwell Road next to Sainsbury's.

Leadbury, on the far side of the street, stood in exactly the same position, taking a great interest in the fingernails of his left hand. He would be the least of Newman's problems. He dialled 155, gave the name and address of the Hotelli Kalastajatorppa from the outside of Alexis's envelope containing the last letter he would ever receive from her. The girl gave him the number. He dialled it.

The chief of reservations spoke perfect English. He was sorry but for the next three days they only had a suite. Price one thousand markkaa per night. Something about 'the football match between Finland and Sweden'. Newman said he would take the suite.

He was dialling British Airways when he saw the cab stop a few yards beyond Leadbury. The cab waited while a plump, middle-aged woman wandered towards Leadbury, peering inside her bandbag. Newman froze. Monica, Tweed's asistant. She was dangerous.

He continued watching through the heavy net curtains when she stopped next to Leadbury and started talking to him. He felt inside his trouser pocket while she held a banknote. Oh, yes – dangerous. She was pretending to ask him for change. If Newman hadn't been watching through the window he would have missed the waiting cab.

After less than a minute's conversation she crossed the street and began talking to Sergeant Peacock who stood at the top of the steps. She smiled and listened. Not once did she glance towards the windows of Newman's ground floor flat. Then she was smiling again, as though thanking Peacock. She wandered back to the cab, got inside the vehicle and it drove off. Behind the curtain Newman swore. With Tweed on his heels he had less time than he had hoped for: the trackers Tweed used were far more difficult to elude than Leadbury.

Newman redialled British Airways and a girl

answered almost at once. Yes, she could help him with flights to Helsinki for today. There was Flight BA 668, nonstop to Helsinki, departing 11.15, arriving 16.10, local time.

'They're two hours ahead of us at the moment,' she continued.

'Get me Club Class, if you can. I'm ten minutes' walk from you. How much is it? I'll pay cash.'

'Could you wait just a moment, sir.'

He had a picture of her checking BA 668 on the console. He looked at his watch. He was going to have to move – to escape Tweed, to catch the goddamn flight. She came back on the line.

'You have your reservation, sir.'

He gave her his name, said he'd be with her in thirty minutes and replaced the receiver. To travel abroad you need four items. Passport. Air ticket. Preferably a hotel room waiting for you – it's surprising how many major cities can be packed out with a fashion show, an engineering exhibition – or a football match. And money.

As a foreign correspondent Newman always carried his passport. He'd booked his air ticket, reserved a hotel room. And he was a walking bank. In his wallet he had high denomination Swiss franc and German mark traveller's cheques – and dollars. The three hardest currencies in the world in August 1984. He also had French francs left over from a recent trip to Paris. He even had a little British money.

He opened the sitting room door quietly. The lobby

was empty. Peacock was presumably holding vigil on the doorstep, waiting for the fingerprint boys and the rest of the useless public relations exercise the police employed for break-ins. The main bedroom at the back was also empty – and a mess.

Newman always kept a suitcase packed for instant departure. Every night he repacked it to keep the contents fresh and unrumpled. It was perched on the dressing table with the lid open. The contents had not been touched. The intruders must have been disturbed and fled before they'd had time to check the case. He snapped the catches shut, locked it and carried it to the end of the entrance hall and ran down to one of the basement flats.

Julia, a thirty-year-old girl with thick blonde hair who was something in the entertainment business and didn't start work until ten o'clock, recognized his tapping and opened the door.

'A favour, please,' Newman began. 'I'm in one hell of a rush to catch a train north – '

'I've heard about your flat.'

'That's why I need your help.' She had ushered him inside and closed the door. He extracted a card from his wallet. 'You know this chap, Wilde, the carpenter and locksmith – jack of all trades. Would you phone him, get him to fix my place up, then give you the new keys to keep for me till I get back?'

'My pleasure. What about a cup of coffee? No? Suppose Alexis gets back while you're gone? Will she know – '

His face went blank, then he forced a grin. She pulled the long curtains of hair back from both sides of her face and peered at him more closely. Julia was very quick at spotting men's reactions.

'Is something wrong, Bob? Just for a moment you looked as though – '

'Of course something's bloody wrong. I come back from breakfast at the Forum and find this mess – just when I have to rush off.'

'Sorry. I'm pretty dim first thing.'

'Dim you are not. And Alexis won't be back before me – she's on an overseas assignment.'

'Look, Bob, you push off. I'll handle everything. Can I go into your flat and do a bit of clearing up?'

'Anyone ever tell you you're an angel?'

'Lots of men. They always follow it up with a suggestion not normally associated with angels. Push off, Bob. Julia always copes.'

Running back up the staircase to the entrance hall, Newman concentrated on the next problem. Leadbury. An ex-policeman whose main asset was total loyalty to Howard to whom he reported all the office gossip, which included staying late at the office to poke around people's desks in the hope of locating a tasty bit of info for his chief. There is one in every organization.

Peacock, standing straddle-footed at the end of the hall, his hands thrust into his jacket pockets, didn't help. He turned round, stared at Newman's suitcase and made his pointed comment.

'That's a large bag for a quick trip up north.'

'Ever heard of a man who changes his shirt three times daily?'

'Where can we contact you? And what about that door?'

'The blonde-haired girl downstairs is getting that fixed up. She has complete access to my flat until the job is done.'

'Not until Fingerprint Fred arrives, she hasn't. And we'll need yours – for elimination purposes, you understand?'

'I never agree to be fingerprinted – and you can't do anything about that. You can't contact me either – I have to find a hotel. I'm back tomorrow so I'll call the local station.'

'I don't find that entirely satisfactory, sir.'

'I often have the same problem. The blonde girl's name is Julia. Now, if you don't mind, I have a train to miss.'

Walking down the three worn, stone steps into the street, he wondered how he managed to appear so normal, to talk in such a flippant way. He pushed away the nightmare which hovered at the back of his mind and devoted his attention to Leadbury: to losing him fast.

Newman hailed a cab coming over the intersection from the direction of Fulham Road and was disgusted to see another cab, which was also free, following the first cab. It occurred to him he had almost missed an excellent opportunity to achieve his purpose. He signalled the first cab, carefully not looking at the far side of the street where Leadbury was watching.

'Harrods, please,' he told the driver.

He glanced through the rear window as the taxi proceeded along Beresforde Road. Leadbury was climbing inside the other taxi which then started following Newman's cab. Satisfied that his stratagem had worked, Newman settled back in his seat and extracted a bank note from his wallet.

The lights were red at the Cromwell Road intersection and his taxi stopped. Newman glanced back again. There were two cars between his cab and the one occupied by Leadbury. He leaned forward, pulled aside the window separating him from the driver and held out the note.

'Here's a fiver. My wife has a detective following me in the cab behind us. When we hit a traffic jam I'm getting out – you keep the change. OK?'

'OK, sir!'

The driver stared at Newman in his rear view mirror and winked. It was a situation he was not unfamiliar with. The lights turned green and he swung along the Cromwell Road into heavy traffic. They drove at a reasonable pace until they were close to Harrods. Newman glanced back a third time. The other taxi was still two cars behind them. His own cab stopped in the snarl-up of vehicles. Newman opened the door, dived out, slammed the door shut, threaded his way between the stationary cars and walked rapidly down Beauchamp Place.

Ahead of him a cab was dropping a woman passenger he guessed was about to embark on a shopping spree inside the huge store. He waited while she paid, glancing back up the street. Not a sign of Leadbury who would now be trying to work out his next move – whether to stick with his cab and try to follow Newman, or to pay off the driver and attempt to catch up with his quarry on foot.

'Where are you going, sir?' the cab driver asked.

'Sainsbury's in Cromwell Road. Take me along Walton Street and up past South Ken. station. I'm in a hurry.'

'They all are.'

He stopped speaking as Newman handed him a five pound note from inside the cab. The vehicle started moving without further conversation. Behind them in Beauchamp Place there was no sign of another taxi, of Leadbury.

Newman's route was following an approximate circle – taking him back to where he had started from. It was the last manoeuvre his muddle-headed tracker would expect him to carry out. Had it been Tweed at Newman's heels the outcome might have been very different – and all that followed might never have happened.

Chapter Two

Tweed put down the phone and looked at Monica, his expression grim. He got up from behind his desk, walked across the room to the cupboard containing his raincoat. Taking it off the hanger where Monica had carefully hung it, he folded it over his arm, talking as he did so.

'That was Howard's secretary – Howard is in a huff so I don't think we're on speaking terms. It's that new directive from the P.M., of course.'

'If you pull this off – ' Monica's grey eyes sparkled at the prospect ' – you could be sitting in Howard's chair. This is the second time the P.M. has bypassed him and given you her full confidence.'

'I don't want his chair,' Tweed responded irritably, blinking behind his spectacles. 'And I'm not at all happy about this assignment. Still, there we are. Leadbury has lost Newman. Of course. Something about switching cabs near Harrods. Now, tell me again about that police sergeant you tricked outside Newman's flat.'

'He told me the local postman had been attacked. I told him I was the postman's sister – so I got out of him the fact that they've taken the postman to St Thomas'. A minor head injury. You're going to Newman's flat?'

'No. St Thomas'. Our only lead is that postman. I'm very worried about Newman. Leadbury saw him leaving Chasemore House carrying a suitcase. My bet is he's leaving the country. The question is – which destination is he heading for? God knows what danger Howard has sent him into.'

Their eyes met and Tweed knew they had the same thought. It happened frequently. They had been together so long their mental processes ran along the same railway lines.

'Heathrow?' Monica queried.

'It's our only hope. Get on to Security. Have them check every flight.'

'That will take time,' she warned. 'It's still the holiday season . . .'

'And time is something we haven't got. We can only try. I must rush over to St Thomas'.'

'Can you give me any idea what this Procane business is in aid of?'

'I'm sorry. No.'

Arriving at St Thomas' Hospital, Tweed showed his card to a senior consultant who immediately located the general ward where the postman, a George Young, had been taken.

'Can you have him moved to a private room while

I interview him, please?' Tweed requested. 'And it's very urgent – we're concerned this could link up with something rather big.'

Five minutes later Tweed sat down by Young's bedside in a private ward. The postman's face was colourless, haggard and drawn. He'd been X-rayed and there was no skull fracture. He was thin and bony. Tweed proceeded carefully.

'How are you feeling? You had a nasty experience, I gather?'

'Like my house fell on me. Good job it wasn't the Empire State Building. Who are you?'

'I'm from Special Branch. Are you up to answering a few questions?'

'Fire away, mate. Special Branch? What's the score?'

'It's just possible – no more than that – that the people who attacked you may be linked with a terrorist cell we're after. At Chasemore House a man's flat was broken into.'

'Mr Robert Newman's place. I woke up inside it with those two ambulance chaps bending over me. He's one of the best is Newman. Gives me a Christmas box every year. Not many do that these days. Used to live round the corner from where he is now. A real gent. Funny thing, I met him in the street only a minute before those sods coshed me.'

'You saw your attackers?'

'No, but that policeman told me a cleaning woman saw two men getting out of a parked car and following me across the road. Couldn't describe them, of course. Useless old cow. I'd have described them if they hadn't come up behind me as I was pushing the mail through the letter box. The door wasn't closed properly, which is how they got me inside. People are careless. You've got to watch it these days . . .'

He was rambling on. Coming out of a state of shock, Tweed guessed. He interrupted gently, his manner casual as though the question wasn't all that important.

'You say you met Newman in the street? Coming back to Chasemore House, you mean?'

'No. Walking away from it towards the Forum Hotel. I gave him his mail.'

'Did you now?' Tweed carefully suppressed his excitement. 'Postmen have good memories. Can you possibly recall anything about the mail you handed him?'

'Three envelopes,' Young said promptly.

'Can you give me some detail about those envelopes?'

'Don't think I can. Just post. A couple in brown envelopes that looked like bills. Hang on.' Young crinkled his forehead between the bandages. 'The third one was a long white envelope from overseas with a blue air-mail sticker. And she'd written the address in a rush, I thought.'

'What made you think that?'

Tweed leaned back in his chair and clasped his hands in his lap, outwardly the soul of relaxation. He was scared stiff of breaking the spell. At any moment, from his experience of casualty cases, Young would start feeling tired, would lose the thread.

'The way she'd written the address – great sprawling sort of handwriting.'

'You said "she".'

'The writing sloped backwards. I've noticed a lot of women write like that. Men are more inclined to write with the letters sloping forward.'

'Quite right. The foreign stamps probably showed you which country the letter was sent from?'

Always phrase a question positively. Use a negative approach and you're asking for a negative answer.

'There weren't any stamps. It was franked. I can remember that much. And there was the name of a hotel printed in the upper left-hand corner.'

'Was the franking – which would show the city – clear?'

'Yes, it was. Don't ask me the name. You know how many letters I deliver on an average morning?'

'A large number, I'm sure.' Tweed leaned forward. 'You have a quite exceptional memory. You'd make a marvellous witness. One in a million. Now, the franking was clear. I'm going to give you a few names of cities – see if any of them sound right. For starters, Copenhagen?'

'No, it was shorter – at least the top one was.'

'The top one?'

'There were two names inside the franked circle.

31

One at the top, one at the bottom, with the date of posting in the middle. And don't ask for the date – I'm not Mastermind.'

'Helsinki?'

'Yes!' A flush of colour came back into Young's face. He was taking an interest in life again. 'Helsinki it was.'

'And the name below the date was Helsingfors.' Letter by letter, Tweed spelt it out. 'You see, ten per cent of the population in Finland is Swedish-speaking – so they pay them the courtesy of putting names first in Finnish, then in Swedish.'

'It was something like that – but I can't remember exactly what.'

'Now, let's try one more thing. The name of the hotel you said was printed in the upper left-hand corner of the envelope. Can you recall that?'

'No way.' Young shifted his position in bed. It was the first movement he had made since Tweed entered the room. 'I know it was a long name,' he continued, half-closing his eyes as he tried to see the envelope in his mind. 'Tell you what – I'm pretty sure it started with the letter "K" – a real jaw-breaker, I do remember that.'

'I think I've taken up enough of your time.' Tweed rose to his feet. 'You've been very helpful. I'm most grateful. I hope you're soon on your feet and this unpleasantness is only a fading memory. From what the doctor told me, that will prove to be the case.'

'You wouldn't have a fag on you?'

'The doctor will kill me.' Tweed reached in his pocket and took out a packet of Silk Cut. He didn't smoke but he always carried a pack – it could be the most persuasive weapon during an interrogation. He gave the cigarettes to Young, lit one for him with a bookmatch which he left on the bed. 'You can use that saucer on the bedside table as an ashtray. And those are cigarettes you brought in with you.'

'They're even my brand. Hope you catch those bleedin' terrorists. They should be strung up.'

'If you keep this conversation strictly between us you'll increase my chances of finding them one hundred per cent,' Tweed assured him. 'I have to make an urgent phone call now.'

The consultant loaned him his office and discreetly left Tweed to make his call on his own. As he dialled Monica he checked in his mind what Young had told him. A hotel beginning with the letter 'K'. That made sense. Without that letter the Finns wouldn't have a language to speak: and the reference to the hotel name being a 'jaw-breaker' only confirmed further it was Finland where the letter had been posted.

'Monica,' he began, 'I'm on an open line from St Thomas'. Any luck with Heathrow?'

'They just came through. The subject is taking Flight BA 668 to Sibelius land.'

'Can we stop him, delay him on some technicality?'

'The flight departs 11.15 hours.'

Tweed, who had lost track of the time, checked his watch and swore inwardly. Of all the rotten luck. It was 11.25 a.m. Newman was already airborne. Monica came on the line again.

'I've just looked at the clock.'

'I know. He's gone. Where does that flight put down before it reaches its ultimate destination?'

'It doesn't. It's nonstop. Arrives 16.10 hours, local time. They're two hours ahead of us at the moment.'

'Wait a minute. Let me think.' Tweed was appalled. The wrong piece on the board at the wrong time, as he had told Howard. 'Monica, I calculate I have less than three hours before he lands?'

'That's correct.'

'I'm coming straight back to the office. Look up the number of that girl in Sibelius City who was so helpful a couple of years ago. Have it ready for me when I get back. No, this I'll deal with myself. It's the only chance I have of saving the man aboard that flight from God knows what.'

Chapter Three

Flight BA 668 had reached its cruising speed of 500 mph, its cruising height of 35,000 feet, as it headed over the North Sea towards the Baltic. They were serving drinks in Club Class but Newman asked only for a glass of orange juice and a glass of water. He never drank alcohol when flying – it speeded up the process of dehydration which, despite the so called pressurization, was encouraged by the great altitudes at which modern aircraft flew.

He sat in a window seat on the starboard side, totally unaware that the Boeing Super 737 was flying over an ocean of cloud that made it impossible to observe the sea far below. Since boarding the aircraft he hadn't glanced once out of the window. When the stewardess emphasized that the alcoholic drinks were free he had another pang. An argument he had always had when he was flying with Alexis.

'Alcohol dehydrates – '

'So, what makes the difference?' she had flared. 'You surely understand by now that I am scared of flying. Only a drink can dull that fear.'

'Have it your own way.'

'I intend to! Because we are married you think you own me? *Comprenez?*'

'Yes, I *comprenez*,' he would reply.

'So, I drink and drink and drink until I am floating like the bloody plane. Then when we land – if we land – you carry me off like a piece of Vuitton luggage. That is OK with you?'

'Drink what the hell you like.'

'I do that. Drink what the hell I like. *Chéri!*'

She was very French. He was very English. Fire and water – not the best combination. Had they married in a fit of mad passion? Did most marriages start that way? And she was competitive. And they competed in the same field. She was foreign corre-spondent for *Le Monde*. Her by-line was smaller than his, much smaller. That rankled.

A quick movement across the aisle caught his eye. A dark-haired girl was tossing off her drink. Another memory. After the argument, Alexis shaking her long black mane as she tossed off a drink with a defiant gesture. One blessing – the seat alongside him was empty. On this trip he could do without company.

He reached for the briefcase he always took aboard a plane, the briefcase containing those few things he wouldn't want to lose. A very compact Voigtländer camera. Spare films. His notebook. His address book. Taking out a large cardboard-backed envelope, he extracted the photo of Alexis he had slipped out of the silver frame on the sideboard in the Beresforde Road flat. Her face stared straight at him.

He would need that for identification when he tried to backtrack her last movements in Helsinki. That and the maiden name she used professionally. Alexis Bouvet. He returned photo to envelope, envelope to briefcase. He checked his watch. Another couple of hours and he would be landing at Vantaa, the airport north of Helsinki. Would the place have changed since his previous visit two years before? He doubted it. He stirred irritably in his seat as they came along with the food. He still did not look out of the window.

'The girl in Sibelius City – Helsinki – is Laila Sarin,' Monica told Tweed, as he carefully put the old Burberry he had carried on the hanger. He was sweating with the heat – the temperature had already climbed to 81°. The only reason he took the Burberry was in case he wanted to change his outward appearance. He carried it folded with the distinctive pattern of the lining showing; if he put it on he became a nondescript character in a worn blue raincoat.

'Yes, I remember her well. It's her phone number I need. I can dial it myself.'

'Which is on the piece of paper on your desk. Also the name of the newspaper she works for – which I can't pronounce.'

Tweed sat behind his desk, glanced at the note and reached for the phone. The fact that he insisted on dialling the number himself told Monica he was working under tension. The name of the newspaper was *Iltalehti*.

'How long do we have?' Tweed asked.

'Newman lands two hours from now. Is the airport a long way out?'

'Only a twenty-minute ride to the centre of Helsinki.'

He was dialling the complex number. When the switchboard came on the line he gave the extension number and asked for Laila Sarin. Of course, she'd be out on some assignment. He drummed the fingers of his left hand on the desk and then stopped. It was an excellent line and he remembered her distinctive and soft voice.

'Laila, this is Tweed calling from London. Can you do me a great favour at very short notice?'

'Wonderful to hear from you. My notepad is ready. Tell me what I can do.'

He explained it as briefly as possible. She kept saying, 'Yes, I understand. No problem.'

He gave her Newman's description, told her the flight details, warned her that Newman was very astute and would soon spot anyone following him. She made an unusual suggestion.

'Could I not introduce myself, using your name in some indirect manner? Does he work alone – or might he welcome some help under the circumstances? He will be in a state of great emotional shock due to his wife's death. We have the story in today's edition.'

'You have?' Tweed gripped the receiver more tightly. 'May I ask where you obtained the information from?'

'A photo was delivered to our offices. We have seen enough pictures of Alexis Bouvet to recognize her. But, in any case, there was a note with the photograph. Now, can I make the approach to Newman when he comes off the plane?'

'You can reach Vantaa in time?'

'No problem. I only have to mention the name, Robert Newman, to my editor, and he will smell a good story.'

'He may brush you aside,' Tweed warned.

'Oh, I have already foreseen that. I have a friendly taxi driver who will be waiting and will follow him if that happens.'

'Laila, I think I'd better leave everything to you.'

'I meet the plane, Mr Tweed. You can rely on me. And how do I contact you?'

Tweed gave her a number which was not the number on his own phone, a number which was nominally an insurance company in the same building. He thanked her and replaced the receiver, looking across at Monica.

'Her English is good, then?' Monica enquired.

'Many Finns speak excellent English. They are a very realistic people. Who else in the world understands their language? It's a form of Finno-Ungarian – it's akin to Hungarian. No one really knows where

39

those two peoples originated from. Plenty of theories. No proof. Now, my next trip must be to look at Newman's flat. There might just be something.'

'I've got your air tickets for Paris, Frankfurt, Geneva and Brussels. You haven't much time to catch the Paris flight this afternoon.'

'With the Procane project I haven't much time for anything . . .'

When he walked into Newman's flat a man was repairing the main door leading to the inner lobby. Tweed reached the entrance to the sitting room and stopped. Howard, looking rather aimless, stood in the middle of the room sipping a cup of coffee. He raised the cup.

'The girl downstairs made it for me. She's rather nice.'

Tweed kept his expression blank. Howard's normal public school accent had softened to an almost wistful note. It was well known that he was not getting on too well with the rich county girl he had married.

'Why did you come here?' Tweed asked. 'And, since you are here, have you found anything?'

'Nothing to find. Newman is an artful sod – not a notebook or piece of paper in the whole flat which gives a clue. As to why I am here – ' the upper crust accent returned with a vengeance ' – he gave Leadbury the slip.'

'Not an impossible achievement.' Tweed began to

walk slowly round the large room, touching nothing, seeing everything. 'Why is that plain-clothes police-man still hanging about on the doorstep?'

'Peacock? Not too bright, like so many of them. The fingerprint brigade have still to come. Apparently there was a spate of break-ins last night. Something caught your attention?'

'Just looking.'

Tweed was staring at the top of the Regency sideboard at the inner end of the room. A fine film of dust coated the surface. Housework had never been Alexis's strong point. Two lines were clearly delin-eated in the dust, one behind the other. Tweed opened the drawer in front of the lines, grasping the metal handle which wouldn't take fingerprints.

'You won't find anything in there,' Howard assured him airily. 'I've been through the lot.'

Tweed stared down at the empty silver frame which must have recently stood on the sideboard, the kind of frame which contains a photograph. He closed the drawer and walked across the room to mount the two steps to the kitchenette. Glancing around, he left the room and walked into the bedroom at the back – the smaller room leading off the sitting room at the front was the study Newman used for working. There would be nothing in there.

He searched the bedroom carefully, even peering under the two beds. It was hot as hell in this room. He mopped his forehead and wondered what fantastic heights the thermometer had climbed to. Would this bloody heatwave last forever? Tweed hated the big heat. Give him the invigoration of really biting cold weather any day.

'Nothing?' Howard enquired from the doorway.

'Nothing.' In an odd way he was telling the truth. 'I'd better get moving,' he decided. 'I have a plane to catch.'

'To Paris? You think *Le Monde* might be able to tell you something about Alexis?'

'It's doubtful. I must rush. Excuse me.'

'You're not going to tell me anything about Procane?'

'I wish I had something to tell. It's just a name. The odd thing is there is no one in Washington in a key position with that name. Curious, isn't it?'

'Your suitcase is in the coat cupboard, the air tickets and traveller's cheques plus about a hundred pounds in French currency are in that envelope on your desk,' Monica announced as Tweed came into his office. 'You do have your passport?'

'For God's sake, stop fussing. You know I always carry my passport.'

Tweed regretted his outburst the moment he sat down behind his desk. Monica looked hurt and opened a file, bending her head over it. He took a deep breath and spread both hands on the top of the desk as he pressed his back against his swivel chair.

'I'm extremely sorry. That was unforgivable. I'm most grateful for the way you always look after me so well.'

'Something about this assignment is worrying you?'

'I dislike the whole business, but it has to be done.'

'You found something at Newman's flat?'

'I found Howard standing there like God. He had no right to go there – but I kept my mouth shut.'

'Good for you. What *did* you find?'

'It's what I didn't find that is so disturbing. The absence of two items. Howard hadn't noticed either, of course. People never do see the *absence* of something.'

'What was missing?'

'A photo of Alexis. I found the empty frame in a sideboard drawer. Newman has taken the photo to show it to people in Finland. He's trying to trace her last movements. And the case he always keeps packed for quick departures had gone. There is no doubt any longer – he's gone off to track down the killers of his wife.'

'And that could be dangerous?'

'Very. Finland is a fascinating country – but it also lies under the looming shadow of Soviet Russia. The Finns play it with exceptional skill – walking the tightrope, keeping on friendly terms with the Kremlin while still determined to preserve their independence. I admire them enormously. But I fear Newman in his

43

grief and rage underestimates what he has walked into.'

'And that is?'

'The gigantic No Man's Land of Western Europe.'

Chapter Four

The gigantic No Man's Land of Western Europe.

Flight BA 668 was losing height rapidly, the machine swinging in a huge curve as it continued its descent. For the first time Newman looked out of the window, stirring himself from the stupor brought on by the Boeing's monotonous engine drone. Suddenly, the plane broke through the heavy cloud and there it lay below him. Finland!

Open country, a handful of neat, red-roofed houses – buried inside islands of dense, dark forest. In the long winter it must be claustrophobic living in those lonely homes – so many isolated inside the firs and pines with no more than a thread of track leading to them from the nearest road. Small lakes, leaden-coloured, were scattered across the flat landscape.

Then they were landing. The massive fir forest skimmed past his window. A gentle bump as the wheels touched down on the runway. The sudden slowing as the flaps were lowered and the tremendous power of the engines strained against the application of the braking. They were gliding along now, losing speed every second. The view from the window reminded Newman of Arlanda – the much bigger airport outside Stockholm which is also surrounded with dense fir forest.

As the machine stopped he unclipped his safety belt, thanked the stewardess for bringing him his British Warm, struggled inside it and moved into the aisle, clutching his briefcase. He remembered the same pulsating feeling of excitement he had experienced on his first visit to Finland. He was a long way east – as far east as you can go without landing in Russia.

In his impatience he was the first passenger to leave the aircraft. No telescopic corridor had been attached to the exit – he walked out on to the head of a mobile staircase leading to the ground. Close by was the main airport building, comforting in its smallness with its identity emblazoned in large letters. *HELSINKI – VANTAA.*

As he walked the short distance between aircraft and airport building he breathed in the biting fresh air. He had left behind a heatwave in London; now he was in a different world. He felt oddly thankful, relieved to be away from familiar things.

Overhead was a dark, brooding sky but somewhere it had thinned. The sun broke through, a vague, misty disc no larger than a five-markkaa Finnish coin. All those 'k's', Newman thought wrily as he entered the building. He was going to see plenty of them.

Vantaa is like Cointrin Airport at Geneva – or

Kastrup at Copenhagen. Compact and cosy. A world away from the sprawl and thunder of Heathrow. Newman had forgotten another distinction as he passed through Passport Control and waited by the carousel for his suitcase. At Vantaa there is none of the endless vinyl which makes other airports so anonymous. At Vantaa the floor is paved with wood blocks. They have a lot of timber in Finland.

The girl came up to him as he walked through the reception hall, heading for a taxi. In many ways she was typically Finnish. The lint-coloured hair he was to come to know once again so well. Slim, about five feet six, she wore a very clean pair of blue jeans tucked into leather knee-length boots. The upper part of her body was clad in a white woollen sweater decorated with blue diamond symbols. He later observed it was the popular fashion that year. She held herself erect and looked directly at him through her glasses.

'Mr Robert Newman?'

He was immediately wary and hostile. Dammit, he just wanted to be alone. He nearly walked straight past her without replying, then decided he'd better find out what she was about.

'I don't know you,' he said shortly, 'and I'm in a hurry. Do you normally accost strangers?'

'Only when they're wearing a tweed suit.'

Her right hand briefly fingered the lapel of his heavy, navy blue suit inside his open overcoat. She had emphasized the word tweed. He hesitated, thinking rapidly. How the hell had Tweed traced him so quickly? He decided to make sure.

'Except that I'm not wearing that type of suit.'

'I know. But Tweed is the right name, isn't it?'

'Who are you, anyway? And I'm tired and short of time.'

'Laila Sarin. I am a reporter on the newspaper *Iltalehti*.'

'Get lost.'

'I beg your pardon. I'm sorry.'

He still hesitated. What the devil was the matter with him? He couldn't even take a simple decision. And his course of action was obvious: he had to find out what this girl was up to – so he could checkmate her, lose her.

'That was rude of me,' he said. 'I apologize. I'm on my way to this hotel.' He showed her the envelope containing the letter from Alexis. 'I was going to show it to the taxi driver. I can't pronounce it. Come along with me.'

'Let me tell him.' She hooked her large handbag more firmly over her shoulder by the long strap. She had looked so disappointed he began to think he'd taken pity on her. He'd better watch this: maybe the girl was better at her job, cleverer at handling men than he'd suspected.

They walked out of the entrance and she spoke in Finnish to the driver who put Newman's suitcase in the boot of the Mercedes while they climbed into the back. He was aware that she was watching him out of the corner of her eye as the vehicle moved off.

'Let me just say one thing,' she remarked. 'It is a really nice hotel you have chosen. It is just outside the city of Helsinki – very quiet and restful. A good place to think, to relax.'

She left it at that as they drove at speed along a straight, four-lane highway lined on both sides with copses of firs and here and there an outcrop of rugged granite. No sign of a city. Now he remembered the granite – the soul of Helsinki. A tough people, the Finns. They had literally hewn their capital out of the solid rock.

It was still daylight but all the cars driving in the opposite direction had their headlights on – another intriguing aspect of Finland which came back to him. It was the law – you had to drive with your headlights on all the time unless you were in the centre of a city, when it was optional. This gives a weird impression that, no matter what time of day it is, you always feel it is close to nightfall.

'You should see this,' she said, handing him something.

It was her press card. She was establishing her identity – in another attempt to reassure him. He should, of course, have asked to see it back at the airport. Christ, he did need a few days to think, to relax. Wasn't that what she had said? She seemed very intuitive. Could she know about Alexis and carefully have made no reference to it?

49

'We don't go into the city to reach your hotel,' she said as he stared out of the window, not looking at him. 'And I hope you have a nice room overlooking the sea.'

'They only had a suite, so I took that. The hotel is on the coast?'

'Yes, but you won't feel it is. That part of the sea is more like one of our Finnish lakes. With a suite you will have the view. I would like to talk to you, Mr Newman. Is it possible for us to have dinner this evening?'

'I don't know. I may want to go straight to bed.'

'I should have thought of that – you have had a long and tiring flight. I am sorry.'

'No need to be.' He paused. 'We'll see – how I feel when we get there, I mean – '

'I do understand,' she replied evenly and with the same patience.

Newman realized he was letting his irritability show, that he was not being very kind to her. He glanced at Sarin who was still gazing out of the window on her side. She would be about twenty-seven, he estimated. No rings on the third finger of her left hand. She was not all that attractive by conventional standards, but there was something in her personality he found soothing despite his foul mood.

She turned slowly and from behind her glasses her blue eyes stared at him. He gazed back without any particular expression and then looked out of his

50

window again. They were coming into the outskirts of the city. The buildings here were nondescript blocks, giving the strange impression they had finished creating Helsinki only a few months ago.

Then they drove through an area of parkland with, here and there, a strange piece of sculpture rearing up amid the trees. The cab swung round a curve and Sarin looped the strap of her bag over her shoulder.

'We have arrived.'

With his memories of the hotels in central Helsinki, the Kalastajatorppa was a shock for Newman. Perched at the top of a slope rising up from the sea shore, the hotel complex was a series of three- and four-storey concrete blocks of considerable size – one block sweeping in a long curve. The rooftops were flat.

Newman stared out of the window without moving. Finnish architects are cunning, even ingenious. This architect had merged the concrete with the large granite massifs rearing up out of the ground so it appeared to grow out of the rock itself.

The hotel was situated in separate sections on either side of the quiet country road leading through pine trees. To his right he saw the calm, leaden grey of the sea and beyond that, in the distance, the element which is never far away in Finland – the dark, endless swathes of the forest like great arms strangling the bay.

'It is different? Yes?' enquired Sarin.

'It is extraordinary,' Newman agreed.

He paid the cab driver and they walked into the

spacious reception hall. They didn't count the cost of cubic areas in Finland. The generous sweep of the architect's vision was everywhere in the clinical spotlessness of the place. It was quiet; only a handful of people sitting in the comfortable chairs in front of the reservations counter.

Newman registered and a porter took them up in the lift to the suite on the second floor. It seemed quite natural that Sarin should accompany him. The suite was a large bedroom with twin beds, a bathroom and a door leading to the adjoining sitting room. When they were alone Newman sank onto one of the beds, feeling unutterably weary.

He had driven himself from the moment he had watched that horrific film of Alexis's murder with Howard in the cinema in Park Crescent. How long ago was that? Christ! It had been the morning of this same day. Now he was in faraway Finland. Laila Sarin ran over to the large picture window and called out with almost childish enthusiasm.

'Mr Newman! You do have the view! Come and look.'

'OK. Coming.'

Something in his tone of voice made her swing round as he came to stand beside her. She asked him if he would like coffee and he nodded. He stood and gazed out across the flat roof which projected over the reception area, as she called room service and spoke in rapid Finnish.

Yes, she had been right, this was Finland. Perched

above the buildings on the other side of the road, he had the most magnificent panorama of the bay – which did look like a lake. A wind was ruffling the surface of the sea now which crawled towards the deserted shore in an army of wavelets.

Always in Finland you are conscious of the vast sweep of the sky, a sky seen nowhere else in Europe in its clarity and feeling of immensity, of going on forever. The sun broke through like a murky search-light, illuminating a small patch of water. Then the wind dropped and the surface of the sea was still.

He stood watching the sheer peace of the view, the absence of a single human being anywhere. Just the sea, the darkening sky, and the forest. His legs felt like jelly. But the beauty of the scene held him as Sarin came back and stood beside him. He put his arm round her shoulders and felt her relax against him.

'Coffee is coming,' she said as they stood there in the semi-dark. 'And you can call me Laila, if you like.'

'I'm Bob. From now on you can cut out the Mr Newman stuff. Laila, I'm dropping.'

'Go lie down until the coffee arrives. It won't be long.'

He walked to the bed nearest the door, sagged onto it, removed his shoes, swung his legs up and flopped. She eased the pillow under his head, undid his tie and collar. He fell fast asleep.

She didn't wake him when the coffee came. Pouring herself a cup she carried a chair to the window, sat down and watched night fall as she sipped at her coffee. An hour later she had emptied the coffee pot and Newman slept on, his breathing even. She switched on the other bedside light, propped up the pillow, took off her boots and stretched her long, slim legs on the second bed.

Through her glasses she watched this stranger from across the seas, the Englishman who, from her first sight of him at the airport, had reminded her of a lost soul.

Chapter Five

Tweed walked out of the reception hall of that strange, twenty-first-century-style airport, Charles de Gaulle, just after 5.30 p.m. After disembarking from Air France Flight 815 he had wasted no time waiting for the arrival of a suitcase at the carousel. He always travelled light, taking aboard the aircraft his only luggage, a small case.

This technique gave him one great advantage. Anyone following him was left behind at the carousel while they waited for their own luggage to be unloaded. Speaking French, he gave the cab driver his instruction.

'The Hotel Bristol, if you please.'

It is often assumed that if you wish to visit Paris unobserved it is best to stay at a small and obscure hotel on the Left Bank. This is a mistake committed frequently by so-called experienced travellers.

The *concierges* of these small – and often shabby – establishments make a habit of spying on their guests. For a fairly modest sum they will report the presence of a visitor to anyone interested. A further danger is the underground network of contacts these *concierges* maintain with each other.

A very different outlook prevails at the majestic hotels to be found on the Right Bank – prominent among these being the Bristol. Here the chief *concierges* make a great deal of money serving the whims of their well-oiled clientele, not the least of these being the Americans – especially in 1984 when the strong dollar meant everything was being given away to *Les Yanks* for a song.

No *concierge* at a de luxe hotel would dream of endangering his lucrative income by selling information about his guests, no matter how great the inducement offered. Tweed was only too well aware of this economic fact of life.

He paid off the cab in the rue du Faubourg St Honoré, let the porter take his case, and entered the Bristol, which is a stone's throw from the Elysée Palace and the Ministry of the Interior in the Place Beauvau.

Anyone who had followed Tweed – and no one had yet achieved this feat without his knowledge – might have been surprised at his choice of place for dinner on the evening of 30 August. While – a thousand miles away to the north-east, Newman lay in a deep sleep in Helsinki, watched over by Laila Sarin – Tweed swiftly unpacked his case. He had a wash, and then walked into the corridor after making a local phone call.

He left a *Please Do Not Disturb* notice hanging from the outside of his bedroom door and kept his room key in his pocket. It was muggy and airless as he strolled along the Faubourg St Honoré. He crossed the Place Beauvau, past the entrance to the Ministry of the Interior where the grille gates were closed and police guards with holstered pistols stood, and continued along the pavement past the Elysée Palace.

Paris had changed since his last visit – and not for the better. Even opposite the Presidential residence the paving stones were slanted at different angles and there was a general air of decrepitude and neglect. Paint peeled from walls, the city had a look of shabbiness and neglect.

Stopping occasionally to glance in a shop window, he only took a taxi when he was satisfied he was not accompanied by trackers. He directed the driver to take him to the rue des Pyramides, a side street leading off the rue St Honoré and connecting with the rue de Rivoli. It was only a short distance and he compensated the driver with a generous tip, which was not acknowledged.

Trudging along the street, he paused again, but there was no sign of either a pedestrian or a vehicle following him. He turned into the Restaurant aux Pyramides, ordered a Pernod at the bar counter and asked for the phone. His second call was to the same number and this time he made the rendezvous after checking his watch. He sipped at the Pernod for appearances' sake and walked out, leaving most of the contents still in the glass.

The second cab dropped him outside Bastille Metro station. He walked again, a small, ordinary-looking man, hatless as he moved at a brisk pace down the rue St Antoine and turned right down the side street which leads to the renowned and once-elegant Place des Vosges. The Place, only a few years before the residence of the very rich, gave him a shock.

The de luxe apartments above the arcades were shuttered and had an unoccupied look. The rich are mobile and they had fled from Mitterrand. They were now residing in apartments in New York or Switzerland. The vaults of the banks in Basle were stuffed with billions of French francs – moved out of France by the canny on the eve of the Presidential election when Giscard had been defeated by Mitterrand.

Their absence showed even at La Chope, the restaurant Tweed was making for. There were still tables on the pavement outside the restaurant at the northeast corner of the great square, but the clientele had changed. Tweed took it all in at a glance.

The chic women dressed by Paris's leading couturiers, their men friends who had inherited fortunes, the occasional wealthy husband and wife – normally exchanging hardly a word. All were gone.

Instead the people sitting drinking and eating were lower middle class or upper working class (Tweed never knew where one division started and the other ended). He checked his watch. It was exactly 7.30 p.m. At an isolated table for two at the corner sat a huge-stomached man of about fifty. Tweed gazed round with a resigned expression at the other full tables.

'Excuse me,' he said in French, 'may I sit here? There doesn't seem to be much room this evening.'

'Seat yourself,' invited André Moutet.

The sun beat down from above the rooftops on the opposite side of the square. Tweed shaded his eyes from the glare and twisted his chair closer to the other man as a waiter offered him the menu.

'You still have veal?' Tweed enquired.

'Of course, sir. Something to drink?'

Tweed ordered a carafe of the house wine and they were alone again. Moutet had put on even more weight. As Tweed watched him shovelling potatoes inside his cavernous mouth he thought he understood why. A good trencherman, André Moutet. They began talking in low tones. Not that Tweed was bothered that they might be overheard – the other diners were totally preoccupied in themselves and what lay on their plates and inside their bottles.

André Moutet was heavily built in every region of his ample anatomy. The dark hair on top of his large head was cut *en brosse*, his jaw was well jowled, his lips full and deceptively slack. His official profession was that of racing tipster, an occupation which permitted him to mix with the low life of the city unnoticed. On the odd occasion he had brief conversations with some very well-heeled people who gambled in vast sums at Longchamps. He even numbered among his connections certain *comtes* – not to say, *comtesses*.

'Comtesses,' he had once confided to Tweed contemptuously, 'are the worst of the lot. If they can't screw any more out of their husbands, they can be found earning the ready, aiming, of course, to recoup their huge losses, by hiring themselves out to the more exclusive *salons*. You know what I mean?'

He had winked. And Tweed knew what he meant. But this was the surface Moutet. His real source of income lay in a quite different direction – although it still involved the collection and passing of information.

Moutet was on good terms with the porters and cleaners in every foreign embassy in Paris. From these lowly sources it was surprising how much highly secret information he obtained for comparatively small sums of francs. His mark-up, when it came to relaying such information to interested parties, was in the region of ten thousand per cent. Cash only, of course. The tax man never saw a sou from this income.

As he ate his veal Tweed listened to Moutet. Then Moutet listened to Tweed. At the coffee stage Tweed hauled a copy of *Le Monde*, a discarded newspaper he had picked up off one of the tables in the Restaurant aux Pyramides, out of his jacket pocket. Tweed showed Moutet an item on the still-folded paper which the Frenchman glanced at, nodded, and then thrust into his own pocket as though he were going to read it more carefully later. The envelope containing two thousand francs was concealed inside the folds of the paper. Moutet leaned forward and whispered as he picked up a toothpick.

'The bars. Those are the best channels. Bartenders love a bit of dirt for their customers. You might find them very useful. I'll be busy for you all next week. But you might wish to start tonight. Which way do you go home?'

'Towards the Elysée,' Tweed replied cautiously.

'Couldn't be better. The higher levels of society, shall we say? I'll give you a short list. You agree? Good. I'll go down into the sewer.' A wisp of a grim smile crossed the fat man's face. 'Hardly your *milieu*? Although – don't misunderstand me – I know you could handle that if you had to. You're a bloody chameleon, you are.'

The bloody chameleon nodded in agreement, blinked once and glanced at the nearest table to his left. A fresh couple had just taken it, the girl about twenty, the man in his forties. She faced Tweed as she closed in an embrace with her partner, taking the proffered menus from the waiter with one hand and closing one eye. Tweed smiled at her: it seemed to be an evening for winking. He decided it must be the atmosphere – the air was now balmy and relaxing.

Moutet was scribbling down his list of bars and their addresses. Tweed caught the waiter and paid the bill for both meals. Moutet appreciated little perks like that. The fat man folded his grubby piece of paper and handed it to Tweed, then stared at the carafe of wine which was almost full.

'You're leaving that?' he enquired in Gallic amazement.

'You know I don't drink much. Help yourself. And now, I am leaving. I may need you to come and see me for a day in a week or two. I'll let you know.'

'Always at your service.'

Moutet raised his glass, refilled from Tweed's carafe. Tweed glanced again to his left as he rose from his chair. He appeared to be looking at the couple at the next table who were still entwined in a serpentine embrace. In fact, he was looking at a small, swarthy-faced individual smoking a cheroot who had sat at another table by the wall ever since Tweed had arrived. Moutet was still using the same bodyguard, the man he called The Corsican.

Tweed spent a long, diligent and punishing evening after leaving the Place des Vosges. He visited every bar on Moutet's list. Most of them were in side streets leading off the rue St Honoré. A few were in the main street itself.

Always his routine was the same. He entered a bar, stood near the entrance, patting his jacket pockets as though searching for something while he checked the people inside. Then he walked up to the plastic-covered counter – the old zinc tops which gave such character to Parisian bars have long since given way to the march of science, and economy.

'A Pernod,' he would order from the bartender, leaning against the counter.

Then he chatted for a few minutes, listened to a tale of gloom and doom. As one bartender told him, 'La Belle France is no longer belle.'

Tweed then started chattering away himself and always the bartender would stop polishing the counter or glasses while he listened with great interest. It is doubtful whether Tweed, even with his fluent French, passed for one of the locals, but occasionally he laced his conversation with an apparent slip of the tongue, inserting a brief Spanish word.

It was close to midnight when he arrived back at the Bristol and went straight up to his room. He undressed rapidly, put out his fresh clothes for the morning, set his travelling alarm clock for 6.00 a.m. and flopped under the sheets.

The following day he was in Frankfurt, West Germany.

Wunderbar! Frankfurt am Main is a good place to witness the West German industrial machine humming into higher and higher gear. The contrast with the seedy France Tweed had left behind was staggering.

Instead of drooping shoulders, sagging expressions and an air of mourning for the past, the Germans walked briskly, confident of their present and future.

It is possible to walk along any street in the power-house city without the ankle-breaking experience Tweed had endured in the rue St Honoré.

The cab from the huge airport deposited him at the Intercontinental Hotel in time for lunch. Like the Kalastajatorppa in distant Helsinki, the Intercontinental has separate buildings on either side of the street – but, except for the underground tunnels linking the buildings, here the comparison ends.

The Intercontinental comprises two huge sky-scraper blocks. Tweed found himself being escorted in the high-speed elevator to Room 1467. After giving a tip to the porter who had insisted on carrying his small case, Tweed spent a few moments looking out of the huge picture window which spanned the outer wall.

The view reminded him of Los Angeles. At noon the city was still enveloped in a grey, sea-like mist. Out of this mist loomed more skyscrapers and he could just make out the pole-like tower which, from a previous visit, he knew was topped with what had once been among the first revolving restaurants in Europe.

He didn't hurry unpacking his case and having a wash. He took some care over his appearance, brushing his dark hair carefully to make himself presentable for his lunchtime guest. He had phoned her from the Bristol before leaving Paris and she had immediately and enthusiastically agreed to keep the appointment.

'It is a quiet time of the day for me, as you know,'

she had explained. 'Dinner is always difficult – business comes first in the evenings.'

'Of course,' Tweed had agreed tactfully.

At 12.45 p.m. – fifteen minutes before his lunch engagement – Tweed went down to level 'U', the basement area where a tunnel leads underground to the main building. While waiting for the elevator, he looked out of the window. Through a gap between two buildings he could see people walking along the banks of the river Main, a slow-flowing stretch of water.

Arriving at 'U', he trotted along the tunnel and up the escalator into the huge reception hall. It was alive with activity. People arriving; other guests, their expensive luggage stacked on trollies, departing.

He went along to the top-class restaurant, the *Rotisserie*, and he checked with the Maitre d' that he had been given the secluded corner table he had reserved on arrival. The table was perfect. Of course! He went back into the lobby to wait.

Promptly at one o'clock, Lisa Brandt arrived, saw Tweed and flew along the hall to fling her arms round him. No one ever described Tweed as tall but Lisa was only five feet three high. In her early forties, with long auburn hair beautifully coiffeured – Tweed suspected she had come straight from the hairdresser – she was slim and vivacious, brown-eyed, intelligent, and had a wicked sense of humour. They greeted each other in fluent German.

'Darling! It has been so long!' She hugged him with

genuine affection. 'You have time for some fun while you are in Frankfurt?' she suggested. 'Let us make this a day to remember.'

'Now, now,' he chided her. 'You know I never participate in the delicacies you have to offer.'

'Tweed!' Her tone was mock-indignant. 'I am talking about myself!' She stroked his chubby cheek. 'Once, there was a time – or have you forgotten?'

'Lunch is waiting.' He escorted her to the table and she stopped suddenly.

'Champagne! You know I love it!'

The head waiter, who had remained discreetly in the background, came forward. He pulled out her chair, bowed, treated her like royalty. He had little idea that his guest was the madame of the most exclusive brothel in Frankfurt.

'I have to board another plane late this afternoon for a fresh destination,' Tweed told her as they clinked glasses. 'I'm very sorry. Truly, I am. I need a favour from you.'

'My favours are at your disposal,' she told him archly.

Tweed cosseted her, treated her playfully, and she loved it. Had Howard, who fancied himself as a bit of a ladies' man, been able to witness the lunch, he would have been stupefied. This was a side of Tweed people rarely saw. He flattered her outrageously and she drank up every drop – knowing exactly what he was doing.

As with André Moutet, Tweed listened to her and later she, in her turn, listened to him as they dined off some excellent salmon. 'Flown in direct from Scotland,' the head waiter told them.

'I am sure I can help you, Tweed,' Lisa remarked at one stage as she held her glass in her slim, small hand and watched the bubbles rising. 'I have very high-level clients – ministers, members of the Bundestag, even a couple from the BND between you and me.'

The BND was the Federal Secret Service, and Tweed nodded his approval at her reference to these august personages who patronized her establishment. Again, as with Moutet, he raised the same point with her at the coffee stage.

'In a week or two I may need you in London for the purpose I mentioned earlier. You can fly over and back in a day.'

'Of course – you only have to phone me.' She stared at her coffee while she stirred it slowly. 'How is your wife?'

'I have no idea where she is.'

'Or who she is with?'

'I'm not interested. It's over. Lisa, have you ever walked through the streets of a well-to-do suburb at night – any suburb for that matter? If so, have you wondered just how many men and women behind those drawn curtains are quietly murdering each other day by day?'

'And why do you think I'm still single, you silly man?' she asked, staring straight at him. 'God knows I've had enough offers in my time. Running the sort of establishment I do, can you imagine the kind of conversations the girls report to me after a client has left? Marriage is a booby-trap, Tweed, a minefield you walk through every day. For the woman, for the man. When I come to London, do you want me to stay overnight?'

'No! That may sound cruel – but this business I'm engaged in is going to take every ounce of energy and concentration. I wouldn't admit it to anyone except you – but I'm not sure I can manage it.'

'It sounds dangerous. Take care, my Tweed.'

'I've had rather a lot of experience doing just that.'

Frankfurt was Friday, 31 August. Saturday, the first day of September, found Tweed in Geneva. He had stayed overnight at the Richmond, one of the most exclusive hotels in the Swiss city. Before leaving Lisa Brandt, he had been extremely tactful in dealing with the financial question. He had handed her an envelope containing deutschmarks of high denomination with no attempt at concealment. Earlier, in his bedroom, on a hotel envelope, he had written her name and address on the outside illegibly. The postage stamps affixed to the upper right-hand corner he obtained from the *concierge*. Anyone seeing the transaction at their table would have assumed he had given her an envelope to post.

In Geneva he was much more direct as he sat at a corner table at four in the afternoon, inside the Brasserie Hollandaise on the Place Bel-Air. His companion this time was a thin-faced man of forty. Alain Charvet was an ex-policeman who had resigned when he was passed over for promotion by a jealous superior. Charvet had promptly set up a discreet private investigation agency.

'There is the money,' said Tweed in French, pushing an envelope across the table. 'A thousand Swiss francs.'

Charvet whisked the envelope into his pocket and clasped his long, bony fingers on the polished wooden table top. Tweed explained what he wanted and Charvet nodded, then sipped his coffee. Their conversation took no more than ten minutes and Tweed then stood up to go, glancing round the curious relic from the past.

Very Dutch-looking, this café. Not at all Genevoise. Dark brown leather banquettes topped with brass rails, the place was illuminated by large milky globes supported on brass pillars. Tweed walked out into the overcast Place Bel-Air and crossed a bridge spanning the Rhône.

Charvet's main source of income was unusual. He 'stood in' for foreign agents who were supposed to be keeping track of the movements and contacts of certain subjects. It was a boring job and hardly surprising that a number of these agents preferred to spend the time with their mistresses.

They, therefore, 'sub-contracted' these assignments to Alain Charvet who, in any case, knew the city far better than they ever would. Charvet would take a sheet of blank paper in gloved hands and insert it into an ancient Olivetti Lettera 22 which he kept for this purpose only.

He would then type a detailed report on the movements and any contacts he had observed by the subject he'd followed. For this service he was often paid surprisingly large sums of money. The use of gloves was to ensure his fingerprints never appeared on the typed sheets he handed over.

Charvet was a cautious man and knew that some of these assignments could be dangerous. He even took the precaution of storing his portable typewriter in a bank vault – experts can easily tell if a page of typing has been produced on a particular machine.

He worked not only for Soviet and American agents. He took a further precaution. Occasionally when his experience as a policeman told him the information concerned Swiss security, he'd type a separate copy. This he passed to Swiss counter-espionage – for no payment.

Theoretically he was now covered on all fronts. But for Tweed he was an excellent instrument to exploit because of his contacts with foreign agents. The following day was Sunday, 2 September. Before midday

Tweed had settled himself in his room at the Hilton in Brussels on the Boulevard Waterloo.

'You do understand how I want you to operate, Julius?' Tweed probed as he looked round the buffet in Brussels Nord station.

'It is perfectly clear,' Julius Ravenstein replied in English. 'And I will hold myself available to make a one-day visit to London when you call me.'

'Good. Then I don't think I need detain you any longer.'

He watched the portly, fifty-two-year-old Belgian as he pushed back his chair. Ravenstein had the neat, well-fed appearance of a man who has prospered, which indeed he had. Once numbered as one of the world's most skilful diamond-cutters, Julius had the misfortune to develop a bad case of arthritis. His lucrative days as a diamond-cutter were ended.

When a man is desperate his brain can work overtime. Julius came up with an idea which appealed to his employers in Antwerp. He suggested he should penetrate the underworld and pretend to set up as an adviser on the best 'fences' to approach for criminals planning a diamond raid, a never-ending anxiety to the Antwerp diamond community.

His 'cover' was planned carefully. His sister, who sang in a Brussels nightclub, complained to anyone who would listen how badly her brother had been treated by the diamond industry.

'He's been dumped on the garbage heap by those bastards,' was her constant refrain. 'After a lifetime of learning about diamonds, the buyers and the sellers – *and* the security techniques they use . . .'

This last bit was thrown in as an afterthought – and it wasn't long before interested parties latched on to the possibilities of the afterthought. Julius found himself approached by men of different nationalities he had never met before. He listened and then said, 'Thanks, but not interested. I don't see the future in anything like that.'

It wasn't long before a Dutchman from Amsterdam outlined for Julius a future which could prove very profitable indeed. The 'fences' who took stolen diamonds off the hands of gangs which raided the factories paid widely differing amounts for the 'delivery'. It was no secret among the Antwerp dealers who these fences were – but knowing something and *proving* it to the police were two rather different matters.

So Julius Ravenstein – who had a wife and her aged relatives to support – went into business in a dual capacity. On the one hand he advised very anonymous individuals who approached him *before* a raid on the best fence to handle a particular type of 'merchandise', as it is known in the trade.

He then immediately sent out a 'White Star' alert to Antwerp that a raid somewhere was imminent. Security was tightened one-hundred fold in the factories. Sometimes the raiders were trapped and put away for a long time. Sometimes they escaped.

The outcome made no difference to Julius. He was making more money than he'd ever seen in his life. The raiders paid him a handsome sum for his advice on which fence to choose – always cash in advance. On top of this 'cream cake' income, he secretly received a regular monthly 'bread and butter' salary from the diamond dealers who regarded 'White Star' – his code-name – as the best insurance they had ever bought.

Ravenstein was the last contact Tweed talked with and instructed before returning to the Brussels Hilton prior to catching a plane back to London. He used room service and ate his lunch alone while he assessed what he had accomplished. It was years since he had personally engaged in such frenetic activity.

In every conversation the name Adam Procane had been repeated several times. As he ate his *sole meunière* – Tweed was fond of fish – he decided his best bet was Lisa Brandt in Frankfurt. Ravenstein was a gamble. In exceptional circumstances stolen diamonds were used by both American and Soviet agents to pay high-level informants who deposited their loot in private safety deposits. This meant the payment of a large sum in cash would never show up on their bank statements.

The one piece on the board in the huge game which was developing that worried Tweed was Bob

Newman, who had flown to the most sensitive area – Finland. He could prove to be the joker in the pack – and Tweed was genuinely concerned for his safety.

He drank more Perrier water as his mind roamed over his four informants. Ironically, Tweed had underestimated the skill of the one informant he devoted least thought to. Already rumours were flying round Paris as a result of the efforts of André Moutet. Even as Tweed finished his lunch these rumours had reached the ears of the military attaché at the Soviet Embassy in Paris.

But still no one had any inkling of what Tweed had so deviously achieved. He had lit a fuse leading to two powder kegs which were on the verge of exploding.

Chapter Six

'The information comes from Paris,' General Vasili Lysenko informed his subordinate abruptly. 'If this Adam Procane crosses over to us before the American Presidential election in November can you imagine the effect it would have? This could stop that hard-line bastard Reagan getting a second term. You *do* see now why it may be one of the events of the century?'

Lysenko had just flown from Moscow to Tallinn to make sure Colonel Karlov grasped the significance of his news. Tallinn is a city few people in the West could place within a thousand miles of its location.

Capital of the Baltic state of Estonia, it lies on the Gulf of Finland and faces Helsinki which is only forty miles away on the opposite shore. For Moscow this tiny Baltic republic is a potential powder keg. The Estonians detest the Russians and regard themselves as under foreign occupation.

Television does not help the situation – because the Estonians are close enough to Finland to watch on their screens the programmes beamed from Helsinki. They see portrayed a very different, richer, freer life.

Ironically, during the 1984 Los Angeles Olympic

Games the city was flooded with high-ranking KGB and Communist Party officials who flew from Moscow to Tallinn – so they could watch the Games televised from Helsinki. It was because of this general situation – and other more immediate and dangerous incidents – that Colonel Andrei Karlov of the GRU had been despatched to Tallinn earlier by his chief, General Lysenko.

The General was short and stockily-built, not unlike Marshal Zhukov of World War Two fame. And, again like Zhukov, Lysenko carried himself with a brutal self-confidence and, at times, displayed a coarse sense of humour, often at the expense of his inferiors. He was sixty-seven years old.

Andrei Karlov, only forty-two years of age, was a man of very different calibre – one of the new breed who secretly thought the older generation had fossilized. Karlov was also very different in appearance.

Tall and slim, with a long thin, clean-shaven face, he had a prominent jaw and wary, foxy eyes. When Lysenko wished to get under the skin of his subordinate, he would refer to him as The Fox.

Both men belonged to the GRU – Glavnoye Razvedyvatelnoye Upravleniye – or the Chief Intelligence Directorate of the Soviet General Staff. In Britain they would have been chiefs of Military Intelligence.

They faced each other across the table in the office on the first floor of a building in Pikk Street, which Karlov had requisitioned on his arrival in Tallinn several months earlier. Both wore civilian clothes instead of the normal GRU military uniform – for reasons of self-preservation.

Lysenko's attitude was arrogant, verging on contempt. Karlov was outwardly respectful, careful to give his chief no opening for reprimand. Inwardly he was seething with suppressed rage. There was no love lost between the two men who were supposed to be working in harmony on a mounting crisis. It was Lysenko who spoke again.

'I asked you a question, Comrade.' The last word an after-thought.

'I was thinking of the implications – to give a correct response. When I was at the London Embassy I received – from an unknown source – a number of items of information concerning the American MX and so-called 'Star Wars' military projects from this man who calls himself Adam Procane. I forwarded all this information to Moscow where I understand it was received as valuable. The type of information could only have originated from a very high source – as high as the National Security Agency or the CIA.'

'And yet,' Lysenko objected, 'we put a trace on all possible personnel staffing not only the NSA and CIA but also the Pentagon. No such person exists.'

'So, clearly, Procane is a code-name,' Karlov observed. 'I would be interested to hear of this latest information which you have received via Paris.'

'No more than a rumour – but a strong one. Adam Procane is preparing to cross over to us with a whole cargo of data on the latest American military projects.'

The burly Lysenko leaned his short, thick arms on the table and spread his hairy-backed hands. 'It has been decided that you will be in charge of the operation to make sure Procane crosses over safely.'

'Why me, for God's sake?'

'For the Party's sake. God got lost long ago!' Lysenko gave a deep rumbling laugh at his own joke. 'You have lost the little colour you ever had, Comrade. It is an honour which has been conferred on you.'

'Again, please, why me?' Karlov persisted.

'Obvious, I should have thought. You had the first contact with this Procane, whoever he may be. When he arrives there will be a great conference in Moscow – for all the reporters from the Imperialist press. Imagine the sensation in Washington! Such a defection will topple Reagan – '

'I return to Moscow?'

'No!' Lysenko thumped his clenched fist on the table. 'You stay here, continuing your present duties.'

'Again, may I ask why?'

'Because the report from Paris hinted at the route Procane will cross over by – through Scandinavia! So, you are waiting for him here. On the doorstep!'

'This is not Scandinavia,' Karlov pointed out.

'Close enough.' Lysenko switched the angle of his conversation, a favourite gambit to keep his subordinates off balance. 'Do you see that man from the Finnish counter-espionage unit in Helsinki still? Their so-called Protection Police?'

'We keep in touch,' Karlov replied cautiously. 'We

maintain a friendly relationship. But you know the Finns – it's a bit of an arm's length business.'

'His name?' Lysenko snapped his thick fingers as though summoning a waiter.

'Mauno Sarin. He is chief of the Protection Police – and very shrewd. We have to be careful – '

'How and where do you meet?' Lysenko interjected.

'Tourist ships sail across the Gulf – '

'I know that! The list of passengers lands on my desk.'

'I was going to explain,' Karlov continued patiently, 'that he comes across anonymously from Helsinki as a tourist. He slips away from the conducted tour – which lasts two hours – and for an hour or so we talk here. Then he discreetly rejoins the tour on its way back.'

'Tell him nothing about Procane! There may come a time when you should pay him a return visit – find out just what is going on among that nest of spies across the Gulf.'

'Understood.' Karlov paused, cherishing the moment before he dropped his bomb. 'There has been another murder of a GRU officer. I was going to report it when I heard you were on the way here.'

'Another one! That makes two majors and one captain.'

'Two majors and *two* captains,' Karlov corrected him.

'My God, this place is getting out of control! Why

is it always GRU personnel? Why not the KGB? Bloody hell, man, that is why you were kept here in the first place – the first killing happened while you were on holiday. How did he die?'

'The same timing – in the middle of the night according to the doctor. The same technique – garrotted from behind with a wire,' Karlov added sombrely. 'This time his neck was almost sliced through.'

'And he was drunk at the time, I assume?' Lysenko demanded savagely.

'He stank of vodka.' Karlov hesitated. 'The autopsy did show that a small amount had been consumed shortly prior to the murder – but the criminal police team sent from Moscow to assist me are convinced he was *not* drunk. They say vodka was poured inside his mouth and down his uniform after death.'

'Really?' Lysenko jumped up and walked to the window where he stood staring down into the old street, hands clasped behind his back. 'That tells me something highly significant – the hell of it is I can't put my finger on what it is. Later, it will come back to me. They are still assuming the killings are the work of some swine from the Estonian bandits – the so-called protest movement?'

'I don't think they know where they are yet.' Karlov changed the subject. 'That so-called execution of the French journalist, Alexis Bouvet, carried out by Captain Poluchkin was pretty damned stupid.'

'But he is your second in command, your deputy!' Lysenko moved away from the window and laid a hand on Karlov's right shoulder, a gesture Karlov disliked intensely. It portended anything but friendship. 'So, if there is any backlash surely the responsibility is yours.'

He removed his hand and used it to insert a cigarette with a cardboard holder between his thick lips. He sat down again in the chair facing his subordinate and waited for his reaction – a reaction which startled him.

'That is simply not true, General, and not only do you know it, but the facts are also on record. Poluchkin acted without consulting me. He set up the whole macabre incident without my knowledge. And he could not have flown in the unit which filmed the murder without the specific backing of the Politburo. My report disassociating myself from his act of gross insubordination is on file. It was madness – further compounded by sending a copy of the film to London.'

'You question the decision of the Politburo?' Lysenko enquired softly.

'I simply recall the facts. What could possibly be gained by such an outrage?'

'To serve as a deterrent, Comrade. You really think we want foreign reporters poking their snouts in our backyard? There can be little doubt that rumours of the murder of several GRU officers in Estonia had reached the ears of this French cow. She came over on one of the tourist boats from Helsinki to investigate.'

'Had Poluchkin informed me of her presence I

could have had her escorted back to the ship.' Karlov persisted. 'We would have searched her – maybe found some incriminating document we had planted on her. That would have been deterrent enough.'

'I must go.' Lysenko stood up and continued speaking with the cigarette in the corner of his mouth 'You might have a point in what you've just suggested. And how are you proceeding in your efforts to trace the bandit – or bandits – who are killing our men with complete impunity so far?'

'By setting nightly traps.' Karlov had also stood up as he explained. 'Every night a GRU officer is used as bait – following a pre-arranged route. He walks through Tallinn as though drunk. At regular intervals along that route I have plain-clothes men disguised as Estonians, heavily armed. So far, none of the tethered goats has been attacked. I shall persist. Soon, we must get lucky.'

'The sooner the better.' Lysenko extracted a sheet of folded paper from his jacket pocket and dropped it on the table. 'That is your directive, signed by myself, giving you total control on a temporary basis of the operation to bring in Adam Procane alive and well.'

'I have no idea who this American is.'

'So, keep in touch with Mauno Sarin in Helsinki. He is the man who knows everything that is happening in Scandinavia. The man most likely to hear that Procane is on his way. The Fox will bring off this huge coup.'

Lysenko left the room with this final, insulting

thrust and Karlov gritted his teeth. When he had been recalled to Moscow from the West he had fully expected a vertical promotion – that he would be sitting in the chair in Moscow occupied now by that political manipulator, Vasili Lysenko.

Karlov had good reason to expect such promotion during his flight back to the motherland. A brilliant mathematician, he was also a superb military analyst and probably one of the best strategic planners in the Red Army, with an intimate knowledge of the latest technical advances. But Lysenko had smeared his erstwhile rival with the label, The Fox.

Capable? Of course. Enormously so. Trustworthy? Loyal to the Party? That was another question. And so the laurels had been handed to Lysenko. Which was why Andrei Karlov hated his guts.

Lysenko climbed into the rear of the limousine and the man in chauffeur's uniform, a lieutenant in the GRU, ran round to the front and got behind the wheel. He drove at high speed to the airport.

The chauffeur was secretly amused at the whole charade – in Moscow Lysenko had boarded his aircraft in full uniform, only changing into civilian clothes when the plane was airborne. The chauffeur knew his eminent passenger was shit scared about the mysterious series of murders which had occurred in Estonia – and regarded a ranking general as a prime target for the unknown assassins.

He also knew that as soon as the plane left the ground once more, heading back for Moscow, Lysenko would immediately change back into uniform. No point in letting an observer report to the Politburo that a GRU general hadn't the nerve to walk the streets of Tallinn in full uniform.

In the rear of the car Lysenko patted his stomach with satisfaction. He had dumped the whole Adam Procane affair in the lap of Karlov. Fully confident of the outcome, Lysenko was still cautious enough to let a subordinate handle the earlier stages. And he was also confident Karlov had not spotted the time trap inserted into his directive. In this assumption General Lysenko was dead wrong.

... *giving you total control on a temporary basis of the operation to bring in Adam Procane alive and well.*

Karlov sat reading this extract from Clause Eight of the directive handed to him by Lysenko. They were the exact words Lysenko had casually used in conversation. The bastard!

Karlov pushed his chair back from the table in his office and pursed his lips. His cold, analytical mind had immediately riveted on this phrase as the key wording in the document. The word which really counted was *temporary*.

This, Karlov understood only too well, would enable Lysenko to take over direct control of the operation at the last minute, presumably when Procane had safely crossed over into Russia – thus claiming all the credit for the tremendous coup. Well, Comrade, Karlov said to himself, it may work out differently from how you expected. He decided his first move would be to make direct contact at the earliest possible moment with Mauno Sarin, Chief of the Protection Police in Helsinki.

In the meantime another report expressing his doubts about the value of the information provided so far by Procane would be a good idea. Going to a cupboard, he took out his typewriter and settled behind it at the table. His previous reports on the same lines had only whetted Moscow's appetite. He had little doubt their reaction to this fresh report would be the same.

Chapter Seven

While Tweed was flying across Western Europe, questioning and instructing his informants, Bob Newman spent three quiet days at the Kalastajatorppa Hotel on the fringes of Helsinki with Laila Sarin. He had a nasty shock on the first morning when Laila returned to join him for breakfast.

Walking out of the elevator into the lobby, he caught sight of a Finnish newspaper someone had left on one of the glass-topped tables. *Iltalehti*, the leading evening paper. Staring up at him from a picture on the front page was Alexis.

He picked up the paper, still feeling numb, and frowned as he examined the photograph. It had been taken from the vile film Howard had shown him in the basement of Park Crescent – but this picture was trimmed so it showed only Alexis, holding up her hand as the headlights of the car shone full in her eyes. No background, no sign of the weird castle perched high up. He glanced down to the bottom of the article, headlined, *Well-Known French Journalist Dies in Car Accident?*

At that moment, unable to read Finnish, he couldn't

translate the headline, but he could read the name of the reporter who had written the article. Laila Sarin.

'Good morning, Mr Newman. How are you feeling?'

He looked up and Laila Sarin stood in front of him. Despite his fatigue he had noticed how silent she was in her movements. You never heard her coming. With a grim expression he held out the paper.

'I'm sorry,' she continued in her soft voice, 'but I didn't think you would want to see that last night. I even had the bookstall manager at Vantaa Airport remove all copies until we were well clear of the place.'

'I have some questions to ask you over breakfast,' he said and then remained silent until they were seated in the restaurant and had been served with coffee and rolls.

'You slept well?' she ventured. 'I was worried about leaving you after we had dinner.'

He nodded. No point in telling her he had woken in the middle of the night yelling at the top of his voice. He had dreamt he was watching the film again, that he had heard Alexis screaming, followed by the thump of the car rolling over her prostrate body. His tone was terse as he asked the question.

'Where did you get the copy from to write that article? Also that picture – how did you get hold of it? And what does the headline say?'

She translated the headline for him and continued explaining. 'A messenger delivered an envelope at the office addressed to me. It contained that single photograph.'

'You trimmed it down before you printed?'

'No. That is the glossy print which came inside the envelope. Why do you ask that?'

'Only because I know it often happens. Do go on.'

'There was also a sheet of paper with a brief account of the story as I have reported it.'

'This account – was it typed or hand-written?'

'Typed – by someone not used to a typewriter, I think. It had a lot of mistakes. An old machine, I imagine.'

'What language?'

'In Finnish. If you will just eat your breakfast and listen, I will tell you. Your wife stepped out off the verge on a lonely road outside Helsinki. The driver was unable to stop and she was run over. This must be very painful for you.'

'Never mind about that. Just get on with it.'

'That was all there was in the account. My article reports the accident as it was typed in the story delivered to me. Of course, I made it longer – the editor wanted it as the lead story. But that was all the information I had to work from. You see, Alexis Bouvet visited me when she arrived here a week ago.'

'Has the body been discovered? You mentioned a lonely road outside Helsinki.'

'No, it hasn't, which is worrying the police. They think the hit-and-run driver may have dragged it off the road and left it in the forest.' She paused. 'It could be months before she is found.'

'And on the basis of this flimsy evidence – no body, no corroboration – you print this as a lead story? Is that how you conduct journalism in Finland?'

She flushed but kept her temper. Newman was under appalling strain, she reminded herself. She dabbed at her full lips with her napkin before replying, keeping her tone steady and detached.

'First, there is a query mark at the end of that headline – it is asking a question, not making a statement. Second, if you were able to read the text I wrote you'd see I make it a mysterious incident. I do not accept the fact that there is positive evidence that your wife is dead. Third, besides the photo and the typed statement there was another item inside the envelope.'

She reached inside her shoulder bag and brought out something she concealed in her hand. Newman drank more coffee and Laila watched him sympathetically.

'Before I show you this, prepare yourself for a shock.'

'I'm prepared. Get on with it.'

'You could be nicer to me – I am trying to help you.'

She opened her hand and passed to him a piece of costume jewellery, a brooch in the shape of the French Cross of Lorraine. Newman took it and his expression was blank as he stared at it in the palm of his own hand. He felt an awful pang.

'You say this was inside the envelope which arrived at your office? What does it prove?'

'When Alexis Bouvet visited me she was wearing that brooch. I deliberately did not mention the brooch in my article. You recognize the brooch?'

'Yes,' Newman admitted. 'She was an ardent Gaullist.'

'Ardent?'

'Enthusiastic, loyal. A great admirer of Jacques Chirac. It is the custom in Finland for hit-and-run drivers to report their crime to a newspaper? I assume it is a crime in Finland?'

'You are an impossible man!' He had at last got under her skin. She dropped her piece of roll on the plate and reached for her bag, prior to leaving.

Newman leaned across the table and took hold of her hand, detaining her. Apart from the letter Alexis had written him this girl was so far his only lead. He smiled and phrased his apology carefully.

'I'm sorry. You have been very good to me ever since I arrived. You even watched over me in the bedroom last night until I woke up and we came down here for dinner. But, as a journalist, I can tell you're experienced enough to be sceptical of anything you're told – '

'Now he flatters me!'

'Please! Hear me out. You said a moment ago you

were trying to help me. I think maybe you are – but I don't know a thing about you.'

'I told you Tweed, the insurance and security specialist in London, phoned me.'

'Yes, you did.'

Newman paused, working out what he should say next. And it was interesting that, like so many of Tweed's contacts, she thought he was the head of an elite and exclusive insurance outfit which, in exchange for large premiums, and in combination with a security outfit, looked after men and women who could be targets for kidnappers. It was a very convincing cover story. Among other things it explained why he had so many international connections, why he occasionally travelled extensively abroad. And why his work was shrouded in discretion and secrecy.

'If I'm going to confide in you I would like to know something more about you,' he suggested gently, still holding her hand.

'You think I'm just trying to steal your story, the one you're working on?' she challenged him. 'You are the great Bob Newman, the famous foreign correspondent who wrote that international bestseller, *Kruger: The Computer That Failed*. Is that what you think I'm doing?'

'When you Finnish girls let rip you really go through the roof, don't you?'

'Go through the roof?'

'Explode! Like a bomb. *Boom!*'

He grinned and her hand went limp in his grasp as she laughed. She relaxed in her chair, let go of her bag with her free hand. Behind her glasses her intense blue eyes regarded him keenly.

'May I have my hand back to finish my breakfast? I do only have two of them. And you are right. About the Finns, I mean. The men as well as the girls. It takes a lot to make us angry but when we do get angry, *Boom!*'

Newman released her hand and drank some orange juice. He had thought he had lost her – and he realized that would have been very stupid. He sensed she was making up her mind about something so he kept quiet and continued with his breakfast until she suddenly looked straight at him.

'I do understand that you should know more about me. And I am sure you would find out by yourself, being what you are. I am the daughter of a man high up in the Protection Police.'

'How high?'

'He is chief of the unit. Mauno Sarin.'

'My editor told me I could stay with you for several days – he's hoping I'll get a story out of you,' Laila said impishly.

'That's all editors ever think of,' Newman replied absent-mindedly.

They had put on raincoats and Laila had led the way across the empty road to the opposite building of the Kalastajatorppa. Again Newman was intrigued by the way the concrete blocks seemed to grow out of the granite crags. They went inside the building and it was deserted.

Newman followed her along a devious route which led down inside a circular, dimly lit room. 'The nightclub,' Laila explained. They climbed a curving staircase to ground floor level, and she opened a door to the park-like grounds beyond, which sloped down to the water's edge.

They descended a wide flight of shallow stone steps into the parkland which was also deserted. A light drizzle like a sea-mist drifted down and moistened their faces. The grey, leaden-coloured water stretching away to the distant shore was like a typical Finnish land-locked lake and Newman had to remind himself he was looking at a bay of the sea.

'When Alexis visited you at your office,' he began, 'had you any idea what she was looking for?'

'I was going to tell you. She was looking for an American, a man called Adam Procane. She had visited the big American Embassy and had somehow found out they had no one of that name on their large staff.'

'Why large?'

'Because this is Finland. The Russians also have a big Embassy. They watch the Americans and the Americans watch them. It is a kind of game they play. You must remember the Russian border is only two hundred and fifty kilometres east of Helsinki.'

'This American – what did you say his name is?'

'Adam Procane. According to Alexis he is very important – very high up. She did not say so, but I had the impression he is not a member of the embassy staff but is someone who will be visiting Helsinki soon.'

'I seem to remember from when I was last here that you have a lot of big passenger ships – liners, in fact – sailing from Helsinki.'

'That is so. They go to many places. To Stockholm, to Leningrad. They are Finnish ships. Then there is the Estonian Shipping Company which has frequent sailings for tourists to Tallinn in Estonia.'

'If I said the word *archipelago*, what would you immediately think of?'

'Two archipelagos,' Laila replied promptly. 'First, the Turku archipelago – that is a port to the west of Helsinki where the coast turns north into the Gulf of Bothnia. It is the second largest archipelago in the world, the first being the Greek archipelago. Geography was one of my better subjects at school,' she added modestly.

'And the other one? You said *two*.'

'The Swedish archipelago stretching out from Stockholm – it reaches out like a great arm to clasp hands with Turku, but there is a gap of clear sea between the two.'

'What is it like there out in the Turku archipelago? Have you ever been there?'

'Oh, yes. A boy-friend I once had was mad on

sailing. I have never seen anything like it – there are thousands of islands, some quite big. One has the capital of the archipelago which is called Maarian-hamina. Strictly speaking it is the capital of a group of islands called Ahvenanmaa – the Åland Islands in Swedish.'

'I think I find Swedish easier – and I can't speak that.'

'So we speak English and understand each other! This is where the helicopters – choppers, yes? – land.'

They had walked down a broad path to two land-ing-stages, one a fixed edifice of wooden planks leading to the second, a floating landing-stage which Newman walked out on to. It bobbed up and down slowly beneath his feet. To his left was a dense tangle of reeds growing in the sea like a small jungle.

The drizzle had drifted away now and he stood, feeling the undulation as the stage swayed in the water, staring out across the water where a distant patch of white moved at speed, leaving behind a streak of white wake. A large power-boat heading south.

'Let us go sit on that seat,' suggested Laila who had come up behind him.

When they had sat down she produced a thick folded map from her bag. Opening it section by section, she spread it across their laps.

'I thought this might be useful. As you see, it is a street plan of Helsinki. You may keep it, Bob.'

'Thanks.' Newman was studying it with interest. 'Helsinki is one of the strangest cities in Europe.'

'I like it! I was born here.'

'Don't be so touchy. I meant fascinating. Its geography – you told me you knew about geography – '

'So why is it strange – fascinating?'

'Well, for one thing it's built on a long peninsula – which means it's surrounded on three sides by water. For another, it has more than one harbour – North Harbour, South Harbour – '

'South Harbour is where those ships sail from I was talking about. According to your destination, you leave from a different wharf – or dock – '

'This one here, Laila?'

'Estonian Shipping Company.'

'So I could find sailing times of all the ships by going to the harbour? An obvious question, really.'

'I could do that for you. I think you are very tired – why not stay here away from Helsinki for a few days and have a rest? It is very peaceful.'

It was very peaceful. As they sat, the only sound was the gentle splash of tiny waves lapping on isolated spits of dirt-grey beaches protruding into the lake – the bay, Newman reminded himself. Here and there more landing-stages projected into the water. Moored to one was a rowing-boat rocking slowly, a rowing-boat with a bright red trim.

'Did Alexis talk about anything else besides this Adam Procane?' he asked.

'Yes, she did.' Laila screwed up her eyes in concentration behind her glasses. 'It was a funny conversation – she jumped backwards and forwards. She said she'd heard rumours that a number of Russian Military Intelligence officers had been murdered – strangled – across the water.'

'Where was she referring to?'

'She didn't say – just across the water. That would be in Estonia. We also have heard these rumours. I tried to follow them up, sensing a story. I tried to question one of the crew who came off an Estonian boat and he looked frightened and wouldn't talk about it.'

'Military Intelligence? The GRU, you mean?'

'That's right. Then Alexis switched again and asked me almost the same question about the archipelagos you asked.'

'You said there are thousands of islands.'

'Yes. Many of them are little more than smooth, rounded rocks sticking up out of the sea. Sailing in those channels can be dangerous – and you can easily get lost unless you are with one of the fishermen who knows his way round every rock.'

'You know someone like that?'

'Yes, I do. He's a close friend. Why?'

'You could introduce me to him if I wanted to ask him a few questions?'

'No problem. But I still think you should have a quiet weekend. You look exhausted.'

'I think I agree. One final question. Alexis was supposed to have been knocked down by a car on a lonely road outside Helsinki. Do you know a weird-looking castle, very old with turrets and perched high up – somewhere outside Helsinki?'

'A castle? You mean like one of your English castles? I once visited England and I saw Windsor and Warwick Castles. They were wonderful – but we do not have anything like that in Finland. I think you would laugh at what we call a castle.' She twisted on the seat and her shoulder pressed against Newman's. 'It is very odd – but this conversation reminds me of the one I had with Alexis Bouvet.'

'I suppose we naturally talked in the same way,' he said easily, fending her off.

He was thinking of a phrase Laila had used earlier about Alexis – *she jumped backwards and forwards*. He was pretty sure he knew what Alexis had been doing. She had muddled up the conversation – so Laila couldn't see what she was really after. He sat watching the sea as he tried to put the pieces together.

The murders of the GRU officers in Estonia. The reference to Adam Procane. The questions about the archipelago. What had he got? None of it seemed to link up. The topics appeared to be isolated, random, not to connect.

'It's going to rain heavily,' Laila remarked. 'Maybe we had better get back to the hotel.'

'That's OK by me – how do you know?'

'Look across the bay – you can see it coming.'

'The weather here changes fast.'

'That's Finland. You get a heavy shower, then it stops and it is beautiful again.'

Above the distant shore banks of low clouds, black as the fir forest walling in the bay, moved rapidly eastwards towards Helsinki and the hotel. A dark, veiled curtain showed it was already raining heavily on the opposite shore. They hurried back along the wide path under the pine trees and Laila pointed to a strange, many-sided building with a circular roof like the top of a huge pagoda.

'That is the Round House restaurant. It would be very nice for you to have dinner there tonight.'

'Only if you will join me.'

'I would love to. I think I will now catch the No. 4 tram into Helsinki and check on those sailing times. You stay here and rest?' she enquired anxiously.

'Anything you say.'

'You see that building beyond the Round House?'

She indicated an ancient, single-storey structure which reminded Newman of a large cabin. It was the oldest part of the hotel.

'That is the original Fisherman's Cottage,' Laila explained. 'It was standing here long before they built the hotel. The architect was clever enough to leave it – he simply made the inside modern.'

They ran up the broad flight of steps leading to the hotel as large spots of rain began to fall. Inside, Laila showed Newman the way to the tunnel linking the two buildings and they parted.

The underground tunnel which ran beneath the road was very strange. On either side it was moulded into rounded rocks of mock limestone, so Newman had the sensation he was walking inside a glacier. Emerging at the far end into the main building, he fetched the envelope containing the photo of Alexis from his room and returned to the reception counter.

'A close relative of mine stayed here very recently,' he explained to the man behind the counter. 'Her name is Alexis Bouvet. Did she leave a forwarding address?'

The man's expression became wooden: he was not enthusiastic about the question, about giving out information concerning guests. He consulted the register, possibly remembering that Newman was paying for a suite, then shook his head.

'No one of that name, I am afraid, sir.'

There was nothing more Newman could do but come out into the open. He produced the copy of Laila's newspaper and spread out the front page on the counter top. To this he added the glossy print taken from the silver frame in his London flat.

'I'm talking about my wife,' he said quietly.

'I am sorry, Mr Newman.' The receptionist only glanced at the print. 'Yes, this lady did stay here for the week before you arrived. I remember her well – a most handsome woman, if I may say so. She paid for the whole week in advance and one night she did not come back – two days before her reservation was ended. She left some effects in her room.'

'May I see them? I am talking about my wife.'

'I understand that, sir. I did not recognize the name you gave me first – you see, she registered as Mrs Alexis Newman.'

'And these effects?'

The receptionist looked uneasy. 'They were collected a few hours before you arrived by some officials from Helsinki.'

'The police – from headquarters at Pasila?'

'No, sir.' The receptionist's discomfort increased. 'It was two officials who carried written authority to take away Mrs Newman's effects.'

Then Newman guessed what he was talking about but did not wish to put into words. Two officials. From the secret police, the Protection Police. Of course. At Ratakatu. He dropped the subject and switched his angle of interrogation.

'Can you tell me anything particular she did while she was staying here? Anything a little out of the ordinary?'

'One morning, soon after her arrival, she made use of the helicopter service. There is a helicopter which takes off from near the landing-stage on the other side of the hotel by the sea.'

'Yes, I know. You mean this outfit over there?'

Newman gestured towards an enclosed, box-like office inside the reception hall. The receptionist nodded and Newman collected his photo, the newspaper, and went across to the office. A dark-haired girl looked up from her desk as he entered through the open doorway. He dropped both the photo and the newspaper on her desk and spoke firmly, making statements rather than asking questions.

'The receptionist has just told me my wife, Alexis Newman, hired one of your choppers. I need to know where the pilot took her.'

'Yes, that is correct, Mr Newman. I remember her – but she didn't want the usual tour. She hired our machine for some special trip. In this helicopter.'

She handed him a large colour photo of a Hughes 500 D, one of the smallest helicopters. The interior looked very cramped and the picture showed the machine airborne, hovering while the pilot operated a camera.

'Where did she go?' Newman asked.

'I do not know. I booked the machine, she paid a deposit, and it was agreed she would pay the rest of the fee when she returned.'

'Could I book the same machine – with the same pilot?'

'No problem, sir. But Monday would be the first day when he will be available.'

Newman paid his own deposit and she wrote her phone number on the brochure. 72 72 57. As he was leaving, he turned back at the doorway and asked again if she had any idea of the destination.

'She did say something about South Harbour, sir.'

*

Laila took the No. 4 tram from its terminal point, which was five minutes' brisk walk from the Kalasta-jatorppa, and was the only passenger to board the tram. It wended its way through a pleasant upper-class residential district of small apartment blocks erected many years ago amid the trees.

She stayed on board until it reached a stop on Mannerheimintie, the main street leading into the city, and got off near the Hesperia Hotel, a curved, multi-storey block looking out on to a modern Finnish sculpture made of pieces of metal which revolved in the breeze like a giant *glockenspiel*.

Plunging uphill into the back streets which are lined with old and less exclusive apartment buildings. she let herself into her first-floor flat and picked up the phone the moment she had dropped her shoulder bag. She dialled the number Tweed had given her of the London and Cumbria Assurance Co.

'I am afraid he is not available today,' Monica informed her. 'Who shall I say called him?'

'Just a friend,' Laila replied and broke the connection.

She left her flat again and walked deeper into the city, past the two sculptured stone vertical slabs which are supposed to represent President Kekkonen. At the Ageba Travel Agency she obtained a list of the sailings of all ships from Helsinki to Leningrad, Tallinn, Stockholm and – as an afterthought – Turku.

She then walked into the bar of the nearby Hotel

Marski and sat drinking a cup of black coffee. Laila was worried. Instinctively she felt she had somehow to keep Bob Newman out of circulation until she was able to talk to Tweed. The trouble was – she knew from the questions he had asked – the aggressive Englishman had already started his investigation into how his wife had died and who was responsible for her death.

Chapter Eight

In his shirt-sleeves, Newman paced the sitting room of his suite like a caged tiger. It was more like a conference room than a sitting room. There was a large rectangular table in the centre surrounded with chairs. Furniture designers in Finland, like their fellow architects, were keen on rectangles.

The cupboards in his bedroom, made of dark wood, were a series of rectangular boxes. The same rectangular motif was repeated in the so-called sitting room. On the table lay his scribbling pad with a felt-tip pen thrown down on top of it.

The Finnish weather had changed again. He stopped for a moment to stare down across the flat roof which was puddled with recent rain. The clouds had evaporated – so it seemed. The vast blue sky was clear, the bay was a sheet of calm, unruffled water. What had he got? He went back and stared at the pad where he had scribbled at odd angles the facts he had accumulated.

A boat which left somewhere at 10.30 a.m. South Harbour? An American called Procane – who apparently didn't exist, but who 'has to be stopped'.

Stopped from doing what? Only Alexis had known. A weird castle perched high up – and Alexis was supposed to have died on a lonely road outside Helsinki.

'A castle . . . but we do not have anything like that in Finland.' Or so Laila had said, and she ought to know. Newman stared at the sketch he had drawn of a castle on the pad from his memory of the background to that hideous film. Like his brief notes on the other items, he had circled the castle.

He was looking for a pattern – some way he could draw lines from one circle to another, to create links. And there weren't any. He lit a cigarette. Inside another circle he had written the words, *murders of GRU officers in Estonia?* That could so easily be pure rumour. God knew, from his last visit to Finland, the place was alive with rumours – often spread by staff from the American and Soviet embassies.

Police Protection Unit. Inside another sweeping circle on his pad. A fresh fact. Why were they so interested in Alexis? Newman strongly suspected they had collected the things left by Alexis in her room to erase all traces of her visit to Helsinki. If so, they had blundered – not that they could have foreseen Newman would turn up so quickly at the hotel where she had stayed.

The Finns were in a difficult position internationally. They had the giant shadow of Russia looming on their eastern border. The Soviets supplied Finland with all its oil – in return for a flow of Finnish manufactured goods. Theoretically, the Kremlin should have a stranglehold on Helsinki.

But the Finns walked their tightrope between East and West with great skill. They maintained their precarious independence by refusing to become a Soviet satellite – by cultivating trade with the West to counterbalance the Bear.

Newman sat down at the table and stared at two more facts he had scribbled on his notepad and circled. *Ratakatu*. The headquarters of the Protection Police, which is located in a quite different part of the city from Helsinki's police headquarters at Pasila.

That item worried him. Laila had admitted her father was the chief of the secret police unit. Was she, at this moment, reporting to him her conversations with Newman?

But there was a contradiction here: Laila had written the article about Alexis's alleged fatal accident outside Helsinki. Surely Mauno Sarin – whom Newman had met on his previous visit – would not be pleased about that? Which cancelled out the idea that Mauno had his daughter in his pocket.

The chopper. This was a fresh piece of information Newman had stumbled on by his persistent questioning of the receptionist. Where had the Hughes 500 D machine flown her to? He should know all the details of her flight on Monday. Newman was convinced that if he could only track Alexis's last movements he would be closer to the truth. Patience. It was so often the key to success when a foreign correspondent was digging out a story.

'Here is the list of ship sailings and times from Helsinki,' said Laila and handed Newman a sheet of paper across the table.

They were having dinner in the upper level of the Round House reached by a curving staircase. They had a ringside table looking straight down on to the tables below. Newman took the paper and glanced down the sailing times written in a neat script.

'You don't waste much time, do you?' he commented.

'In my job you have to get on with things at once.' She flushed when she realized what she had said. 'But, of course, you have known that for years.'

'I'm congratulating you.'

'Is there anything there which helps?' she asked before continuing her meal.

'Even negative information can be useful,' he replied.

'So, what you were looking for is not there?'

'Look, Laila, you know as well as I do by now that if you can eliminate certain leads, this points you in the direction of the other leads you should follow up.'

Newman poured more Chablis into their glasses to conceal his excitement. Among the various sailings there was only one ship which departed at 10.30 a.m. – the *Georg Ots*, sailing for Tallinn, Estonia.

It sounded like some kind of tourist ship, arriving at Tallinn at 15.00 hours. It then departed from Tallinn at 19.30 hours, arriving back at Helsinki at 22.30 hours. What especially intrigued Newman was that Laila had first written the name of the shipping line as Oy Saimaa Lines Ltd – which sounded comfortingly Finnish. But in brackets she had added Estonia Shipping Company – which meant the *Georg Ots* was probably a Soviet vessel.

'Where did you get this information from?' he enquired.

'The Ageba Travel Service. They have an office close to the Marski Hotel – only a few metres further down the main street.'

She reached for the piece of paper and wrote something extra at the bottom. He looked at the addition. *Ageba Travel Service, Pohjoisranta 4.* Thank God so many of the Finns spoke English.

'Is there further information you need?' she asked.

'I don't think so.' He stared at her across the table and realized she had taken trouble over dressing for her dinner with him. She was wearing a clinging, black dress decorated with small gold dragons. It had a mandarin collar which emphasized her firm and shapely chin.

'You really are a very beautiful girl,' he commented.

'Thank you, Bob.' She looked shy and pleased.

'Seen your father recently? Or had any contact with him?'

'Why do you ask that?'

She dropped her knife and fork on her plate and her expression stiffened. The glow of pleasure had gone and was replaced by a mood of annoyance and indignation reflected in the way she had asked the question.

'I just assumed you had regular contact with your father.'

'In his capacity as chief of the Protection Police?'

She had lowered her voice, leaning across the table towards him, and her voice was as cold as the ice in the glasses of the American couple at the next table. Newman realized another Finnish sonic *Boom!* was on the way. Her expression mirrored her tone.

'Simply in his capacity as father to daughter,' he replied.

'I think not! You believe I have been reporting to him all we have talked about together? You think *that* was why I met you at Vantaa when you came off the plane? You trust me that much? Well, Mr Newman, I have news for you. I do not get on too well with my father. I became a newspaper reporter against his wishes. I have not seen – or talked with – him for over two months. And I am no longer hungry. Just coffee, please – and then I go home.'

Newman made no attempt to get Laila to change her mind. He was in a pretty grim mood himself, but his brain overrode his emotions. She was either lying – in which case she had missed her vocation as an actress – or she was genuinely upset.

He had to be sure the latter was the case; if it was, she'd go home. They drank their coffee in silence, he signed the bill and Laila stood up and slipped on her coat before he could assist her.

At the other tables couples were now in a mellow mood, chattering happily and drinking large quantities of alcohol as Newman and Laila left. He escorted her outside where several cabs waited. One of them had the Finnish *Taksi* sign lit up, the others had the more simple *Taxi*.

She thanked him politely but formally for the dinner, said good night and drove off inside a cab. Newman shrugged his shoulders and walked slowly back across the road to his room in the main building. He was a loner by nature, even more so when engaged on a job. And he was engaged on the most bitter job of his life so far. Better alone.

On Saturday, 1 September – the day Tweed spent in Geneva meeting Alain Charvet, the ex-policeman who ran a private investigation agency – General Lysenko flew from Moscow to Leningrad, which he called his 'advance base'.

Lysenko liked to lace his conversation with military terms and regarded Leningrad as the ideal location from which to conduct what he now called 'Operation Procane'. With him travelled his chief aide, Captain Valentin Rebet, known in Moscow circles as 'Lysenko's shadow'.

Rebet was a tall man of thirty-five with trim black hair and an encyclopaedic memory. He was also a first-rate administrator and complemented his more boisterous chief who disliked desk work. Lysenko asked Rebet the question as soon as they were settled in his office, which was on the second floor of a grey slab of a building overlooking the river Neva on Arsenal Quay near the Finland Station.

'Well, Rebet, what have we got?'

Rebet pushed his rimless glasses to the top of the bridge of his long nose and opened a file.

Lysenko was a very physical man, never happier than when he was flying or driving to a new destination, bombarding his subordinates with questions. He consumed large quantities of vodka and *lakka*, the Finnish liqueur distilled from cloudberries. He had an equally large appetite for women. As Rebet had once observed to a colleague, 'When you see his wife you can understand why.'

Valentin Rebet was the intellectual side of the duo, a man who could sit up half the night studying files and agents' reports. If anyone could arrange a series of apparently unrelated facts into a coherent picture, that man was Rebet.

'First, we have the mysterious series of murders of GRU officers in Tallinn,' he began, 'murders which, on the surface, appear without motive.'

'They are obviously the work of the so-called Estonian resistance movement.'

Lysenko jumped up and stumped across to stare

out of the window on his stocky legs. Rebet glanced up and narrowed his eyes, then continued.

'There is no evidence to support that conclusion. There is something very strange about these macabre killings. Four men garrotted – and all GRU officers. Why GRU? Then we have the eminent Colonel Andrei Karlov sitting in Tallinn who now has a dual task.'

'Eminent?' Lysenko roared out the word. 'He's a lickspittle who crawled on his belly to his superiors in the hope of gaining promotion.'

'Karlov is one of the most eminent military analysts in the Red Army,' Rebet persisted. 'And have you seen his latest report which has just come in – again casting doubts on the true value of the information supplied by the mysterious Procane?'

'He's covering himself – because he was the conduit in London who passed on that information. Moscow is convinced Procane is potentially the most important catch we could lay our hands on since the end of World War Two.'

'I think it was a mistake to put him in charge of the investigation of the GRU assassinations. He should be concentrating on helping the unknown Adam Procane to cross over. And a second report has already arrived from the military attaché at our Paris Embassy – that Procane is on his way.'

'So, what is our next move, Comrade?' Lysenko demanded.

'We should inform all the embassies in Western Europe – and particularly unofficial contacts – to report immediately the arrival of any senior American diplomat, Intelligence or military man. Procane will have to invent a convincing reason for crossing the Atlantic – the first stage of his journey to reach us. According to his initial destination we may be able to predict the route he will take across Europe.'

'I will send out an immediate alert,' Lysenko agreed. He lit one of his cardboard holder cigarettes, which meant he liked the idea. Action! That was Lysenko's forte.

'In the meantime, there is a third factor – which I mentioned to you before. The killing of the French woman journalist, Alexis Bouvet, by that mad sadist, Poluchkin. Plus the further madness of sending his film of the murder to London and the photograph with a report to a Helsinki newspaper. More madness.'

'Leave matters of high policy to those who understand them. Anything else you have an observation to make on? If not, we must attend to sending out the general alert for an American. A sound idea, that, Comrade.'

Lysenko was only too aware that Rebet was invaluable to him, that he had the ideas. He was the only subordinate Lysenko occasionally patted on the back. Not too often, mind you – no point in giving a man the sense that he was indispensable.

'I am worried about the whole series of events in Estonia,' Rebet repeated, 'because I cannot yet link these incidents together.'

'They have to be linked?' Lysenko questioned abruptly.

'I just don't believe in coincidence,' Rebet told him.

That was Saturday. On Sunday afternoon Tweed flew back to London from Brussels after his meeting with Julius Ravenstein, the man known as 'White Star' to the Antwerp diamond industry.

On Monday, 3 September he arrived late at Park Crescent, and the moment he entered the building he sensed something had happened. Monica was waiting for him impatiently behind her desk and watched him as he took off his Burberry. The two-month-old heat-wave had broken and it was much cooler with a light drizzle falling.

'There have been urgent phone calls for you,' she reported. 'From Paris, Frankfurt and Geneva.'

'The pot is beginning to simmer.'

'What pot? What is going on?'

'I can't tell you. I'm sorry. From now on you will, I regret to say, be working entirely in the dark.'

'Lovely. That will be a new experience,' she said tartly.

'It's that directive,' he soothed her. 'I have to work on this one entirely on my own. Eventually you will see why.'

'Can't wait!'

She pretended to busy herself examining a file. Tweed swore inwardly. Over the years she had shared

115

every detail of what was going on, no matter how high risk the undertaking. He began to hate the Procane business a little more. Monica spoke rapidly, not looking at her chief.

'All data on those calls are on your desk. No one would talk to me. The one from Frankfurt was a woman, the other two were men. They wanted you to call back urgently.'

'I'll get on with it now.'

'Should I leave the office?'

He looked at her over the rims of his spectacles, then shook his head. She burst out again.

'I hate you when you look at me like that!'

He called Frankfurt first. After he had dialled, there was a brief pause and then Lisa Brandt's lilting voice came on the line. He suspected she had been waiting by her phone for his call.

'I'm recording this conversation,' he warned, and pressed a button on the instrument which activated the tape-recorder concealed in the third drawer down on his right.

It was mostly a one-sided conversation. Lisa talked and he listened. Occasionally he asked a brief question. Her report was concise and businesslike – very different from their chatty conversation over lunch at the Intercontinental. He thanked her and replaced the receiver.

'Who types the recording?' Monica asked more quietly.

'I do,' said Tweed, and left it at that.

He repeated the same exercise with André Moutet in Paris and then with Alain Charvet in Geneva. They were both waiting for his call. When he had completed his phoning he collected his old Remington portable from a cupboard, fed a sheet into the machine, used the ear-phones from the tape-recorder and typed a report of all three conversations. One copy only. He shredded the three backing sheets he had used, aware that Monica was deliberately not watching him.

He then inserted each report into a zip-up file and arranged the three files in a neat pile on his desk. The job completed, he took off his glasses and started cleaning them. Monica, reading his signal, closed her file and waited. He cleared his throat before he began speaking.

'I'm keeping you out of this thing because it's quite the most delicate problem I've handled since I came here. If it should backfire I don't want you involved.'

'Backfire?'

Monica's indignation and disappointment evaporated. It was replaced by anxiety, genuine concern. She stared hard at her boss.

'It could backfire – very easily,' Tweed told her. 'If the whole thing blows up in my face I don't want any of it rubbing off on you. Howard isn't too fond of you – but he's fair.'

'But I expected – hoped – this could lead to promotion –'

'I'm walking a tightrope over an abyss. Better not to forget it . . .'

Her anxiety increased. Howard chose this moment to walk into the office and say exactly the wrong thing. His smooth face was flushed, excited, and he was at his most pompous.

'I need a word with you alone.' He glanced at Monica. 'I did say alone.'

'If you ask her nicely, she will respond. Please don't forget she is a trusted member of staff,' Tweed said waspishly.

'Maybe that was a bit blunt.' It was the nearest Howard could bring himself to an apology. 'Something serious – very – has happened. I need to take Tweed's personal advice on the development. Thank you, Monica.'

. . . *to take Tweed's personal advice.* Inwardly Tweed winced at this typical Howard language. Sounded as though he was consulting his bloody doctor. He sat quite still when they were alone as Howard poured out words.

'I've just had on the scrambler the last person I want to hear from. He must have got up in the middle of the night to call me. Sometimes I think he never goes to bed. God, someone has put the proverbial cat among the damned pigeons. To hear him go on you'd think World War Three had broken out – '

'Who are we talking about?' Tweed interjected.

'Cord Dillon! In person. He's actually flying over here today. You'll meet him at Heathrow, of course. I can give you the details of his flight.'

'No,' said Tweed.

118

'I beg your pardon?'

'No. I won't meet him at Heathrow.'

'Someone has to.' Howard sounded distraught. He sat down in Tweed's comfortable leather armchair and ran his hands through his hair. 'Why won't you do the honours?'

'Bad tactics.'

Cord Dillon. Deputy Director of the CIA. Howard loathed the man – basically, in Tweed's view, because he couldn't handle the fiery American. He recalled Dillon's previous encounter with Howard in his presence.

'You Brits had better get off your asses and make some waves. We can't do the whole goddamn job ourselves – but I guess the way things go over here we're going to have to. Why can't you make waves?'

'Because we don't happen to be King Canutes,' Howard had responded stiffly.

'I thought that guy was trying to stop them coming in,' Dillon had snapped back.

This was the American crossing the Atlantic to thrust his highly unwelcome presence on them. Howard again asked Tweed if he would meet Dillon and Tweed again refused. Something in Tweed's manner made Howard suspect he was secretly pleased with this development.

'Why,' he asked Howard, 'are we so honoured?'

'Because he's had reports from Paris that an American called Adam Procane is about to go over to the Soviets. You know what he's like. I could hardly get a word in edgeways.' He stood up and grasped the bottom edges of his jacket, straightening it. 'I suppose I'll have to go and meet him myself then.'

'That's up to you.'

'*You* are in charge of the Procane investigation,' Howard complained somewhat petulantly.

'Which is why I am not laying out any red carpets for Dillon.'

'Anything you would care to tell me about what is going on? I hear the switchboard wires are burning with messages from the continent.'

'You might care to read these reports.'

Tweed handed the three zip-up files to his chief and sat back while Howard read the reports standing up. His expression of gloom and irritation deepened as he scanned the three sheets and then dropped them back on the desk.

'Jesus Christ, Tweed! Paris, Frankfurt and Geneva are all reporting the same message – that Procane is expected in Europe on his way to Russia.' He sank back into the armchair and threw out his hands in a gesture of despair. 'You do realize the implications behind this? With Reagan up for re-election in November, can you imagine the effect if the news of a major spy scandal broke? It could lose him the election. It begins to look as though Washington has a rotten egg who could be much bigger than Philby. You do realize the implications?' he repeated.

'Perfectly. I have just returned from visiting all those cities – also Brussels. I have contacted my main informants who are now checking any rumours re Procane. The results – much quicker than I expected, I admit – are in those reports.'

'And just who are *A, B* and *C*?'

'My informants. They have to be protected up to the hilt. If the Russians get wind of this – and they will – they might try to kidnap one or more of my informants to pressure them for information. *D* I'm still waiting to hear from. That informant is in Brussels.'

'And the object of the exercise?'

Tweed pressed a switch on his intercom. 'Monica, you can come back now. It's quite safe.'

He waited until Monica had returned and sat behind her desk. Howard frowned but made no comment. As Tweed expected to be out of the country again, he had decided she must have some idea of what was going on. And Howard was now a witness to the fact that she was only in possession of certain aspects of the operation.

'The object of the exercise,' Tweed explained, 'is the hope – and it is a pretty slim one – that we can stop Procane before he takes off for Moscow. If we do succeed, imagine the amount of credit we'll build up with Washington. They always think we muff everything. It's time we built up a very large credit balance.'

'But we haven't any bloody idea who Procane is,' Howard objected. 'Or have we?'

'No idea at all. I told you it was a pretty slim hope, so we can but try.'

'And may I be so bold as to enquire how we go about the job?'

'My first move I explained a few minutes ago. The next step is to issue a general alert to our entire network on the continent, instructing it to watch all likely routes Procane might use to proceed to Russia. One obvious possibility is Antwerp – I happen to know the Soviet freighter, *Taganrog*, has berthed there very recently for so-called repairs. That's the way Burgess and Maclean got out.'

'A bit obvious, as you said.'

'They might think we'll overlook the obvious.'

'And how do we go about detaining any American approaching the Antwerp docks?'

'The Belgian counter-espionage people would arrest him on some phoney charge. Papers not in order, something like that. If a real emergency arises we can have the traitor kidnapped – then brought here for interrogation.'

'That's pretty strong stuff.'

'You think Cord Dillon would object?'

'No, I suppose he wouldn't. He's sailed pretty close to the wind in the past. You don't propose to show him those – '

Howard gestured towards the files on Tweed's desk as though they were sticks of suspect gelignite. Tweed put them away in a drawer which he locked before replying.

'I shall most certainly show him those papers. Co-operation is something the Americans appreciate.'

'He'll blow his top!'

'That, I think, I may be able to endure. What I do find hard to endure is the joker you've slipped into the pack.'

'What the hell are you talking about?' Howard demanded.

'Bob Newman. You showed him that film and now he's rushed off to Finland. You know Newman once he's roused – he's not easy to control. And you did mention the name Procane to him. I have to say I think that was a major mistake which is in danger of gumming up the whole works. To say nothing of the danger Newman himself may walk into.'

'I think,' Howard announced, standing up, 'that I had better check my desk before I push off to the airport to meet Dillon.'

'When does he arrive?'

'18.10 hours this evening. He's aboard BA Flight 192 – Concorde. I'll bring him straight here and dump him in your lap.'

'Not the latter bit – he's the wrong sex.'

There were times when Tweed displayed a quirkish sense of humour which never ceased to surprise even his closest friends. The reply did not appeal to Howard.

'Can I help?' asked Monica when they were alone.

'Yes. And it will keep you busy all day. Alert the whole network about a senior American official – CIA,

NSA, the Pentagon, the lot. Anyone trying to follow a route which would take them to the USSR. My guess would be seaports where there are ships berthed from any Eastern bloc country – and all airports.'

'What about trains?'

'I don't think he'll use them. He'll want a quick getaway, transport which gets him behind the Iron Curtain fast '

'Any particular area to concentrate on?'

'Yes. Scandinavia.'

The call from Laila Sarin came through about an hour later.

'Mr Tweed? This is Laila.'

She sounded nervous and upset. Tweed gripped the receiver more tightly. He immediately set about reassuring her, talking to her like a favourite uncle.

'Laila, I'm delighted to hear from you so quickly. I'm afraid I've given you a very difficult assignment this time. Why do I say that? Everything you've done for me has been difficult – '

'I tried to call you earlier. Before the weekend. Some woman answered and said you weren't available.'

'She was telling the truth. Now, how are things going?'

'Very badly. I have let you down. I am so sorry. I met the Englishman as requested – at the airport. I persuaded him to let me accompany him to his hotel – the Kalastajatorppa.' She spelt it out for him and he scribbled it down on his notepad. 'I spent quite a lot of time with him and told him about how his wife visited me at my office ten days ago. He asked me a lot of questions about what she had said.'

She gave the details concisely and Tweed scribbled furiously on his pad. Everything Alexis had mentioned or asked. Then the details of her conversations with Newman. He went on scribbling. He could have recorded the conversation but he didn't want her to know he had this facility – and it seemed unfair to record without informing. Tweed had a soft spot for the Finnish girl. Then came the nub.

'Mr Tweed, I went back to his hotel this morning to make my peace with him and he was no longer there. He flew off in a helicopter – a private one – and took his bag with him after he had paid his bill. I've no idea where he is.'

'Where are you calling from?'

'My flat. I waited for the helicopter to return and the pilot was alone. I couldn't get him to say what had happened. I think Bob – Mr Newman – had paid him enough to keep his mouth shut. I really am so sorry. I have never let you down before but this time I feel awful.'

'You've done better than you realize. I'm wiring you some money. Same bank as before?'

'Mr Tweed!' Her voice rose several decibels. 'I have

just started. You don't think I'm going to let Mr Newman get away with this, do you? I'll tear Helsinki apart until I find him again – and this is *my* town.'

Tweed was taken aback by her vehemence, by her determination to go on. He had badly underestimated this girl's tenacity and character. He blinked across at Monica who was watching him.

'I'm still sending that money – maybe a little more than I'd decided. You'll need funds.'

'As before, you will receive a careful account of all expenditure,' she said primly. 'I'll report back the moment I have located him. Goodbye – for now.'

Tweed replaced the receiver and marvelled. He started polishing his glasses furiously. Was this going to turn out to be a case where the amateurs beat the pros? It had happened before.

'Something wrong?' Monica enquired tentatively.

'My worst fears realized. Newman has gone missing.'

Chapter Nine

It was the morning of Monday, 3 September in Leningrad. General Lysenko, in full uniform, walked into his office and threw his greatcoat down on a shabby leather couch. Captain Valentin Rebet was already working behind his own desk, studying some sheets which Lysenko noticed were stamped with a top security classification.

'There have been developments,' Rebet informed him. 'Serious ones.'

'And so the week will go on, crisis upon crisis . . .'

Lysenko looked round his office and lit his third cigarette of the day. The walls were lined with grey filing cabinets which matched the grey tiles on the austere floor. Lysenko was a man indifferent to all forms of comfort. The cabinets were Rebet's. The General had very little idea of their contents – and no clue as to the filing system which Rebet had organized.

'Tell me the worst,' he growled.

'It appears Colonel Karlov is wrong in expressing doubts about Adam Procane. I have three separate reports which came in over the weekend – all speak of Procane being on his way here, all from reliable sources.'

'What sources?'

Lysenko took up his usual stance by the window. People were trudging to work across the river, huddled against the rain drifting in from the Baltic. It was a dreary morning, reflecting Lysenko's Monday mood.

'The embassy in Paris, the consulates in Frankfurt and Geneva,' Rebet informed him in his precise manner. 'The military attaché in Paris refers to an unimpeachable source. It's the same story from Germany and Switzerland.'

'Inform Moscow.'

'I have already done so. Under your signature,' Rebet added.

'Good. Good. Any reference to his real identity?'

'None whatsoever.'

'He's a careful bastard. That's good, too. Any indication as to the route he will take? Maybe we ought to make plans about that?' Lysenko suggested.

'How can we at this stage? We are dealing with a man of glass.'

'We can alert every embassy and consulate in Western Europe to prepare contingency plans.'

'That might be very unwise. Think of how many people would then know about Procane. Someone would let something slip – and it would get back to Washington. I suggest we wait a while. We could consult Karlov – he was the original contact with this man of glass.'

'You mean phone Tallinn?'

'With respect, I think that would also be unwise, General. We are still not sure how far the American satellites have penetrated our telephone system. It might be better if I flew to Tallinn and talked to Karlov personally.'

'I agree. With reservation. But for the moment, I leave you to take all decisions concerning Procane. While you are away I will put that in writing. No, better still, I'll dictate the directive and you can take it with you.' Lysenko became bluff and cordial, hammering Rebet on the shoulder. 'It will give you more authority when you meet Karlov.'

'Thank you.'

Rebet's expression was blank. Lysenko was up to his old tricks. Put it in writing that a subordinate is in charge of an operation that could go wrong; as Lysenko knew only too well *all* operations could misfire. That was the moment to dump someone else in the shit. If he was anything, Lysenko was a practised wheeler-dealer. Always guard your back. How else do you become a general?

The chopper pilot's name was Jorma Takala. He arrived at the Kalastajatorppa at nine on Monday morning and Newman, who had already paid his bill, took him into the breakfast room for a cup of coffee. Dumping his bag beside him, Newman was relieved to find that, like many Finns, Takala spoke excellent English.

'This is the girl I'm talking about,' Newman explained and showed Takala his picture of Alexis. 'Recognize her?'

'I remember her well – a beautiful woman who knew exactly what she wanted. Your girl-friend?' he enquired cautiously.

'My wife. She probably gave her professional name, Alexis Bouvet.'

'Yes, she did.'

The pilot hesitated, studying Newman. He would be about thirty, Newman estimated; a tall, blond-haired man wearing a blue jumpsuit and track shoes. Takala drank some coffee before he continued.

'I read the story in the paper. I am very sorry your journey to Finland should be such a sad occasion.'

'Thank you. Now, let's get on with it. I need to know where you took her – I not only want you to follow precisely the same route, I want the same timing. Can you manage that?'

Takala nodded. 'Funny you should ask that – your wife also was very particular about both timing and route. Maybe I just show you? OK. Then we have time to drink a lot of coffee – we took off at exactly ten in the morning. My machine is waiting at the other side of the hotel.'

'I've seen the pad where you land. One other thing,' Newman produced a sheaf of bank notes. 'That's extra to the flight fee. A girl reporter may try and question you – she's made herself a perfect nuisance since I arrived.'

'Not very considerate. But reporters – ' Takala made a throwaway gesture as though he'd like to drop all newspaper reporters into the sea. He poured himself more coffee and Newman remembered the Finns drank the stuff by the litre.

'I will tell her nothing,' Takala went on. 'No details about route or timing. And this tip is too much – '

'Keep it. Tell me something about your job.'

They chatted until it was time and then, at Newman's suggestion, used the underground tunnel to reach the other building. He had an instinctive feeling that Laila might turn up this morning. He had no compunction about tricking her: Newman was in a cold and clinical mood now that he had a positive lead to follow.

The Hughes 500 D looked like a large toy when they emerged at the head of the steps. It stood on its landing skids beyond a chain Takala had raised across the wide path at the edge of the landing-stage.

Seated next to the pilot, Newman put on the headset which had earpieces and a microphone close to his mouth. When the rotors started roaring, this would be his only means of communication with Takala.

The Finn was very careful, checking his watch until the second hand showed it was 10.00 a.m. Switching on, he warmed up and then lifted off. The vibration was considerable and the Hughes felt as if it was shaking itself to pieces.

Takala guided them out over the bay and the

intense blue of the water receded below. It was a perfect morning for observation – the sun shone out of an azure sky and the clarity of vision was something Newman had only experienced in Finland.

He looked back and the Kalastajatorppa was like an architect's model, the most prominent building a curving sweep of concrete. They gained more height and Newman began to see Helsinki's layout – again like an architect's model. He had studied the map Laila had given him and from the air there was an intriguing feeling that he had viewed it from above before.

The peninsula on which the city is built spreads out towards the Gulf of Finland like a mis-shapen, three-fingered hand. The bays surrounding it on three sides are peppered with many islands of all shapes and sizes. Newman thought it was one of the most intriguing cities he had ever visited, an archipelago like the giant ones Laila had described. Takala began commenting.

'Your wife did not take much interest in what we were passing over yet. She kept checking her watch. And I made this wide sweep to the west so I would arrive at the objective when she wanted me to.'

'What objective?'

'You may get a better idea of the trip she made if you wait a few minutes.'

'There's a big park at the top of the peninsula – where Helsinki reaches the sea. What is that?'

'Well Park. A long time ago there was a well the

inhabitants used for their water supply. They shot some of that film which was supposed to take place in Russia down there – the film starring Lee Marvin.'

They were over the sea now and the pilot checked his watch, changed course and began to lose height as he turned north towards the mainland. Below, small vessels were plying their lawful – or unlawful – trade. Newman folded his map and concentrated on the panoramic view.

'That's Estonia over there on the horizon,' Takala commented.

Away to the south on the far side of the Gulf of Finland, Newman could make out a long grey smudge of coast. Estonia. Soviet Russia.

'Those are the shipyards,' Takala's voice continued in his earpiece. 'We're very close to the objective now. This is the point where your wife pressed her face against the window and stared down for the next few minutes.'

They were crossing over Well Park, low enough for Newman to see its intricate network of paths winding amid pine trees as several pedestrians stopped and gazed up at the chopper. They were now flying due north just beyond the fringe of the mainland. More islands, several shaped like pear-drops. Takala gripped Newman's arm with his free hand, showing him his watch. It was exactly 10.30 a.m.

'Look straight ahead,' the Finn advised. 'There is the objective – the Silja Dock.'

'What was the significance of the time?'

'Look down at that ship – it is the *Georg Ots*, just sailing for Tallinn in Estonia.'

He handed Newman a pair of field-glasses, saying that he was doing everything he had been requested to do by Alexis Bouvet. Newman took the glasses and focused them as Takala lost even more height so they had a perfect view of the vessel as it left Silja Dock.

It was a bigger passenger ship than Newman had expected, almost a small liner, with a gleaming white hull and a blue trim line. Very modern with the normal contemporary squat funnel amidships. At first glance it could have been a Finnish ship and then his glasses focused on the red band round the square funnel. The band carried a small yellow hammer-and-sickle emblem. It was Soviet.

Through his glasses he saw an officer on deck also using a pair of binoculars to study the chopper which was now hovering. Below it the vessel sailed through a narrow channel between the mainland and an island with a strange, Disney-like house perched on it.

'What is this area called?' he asked Takala.

'South Harbour.'

Newman's expression was frozen as he watched the ship pick up more speed, leaving the channel behind and head for the open sea. An extract from Alexis's brief letter given to him by the postman in London came back to him with poignant fatality. *In*

one hell of a hurry to catch the boat – it leaves at 10.30 . . .
on my way to the harbour . . .

'Is there somewhere else you can land?' Newman asked. 'I don't want to go back to the Kalastajatorppa.'

'That could pose a problem,' Takala replied dubiously.

'I want to change hotels.'

'There is the Hesperia on Mannerheimintie. Helicopters do land and take off from there to take guests on tours. I would have to use my radio.'

'Use it. A reservation for five days. A double room if they can manage it.'

'Give me a minute. That's the Cathedral down there at the top of South Harbour.'

Newman continued using the glasses to study the area while Takala operated his radio, speaking in rapid Finnish. Newman couldn't understand a word. Then Takala nodded and changed course again to a north-westerly direction.

'We can land, Mr Newman. And you have your double room.'

It was a rainy noon in London when Monica put down the phone and ticked off a name on her pad. The list of names was long and covered most of Western Europe. Sighing with relief, she put down her pencil and looked across at Tweed.

'That was Pierre Loriot of the Direction de la Surveillance du Territoire – ' she was referring to French counter-espionage ' – and he was very co-operative. He's going to concentrate on the airports – all flights from the States. Also, he's checking every seaport from Marseilles to Dunkirk for any kind of ship bound for an Iron Curtain destination. Any such vessels will be watched closely. And Loriot was my final contact. Europe is sealed off – with the exception of Finland which you asked me to leave off the list. Why? I could have called Mauno Sarin of the Protection Police in Helsinki. Or is it a state secret?' she ended with a wistful note.

'Now, now. And it is not a secret. But the Finns are in a difficult position. They have an arrangement with the Russians that any defector from the Soviet Union is to be handed back. So, any American crossing over to Moscow who reaches Helsinki is safe. The Finns would be forced to assist the final stages of his passage. Which is why I'm handling Sarin myself.'

'SAPO in Stockholm – ' she was referring to the Swedish Secret Police ' – were very helpful.'

'Sweden is a different world. Soviet defectors who reach it are never handed back. Procane may fly the polar route and head for Stockholm. If he does, a reception committee will be waiting for him at Arlanda.'

'So I've done the job? Or is there anything else before Monica staggers off to lunch?'

'One more thing I'd appreciate. Call the Chief

Customs Officer at Harwich. Chap called Willie Fairweather. Quote the code-name Brown Seal – that's me. You're allowed to giggle. Tell him that within the next week or so an Estonian trawler called *Saaremaa* – ' he spelt it out for her ' – may put in to Harwich for engine repairs. The moment he gets the radio request to berth at Harwich could he please call me?'

'Consider it done.'

Tweed was grateful that she asked no questions. Few people know that the Estonians fish not only the Baltic but also, not infrequently, the North Sea and the Atlantic. The crews of these vessels are vetted by the Russians – but the Estonians are a wily people and adept at fooling those they secretly consider 'the Soviet occupiers'.

Tweed pretended to be absorbed by his reading of a file, but he listened while Monica called Fairweather. He felt a sensation of great relief when she had accomplished her task. The trawler – named after an island off the Estonian coast – was a very important piece on the gigantic board he was working on.

It was a few hours later on the same day, aboard the trawler *Saaremaa*, rolling in a heavy swell thirty miles east of Harwich, that the Chief Engineer appeared on the bridge and reported to his skipper, Olaf Prii.

'Serious trouble with a boiler, sir.'

'Can't you do anything about it?' demanded the

tall, lean Prii, a man of fifty-five with prominent cheekbones.

'Not a thing. We must put into port for help.'

'Very well. I'll radio Harwich. You can get us into port, I take it?'

'Limping on one foot, but we should make it.'

The helmsman had his back to both men – so he missed the wink Prii gave his Chief Engineer before walking to the front of the wheelhouse, wearing his normal forbidding expression.

Chapter Ten

Enter the whirlwind. Cord Dillon was shown into Tweed's office at 7.30 p.m. Howard mumbled something about 'you know each other' and left the room, closing the door behind him. *He's all yours, thank God*, his expression said.

The Deputy Director of the CIA was a tall, well-built man of fifty with a craggy face. He had a shock of thick brown hair, was clean-shaven, and above a strong nose his eyes were a startling blue, and ice-cold.

Sunken cheeks emphasized his cheekbones and the mouth was thin and tight-lipped. His eyebrows were thick and, for a large man, he walked as though he had springs in his feet. Like Lysenko, he exuded an aura of great physical drive, but unlike the Russian, his energy was controlled and disciplined.

He wore a dark grey suit, a white shirt and a plain dark grey tie. His clothes were neat and well-pressed but he was hardly a picture of sartorial elegance. He wore his clothes like a man who finds them a necessary appurtenance but unimportant. His manner was self-assured and brusque. He dropped his bag on the armchair and Tweed realized he had not even bothered to call in at his hotel. Business first with Mr Dillon.

'We need to talk alone,' he told Tweed, glancing at Monica.

'When I'm not available, your contact is Monica,' Tweed replied amiably, standing up to shake hands. 'Monica, this is Mr Cord Dillon. Say hello to Monica, please.'

'Hello.' Dillon nodded, hauled a chair closer to Tweed's desk, sat down and lit a cigarette. 'Howard tells me you're in charge of locating this Adam Procane.'

'Mr Howard is correct.'

'That's the first bit of good news I've had since I left DC. Made any progress?'

'I suggest you read these four preliminary reports which came in from Europe today.'

Tweed handed over four zip-up files and waited, hands clasped in his lap while Dillon perused them. The American was a high-speed reader. Within a matter of minutes he replaced the sheets inside the files and handed them back. Then he stared up at the ceiling and puffed at the rest of his cigarette before stubbing it out in an ashtray Monica placed before him.

'Who are these people you've designated with initial letters? The usual type of payroll informants who feed you crap to justify their expenses?'

'Not at all. They are high level.'

'How do you define high level over here?' Dillon demanded.

'One is the proprietor of a classy establishment patronized by politicians and – more important – members of that country's counter-espionage organization.'

'A bordello, Tweed?'

'You could call it that. Another runs a private detective agency which numbers among its most profitable clients certain agents who hire it to do the work they should be doing – '

'While they chase women?'

'Exactly. The third has contacts with various embassies in the country concerned. Money changes hands – '

'You can't beat money – unless you use women,' Dillon agreed.

'The fourth – because of his peculiar role in connection with a worldwide industry – also has contact with certain agents – like the private enquiry agency. Soviet agents.' Tweed unclasped his hands. 'American, too.'

'I'd love a list of those bastards.'

'Out of the question.'

'I guessed it would be. OK, so you're playing it close to your vest, which is also OK. Care to say which countries you are referring to?'

'Belgium, Germany, Switzerland and France.'

'That tallies.'

'I don't quite follow,' Tweed commented.

'What brought me here like a homing torpedo was reports which came in from our Paris Embassy. My chief operative heard that Adam Procane is expected in Europe. Arrival imminent. The next report came from Geneva. Same message. You gotten any ideas on the identity of this Adam Procane?'

'I was hoping you would help there. After all,' Tweed pointed out, 'we are talking about an American high up in the government, Intelligence or even the Pentagon.'

Dillon leaned his elbows on the desk and spread his large hands flat on the surface. He studied them as he talked.

'I won't hide from you the fact that this Procane thing is making Washington sweat. The one thing that could stop Reagan – make the polls turn a somersault – would be the defection to Moscow of an American Philby.'

'You've had time to check possibilities?'

'That's going on at the moment. No dice, so far. It may be early days – but November and the Presidential election are coming with seven league boots. What kind of data has Procane handed over to Moscow so far? Or don't you know?'

'Unconfirmed reports – how can we confirm them? – speak of information on the new MX defence system. *And*, the so-called Star Wars programme in space.'

'Again that tallies. Creepy, isn't it? The atmosphere in Washington is hellish. A few top men are keeping the lid on this – and their mouths shut. So far. Can you imagine how those few top men are looking over their shoulders at each other? Is *he* the one? Suspicion can destroy a nation's whole security system. Can we take any action at this end?'

'Already done,' Tweed said crisply. 'A general alert has gone out all over Western Europe. They're concentrating on seaports and airports. What I need is some lucky break which will give me a hint of the route he – if Procane is male – will follow to get to Moscow fast.'

'You think Procane could be a woman?'

'I'm intrigued that the Christian name, Adam, is stressed whenever Procane is mentioned,' Tweed replied and left it at that.

'I thought a lot about the route on the flight over. My best bet would be Vienna. No one has gone that route yet.' Dillon paused. 'Not even any of your people.'

'We'll bear it in mind.'

'One more thing before I go to my hotel. You may just find The Vulture perched on your shoulder if this thing develops. I hear the President is waiting a little longer to see what happens. His normal technique.'

'The Vulture?' Tweed enquired innocently.

'You know who I'm talking about. The most powerful man back in Washington next to Reagan. His favourite National Security Adviser. Stilmar.'

'You mean he might fly to London?'

Stilmar. The legendary aide to the President. The

man always referred to only by his surname. Tweed concealed his surprise at Dillon's announcement. Stilmar had never left the States during the whole of the four years of Reagan's presidency.

'Are you sure this could happen?' Tweed probed.

'It was discussed seriously at the last meeting I attended before I flew over. The trouble is Stilmar is brilliant when it comes to military problems – he's the prime mover in the Star Wars project. But his security knowledge is plain lousy. He's basically a scientist. Just thought I'd warn you. And I plan to fly to Paris tomorrow to check personally that information which came in from the embassy. Just the round trip. See you, Tweed. And I'm staying at the Berkeley.'

'Not the Hilton?'

'Too obvious.'

'What was all that about?' Monica asked when they were alone. 'And in my book he doesn't score top marks for manners.'

'Don't underestimate Dillon,' Tweed warned. 'He's terse but he's also very shrewd. And I want him tracked by the best team available. All the way to Paris. Also, when the trackers know his flight they are to phone you immediately. You then call Loriot in Paris. He will take over until Dillon boards his return flight.'

'What worried you about his conversation?'

'The reference to Vienna. No mention of Scandinavia. Vienna is about as far south as you can get away from Scandinavia and still cross into the Soviet bloc easily.'

'You think he was diverting your attention from the North?'

'I don't think anything. I'm just taking nothing for granted.'

Half an hour later, at 8.15 p.m., the call came through from Fairweather, Chief Customs Officer at Harwich. The Estonian trawler, *Saaremaa*, had just berthed for urgent repairs to its engine-room.

'I'm leaving for Harwich,' Tweed said as he put the phone down.

It is depressing travelling on a train late in the evening by yourself, and Tweed was alone in his first-class compartment as the train approached Harwich. He glanced out of the windows at rectangles of darkness and absorbed himself in studying the notes he had made during his phone conversation with Laila Sarin.

Alexis. Enquired re Procane at American Embassy. Not known. Murders of GRU officers – strangled. Estonia? Archipelagos. Turku? Swedish?

Newman. Adam Procane. Had never heard of him (so he said). Archipelagos (again). Estonian Shipping Company.

Tweed was trying to spot some coherent pattern between what both Alexis and Newman had known independently. He couldn't see one. The factors mentioned appeared random. Except in the case of two factors – archipelagos and *Estonia*.

He slipped his notebook into his pocket and rested his head against the small pillow, closing his eyes as he thought of how he had first encountered Captain Olaf Prii, skipper of the trawler, *Saaremaa*.

It had started with a chance meeting when Tweed was visiting Helsinki two years earlier. There had been a great storm in the Gulf of Finland. The *Saaremaa* had taken shelter in Helsinki's South Harbour and Prii had seized his unique opportunity.

Going ashore, he had made his way to the British Embassy – he'd had enough sense not to seek out the help of the Protection Police, who would have been obliged to report the incident to Moscow.

The Embassy people hadn't known what to do with him or what he wanted. Tweed, who happened to be at the Embassy, had been asked to help. Without speaking a word of Finnish or Estonian – the languages are not entirely dissimilar – Tweed had found he conversed easily with Prii in German.

The Estonians are Balts rather than Slavs historically, and some understand German. Prii explained their attitude pungently.

'During the war the German Wehrmacht came to Estonia. They drove out the Soviet bastards who had occupied us in 1940. We were treated well by the Germans. We would have been happy for them to stay for ever. Then later, as you know, the bloody Red

Army returned. We have been prisoners ever since. I will help the British with information whenever I can.'

'How can you communicate with us?' Tweed had asked.

'By my ship's radio, of course! We fish the North Sea. So, we arrange a signal and you know I am close to Freedom Island.'

'Why not slip ashore in Britain and stay there?'

It was a test question. Tweed was still suspicious that Prii might be a Soviet 'plant'. He had watched the Estonian closely when he replied.

'Because my wife and two daughters can never sail with me. We are watched carefully before we put to sea.'

They had arranged the code signal *Great Elk* which Prii would broadcast five times at three-minute intervals. When Tweed returned to London he had arranged with the vast radio listening complex at GCHQ, Cheltenham, to inform him immediately it picked up the signal. Harwich was to be the rendezvous. And this was the first time since their original meeting in Helsinki that the signal had come through twenty-four hours earlier.

It seemed an odd coincidence, Tweed reflected, as the express slowed down and the first lights of Harwich appeared outside the windows. But, linked with what he had just read in his notes, it might not be a coincidence. He would know more when he interrogated Prii.

147

He reached up for his small case on the rack. When the train pulled up in Harwich station he was standing by an exit door in the corridor.

Fairweather, the Chief Customs Officer, a bluff, red-faced man of forty-five, with twinkling blue eyes, would have made an excellent member of Tweed's staff. He had handled the problem of separating Captain Prii from his crew firmly and discreetly.

Visiting the Cold Horse, the waterfront hotel where the crew of the *Saaremaa* had been put up for the night, he explained that the Chief Customs Officer was not satisfied with the sudden appearance of the Estonian vessel. He had questions to ask the skipper who was to accompany him immediately.

When Tweed arrived he was shown into Fairweather's office. Olaf Prii was sitting at a table drinking a mug of steaming black coffee. He stood up the moment Tweed entered and his relief was only too apparent. Fairweather gestured for Tweed to sit down after his two visitors had shaken hands warmly.

'Coffee for you, sir?' he asked Tweed, not using his name.

'No, thank you very much.'

'Then I'll leave you two on your own for a nice cosy chat. You can stay here all night if you wish. When you're finished, my bedroom is the first door on the right as you leave this room. I'll accompany

Captain Prii back to his hotel – just for appearance's sake.'

Prii was taller than Tweed remembered. His skin was tanned to the texture of leather, the penalty of God knows how many storm-ridden nights on the bridge of his vessel. His hooked nose expressed considerable strength of character and his eyes were alert and watchful.

'I came as soon as I could,' Tweed said in German. 'Also I am most glad to see you. Our system works. Now, what have you to tell me?'

'Bad news from Estonia, I fear. The situation gets worse as each day passes. Did you know that sixty per cent of our Estonians have been removed from Tallinn? God knows where they are now. The Soviets have replaced them with strange people like Moldavians and other nationalities from different parts of the Soviet Union.'

'I am so sorry. Life must be very difficult.'

'But that is not why I decided we should meet. Very strange events are taking place in Tallinn. Three officers of the Soviet Military Intelligence have been murdered – '

'The GRU, that is?'

'Yes. The murderer is clearly the same man in all three cases. He uses the same technique and timing. Always after night has fallen. Some kind of wire garrotte is used. The GRU are now setting traps for the killer – sending a GRU officer to walk the streets while he is watched. It is a crude operation – we even have kids who prowl the streets and catcall the watchers. "How much for another Russian head?" They have put a Colonel Karlov in charge of the investigation.'

'Who?' enquired Tweed.

'Colonel Andrei Karlov – who has set up his headquarters in Pikk Street a few doors along from St Olaf's Church, the same name as my own. He has an office on the first floor overlooking the street. His superior, General Lysenko, visits Tallinn frequently to see how things are going. In a macabre way, it is funny. Lysenko is so gutless he travels to Tallinn in civilian clothes, hoping no one will realize he is GRU. He always flies in after daybreak and leaves for Moscow well before nightfall! There is a bad atmosphere in Tallinn because of these murders – which have nothing to do with the underground. You would like some photographs we have taken of these men?'

'Yes, please.'

'You excuse me? I have to lower my trousers.'

Tweed was bewildered. The amount of information was astounding. He had no doubt that Prii was a member of the Estonian underground but carefully refrained from referring to the fact. Prii turned his back, undid his belt and lowered his trousers. Attached to his backside with surgical tape was a large green waterproof bag which he ripped loose and then made himself respectable. He dropped the bag on the table.

'Go on, my friend. Take a look.'

Tweed unfolded the bag, which was rather like a large envelope. He took out several photos and immediately recognized them as Polaroid prints. Again he was amazed and could not resist asking the question.

'Where on earth do you get a camera like that – and the film? If you don't mind the question.'

'Smuggled in from Helsinki, of course. Aboard the tourist ships – the Estonian Shipping Line. The first two are of Colonel Karlov.'

The prints were taken close up and Tweed wondered how the devil they had managed it. In both shots Karlov, wearing civilian clothes, was looking sideways rather than direct at the camera. He had just emerged from the doorway of an ancient building – his office in Pikk Street, presumably.

'I'm full of admiration,' Tweed commented. 'Someone took their life in their hands to get these.'

'It is easy – if you are careful.' Prii's tone was contemptuous. 'They are not so clever. When he came out of the building a boy was waiting and shouted an insult. He looked sideways and a man on a bicycle with his camera concealed inside a canvas bag took the pictures. Look at the next one.'

Tweed stared at the print and kept his expression blank. Again he was taken aback and had trouble not showing it. He looked up at Prii, who explained.

'That is Mauno Sarin of the Helsinki Protection Police. Very occasionally he crosses on one of the tourist boats and visits Karlov. The Finns have to play it carefully.'

Yes, it was Mauno Sarin. Taken as he was entering what seemed to be the same building. Tweed had recognized him the moment he first looked at the print. He turned to the next one.

'And that is General Lysenko,' Prii explained. 'As you see, no uniform! That impresses the hell out of us Estonians. A general and he hides himself for fear of being murdered in broad daylight! The last print is of a man who is a candidate for murder. Captain Oleg Poluchkin, also GRU. That man is a beast, a mad beast. He killed a French woman journalist who was foolish enough to visit Tallinn, slipped away from the Intourist guides and was caught. He had her killing filmed.'

'Sounds psychopathic,' Tweed commented in a neutral tone. 'May I ask how you found all this out?'

'The underground people are everywhere. A six-teen-year-old boy watched it happen from behind a hedge. Poluchkin drove the Chaika which ran the poor woman down. They made her stand in the road at gunpoint. We heard that Colonel Karlov was very angry when he heard about the murder – even though Poluchkin is nominally his deputy.'

'Nominally?'

'He is Lysenko's personal spy in Tallinn. That is the way the Russians work – they don't even trust each other. Always someone is watching someone else.'

Tweed stared at the Polaroid print of Oleg Poluchkin. Short and fat, wearing GRU uniform, his fleshy chin was jowly and he gave the impression he was about to burst out of his tightly belted tunic. A very unpleasant-looking character.

'May I keep these photos?' Tweed requested.

'That is why I brought them here. The KGB are also present in Tallinn, but the investigation into these strange murders is being conducted by Colonel Karlov – probably because GRU officers are the victims. The trouble is Moscow blames the underground for the killings, but I can assure you that they have nothing to do with them. It is both mysterious and dangerous.'

'Have you heard any rumours that someone important is expected to arrive in Estonia?' Tweed enquired.

'Yes. Mauno Sarin, chief of the Finnish Protection Police. When times are tense Sarin tries to quieten things down.'

'Does the GRU ever visit Helsinki? Colonel Karlov, for example? He appears to be in charge in Tallinn at the moment.'

'Very rarely. And permission has to be obtained from Moscow. Karlov could not visit Helsinki without Lysenko's agreement. Even Lysenko, I suspect, would need Moscow's sanction for such a visit.'

'And can people from the West visit Tallinn on these tourist boats?'

'There is only one ship – the *Georg Ots*. Yes, western tourists are welcomed, provided they have obtained a visa. You see, the Russians try to present Estonia as a model republic, a showcase, if you like. They organize two-hour tours of Tallinn – but during those two hours the Intourist guides never leave their sides. You are not thinking of visiting Tallinn, I hope? I would strongly advise against it.'

Tweed smiled drily. 'You're not likely to see me within a thousand miles of Finland. My job keeps me in London.'

'So, now you know the chief figures of the enemy in Tallinn at the moment. Karlov, Lysenko and Poluchkin, Lysenko's lackey . . .'

They chatted for another half-hour and then Tweed decided Prii had been away from his crew long enough. He summoned Fairweather, thanked him for his co-operation, and asked him to see Prii safely back to the Cold Horse.

'One thing you have to tell him,' Fairweather said briskly, 'so maybe you'd interpret. When he gets back I suggest that Captain Prii complains about the rigorous interrogation he was subjected to. I wasn't satisfied at first with his explanation about engine trouble. On the way back we'll visit the trawler and I'll go down into the engine-room. Then I'll say I am satisfied, but he must leave at the earliest moment. I can say I found a friend at Norwich University who speaks excellent German and acted as interpreter. OK?'

'You really have missed your natural vocation,' Tweed observed and proceeded to translate what Fairweather had said to Prii.

Tweed waited for a few minutes after the two men had left and scribbled in his notebook a shorthand version of what Prii had told him. He was confident the Estonian had not realized the reason for certain questions.

The interview had not reassured Tweed. Rather the reverse. He was thinking of Newman wandering about on his own up there in the Far North. The one common factor which had appeared in Laila's reports on her conversations with Alexis and Newman – apart from archipelagos – was Estonia.

If Newman, in his present mood, boarded the *Georg Ots* for Tallinn, Tweed had little doubt he would never be heard of again.

Chapter Eleven

Mauno Sarin stood up behind his desk stiffly and with a wary expression as his daughter walked into his office. The chief of the Protection Police was a six foot tall man in his early forties with dark brown hair and a fringe beard linking up with his sideburns. Behind his spectacles his blue eyes normally sparkled with a hint of humour. The humour was noticeably absent as he pulled out a chair for Laila.

'You do realize,' he began, 'that you are causing me a lot of trouble with your newspaper articles? Not just one – but two.'

'I am only doing my job,' Laila replied tightly. 'And I do resent your phoning me at my flat and summoning me here like a criminal.

'Now, Laila, that's nonsense.' Sarin sat down behind his desk in his first-floor office and his voice was persuasive and amiable. 'I asked if you would come and see me – it is a long time since we have had a talk.'

'And that talk turns out to be an interrogation. Specifically, what have I done to displease the secret police?'

'You, of all people, know that Finland is in a difficult position *vis-à vis* the Russians. First, you slant your article on the death of that unfortunate French journalist – '

'I do not *slant* articles!' she burst out. 'I write only the facts.'

'You hinted that Alexis Bouvet might not have died on some lonely road outside Helsinki. You made a big thing about the missing body?'

'Well, where is it?'

'I have no idea,' her father confessed. 'God knows the police have searched for it. But you know what the forest is – it goes on for ever.'

'And so does your dislike of my job!'

'Laila, we all have to compromise. Finland only exists as an independent country because we have learned how to compromise with Moscow.'

'A reporter does not compromise with the facts.'

'What facts?' His tone was still quiet and genial. 'Let us take the new story – the one about rumours of a series of brutal murders of GRU officers in Estonia. Rumours are not facts.'

'And you have heard nothing about these murders?'

Sarin hesitated. He was dressed informally, wearing a pair of dark brown corduroy trousers and a windcheater which he now took off and looped over the back of his chair. It gave him time to think.

'Have you now had time to work out your answer?' Laila enquired.

'That wasn't nice, but let's forget you said it. Yes, I have heard the rumours. If I tell you something will you promise not to report it?'

'No! I will not be gagged.'

'Have your own way.' The ghost of a smile crossed Mauno's face. 'You usually do. Which is fair enough. We are two adults talking on equal terms.'

'What are you up to now?'

'Nothing. Laila! Will you never be able to separate my job from my relationship with you?'

'I am busy. Tell me why you summoned – asked – me here and then I will go.'

'I need the source of your information concerning the rumoured GRU murders.'

'Never reveal my sources.' Her mouth clamped shut.

'The government is extremely concerned.'

'Stuff the government!'

'You may find yourself in a difficult situation where I cannot help you.'

'Has Moscow denied the story?' she demanded.

'No, not yet,' he admitted.

'Normally they'd issue a denial within hours of the story appearing. They're being clever for once. They hope if they ignore the whole thing it will go away. They don't want to frighten people from making trips to Estonia. They need the currency.'

He sat watching her without replying immediately. What she had just said coincided exactly with his own thinking. The girl was bright, thank God – even if she did create problems.

'The trouble is, Laila,' he said quietly, 'you and I are too alike. Obstinate, independent – and self-willed – '

'That's the first thing you've said since I arrived that I agree with. Can I go now?'

'I have a favour to ask.'

'I'm listening. No promises.'

'If you hear anything – even a rumour – that an American called Adam Procane has arrived on Finnish soil, could you warn me?'

It was a plea. Laila was shaken but kept a grip on herself. Her face was expressionless when she replied.

'I'll remember what you said. I can't give you any more.'

'I don't ask for more.'

When she had left, Mauno stood up and paced round his office, hands thrust into his trouser pockets. Sometimes he hated his job. He had just attempted to use his own daughter – because if Procane existed, if he turned up in Finland on his way to Russia, Mauno would have only one course of action. To assist Procane to cross over the border.

It was 9.00 a.m. when Laila left the building on Ratakatu and took a tram heading north into the city. The fourth hotel she checked for Bob Newman was the Hesperia. On impulse, instead of once again going to reception, she took the elevator to the first floor where guests had breakfast.

The elevator doors opened and she saw Newman serving himself from the buffet to breakfast. She picked up a plate and stood beside him, helping herself to cheese and ham.

'So, you caught up with me,' he said over his shoulder.

'After checking three other hotels. I needed the exercise, so you did me a favour. Try the brown rolls – they're better for you. They also taste good.'

'The second reason impresses me.'

They chose a quiet table at the side of the room and started their breakfast like a couple staying together. Laila carefully said nothing which might be provocative, which meant she said nothing. Newman could make the running.

'I suppose you think I treated you badly,' he remarked when he had finished his main course and started on rolls and marmalade.

'Not really. I haven't taken out a mortgage on you.'

'For this time of day you're in a very good mood. Have you enjoyed your weekend?'

'I haven't enjoyed my morning so far. I've just come from seeing my father. From Ratakatu. He's furious with me – not that I care.'

'Your two articles in your paper?'

'As a matter of fact, yes. He was very artful in trying to get me to talk. Can I have some of that marmalade? Thank you. I forgot to mention that you are in town. I don't think that he knows yet.'

'So now I owe you – '

'I don't think like that – credits and debits. He must find out things for himself – just as I have to. I can't tell you what he spoke to me about.'

'I wasn't going to ask.'

'If we go on like this we'll get on fine together. An English girl once told me it's what she calls a negative relationship. No quarrels, no talk – no bloody communication at all.'

Newman choked on his coffee and then they both looked at each other and laughed. It was Newman who brought up the subject when he had collected them a further supply of rolls and marmalade. The rolls were crisp and he was famished.

'Did you try and find out where I'd gone after I left the other hotel?'

'Of course! I questioned the chopper pilot. I even showed him a lot of my legs. I could see he was tempted but you must have paid him a big bribe.'

'I did. Alexis hired that chopper. Do you want to know where she flew to?'

'Only if you want to tell me. Are you going to ask me to keep it a secret?' Laila enquired.

'No. I just don't think you'll print it.'

'Moral blackmail.'

'For Christ's sake!'

'Sorry! Sorry! Let's get negative again. It was a joke – ever heard of a joke?'

'My sense of humour got left behind in the shower. Alexis got that pilot to fly her out over the sea and then back again over South Harbour. She asked the pilot to time their trip so they arrived over the Silja Dock at exactly 10.30 a.m.'

'That's when the *Georg Ots* sails for Tallinn.'

'And that was the object of the trip. I think a couple of days later she sailed herself on the *Georg Ots* – and never returned from Estonia.'

'Then she must have planned her trip before she arrived here.'

'What makes you think that?' Newman asked.

'Because all passengers have to apply for a visa two weeks in advance. You send three photos of yourself with the application – '

'Which gives Moscow plenty of time to run all passengers for Estonia through their computer.'

'That's what I think.' She glanced at him and he was holding a piece of roll and staring into the distance. When she spoke again there was concern in her voice. 'Bob, you're not thinking of visiting Tallinn yourself, I hope?'

'That would be a crazy thing to do.'

'But I get the feeling you are a bit crazy – not normally but with this mission, yes. You get a very grim look on your face when you talk about Alexis.'

'We were very close to breaking up – ending the marriage.'

'That wouldn't make any difference to a man like

you. Not if you thought someone had murdered your wife.'

'Get on with your breakfast, girl.'

'Why have you suddenly started to tell me things – to trust me?'

'Because you didn't tell your father I was in Helsinki.'

'So you believed me – all I said?'

'It's my job to know when people are telling me the truth. Incidentally, I may decide to get in touch with your father again. I met him last time I was here and we got on well together.'

'You won't tell him we know each other?'

'Of course not. That's strictly between you and me – whatever we do together.'

'That sounds as though our relationship could become – interesting.'

'Laila, I noticed your legs the moment we first met out at Vantaa Airport. Don't get me wrong – but at the moment girls are the furthest thing from my mind. I have a job to do – and I'm going to do it.'

After breakfast Laila excused herself while Newman went up to his bedroom, No. 817, which overlooked the weird *glockenspiel*-like sculpture, the Mannerheimintie, open grassland beyond and an arm of the sea beyond that.

Laila darted down to the ground floor, found a

phone, and called the London number of the General and Cumbria Assurance Co. She was put through to Tweed without delay.

'This is Laila. I've found Bob Newman again. He moved to the Hotel Hesperia. Have you got that? Listen. He's found out that Alexis went across the water by boat. Do you understand?'

'Yes,' replied Tweed. 'You sound worried.'

'I'm scared Newman will try and go to the same place. I'm sure I can't stop him – he's like a police dog who's picked up the scent.'

'How imminent is the proposed trip?' Tweed asked crisply.

'I don't think he'll go yet. There will be visa problems. But he's clever. He could find a way. I'd better get off the phone. He'll be coming down from his room any moment now. I really am worried.'

'Leave it to me. And thank you, Laila. You did the right thing – warning me. Keep in touch.'

'Oh, I sent you copies of my two articles by express post. You should get them quickly. They're in Finnish, of course.'

'I have a friend who speaks the language. Thanks again – and keep me informed of all developments.'

When Newman arrived in the large reception hall Laila was sitting waiting with her long legs, sheathed in sheér black tights, crossed. You could never tell when a man's attention could be diverted into a certain direction.

'Ready?' Newman greeted her. 'We're going to the Russian Intourist office on the Esplanade. Let's see how much information they provide. Damn all would be my guess.'

After his phone conversation with Laila Sarin, Tweed sat at his desk with his hands clasped, gazing into space for five minutes. Monica stopped typing and pretended to check a file, quiet as a mouse. When Tweed cleared his throat she looked up.

'Laila Sarin,' Tweed began, concentrating his thoughts by talking the problem out with her, 'is very worried that Bob Newman is running wild. Does that really sound like him?'

'No. He will be under tremendous stress – but that's when he is at his best.'

'His wife has recently been murdered,' Tweed reminded her.

'I stick by what I said.'

'I'm not so confident. He took off for Helsinki like a bat out of hell. I'll never forgive myself if I don't take precautions.'

'And just what precautions can you take from here?'

'Contact Mauno Sarin.'

'Newman will be blazing if he ever finds out . . .'

'I'm calling Sarin,' Tweed decided.

He picked up the phone, checked the number in

his worn and tattered address book, and dialled the number himself. When he announced his name he was put straight through to Sarin.

'Tweed, my friend, it is a long time since we met. Too long. What can I do for you?' Sarin asked.

'Mauno, this is a delicate matter. If the subject ever knows I have called you he will not forgive me. But I know you will handle it with discretion.'

'The subject is?'

'Robert Newman . . .'

'He is *here*! In Helsinki?'

'You know his wife was recently killed?' Tweed asked, leading up to his request cautiously.

'Yes. And some idiot reporter did a story on it in one of our leading newspapers.'

Tweed smiled to himself. It sounded as though the relationship beteen Mauno and Laila had not improved. Rather the reverse. He continued carefully.

'Somehow Newman has – rightly or wrongly – placed the murder in your area.'

'Murder? You did say murder?' Mauno queried.

'That's what Newman believes. As you know, he is enormously reliable and always in the past has proved right in the long run. You remember the Kruger business? No one believed he was on the right track until the climax to that affair.'

'So, he will be in an emotional state,' Mauno commented, 'and that could affect the judgement of any man.'

'Any man except Newman. He is staying at the

Hotel Hesperia. Is there any way you can have a talk with him? Without letting him know we have talked, of course.'

'That damned newspaper article! Maybe it will serve a useful purpose after all. God knows it has caused me trouble enough up to now.'

'He is very shrewd. You'll have to think of a reason as to how you know he's at the Hesperia – especially as he recently changed hotels.'

'Why did he do that?'

'I have no idea. But I do know in the past he has made a point of moving around to conceal his presence.' A thought occurred to Tweed. 'His hotel registration – you could use that. Pretend you were looking for another person and stumbled on it.'

'I'll think of something. I'll let you know . . .'

'I think I'd better go into Intourist on my own,' said Newman as he glanced inside the large window fronting onto the tree-lined boulevard known as the Esplanade. 'Can we meet somewhere in about half an hour?'

'I have some shopping to do. You know the bar at the Marski?'

'I got to know it rather well when I was last here.'

'We meet there, then.'

They had walked past the Intourist entrance and Newman paused to light a cigarette while he watched Laila cross the street. He stood smoking to see where she was going. She disappeared inside a large department store. Stockmann's. About the only name in Helsinki Newman could pronounce.

A smartly dressed, well made-up brunette greeted him inside the large Intourist bureau. He guessed she was Russian but she spoke good English. No sign of anyone else about the place.

'I understand you can take a day trip by boat to Estonia,' he opened. 'Have you got any brochures?'

'Yes, sir. All the details are in here.'

Her dark eyes studied him as though she were trying to recall where she had seen him before. She handed over a colour brochure with a picture on the front of the *Georg Ots*, a three-quarters view taken from the stern.

The come-on at the top of the brochure read in English, *What an opportunity – and what a price! Helsinki-Tallinn. FIM 210. Make the best of this opportunity and combine a one-day cruise to the beautiful Hansa town of Tallinn with your trip to Helsinki.* At the bottom the same message was repeated in German.

He opened the brochure and studied the timetable inside which showed the ship did depart at 10.30, returning to Helsinki at 22.30. You got exactly two hours ashore in Tallinn. Most generous. He looked up at the girl who was smoothing her black dress over her well-shaped hips. Her attitude underwent a complete change when he asked his next question.

'Have you a map of Tallinn?'

'A map?'

'Yes, a map of the town. A street plan. Also any photos?'

'We have no maps. No photos. You have the brochure.'

Her manner was suddenly neutral, even hostile. Newman grasped what was going on immediately. The Soviets were paranoid about maps of their country. She probably thought he was a spy. And she was almost certainly a member of the KGB. Who else would be allowed out in the West? She would also make a superb honey-trap.

'Thank you very much,' he said. 'You've been most helpful.'

Tucking the brochure into his pocket, he walked out and turned left, heading back along the Esplanade for the Marski. Behind him the street led direct to South Harbour; that could wait. He noticed across the street the wide frontage of Akateeminen, the largest bookshop in Scandinavia.

The very modern and spacious bar at the Marski is in the basement, which gives it a hidden-away-from-the-world atmosphere. As he drank his coffee from a table where he could watch the entrance, he thought about Laila Sarin.

Since he had boarded the plane at Heathrow, Newman had adopted the mood of wariness and mistrust common to foreign correspondents. You accepted nothing you were told until you had independently checked the facts.

Why had Tweed foisted Laila on him from the

moment he emerged from Vantaa Airport? Tweed was not a man to waste personnel on errands of sympathy. He had to be working on some problem that involved Helsinki. What problem? Like Howard, Tweed must have seen the horrific film of the killing of Alexis. Could there be a link between Alexis's journey to Finland and Tweed's problem?

Newman had deliberately assumed a friendly, apparently frank, attitude with Laila over breakfast. The way to make Laila let down her guard was to show an apparent trust in the girl after his earlier flight from her. Keep her off balance. Christ! At the moment he didn't trust his own shadow. The thought had just crossed his mind when Laila arrived, carrying a plastic bag with the logo, *Stockmann*.

'Did you get what you wanted?' she asked cheerfully. 'Yes, I'd love some coffee. No, nothing to eat – I'm watching my figure.'

'I expect a lot of men are doing just that.'

'God, the man's human.'

'Intourist are loaded with information. A huge room and I get this.'

He gave her the single brochure, ordering her coffee as she studied it. She went through it very carefully, puckering her thick eyebrows in her concentration.

'You see,' she pointed out, 'you do need a tourist visa for Tallinn. And you have to apply not later than two weeks before you want to make the crossing. And they want a photocopy of your passport and three photos. You'd think you were travelling to Vladivostok!'

'It's the system,' he replied casually. 'When we've had our coffee I want to visit Akateeminen. You can come with me if you like.'

'Can I ask what you need? Something to read?'

'Everything they've got on Estonia. I'm hoping they'll have illustrated books, heavily illustrated.'

'Estonia again?' She stared at him through her glasses with no particular expression. 'I'll look, too. I know that bookshop well. If we can get hold of a Miss Slotte she'll be very useful.'

The bookshop was enormous. Newman had been impressed by the length of the frontage. Once inside, he realized it spread back a far greater distance. There was even a gallery on the first floor overlooking the main bookshop below and approached by staircases. Miss Slotte, a handsome, fair-haired girl, ran backwards and forwards searching the stock for books in English which might contain data on Estonia. It was Laila who had the idea of checking children's books, who brought one book to Newman which he flipped open idly and then froze.

Page thirty-six. The small top photograph captioned *The old town, Tallinn.* Had he found the weird castle perched up in the background of the film showing the slaughter of Alexis? He couldn't be sure that this strange and ancient edifice was the same.

171

'What's the matter, Bob?' Laila enquired anxiously. 'You've lost all your colour.'

'A touch of indigestion. Your Finnish coffee is pretty strong.'

'We could get you something at a pharmacy.'

'It's going. I'm buying some of these books.'

He flipped over the page quickly and examined more pages. Laila found him another book. He bought five books altogether – all on Russia. There was no volume on Estonia alone.

'It is only a small republic,' Miss Slotte explained.

When they walked out of the bookshop Newman made a tremendous effort to carry on a normal conversation. Laila had to call in at the newspaper office, so they arranged to meet for lunch and Newman boarded a tram back to the Hesperia.

They had cleared his spacious and comfortable room when he got back and he dumped the books on the bed. Lighting a cigarette, he stared out of the window at the end of the room, across to the arm of the sea which looked like some sort of backwater. A railway bridge from the main station crossed the lake-like bay and he watched a long train crawling over the bridge heading away from the terminus. He would wait a few days before he decided on his next move and in the meantime study his books.

From a few fragments of information contained in the last letter Alexis would ever write him he was building up a picture of what had happened, linking up seemingly unconnected pieces.

In one hell of a hurry to catch the boat – it leaves at 10.30. Now he knew – from his flight in the chopper with Takala – that 'the boat' was the *Georg Ots* bound for Tallinn.

Will post this on my way to the harbour . . . That was South Harbour. Again the chopper trip with Takala was conclusive.

The castle in the background of the film when she was run down – and run over again – by a car. The picture in the children's book on the bed showed the crime might have been staged in Tallinn. They had sent the film to Park Crescent in a hurry.

Later, someone more careful had trimmed the print delivered to Laila's newspaper office. Had it occurred to them that with the Finns being so familiar with Tallinn, someone would soon have pointed the finger at the capital of Estonia? Always Tallinn . . .

That left two floating items in Alexis's letter which Newman couldn't link up in the general pattern. *Adam Procane has to be stopped* . . . But Alexis had told Laila she had enquired at the American Embassy and no one of that name existed. Why make the gratuitous point unless she had been speaking the truth? Who the hell was this Procane? That was something to check on before he even thought of visiting Tallinn. Time to slow down for a few days.

Archipelago is my best bet . . . Equally meaningless and without any link to the general pattern so far. Something stirred at the back of Newman's mind and then he lost it. Forget about it – he knew it would come back to him later. That was when the telephone rang.

'Excuse me, sir,' the concierge reported, 'but I have a gentleman here to see you. Yes, here in reception. He says it is very urgent. A Mr Mauno Sarin . . .'

Chapter Twelve

Stilmar, top National Security adviser to the American President, arrived unannounced at Park Crescent on Wednesday, 5 September, the day when Mauno Sarin called on Newman at the Hesperia.

Again, Howard brought him to Tweed's office, after explaining his deputy was in charge of the Procane investigation This time Howard was more polite. This American stood so close to Reagan he had been nicknamed the 'President's ear'. He was a very different personality compared with the abrasive Cord Dillon.

'I am so pleased to make your acquaintance, Mr Tweed,' he opened as Howard left the room. 'Your reputation stands very high in Washington.'

'Please sit down,' Tweed responded after shaking hands. 'A cup of coffee? And this is Monica, my right arm. In my absence you can talk with her as though you were speaking with me.'

'Ah! The woman behind the man.' Stilmar stood up and shook Monica by the hand. 'And some coffee would be most welcome.'

Stilmar was an impressive figure, the kind of man

who stopped conversation when he entered a crowded room. Six foot tall, he was in his mid-forties, his jet-black hair was neatly brushed and perched on the bridge of his hooked nose was a pair of gold rimless spectacles.

The eyes behind the lenses were dark and quick-moving, taking in everything at a glance. Clean-shaven, his face was smooth and pink-skinned, his mouth firm and with a hint of humour, his chin well-shaped. Like his manners, his garb was faultless. He wore an expensive, dark blue pinstripe suit, and his voice was deep and deliberate.

'Can I go straight into it and ask – what information have you gathered so far on this mystery man, Adam Procane? We are already getting very disturbing rumours coming in from Paris, Frankfurt, Geneva and Brussels. What we lack is any kind of description of Procane. He's like a shadow man someone has invented.'

'Vague descriptions *are* coming in from the continent,' Tweed told him. 'The trouble is they all seem to conflict.'

'Not four Procanes, please!' Stilmar raised his slim hands in a gesture of mock despair, a graceful movement like that of a conjuror. 'One is one too many!'

'It's early days yet. We must wait until the fog surrounding this man begins to clear – and clear it will. When we get to the stage of really positive data I may ask my informants to visit London. We'll arrange for each separately to have a session with Freddie.'

'And who is Freddie?'

'An artist who verges on genius when it comes to building up an Identikit picture. When that stage arrives I'll show you the results and see if the sketches remind you of someone.'

'May I ask where these present vague descriptions come from?'

'From contacts known to my informants – so they originate via third parties. I find that unsatisfactory. We do have until November, Stilmar.'

'Which is racing towards us at jet speed,' the American replied wrily. 'What route do you expect Procane to follow on his way to Russia – assuming, that is, that Adam Procane exists?'

'Through Vienna has been suggested.'

'I don't think so.' Stilmar's eyes gleamed behind his spectacles. 'So far Paris, Geneva, Frankfurt and Brussels have been mentioned as rumour sources. Don't you think it might be possible our attention is being deliberately diverted from a quite different route? Further north, maybe?'

'How much further north?' Tweed asked quietly.

'Scandinavia. Once beyond Denmark, moving east, we are in the neutral zone of Sweden. Beyond Sweden lies Finland.'

'You have heard something?' Tweed enquired.

'I simply make an observation,' Stilmar replied.

'And you should know I am staying at the Dorchester – under the name David Cameron. That is the name I shall use when I travel to Paris, Geneva, Frankfurt and Brussels to find out for myself what is really going on.'

'Surely you will be recognized,' Tweed objected.

'You think so?'

Stilmar stood up, asked Monica for a mirror and perched a hand mirror she produced from her handbag on a shelf. Standing with his back to them, he used a comb on his neat black hair. Next he removed his rimless glasses and replaced them with a pair of horn-rims. He then stripped off his tie, took a speckled bow tie from his pocket and donned it. When he turned and showed himself Monica gasped in disbelief.

The transformation was extraordinary. Stilmar now had a fat-faced appearance, emphasized by his new centre parting, the bow tie and his horn-rimmed glasses – all of which visually widened his face. The newspaper shots of the long-faced elegant Stilmar bore no relationship to the man who stood before them with shoulders hunched, legs slack.

'Remarkable,' commented Tweed with great sincerity.

'I once indulged in amateur theatricals as a young man,' Stilmar explained. 'I wasn't much good – but I met a make-up artist who taught me that to change your appearance you didn't resort to tons of make-up

– padded cheeks and all that nonsense. Just a handful of props would effect marvels.'

'I doubt if anyone would recognize you now,' Tweed admitted.

'So, we have had our preliminary meeting. I'm sure this will be the first of many. I will now take my leave of you. This afternoon I leave for Europe. If you would just give me a number if I wish to phone you, please – '

Tweed scribbled a number on his pad, tore off the sheet and handed it to the American. He glanced at it and gave the sheet back to Tweed. The moment he had left the room Tweed moved.

'Freddie,' he said rapidly into the phone, 'there's a fat-faced man wearing a bow tie and horn-rims just about to leave the building. I need photos of him – but he must not know you are taking his picture. You've no time at all to do the job.'

Monica stared at him as he replaced the receiver. Tweed took off his glasses and laid them on the desk, rubbing his eyes. He sat up straight and winked at Monica.

'What was all that about?' she asked.

'When Freddie has taken his pictures I want him to make five copies. Book him on the earliest possible flights to Paris, Geneva, Frankfurt and Brussels. I'll write out the addresses he has to deliver one copy of each photo to – so he takes four of the prints with him. The fifth I want for my files. He'll keep the negative, of course.'

179

'I'd better go down and wait in his office. I can book his air tickets from there.' She paused, halfway to the doors 'You wouldn't like to tell me what the hell is going on?'

'What did you think of Stilmar?'

'Looks superficially more like a successful businessman than a scientist. Very clever. A regular brainbox would be my estimate. He knows it, of course – but a brilliant man always does. What puzzles me is why did he walk out still in disguise? He could easily have changed back to his normal appearance.'

'God! I must be losing my grip.' Tweed was galvanized. 'Check right now – is there a flight for Paris he could catch if he went straight to Heathrow?'

Monica ran back to her desk, opened a drawer, flipped through an index she had compiled of flights to major European cities. She nodded.

'Yes. One departs just about ninety minutes from now.'

'That's why he put on that performance! So he could walk out of here wearing his disguise and jump into a cab for Heathrow. I bet on his way in he deposited a small case in one of the lockers.' He grabbed the internal phone, dialled a number. 'Fergusson? Tweed here. A man is leaving the building, may already be in the Crescent – ' he gave Fergusson the same concise description he had given Freddie ' – I want you to follow him. He's supposed to be heading for Heathrow and then Paris. You've got your passport? And money? Get after him. Keep on his tail across the whole of Europe if necessary. Report back to me when you can . . .'

He replaced the receiver and mopped his forehead with his handkerchief. He was sweating – not with the effort but with apprehension and self-disgust.

'Thank you, Monica,' he said. 'You spotted something that I should have seen for myself. Stilmar lulls you into a false sense of security with that bland manner. A regular brain-box, you said. He damned near fooled me.'

'Why are you so worried about Stilmar?'

'Because he's a top-level American, because he's arrived in London, because he's now on his way to Europe. That makes him Candidate Number Two for Adam Procane.'

Ian Fergusson was a dry, cynical, lean-faced Scot of thirty-three who spoke French, German and Italian fluently. At a pinch he could bluff his way with a Spaniard if he pretended he'd had a few drinks.

He was chief international tracker for Tweed and had never lost a target yet. He kept a bag packed by his desk, his passport in his pocket and his wallet contained a small fortune in American Express dollar cheques, currency for France, Germany and Switzerland. He was outside the building thirty seconds after putting down the phone, raincoat folded over his left arm and carrying his case. He caught up with Fat-Face – as he had christened Stilmar – halfway round the Crescent, sensed he was looking for a cab, sprinted to the opposite side of the road and flagged down the taxi the American was hurrying to hail.

He was giving the driver careful instructions while the vehicle remained parked at the kerb as Fat-Face stood a few yards ahead on the main road. He handed the driver a fistful of pound notes as a tip and settled back and relaxed.

Stilmar found his own cab and headed west towards Baker Street, which was the right direction. His own driver eased his way one car behind Stilmar's taxi and Fergusson lit a cigarette. Things had been quiet recently. He was glad to be on the move.

'He's a regular comic is Fat-Face,' Fergusson reported from the telephone at Heathrow.

'Yes?' queried Tweed.

'First he collects a case from the locker, then he heads for the gents and disappears inside a cubicle. Can you hear me – I'm not in a rush. Yet . . .'

'He *did* have a case in a locker,' Tweed informed Monica with his hand over the mouthpiece. 'Loud and clear,' he resumed his conversation with Fergusson. 'What then?'

'Comes out three minutes later – I timed him. Talk about a quick-change artist.'

'Tell me.'

'He goes in wearing a navy blue business suit. Very posh. He comes out wearing a loud check jacket and slacks. A sports shirt, too. Thick brown woollen tie. All in three minutes. Fat-Face is good.'

'Where is he headed for?'

'Paris. Next flight. Leaves in forty-three minutes. And he's travelling Economy. That way he merges with the crowd. I'm booked on the same flight. No, he hasn't spotted me. Now, was that question really necessary? Remember me? Fergie?'

'Sorry,' said Tweed. 'Also, my apologies for sending you off just after your fortnight's leave.'

'I was bored stiff. Ever spent a week on the beach at Bognor? I must go. Fat-Face is moving. I'll report back when I can . . .'

Tweed put down the phone and thought about how much of his life he spent behind his desk on the phone. He envied Fergusson. His recent European trip had made him restless for more fieldwork.

'Any news?' Monica asked.

'Stilmar is on his way to Paris. Who were you talking to when I was on the phone?'

'Cord Dillon left a brief message. He's back in London. And he's on his way to see us.'

Tweed frowned. 'That's out of character. Dillon is the kind of man who just breezes in without warning.' He looked up as Freddie entered his office holding a batch of prints. 'How did it go, Freddie?'

'Pretty good. Judge for yourself.'

Freddie, a small, gnome-like cockney who never let anything disturb him, placed the prints on Tweed's desk. He had caught Stilmar with an excellent three-quarters view. The photos were very good. Tweed slipped one in a file and returned the others to Freddie as he talked.

'Here are the addresses in Paris, Geneva, Frankfurt and Brussels. Deliver one print to each of these people. I have called them so they know what to expect. Monica has your air tickets. It will be a bit of a rush – but we have allowed enough time for you to take a cab from the airports, to deliver the photos and get back to the airport for the next flight.'

'Roger.' Freddie glanced down the list. 'Just to check – are any of these airports miles outside the city concerned?'

'Paris and Frankfurt – as you know – but we've allowed extra time. Geneva and Brussels are close in. The man you've photographed will be in Paris before you – he's just boarding his flight at Heathrow as we talk. But from there on you should arrive ahead of him. You know where the rue des Saussaies is?'

'Close to the Elysée and practically next door to the Ministry of the Interior. I'll hold the cab there while I deliver and head straight back for the airport. No need to report back I take it?'

'Just do the job. And thank you.'

Monica waited until they were alone before she asked the question. 'What are you up to now?'

'Sending photos of the theatrical Stilmar to people like Loriot of French counter-espionage. He already has men watching the airports and within hours they will be on the lookout for Stilmar. If he tries to board a plane for the East he will be stopped on some pretext.'

'My God! That would cause a sensation.'

'No sensations,' Tweed replied. 'He will be brought back to London under escort and put aboard a flight back to the States. Very quietly, very discreetly.'

'You really believe he could be Procane?'

'Anyone could be Procane.'

Half an hour later Cord Dillon arrived.

'The information is positive,' Dillon told Tweed as he settled himself in the leather armchair and cocked one leg over an arm as he lit a cigarette. 'I've sewn up the Paris Embassy tight. Only two people even know about the name Procane – the military attaché and my chief operative.'

'What information?' Tweed asked.

'The attaché has contacts he meets in the bar of the Meurice. One of them is an André Moutet, a bookie's runner and racing tipster. His real income is from tips he gets from staff at the embassies. A lot of money can change hands according to this attaché. The Soviets are expecting Procane to go over. But we've been on the wrong track. He's crossing over through Scandinavia when he arrives. I've already transferred operatives into Denmark and Sweden. As you probably know, we have a close relationship with SAPO, the Swedish Secret Police.' Dillon took a deep drag on his cigarette. For the Deputy Director it was a long speech. 'I think my trip was worthwhile,' he concluded.

'It sounds as though it was – providing this man, Moutet, did you say? – is reliable.'

'The attaché says he's pure gold.'

'So, what is your next move?'

'I'm booked on tonight's flight for Copenhagen.'

'And points east?'

'May I mark that wall-map?'

Dillon stood up, produced a felt-tipped pen and walked over to the wall-map. He drew a line which followed the eastern coastline of Sweden facing the Gulf of Bothnia with Finland across the water. Standing by the map he went on talking.

'Before I came here I called Washington. That is the demarcation line no American from the States from now on can cross.'

'Finland?' Tweed queried.

'No-go territory – too close to Russia. We have to find and stop Procane before he leaves Stockholm. That's it, Tweed.'

At the Hesperia in Helsinki Newman heard the gentle tapping on his door and unlocked and opened it. Mauno Sarin smiled, slipped inside and held out his hand.

'It must be two years since we last met, Bob.'

'It is. And what do I owe this visit to? You didn't

take so long finding out I was here,' Newman remarked.

His manner was cold and unwelcoming. He remained standing as Mauno glanced round the bedroom. The Finn hadn't changed since they last met; if anything he looked ten years younger.

'I stumbled over your name checking the hotel register in the lobby. There are four main hotels in Helsinki – the Marski – which I checked first – then the Intercontinental, this place and the Kalastaja-torppa. I'm trying to trace an American called Adam Procane.'

'What's he done?' asked Newman in a bored tone.

'Nothing. Yet.' Sarin was at his most amiable. 'But you know the games we play here. The Russians watch the Americans, the Americans watch the Russians – and we try to watch them watching each other.'

'You'd better sit down.'

Newman led the way over to the big window and chose the chair in the shadows, compelling Sarin to sit down in the opposite chair in the full glare of the clear Finnish light pouring in through the window. He forced himself to relax but he was furious. He didn't believe Mauno's ingenious excuse. Laila had betrayed him, had told her father where to find him.

'I was very sorry to hear of your wife's death. She truly was a remarkable woman,' Sarin commiserated.

Newman picked up the phone. 'You'd like some coffee. Still addicted?'

'Twenty-four cups a day! I have counted them. My job can be very arduous. And I am not pleased with Laila's performances as a journalist at the moment. That story about your wife was iniquitous.'

'And you must have loved her next one about the GRU murders in Estonia,' Newman commented as he put down the phone after ordering coffee for two.

'How did you learn about that? You don't speak a word of Finnish.'

Newman sagged in his chair and crossed his legs. He reminded himself to watch it. Mauno was sharp as a tack.

'I saw her by-line, so I asked the waitress at breakfast who translated it for me,' he lied easily.

'Yes, I was not pleased.'

'But is it true?' Newman pressed. 'About these GRU officers in Tallinn being strangled – and always after dark?'

'We are not conversant with daily happenings in Estonia.'

'I was asking about nightly happenings, Mauno.'

'Well,' Sarin hesitated. 'Yes, there have been strong rumours that some maniac is loose. Unconfirmed reports, that is – from people like the crew of the boat which sails between here and Tallinn with tourists.'

Liar, thought Newman. Laila had tried to question a member of the crew of the *Georg Ots* on this very subject and he had clammed up. Then it occurred to him that Mauno might well have his own contacts in that direction.

'But who could be responsible for such murders?' he persisted. 'And how many murders so far? That must be causing one hell of a hullabaloo back in Moscow.'

'You're not going to print any of this, Bob? Good. I had to check – it might have been why you are here. Two or three murders. At least, that is my uncon-firmed information. And yes, naturally it is a cause for concern in Moscow. So much so that they have appointed one of their top men to investigate the whole affair. A Colonel Andrei Karlov. I am surprised – he is one of their most brilliant military analysts. I heard that when he returned from a tour of duty in the West, he was tipped for promotion to their equiv-alent of the General Staff. You see how I trust you, my friend.'

He broke off as the waiter arrived with a tray of coffee. While he poured, Newman reflected that he would never normally have extracted so much infor-mation so easily from Mauno – who had to be covering up something else.

'You are adopting my parlour tricks,' Mauno remarked and he pulled the curtain partly across to shield his face from the glare of the intense light. 'And thank you. My sixth cup.' He checked his watch. 'Not bad so far. Why are you here?'

'Because I want you to help get me across the Gulf so I can look at Tallinn without the visa nonsense.'

Newman threw it at him without warning and Mauno choked on his coffee. He put down the cup hastily and dabbed at his lips with his handkerchief, staring at Newman.

'That is quite impossible. You are not contemplating something dangerous, for God's sake?'

'I bet you keep in touch with Tallinn, make the occasional trip over there in the course of your duties. I want you to take me with you.'

'Quite impossible,' Mauno repeated.

'I'm a British journalist – not American. And if they file everything written about them – as I know they do – they'll come up with an article I wrote a few months back with the headline, *Whose Encirclement?* I argued they had a case for being worried with Europe to the west, China to the east, and US space stations soon circling overhead.'

'I'm sure you had some devious reason.'

'Oh, yes. I wanted a visa for Leningrad where I had a contact. But that's irrelevant. The point is the article is on file. The Russians may soon wish to soften their hard line with the West. A sympathetic report on their model republic, Estonia, might be very useful to them.'

'And why do you want to go to Tallinn?'

'I'll tell you that when you've fixed up the trip.'

'Which will be never! I am sorry, Bob, but this I cannot do. But there may be some other way I can help you. Unofficially, you understand? If so, you call me at once. Same number as before. I'm sure you still have it,' he added with a dry smile.

'I'll bear it in mind.'

'And soon we have lunch? I can reach you here? And I am not checking your movements,' Mauno lied with the same ease as Newman.

'That's a date.'

General Lysenko, who had just left his Leningrad girlfriend, stormed into his office in a towering rage. His heavy boots clumped the floor, he tore off his greatcoat and flung it down on the couch.

'Rebet! What is so urgent that you have to call me from an important meeting?'

'Thank God you have arrived,' Rebet replied calmly. 'They said they could reach you. Our London watchers at Heathrow have reported the arrival of not one – but two – high-ranking Americans. Cord Dillon, Deputy Director of the CIA – and the highly influential National Security Presidential Adviser, Stilmar.'

'They came in together?'

'No. Separately. Dillon arrived Monday, Stilmar came in today. There was some bureaucratic delay in London reporting on Dillon. The radio signal from the Embassy in Kensington Palace Gardens reached Moscow an hour ago and they immediately phoned the news to me.'

'So!' Lysenko strutted to his favourite position and stood by the window. 'I was right to order close surveillance on all flights arriving from the United States. In this business, Comrade, you have to learn to out-think the enemy first!'

'I've transmitted the information to Colonel Karlov in Tallinn,' Rebet informed his chief.

'Why the devil did you do that?'

'Because you told me you had put Karlov in charge of the Procane investigation,' Rebet replied quietly. 'One of these men – Dillon or Stilmar – might be Adam Procane. Surely Karlov can only do his job if he has all the latest data?'

'In future, check with me first before you transmit information to Tallinn. It is one hell of a long way from London to Tallinn.'

'Not really,' Rebet responded. 'British Airways have a direct, nonstop flight daily to Helsinki. The Finnish capital is just a boat ride away from Tallinn. Shouldn't we prepare a visa in a British name, ready in case Procane does arrive in Helsinki? We could leave the photo blank for the moment.'

'An excellent suggestion. Have the visa prepared at once and send it by air to the Embassy in Helsinki. How did Karlov react to your phone call?'

'Sceptically. He said neither American visited London while he was at the Embassy.'

'Karlov is covering himself again!' Lysenko left the window and he hammered one chunky fist into the palm of the other. 'I seem to recall there were inter-mediaries who handed the data to Karlov – a different one each time. These go-betweens could have travelled backwards and forwards to the States, collected the data and dumped it in Karlov's lap.' His voice dripped sarcasm. 'And what does my so precise assistant think?'

'I also am not sure. I have asked Moscow to hand all the information from Procane to another top analyst for his opinion.'

'Without my sanction?'

'To protect your back . . .'

'None of you would achieve a thing without my drive! Think of it – if either Dillon or Stilmar turned up in Moscow, it would destroy that aggressive swine, Reagan.'

Chapter Thirteen

Mauno Sarin sat behind his desk and studied the envelope which was typed and addressed for his personal attention. He slit it open carefully with a knife and extracted the thick sheet of expensive note-paper inside which had been folded once. He read the few typed words and swore aloud.

It would be useful if we could meet here within the next week or two. Time to compare notes possibly? Andre Karlov.

No signature. Even the name was typed – and wrongly spelt on purpose. *Andre* instead of *Andrei*. He held up the sheet to the light pouring in through his window and examined the watermark. Just as he had expected – it was Finnish paper, as was the matching envelope.

Karlov was a cautious and ingenious operator. No one could ever prove the communication had originated from Tallinn – and the deliberate misspelling of the name suggested it was a hoax, which Sarin knew it wasn't. It was the way the system worked over there – if you were to survive. Never put anything down on paper which might be used in evidence against you at a later date.

The envelope was postmarked *Helsinki*, so Sarin guessed it had been posted by a reliable aide of Karlov's who had crossed on the *Georg Ots* for the sole purpose of posting the letter. The question which worried him was why had Karlov chosen this particular moment to suggest a meeting?

The GRU murders? Most unlikely – he would want to hush them up, not broadcast the fact that they couldn't protect their own officers in their 'model' republic. Adam Procane? Also unlikely. That left Laila's articles on the death of Alexis Bouvet and the same GRU murders.

Mauno reached inside a drawer and brought out a copy of *Le Monde*, the French newspaper Bouvet had worked for. Attached was the text translated for him into Finnish by one of his staff. They had picked up Laila's story and given it banner headline treatment.

French Foreign Correspondent Assassinated in Finland? The story generally followed Laila's – with the normal Gallic exaggeration and dramatization. Yes, it could be this which was bothering Karlov. The Russians were beginning to get a very bad press internationally. Mauno had no doubt the German and British press would soon pick up the story, with further embroidery.

Mauno was an excellent tactician in the tricky business of dealing with Moscow. The best response to Karlov would be to throw him off balance with a fresh angle – something he'd have to refer back to Moscow. He left his desk and ran down the staircase into the basement where the communications complex was housed. He approached the small cubby-hole offfice which accommodated the radio-telephone operator.

'Pauli, try and get Colonel Karlov on the phone in Tallinn. If you get through, could you please leave me alone? This conversation is confidential.'

It took Pauli only three minutes to reach Tallinn. He handed the instrument to Mauno, left the cramped room and closed the door. Mauno settled himself into the secretary's stool with the adjustable back.

'Andrei? Mauno Sarin here. I have a suggestion. Reports are now starting to circulate in the West about a series of alleged murders of GRU officers in Estonia. *Le Monde*, the newspaper Alexis Bouvet worked for, is calling her death an assassination.'

'But that happened in Finland,' Karlov reminded him coldly.

'They have picked up this story. In the same Helsinki paper on the following day there was another major article on the so-called GRU murders. How long do you think it will be before they print that in Paris and God knows where else? New York, next,' suggested Mauno, putting on the pressure. 'I am trying to help you.'

'Oh, yes? How?'

'A famous British foreign correspondent, Robert Newman, has just arrived in Finland.' Mauno was careful not to say *Helsinki*. 'If I brought him over for a day he could see that all is well in Estonia – if all *is* well. A story from him would counter any other unpleasant reports.'

'No! Western correspondents are not permitted here. They only tell lies, make provocations.'

'Put Newman through your computer. Check his track record with Moscow.'

They were conversing in English. Mauno spoke Russian but he knew Karlov welcomed any opportunity to practise his English, to keep up the fluency he had perfected during his tour of duty at the Soviet Embassy in London.

'I do not think for one moment they would agree.'

'There would be conditions for his visit – '

'No preconditions!'

'The conditions would be a guarantee of safe conduct signed personally by General Lysenko,' Mauno persisted. 'Also we would spend only one day in Tallinn – sailing on the *Georg Ots* and returning on the same day. That, also, I would need in writing.'

'None of this is acceptable.'

'One more condition. You would have to rush through a valid visa for Newman.'

'This Newman – he would be willing to visit Tallinn?'

'I would have to persuade him,' said the wily Mauno. 'If I knew you had invited him – strictly under the conditions I have laid down – it might make my task of persuasion easier.'

'I think the whole idea is unlikely to meet with acceptance in Moscow.'

That was the moment when Mauno knew the fish had taken the hook. They exchanged the normal arm's length polite conversation and then Mauno put down the instrument. For a few minutes he remained in the chair, staring at the wall. The confined space helped concentrate his thoughts.

It was a long shot, but he knew Karlov would feel compelled to pass on his suggestion to Lysenko – he simply dare not risk suppressing the phone call. Mauno was motivated by different considerations.

On the one hand he was convinced Newman – for some unknown reason – was determined to visit Estonia. And he could attempt the passage across the Gulf of Finland illegally. There were fishermen with boats who would agree – for a substantial fee – to sail him across after dark and put him ashore before daylight.

If the Russians caught him, there were two possible outcomes – both equally unpleasant. Newman might simply disappear. Or, worse still from Helsinki's point of view, he might be paraded at a Moscow press conference as an alien intruder, a Western spy caught in the act.

From his official position the second outcome would be appalling. It would give Moscow a lever to exert pressure on Finland. 'Harbouring *agent-provocateurs* to stir up dissidents and spy on the motherland . . .' That would be the line they'd take. Understandably – from their point of view.

The course of action Mauno had suggested would

kill two birds with one stone. Newman would get out of his mind what Mauno was convinced had become an obsession. And the Finn had no doubt that – whatever the truth about Estonia – Karlov would stage-manage their visit in a way that would enable Newman to write a story which gave the republic a clean bill of health. Any tension caused by Laila's crazy article would evaporate.

'I must just pray that it comes off,' he said to himself and left the tiny room, calling out to Pauli his thanks and that he was finished now. God, I'm walking a tightrope on this one, he thought as he mounted the stairs back to his office.

'Tallinn is beginning to smoke. Soon we may see fire.'

Lysenko made the remark with great satisfaction and rubbed his chunky hands together, staring at the phone he had just put down. *Action!* That was what he craved. The smoke of battle, the firing of big guns. The thought had made him phrase his remark in the way he had.

'A further development?' Rebet enquired, looking up from the fresh report he was studying on the Procane data which had just been flown in from Moscow.

'Karlov. He has just had the most provocative conversation with Mauno Sarin in Helsinki. Can you imagine what Sarin has suggested? That he brings to

Tallinn a Western reporter who would write an article on peaceful Estonia!'

'Which reporter?'

'An Englishman. Robert Newman. What does he think we are running? Celebrity tours to Tallinn?'

'I seem to recall this Newman is objective,' said Rebet, who was widely read. 'We ought to check him out on the computer in Moscow.'

'You mean let him come!'

'Look again at that copy of *Le Monde* and the translation on your desk.'

'But it refers to the killing of Alexis Bouvet.'

'Which they have obviously obtained from that Helsinki newspaper report. And the following day that same newspaper carried unconfirmed reports of the murders of the GRU officers in Tallinn. Can't you imagine the next big story *Le Monde* will feature?'

'We shall deny everything. We always do.'

'And how much weight do you think that carries any more in the West?' Rebet demanded without concealing his irritation. 'But, if feasible, a story from a much-respected British reporter is going to confuse the whole issue.'

Rebet was an unusual man. An expert administrator – without him Lysenko's department would have been chaos – he also had a fingertip feeling for propaganda. Far better than issuing the tired blasts from *Pravda* if you could manipulate the Western press into doing the job for you.

'We'd better forward this whole question on to

Moscow,' Lysenko decided. 'Inform them at once, have Newman checked on the computer. Above all, emphasize this idea was transmitted from Colonel Karlov in Tallinn –'

Which covers every angle, especially your own position, thought Rebet, as he reached for the phone.

The intriguing aspect was that it never occurred to either of them that *they* were being manipulated. Back in Helsinki Mauno Sarin had worked out all the angles as he sat for a few minutes in Pauli's chair in the basement. Offer the Bear a choice enough morsel and the chances were it would swallow it at one gulp.

Sometimes you get lucky. In Geneva Alain Charvet, the head of the private detective agency whom Tweed had visited, was phoned at his office by a stranger speaking French with a Russian accent. His caller explained he had just arrived to take over from a client of Charvet's who had returned 'home' – which Charvet interpreted as Moscow. They arranged to meet at a small café near police headquarters in the Old City.

Charvet was secretly amused at this new client's name. His command of English was excellent and over the phone – for God's sake – he had announced himself as Lev Shitov. Charvet already had a mental picture of Shitov when he entered the café and the reality was even worse than his imagination had conjured up.

Coarse. That was the word which had sprung to mind. If anything it was an understatement. Shitov was sitting at a corner table, pretending to read a copy of the *Journal de Genève* with a bottle of unopened beer perched in the middle of the table as Charvet had instructed. He sat down opposite the Russian.

Shitov was already half-drunk. Charvet could smell the fumes wafting across the table. Also, Shitov had trouble folding his newspaper which ended up a crumpled mess. It was not the only crumpled mess present.

Lev Shitov was short and fat with greasy, untidy black hair. A man in his late thirties, Charvet judged, he had a plump face, baggy eyes and slack lips. He wore a crumpled raincoat and the belt was twisted, pulled tight, so Shitov bulged above and below it.

'I'm Charvet. It is too early for snow on the mountains.'

'But the Rhine flows fast here.'

His speech was garbled and he should have said 'Rhône'. He produced a stained pocket flask, unscrewed the cap with difficulty and drank heavily from it. Then he extended the flask towards Charvet.

'Vodka,' he whispered. 'Help yourself.'

'Later, thank you.'

'Want you to follow a UNESCO official – English. Man called Peter Conway,' the Russian mumbled.

'Where he goes. Addresses he calls at. How long he stays. Who he meets. Photos – if possible. Women especially?'

202

Charvet reeled off the requirements from long experience. He could see that Shitov needed help with the conversation. And his mention of women pressed the right button. Shitov winked ponderously with his baggy right eye and helped himself to more sustenance from his flask.

'Women,' he repeated. 'Man I am replacing was helpful with addresses. He says Marie-Claire Passy is something no man must miss. She has boobs like cannonballs. I have an appointment. Phoned her soon as I'd called you. She's waiting. Peter Conway is in this building.'

Charvet was amazed. The fool had committed the name and the address to paper, a grubby slip which he pushed across the table with no attempt at concealment. Charvet's hand closed over it and it vanished. Shitov smiled fatuously as he glanced round the café.

'This is better than Tallinn. And working under that bastard Karlov. With luck he'll be murdered next before he ever finds Procane. I like this bar,' he maundered on, looking round again. 'Any idea of the time?'

'Exactly 4.15.'

'Oh, mother, my appointment with the Passy woman is now.'

'I'll show you how to get there. You've paid for the beer? Come on.'

Charvet had taken a swift decision. He doubted whether Lev Shitov would find his way to the address in the Old City by himself – and he could be questioned by the police on the way.

He guided Shitov by the arm out of the café and up the steep pavement high above the curving, cobbled street below. Charvet had known Marie-Claire Passy since his days with the police and he stopped in front of a crooked old building and pressed the bell. He pushed Shitov's head close to the speakphone as the clear, sharp voice of a girl asked in French, 'Who is that?'

'It's Lev – phoned you – '

'Come on up. First floor.'

Charvet pressed the door open after the buzzer sounded and thrust Shitov inside. He followed him a few steps to point him up the rickety staircase and whispered, 'First floor.'

When the door had shut on its automatic spring, Charvet rushed back down the street to the nearest telephone booth. He looked up Passy's number and dialled. She answered at once in her clear, sharp tone.

'Who is it?'

'Alain Charvet. You have a customer. Can he hear us?'

'You must be joking, Alain. He couldn't hear the crack of doom. And he's in the bathroom.'

'A favour. Pillow talk after the great experience. Try and get him to talk about Estonia.' He spelt out the name. 'And a man called Karlov.' Again he spelt it. 'He worked under him and hates the bastard – his own words. Also, if you can, find out what Karlov's job is. Shitov, your customer, is a new boy.'

'You have to tell me that?'

'I'll call you later.'

'Could this be dangerous?'

'Not if you keep him drunk. Vodka. He carries his own flask. And he's close to a blackout. In the morning he'll never recall what he told you.'

'Leave him to me.'

Charvet next consulted the directory again for the number of the UNESCO section Peter Conway worked for. He dialled the number and asked to speak to Conway, ready to break the connection if the Englishman came on to the phone.

A girl informed him Conway was in a meeting which was not expected to break up before seven in the evening. Charvet said there was no message, thanked her and put down the receiver. That gave him plenty of time to be at the UNESCO office later when he would do the job of following Conway.

Shitov . . . is a new boy. Charvet was familiar with the type. Certainly he would have received intensive training before he left Russia. In one of the special camps the Soviets ran he'd have been taught not only French but, probably, German. Far more important, he'd be shown how to dress, instructed in the habits and customs of the Swiss way of life.

He would be made familiar – not only from maps but also a large-scale model – with the layout of

Geneva. He would be introduced to a whole bag of tricks about the mechanics of his new craft. He would be warned against the temptations of the decadent West.

And that, as Charvet knew only too well, was the one thing which no amount of training could guard against one hundred per cent. The shock *impact* of leaving the austere motherland and being confronted overnight with the luxuries available in all forms in the West.

The women! The chic girls with their shapely legs clad in sheer black tights. And that was precisely what Shitov had gone overboard for – probably within days of his arrival. He'd gone hunting for a woman – her name and address helpfully provided by his predecessor who had also availed himself of the facilities.

It didn't always happen. Many Russians were too frightened to risk it. And, after a few weeks, Shitov would possibly grow more cautious. Charvet had noted that over the phone his French had betrayed traces of a Russian accent – whereas in the café his French had become more fluent, more accentless. But for the moment Shitov's manly instincts were in the ascendant: he was at his most vulnerable.

And Charvet's own reaction, his handling of the situation, was almost unique. It was Shitov's slip in mentioning the name, Procane, which had decided him to follow a course of action quite foreign to his normal pattern. Because Procane had been mentioned several times by Tweed during his visit to Geneva. If

Passy did pull off a hat trick then Tweed must be informed immediately.

The following day Tweed arranged to meet Alain Charvet. Charvet had – typically – called him from Cointrin Airport. He had timed the call so he could board a Swissair plane for London inside forty minutes. Tweed had agreed after hearing Charvet's coded message. Their rendezvous would be the Penta Hotel at Heathrow Airport.

Arriving at Heathrow, Tweed waited by the passenger exit barrier until he saw Charvet emerging. He noted the Swiss carried a large suitcase as though he was making a prolonged visit. Tweed wandered away towards the large Smith's bookstall and stopped at the paperback section.

He chose a position at one end away from other customers, his small ballpoint pen concealed in his hand. Hc glanced at several books as Charvet strolled up behind him and gazed vaguely at the vast array.

Tweed chose a paperback at random, a copy with a near-nude girl on the jacket. He opened it idly and wrote 134 in his neat handwriting on the end-paper, then returned the book to the shelf and walked away.

Charvet picked up two books, glanced at them, returned them to the shelves and then selected the paperback Tweed had looked at last. When he went to pay for it Tweed had vanished. Charvet walked across the hall and left by the exit where taxis queued.

'Penta Hotel,' he instructed the driver when he was inside.

As the taxi drove off he looked inside the paperback and pretended to read it. At the Penta Hotel he paid his fare, walked inside, glanced at the reception counter, saw that all the staff were busy and entered a waiting elevator. When he rapped quietly on the door of Room 134 Tweed opened the door and closed it as soon as he was inside.

'Good of you to come, Charvet. Something has happened in Geneva?'

'A new boy, Lev Shitov, arrived,' reported the Swiss in his precise fashion. 'He was so drunk when he called me he gave me his real name. We met in a café and he gave me a job to do – what is irrelevant. The main thing is he mentioned Procane.'

'Could it have been a trap?'

'No. I can tell when a man is raving drunk. And who knows I am working on this project for you?'

'Only me,' Tweed admitted. 'I must be getting tense to have asked you. Come and sit down and tell me what it's all about.'

'As I said, he's a new boy – just arrived in Geneva. Mad for a girl. The man he's replaced gave him an address and a name – luckily I knew the girl. From my police days I still know most of them. This girl, let's call her Celeste, really got him talking at her place. Previously he worked for Andrei Karlov, a colonel in the GRU in Tallinn, Estonia. Have you ever heard of him?'

'I'll check up on him when I get back. Do go on.'

'The reason I didn't use the phone – we can never be sure how far Washington has gone with using their orbiting satellites to tap landline telephone conversations – is that Celeste got out of Shitov the information that Karlov has been put in charge of the job of bringing Adam Procane safely across to Moscow.'

'This Karlov is still operating from Tallinn?'

'According to Shitov, yes. He overheard something when he was getting his final briefing in Moscow before departing for Geneva. Sometimes we overestimate Soviet security.'

'Please continue.'

'Karlov has a lot on his plate. A General Lysenko put him in control of the Procane operation – so it sounds as though they expect Procane to cross over via Scandinavia. But, incredible as it sounds, Karlov is also in charge of a major investigation into the murder of several GRU officers in Tallinn.'

'There's a story about that in *Le Monde*, the Paris daily, this morning. The alleged murder of GRU officers,' Tweed remarked. 'Do you think it's true?'

'Today's *Journal de Genève* also carries a small, unconfirmed report on the same topic. Estonia is becoming a seething cauldron. I remember at the beginning of August Enn Tarto, a leading nationalist, was sentenced to a long term of imprisonment. Then, in the middle of August, the Estonian Deputy Minister of Justice and his wife defected to Sweden. This Colonel Karlov is in a hot spot, which is odd.'

'Why odd?'

'Because he has the reputation of being a brilliant analyst according to what Lev Shitov told Celeste.'

'Any news of how Karlov gets on with his boss, this Lysenko?'

'Ah, there we may have the reason. Shitov detests Karlov. But he also let slip he was sent back to Moscow at Karlov's request for incompetence. As to Lysenko, Karlov apparently hates him even more than Shitov dislikes Karlov.'

'Happy families.' Tweed sighed and wished he could order coffee – but it wouldn't do for anyone, even a waiter, to see him talking with Charvet. 'Why,' Tweed continued, 'do we always consider that trouble is something we only have on our own doorstep? And I wonder why they let this Shitov out of Russia if he's so incompetent?'

'I think because he probably knows the right people – including General Lysenko, who recommended him for overseas duty. One more thing, Karlov apparently was the original contact with this Adam Procane while he was seconded to the Soviet Embassy in London. That might well explain why he's in control of the operation to see him safely into Russia when the time comes.'

'Lev Shitov does seem to have talked his head off to your Celeste,' Tweed commented, staring at the blank wall as though his real thoughts were miles away. 'Isn't that potentially dangerous for the future?

Is there some way we can shut him up? See he doesn't talk about this to anyone else?'

'Is that likely? If he told his own people they'd whisk him straight back to Russia.'

'He drinks heavily,' Tweed reminded him. 'He might confide in the wrong person. You need to frighten him. Isn't there some way you could scare the living daylights out of Lev?'

'That's a tall order.' Charvet leaned back in his chair and frowned. 'I've got it,' he said suddenly.

'Really frighten him,' Tweed stressed.

'I'll warn him I've just discovered Celeste is a member of the DST. The thought that he's talked to French counter-espionage will seal his lips for ever.'

'Excellent.' Tweed stood up. 'Your trip was well worthwhile. It gives me some more key pieces for the jigsaw I'm trying to put together.' He took a fat envelope from his breast pocket and handed it to Charvet. 'Swiss francs. They'll cover your fare and pay for your valuable services. You are catching the next flight back to Geneva?'

'Not the *next* flight,' Charvet corrected him. 'That might be the plane which brought me here. I'll have lunch at the airport and take the following flight.'

Tweed nodded. Charvet was a man who never missed a trick. There would be no witnesses to the fact that he had ever left Switzerland. Tweed picked up Charvet's large case.

'I'll carry this while I pay for the room. If they see

you carrying it out they might think you're skipping without settling your account. Wait by the taxi rank and I'll bring it out to you.'

'I'll keep working on Procane – and report the moment anything else develops.'

After leaving Charvet, Tweed did not immediately return to London. He caught the airport bus from Terminal 2 to Terminal 3, which handles transatlantic flights. Wandering over to the exit for passengers from the US, it took him only a few minutes to spot what he was checking.

A slim reed of a man wearing a raincoat and a porkpie hat stood chewing a matchstick, hands thrust inside his pockets. His clothes were British-made, he looked inconspicuous – but why, Tweed wondered, did Soviet watchers so often favour the porkpie hat? They were still checking on arrivals from the States.

On his way back to Park Crescent in a taxi, Tweed ran over in his mind what Charvet had reported. Colonel Andrei Karlov was supervising the arrangements for the reception of Adam Procane from remote Tallinn. So, Stilmar's contacts were seemingly reliable. It was Stilmar who had first suggested the crossing would be through Scandinavia. The GRU murders were an odd complication which Tweed didn't understand.

It could be the Estonia underground who were responsible, but Tweed didn't think so. He had never believed in coincidences. All the arrows were beginning to point towards the Baltic, to Estonia. He began to worry all over again about Bob Newman.

The next day he had something else to think about. A third American arrived aboard Concorde, a very big fish indeed.

Chapter Fourteen

'Did you realize Helene Stilmar is in London?' Monica enquired casually as Tweed walked into his office.

'No, I didn't – and you know it. What more have you up your sleeve?'

'It shows?'

'I should know your expressions by now.'

'Well, Helene is waiting to see you. Howard is out for the day so I put her in his office. I thought you might want to gather your strength, straighten your tie, brush your hair – things like that.'

'She's a stunner?'

'A very beautiful woman. Used to getting her own way, in the nicest possible manner. Clever at handling men. You'll need your wits about you,' Monica added with a hint of waspishness. 'Her file is on your desk. She's also one of Reagan's aides.'

Tweed walked round his desk and flipped through the file as he absent-mindedly checked the knot on his tie. Helene, the wife of Stilmar. Age: early thirties. Married six years. Responsibilities: Europe, with special attention to the woman's angle. Previous experience: assistant in State Department.

He guessed that was probably how she had met Stilmar. The main thing was she had spent time on the Washington circuit. She'd be *au fait* with the kind of wheeler-dealing which got things done in DC. Tweed closed the file and went to the wash-room to tidy up. When he came back Monica glanced up.

'Ready to do battle?'

'Wheel her in, as the Yanks are alleged to say.'

'Anyone less in need of a wheelchair I haven't seen for a long, long time.'

Helene Stilmar was slim, very erect, and had long, shapely legs with clinging sheer black stockings and expensive, high-heeled shoes. Her thick, chestnut-coloured hair was shaped so it displayed to advantage her superb neck.

She had strong bone structure, a prominent but delicate nose and a well-formed chin expressing energy and determination. She walked forward, hand extended, her grey eyes staring straight at Tweed as she gave him a smile which drew him to her immediately.

'Mr Tweed, I've heard so much about you from my husband – and he is a man who is not easily impressed.'

'I can see why he was impressed by you.'

Out of the corner of his eye Tweed saw Monica's head jerk up in blank astonishment. This was yet another side of her chief people rarely saw. He remained standing and threw her off balance with his next comment.

'It's nearly time for lunch. I know a place I think you might like. The Capital. It's close to Harrods. The food is quite excellent, the atmosphere intimate, the wine good. You will join me, I hope? With you as my dining companion everyone is going to look at my table. I shall enjoy that.'

'Mr Tweed . . .'

'Just Tweed will do.'

'Tweed. I like your name, too. I think that's a really lovely idea. Of course I'd be delighted to join you.' She smiled her warm smile again. 'I'm sure you and I will find plenty to talk about.'

'Book us Table Seven, please,' Tweed requested of Monica, without looking at his assistant.

'What have you done with my husband, Tweed? He's disappeared.'

As she asked the question Helene watched her lunch companion over the rim of her glass of dry white wine. She had the most compelling eyes and her voice was feminine and enticing. She's sexing me up, Tweed thought as he sipped at his own glass.

Her beige dress had a high collar and she wore a scarf of the same material looped over her left shoulder. At the Capital, Table Seven is at one end of the long room, next to the window and with its back to the wall. They sat alongside each other on the banquette and Helene was turned sideways to observe his reaction.

'My impression is your husband goes his own way.'

'So,' she pounced, 'you have seen him since he arrived here?'

'Only briefly.'

'We have no secrets from each other,' she pressed.

'That's a nice relationship.'

'Tweed, talking to you is like addressing the Berlin Wall.'

'I'd sooner talk about you. You like government work? And what exactly do you do? Or is that a state secret you only share with your husband?'

'Touché!' She played with the stem of her glass. 'What do I do? Well, the President believes that women are playing a more and more important part in influencing opinion. He also believes the same thing is happening in Europe. I'm a first-generation American, Tweed. The President thinks I have what he calls a fingertip feeling about European women. So, I advise him on how they will react to a particular policy. It's as simple as that.'

Not quite, Tweed said to himself. The file on Helene Stilmar had recorded she was of Swedish origin. A Swedish mother and an American father. Scandinavia again.

'And what are you doing on this trip?' he enquired, glancing out of the window.

'Visiting various European capitals to check on present opinion.' She stared straight at him and smiled. Tweed felt himself being drawn towards her vibrant personality. This woman is dangerous, he thought as he gazed back. 'There is a growing amount of talk – and anxiety – in Washington about some person called Adam Procane.'

'Man or woman?' he asked promptly.

'A man, I presume.' Her voice showed surprise at the question. 'With a name like that.'

'A code-name could conceal a woman.'

'You think it is a code-name, then?'

'You know someone of that name in Washington? Or anywhere else?'

'They said you were a top professional,' she observed and helped herself to some smoked chicken which had just been served during a pause in the conversation. 'No, I don't know anyone called Procane. The worrying thing is neither does anyone else.'

'That suggests it is a code-name – if Procane does exist. I was going to ask you which part of Europe you have on your programme. A highly organized woman like yourself will have mapped out every hour of your visit before you left Washington.'

'You know just what to say to a woman, don't you? That was something they didn't warn me about.'

'And you still haven't answered my question.'

'You have, of course, heard about the Soviet mini-submarines penetrating the Swedish archipelago close to an important naval base? Our information is that the Swedes are becoming a little less neutral – they are so furious with the Russians. I have an idea. Why don't you come with me?'

'Where to?'

'Stockholm. I fly there tomorrow.'

'Did you succumb to her charms?' Monica enquired when Tweed returned to his office just before five o'clock. 'You have a very dreamy look.'

'She wants me to fly with her to Stockholm tomorrow.'

'Oh, I see.'

Monica suddenly found something among her papers which she studied intently. Tweed took off his damp Burberry – it had started to drizzle, a sea-mist type of drizzle which made his face moist. He sat down behind his desk.

'No, you don't see at all. It means a hell of a lot more work. The compass needle is swinging madly in the direction of Scandinavia. Now we have Cord Dillon on his way to Copenhagen. At lunch I hear from Helene Stilmar the fact that she is going to Stockholm. That makes two potential Procane candidates heading for the Scandinavian route towards Russia.'

'Surely Procane can't be a woman?'

'Can you imagine how much information Helene may be carrying in her beautiful head – remembering who her husband is?'

'Stilmar won't talk to her about his job,' Monica commented firmly.

'You can never be sure. She's his second wife.'

'What's that got to do with it?'

'I've noticed men are more likely to confide in their second wives. It's what the Americans call starting over. And she is a very attractive woman.'

'You really are smitten.'

'You might not think so if you'd overheard our conversation at lunch. It was like a fencing match – and she's an expert when it comes to fencing.'

'There you go again.'

'And there's more. I urgently need a good photo of Helene – for widespread distribution. Head and shoulders – it will have to be a blow-up. Our photographer will never get that close without her knowing.'

'I don't see how he's going to get anywhere near her.' Monica looked up from her notebook where she had been making brief notes.

'That's easy. We'll use the double act technique. Freddie is still away delivering the Stilmar pics. Is Harry Butler available?'

'Yes. And he happened to be in the hall when she arrived and brought her up, so he knows what she looks like.'

'Better and better. He's good with a camera. Now, she'll be at the Dorchester – Stilmar said he was staying there. So, I think I'll send her a huge bunch of flowers.'

'Accompanied by a *billet-doux*? "With all my love"?'

'Not quite. The card should simply read "Bon

voyage. Tweed". And I want that card buried in the bouquet so she has to search for it.'

'What are you up to now?'

'Harry, the cameraman, takes along a partner. Adams for preference. Harry follows Adams into the foyer of the Dorchester. Adams asks for Helene Stilmar and insists she has to come down to the foyer. He's parked his van awkwardly – he'll think of something. Adams is the florist's delivery man – he presents the bouquet and says he must have a receipt. Knowing Helene a little now, she'll be consumed with curiosity as to who has sent the flowers. You would be yourself. She'll burrow away for the card. All this will give Harry plenty of time to take his pics without her knowing.'

'I don't remember our using this one before.'

'We haven't. I just thought it up.'

The brief shower stopped and the sun shone down on Helsinki's South Harbour as Newman stood on the pavement opposite Silja Dock and took photos with his Voigtländer like a tourist. It was 10.28 a.m. and going to be another lovely autumn day.

The *Georg Ots* was about to sail as Laila chatted at the dockside with a young seaman unfastening a mooring rope. In her right hand she held a large carrier bag and she looked round and up at the ship before pulling out a package and slipping it to the seaman. He concealed it under his heavy jacket, threw the rope down and headed for the gangway as Laila crossed the road and wandered off along the waterfront away from the city. Newman strolled after her, only catching up when they were out of sight of the ship.

'I really didn't think it would work,' Laila admitted. 'But when I tried questioning one of them I never thought to offer that kind of present.'

Inside her carrier bag she had hidden at Newman's suggestion a choice collection of pop records – wrapped in the package she had just passed over to the seaman. In case the man had been older, her carrier also contained a box of Havana cigars and several cartons of cigarettes.

'Find out anything?' Newman enquired.

'Yes. To start with he wouldn't give out any information until I told him about the records; ABBA, Michael Jackson, and so on. He couldn't resist *that* bait.'

'And he told you what?'

'You were right. They know everything about all the passengers before they ever get near the ship – because they have checked the visa applications carefully. At least I think he said that – it's not easy to understand every word of Estonian.'

'Anything else?'

'You were right again. During every crossing they have one GRU man in plain clothes aboard checking and watching the passengers. And it will be nice and quiet if we walk in here.'

They turned away from the curving waterfront road, entering the large, hilly park Takala had pointed out from the chopper. What had he called it? Well Park.

A whole network of pathways curved up and down between pine trees. Young girls and men, jogging, kept passing them. Laila led the way up to the highest point at the very tip of the peninsula and they paused to take in the panoramic view of harbour and open sea dotted with islands.

'Better watch your footing here,' Laila warned.

They were perched on a granite cap and a fresh breeze blew her hair. Newman took several cautious steps forward and saw the reason for her warning. They were standing at the edge of a massive rock bluff which ended precipitously. Beyond there was nothing but space as the bluff descended vertically about seventy feet to a hard, tarred path winding down to the road which fringed the peninsula. It was very quiet, very remote, and there was no one else about.

'You see what I mean?' Laila called out. 'One step further and we never talk together again. There have been accidents – drunks coming up here at night and stepping into eternity.'

It was a remark Newman was to recall later.

Chapter Fifteen

'The prints of your Helene are ready for despatch,' Monica informed Tweed. 'And really, it is quite a good likeness.'

'Send them off by courier at once, please,' Tweed requested.

He had kept one print which he inserted carefully inside a cardboard-backed envelope and slipped into a drawer. Monica watched this with scarcely-concealed amusement.

'Shall I get it framed for you?' she enquired. 'I'm sure it would look nice in a silver frame. I know a – '

'Stop larking about and get those prints off,' Tweed told her brusquely. 'She's flying to Stockholm tomorrow so I want the prints to arrive ahead of her. There will be a messenger at Arlanda Airport to collect them from our courier. Password "Golden Girl". I've already phoned Stockholm. Give me details of the flight and I'll phone them also.'

'Golden Girl. My – '

'I thought you'd rise to that one.'

'And what purpose will the photos be put to?'

'Distributed to airport security, the Coastguard

people, the Stockholm police. And SAPO, of course. They're in charge of letting the others know the score.'

'And what is the score?'

'You see this line Dillon drew with his felt-tip pen,' he walked across to the wall-map and his finger followed the dark line along the eastern coast of Sweden the American had drawn.

'Yes. So?'

'If Helene attempts to cross that line she will be arrested at once. They'll trump up some charge. Suspected of dealing in drugs, anything that works.'

'You really are ruthless,' Monica commented with feeling.

The Estonian trawler, *Saaremaa*, was now sailing deep inside the Kattegat between Sweden and Denmark. Having returned from the North Sea she was proceeding on a southerly course, heading for the Öresund – the narrow channel dividing Sweden from Denmark.

Once she passed Copenhagen, the open Baltic and distant Estonia lay before her. In the wireless room the operator was just completing sending a long, high-speed signal on his modern transmitter. As he ended the signal the door to his cabin opened and Captain Olaf Prii's tall figure stood there motionless. The operator looked up.

'I have now sent the coded message, sir,' he reported.

Prii nodded, closed the door and returned to his

bridge. A plane with Danish markings was over-flying his vessel and he watched it fly away towards Kastrup Airport. He smiled grimly and gave the order to increase speed.

Despite the speed of the transmission, it was clearly picked up and recorded at GCHQ, the superbly-equipped listening post at Cheltenham in England. Within an hour a report about the transmission was lying on Tweed's desk.

At almost the same time a further report came in, this time from Danish NATO Intelligence. The message recorded the exact position and approximate speed of the *Saaremaa*. Tweed got up from his desk, walked over to the wall-map and grunted as he placed a pin in the map.

He walked back to his desk and read again the report from Cheltenham. '... *first indications suggest high-speed transmission in Soviet one-time code*...' Which meant it was practically unbreakable – impossible to decipher.

The position and probable future course of the *Saaremaa* did not surprise Tweed. What might have intrigued him if he could have read the message was the destination and the recipient. The signal had been sent to Tallinn. It was addressed to Colonel Andrei Karlov.

An hour later Monica returned from her mission at the Dorchester Hotel. She gave Tweed a certain look as she unwrapped her damp scarf from her head – it was drizzling outside – and took off her raincoat with irritating slowness.

Tweed watched her and was careful not to say anything. From her expression he knew she had discovered something and was teasing him by taking her time. It was her way of paying him back for keeping her in the dark about Procane.

'Helene Stilmar lied – by omission,' she announced while she settled herself behind her desk. 'I told reception at the Dorchester a friend wanted to phone her urgently – that the friend had tried to contact her for several days.'

'Do get to the point, Monica.'

'I believe you are under the impression Stilmar and his wife travelled together across the Atlantic.'

'Of course they would.'

'But they didn't! Helene arrived the day before her husband. Stilmar followed her on another flight the next day.'

'*Followed?*'

'The word has two meanings – to join someone later by mutual arrangement – ' she paused, ' – or to keep track of what the other person is up to.'

'I am fairly fluent in English.'

'I also learnt,' Monica continued, ignoring the remark, 'that Helene Stilmar is flying to Stockholm on the direct flight *today*. I got on rather well with that receptionist. He said my friend would have to phone quickly to catch her.'

'She did tell me she was going there – you know that.'

'Women sometimes tell a man something to conceal the fact they are planning something else they haven't told him.'

'She even suggested we fly there together,' Tweed persisted.

'You'll have to run fast to catch her. Her plane took off from Heathrow at 11.35. She's in midair now.'

'What times does that flight reach Arlanda?'

Tweed was unlocking a drawer and taking out a small address book. Monica bent over a fresh file she was compiling, a file headed *Helene Stilmar*.

'15.30 hours, local Swedish time,' she told him. 'Don't forget Sweden is one hour ahead of us.'

'Then I may just be in time,' Tweed commented as he reached for the phone and began dialling.

The university town of Uppsala is about six Swedish miles north of Stockholm. One Swedish mile equals seven English – so Uppsala is approximately forty miles from the capital.

It also has a cathedral and a grimmer establishment. At Uppsala is located the seismological institute which records earth tremors. At intervals this institute hits the world's headlines when it reports the location and magnitude of an atomic device tested somewhere in the world.

Ingrid Melin lived in a large ground-floor apartment on the outskirts of the town. A brunette of thirty-two, she was five feet seven inches tall – but her exuberant personality made her seem taller. Her dark hair was trimmed well back above her high forehead and draped to shoulder length. Her nose was straight, her eyes brown, her gaze wary.

Married twice, she often joked, 'Third time, unlucky again.' With another girl she had founded a photocopying service which had expanded over the years and was now very profitable, the main business coming from her Stockholm office. Which wasn't bad, considering they had started with one second-hand machine. Dripping wet, she ran from the bathroom to the phone in her living room and lifted the receiver on the sixth ring.

'Ingrid Melin.'

'Tweed here. Speaking from London. How are you?'

'Marvellous! Now I hear from you. You have work for me?'

'Urgent work. A flight from London – nonstop – arrives at Arlanda at 15.30 hours. There is an American woman aboard . . .' Tweed gave a careful description of Helene Stilmar and Ingrid's reaction was immediate and positive.

'I shall know her.'

'Can you get to Arlanda in time and follow her?'

'Of course! I take a taxi direct from Uppsala to the airport. There is good time. No problem!'

'Use some of the money I deposited in your bank.'

'Every krona is still there.'

'I knew it would be. I may send you more. The woman's name is Helene Stilmar,' he spelt it out. 'I need to know where she goes, who she meets. Most important, Ingrid – if she buys a ticket for Finland to go there by boat or plane you call me at once. If I am not here give the news to Monica.'

'Monica. I do that. Tweed! You will come to Stockholm to see me? Maybe?'

'I do not know. If I can, I will.'

'Please come! If you can. Now I will do the research for your insurance. I must go. I have to call a taxi.'

'Ingrid. Take care.'

'I will do that. Goodbye!'

Tweed replaced the phone and stared into the distance. He had been careful to use simple language. Ingrid had few opportunities to speak in English.

Tweed had a whole network of girls in Western Europe he used to obtain information. As he had once said, 'Women are more loyal than men if they trust you.' And among the string of girls he had built up Ingrid was probably the most reliable and resourceful. A very practical girl who worked out things for herself. Monica made the remark with her head bent over her new file.

'You could have given her a hint you're going to Stockholm. She likes you a lot.'

'You know I never give anyone advance notice of my movements if I can possibly avoid it.'

'She's very security-conscious.'

'She's very good,' Tweed agreed, still staring into space. 'She even made a reference to doing research for my insurance work – just in case someone was listening in. I do believe she's the only one who suspects what my real job is.'

'Is there any danger for her?' Monica asked.

'There is always danger – mostly when you least expect it.'

'Tweed, you look after that girl. If anything happened to her I would never forgive you.'

He gazed at her in astonishment. In all the years they had worked together Monica had never said anything like that to him before. The remark unsettled him. He began to worry and took a sudden decision.

'Arrange it so I can catch a plane to Stockholm any day at a moment's notice.'

The following morning Tweed heard news that increased his anxiety – as Monica noticed from his change of attitude. It was, of course, Howard who brought the good news. He strolled into Tweed's office, closed the door, perched his backside on a corner of his deputy's desk and folded his arms.

His manner was affable but Tweed, who leaned back in his chair and clasped his hands in his lap, detected hostility beneath his chief's amiability.

'I understand,' Howard began, 'unless I'm way off

beam – which I may well be. After all, I don't know what this Procane business is really about. Which makes it a trifle difficult for all of us.'

He was studying the fingernails of his right hand now. For God's sake, get on with it, Tweed thought, but he remained silent.

'I understand,' Howard began again, 'that you're interested in any high-ranking Americans who visit our shores at this moment in time.'

Tweed saw Monica wince behind Howard's back at the pompous phraseology. He nodded to encourage Howard to stop creeping round the mulberry bush.

'So,' Howard went on, 'you might care to know that General Paul Dexter, Chief of Staff of the United States Army, came in this morning aboard a special aircraft which landed at Lakenheath in East Anglia. Relevant?'

Tweed got up slowly and walked round his desk. He stood with his back to the wall-map. His expression gave no clue as to what he was thinking.

'Do we know why he is here?' he asked.

'Tour of inspection. He's going on to look at various NATO units in Denmark and Norway. But first he wants to meet you. Ministry of Defence. Lanyon's office. This morning. Eleven o'clock prompt.' He walked to the door and paused before opening it. 'He's a stickler for punctuality, I gather.'

'The arrogant sod,' Monica muttered when the door had closed. 'He knows you're always prompt.'

'Not in a good mood,' Tweed commented as he stared at the map.

'You do realize he's so hopping mad about the P.M.'s directive, he hopes you're going to fall flat on your face so he can get rid of you.'

'I don't know about that.'

'I do. What's the matter? You look as though a bomb had just exploded.'

'Scandinavia again. Another top-flight American.' Tweed appeared to be voicing his thoughts aloud as he went on gazing at the map. 'This is getting very dangerous.'

'You know the time?'

'Yes. Howard has deliberately given me the minimum warning to get to the MOD for my appointment.'

Tweed was escorted by a uniformed major to the door of Colonel Lanyon of Military Intelligence. When the major opened the door and Tweed entered the room Lanyon was nowhere in sight. A keen-eyed American in his early fifties and his shirt-sleeves rose to greet him from behind Lanyon's desk.

'Good of you to come and see me, Mr Tweed.' They shook hands and General Dexter ushered his visitor into an armchair, then pulled his own chair from behind the desk and sat alongside Tweed.

'They've handed you the grenade with the pin

pulled, Tweed. You are running the operation to find this Adam Procane before it's too late. Right?'

'That is so. Yes.'

'I won't hide from you that the Pentagon is shit-scared about one of our people crossing over to Russia at this stage. At any stage it would be a disaster. At this stage – with the President coming up for re-election in November – it would be a catastrophe. Who is Procane, Tweed? Any ideas? And this conversation is just between the two of us. I give you my word.'

Tweed hesitated, looking at the American. Dexter was a vigorous man, both physically and mentally. Thinning brown hair with streaks of grey receded back over a high forehead, the hair trimmed short. Above a strong nose his dark eyes stared back as he studied the Englishman. A very strong, decisive man.

'I regret to say I have no idea yet,' Tweed replied.

'A man like you will have thoughts. Maybe even suspicions. I also know you've been very active – recently you visited Western Europe. We do know you have a most unusual organization with agents all over Europe. Give, Tweed.'

'Being American,' Tweed began slowly, 'it is clear that whoever Procane is must first travel to Europe on his way to the Soviet Union. And the compass needle is now pointing more and more towards Scandinavia.'

'Which is where I'm headed for,' Dexter gave a low rumbling chuckle. 'So that puts me on your list of suspects.'

'Is that a statement or a question?'

'A statement! Quit stalling me.'

'Quite a few top people from Washington have chosen this moment to arrive in Europe.'

'That I know. You Brits think we're naive in Washington?'

'I never thought Americans were naive – unlike some of my colleagues,' Tweed admitted. 'I have never made the mistake of underestimating our friends,' he added.

Dexter laughed again. 'Let's get straight down to the bottom line. You're thinking of Stilmar and Cord Dillon. They are over here on the same mission.'

'You've left out Helene Stilmar.'

'Helene? Now there's a woman. All woman. Did you know she worked as liaison between State and the Pentagon before Reagan took her on as adviser?'

'I didn't know that.'

'She is good, very good. Competent as hell. Why add her to the list? Procane is a man.'

'How do we know that?' Tweed challenged. 'It's obviously a code-name. What better cover than using a man's name for a woman?'

'You don't trust anyone, do you?'

'I don't rule out anyone until I know. General, where are you going to in Scandinavia?'

It was Dexter who hesitated now. Again he studied Tweed, who remained silent. There was no better way of encouraging a confidence. Dexter flexed his long, wiry hands and sighed.

'Better you know – you'd find out anyway. Officially I'm making an inspection tour of units in Denmark and Norway. My main job on this trip is to travel secretly to Sweden for consultation with certain military chiefs. I fly in a Swedish plane in civilian clothes to an airfield at a place called Jakobsberg. That's just outside Stockholm.'

'I know it. The Swedes have Drakens there.'

'A fine warplane, the Draken. You certainly know your Europe.'

'I'm surprised the Swedes agreed – even astounded. If your visit was discovered by the Russians there would be all hell to pay.'

'Which is why my visit has been so carefully planned. I've got a double, a guy who looks just like me. While I'm talking with the Swedes at Jakobsberg, my double in full uniform will be inspecting NATO units in full view in Norway. Moscow will be checking my movements like a cat watching a mouse. That way we throw dust in their eyes. The Swedes are getting nervous – those Soviet mini-subs testing their naval defences in the archipelago were a mistake . . .'

'They'll never join NATO,' Tweed observed.

'We don't want them to. They're very neutral, as you know – which is their affair. I'm taking with me a submarine warfare expert. He might give them a tip or two about bringing those subs to the surface. Maybe they'll give us a tip or two. They're very good at their job.'

'When are you flying to Jakobsberg?'

'The trip is still being finalized,' Dexter went vague for the first time. 'Within the next week or two, I'd guess.' He stood up and Tweed heaved himself out of the deep armchair. 'It's been good talking with you, Tweed. I just feel a little less unhappy about this mysterious Procane thing now we've met. You really think he exists?'

'Don't you?'

'More and more reports keep coming in from Europe about him. But no description. Just zilch.'

'I don't promise,' Tweed said cautiously, 'but I might just have some kind of a description in the not too distant future.'

'You'll pass that on to our people?'

'They'll know about it as soon as I do.'

'Then, good luck, Tweed. Hope to see you again.'

They shook hands. As Tweed opened the door to leave he turned back briefly. The American was smiling. Paul Dexter was the very prototype of a US general. Unlike the bland Eisenhower Tweed had watched on films, Dexter was direct and forthright, a man with no time for *finesse*. He probably had a contempt for most diplomats and politicians. Tweed thought about him as he walked down the staircase to where his escort, the major, waited for him. Prototypes always worried Tweed.

'A signal has just come in from Danish Intelligence,' Monica announced as Tweed returned to his office.

'Let me get my coat off. Please,' he said.

'Cord Dillon has just left Copenhagen on a flight bound for Stockholm,' she continued remorselessly. 'He's travelling under the assumed name of Alfred Mayer.'

'Warn Gunnar Hornberg of SAPO. The usual routine. Let Gunnar have a description. Has he time to send people to Arlanda to see where Dillon is heading for?'

'Yes. If I call him now. It's thirty minutes from Stockholm to Arlanda, isn't it?'

'More like forty-five. In any case Gunnar can use airport security.' Tweed's eyes turned automatically to the wall-map. 'The pace is accelerating. All roads lead to Stockholm.'

'Of course,' Monica surmised as she began dialling, 'Dillon may be on his way to see Hornberg. We know SAPO have discreet links with the CIA.'

Which was true, Tweed thought as he sat behind his desk. For years, SAPO had kept in close touch with their opposite numbers in Washington – all despite Sweden's genuine stance of impartial neutrality.

'Tell Gunnar,' he said as she completed dialling, 'that if he finds Dillon making any attempt to go further east to Finland he must stop him at all costs. It would involve political complications – that sort of thing. Tell him to hold everything until I reach Stockholm.'

'When are you going? The line is engaged.'

'Today. If possible.'

'Flight SK 528. Departs Heathrow 18.30 hours. Arrives Arlanda 20.40,' Monica said promptly. 'I'll book you on that flight. A packed suitcase is in the cupboard as usual.'

'Also put three watchers on General Paul Dexter. That, too, is urgent.'

'What isn't?' She was dialling the SAPO number again. 'Do I take over while you're away? If so, better tell Howard.'

'So many pieces on the board,' Tweed remarked, still staring at the wall-map. 'And Bob Newman is still out there in the wilderness – in more ways than one.'

'That was the other thing I had to tell you. Laila Sarin was on the phone. Newman is still at the Hotel Hesperia on the Mannerheimintie. Laila is having a tough time – but she's sticking to Newman like glue. Her expression, not mine. God, you work these girls, Tweed. What with her in Helsinki and poor Ingrid in Stockholm.'

'I know. It bothers me at times. At least I'm going to join them.'

'You'll be back in your element. Fieldwork again.'

'If I haven't lost my grip.'

Monica snorted, then began talking to SAPO head-quarters. As she talked, Tweed revolved in his mind the movements of all the characters involved. Everything was now pointing to Procane crossing via Scandinavia. Monica asked the question as she put down the receiver.

'Hornberg alerted. Do you mind telling me exactly what this Procane thing is all about? You know something? You remind me of a conductor guiding a great orchestra through an intricate symphony.'

'What a weird remark. And you are in charge while I'm away. I will tell Howard before I leave. Incidentally, I saw him on my way upstairs after seeing Dexter. He told me Stilmar has returned from Europe. He's at the Dorchester. Have him watched, too.'

'You do realize we're stretched to the limit? I'll manage something. And you still haven't told me about Procane,' she reminded Tweed who had left his desk to collect his packed case.

'Let me recall something if you'll promise not to fly into a rage.'

'Which means I'm not going to like it.'

'A secret remains a secret only when one person alone knows it.'

Part Two

STOCKHOLM

The Forward Area

Chapter Sixteen

As the plane descended, broke through the overcast cloud and began its final run-in to Arlanda, Helene Stilmar peered out of the window. Sweden lay only a few hundred feet below.

Huge copses of fir forest were scattered over the flat landscape. Here and there clusters of great boulders created the impression of a desert area. Then there was the occasional road, the occasional car or truck seeming to crawl along its surface.

The ground came up swiftly to meet the aircraft. The concrete runway appeared and Helene braced herself. The wheels of the machine kissed the runway. A dense wall of fir trees rushed past the window. The plane lost more speed, cruised and then crawled to where the telescopic passenger exit waited to nose its way against the exit door. She was in Sweden, home of her ancestors.

In the reception hall Ingrid Melin was standing and staring at the point where the Stilmar woman would appear. Hatless, she wore a powder blue pant suit, looking very slim and erect. To make herself inconspicuous, she had taken up a position behind a family also waiting for arrivals off the flight. Then she saw Helene Stilmar.

Tall, chestnut-haired, confident with her brisk stride, she wore an expensive cream suit which looked as if it had been bought from a couturier. A porter relieved her of the three large cases she had been pushing on a trolley and led her outside. Ingrid followed, saw that she was taking a taxi and ran to the Volvo she had hired.

The road linking Arlanda to distant Stockholm is a magnificent six-lane highway which passes through open country for a good fifteen minutes before the suburbs of the city begin to appear.

It is rocky country and frequently the highway passes between granite gulches and past huge outcrops. Ingrid drove a large four-seater Volvo and crouched over the wheel with intense concentration as she kept one vehicle between herself and Helene's taxi. Her head hardly moved as she drove with an expertise a man might have envied.

On the passenger seat beside her rested a suitcase. She expected Stilmar to go to one of the top hotels but that was only an assumption. She might be staying in a friend's apartment – anywhere.

Ingrid had changed her mind about using a taxi from Uppsala almost as soon as she ended her call from Tweed. She had hired a car because this gave her so much more mobility. It was also an assumption that Stilmar was heading for Stockholm – she might be travelling to a quite different destination.

It was with a sense of relief that Ingrid followed the taxi across Sergels Torg, the main square in the centre of Stockholm with its curious sculptured column made of a glass-like substance. It was with an even greater sense of relief when she saw the taxi pull up outside the Grand Hotel.

Ingrid drove the Volvo straight into the one remaining parking slot outside the hotel. Another vehicle must just have departed. She locked the Volvo, attended to the meter, then walked ahead of Helene up the steps into the hotel, carrying her case.

She had been able to execute this manoeuvre because Helene had those three large cases which had to be unloaded from the taxi and taken inside by a porter. Curious, Ingrid was thinking – that she should need so much luggage for a short stay, which was the impression she had received from Tweed.

Ingrid stood with her case at her feet as though waiting for someone close to the reservations counter while Helene registered. She heard the receptionist tell the new arrival her room number on the sixth floor. She watched as Helene walked inside the oldest of the three elevators, a gilt cage with walls of padded red leather. When the doors closed she walked to the concierge's desk, speaking in English.

'I need to put in a long distance call. London. Here is the number. Please check the cost – I will pay when I have made the call.' She paused. It was a very public place from which to phone Tweed. 'No, I have changed my mind. I'll make the call from my room.'

Picking up her case, she walked the few steps to reservations, at the rear of the reception hall. A girl came forward and asked could she help?

'I'd like a room for three days, please. Have you something on the sixth floor? At the front. I like the view from up there . . .'

'Only a double. The price is one thousand kronor per night. That includes breakfast.'

'I'll take it.'

'Room 634.' The girl was writing the room number and the price on a small blue folder which carried a colour picture of the Grand Hotel on the front cover, a picture taken at night with reflections from street lamps like stabs of light in the still waters. She added the dates of the visitor's stay.

'A porter will take – '

'I don't need one,' Ingrid interjected. 'I can carry my own case and I'm in a hurry.'

She took the room key from the girl's hand and walked inside the same lift which had transported Helene Stilmar up to her room. Arriving at the sixth floor, she checked the wall-plates which indicated the directions of the various rooms, walked across the deserted hall which was furnished with several comfortable chairs, and inserted her key into the door of Room 634.

'Tweed is not here, Ingrid,' said Monica on the phone. She kept talking to reassure the Swedish girl. 'He knew you would call and asked me to take a message. I can't call him but he'll be phoning me. He has left me in charge – I am sitting behind his desk. He will want to know how you are getting on. He said that to me just before he went away.'

Like Tweed, Monica was careful to use simple English. God, she thought, we British are awful the way we don't learn other languages. We leave the foreigners to learn ours. Ingrid began talking, phrasing what she said carefully because the call was passing through a switchboard.

'I picked up the subject of our research at the airport. The subject has booked a room at the Grand Hotel for seven days. Room Number 636. The subject has a lot of luggage – she has three large bags.'

'Where are you calling from, Ingrid?'

'A room I have booked at the Grand Hotel. My room number is 634. If I am not here when you telephone, please leave a message with the porter's desk. Make sure to tell them not only my name but also my room number. The Grand Hotel telephone number is 08 22 10 20.'

'I understand, Ingrid. Be very careful.'

'Will he be coming here?'

There was a note of anxiety tinged with hope in her voice. Monica thought quickly before she replied.

'You never can tell when he will turn up, my dear.'

'Thank you. I will keep you in touch with what happens.'

Monica replaced the receiver, picked up her biro and revolved it between her teeth. Strictly speaking, she shouldn't have made that last encouraging remark, but it could be very lonely – working on your own in the field. And Monica could not rid herself of the feeling it could also be dangerous. What the hell was Tweed up to?

'Any developments?' General Lysenko asked breezily as he walked into his office in Leningrad.

'Yes,' replied Rebet. 'Very strange developments. The Americans are coming to Europe in force. Two reports have just come in. General Paul Dexter, Chief of Staff of the United States Army, took off from Andrews Air Force Base in a military plane yesterday.'

'How do we know that?' rapped out Lysenko.

'We have a mechanic we pay for information at Andrews – he helped service the machine and overheard that the plane was bound for England. Later he saw Dexter boarding the aircraft which immediately took off.'

'And the second report?'

'Our watcher near the British Ministry of Defence in London Whitehall saw Dexter go inside the building. Our people at Heathrow have been warned to look out for him in case he takes a flight to Europe.'

'They saw Dexter arrive there?' Lysenko pressed.

'No, they didn't. But it was a military aircraft he travelled aboard. That suggests it would land at one of the American air bases in East Anglia. So he tried to arrive secretly.'

'Impossible that he could be Procane,' Lysenko mused aloud.

'He would have access to all the information provided by Procane,' Rebet pointed out.

'And the Kremlin have just told me they regard that information as genuine,' Lysenko responded with a note of triumph. 'So that is one in the eye for Colonel Karlov and those bloody sceptical reports he tries to bury me under. Procane exists. Procane is coming. Tell that to Karlov. Tell him to arrange a meeting with Mauno Sarin in Tallinn as early as possible. Sarin will know the moment one of these Americans slips across from Sweden into Finnish territory. He must tell Sarin we shall regard it as a hostile act if he does not inform us immediately this *agent-provocateur* arrives in Finland.'

'*Agent-provocateur*? Procane? I do not understand.'

'That is because you do not look at the other side of the hill – like the British Duke of Wellington always did.' Widely read in military history, Lysenko never lost a chance to show his erudition.

'I still don't understand,' Rebet persisted. 'Procane is our man.'

'But we do not let that wily Finn, Mauno Sarin, know this. We make him think Procane is an American agent who has had the audacity to risk compromising Finnish neutrality. Then he will not hesitate for one second to hand him over to us.'

Rebet nodded. Lysenko was full of surprises. At times he displayed extraordinary cunning in manipulating people. It was, Rebet admitted to himself, a clever ploy.

'But we still don't know who Procane is,' he reminded his chief.

'We have plenty of candidates for the role. We know Cord Dillon has flown to Europe – that shortly afterwards Stilmar arrived from Washington. Now we have the illustrious General Paul Dexter paying a visit to Europe – and yet he was over here only two months ago. Why this second, sudden visit? Mark my words and remember them well, Rebet. One of those three is Procane. And now? Phone Colonel Karlov.'

At this stage of the game Lysenko was – from his point of view – correct. He had only overlooked one further candidate. Helene Stilmar.

Chapter Seventeen

'I know where Alexis was murdered,' Newman said to Laila.

His voice was flat, his face frozen in a hard expression. He was sitting in his double room at the Hesperia Hotel in Helsinki. Laila was snuggled up close to him, perched on the arm of his chair.

Their relationship had grown closer during the days they had spent together – tramping the streets of the city. They had not slept together – the Finnish reporter was too young for Newman. At least that was what he told himself. The truth was he did not feel like intimacy with any woman. He had grown tough and remote, his whole mind focused on one objective – locating the man who had killed Alexis, the wife who had no longer loved him weeks before her last journey to the Baltic.

'How do you know that?' Laila asked.

'This new book on Russia I picked up from Aka-teeminen today.'

A travel guide to the Soviet Union, it was heavily illustrated. Newman turned to a page on the Estonian Republic. He pointed to a large photograph of Tallinn showing the old city and handed it to her. He lit a cigarette.

'I don't understand,' Laila commented, staring at the photo.

'Someone in London showed me a film of the killing, a film obviously sent from Moscow to warn off anyone from following Alexis. Some brutal idiot sent it as a deterrent. Normally the Russians wouldn't have made that mistake. I wouldn't mind betting whoever did send it is now in Siberia.'

'I still don't understand.'

'This strange castle perched high up – ' he pointed at the photo, ' – I saw it in the background of the film when a car ran over Alexis. I knew I'd seen the damned thing somewhere. Probably in another picture. A foreign correspondent needs a photographic memory. Literally.'

'I know it. I've been there. It's called Toompea Small Fortress. There are three great towers – Tall Hermann, Pilsticker and Landskrone. It's near the Dome Church and looks down on Lossi Square. What are you thinking of doing, Bob?'

'I'm going to do something about it.'

Her voice was full of anxiety as she squeezed his arm to get his attention. She didn't like his expression.

'If you find the man responsible for your wife's death you are going to kill him, aren't you?'

'I didn't say that – ' Newman pulled himself free of her grip roughly, stood up and walked over to the small cupboard where the telephone was perched. He opened a drawer and lifted out the Helsinki telephone directory.

'I want to hire a car. Who are the best people in town?'

'Hertz would be the best, I imagine. They have an office inside the Intercontinental next to us.'

'Got them. 44 69 10.' He scribbled the number on the pad provided by the hotel. 'Time for lunch. I'll call them when we've eaten.'

'Where are you going, Bob? Can I come with you?'

'To lunch, yes. With me in the car, no. Don't argue,' he went on in the same flat voice. 'Go back to your office this afternoon.'

'They don't expect me. I've taken some of my holiday to be with you, Bob.' Her voice had a pleading note.

'Then find something else to do. Now, are you hungry? If so let's go down and sample their excellent buffet.'

In the large, comfortable dining room on the first floor which overlooks the Mannerheimintie, they ate their main course in silence. Laila ate automatically, glancing across the table frequently at Newman who still had that frozen look which so worried her. She had a difficult decision to make. They were walking back to the large buffet table to choose from the variety of desserts when she spoke.

'Bob, back in a minute. I have to go to the powder room.'

'Take your time.'

She hurried out of his sight, then ran down to the ground floor by the staircase – he might have spotted her if she had used the elevator. She dialled Ratakatu – headquarters of the Protection Police – and asked to speak to her father. Mauno came on the line almost at once.

'What is it, Laila?' he asked abruptly.

'I'm calling from the Hesperia. I am terribly worried about Bob Newman, who is here in Helsinki – at this hotel. He has found out where his wife died. Across the water. After lunch he is hiring a car. He won't tell me where he is going.'

'Newman is here? Really? Who is he hiring the car from?'

'Hertz. At the Intercontinental. He won't let me go with him. Can you do something?'

'I think so. Is that all? Good. Thank you for calling me – you were right to do so. Don't let him know you've told me.'

'Of course not. He'd think I had betrayed him. Which, in a way, I have.'

'You may have saved him. I must make a call. Thank you again. Be careful he does not suspect you have been in touch with me. Goodbye for now.'

Laila put down the receiver and sighed. She felt like a traitor. She walked quickly to the powder room to make herself up – she must seem normal when she returned upstairs.

At Ratakatu, Mauno Sarin was already calling the Hertz Agency. He gave them very precise instructions and they promised to call him back. Sarin then called for a car with radio equipment.

Porvoo is a small and ancient town some fifty to sixty kilometres east of Helsinki. It is reached by driving along a modern highway which continues further east until eventually it crosses the Finnish-Soviet border and proceeds on to Vyborg, now inside Russia since the settlement agreed at the end of the Continuation War in 1945.

Newman drove the Ford he had hired from Hertz across the bridge which spans the river leading south to the sea not far away. He found a place to park the car, fed coins into the meter, and began walking as though exploring the place like a tourist.

He walked up a narrow cobbled street – the cobbles so uneven they were ankle-breakers – and reached the Town Hall square. This was old Porvoo, a collection of wooden single-storey houses painted a bright rust-red.

But these houses are no museum pieces as they are in Turku to the west of the capital. People lived in them as their forefathers had lived there when Porvoo was part of the Grand Duchy of Russia in Tsarist times. As he walked Newman kept glancing round and behind him but there was no sign he had been followed.

Retracing his steps, he followed the route he remembered from his previous visit to Finland parallel to the river, until he reached the area where several battered fishing boats were moored.

Before leaving the Hesperia – and after seeing Laila off the premises – he had changed American Express traveller's cheques into a great deal of Finnish money, mostly in high denomination notes. He turned down a narrow side street, little more than an alleyway, and came to more old buildings at the river's edge. Several fishermen sat on wooden barrels, tending their nets.

His nostrils picked up a mixture of aromas – rotting fish, diesel oil and the faint tang of salt water from the invisible Gulf of Finland. He spent some time strolling along the riverside, studying the fishermen until he spotted one man, middle-aged like the others but who sat alone.

'Do you speak any English?' he asked the walnut-faced man.

'A little.'

'Is that your boat?'

It was a weatherbeaten old craft with a small wheelhouse amidships but it looked very seaworthy. And the man he was talking to had the look of a fisherman who knew what he was about.

'Yes,' the fisherman replied. 'You want something?'

Newman paused. The Finns were a sturdy people with a direct outlook on life. No Mediterranean-type haggling here, he decided. Tell him what you wanted, state the price and he would say 'Yes' or 'No.' Don't beat about the bush. Not in Finland.

'Could you take me out to sea? I want to cross to Tallinn. After nightfall. Can you land me on a quiet part of the Estonian coast so no one sees me?'

'The Russians have patrol boats. The patrol boats have the radar.'

'I know. But will you do it? For seven thousand markkaa?'

Newman produced a sheaf of folded banknotes and counted as the fisherman watched him, the net still in his gnarled hands. He had just finished counting when a hand fell lightly on his right shoulder. He swung round. Mauno Sarin could move like a cat.

'Wait for me, please, Bob. My car is the blue Saab parked at the top of the alley you've just walked down. And could you please give me the keys to your hired Ford? One of my men is waiting with it. He will drive it back to Helsinki behind us.'

'Supposing I refuse?'

'You can't. You're under arrest and I'm taking you back to Ratakatu for interrogation.'

'On what charge?'

'You need me to tell you that?'

'Yes, I do.'

'For attempting to leave Finland illegally for the purpose of entering the Soviet Union, also illegally.'

'Illegally?'

'You have a visa for Russia?'

Mauno pulled at his fringe of beard while he watched Newman with no sign of friendliness in his piercing blue eyes. He was very much the chief of the Finnish Secret Police.

'I'll wait in your Saab,' said Newman.

'You're crazy, Bob, crazy with fury. Trying to bribe a Finn to land you in Estonia.'

They were driving back along the same route Newman had followed to Porvoo. Behind them a man in plain clothes drove the hired Ford. Mauno drove at speed along the countryside highway, then slowed briefly before accelerating again.

'How much did you offer that fisherman?' he asked.

'Seven thousand markkaa.'

'Maybe you give me the money and I take you to Tallinn?'

Newman turned and stared at Mauno who was grinning mischievously. The Finn winked at him and then turned to swerve as a huge trailer truck's rear rushed towards them.

'You're a bit crazy yourself the way you drive,' Newman observed while he digested Mauno's remark. 'And why did you slow down briefly a few kilometres back? There was no traffic about.'

'The police often have a speed trap there. Imagine it! The chief of the Protection Police hauled up for speeding! That would make a story for Laila's rag! And she would write it. I wonder what she is doing?' He looked at Newman. 'Have you seen her?'

'If I had, I wouldn't tell you.'

And that little exchange, Mauno thought with satisfaction, protects Laila nicely from any suspicion Newman might have had that she was my informer.

'How did you get on to me at Porvoo?' Newman enquired. 'Or is that a state secret?'

'I had you watched! Of course! Knowing the mood you are in.' Mauno's voice changed, became sympathetic. 'If it were my wife I would probably react as you have – but to attempt to go to Estonia that route was madness.'

'Is there any other route? Or were you joking again when you said you would take me to Tallinn?'

'Not entirely.'

Mauno was suddenly concentrating all his attention on driving. Newman stared hard at the Finn. His left leg felt cramped and he was going to ease it when he remembered the hunting knife concealed inside his sock, the knife he had purchased in Helsinki before leaving for Porvoo.

'And what does that imply?' he enquired.

'This is confidential. You never print it. OK? Good. I have been in secret communication with the Russian GRU colonel in charge of security in Estonia. Andrei Karlov. He is based in Tallinn. He wants me to cross the Gulf on the *Georg Ots* to meet him. He also suggested that he might be willing to see a responsible Western journalist and show him over Tallinn. I suggested your name.'

'Why me?'

'Because I have had you watched from the moment I knew you had arrived here. You have shown an unhealthy interest in Estonia – unhealthy not only to yourself but also to me. The incident at Porvoo proves that. The Russians would blame us if you did something crazy – and had travelled from Finland to do it.'

Which means, Newman thought, Mauno has been questioning Takala, the pilot of the chopper which flew me from the Kalastajatorppa Hotel over South Harbour when the *Georg Ots* was sailing for Tallinn. He didn't blame Mauno – he had a job to do.

'You are seriously suggesting I travel with you to Tallinn?' he asked.

'If you wish to – and if Karlov agrees. I would insist, of course, that they give you a safe permit to return the same day with me, a permit signed by General Lysenko at least.'

'And who is this Lysenko?'

Mauno paused again. 'This is very confidential – but we do have ways of knowing what is happening over there. Lysenko has overall GRU control of security in the Baltic republics – Latvia and Lithuania as well as Estonia. He got the job Karlov was hoping for when he returned from his London posting.'

'I still don't see why Karlov wants a visit from a Western journalist.'

'Because there have been so many rumours of unrest in Estonia – rumours which have appeared prominently in the press in Europe and America.

Karlov thinks – I am guessing but I know I am right – that if an impartial journalist who carries a lot of weight visited Tallinn and found everything peaceful and calm, then wrote an article which would be widely syndicated, this would kill the rumours.'

'Again, why me?'

Mauno chuckled as he reduced speed while they entered the suburbs of Helsinki. 'Obviously they have put you through the computer in Moscow and you have come up neutral.'

'Hardly pro-Soviet.'

'Karlov wouldn't want that – it would not be convincing. You always write the truth as you see it. So – '

'How soon would this trip be – assuming it comes off?'

'Impossible to say. Karlov will give us very little notice or advance warning. So, Bob, do me a favour – if you're willing to come with me. Keep yourself available at the Hesperia. And no more sailing adventures in the Gulf of Finland! You will come if the chance arises?'

'Assume I will.'

'Great! Now, to celebrate our agreement, we will forget to go to Ratakatu. I'll just pull in here and tell my man to drive your Ford back to the Hesperia. Then we go and have a drink at the Marski Hotel. Where the spies are!'

*

Mauno stopped sipping his glass of dry white wine and stared across the large basement room which is the bar at the Marski. He stared for only a few seconds and then turned to Newman.

'That's extraordinary. You remember the little joke I made about the Marski where the spies are?'

'Yes.'

'Don't look for the moment. But you see that dark-haired man in a grey suit sitting by himself on a banquette in that corner opposite? Greasy black hair smoothed down over his forehead. A slab-faced man wearing a grey suit, a white tie and a blue shirt?'

'I noticed him a few minutes ago. He was watching us.'

'That is Oleg Poluchkin, one of Colonel Karlov's aides.'

'I don't much like the look of him.'

'He is a captain in the GRU. He must have been sent over by Karlov to sniff around before they make the final arrangements for my visit. He has a bad reputation. A bit of a brute.'

Newman studied Oleg Poluchkin by glancing slowly all round the bar. The Marski bar is one of the best in town. Spacious, discreetly lit, there are comfortable chairs which look as though they're made of leather. On a Friday night it was full. Boys with their smartly-dressed girl-friends. Older men with their equally young girl-friends. Most of the girls had that special, lint-coloured hair you find only in Finland. Above the clink of glasses there was the animated chatter of people but it was not noisy. The customers were served by waitresses as attractive as the girl-friends sitting down.

Oleg Poluchkin would be about forty, Newman guessed. The Russian was heavily built, his clean-shaven, plump face had a sallow complexion. His mouth turned down at the corners which did not help to make him a pleasant-looking personality. His dark eyes, under thick brows, moved slowly. When they caught Newman's they reminded him of a lizard. Cold, remote. Not a man to meet in a deserted alley after dark.

All his movements were deliberate, calculated. He wrapped the fingers of his pudgy left hand round a glass and lifted it slowly to his thick lips. After drinking, he placed his glass back carefully on the table in the same position he had raised it from.

His blank eyes met Newman's again, gazed at him for a few seconds, then swivelled his attention to an attractive girl sitting with four men at the next table. She caught his look, stared back and then turned away. She didn't like him.

'Where is your own man?' Newman asked casually as he lifted his glass.

'My own man?' Mauno asked in a puzzled tone.

'Oh, come on! This is your town. You have a man somewhere in this place watching Poluchkin.'

'Actually, it's a girl.'

'She'd better watch it – following that around.'

263

'She can handle herself – she's a judo expert.'

'I still say she'd better be good. I've learned to spot a member of the heavy mob. Your friend Poluchkin is no pussycat.'

'You must remember this is Helsinki. There is little violence here compared with other countries. Our President walks in the streets without guards – unfortunately, that does not apply to your Queen. You don't shoot people in Finland. And the Russians know the rules of the game. They keep to them.'

'There's always the maverick,' Newman responded, watching Poluchkin again.

'Maverick?'

'The loner who runs amok.'

'You are referring to yourself?' Mauno enquired genially.

'I'm referring to that very nasty piece of work who is just leaving.'

Poluchkin had stood up from his table and was slipping on his lightweight camel-hair coat. Thrusting both hands into the pockets, he sidled away slowly between the tables towards the exit. A fair-haired girl who had been drinking alone stood up, put on her windcheater and also left the bar.

'Your girl?' Newman enquired.

'You are very observant.'

'In more ways than one, Mauno.'

'And what do you mean by that, my friend?'

'The little comedy has been played out now, hasn't it? You brought me to this bar after arranging with

Poluchkin to be here waiting. Now he's had a good look at me and can report back to Karlov.'

'What a fertile imagination you foreign correspondents have!'

'Why was that necessary?' Newman demanded with an edge to his voice. 'And I would have appreciated your warning me before we came here.'

'Had I done that, Bob, you might have found it difficult to act naturally. Karlov has still not agreed that you will be permitted to visit Tallinn.'

'So, everyone watches everyone else?'

'This is Finland. We can only hope Poluchkin's report to his chief is favourable.'

Outside in the darkness Poluchkin strolled slowly south into the heavily built-up area which lies at the head of the peninsula. He could have taken a taxi from the nearby rank but he preferred to walk, to make sure he was not followed.

Half an hour later he arrived at the very large old building which stands in grounds behind a wall topped with railings. Tehtaankatu 1. The Soviet Embassy. Like the American Embassy, situated in the same district but housed in a far more modern building, the Russians have a huge staff.

Once inside the office allocated to him, Poluchkin took off his coat and asked the operator to call Tallinn. He used the scrambler phone to speak to Andrei Karlov.

'I have seen this Robert Newman,' he reported. 'I have had a good look at him – the arrangement was made by Sarin. I do not like the look of the Englishman.'

'God Almighty!' Karlov exploded. 'You were not sent to give your opinion. You were sent to identify that this man really is Robert Newman. Is he?'

'From the photographs shown me and the few shots of him on film I watched I would say this is Robert Newman, yes.'

'You are positive? Bearing in mind you have not met him – before you say that,' Karlov rapped out. 'Relying solely on the photos and the film, you are confident the man you saw is Robert Newman?'

'I am confident.' There was a sullen note in Poluchkin's voice. 'But I would still like included in my report to Moscow that I do not trust this man.'

'*Your* report! Captain Poluchkin, *you* are reporting to *me*. Is that clearly understood? A positive answer.'

'It is clearly understood. Now I can return to Tallinn – '

'No! You cannot! You stay where you are – and keep your eyes open. Is that also clearly understood?'

'It is clearly understood, Comrade.'

'Finally, you might be interested to know that during your absence there have been no more murders of GRU officers.'

Karlov slammed down the phone. In Helsinki Poluchkin was ashen-faced as he replaced the receiver.

*

Behind his desk in his office in the old building on Pikk Street, Colonel Karlov rubbed the end of his long nose as he stared at his girl assistant. The dark-haired, attractive girl watched her chief, waiting for his instruction.

'Raisa,' Karlov began, 'that conversation was taped?'

'As you requested.'

'Put the reel in a sealed envelope and store it inside the safe. That man makes me sick. He is arrogant beyond his means. Now, is my secret visitor waiting?'

'I asked for Mr Davidov to be shown into your private waiting room.'

Raisa indicated the closed door leading into the next room. Karlov thanked her and suggested she should go home after dealing with the tape. When Raisa had closed the safe she said good night to her chief and left.

Karlov immediately jumped from his desk, walked over to the waiting room door, unlocked it and threw it open. He gestured to 'Davidov' to enter. Captain Olaf Prii, skipper of the Estonian trawler, *Saaremaa*, walked into the office and sat in the chair facing Karlov's desk.

'Now, Prii, tell me about your visit to England.'

Chapter Eighteen

Ingrid Melin sat in an armchair in the sixth floor lobby of the Grand Hotel in Stockholm facing the elevators. She wore horn-rimmed spectacles and was pretending to read one of the Swedish fashion magazines she had picked up from a table.

The spectacles alone altered her appearance but she had also changed her clothes. Instead of the powder blue pant suit she had worn when she waited for Helene Stilmar to appear at Arlanda, she was now clad in a red two-piece suit with a white pleated blouse.

By her side, folded over the arm of the chair, was her camel-hair overcoat. Concealed beneath it was a head scarf. She was waiting – hoping – for Stilmar to appear. And with her legs crossed and her relaxed manner, she looked like a girl who was waiting for her man to arrive and take her out to dinner.

Earlier she had seen room service deliver a tray to Stilmar's room. The tray contained one open ham sandwich and a pot of coffee. This suggested Helene Stilmar was going out to dinner later – that she had ordered a snack to keep her going.

Later she had watched out of the corner of her eye while Stilmar opened the door of her room and put the tray on the floor outside. She had been wearing a silk dressing-gown – probably she was taking a bath prior to going out.

Ingrid heard a door open and close half an hour later. The American woman, wearing an emerald green dress and carrying a mink jacket, walked across the lobby and pressed the button to summon the elevator. She hardly glanced at Ingrid, intent on where she was going. As the elevator doors closed Ingrid moved.

Grabbing her coat and scarf, she ran for the staircase and dived down the steps, taking them two at a time. As she ran she slipped on her coat, then wrapped the scarf round her head and draped it over the back down her neck to conceal her hair.

Arriving in the main entrance hall she was just in time to see Stilmar walking down the steps to the exit doors. Ingrid produced a pair of dark glasses and put them on in place of her reading glasses.

The impressive doorman, a six-foot-two, bearded giant who looked like Orson Welles, was summoning a taxi. He stood outside with a whistle in his mouth and gave a piercing blast. A passing taxi curved round to pull up in front of the Grand.

Ingrid slipped behind the wheel of her hired Volvo – thankful she had changed her mind and had not used a taxi from Uppsala to Arlanda. Turning on the ignition, she crouched over the wheel, concentrating on two things – driving the car safely and following the taxi which was pulling away from the Grand.

It was daylight, 18.30 hours, and the traffic was light. On the far side of the water between the passenger boats moored in front of the hotel, were glimpses of the Royal Palace and the Houses of Parliament. Typical, solid-looking buildings which make Stockholm one of the stately cities in the world.

Again she began to worry that she might lose Stilmar's taxi. None of this anxiety showed in her calm expression as she coolly manoeuvred her way through the older part of Stockholm. She appeared to be heading for one of the more exclusive districts, not so far from the centre and occupied by old and expensive apartments.

She knew she had guessed right when the taxi turned along Karlavägen where there was hardly any traffic at all. Slowing – to put more distance between herself and Stilmar – she cruised to a stop as she saw the taxi turning into the kerb.

It had obviously never occurred to Helene Stilmar that she might be followed. Alighting from the taxi, she paid off the driver outside an apartment entrance, climbed the few steps, inserted a key and dis-appeared inside. Ingrid had now left the Volvo, walked briskly along the pavement and was close enough to realize Stilmar had used a key instead of the speakphone.

The key! Sitting in her armchair in the sixth floor lobby of the Grand, she had seen a messenger from

the porter's desk deliver an envelope to Helene
shortly after the arrival of the room service snack.
Had that envelope contained the key, the address and
a message? Maybe.

Karlavägen 72C. That was the address the American woman had entered. Ingrid had a thought and
darted across the deserted street. She peered up at the
building – just in time to see a light come on in two
third-floor windows. Behind the heavy net curtains
she saw the silhouette of Helene passing one of the
windows.

Ingrid had once been inside one of these apartments further down the street. She remembered it was
spacious – and it ran the full depth of the building
from front to rear. She retraced her steps across the
street to see who occupied the third floor. *B. Warren.*

The name meant nothing to her. She thrust both
hands inside her coat pockets and walked slowly back
to where she had left the Volvo. There were two
problems needing a quick decision. Helene had
walked out of the hotel wearing fresh clothes –
evening clothes. To Ingrid that meant only one thing.
She was expecting a man. It might be important to see
who the man was.

He could, of course, already be inside the apartment. Mr B. Warren. But Ingrid didn't think so. The
heavy curtains had been left drawn back. And, if he
was waiting for her, why give her a key? He could
have let her inside when she called him on the
speakphone. Or given her the code which automati-

cally opened the front door – there had been a code system above the speakphone, the numbers ranging from 1 to 0 through 9.

The second problem was the Volvo. Parking was restricted in this part of the city. If the police came along she was in trouble. Reaching the Volvo, she lifted the bonnet as though something were wrong with the engine.

As she stood by the bonnet she extracted the small camera Tweed had supplied her with for an earlier mission. It was very compact. A Voigtländer, model Vitoret 110. She slid the white safety bar across for instant action. At that moment a taxi drove past, slowed down and stopped. In front of No. 72C.

A man got out and paid the driver. His attention was occupied with the job in hand for the moment. She raised the camera and took three shots in rapid succession. She waited until he had gone inside the building and ran back along the pavement. Again she crossed the street and looked up at the windows on the third floor.

Helene had just turned away – after looking out when she heard the taxi stop, Ingrid guessed. A man appeared, threw his arms round her and they embraced passionately. Then, as Ingrid moved back across the street he remembered the curtains and drew them.

Ingrid hurried back to the Volvo and was closing the bonnet when a patrol car pulled up alongside her.

She got in behind the wheel as a uniformed policeman got out.

'No parking here.'

'I'm not parking here. I'm breaking down.'

She gave him her best smile as she switched on and the engine fired. He stood with his hands on his hips, uncertain what course of action to take.

'It's OK now,' he said.

'Thank God. I'm late for an appointment.'

'He's a lucky guy.'

'Thank you, officer . . .'

'Next time you break down, just make sure I'm around.'

'That's a promise. May I go?'

'Have fun. You will. Always.'

The shock was waiting for her shortly after she arrived back at the Grand.

Captain Olaf Prii settled himself comfortably in the chair facing Colonel Karlov's desk, took out an old pipe and asked for permission to smoke.

'Of course,' Karlov agreed, sitting back in his own chair. 'Now, I am listening. I received your coded signal. Everything went well, I gather?'

They were conversing in German, their only common language. Prii had become fluent in it during the Wehrmacht's occupation of Estonia in 1942. He had co-operated with the Germans: Prii was a survivor. He puffed at his pipe and watched Karlov's lean, alert face through the smoke.

'We put into the port of Harwich. We faked engine trouble.'

'Excellent. Who came to meet you?'

'A man called Tweed.'

'Ah, Tweed! A clever man – a dangerous man. Has he fallen into my trap?'

'I don't know. He gave no indication he would visit the Baltic. As you suggested, I told him about the murders of your GRU officers. I also told him you were here in Tallinn in charge of the investigation.'

'Good! Good! And what else?'

'I told him about that Finn, Mauno Sarin, and his visits to see you in Tallinn.'

'Tell me something else.' Karlov picked up a round ruler like a baton and revolved it slowly between his long fingers. 'Did he mention an Englishman, a newspaper reporter called Robert Newman?'

'No, not a word. He did, however, near the end of the conversation, mention an American called Procane,' Prii spelt out the name. 'It was just a casual question.'

'And you replied?'

'The truth. I have never heard of anyone with that name.'

'No matter. This Tweed who interrogated you – did he seem tense, anxious to get every bit of information out of you he could? What was his general attitude?'

'Very calm. As though interviewing me was a routine assignment, something that happened every day. Almost as though he was carrying out a chore he could have done without.'

'Clever. Very clever.'

'I thought he was rather stupid.' Prii used a nicotine-stained knuckle to tamp down his pipe. 'I have something else for you, Colonel, something I obtained from a member of the Estonian underground. Three photographs taken with the special camera you gave me.'

'Taken when?'

'Not so long ago.'

Taking a cheap envelope from inside his thick seaman's jacket, Prii extracted three photographs and dropped them on the desk. Karlov picked them up and arranged them side by side. He stared at them for a long time, his expression intent and bleak.

'The man who took these – he will keep his mouth shut?'

'You can rely on that – it is more than his life is worth to talk about them.'

'I will keep these.' Karlov glanced towards the safe and then changed his mind. Pulling out his wallet, he inserted the three photos inside and returned the wallet to his pocket. 'These photographs do not exist. They were never taken. You understand, Prii?'

'Perfectly. May I go now? The same way I came in?'

'Yes. You have to be careful.'

Prii doused his pipe with his thumb, replaced it inside his pocket and left the room by the side door. Leaving the secret waiting room, he walked down a twisting staircase. It was very old and centuries of footsteps had worn a shallow trench in the centre of each stone step. Curious the way people always walked down the middle of staircases. On board his trawler Prii was accustomed to stepping down the side of a companionway – especially in rough weather – so he could hold on tight to the handrail.

He emerged cautiously into Pikk Street, looked both ways and saw it was deserted. Before resuming his walk back to his lodgings, he turned and spat viciously on the entrance steps to Karlov's building.

Four hundred kilometres away across the Baltic, Ingrid sat on the edge of her bed in her room at the Grand, completing a coded record in her small notebook of recent events, including precise times. She closed the book, yawned, rubbed her tummy and realized she was very hungry.

She liked this double room perched up in the roof. There were two large dormer windows – to see out properly over the panoramic view of Stockholm at night you had to walk inside an alcove. It was cosy and very quiet. The thought had just crossed her mind when she heard the tapping on the door.

She opened it cautiously – with the safety chain on – gazed out and then tore at the chain to release it.

Discreetly she said nothing until her visitor was inside the entrance lobby and she had closed and locked the door.

'Tweed! Oh! How glad I am to see you again – '

She threw her arms round his neck and hugged him warmly. Normally he would have been embarrassed but instead he squeezed her slim waist and hugged her back, still wearing his battered old trilby and clutching his briefcase.

'Trouble?' he enquired as they released each other and she led him into the bedroom, then helped him off with his coat and removed his hat. The coat was carefully arranged on a hanger as she told him to sit down.

'When did you arrive, Tweed? Have you come straight here? How did you know where I was?'

It was typical of Ingrid – the exuberant flow of relevant questions, the aura of excitement and sheer pleasure at his arrival. Tired by the nonstop flight from London and the longish drive-in from Arlanda, he already felt fresher because of the warmth of her welcome.

'I'd better put on the radio,' she whispered. 'I am certain no one followed me – but I still put on the radio.'

He watched her dance across the room and switch on a station playing pop music. In the unlikely event that the room was bugged the music would scramble their conversation. She had no experience of this kind of work when he had first met her by chance at a party in Stockholm – but she had picked up all the tricks more quickly than any professional agent he had ever known.

'When did you last eat?' he asked her.

'Not for a time but – '

'No "but's" – we'll use room service and order a feast.'

'It is all right. Do not get up. I know where the menu is. They have smoked salmon. I love smoked salmon.'

They studied the menu together and then she picked up the phone and ordered their meal, including a good bottle of white wine chosen by Tweed. While they waited for the meal, she told him everything that had happened since she arrived at Arlanda.

Tweed was silent, watching her relaxed in the chair she had pulled up close to him, her legs tucked up beneath her. He was a good listener and she had an amazing facility for presenting facts in order and concisely. When she came to the incident of the parked Volvo and the policeman she laughed as she produced her camera.

'I think that policeman would have liked to ask me out for dinner.'

'His bad luck is my good luck. Now, to answer your questions. I arrived at Arlanda and took a taxi straight here. I knew you were at the Grand because of Monica. You told her on the phone and I called her from the airport. I booked a room at the Diplomat –

but I've decided to move over here at once, even if I have to sleep in the entrance hall.'

'That's wonderful. But don't you usually stay somewhere different from your helpers?'

'The Grand is more central.'

The truth was he had remembered Monica's warning that there might be danger for Ingrid. And that wasn't the entire truth, he admitted to himself. He was breaking one of his cherished rules of procedure in the field because he wanted to be near Ingrid.

'This man you saw going into Karlavägen 72C,' he said, resuming the business in hand. 'I have some photos here. See if you can spot him – or anyone else – from these pictures.'

'Spot?'

'Recognize. "Spot" is slang.'

'Now I have a new word!'

He opened his briefcase, took out a large cardboard-backed envelope. From the envelope he extracted several glossy prints and spread them out on a low coffee table.

Ingrid picked them up and assumed a characteristic attitude Tweed recalled well. She had a mobile face and many different expressions. She cocked her head to one side and stared seriously at the prints. Her fine bone structure became marked, almost like a frozen mask.

'This is the Stilmar woman I met and followed from the airport.'

She handed him the picture Tweed's men had taken of Helene holding a bouquet of flowers in the entrance hall of the Dorchester Hotel in London. One slim hand was searching for the gift card.

'That's her,' Tweed agreed. 'Anyone else?'

There were pictures of Helene's husband mixed in with other photos Tweed had chosen at random. Ingrid sifted through the collection and stopped suddenly. She bent forward so Tweed could see only the crown of dark hair, holding a print under the table lamp to see it more clearly.

'This is the man I have three pictures of in my camera, the man who came to Karlavägen to meet her, the man who embraced her passionately in front of the window as I told you.'

'Let me see.'

Tweed gazed at the print she had chosen. He nearly asked if she was sure, then remembered this was Ingrid he was talking to. It was a very good likeness. The man who had arrived at Karlavägen was Cord Dillon, Deputy Director of the CIA.

Chapter Nineteen

'This is now the forward area,' said Tweed.

'And what does that mean?' asked Gunnar Hornberg, chief of the Swedish Secret Police – SAPO.

'That Sweden is the last stage before Adam Procane crosses over into No Man's Land – Finland. We have to stop him – or her.'

'One thing I can always count on when you arrive,' Hornberg commented. 'Plenty of activity – not to say action.'

It was after ten o'clock at night. After dining in Ingrid's bedroom, booking himself a room at the Grand and moving from the Diplomat, Tweed had taken a taxi to police headquarters inside the new complex on Polhemsgatan.

Built about three years earlier, the vast new seven-storey complex is an extension of the old building on Kungholmsgatan. The entrance to the Criminal Police department is at No. 30 on Polhemsgatan and faces a large park. Installed inside this complex, discreetly situated on the fourth floor, is the office of the SAPO chief.

Typical of the man occupying this office, there are

no frills. The oblong-shaped room is illuminated by shaded, white fluorescent strips suspended from the ceiling. The furniture is plain and austere – hard-backed chairs, while the walls are lined with steel filing cabinets.

Gunnar Hornberg was a man of fifty-eight, heavily-built, with a large head covered with a mane of thick grey hair. His glasses were pushed back over his high-domed forehead. His grey eyes were shrewd but kindly, the eyes of a man who has seen all humanity, the good and the evil. His voice had a deep timbre.

'As usual, Tweed,' he observed, 'you are three jumps ahead of me – and here I sit, trying to catch up with you. We are watching out for all of them – those Americans – as you requested.'

'And who do you list as all of them?'

'Here we go,' Hornberg smiled and his normally stern expression glowed. 'Playing games. So, let us play. Stilmar, National Security Adviser to the President. Cord Dillon, CIA. And General Paul Dexter. Three candidates, as you said, for the role of Adam Procane.'

'You missed a fourth candidate.'

'Here we go again. And I noticed you said "or her". More mystery.'

'Candidate Four. Helene. Wife of Stilmar. One-time liaison officer between the State Department and the Pentagon. A sensitive post, wouldn't you agree?'

'I agree. But you're leading up to something. I

know you – where does this Helene fit into the Procane business?'

'She arrived from Heathrow at Arlanda this afternoon. She took a cab to the Grand Hotel, dumped her bags – a lot of luggage – in her room. Later she paid a clandestine visit to Karlavägen 72C. Who lives there, I wonder? The name on the outside plate for the third-floor flat is B. Warren.'

'Bruce Warren,' Hornberg said promptly. 'Chief agent of the CIA for Scandinavia. Holds some innocuous post at the Yank Embassy. Just for cover. He could have loaned his apartment to Cord Dillon. We did see Dillon come in through Arlanda,' he added casually. 'And followed him to Karlavägen – the address you mentioned. It intrigued us – we expected him to go to his Embassy in the Diplomatstaden district – not far from the Diplomat Hotel you left when you moved to the Grand – '

'So it was your men who followed me?'

'You see, Tweed, I am now only two jumps behind you. But we missed this Helene Stilmar. Is she a brunette by any chance? My people spoke to such a girl near 72C who said she couldn't start her Volvo.'

'The description is wrong,' Tweed replied with a blank face. 'Your people must have scared some innocent person.'

'I don't think we scared anyone. My men wore traffic police uniform. It is a useful trick. Then if they find themselves in a quiet area – like Karlavägen at night – they are not in any way conspicuous. You have something for me?'

Tweed produced his envelope from the briefcase. He found the photo of Helene Stilmar and handed it to Hornberg. The Swede pulled down his glasses on to the bridge of his large, strong nose, studied the photograph and grunted, nodding his approval.

'I would say that is some woman.'

'She was seen clasping Cord Dillon in her arms – before they remembered to draw the curtains.'

'So,' Hornberg peered over his glasses at Tweed. 'They are having an affair. They are discreet – this woman would be. They come to Sweden where no one will know.'

'Or one is using the other – to cross over to Finland on the way to Russia.'

'What a devious mind you have, my dear chap.' Hornberg liked to lace his excellent English with upper-crust phrases.

'This is a devious business.'

'Your watcher glimpsed this display of intimacy?'

'I didn't say that.'

'Let us deal with something else while I remember it, something important.' Hornberg pressed down a switch on his intercom, then spoke in English. 'You can come in now, please. Mr Tweed is here.'

When the door opened a small, roly-poly faced man wearing spectacles walked in smoking a pipe. He had a Pickwickian appearance and Tweed, who had turned round, liked him at once.

'This is Peter Persson, a very nice person,' Hornberg introduced with his little joke. 'Meet Mr Tweed. He is my favourite bloodhound,' Hornberg continued, 'the best tracker I have ever known. Also a formidable bodyguard. He is yours while you are in Sweden – you only have to phone me. I would not like anything unpleasant to happen to you, Tweed. And this – ' he pressed a finger against the left side of his large nose ' – smells danger. Russian agents are watching all arrivals coming into Arlanda. They probably know already you are here, Tweed.'

'Thank you. I will bear it in mind. You work with a team?' Tweed asked Persson.

'Never! Always by myself. That way I do not have to worry about anyone except the target I am following – and myself.'

That was interesting, Tweed thought – he had put himself second. This man was a pro. Persson's eyes had never left him since he entered the room. Tweed realized Persson was imprinting his image in his mind.

'That must be difficult,' he observed. 'Supposing you have to follow someone into a shop with several exits – and they don't leave at once?'

'I buy something,' Persson replied immediately. 'Pay for it. Tell the salesgirl to gift wrap it and I'll call back later. I am inconspicuous – I have gone into the shop for a purpose.'

'Very good. Except that sooner or later your appearance will give you away – working on your own.'

'You think so, Mr Tweed? Why do you think I smoke a pipe? The pipe disappears, I remove my glasses – '

He took them off, placed the pipe in an ashtray on Hornberg's desk, produced a crumpled hat from his pocket and rammed it on his head. What astounded Tweed was the change in his face, which seemed to be made of rubber. He assumed a different expression and was scarcely recognizable as the man who had originally walked into the room.

'I'm impressed,' said Tweed.

'So, Mr Tweed, in case you need me, where are you staying? What is your room number? What time do you get up? Do you have your breakfast in your room?'

'Grand Hotel. Room 632. Seven in the morning. Breakfast in the dining room. Anything else, Mr Persson?'

'That will do very nicely, thank you.'

Persson stuffed his hat back inside his pocket, picked up his pipe, and left the room.

'I like him,' Tweed told Hornberg. 'One more thing before I go. If you were leaving Sweden secretly for Finland what route would you choose?'

'The archipelago. Cross over by small boat from one of the many islands in the Swedish archipelago – I would choose the large island of Ornö – almost on the edge of the Baltic. From there it is only a few hours to the Abo archipelago in Finland. The only problem is we are watching that area very closely because of the Soviet mini-subs testing our naval defences. God knows those mini-subs have made the world's press.'

'Any other route? A faster one?'

'Bromma Airport – here in the middle of the city,' Hornberg suggested. 'A light aircraft – a private job – could fly out and land at the airfield near Abo – Turku as the Finns call it.'

'So, you keep up the close watch?' Tweed remarked, standing up.

'Surveillance on Dillon and Helene. Continuous check on all entry points for Stilmar himself – and General Dexter.'

Hornberg, with his great height – over six foot two – and his mane of hair, towered over Tweed as he also stood, holding out his hand. Tweed paused at the door. He always kept the most important remark for when he was leaving – the last thing you said was the subject which stayed in a man's mind.

'Has it occurred to you this Russian mini-sub business just could have a different purpose from testing your defences?'

'What other purpose?'

'To have a mini-sub waiting to pick up Procane. I'd like to take a look at that island of Ornö if you can fix it for me.'

Chapter Twenty

'I think the time has come to send the Executioner into Sweden,' Lysenko announced as he gazed out of the window of Karlov's office down into Pikk Street.

'Captain Oleg Poluchkin? Why?'

Karlov was appalled at the statement. Lysenko had flown into Tallinn without warning from Leningrad. It was one of the General's favourite tricks – to arrive unexpectedly and check up on his subordinates. Suspicious of everyone, trusting no man – or woman – he liked to move secretly. Even Rebet, back in Leningrad, had not been informed. He swung round and stared at the colonel.

'You are questioning my order?'

'Yes, I am.' Karlov stood up behind his desk. 'We have a delicate operation under way – to bring Procane safely across. Violence could ruin everything.'

'Poluchkin is trained for the job,' Lysenko continued. 'He will contact that Roumanian woman, Magda Rupescu, who entered Sweden as a refugee from Bucharest. They will work as a team.'

'She is even worse than Poluchkin,' Karlov protested. 'A hideous woman who enjoys her work.'

'And is very good at it. Also they both speak fluent Swedish. Phone Poluchkin at the Helsinki Embassy this morning and give him his marching orders.'

'Why? I ask you again. Why?'

'Someone has to be there to help guide Procane into Finland when he surfaces. And because of what you have just told me. The operation is approaching a climax. I feel it in my old bones, Comrade.'

'You mean the news that Tweed and Cord Dillon have been seen arriving by our watchers at Arlanda? Is that a good enough reason to send killers?'

'The arrival of Tweed is. That man is very dangerous.'

'Killing him would be even more dangerous. Just supposing anyone could do that. Which I rather doubt.'

'Oh, I don't know whether that will be necessary.' Lysenko punched one clenched fist into the palm of his other hand and then placed an arm round Karlov's shoulder. 'If all these new developments worry you, why not send a report to Moscow saying you carry out these orders under protest? Eh?'

Karlov sensed a trap. The arm round his shoulder felt like a noose. He shook his head and sat down again, which forced Lysenko to drop his arm.

'I am not sending any such report,' he replied, watching his chief closely.

'Good! Good! I forgot to tell you that these instructions originate from the highest authority. So, you phone Poluchkin. Magda Rupescu is living in the

Solna district of Stockholm and she has a job with a secretarial agency. Her address is Bredkilsbacken 805, 171 57 Solna. I will write it down for you – and her telephone number. You pass this on to Poluchkin on the scrambler. Tell him to leave at once.'

'By what route?'

'By plane from Vantaa Airport, of course. He speaks fluent Swedish and has a passport in another name for that country – he will pass through the controls by simply speaking Swedish.'

'And his precise instructions?'

'To contact Rupescu. I have already spoken to her.'

'From Leningrad?' Karlov's tone expressed alarm.

'Of course not! I crossed the border to the Finnish town of Imatra and phoned her from there.' He slapped Karlov on the shoulder. 'You forget, I am an old dog at this game.'

'With those two loose in Sweden there will be violence. I still do not like it.'

'Karlov, the instruction from Moscow does not include any reference to your having to like it.'

'And what about the plan to bring over Mauno Sarin to Tallinn together with that English foreign correspondent, Newman – so he can see that every-thing is supposedly quiet and peaceful here?'

'I have not sanctioned that yet. We must get the timing right. Let them wait. They will be more eager to come if we leave them kicking their heels in Helsinki. First, Poluchkin must find out what is happening in Sweden. By the way, how did you hear that Tweed is involved in this Procane operation?'

'You know the rules, General,' Karlov replied, 'the informant's identity must be known to only one person.'

'Correct.' Lysenko knew he was checkmated. Since the leaks to the West from Moscow, they had reverted strictly to the cell system – only one man to know the identity of an agent in the West. Again, Karlov had avoided a trap. Lysenko reasserted his authority. 'So, despatch Poluchkin. I want him in Stockholm today.'

The heavily-built man with the sallow face who wore Swedish clothes paid off the taxi outside the block of flats in Solna. Oleg Poluchkin fiddled with the belt of his raincoat until the taxi had disappeared.

Before leaving the Soviet Embassy on Tehtaankatu in Helsinki he had been kitted out from the extensive collection of Swedish clothes kept in the basement. Picking up his case, he entered the modern block of flats. Once inside, he checked for a rear entrance and then climbed a staircase to the third floor. Outside Flat No. 805 he put down the case to keep his hands free and pressed the bell. Magda Rupescu did not open the door immediately and Poluchkin shuffled his feet impatiently.

Then he spotted the spyhole in the centre of the

door at eye level. He waited while three separate locks were opened. He heard a safety chain being removed. The door opened and he sucked in his breath. Magda looked even more desirable than he remembered.

Her thick red hair hung to her shoulders. Thirty years old, she was a slim, but full-figured, five foot eight inches tall, and her complexion was dead white. The whiteness was emphasized by the bright red lipstick, the only make-up she wore. She stared at him through her dark glasses.

'Are you going to stand in the corridor all day?' she asked in Swedish.

He walked inside the flat slowly, brushing her left breast and put down his case, glancing round the flat. It was more spacious than he had expected – the apartment block was only a little over a year old.

Behind him she slammed the door shut. Her long, nimble fingers attended to the locks, put back the chain. Removing her glasses, she swung round and gazed at him, her greenish eyes hard and cold. She put her hands on her hips before she spoke.

'You touch me again like that and I will kill you – '

'You kill me!'

His tone was mocking, his slack lips smiled unpleasantly. Her right hand moved swiftly, produced something from inside the pocket of her loose-fitting black dress and he felt the point of a sharp instrument tickle his throat. He stood very still. She was holding some kind of stiletto.

'Yes,' she repeated, 'I said I kill you. We are here

on a job. All our energy and concentration is focused on that. Do you understand?'

'No need to blow your top. We're supposed to work together.'

'Not in bed. You understand? Your bedroom is behind the door over there. Mine is behind that door. I don't lock it when I sleep. You come creeping in there and I rip you open. You understand, Poluchkin?'

'I understand. And I'd just as soon you put that thing away. What is it, anyway? I've never seen anything like it.'

She put down the weapon, and her manner became instantly normal, her voice detached. She demonstrated, squeezing the bottom of the handle. The steel needle retracted and Poluchkin realized it was spring-loaded.

'You would never guess where it comes from,' Magda remarked in a soft voice. 'England! They call it a Corkette. It is for taking corks out of wine bottles. You press the needle into the cork and use a pumping action. The cork slides out. One of our technicians adapted it. Who is going to suspect it is a weapon?'

'You can't ram that into someone's throat in a crowded street,' the Russian objected.

'But you can ram it into your target's spinal cord from behind, retract the needle and walk on. Especially in a crowded street. I carry it everywhere. Even when I go to bed,' she added. 'And what name are you travelling under?' she enquired in a business-like tone.

293

'Bengt Thalin. Travel agent for a dummy firm in Helsinki.'

'Show me your passport.'

'Don't you believe me? And we're supposed to work as a team. So cut out the bossiness – '

'I am in charge of this operation. You were told that by our superior. He phoned me while you were on the way to Arlanda. Show me your passport.'

Reluctantly he hauled the passport out of his pocket and she took it over to the window to examine it more closely. This infuriated Poluchkin who followed her.

'Why the check? Our people know what they're doing.'

'I was once in charge of Personal Credentials Section in Moscow. As you know, that covers manufacturing all identification papers for agents going abroad. Including passports. Sometimes they are not too bright – they make mistakes.' She handed back the passport. 'That's satisfactory.'

'Thank you very much,' Poluchkin replied with an ironical note.

'Don't get sarcastic with me. My skin is at risk, too. If Hornberg's men pick you up they could grab me.'

She sat down, crossed her long legs and lit a Blend cigarette. She waved the cigarette at him.

'Swedish. Now, let's get down to business. I'm operating here under the name Elsa Sandell – ' she spelt out the surname ' – and I run a small secretarial agency. Officially another woman, Swedish, is in charge, but she doesn't know her ass from her elbow. So I run the place. She has no idea of who I really am, of course.'

'Name of agency?'

'That need not concern you. Nominally – I empha-size the "nominally" – you're my boy-friend and we're living together. Our first priority is to identify and then contact Adam Procane. I have been told he is probably one of three people. Cord Dillon of the CIA – who has arrived secretly in Sweden. Our people at Arlanda saw him come in and then lost him at Sergels Torg in Stockholm. That's the square in the middle of the city – '

'I know this place – '

'Please shut up while I continue the briefing. We now have people watching the American Embassy. He's bound to surface sooner or later. Then there is Stilmar, National Security adviser. So far no sign of that one. Finally, General Paul Dexter. He was seen going into the British Ministry of Defence in London. Again, he hasn't shown here. Yet. Questions?'

Magda blew a smoke ring and watched it float towards the ceiling. Every gesture, her tone of voice, was calculated to indicate she was addressing a sub-ordinate. Screw you, Poluchkin thought, and maybe I will, but he kept his temper as he spoke.

'What route do we use to get Procane out once we have found him?'

'That you will learn after we've located him. One

thing at a time. And there is a man we may have to deal with if he gets in our way when that time comes. Peter Persson – '

'Who is?'

'Gunnar Hornberg's best tracker so far. I have a photo I'll show you in a minute. Don't underestimate Persson. It could be your last mistake. Also you need to look at photographs of Stilmar, Dillon and Dexter.'

She stood up, holding the cigarette between her red lips and unlocked a filing cabinet standing in a corner of the living room. Taking out a file, she sat down again on the sofa and carefully peeled three small photos from different sheets.

'Records of temporary secretaries my agency uses,' she explained. She handed him the pictures of three girls and he looked puzzled. 'The backs,' she said impatiently. 'Look at the back of each photo and show them to me one by one.'

On the reverse side of the first photo of a girl was another photo, a picture of a man. He showed her the print without saying anything. Let the bitch do the talking: he'd bring her to heel in time.

'Stilmar,' she said. 'Next – that's Cord Dillon. So the third has to be Dexter.'

He nearly said I had worked that out for myself. Instead he clamped his lips tight and spread out the three photos, studying them for a short time. From under a cushion Magda produced her handbag, opened it and extracted a fourth print from a secret pocket. She flung it on a table with the others.

'And that is Peter Persson.'

'Looks harmless enough.'

She leaned forward, staring at him and then she erupted. 'I don't think you've listened to one bloody word I've been saying, you cretin.'

'You can't talk to me like that.'

'Can't I? Don't you realize who sent me here? Who my superior – my protector – is? Well, he somewhat outranks you, Poluchkin. He could grind you to dust under one boot. Now, you listen – and listen well. Peter Persson fools almost everyone. His appearance has fooled you. He is very dangerous. He is the man Hornberg will choose to track Procane if that wily Swede discovers who Procane is.'

'If that happens, we deal with Persson.'

'No! I deal with him,' Magda produced the Corkette needle again. 'With this. If we have to dispose of the body that is your job. And I have a funny feeling that is what is going to happen.'

The phone rang early the following morning inside the flat in Solna. Magda hurried to answer it, tying her dressing-gown round her slim waist. The door to Poluchkin's bedroom opened and the tousle-haired Russian stood in the entrance to listen.

'Yes, I was fast asleep – in the middle of a dream,' Magda said, identifying herself by her coded remark. 'No, the post has not yet arrived. It is too early. This Englishman ... already in Stockholm, you say? He needs three secretaries. Certainly I can help. I will wait for him to contact me. Yes, I will give him top priority. Thank you for putting the business my way. Goodbye.'

She put down the phone and stared grimly at Poluchkin. She was on her way back to her room when he asked the question.

'What was all that about?'

'Big trouble. Wait for the post to arrive.'

She slammed the door in his face, locked it to vent her feelings and lit a cigarette. Bathing and dressing quickly, she spent the next half hour pacing her room, chainsmoking.

The two of them were eating breakfast in heavy silence in the dining room which led – open plan – off the living room, when she checked her watch. She stood up without a word, collected her handbag and left Poluchkin staring at the front door she had slammed shut, wondering where she had gone.

Within a minute she returned from the row of mail boxes on the ground floor. She dropped two advertising circulars in a basket and sat down to open a stiff, brown envelope. Addressed to Elsa Sandell and postmarked *Helsinki – Helsingfors*, it contained two identical photographs.

She handed one to Poluchkin after reading the brief description on the back. *This is the man requiring the services of three secretaries. Your friend.*

The last two words were in a handwriting she recognized. General Lysenko's. They must have rushed the photos from Tallinn across the Gulf of Finland to Helsinki aboard a Soviet patrol-boat, she guessed.

'Who the hell is he?' growled Poluchkin.

'An Englishman called Tweed. Their best operative is how he was described to me. He has just arrived in Stockholm.'

'And you call him big trouble?'

'You really are an idiot.' She sighed. 'This Tweed knows me. It was a few years ago in Bonn. That damned computer the Germans have in Dusseldorf caught up with me. While I was waiting for deportation, the chief of the BND brought in this Tweed to see me. He would know me again.'

'Then you have to see him first.'

'I have to see him first,' she agreed.

Chapter Twenty-One

'What is Newman doing now, Laila?' Tweed asked over the phone in the privacy of his own bedroom at the Grand Hotel.

'I hope you don't mind my phoning you,' Laila replied. 'I got your number from Monica. I'm so glad you are closer to me. It is only a fifty-minute flight from Stockholm to Helsinki. Can you come here at once?'

'Tell me what Newman is doing,' Tweed repeated. 'And I don't mind you calling me – I want to know what is going on – '

'I'm in my flat. Newman is trying to cross the water. Do you understand me?'

Oh, Christ! Tweed said to himself. He made a great effort to keep his voice calm. He had to soothe the girl down. A crisis was building up: he could tell that already.

'I understand,' he replied. 'Can you delay him in some way? I will try to come but I cannot promise. Why does he want to do a mad thing like that? It's not like him.'

'He is convinced he knows where his wife, Alexis, was killed.'

'Across the water?'

'Yes. He is very cold. No more jokes.'

'Do you think he is right, Laila?'

Tweed was keeping the conversation going while his mind raced. He was caught in a time trap. Things were developing in Sweden which meant he had to stay a little longer. Other things were happening in Finland too quickly. The timing was going all wrong.

'Yes,' Laila said after a pause. 'He has convinced me. Do please come quickly, Tweed. Otherwise it may be too late.'

It was a struggle for priorities. Tweed sensed the situation was getting wildly out of control. There were two main problems. Procane. And Tweed had to wait in Sweden until events moved in a certain direction.

The factor he had not foreseen – could not have foreseen – was the arrival of the rogue elephant in Helsinki. Bob Newman. Normally so reliable, he had become totally unpredictable – due to the murder of his wife. Tweed took a quick decision.

'Are you still there?' asked Laila.

'Yes. This is what you do. First, keep your nerve. Use every feminine wile you can summon up to keep Newman in Helsinki. Second, I want to talk to Newman on the phone at the earliest possible moment. If he won't call me, trick him – phone me when you've got him back in his room at the Hesperia, then hand him the phone.'

'I think that I might manage that,' Laila replied. 'I cannot say when – '

301

'Today, Laila, *today*. I'll try and stay here at the Grand until you work the trick.'

'I will do my best.'

'You may be saving his life,' Tweed warned her grimly.

'I will do more than my best. Goodbye.'

Tweed sat by the telephone after replacing the receiver. He needed more help. Time was running out. He had known this stage in a major operation before – suddenly the tempo speeded up. Everything started happening at once. At this point control had to be firm and decisive.

He picked up the phone again and dialled Park Crescent. He was put straight through to Monica. She knew him so well she detected something in his voice.

'Trouble?' she enquired.

'Maybe. I need back-up. Fast. Two men.'

'Harry Butler and Pete Nield?'

'Perfect. How quickly can they get here?'

'Today. They can just catch the 11.35 nonstop flight – so they'll arrive Arlanda 15.30 your time.'

'Send them. I'll get off the line.'

Tweed put down the phone and sighed with relief. Butler and Nield. The perfect combination. Harry Butler, the man who had photographed Helene Stilmar at the Dorchester Hotel in London, was phlegmatic and cautious, a Scot from Edinburgh. Nield had a more electric personality, a man for an emergency.

Tweed picked up the phone for the third time and booked two rooms. He was breaking another of his maxims – never house more than one person in the same hotel. But intuitively he felt the crisis was approaching. Better to have the whole team where he could contact them at a moment's notice. His judgement was confirmed within minutes of his taking his decision.

In the entrance hall of the Grand Hotel Magda Rupescu walked confidently up to the reception desk. She wore a light, beige-coloured raincoat and a head scarf which almost completely concealed her flaming red hair. She chose a male receptionist to talk to.

'I run a secretarial agency. A Mr Tweed who is staying here asked me to send him a secretary at midday. The girl who took his call foolishly lost her note of the conversation. Can you give me his room number, please?'

She gave him her most winning smile, leaning both forearms on the counter. Her whole manner suggested there was no doubt he would provide the information.

'Just a moment, madam.' The receptionist checked his records. 'Mr Tweed is in 632.'

'Thank you so much.'

She turned away, walked past the more old-fashioned and elegant elevator, and, very erect, continued towards the flight of steps which lead down to the exit. Behind her the elevator doors opened and Tweed stepped out.

He saw her immediately. It was over three years since he had studied her at the interrogation room in Bonn prior to her deportation by the German authorities. But during that encounter he had followed his usual practice of walking casually round her. He had also watched her when she walked out of the room.

However much trouble a person takes to change their appearance they rarely succeed in altering the way they walk. Tweed recognized her as Rupescu at once. Also, below the head scarf the bottom of her red hair showed. He walked after her.

Outside the hotel she climbed behind the wheel of a two-door Volvo, started the engine and drove off. Tweed stood on the pavement, memorizing the registration number, then returned to his room.

Sitting in a comfortable armchair, he took out his small notebook and wrote down the number. It had seemed like a fortunate coincidence. But when he was thinking out a problem Tweed's habit was never to isolate himself in his room. He thought more swiftly in a public place – a restaurant or a hotel lobby. He moved about a lot when he was in the field.

As he sat considering the implications of this new development, Rupescu was driving back to Solna with a feeling of triumph. The Grand was the fifteenth hotel she had called at, using the same psychological trick at each place. Never ask a question when you are seeking information. Always make a positive statement. *A Mr Tweed is staying here . . .*

Put that way, the person you are talking to was prepared to confirm the statement if it were true. It was a trick practised by Intelligence services all over the world and was the basic starting point of all interrogations.

She had started with the smaller hotels – working on the normal assumption that agents hid themselves away in anonymous hostels. Even as she drove on to Solna she was surprised Tweed had chosen the Grand. And as she drove, Poluchkin was searching in another part of the city for Tweed's hotel. She had drawn up a list and split it between them. Now we know where the enemy is, she thought as she pulled up in front of the Solna apartments, but he doesn't know that we know . . .

Gunnar Hornberg came back on the phone with the answer to Tweed's question very quickly. Tweed was doodling pictures of five-pointed stars in his notebook, relaxed in the armchair in his bedroom, when the phone rang.

'Vehicle Registration have come through with that Volvo registration number data,' he informed Tweed. 'Would you care to tell me what this is all about?'

'Not over the phone.'

'And probably not when we next meet. I do not

know why we accommodate you so generously, Tweed.'

'Because I have been so useful in the past to you.'

'It has something to do with our discussion in my office?'

'Actually, no,' Tweed lied. 'I'm ready with my notebook.'

'The address is Bredkilsbacken 805, 171 57 Solna. That flat is occupied by an Elsa Sandell – two "l's". We charge a fee, of course.'

'Put it on my account,' Tweed joked back, then he thanked Hornberg and hung up before the Swede could think up more questions.

All of which was rather satisfactory, Tweed thought. Now he only had to wait for the arrival of Butler and Nield before he put the Solna apartment under surveillance. He doubted whether Rupescu was working alone.

'Tweed has been located in Stockholm,' General Lysenko told Colonel Karlov with a note of jubilation in his voice.

He made the announcement as he walked into his subordinate's Tallinn office and stripped off his coat which he flung over the back of the nearest chair. Karlov, who had had no warning of Lysenko's visit, pursed his lips. The trouble was Tallinn is only two hundred miles west of Leningrad which made it only too easy for Lysenko to jump aboard an aircraft and fly to the Estonian capital.

'Are you sure?' Karlov asked.

'Of course I'm sure!' Lysenko bellowed. 'He is staying at the Grand Hotel. I was informed only this morning.'

'By whom?'

'Magda Rupescu. You know we placed her in Sweden one year ago. That girl is good – she always delivers. And you know Oleg Poluchkin is assisting her.'

'She'll enjoy that,' Karlov commented. 'And they'll make a pretty pair – those two.'

He looked up as someone knocked on the outside of the closed door. Before he could react Lysenko swung round and shouted at the door.

'Come in, Rebet!'

Lean-faced and studious, Captain Valentin Rebet came into the office, closed the door and took off his own coat. He nodded to Karlov and spoke politely.

'Good to see you again, Colonel.'

'Just stand there and listen,' Lysenko told him.

He swung back to Karlov, placed both hands on the desk, bent over and stared hard at the colonel. His thick eyebrows bristled as he began speaking with great deliberation.

'Do you not appreciate the significance of Tweed's arrival in Stockholm? He is trying to stop Procane reaching sanctuary in the motherland. The British are always sucking up to the Americans. What a feather in their cap if they could stop a major Washington defector crossing over to us! That is why that dirty swine Tweed is in Stockholm. Which means he must know – or suspect – that Procane has arrived in the Swedish capital. Or is due there shortly . . .'

'Possibly – '

'No! It is a certainty. You have warned Mauno Sarin of the Finnish Protection Police you would like to confer with him here in Tallinn soon?'

'Yes, General – '

'And that British foreign correspondent, Newman, will come with him?'

'So he says. I have Newman's visa in my desk.'

'Send it to the Embassy in Tallinn. Today! This way we'll kill two birds at once.'

'Exactly what does that mean?' Karlov asked quietly.

'We show the outside world that everything is peaceful here, that Estonia is a model republic. If I finally decide he can come, you take this Newman on a conducted tour round the city. I have read his file. He is an independent swine. Good for us because he will write what he sees – but he will try to break off the arranged route. Let him!'

Lysenko was striding round the room, waving his short, stocky arms. He liked nothing better than to lecture his subordinates, to demonstrate his points. He continued in full flood.

'Previously you will have cleared the side streets

of anyone suspect. Fill them with our tame Moldavians. He won't be able to tell the difference. I can hardly tell it myself! That is the first bird you kill.'

'The second?' Karlov enquired quietly.

'Mauno Sarin, of course! You tell him Procane is crossing over through Finland – which I am sure he is. He reports to you immediately any important American who sets foot on Finnish soil. He has him followed, guarded, protected.'

Pulling a folded paper out of his jacket pocket he threw it on Karlov's desk. Then he stared out of the window into Pikk Street. The colonel unfolded the document and scanned it. He was a fast reader and in less than a minute he looked up.

'This is a pass permitting me to visit Helsinki.'

'And you know how few people are issued with that.'

'Except that it is not complete. There is no official date stamp and you have not signed it.'

'For a simple reason, Comrade. The time has not yet come for you to go to Helsinki. You only make that journey when Procane has arrived and identified himself. You escort Procane back to Tallinn and we fly him at once to Moscow.'

Karlov leaned back in his chair, unlocked a drawer and dropped the pass inside. He closed and relocked the drawer. After a glance at Rebet he stared at Lysenko.

'Since I am in charge of the Procane operation I must from now on transmit all instructions to the

Poluchkin-Rupescu team in Stockholm. Further, they will report back to me.'

'They have all their instructions – '

'If my request is not granted, General, I shall immediately forward the strongest protest to Moscow – warning them that this operation is in danger of going wrong because of divided command. And, General, if I may say so, I have a witness to this conversation. Captain Rebet.'

'You threaten me?' Lysenko rasped.

'I used the word "request" – and I need a positive answer at once. Now. Procane may surface at any moment – '

'Request granted,' snapped Lysenko. Being an old soldier, he immediately counterattacked. 'May I remind you, Karlov, you have a dual role here in Tallinn. What have you found out concerning the murder of four GRU officers? That was why you were kept here in the first place.'

You bloody old liar, Karlov thought. I was held here so that I was well away from Moscow and the Politburo. He kept his temper and smiled before he replied.

'I am setting traps, as you know. I pick a GRU officer and he goes out after dark, wandering the streets and pretending to be drunk. He follows a carefully arranged route with my men secreted in positions all along that route. So far our killer has not gone for the bait.'

'You do this every night?'

'Of course not. That would be too obvious. Twice a week is the most we can bait the trap. I am a patient man –'

'I am not!' Lysenko snatched up his coat, his mood still choleric. 'And neither is Moscow. They want results quickly. So, get on with it. Rebet, I will call back for you here later. I'm going to look round this godforsaken, backwoods city myself . . .'

On this aggressive exit line, he left the office. Karlov asked Rebet to sit down, gave him a cigarette and began talking.

'Are you happy about this team of killers they have sent into Stockholm? I know Rupescu was there before but they are now activated.'

'Between you and me, no,' Rebet said promptly. 'But you must be careful, Andrei. There was a lot of discussion in the Kremlin about that decision and the hardliners – headed by Marshal Ustinov – persuaded the First Secretary and carried the day. At least you have that pass in your drawer. Not many people ever get that. Even Lysenko would have to get his own superior to issue such a pass before he could visit Helsinki.'

'Just assuming Lysenko ever signs and stamps it.'

'Oh, he will,' Rebet assured Karlov. 'You are the best choice to escort Procane here. You were the conduit while you were in London who passed the information from Procane back to us. Did you never have any suspicion who Procane might be?'

Karlov sighed and shook his head. 'This Procane is

a careful bastard. Always the information was passed to me in a crowded place – a pub, a railway station when several trains were leaving at the same time. And always a different Englishman. I am quite sure he had no idea of the contents of what he gave me.'

'But was there never the same high-ranking American in London at the times when you received data?'

'I have thought and thought. The answer is, if there was, he kept his presence well-concealed. These Americans do that – a fact unknown to the public in the West. They travel secretly to London, have a meeting with someone high up, maybe the Prime Minister, and return the following day. That way their brief absence from Washington is not noticed.'

'Stilmar, Cord Dillon, General Dexter. If you had to guess, which one?'

'I have no idea,' Karlov confessed. 'One thing I do predict. When I meet Procane face to face I will have the surprise of my life.'

Chapter Twenty-Two

Newman lay sprawled on the bed in his room at the Hesperia, head resting on the pillow, hands clasped behind his head. He was in shirt-sleeves, tie thrown to one side, collar open at the neck.

Laila moved quietly, careful not to disturb the brooding newspaperman who stared at the opposite wall without seeing it. She hauled off her thick, polo-necked sweater over her hair. Next she unzipped her corduroy slacks and slid them down over her long, white-skinned legs.

Easing herself onto the bed beside him, the nimble fingers of her right hand unbuckled his belt before he knew what was happening. He looked sideways and saw she wore only a transparent slip and no bra, stockings and a suspender belt. No essential part was covered.

'What the hell are you up to?' he burst out.

'Isn't it rather obvious?'

He kissed her slowly as she watched him, her eyes staring into his. Their bodies were oily with perspiration. They kissed and felt and fondled each other, her hair splayed over the pillow. Newman sprawled back on the bed.

It had been sheer animal passion for him. All the pressure that had been piling up on him since that distant morning at Park Crescent when he had watched that horrific film lifted, and for the first time he felt limp and relaxed. He lay inert as Laila slid off the bed.

'What are you doing now?' he asked with his eyes closed.

'Using the phone. Isn't that rather obvious, too?'

'In a little while maybe we can – '

'Ready, willing and able. Is that not the phrase?'

Her fingers were dialling the number and he agreed that was the phrase. She lowered her voice as she spoke on the phone and got through to Stockholm. *If he won't call me, trick him* – that was what Tweed had said, although she doubted whether he had in mind what she had just done. The moment he came on the line she said, 'I have someone for you to speak to,' and handed the receiver to Newman. 'It is for you – '

'Tweed here, Bob. I am in serious trouble and urgently need your help. I am speaking from the Grand Hotel in Stockholm.' Tweed was talking fast, not stopping, sensing he had to get Newman reacting immediately. 'You remember that postman who was attacked outside your London flat?'

'How is the poor bastard?' Newman enquired.

'Back on his rounds. Luckily he has a thick skull –

otherwise he'd have ended up in the mortuary. Bob, I really do need your help – I'm short of information. We know you met that postman before he reached your flat, that he gave you an envelope from Helsinki. Was there information in that last letter from your wife?'

Tweed paused, hoping he had guessed right. There was a silence at the other end of the line and Tweed forced himself to keep quiet. The next move had to come from Newman.

'Information about what?' he asked eventually.

'A man called Adam Procane. Bob, time is running out. This thing is big. I'll get to Helsinki as soon as I can – '

'I'll talk with you when you arrive.'

'That may be too late. Things are running out of control here. I need any information you have now. I needed it days ago.'

Newman was startled. This was not the quiet-spoken Tweed he had known in London – and elsewhere, come to think of it. This was a man who was using every trick in the book to get him to talk. But this situation he wanted to handle in his own way – by himself. Still, he had to give Tweed something.

'I presume it's OK to talk over the phone?' he enquired.

'It has to be,' Tweed responded promptly.

'There was a last letter. She didn't make a lot of sense – it was written in a kind of shorthand style. It took me quite a while to work out even a part of it. She said Procane had to be stopped. Who is this Procane?'

'I was hoping you would tell me.'

'The American Embassy maintains it has no one of that name on its staff – further, they have never heard of him,' Newman added, using the information Laila had passed on to him from her conversation with Alexis.

'Anything else in her letter?' Tweed persisted.

'Yes. A partial sentence that made no sense at all. *Archipelago is my best bet . . .*'

'And what is the significance of that? Don't make me drag every bit out of you. Lives are at stake.'

'I simply don't know. Tweed, I have an appointment.'

'I deeply appreciate your co-operation.' There was a bite in Tweed's tone. Newman was stalling – Tweed hadn't mentioned that Procane was an American. 'Could I have a word more with Laila?'

'She's all yours.'

'Laila,' Tweed said with emphasis when she came back on the line, 'I'm coming, but I can't say when. Do your best to keep Newman in Helsinki until I arrive.'

'I'm doing my very best for you,' she said. 'But I ask you, please hurry.'

'As early as I can. Goodbye. And good luck.'

She put down the phone, swivelled round and Newman was lying back on the bed again, hands clasped behind his head. He was studying her closely as he asked the question.

'What we've just done. Was that Tweed's idea?'

'Would Tweed ask me to do that?'

Newman shook his head as she perched a naked knee on the edge of the bed. He stretched his arms wide for her to come to him. For a few seconds she stayed where she was, then smiled and asked her own question.

'Ready and willing?'

He whipped his arms round her, joined his hands across her back and hauled her down on top of him. She rolled off and lay alongside him, a teasing note in her voice.

'I may be ready and willing – but are you able? Perhaps you just like to rest now?' She peered over his flank. 'No? I thought not . . .'

In his room at the Grand Hotel, Tweed was spreading out a map of Scandinavia on the bed. Seated in a chair, Ingrid was studying the notes of his conversation with Newman.

'Archipelago,' she said. 'Which archipelago? The Swedish or the Abo in Finland? And why is it important?'

'I wish I knew. Come and look at the map with me.'

As she bent over the map her expression was serious, head cocked to one side. She followed his index finger as it traced a complex course which started at Abo on the mainland. The finger threaded its way across the Finnish archipelago, twisting and turning amid the maze of islands, emerged in the open sea, crossed the Gulf of Bothnia and then twisted and turned again, ending at the large island of Ornö.

'You go backwards,' she objected. 'You tell me this Procane will try to go secretly from Sweden to Finland.'

'It sometimes helps to see what might be going to happen if you start at the end and arrive at the beginning. Gunnar Hornberg has promised to take me to the island of Ornö. I think the sooner I look at that place the better.'

'And I come with you? Please?'

'Hornberg doesn't know of your existence, which can be useful to me. Let me think about that.'

'I know those archipelagos. A boy-friend once took me in a boat along that route your finger followed.'

'How long did the trip take – to get across?'

'Only a few hours. It was a big boat with an engine. The small islands are really big rocks. They stick up out of the sea and little grows on them. Often nothing. From what I have read in the newspapers that is the area where the Russian mini-submarines are.'

'Any place in particular?'

'Yes. South of your Ornö island. Near our naval base on the island of Muskö. There.'

'They keep coming into people's conversation –

those Soviet mini-subs,' Tweed remarked as he straightened up and sat down in the armchair, taking off his glasses and inserting one of the handles in the corner of his mouth. Ingrid perched on the arm of his chair as she made her suggestion.

'I have visited Helsinki. Ten per cent of the people there speak Swedish. So, you take me when you fly there. Then I can interpret if you talk with a Swedish-speaking person.'

He glanced up at her. 'You can think of good reasons to stay with me wherever I go.'

'That is because Scandinavia is my part of the world. Is the Sarin girl very beautiful?'

'She is rather young for the job I've given her. Which is why I worry about her.'

'Tweed, that is not the question I asked you.'

'She is attractive, yes.' He chose his words carefully. 'She tries very hard and is good. But for a difficult mission, I would choose you every time. You are more practical.'

'How much younger than me is she?'

'Ingrid, I'm hopeless on ages. The main thing is you are much more on my wavelength.'

'Wavelength?'

'We think in the same way. So ours is a closer relationship. Now do you see the difference?'

'Yes. I like the difference. And you take me to Ornö. Then when you take the plane to Finland, which I think will be very soon now, you take me there so I can see the Finnish girl Maybe I like her. Maybe – '

'Maybe,' said Tweed, and left it at that.

Poluchkin stood by the front of his hired Audi, parked one hundred metres back from the American Embassy. He had the hood of the vehicle open and pretended to fiddle with the engine as the uniformed American soldier walked across the wide open space in front of the Embassy and came up to him.

'You can't park here, buddy,' the soldier informed him.

Poluchkin looked puzzled. He waved his arms about and pointed to the engine. He began talking rapidly in Swedish.

'It's broken down. God knows what's wrong with it. This is the second time this morning. I may have to get a pick-up truck to tow it back to the garage.'

The soldier gazed at him blankly. As Poluchkin had counted on, he hadn't understood a word. He made a gesture for Poluchkin to move on.

'Don't you speak English?' he demanded.

'No English,' Poluchkin broke into another flood of Swedish, repeating his arm-waving exercise. The soldier showed him his watch and indicated a time fifteen minutes from now. Then he again made a gesture for Poluchkin to move away and marched back to his post outside the white building.

Poluchkin was jubilant. Five minutes after his

arrival he had recognized a man who arrived in a taxi, paid off the driver and hurried inside the building at a brisk pace. He was hoping to spin out his illegal parking until the same man emerged from the Embassy.

Ten minutes later he saw another taxi pull up outside. No one alighted. The driver's 'free' light was not illuminated. He had been summoned to pick up a passenger.

Poluchkin closed the hood, got behind the wheel of the Audi and started fiddling with the ignition without firing the engine. Out of the corner of his eye he saw the soldier who had tried to move him on turn his head away. A minute later the man who had earlier entered the building appeared and climbed inside the waiting taxi. Poluchkin fired his engine.

He followed the taxi back into the centre of Stockholm where the driver dropped his passenger outside a travel agency near Sergels Torg. Poluchkin just managed to beat another car into a parking slot, locked his car and fed coins into the meter.

The American was leaning on the counter, talking to one of the girls. Poluchkin chose the girl next to them and enquired about package deals to Cyprus. As the girl explained what was available he listened to the American's conversation.

One aspect of Poluchkin's training at a camp west of Moscow had been *concentration* – the ability to talk to one person as his mind recorded all details of another conversation carried on at the same time. It was one of the less unpleasant skills taught him at the camp, but he had found it one of the most difficult.

Five minutes later the American left the agency, Poluchkin thanked the girl who had served him and hurried out with an armful of brochures which he threw on the back seat. His target was hailing a fresh taxi. Poluchkin sat behind the wheel and again followed the American.

This was about a ten-minute journey because of the traffic, but Poluchkin had no trouble keeping up with the taxi, always driving with one vehicle interposed between himself and the American. Another technique drilled into him at the camp.

The taxi turned into a wide street where the traffic was quieter and pulled up outside the entrance to an old apartment block. Poluchkin continued slowly past the taxi as the American turned away and ran up a short flight of steps. The Russian parked by the kerb and strolled back. Karlavägen 72C. That was the address the American had gone inside. Poluchkin decided he had pushed his luck far enough. Returning to his car, he headed back for Solna.

Inside the third-floor apartment at Karlavägen 72C, Helene Stilmar sat on a couch in the living room, stroking one of her crossed legs with her slim hand while she listened.

'I've gotten a lovely idea, darling,' said Cord Dillon. He sat beside her, grasped her knee and pushed his hand under her pleated skirt. Helene leant back against a cushion and they kissed for a long minute. Then she stopped his hand exploring further, pushed him gently away and smoothed down her hair.

'OK, Cord, let's have the lovely idea. You're full of them. Incidentally – ' she lit a cigarette ' – did you hear anything interesting at the Embassy? About Adam Procane, I mean.'

'There's a wild rumour that Procane has already arrived in Stockholm.'

'Wild?'

'Shit! It's just a rumour. No solid evidence to back it up. When I asked for hard facts they went all vague. Those boys are as nervous as a woman about to give birth. What is really scaring them is that Procane will slip through the net and they'll be held responsible. So they feed me any crap so they can say afterwards they warned me.'

'And how do you handle that?' she enquired, blowing smoke into the air.

'You smoke too much.'

'You're evading the question, Cord.'

'I asked for an empty office with a scrambler phone and called Washington about the rumour – emphasizing that it is a rumour I hadn't had time to check out.'

'You always cover yourself, don't you? And what is this lovely idea you've come up with?'

He produced a travel agent's folder from his pocket and slapped it down on the couch between them.

Helene looked at the folder without touching it. Dillon was disappointed by her lack of reaction.

'You might show some enthusiasm.'

'About what?' she asked coolly.

He got up and went over to the hi-fi deck. From a collection of records stored beneath he picked a Count Basie, started the machine and adjusted the volume to medium-loud. Then he went back to the couch.

'Why do you keep doing that?' she asked.

'Bruce Warren could have bugged this place before he loaned it to me. That will scramble what I have to say.'

'Great! The way you boys trust each other,' she commented. 'So, surprise me.'

'There are two tickets in that folder for sailing aboard a Viking liner overnight to Helsinki. We could really enjoy ourselves there for a few days – in safety.'

'Except that none of us is permitted to go further east than Sweden. Sometimes, Cord, I think you're a little crazy.'

'It's still a great idea.'

'Unless you're using me – '

'Using you?' Dillon's mood changed to his normal, abrasive manner. Helene watched him through half-closed eyes which usually turned him on. Not this time. 'What the fucking hell do you mean?' he demanded.

'Only that I'd make excellent cover if you are Procane . . .'

*

Poluchkin drove up to the apartment block in Solna, stopped with a scream of brakes and stared through the windscreen. A woman had just walked out of the exit. Magda Rupescu. He jumped out of the Audi, locked it and ran across to her as she was inserting her key into her own car.

'Elsa – ' he began, careful to use her cover name – she had chewed his balls off for calling him Magda inside her apartment ' – let's go back inside. Very interesting developments. I got lucky at the American Embassy – just how lucky is going to knock you out.'

'I rather doubt that, Bengt, but all right, we'll go back.'

Perhaps because of their unexpected encounter neither of them noticed the parked Renault. Inside the car a man, slumped almost out of sight behind the wheel, came to life. He snatched up the camera off the seat beside him and aimed the zoom lens through the offside window he had left open.

Upstairs in her apartment Magda threw down her keys on a table near the door. Standing in front of a wall mirror she started brushing her waterfall of red hair as she talked.

'Tell me – and keep it to the point.'

'That's what I really appreciate – a warm welcome – '

'You want a crack on the skull?'

She swung round and flourished her hard-backed brush. Poluchkin retreated several paces. The bitch was quite capable of carrying out her threat. One day he'd pin her down and give it to her. One day.

'Cord Dillon arrived at the Embassy shortly after I'd parked outside the place.'

'They'd notice that – parking isn't allowed there.'

'For Christ's sake, I know my job. I pretended I'd had a breakdown – that it wouldn't start. Now, can I tell you what happened or not?'

'I'm still listening.'

'Dillon went straight inside the building. He doesn't waste time, that Yank. He was inside ten minutes. Then he left in another taxi and I followed him to a travel agent. Inside the travel agent you will never guess what he bought – '

'We're not in the guessing business.'

'Two tickets for the boat to Helsinki.'

'I see.' Poluchkin had her attention now as she stared back at him in the mirror. 'Return tickets?'

'No. One-way! He said he would phone them the exact date in the near future. I wonder who the other person is?'

'Maybe a girl-friend to give him cover – make it look like a dirty weekend,' Magda suggested at once. 'You've done well, Bengt. Who knows – this might end up in a promotion for you. I'll call Helsinki now.'

'Why not Leningrad?'

'A change of instruction. It's better security anyway.'

She reached for the phone just as it began ringing.

She lifted the receiver, announced herself as Elsa Sandell, phrased a remark about the weather which positively identified herself and then listened. Her side of the conversation was monosyllabic. 'When? Identification certain? He's a very good customer of the secretarial agency.' That ended the call.

She broke the connection and, lifting the receiver again, dialled Helsinki 661 876, the number of the Soviet Embassy. She asked for Arvid Moroz and was put straight through.

'Arvid, did my express letter reach you? I hope I spelt your name right.' Another identification procedure. 'We have news about the Dillon consignment. It will come to you by sea. The Viking Line. Date of despatch I will let you know later. The consignment is definitely booked aboard one of their ships. I must go now.'

Poluchkin stood watching her, revising his opinion of her. She might be a bitch but she knew her job. He decided that in future he would treat her more tactfully. He phrased his question carefully.

'They understood? That was clever the way you told them.'

'Standard procedure.' She studied her blood-red, varnished nails as she went on talking and Poluchkin fought down a rising anger. The bitch was always playing this trick – never looking at you when she was speaking, which made him feel like a serf. 'So,' she continued, 'What is your view of the situation now?'

'I haven't bloody finished telling you what I accomplished. After Dillon left the travel agent I followed him again back to an apartment where I'm sure he's holed up. Karlavägen 72C.'

'You might have told me that before – now I have to phone Helsinki again.'

'Christ! You never gave me a chance. If you go on like this I'm going to complain to Lysenko.'

'No names!' Her voice changed. 'You have performed well.'

And I'd like to do a performance on you, he thought as she went on talking.

'I repeat, what is your view of the present situation?'

'That Cord Dillon is Procane.'

'That other call I took just before I phoned Helsinki. You would like to know about that call?'

'If it affects us.'

'From now on we have two jobs to do – you will keep a close eye on Dillon. I have someone else to watch.'

'Who is that?'

'That call I took was from one of our watchers at Arlanda. Stilmar has just arrived. He appears to be on his way in to Stockholm . . .'

Chapter Twenty-Three

Inside the Renault parked close to the Solna apartment block, Pete Nield had taken two quick pictures of Rupescu and Poluchkin with his camera. He had then waited until they disappeared inside the building before starting up the car and driving off.

Arriving at Arlanda with Harry Butler, the back-up Tweed had asked Monica to send urgently, he had phoned Tweed from the airport. Tweed had given him clear, precise instructions.

'Hire a car. You brought a camera? Of course. Proceed to this address.' Tweed had spelt out the address obtained from Gunnar Hornberg who, in turn, had obtained it from Vehicle Registration, using the car number Tweed had memorized as he watched Rupescu drive away from the Grand Hotel.

Tweed had also given a clear verbal description of Magda Rupescu to Nield. The task Tweed had given Nield was simple and direct. 'When that woman appears follow her . . .'

Nield, twenty-eight years old, dark-haired and with a small neat black moustache, was a man you didn't have to spell out everything to. When he spotted Rupescu leaving the block he had prepared to follow her. When Poluchkin arrived and was close to Rupescu he had taken his photographs. Now he felt it was important for Tweed to see the results quickly.

He arrived at the Grand Hotel about two hours later, booked in, took his case to his room and called Tweed. A minute later he was inside Room 632 and Tweed closed and locked the door, then switched on the radio.

'Something happened?' Tweed asked.

'I think I did the right thing. You can kick my backside if I didn't.'

'I doubt that will be necessary. Harry Butler will be here any moment – I think we should all know what is going on – ' Tweed broke off as someone tapped on the door. He opened it on the chain, saw it was Butler and let him in.

The two men were very contrasting personalities but the main thing was they had worked successfully as a team before. Pete Nield was quick-witted, fast on his feet, and his dark eyes missed nothing. There was a hint of challenge in his makeup. Also he was a snappy dresser. He wore a dark blue, pinstripe suit with a white shirt and a blue tie decorated with flamingoes.

Harry Butler was taller, more heavily-built, a few years older, clean-shaven and a very wary man. He nodded to Nield and sat down on the edge of the bed. He was dressed more casually than his partner in grey slacks and a check sports jacket. He was not a man who thought overmuch about clothes.

'Go ahead, Pete,' said Tweed as he sat in the armchair. 'I want Harry in the picture.'

Nield, who thought better on his feet, gave a brief outline of the Solna episode. He then waved his hands in a deprecatory gesture.

'This is maybe where I get my backside paddled. You told me to keep a watch on the Rupescu woman. Well, after she had gone back inside the apartment block with that thing, I guessed they'd spend some time there. It meant leaving the place unwatched but I thought you ought to see these . . .'

He reached for a large envelope he had dropped on the coffee table and produced two glossy prints. He went on explaining after handing them to Tweed.

'You hadn't mentioned that thug – a nasty-looking piece of work. So I drove to the British Embassy, showed them my card and made use of their dark-room . . .'

'Developing and printing yourself?' Tweed queried.

'Oh, yes. I threw out their technician. He wasn't best pleased but you can't please all of the people and all that jazz. And the negatives are in the envelope. Was it worth leaving Solna unwatched?'

'What do you think, Harry?' Tweed asked, handing both prints to Butler. 'You have more experience than Pete, more memories. Recognize the man with Magda Rupescu?'

'Oleg Poluchkin. And a right royal bastard if ever there was one. Speaks fluent Swedish, Norwegian – and Lapp for all I know. A trained killer, to boot. He is very bad news.'

'So it was worth it?' Nield enquired.

'Well worth it.' Tweed sounded sombre. 'They're bringing in the big guns – literally. Rupescu and Poluchkin are expert with just about any weapon I can think of.'

'And maybe a few we haven't thought of,' Butler remarked. 'I suggest, Pete, that you don't underestimate Magda Rupescu. She is one lovely, highly lethal lady.'

'Now, let's get down to business and make our dispositions,' Tweed said. 'We have the following pieces on the board in Sweden. Cord Dillon, who *appears* to be having an affair with Helene, wife of Stilmar. Then we have the Rupescu-Poluchkin team – Rupescu will be the control . . .'

'Is there someone in the bathroom behind me?' Butler asked. 'Or is it none of my business?'

'Ingrid!' Tweed called out. 'Come and meet our reinforcements.'

'Did I make a noise?' Ingrid asked Butler when she emerged from the bathroom where the door had been three-quarters shut.

'Not even that of a mouse,' Butler assured her as she gazed directly at him. 'I just get feelings about these things. Welcome to the battlefield. This is Pete

Nield, the boy wonder,' he added ironically. 'And I'm Harry Butler.'

Ingrid stared at Nield, who stared back, studying her with interest. She returned the stare with a blank expression and sat on the bed.

'Ingrid knows as much as you do – which isn't enough yet,' Tweed explained. 'She's Swedish and speaks some English – she is also my right arm in this part of the world – ' He broke off as the phone started ringing.

'Ian Fergusson here,' a voice whispered on the line. 'I'm downstairs in the lobby. You have a visitor and I think he's about to contact you. Couldn't phone from the airport – I'd have lost him.'

'Book yourself a room here,' Tweed told him tersely. 'We'll talk later. I'll call you. Let me know your room number.'

He had put down the phone when it rang again. Tweed announced himself and then listened, saying 'Yes,' and 'No.' As soon as the call was finished he jumped up.

'We have a new piece on the board. Stilmar himself is coming up to see me. Nield, make yourself scarce – ' He was still speaking when Nield left the room. 'Harry, you wait by the staircase exit so you get a glimpse of him. Don't let him see you. Ingrid, go and sit in one of those armchairs outside. You will follow Stilmar.'

Butler was leaving. Ingrid whipped a scarf from

inside her handbag, wrapped it round her head to conceal her black hair, and followed Butler. Tweed spread out the map of Scandinavia across the bed and waited. Less than a minute later there was a gentle tapping on the door as Tweed was putting down the phone. Fergusson had reported his room number.

Even after his direct flight from London, Stilmar was an impressive man who looked as fresh as paint. He was wearing another dark blue business suit, this time a bird's-eye which had clearly come from Savile Row. He towered over Tweed as they shook hands and Stilmar studied the Englishman through his rimless spectacles. Tweed ushered him to a chair and sat in his armchair. Again, Stilmar came straight to the point, speaking in his deep timbre.

'You have the radio on but is this room clean?'

'It was flashed by an expert from our Embassy this morning.'

'Flashing' was a term Tweed disliked but it was the latest jargon everyone used for testing a room for bugs. Stilmar pushed his spectacles up on to the bridge of his nose before asking his next question.

'Your expert does the job at the same time each day?'

'No, he doesn't – and that's all I'm telling you about the technique we employ . . .'

'They said you were a tough hombre. Have you identified Adam Procane?'

'Not for certain. Yet – '

'Ah!' Stilmar leaned forward. 'But you're pretty certain of his identity.'

It was a statement, not a question. The well-known Stilmar tactic of putting his opponent on the defensive – throwing him off balance from the outset of a conversation.

'I have four candidates for the role of traitor,' Tweed explained. 'Three of them have already arrived in Stockholm – the last staging post before crossing over into Finland – and once Procane is on Finnish soil he's practically in Russia.'

'Care to name those candidates?' asked Stilmar, still leaning forward so he could watch every expression on Tweed's face.

'I'm not concealing anything from you,' Tweed assured him with a blank expression. 'Cord Dillon, General Dexter, your wife, and yourself.'

'That's pretty goddamn frank – even insulting.'

'Why have you come to Stockholm, Stilmar?'

'The Swedes are getting nervous – and who can blame them? They have Soviet mini-subs sniffing round deep inside their territorial waters. The final straw was the Russian overflight into their air space. It recalled that airliner they shot down off Japan. That overflight – you know about it?'

'Yes. It will soon become public property despite the Swedish government's attempts to hush it up. I understand some British thriller writer is here for the publication of one of his books. He's being interviewed by Radio Sweden tonight and he's going to blow the thing wide open.'

Tweed had first heard of the serious incident from the technician who came from the British Embassy daily to flash his room. A MIG fighter had pursued a Swedish charter flight over the Baltic, only turning away when the Soviet pilot was almost across the Swedish coastline.

'That overflight brought me here,' Stilmar went on. 'The timing was perfect – from our point of view. It decided the Swedes to receive not only me – but also General Dexter – '

'Dexter is on his way here?' Tweed asked sharply.

'He is flying secretly from Denmark in a military aircraft to consult with the top Swedish military brass. He lands at an airfield at Jakobsberg – just outside Stockholm.'

'When?' Tweed demanded.

'The timing was uncertain when I left London, but soon. Again it was the Soviet overflight which made the Swedes change their minds. Tweed, you asked me why I came here. You have a reputation for extreme discretion. Can I take it that what I am going to reveal will remain strictly between the two of us?'

'Yes. I'm listening.'

For the first time Stilmar showed less of his supreme self-assurance. He rubbed the side of his hooked nose with his index finger. He removed his glasses and laid them on the table. He took out a silk handkerchief monogrammed in one corner with the letter 'S' and blew his nose several times. All the signs of a man wondering whether he should take the plunge.

Tweed remained perfectly still, a hand resting on each arm of his chair. He also remained silent, resisting the impulse to encourage Stilmar to talk, which he knew might well have the opposite effect. When Stilmar spoke Tweed had to force himself to show no reaction, to conceal his surprise.

'I am here on official business – as I have just explained. But there is also a personal angle. I think my wife, Helene, is having an affair with Cord Dillon.'

'I could do with a Scotch on the rocks,' were the next words Stilmar spoke.

Tweed maintained his silence while he stood up, walked over to the refrigerator and made the drink. He handed the glass to Stilmar and then sat down again in his armchair.

'You said "think" – don't you know?' was Tweed's response.

'That's the hell of it. Dillon is the craggy, rough-as-an-uncut-diamond-type she goes for. Her previous husband was a perfect specimen of the type. I used your chief, Howard, back in London, to check all flights when I found she'd gone after I got back. He traced her on to a flight to Stockholm.'

'And Cord Dillon?'

'I knew he was on his way here sooner or later –

because of this Procane thing. They're really worried about that in Washington. For obvious reasons. Every day that passes brings the Presidential election a day closer. Do you think your Soviet opposite numbers know your four candidates are here, or on the way?'

'That I can only guess,' said Tweed, playing for time while he decided how to handle Stilmar. 'How did you come in?'

'Through Arlanda – under the name of Ginsburg on the passenger manifest – '

'And then you had a car waiting for you?'

'I may be naive as far as my wife is concerned, but not in my job. I had another man aboard from the Grosvenor Square Embassy. He left the aircraft first at Arlanda where an official Embassy limousine was waiting for him. I waited until the limo was away and followed in a taxi.'

Tweed did not comment that his own man, Ian Fergusson, had tracked Stilmar successfully to the Grand Hotel. Which meant the Soviet watchers had done the same thing.

'What are you going to do about your wife?' he asked.

'That is the point. Should I do anything? Helene may be having a brief fling which will pass.'

'Why not pretend you haven't noticed anything. For the moment?'

As he said the words, Tweed thought of his own experience in the same situation. Here he was handing out advice he hadn't taken himself. Not that it would have made any difference – Lisa had always been a woman who went her own way.

But Tweed was keeping his eye on the ball. His main preoccupation at this stage was to keep Stilmar in a state of suspension regarding his marital problems. Stilmar replaced his spectacles, drank the rest of his Scotch and looked at Tweed.

'I think that is very good advice. Now, when we were talking at Park Crescent, you said you expected to receive soon descriptions of Procane from the continent.'

'Identikit pictures from Frankfurt, Geneva, Paris and Brussels.' Tweed stood up and made for the door. 'They have just arrived by courier.' He gestured towards the map spread over the bed. 'While I go down and get them, perhaps you'd like to study that map.'

Once outside in the corridor he turned left towards Ian Fergusson's room. He had purposely used the phrase 'go down' – knowing Stilmar would assume the person he was visiting must be below the sixth floor. When he returned, clasping a large envelope under his arm, he found Stilmar stooped over the map, studying it carefully.

'This line you've drawn,' said Stilmar, 'running from Ornö island to Turku in Finland. What does it signify?'

'The most likely route Procane will follow when he crosses over.'

'That sounds defeatist.' Stilmar straightened up. 'What have you got there?'

Tweed extracted four sketches from the envelope and spread them on top of the map, then he pointed at each in turn. 'Frankfurt, Geneva, Paris and Brussels.'

'That's weird.' Stilmar stooped over the bed again and Tweed was impressed with the speed of his reaction. 'This one reminds me of no one, this one of Dillon, this one of a woman is like Helene, and this one – '

'Reminds me of you,' Tweed commented. 'Incidentally, who are you meeting in Stockholm?'

'I can't tell you that.'

'What about these sketches. Anything strike you?' Tweed asked.

'Not a damned thing.'

'Are you sure?'

'I'm quite sure.' Stilmar straightened up, shot his cuffs to display his gold links embossed with the American eagle. 'And now I have to go to keep an appointment. I'm staying here, so no doubt we will meet again.'

'No doubt.' Tweed escorted his guest to the door, opened and peered out. Ingrid was still sitting in an armchair in the lobby in front of the elevators. She didn't look up at the sound of the opening door. Stilmar turned back just as he was leaving and lowered his voice.

'Did something strike you then?'

'All the candidates are there with one exception. General Paul Dexter.'

Chapter Twenty-Four

Ten minutes later Ingrid returned to Tweed's room. He could tell she had been rushing. She perched herself in her favourite position on the edge of the bed and began talking, waving her hands.

'I came up by the stairs – all the elevators were occupied. Stilmar is having dinner in the French restaurant. He will be there some time. I am sure that if he was going out soon he would have chosen the quick-service buffet.'

'He is eating alone?'

'Yes. At a table laid for only one person. He is writing in a notebook. He should have asked you to dinner.'

'I gave him plenty to think about.'

Tweed told her everything about his conversation with the American. She listened with her serious expression, saying nothing, and Tweed knew that later she would be able to repeat what he was saying word for word. He asked her the question when he had brought her up to date.

'From your experience of men, how would you expect him to react to his wife having an affair with Cord Dillon?'

'I saw him twice. Only for the few moments. But I would expect him to find her and ask what is going on.'

'I agree. I don't think he is going to do that. Which I find strange.'

'What could be the reason?'

'If he is Procane, the last thing he would do is start a row with Helene. That might lead to complications. He is a forceful, decisive man who is acting out of character. Also, I found it odd that he started talking to me about his private life.'

'Why did he do that, do you think?'

'To stop me guessing why he really is in Sweden. One would be inclined to accept that a man with domestic worries has his whole mind taken up by them – but, as I pointed out, he's not doing anything about his suspicions of Helene.'

'You don't trust anyone, do you?'

'Not where Procane is concerned. Another thing – Stilmar is saying the Swedes finally agreed to his visit because of that Soviet MIG fighter flying into Swedish air space.'

'That makes real sense to me.'

'Unless,' Tweed suggested, 'the Russians deliberately staged that overflight to provoke the Swedes into drawing closer to the United States – so Procane would have a reason for coming here.'

'I think someone is playing games,' Ingrid observed. 'I have the oddest feeling I am watching a gigantic conjuring trick.'

Tweed blinked at her, removed his glasses and began polishing them with his handkerchief. She watched him and he thought about what she had said before he replied.

'Then we'll just have to find out who is holding the hat with the rabbit inside it . . . who the conjuror is.'

It was close to midnight as Cord Dillon walked slowly along Drottninggatan – Queen Street – in the middle of Stockholm. This is a walking street in the Swedish capital, running straight as a ruler from beyond Sergels Torg until it ends eventually at the Riksbron bridge, which crosses the river past the Houses of Parliament and continues on to the island of Gamla Stan.

There were still a few pedestrians about at that hour. Behind him, two dozen paces away, strolled Poluchkin, who kept stopping to peer into shop windows. Several girls hurried past him and were careful not to glance at this solitary man who loitered at that hour.

Only late that afternoon Rupescu had told Poluchkin they were to continue watching the same targets. She would track Stilmar while Poluchkin kept a close eye on the movements of Dillon.

'So, I have the prime target?' Poluchkin had said, watching her closely. 'Dillon is walking round with tickets for Helsinki in his pocket . . .'

'Therefore, don't lose him,' she had replied with her usual *finesse*.

'Have I ever lost anyone?'

'There is always a first time.'

Poluchkin hadn't believed her for a moment. For some reason, which she hadn't revealed, he was convinced that the cunning cat had decided Stilmar was Procane. The Russian was betting that she was wrong – that the American he was following was the true target.

A short distance behind him a roly-poly faced man limped unsteadily. At intervals he staggered inside shop entrances and stared blankly at the windows before stumbling out again. Poluchkin had noticed him. Another drunk wandering the streets – the Russian was observant and had seen the nose of a bottle protruding from the moon-faced man's pocket. Behind Poluchkin, Peter Persson continued his apparently drunken amble down Queen Street.

The Swede had drink on his breath – an aroma produced by the simple expedient of rubbing whisky across his lips and down his chin. He limped inside another shop entrance, waited for less than a minute, then emerged into the street again.

Dillon had reached the bottom of the street and turned left. When Poluchkin reached the same corner he was surprised to see the American over a hundred yards away. He was on the verge of speeding up his pace when the American turned round, cupping his hand, and lit a cigarette. Waiting by the corner, Poluchkin heard the muffled roar of water.

Curious as to what was making the noise – and to

give himself an excuse for lingering – he crossed the street diagonally and peered down into the river over the parapet. At this point, close to the bridge, the powerful flow of the water rushed over a weir. Poluchkin was to remember that weir in the near future.

He crossed back to the other side of the street as Dillon continued walking along the riverside. This action stopped Poluchkin from seeing that beyond the weir a chain of linked buoys was strung across the full width of the river on a cable.

In this part of the city a series of bridges links Stockholm with the island on which Gamla Stan, the old city, stands. Poluchkin reached the third bridge, Strömbron, and Dillon had vanished.

The Russian couldn't believe it. In the distance, further along the waterfront, stood the impressive façade of the Grand Hotel, the orange sun-blinds of its ground-floor windows furled. The front was illuminated, and high up on the roof crouched the dormer windows of the sixth-floor rooms. One window was lit behind closed curtains. Poluchkin had no way of knowing he was staring at Tweed's bedroom.

Poluchkin scoured the whole waterfront area, passing the white passenger boats moored in front of the Grand, and then returning the same way. He had to accept the fact: he had lost Dillon. The American had performed some kind of conjuring trick.

There is always a first time ... Rupescu's mocking words came back to him and he cursed inwardly. Then he decided on his only course of action. He walked rapidly away from the waterfront until he reached Karlavägen 72C.

Poluchkin settled down to wait, huddled inside the entrance to 72B. If the police arrived he would say he was waiting for his girl-friend who had the key. The thought had just passed through his mind when a patrol car slid to the kerb and a uniformed policeman sitting beside the driver stepped out.

'I'd like to see some form of identity,' the policeman said, staring hard at Poluchkin.

The Russian produced his driving licence, made out in the name of Bengt Thalin complete with his photograph. The policeman handed back the licence and leaned one arm against a pillar.

'Care to tell me what you are doing here?'

'It's a little awkward, officer, I'm waiting for my girl – she has the key.'

'Don't look round. What is her name?'

Poluchkin was ready for that one. He had already chosen from the names alongside the bell-pushes Karin Virgin, which he knew would strike the police-man as amusing. But that was his last resort. Never be too eager to impart information to the police.

'It's rather embarrassing,' he began and paused.

'Embarrassing in what way?'

'She's a married woman – and her husband is away.'

'She doesn't trust you with a key?'

'This is only the second time.'

'Just so long as her husband doesn't change his schedule – it has been known to happen,' the policeman warned, went back to the patrol car, and drove off.

Five minutes later Dillon walked down Karlavägen, went up the steps to 72C. Poluchkin heard him fiddling with keys, a door open and shut. He checked his watch. Cord Dillon had disappeared somewhere unknown for exactly twenty-five minutes. Poluchkin decided that in his report to Rupescu he would omit to mention that he had lost Dillon for a short time.

After all, he told himself as he began walking back along the street, Rupescu would make a big thing of it. And he was sure she would report his mistake back to Moscow. What was the point in giving her an excuse to smear him? All for less than half an hour.

But in this assumption Poluchkin was wrong. The missing period of twenty-five minutes was the key to the whole Procane mystery.

Chapter Twenty-Five

The following morning in Tallinn General Lysenko held a council of war, as he termed the meeting. Three men met at 7.00 a.m. in Colonel Karlov's office. Lysenko, his deputy Rebet, and Karlov himself.

The General had moved his headquarters from Leningrad to Tallinn overnight. No warning of his coming to Karlov. He simply descended on the Estonian capital with his staff and installed himself in the building on Pikk Street.

'We are approaching the climax of the operation,' Lysenko began. 'Do you not agree, Colonel?'

'Certainly there is a lot of activity in Stockholm.' Karlov spread out three large photographs on his desk. 'We know both Cord Dillon and Stilmar are in the Swedish capital. There are strong rumours – unconfirmed – that General Paul Dexter is expected to make a secret visit to confer with the Swedish military –'

'And one of those men has to be Procane,' Lysenko said with great emphasis. 'I know where I am putting my roubles.'

Karlov ignored the interruption as he produced a

green file from the drawer which also contained his incomplete movement order to visit Helsinki. From the file he extracted a photograph which he added to the others, then leant back in his chair.

'This file was flown from Moscow by courier at my specific request.'

'What is it?' Lysenko demanded. 'I take it you haven't been going off half-cock again without informing me?'

'You were in midair, flying here with Rebet,' Karlov said in the same level tone. He held up the file so Lysenko could read the name for himself. *Helene Stilmar*. Then he held up her photograph.

'What the hell has that to do with Procane?' asked Lysenko.

'Yesterday I spent a lot of time re-reading all the files. I was struck by something we may have overlooked. Before she became adviser to the American President on women's affairs, Helene was a top liaison officer between the State Department and the Pentagon – '

'So?'

'I have asked the Rupescu team to check all hotels in Stockholm to look for this Helene woman. Stilmar is in the Swedish capital. Maybe his wife is also there.'

'She didn't come in through Arlanda with Stilmar,' Lysenko objected. 'Our people would have reported the news.'

'Suppose she travelled by herself?' Karlov queried.

'Why should she do that?'

'The answer to your question might be significant.'

'We shouldn't miss any fresh possibility,' inter-jected Rebet.

'There is more in her file,' Karlov continued. 'She is a first generation American – with Swedish ancestry. She has a twin sister living in Stockholm. Also a brother – older than her – '

'No one has so far suggested Procane could be a woman,' Lysenko snapped. 'We are talking about *Adam* Procane.'

'Which would be excellent cover for a woman.'

'It is Cord Dillon who has bought two tickets for travel to Helsinki overnight by sea,' Lysenko barked, deliberately losing his temper.

'And Rupescu suggested,' Karlov continued remorselessly, 'the second ticket could be for a woman. That woman could be Helene Stilmar.'

'Theories! Theories!' Lysenko exploded. 'You are guessing into space! No hard facts.'

'I have guessed into space before – with my plans for countering the American Strategic Defence Initiative, the so-called Star Wars programme.'

'On the basis of facts supplied by Procane.'

'There is a fact here you appear to have overlooked. Dillon bought one-way tickets to Helsinki.'

'So? Rupescu made no comment on that.'

'Because, General, she also overlooked something significant. If Dillon is Procane he would have covered his tracks better. He would have bought *return* tickets.'

'Poluchkin is an expert tracker. Dillon probably never dreamt he was being observed.'

Even as he spoke Lysenko realized his argument sounded false. He hoped Karlov would miss the phoney sound of his statement. No such luck.

'The Deputy Director of the CIA?' Karlov enquired with a note of irony.

'Agreed, then,' relied Lysenko, covering his retreat as he changed the subject. 'You instruct Rupescu to search for Helene Stilmar. Personally I think it's a waste of time.'

Which Lysenko, who had been thinking about what the file on Helene had revealed, did not believe. And again there was a witness to the conversation – Rebet – who said little and forgot nothing. Now that Karlov had raised the question they had to check.

'And the GRU murders?' Lysenko went on. 'Are we any nearer to solving them?'

'No. The killer has not fallen into my traps – and there have been no more murders since Poluchkin left Estonia.'

'That is an outrageous suggestion – '

'Merely stating a fact, General. You said that facts were all important.'

Lysenko switched the subject again. 'I think the time has now come when we should invite Mauno Sarin to Tallinn – to have a little chat with him about Adam Procane.'

'And the British newspaper correspondent, Robert Newman?'

'He can accompany Sarin. Since there have been no further murders this would be a good time to show this Englishman that all is well in Estonia. During the next few days, Karlov.'

'We must not forget that Newman's wife, Alexis, was killed while she was here. That still worries me . . .'

'The Alexis woman was killed because she found out too much about the route we planned Procane would use. She got the information from that drunken slob, Nasedkin, who is now in Siberia. She got him drunk – she was too clever. I told you what had happened afterwards. Let me do the worrying – that is why I hold the rank I do. You contact Rupescu, then Sarin. Tell Rupescu Cord Dillon must be protected at all costs.'

'That is a drastic instruction,' Karlov protested.

'Do it!' Lysenko rubbed his hands together with satisfaction. 'We are at battle stations. I have a feeling it will not be long before Procane is safe on Soviet soil. I shall win this duel with Tweed.'

Ratakatu, National Police headquarters, is situated in an old and densely built-up part of Helsinki on the peninsula. Men who know Leningrad say this district is different from the great Soviet port, but not unlike it. It is inside this same building where the forty-man Police Protection Unit is discreetly housed.

Newman walked along the street alone, taking his

time as he approached the street's end. He walked on the opposite side of the street to refresh his memory of the building. It is old, a four-storey edifice constructed of pale-coloured stone. Over the entrance is a square, milky lamp with the number '12' inscribed on three sides.

Two stone steps lead up to the heavy entrance door made of brown, panelled wood and with a metal pull-bar slanted at an angle across the door. Beyond the corner – across the street running at right-angles to Ratakatu – the pink-walled church of St Johan stands, overlooked by windows of the police building which continues round the corner.

He had been summoned to Ratakatu by an urgent phone call from Mauno Sarin. The Secret Police chief had sounded curt and worried.

'Newman, there has been a development.'

'What development?' Newman had demanded.

'Not something I care to discuss over the phone. Please come and see me at my office at once.'

'That's pretty dictatorial. Suppose I don't come?'

'Then I wash my hands of you. Within the next hour, if you please.'

The connection had been broken before Newman could reply. It was so unlike Mauno, the Englishman had slipped on his raincoat and left the Hesperia at once. Laila was due to come and see him so he left her a hastily scribbled message.

He crossed the street and paused outside the door. An engraved brass plate carried a typical Finnish trainload of letters. *Centralkriminalpolisen*. Checking his watch, he walked to the corner and looked up at the street sign. In Finnish first. Ratakatu. Then, below it, the Swedish version. Bangatan. He swung round on his heel and stared along a deserted street. He had not been followed. He walked back and entered the building, slapping his press card down on the reception counter.

Inside his office Mauno Sarin rose from behind his desk and shook hands, gestured towards a chair, sat down and spoke in a businesslike tone.

'Our visit to Tallinn is imminent. Within the next two or three days.'

'For Christ's sake, more hanging about.'

'You are damn lucky they have agreed to let you go to Estonia. From now on I want you to stay in your room at the Hesperia.'

'The *Georg Ots* sails at 10.30 in the morning. So I don't have to stay in my room penned up like a prisoner after that time each day. I assume we are travelling aboard the liner?'

Mauno jumped up from behind his desk and began pacing restlessly round the room. There was an atmosphere of tension inside the place. Both men were keyed up.

'Yes,' Mauno snapped, 'we go aboard the *Georg Ots*. But I do not want you wandering about at this stage. Oleg Poluchkin has disappeared – you remember that man I pointed out to you that evening in the Marski?'

'My job is to have a good memory for faces. What has that got to do with my staying behind bars at the Hesperia?'

'My people lost Poluchkin. A very bad slip, that. While I remember it, before you leave with me for the ship, you have to be subjected to a body search by my people here at Ratakatu. No weapons, no cameras.'

'Like bloody hell!'

'It is part of my agreement with Colonel Karlov.' Mauno was still pacing like a caged animal. 'If you want to come you accept the condition. It is their idea, not mine. Have you seen Laila recently?' He fired the question suddenly.

'She has a job to do.' For the first time in years Newman almost blushed. 'Writing articles you don't like,' he continued. 'Have you seen her?'

'No.' Mauno paused to light a slim cheroot, a sure sign he was under pressure. 'What about the body search?' he repeated.

'If it is the only way I can get there –'

'It is. So, you have agreed to one thing for a change.' He stopped by his desk, opened a folder and produced three photographs. Two were glossy prints, the third a grainy reproduction obviously taken from a newspaper picture – the screen dots showed prominently. Mauno arranged them in front of Newman.

'These are the Russians who run Estonia. Colonel Andrei Karlov.'

Newman stared at the head-and-shoulders picture of a man in the uniform of a GRU colonel. Lean-faced, highly intelligent, alert, the eyes stared straight back at him. Newman, who had an encyclopaedic memory, had never seen the man before. Which suggested the Soviets had taken care that he was rarely photographed. Tactfully, he refrained from asking the Finn how he had obtained the picture.

'This gentleman you know, of course.'

Oleg Poluchkin. Narrowed eyes, a slack, mean mouth, and in this photo the eyes had an odd blank look, the same look Newman had observed in the Marski bar.

'This is General Lysenko who commands all the Baltic States.' Mauno pointed to the grainy print. 'Normally his headquarters are in Moscow but he has moved to Leningrad. You will certainly not meet him. But Karlov may mention him. Now you will know who he is talking about.'

One of the old-style military types. A Bolshevik from his thick neck to the top of his Slavic head. Even from the poor print Newman could sense the man's coarse energy and fiery nature. He was looking away from the camera, like a man who was listening intently. A difficult man to reason with. A man who held to his own opinions as though they were gospel.

'Karlov looks the cleverest man by far,' Newman commented. 'A man who can keep secrets. A loner.'

'That is very perceptive of you,' Mauno remarked as he put away the photographs. 'Now, you get to hell out of it – I have work to do. Why I do this favour for you I do not know myself – '

'Because,' Newman rapped back, standing up, 'you're scared stiff if you don't, I'll find my own way to Tallinn – which is exactly what I would do.'

Inside the flat in the Stockholm suburb of Solna, Rupescu sat swinging her crossed leg, a motion which disturbed Poluchkin as he tried to concentrate on what she was saying.

'New instructions from Tallinn. We have to concentrate all our efforts on Cord Dillon. Plus the additional task of calling every hotel in the city to try and locate Stilmar's wife Helene – which I have just done. First time lucky. She's at the Grand. A courier is bringing her photo in from Helsinki today. Now, last night when you were following Dillon, he appeared to be just wandering round without any purpose?'

'That was my impression.'

Poluchkin answered shortly and was careful not to elaborate. If he said too much Rupescu, who possessed a devilish instinct for knowing when he was lying, might hit on the missing twenty-five minutes when he had lost Dillon.

'So, it was a trial run,' she said as she lit a cigarette.

'A trial run?'

'Don't be so stupid. Tallinn has decided Dillon is Procane. The tickets he bought for the sea trip to Helsinki convinced them. So, what will he do first? Make sure he is not being followed. That explains his midnight stroll.' Her voice took on an edge. 'That man

357

is a professional. You are sure he did not know you were behind him?'

'You are not the only one who knows how to track a man.'

'That is not a direct answer.'

'I am sure,' he replied, fuming inside, staring at her swinging leg.

'And you can get your mind off bed,' she told him.

'Not a hope in hell. Now,' she whipped a photograph from behind a cushion and shoved it at him. 'And are you also sure that Peter Persson was following you in Queen Street?'

'Quite sure. At the time I was concentrating on Dillon – on making sure he didn't spot me. But I noticed this fat-faced little man who appeared to be drunk and walked with a limp. He seemed familiar. As you know, when I got back here from Karlavägen I asked to see this photo again.'

'You have now slept on it. You are still sure this limping drunk was Persson?'

'How many bloody times do I have to tell you?' He jumped up and went over to the sideboard where the drinks were kept. Pouring himself a large vodka he raised the glass to his lips.

'Alcohol and this job don't go together,' she informed him.

'Go screw yourself. Nagging bitch.'

He waited for her explosion, not caring any more, and once again she surprised him. Her leg stopped swinging as she watched him empty the glass and then put the bottle away. She lay back on the cushion, watching him through half-closed eyes.

'You have to keep your nerve only a little longer,' Magda told him, her voice soft. 'And you've done well so far – I've told Tallinn that. You found that apartment on Karlavägen, so we know where we can pick up Dillon. Let's hope we can do just that this evening. He may take the same walk – Dillon is a careful man. I've re-read his file. A real pro – '

'We?'

Poluchkin was thrown off balance by her lightning change of mood. He was still underestimating Rupescu's skill at handling men. She took another puff at her cigarette and paused before replying in the same mellow tone.

'The new instructions say Cord Dillon has to be protected at all costs. At all costs,' she repeated.

'Which means?' he asked truculently.

'Do sit down. Relax. We have a lot to do. And we can't do it without your help . . .'

He shrugged and sagged into the chair. His stiff expression became less hostile. The vodka and her new use of the word 'we' as opposed to 'I' was having its effect, Rupescu observed. She wondered whether a spell in bed would complete the transformation – and immediately rejected the idea. Poluchkin still had to be kept on a leash – a longer leash, but still on a leash like an unpredictable dog.

'It means,' she went on, 'that at the earliest possible opportunity we have to eliminate Peter Persson if he

continues to follow Dillon. That is now a definite
decision. I do the job myself. Let us hope – if Persson
appears again tonight – that Dillon follows the same
route. Which is likely.'

'Why the same route?'

'It will be easy to get rid of the body.'

Chapter Twenty-Six

Newman closed his bedroom door at the Hesperia, walked over to a drawer, opened it to take out his notebook and froze. He walked back to the wardrobe, opened the door and stood looking at his clothes.

He was still staring inside the cupboard when he heard a quiet tapping on the room door. He stood to one side of the door before he asked the question.

'Yes? Who is it?'

'Laila.'

He let her in and closed and locked the door again. She was wearing a pale blue windcheater, dark blue socks tucked into knee-length boots and beneath the windcheater a white blouse with a mandarin collar. She put her arms round him and looked up into his face.

'Something is wrong, Bob? What is it? I can tell from your expression. Are you angry with me about –'

'I just got in myself. While I was away this place has been turned over.'

'Turned over?'

'Searched. By professionals. Everything is as I left

it when I went out – but not quite. What I'd like to know is who is responsible?'

'Someone who knew you wouldn't be here,' she suggested shrewdly. 'Who knew that?'

'No one I can think of,' he lied.

'Your key was gone from Reception when I called earlier. I thought you were here so I came up. As I came round the corner I saw a man in hotel uniform come out of a room – and I thought it was yours, then decided I must be mistaken.'

'Professionals,' Newman repeated. Mauno Sarin's men, was the thought which ran through his mind. At least, he hoped it was the bastard's men. Thank God he kept Alexis's last letter inside his breast pocket.

'You're looking very tense,' she remarked. 'I thought maybe tomorrow we could drive to Turku – get you away from Helsinki for a day. It would do you good. We could start early in the morning.'

'Not early. No,' he answered brusquely, half his mind on the problem of who had searched his room. 'Perhaps nearer to lunchtime,' he went on.

'Why not early?' she pressed.

'Because I'd like to sleep in a bit for once,' he replied, a touch of irritability in his tone. 'That is, if you don't mind my having a say in the timetable.'

'Of course not. We could go to bed now if you like,' she said with a certain look.

'No! That was a mistake.' He felt she was driving him into a corner. 'Look, Laila, finding your room has been searched isn't pleasant. Why don't we meet for lunch in the dining room? I have notes to make – '

'Of course. What time do you expect to be hungry?' she asked with a trace of sarcasm.

'I don't care! Oh, make it noon. I'll see you then.'

'Noon it is.'

She walked out without another word. To give herself time to think she used the stairs. Something was wrong. Why his outburst about not starting early? She was close to the ground floor when she stopped. Oh, my God! That bloody boat for Tallinn left at 10.30. And it must have been the Protection Police who had 'turned over' his room, as he had put it. So he must have been visiting her father. She had to warn Tweed. Newman was in danger. She ran down the remaining steps and made for the nearest telephone booth.

'I sense the hand of my old antagonist, General Lysenko, behind the latest developments,' Tweed told the assembled company in his bedroom.

He was looking again at the photographs of Rupescu and Poluchkin taken by Nield at Solna. Nield himself sat in a chair while Butler leaned against the wall. Ingrid was perched on the bed and a fourth man stood near her.

Ian Fergusson, the Scot who had followed Stilmar from London to Stockholm, was an inch taller than Ingrid.

A wiry, bony-faced man of thirty-three, he was slim and light-footed. Monica had once said that his expressions varied from poker-faced to blank. He wore a canvas jacket and jeans and an open-necked shirt. Outside in the streets of Stockholm he blended with the crowd of students who roamed the city. He looked almost ten years younger than his real age, which had often proved an asset in his profession.

'Why that cunning bastard, Lysenko, Mr Tweed?' he asked.

'Difficult to put it into words. But I would bet my pension Lysenko has now moved from Moscow close to Helsinki. Like me, he will have sensed the search for Procane is coming to a climax. The whole momentum of events is about to speed up. Ingrid, tell us again what you observed earlier today.'

'First, I saw Helene Stilmar coming into the entrance hall downstairs. She has a room here on this same floor – further along to the right as you leave this room.'

'If she is staying here what is significant about that?' asked Fergusson in his Edinburgh accent.

'The fact that when she arrived she spent only a short time here and then moved into an apartment at Karlavägen 72C. I get the impression she was keeping out of sight of people. Now she comes back into public view.'

'Could mean nothing,' Fergusson commented.

'You think so?' Ingrid looked sideways at him. 'Wait until I have finished. After Helene Stilmar had gone up to her room in the elevator I sat down in the entrance hall to see if she came down again. Ten minutes later Helene walks into the hotel a second time! She is wearing a bright red coat and a long red scarf and dark sun-glasses. I could hardly believe it –'

'There is a back entrance to this place?' Fergusson suggested.

'I said wait until I have finished!'

'Sorry, I talk too much.'

'You do! This new Helene wore quite different clothes from the first one. She also went up in the elevator and I watched the numbers. She got off at this floor.'

Tweed caught her meaning first. He leaned forward. 'You are talking about two different women?'

'I think so. They walk a little differently.'

'There's nothing about a twin sister in the file on Helene,' Tweed said thoughtfully.

'The files!' Ingrid was contemptuous. 'All of you keep talking about the files! If everything was in the files you could have stayed in London. We are here to find out what is not in your files.'

Her statement was so profound everyone else in the room remained silent and stared at her. It was Fergusson who broke the silence.

'What game is she playing then?'

'That is most obvious,' Ingrid told him. 'If the real Helene is going to Finland, she leaves her sister in her room here at the Grand. The sister appears in public, maybe has her meals in the dining room. That way we all think Helene is still here in Stockholm. But she is not. She is on her way to Helsinki or some other place.'

'That makes sense,' Tweed agreed. 'The spotlight of suspicion now switches back to Helene Stilmar. Ingrid, you have a new task. Go and sit in the entrance hall and watch for Helene to leave the hotel. Follow her if she does.

'I will keep you supplied with food from room service,' Tweed promised as she stood up. 'And I will come down and check with you from time to time.'

'I will change my position in the entrance hall,' Ingrid replied. 'Then I will not be so noticed.'

She left the room and Butler carefully waited until she had gone for a minute. He cleared his throat and Tweed guessed he was raising an awkward subject.

'Are we sure we can trust Ingrid?' he asked. 'Your security is normally so tight, Tweed, I find it a bit surprising you discuss everything in front of her.'

'She was secretly vetted before she ever undertook any work for me,' Tweed told him brusquely. 'She knows Scandinavia in a way we never shall. We are lucky to have her.'

'If you are happy . . .' Butler ended lamely.

'What I'm not happy about,' Tweed continued, 'is a foreign correspondent in Helsinki called Robert Newman. He is the unknown quantity who could just upset everything – because he doesn't know what is going on. Also, he's in a highly emotional state.'

For Fergusson's benefit, Tweed briefly outlined the history of the murder of Alexis Bouvet and Newman's sudden flight to the Finnish capital, plus his subsequent interest in Estonia. He was coming to the end of his explanation when the phone rang. It was Helsinki, and Laila sounded under strain.

'I said the unknown quantity,' Tweed repeated grimly as he replaced the receiver, 'and time is running out faster than I had feared in Finland. That was the Finnish girl who is keeping tabs on Bob Newman.'

'Another girl?' enquired Fergusson.

'Yes, Ian, another girl.' Tweed stared hard at the Scot before he went on, his tone terse. 'And she was also vetted before I first used her. Because she's in Finland she doesn't know anything like as much as Ingrid. But only a girl could get close to Newman – plus the fact she's also a reporter.'

'You don't mind my asking?'

'Just so long as that is the last time.' Tweed stretched out his arms and flexed his fingers. 'Newman may be visiting Tallinn within the next few days. I just hope I can reach Helsinki before he's gone.'

'Or he'll never come back?' Butler suggested.

'That is certainly on the cards. He's shrewd, experienced – probably one of the best foreign correspondents in the world. What scares me is his emotional state – as I mentioned before. There's only one reason why he should risk going to Estonia – '

'And that is?' asked Butler.

'He thinks his wife was murdered there. It is his shrewdness which worries me most at the moment.'

'I don't follow you,' said Nield, entering the conversation for the first time. Junior to Butler, he was careful to listen rather than talk.

'Supposing he spots the killer of his wife while he's there,' Tweed pointed out. 'Will he be able to keep his normal self-control? If only events here would move faster. I could take the first plane for Helsinki and talk to Newman face to face. Let's hope to God it does work out that way. Now, we must assign targets for you to watch.'

Late that evening Cord Dillon was walking down Queen Street for the second night running. Apparently absorbed in working out some problem, he strolled with hands thrust inside his coat pockets and his head down.

Again there were very few people about at that hour. Behind him Poluchkin followed at the same pace, his rubber-soled shoes making no sound. Peter Persson had lost his limp and wore a short raincoat as he trudged after Poluchkin, stopping to gaze briefly in shop windows where there was an illuminated display.

Magda Rupescu wore flat-heeled shoes and kept stopping to search in her handbag as though she had lost something. She walked about three dozen paces behind Persson and her thick red hair was concealed underneath a head scarf.

Persson was concentrating on watching Poluchkin but he was also aware that a woman was trailing behind him. He glanced back as he stopped in front of another shop window and saw Magda showing a folder to a girl passerby. Another tourist lost in the labyrinth of Stockholm's many streets and islands. At least she had the sense to consult another woman at this time of night.

Persson continued following Poluchkin at a distance. It was becoming significant that it was Cord Dillon who was so closely 'marked'. He thought Hornberg would find that interesting. He walked a little faster. Dillon was close to the end of Queen Street where he had the alternative of three different directions. South across the bridge to Gamla Stan. East towards the Grand Hotel. West away from the centre of the city.

Poluchkin stopped suddenly. Beyond him Dillon had reached the corner and he also stopped, turning as he cupped his hands to light a cigarette. Poluchkin slipped inside a shop entrance. Persson continued walking as Dillon disappeared to the left at the corner and Poluchkin reappeared from inside the entrance.

The Russian did not look back up the street. He appeared to be thinking only of what had happened to Dillon. He reached the corner as Persson crossed one of the side streets after a quick glance to make sure no traffic was coming. It was one of the hazards of proceeding along the Walking Street.

He was passing another shop entrance when the woman with the head scarf came up on his left. He stiffened. She was holding a street plan of the city open.

'Excuse me,' she said in Swedish, 'but I am completely lost. I am looking for a street called Hamngatan. I asked a woman a moment ago but she was from Hälsingborg.'

As she was speaking, holding her handbag and the open map in her left hand, she let the map slip and it fell inside the shop entrance. Persson stepped inside and stooped down to retrieve the map. Too late, some sixth sense warned him.

He was straightening up and turning when Magda rammed the long steel needle of the corkette in a driving upwards movement between his ribs and close to his vertebrae. The needle penetrated up to the hilt. Persson was dead as she put one foot on his slumped back and heaved with all her strength, withdrawing the weapon as Poluchkin arrived.

'That cleaner – ' Magda hissed. 'His bin – the river – '

Poluchkin grasped her meaning at once. A street cleaner clad in an orange jacket and trousers had come round the corner and was pushing a large trolley on wheels used for collecting garbage.

Poluchkin walked straight down the street and as

he drew level the stiffened side of his hand struck the cleaner a hard chopping blow on the neck. The Russian had already checked to see that Queen Street was deserted. He hauled the unconscious man inside a shop entrance, pulled off the cleaner's orange jacket, tore off his raincoat and slipped inside the orange jacket.

It was too big for him so he rolled up the cuffs, stepped into the street, took hold of the wheeled bin by the handles and guided it to the shop entrance where Magda waited with Persson's corpse. He heaved the body inside the bin, draped the raincoat he had carried over his arm across the protruding head and then wheeled it the last few metres to the road at the end of Queen Street.

Glancing to left and right, he saw there was no traffic. He wheeled the trolley across the street and stopped by the stone wall bordering the river. Poluchkin was a man of considerable physical strength. It took only one heave, his hands under the dead man's armpits, to hurl him into the river. The splash was muffled by the rumble of the nearby weir.

He tipped the bin after the body, took off the orange jacket and threw that into the water. Magda, who had held his raincoat, helped him inside it and then they walked side by side along the river front towards the Grand Hotel. He took her by the arm as they reached the Riksbron bridge only a few metres beyond where he had got rid of the body.

'Cut across the street here into the shadows. With a

bit of luck,' he continued as they reached the other pavement, 'come morning that body will be floating in the Baltic. He has all night to swim to the sea,' he added brutally.

'I heard a window open in Queen Street,' Magda said calmly. 'I didn't look up. Did you see anything?'

'Bloody hell, my mind was occupied with other matters. If there was someone, what does it matter? No body, no trouble.'

Chapter Twenty-Seven

It was three o'clock in the morning when Tweed was summoned by the phone call from Gunnar Hornberg. He stumbled out of bed, threw on his clothes, paused before a mirror to straighten his tie, comb his hair. Then he crammed a hat on his head and left the room.

Hornberg was already waiting for him outside the entrance behind the wheel of a Volvo. He was alone in the car. Tweed climbed in beside him and the Swede drove the short distance to Riksbron bridge. Stockholm was deserted, the stately buildings like a stage setting with the street lights reflected in the water.

'Whose body is it?' Tweed asked during the brief drive.

'The Criminal Police say it's Peter Persson. I'm just hoping to God they're wrong. But he didn't report back tonight.'

'Who found the body?'

'A man taking his dog for a late walk. Always it's a man with a dog. Oh, my God! Look at that – trust them to make a major performance out of it.'

Hornberg sounded really angry, which was unusual, as he stopped the car by the river, jumped out and left Tweed to follow him. Parked in the centre of the bridge was a large pick-up truck, its crane swung out over the river, its chain dangling a lifting-hook a few feet above the water.

The chain was supporting something as it elevated slowly. The something was a waterlogged body wrapped inside a canvas cradle. Tweed could see that the body had been lifted from where it must have been caught up in a system of pink buoys floating in the water and linked by a cable.

A police boat bobbed up and down in the black water, kept in the same position by the gentle running of its engine. Five uniformed men aboard the craft stared upwards as the cargo climbed higher into the night. It was a macabre sight.

Parked behind the pick-up truck an ambulance waited with its rear doors open and two white-coated men standing. A third man in civilian clothes, hatless and carrying a bag, stood with them. More men in civilian clothes stood by the river wall, hands in their pockets. A quiet but cutting wind wafted down-stream. Tweed was struck by the silence, the sheer immobility of the men watching.

The suspended cradle reached the level of the bridge and was slowly swung over it and lowered. Tweed walked after Hornberg who was hurrying onto the bridge, his mane of thick hair blowing behind him in the wind. As the cradle was lowered gently onto a trestle stretcher he heard Swedish voices raised. Horn-berg sounded livid. Tweed approached the SAPO chief and the man he was talking to slowly. Hornberg swung round, switching to English.

'Tweed, this is Inspector Holst of the Criminal Police. Holst, meet my friend, Tweed, of Special Branch – '

'A bad night,' Tweed observed, shaking hands and grateful to Hornberg for the anonymity of his introduction regarding who he really was.

'A bloody bad night,' Hornberg agreed savagely and addressed Holst, still speaking in English. 'Why in hell's name could you not have lifted him out of the river from the launch? It is an insult to a man's dignity to hoist him up like a sack of potatoes.' He glanced at Tweed. 'It is Peter Persson.'

'He was a nice man. I am sorry,' Tweed said quietly.

They were unstrapping the canvas cradle which supported the dead man. Persson's eyes were open and he gazed sightlessly at the starlit sky he would never see again. Holst shifted from one foot to another but before he could reply the civilian with the bag introduced himself and answered the question.

'I am Dr Schill, the new police pathologist. It was at my request that the deceased was taken out of the river in this manner.'

'Would you mind telling me why the hell you gave that order?' Hornberg demanded.

Lean-faced, ascetic, a man of about forty, Dr Schill watched the two men closely as they unfastened the cradle while he replied.

'This could be a case of violent death.'

'Could be! Peter Persson is – was – one of my best men. I am Gunnar Hornberg of SAPO. You think one of my people fell over the wall into the river? Of course it is violent death.'

'I shall be able to confirm that after my examination. And if he had been hauled into that launch, valuable medical evidence could have been destroyed. Lifting him out with that cradle is the way we disturb him least.'

'I don't think Persson is too bothered about how he is disturbed now. Please get on with your job. I require an immediate opinion.'

'After my examination back in the laboratory –'

'Examine him now!' Hornberg delved into his pocket and produced his SAPO identity card which he held under the pathologist's nose. 'I said SAPO. I will be back in a few minutes. Come on, Tweed. Before I lose my temper with these bureaucrats.'

'I wouldn't like to see you really lose your temper,' Tweed remarked, trying to calm down the Swede. 'What actually happened – or is it too early to say?'

'He was killed first – that I am sure of – and then tipped into the river here like a piece of rubbish from a garbage bin.' Hornberg turned to one of the plain-clothes men. 'Could I please borrow those glasses again?' He aimed them at a pillar supporting the bridge on the far side of the weir, and handed them to Tweed. 'Look for yourself.'

'What am I looking for?'

'A wheeled garbage bin wedged against the base of that pillar. The people who did this thing do not know Stockholm too well. Certainly they are not inhabitants who have lived here for years. That we do know.'

'How do you know?' Tweed enquired as he trained the night-glasses on the bridge's pillar.

'The killers obviously hoped poor Peter's body would float on down the Strömmen towards the Baltic and maybe never be found. If they were Swedes who lived in the city and knew it well, they would have known about the chain of buoys beyond the weir.'

'Where the body was entangled.'

'Precisely,' Hornberg replied. 'My guess is that it was discovered within hours of his murder.'

'Yes, I can see the garbage bin,' Tweed commented, handing back the glasses. 'Who found the body? You said something about a man taking his dog for a walk.'

'He's over there, sitting in the back of that patrol car. It is always a man and a dog who find trouble at night. Some drug addict lying in a doorway at his last gasp. Or a man who has been knifed in a fight lying in an alley. Often it is the dog, sniffing around, who makes the discovery.'

'Persson was on duty, I take it?' Tweed enquired.

They were standing out of earshot of the others as Hornberg pulled at the end of his nose and studied the Englishman – who knew he was wondering how much to say. Tweed carefully kept quiet.

'Yes,' the Swede admitted eventually, 'he was shadowing Cord Dillon. I want to have a word with him. Did he just walk away from it all? If he did, he's on the first plane out of this country.' He paused. 'Maybe you would like to come with me when I interview him?'

'That's very courteous of you. I accept.'

'Life is funny,' Hornberg ruminated. '"Courteous," you said. I was just about to request *you* to leave Sweden.'

'And why was that, Gunnar?'

'My Minister was getting a fit of the nerves,' Hornberg mimicked his superior. '"After all, we are neutral. I really don't like all these NATO people on my territory." Now I can road-block him,' he continued with savage satisfaction. 'It is the only good thing which has come out of this horrible killing.'

'I don't quite follow you,' said Tweed, although he understood perfectly.

'For God's sake! Some swine has murdered one of my best men. The Soviets invade our territorial waters with their mini-subs. They invade our air space with their MIG fighter. Now they have sent in one of their execution teams – maybe more than one. You think I am going to stand for that? The killing of Persson is clearly linked with Procane. You are directly involved – so you are welcome until we find the killers –'

'Providing Persson was murdered,' Tweed pointed out.

'Then let us see whether that pedant of a pathologist can yet give us an opinion. He's had time now to make a preliminary examination.'

Hornberg marched back onto the bridge where the stretcher with its pathetic occupant had been taken inside the ambulance. The pathologist was stooped over the body. He looked up as the SAPO chief arrived.

'SAPO are taking over this case,' Hornberg informed Inspector Holst.

'I thought that was coming.'

'So.' Hornberg continued, talking to the pathologist, 'Dr Schill, I must have your first opinion.'

'I have only had time to make a cursory examination,' Schill began.

'Tell me,' snapped Hornberg.

'It appears to be murder. There is one lethal stab wound in the back. I find it curious and interesting – the weapon, I mean. At first impression some kind of stiletto.'

'Then it's murder, as I knew it had to be. You see, Tweed, I was – '

Hornberg turned round and Tweed was no longer behind him. He had wandered away from the bridge and started to walk slowly up Queen Street, glancing from side to side. No one else was in sight as he peered into each shop entrance. He paused at one and then stepped inside.

When Hornberg caught up with him, Tweed was crouched on his haunches, staring at the tiled floor. He touched the floor with his right hand and then withdrew it just as the Swede arrived. Tweed remained in his crouched position.

'What are you doing down there?' Hornberg asked.

'There are faint wheel tracks along the street leading from here to the edge of the pavement opposite where the garbage bin was thrown into the river. Traces of some black substance like coke or coal.'

'I forgot to tell you. We found the garbage collector lying unconscious inside one of the shop entrances nearer the river. Minus his orange jacket. He is in hospital, suffering from a severe case of concussion. What about the wheel tracks?'

'I think earlier he wheeled his bin over a spillage of coke or coal – probably dropped by a truck. And here on the floor I think there is a patch of dried blood. Schill had better have a look.'

Tweed pointed with the index finger of his clenched hand concealing the lipstick holder he had picked up off the floor. Hornberg bent down alongside him and nodded agreement before both men straightened up.

'That was clever of you, Tweed. Stay here while I fetch Dr Schill.'

While he waited Tweed slipped the lipstick holder he had palmed into his pocket. The holder was gold-coloured, looked expensive. He decided he would show it to Ingrid at the first opportunity. He now had little doubt a woman had been involved in the murder of Peter Persson.

Chapter Twenty-Eight

During the middle of the same night two women sat in front of the dressing-table mirror in Helen Stilmar's room at the Grand Hotel. The two images in the glass were startling – as though the mirror had in some odd way distorted the images, creating two reflections of the same person.

'Do you really think we can get away with it?' asked Helene's twin sister, Eva.

'We have to – Cord Dillon is going to use that ticket to go to Helsinki by sea. Tweed is here to stop Adam Procane escaping from Sweden. It would be a great mistake to underestimate that mild-mannered little Englishman.'

'He didn't look very formidable when I peered into the restaurant downstairs.'

They were speaking in Swedish and there was an atmosphere of tension in the room. Helene was feeling under great strain. She concealed it well but the sisters knew each other so well they could often read each other's thoughts and emotions.

'I suspect a lot of people have made that mistake,'

Helene replied. 'Don't forget, Eva, I had lunch with him at the Capital in London. He's very dangerous.'

'But you still think we can fool him?'

'Look in the mirror.'

Eva, who lived in Stockholm and was the wife of a financial consultant, stared into the mirror again. She wore Helene's favourite emerald green dress, high-necked and with a scarf looped over her left shoulder.

Early during the previous day both women had visited one of the top Stockholm hairdressers. Helene had made a joke of what they required from the manager.

'We are playing a trick on a man who keeps bothering me. We want you to reproduce for my sister exactly the same hairstyle as mine. We're going to teach him a lesson.'

The hairdresser had grinned. He thought he knew what these two women were up to. And he noticed they spoke in the same way. Even their voice modulations were similar. The only difference he could detect was that the woman who had explained what they wanted had an American accent. How would they get over that problem, he wondered?

Helene had been 'getting over that problem' by sitting up half the night training Eva to acquire an American accent. It was easier than she had imagined. Eva, who travelled all over the world with her husband, was a natural linguist. She spoke not only her native language, Swedish, but also English, French, German and Spanish.

'Goddamn it,' Eve complained, 'I've gotten tired of this endless chatter. I just want to stretch out on that bed and go to sleep.'

Helene clapped her hands, applauding. Standing up, she poured more coffee – the third pot they had obtained from room service. When the waiter appeared Eva hid inside the bathroom.

'That was perfect,' Helene commented as she added cream. 'I doubt you'll have to talk much, but we mustn't overlook anything. When we perform my vanishing trick it has to work – and Tweed is sharp as a needle.'

'Tweed! Tweed! Tweed!' Eva swung round on the dressing-table stool and stretched out her long legs. 'Shit! I'm so fed up with that man's name. You make him sound like a bloody magician.

'He's performed some pretty smart tricks of his own in his time. Just take it easy,' she soothed her sister. 'Drink this coffee – it will waken you up.'

'I don't know why I agreed to this crazy idea,' Eva continued in English with an American drawl. 'And I haven't a hell's tooth idea of what is going on.'

'But you do know what you have to do when the time comes. I wouldn't ask you to do this if you were going to be involved in any danger.'

'But what about yourself, Helene? I don't like the idea of what you propose doing. Anything could go wrong – '

'I can look after myself. Now, the great thing is to

form a daily pattern, a routine which will lull Tweed
into a false sense of security . . .'

'You really think he will fall for it?'

'Results guaranteed,' replied Helene.

Tweed was relieved to find he still possessed his old
stamina, his ability to stay up all night and remain
fresh and alert as Gunnar Hornberg continued his
interrogation of Cord Dillon in his office in the SAPO
section at police headquarters.

The craggy-faced American was displaying the
same stamina under pressure, but he was a younger
man. The one advantage Hornberg wielded over the
American was that Dillon had been unexpectedly
dragged out of bed at four in the morning. Hornberg
himself had driven with an aide to Karlavägen 72C,
waited while Dillon dressed, and had then driven him
back to his office. An hour had passed since the
Swedish Secret Police chief had begun what he cour-
teously termed 'the interview'.

'Mr Dillon,' he repeated, 'one of my best men has
been killed in the middle of Stockholm. That is something which fills me with horror. It is also something
which means nothing – and no one – is sacred.'

'I've told you a dozen times if I've told you once,'
Dillon replied in the same bored tone. He paused to
light a fresh cigarette. 'I know nothing of this Persson
character.'

'But why were you walking round the streets of Stockholm at that hour, Mr Dillon?'

'I've told you that. I walk two miles every day.'

'Always at night? In Washington?'

'Not in Washington.'

'Not at night, you mean?'

Dillon compressed his lips at the Swede's persistence and Tweed, who had sat in silence next to the American on the other side of the SAPO chief's desk, stirred. He asked the question quietly, as though saying something for the sake of speaking.

'Cord, you followed the same route two nights running. Gunnar told me Persson followed you.'

'So what?' the American demanded.

'That is against all your training.' He paused. 'Unless you were checking to see if someone were following you.'

Hornberg, who sat with his forearms steepled on his desk and large hands clasped, his glasses pushed up over his head, leaned forward. He spoke only when it was clear Dillon had no intention of replying.

'Tweed has just asked a very valid question.'

'And I don't have to answer any of these goddamn questions.'

'No, that is true,' Hornberg agreed. His voice deepened in timbre. 'But if you don't, relations between my country and yours will be strained severely. Supposing I was in your position in Washington – and one of your men had been murdered? What would your reaction be?'

'The same as yours, I suppose.' Dillon swivelled to look at Tweed. 'It would be you who noticed that discrepancy in my behaviour pattern.'

'Am I right, then?' Tweed enquired.

'On the nose. Yes, I followed the same route deliberately. The first night I was out for a walk – and I noticed I *was* being followed. The second night I was checking to be sure. And yes, I was being followed.'

'Who by?' Tweed asked in the same gentle tone.

'The man Hornberg showed me a photograph of – Persson. He was pretty damned professional, but I've had a little experience in that task myself. Who do you think killed him?'

Hornberg ignored the question. He remained quite motionless behind his desk, a large, Buddha-like figure, his eyes fixed on the American. Instead, he asked his own question.

'When were you first convinced you were being followed?'

'About three quarters of the way down Queen Street. Not long before you reach the bridge.'

'And who else was following you – or Persson?'

'No one.' Dillon snapped out the reply.

'I see.' Hornberg's tone expressed disbelief. 'A man like you should have seen the killers.'

'You know there was more than one?'

'Yes, we know that. Queen Street is pretty deserted

at that hour. Are you sure you did not see anyone else behind you?' Hornberg pressed.

'No one,' Dillon repeated.

Hornberg sighed, pulled his glasses down on to the bridge of his strong nose and stood up slowly. He buttoned his sports jacket. Dillon carefully did not stub out his cigarette: he was waiting for the other man to make the next move.

'I thank you for coming to see me at this ungodly hour, Mr Dillon. I don't think we are going to get any further – so there is no reason why I should disturb your night's rest any longer.' He turned to Tweed. 'If you could wait a few more minutes I would like to talk to you again about your discovery in Queen Street.'

Hornberg escorted the American to the elevator, waited until it was descending, and returned to his office, shaking his head as he closed the door. Picking up the phone, he ordered a fresh pot of coffee and replaced the receiver.

'He was lying, of course,' he remarked as he settled himself behind his desk.

'Not necessarily,' Tweed objected.

'Why do you say that? You were the one who trapped him into his admission that he knew he was being followed.'

'The killers could have followed them by using the old trick of advance surveillance.'

'Explain, please.'

'They could have been in front of both Persson and Dillon – there are plenty of side streets crossing Queen Street where they could have waited.'

'How would they know the route he was walking along?'

Tweed waited until a girl who had come in with a tray with the fresh pot of coffee left and they were alone again. 'Because they had followed Dillon the night before. This was the second night Dillon walked down the same street.'

'It's possible – but unlikely,' Hornberg commented. 'What motive could Dillon have for lying?'

'Because he's here on a job and doesn't want to get tangled up with the Persson murder. All his instincts would tell him to steer clear of your investigation.'

'You have overlooked the possibility that Dillon has turned sour. Then it all fits. Persson was killed to protect Dillon. We will find out in time – I do not give up. And later today – say mid-morning if you are available – I will drive you to the island of Ornö which seems to fascinate you. I wonder what we will find there that grabs your attention?'

It was just before nine in the morning as Ingrid tapped on Tweed's door. He was up, shaved and dressed despite only having had three hours' sleep after his early hours' vigil with Hornberg. When he let her in he was pleased to realize he was so alert.

'Can we have breakfast together?' she asked, perching on the bed which was still made up.

'I am afraid not.' He saw her expression droop. 'I have a job for you – and from now on we must not be seen together in this hotel by the outside world.'

'What is this job I do for you?'

'You follow Helene Stilmar wherever she goes. Find out who she meets – ' he handed her a bulky envelope. 'There is money for expenses. She might board a plane. You have your passport?'

'I always carry it with me when I work for you.' She patted the handbag beside her. 'Not that I would need it inside Scandinavia.'

'Of course not.'

Tweed had forgotten that Passport Control inside Scandinavia was only interested in foreigners – non-Scandinavians. Ingrid could fly to Helsinki, speaking in Swedish before she boarded the aircraft, and Passport Control would wave her on. She was checking the money inside the envelope.

'The notes inside the clip are your fee,' Tweed remarked.

'It is too much. You know how I like working for you – and I have a staff who look after the business while I am away.'

'Is business good?'

'Very. Clients want top quality photocopies quickly. They get what they want. I still say this is too much – '

'I decide the fee. So you are not allowed to argue. Can you tell me what sort of woman would use this?'

He handed her the lipstick holder he had palmed in the doorway on Queen Street shortly after the discovery of Peter Persson's body in the river. Ingrid took off the top of the gold holder, pushed up the lipstick and stared at it. Tweed was adjusting his tie in front of the mirror as he made the remark.

'In England we would call that colour carmine.'

'Carmine?'

'Crimson, then. A bright red.'

'Possibly a red-haired woman who has very white skin.'

He paused, staring in the mirror. He was wondering how much to tell her. Harry Butler's comment on the need for security had stuck in his mind – one of those annoying remarks which make you wonder about your own judgement. He decided to stop wondering, to follow his instincts.

'Ingrid, it is almost certain that lipstick belongs to a woman who is a murderess – or an accomplice to a murderer. Both of them professionals. The woman's real name is Magda Rupescu, the man's Oleg Poluchkin.'

He described both of them as best he could and Ingrid listened with her head crooked to one side. She stared at the holder as though it had suddenly become evil.

'It is an unusual colour,' she said slowly. 'It might also be used by a woman with chestnut hair. Helene

Stilmar has hair of that colour. I will look carefully at her colour of lipstick when I next see her.'

'Which may well be at breakfast.'

'So,' she stood up, 'I should go down to breakfast, maybe? Here is the lipstick.'

'I think you should,' Tweed agreed. 'But you take great care. One of Gunnar Hornberg's best men was murdered in the middle of Stockholm in the early hours of this morning – it is becoming very dangerous. You take no chances. That is an order. A red-haired woman. Watch out for her.'

'Or even a chestnut-haired woman? Maybe?'

Ingrid walked into the breakfast room – which, in the evening, is the French Restaurant – and then slowed down. At the buffet table Helene Stilmar was collecting bread rolls and the accessories.

The Stilmar woman wore a deep blue pant suit – trousers and jacket – and a cream blouse with a pussy bow at her throat. The normal procedure was to find a table for yourself, tell the Britt Ekland-type waitress whether you wanted tea or coffee, then walk into the rear section of the huge room and choose your food from the buffet.

Ingrid reversed the process. She wandered in a leisurely fashion – quite unlike her usual brisk movement – towards the buffet. The Stilmar woman walked away from the buffet, holding a plate in each hand, and Ingrid frowned.

She selected two brown rolls, one wrapped pat of butter, and a round, shallow canister of blackcurrant jam. Drifting into the front section where the large windows overlooked the waterfront and the white passenger boats moored forward, she paused again.

Helene Stilmar was sitting at a table by herself next to the windows. Ingrid chose a table closest to the buffet area and sat down, facing her target at a diagonal angle. She extracted a pair of light-tinted glasses from her handbag, put them on and drank some of her black tea.

She had checked on the lipstick Stilmar was wearing before putting on the glasses. It was light pink – a mile away from the colour of the lipstick holder Tweed had shown her. What was the name he had used? *Carmine!* Which proved nothing one way or the other.

She was the kind of woman who changed her lipstick according to what she wore, the time of day. A strong red for the evening. And Tweed had picked up the holder in Queen Street early in the morning.

Ingrid frowned again as she buttered her roll and scraped a portion of blackcurrant jam on it. Something was bothering her. She was damned if she knew what it was. She glanced again at the woman who was staring out of the windows with a faraway look.

Very chic. Very American in her style of clothes. Her make-up was a work of art. Fifteen minutes in front of the dressing-table before she let the outside world see her. Ingrid made herself up in thirty seconds. She could change into a different outfit in two minutes. Stilmar would need thirty minutes to bathe and put on fresh clothes.

A quarter of an hour later the tall, elegant, pant-suited woman left the breakfast room. She walked past Ingrid's table without a glance in her direction. A waft of perfume drifted into Ingrid's nostrils and she recognized the aroma. The same perfume she had smelt when Helene Stilmar walked past her to the elevators on the sixth floor several evenings before.

Ingrid picked up her room key – you needed this to show to the waitress when you entered the break-fast room – and collected the light raincoat she had draped over the opposite chair. In the entrance hall Helene walked down the wide steps and out of the exit. The doorman walked into the street to summon a taxi.

Ingrid ran to her parked Volvo, unlocked it and jumped behind the wheel. She swung out just in time to follow the taxi Helene had climbed inside. Crouched over the wheel, Ingrid concentrated on not losing the taxi, on her driving. But still at the back of her mind she was trying to pin down what it was that bothered her. Give it time. She'd put her finger on it. Sooner or later. Better sooner. Maybe . . .

Chapter Twenty-Nine

Early that morning, just after daybreak, a Swedish military aircraft – an SK60 jet – swooped low over Jakobsberg, twenty kilometres from the centre of Stockholm, and landed at Barkarby airfield.

The machine cruised to a stop close to where a black, six-seater Volvo with tinted glass windows waited, a soldier seated behind the wheel. Three men alighted from the plane, all wearing Swedish military uniform.

They walked across the short distance to the limousine, each carrying a briefcase. There was nothing remarkable about the event. Barkarby is a military airfield where such machines are constantly landing and taking off.

There was nothing remarkable about the three men. They all bore the insignia of the rank of a Swedish major. They climbed inside the rear of the Volvo, the doors were slammed shut and the car drove off.

The remarkable thing was the journey they had just completed. First, late the previous evening, they had been driven westwards across Denmark from Copenhagen to the quiet town of Roskilde at the foot of the Roskilde Fjord.

There, at the tiny harbour near the museum which houses reconstructed Viking vessels, they had boarded a power cruiser which had slipped its moorings as soon as they were aboard. The vessel had headed north, left the fjord and continued into the Kattegat where it turned due east.

It landed its three passengers at a quiet point on the Swedish coast where a car was waiting. They were driven to a certain Swedish military airfield in the middle of the night and transferred to the SK60. They changed clothes in midair.

At Barkarby they were driven only a short distance to one of the buildings on the airfield. The three men left the Volvo and disappeared inside the building. General Paul Dexter, US Army Chief of Staff, and two aides had arrived in Sweden.

'Any news yet?' enquired General Lysenko as he entered Colonel Karlov's office on Pikk Street. In was typical that he should start talking almost before he was inside the room.

'No,' Karlov informed him as Captain Rebet followed his superior into the office and carefully closed the door.

'Have we done all we can about setting up a system of communication for Procane?' demanded Lysenko, throwing his coat over a chair.

'Not having the slightest idea who Procane is, there is a limit as to what we can do,' Karlov explained, suppressing a rising feeling of irritation.

In all such operations there came a point where most men began to feel the strain of waiting. It expressed itself in different ways. Outbursts of bad temper. The same questions asked over and over again. The habit of the man at the top to pester his subordinates with more and more frequent – and unwanted – appearances. Anything rather than sit on your own in an office with blank walls.

'Go over it once more for me,' Lysenko ordered, straddling a chair he had turned round so he could rest his arms on the back.

'The Embassy in Stockholm has been given strict instructions,' Karlov began, exerting great patience. 'We assume the only way Procane can inform us of his arrival is to call the Embassy. As he is obviously a top professional – otherwise we would have had a hint of his identity while I was in London – we expect he'll use a public phone box in Stockholm.'

'I know all that,' Lysenko interjected.

Then why the hell are you asking me, Karlov wondered, but he kept his expression blank as he went on.

'Special operators are manning the switchboard at the Embassy. As soon as Procane comes on the line they will switch him through to Helsinki – and Helsinki, in turn, will put him through to me via the radio telephone link. My task will be to instruct him and make sure he is only on the line for the very minimum of time.'

'It's very crude,' Lysenko commented.

'Of course it is! But have you any other suggestions?'

'The man is a ghost,' Lysenko brooded.

'Which is why he has been so successful,' Rebet suggested.

Lysenko jumped up, slapped his arms round himself, went to the window, peered down into the street. He then put on his civilian coat again, thrust his hands into the pockets and stared at the two men.

'It is all down to you, Karlov. Be very careful!'

On this encouraging note he left the room. Rebet shrugged, took off his own coat and sat down. He waited for a minute in case Lysenko returned and then relaxed and began speaking.

'He can't stay in one place for more than a few minutes. It is getting to him. You heard about the killing of one of the SAPO men in Stockholm?'

'Yes.' Karlov looked gloomy. 'It's madness. That will undoubtedly stir up a hornet's nest – and just when we want everything to be quiet in Stockholm. What do you think?'

'Madness,' Rebet agreed. 'The trouble is that mentally Lysenko is still back in the sixties when that kind of thing was normal procedure. Times have changed – but Lysenko has not changed with them. Will these old Bolsheviks never fade away?'

'Not until a new generation takes over the Politburo in Moscow. One old man brings in another. They form a club. And Tweed is in Stockholm. That is the man who really worries me.'

'Don't let Lysenko hear you say that,' Rebet warned. 'He may get the idea of instructing Rupescu to go after him. Now that would be a disaster. Tweed, thank God, was never a man for violence.'

'I could do with a drink.' Karlov produced a bottle of vodka. 'Maybe we could arrange an exchange? Lysenko takes over the British SIS and Tweed commands the GRU? How would that suit you, Comrade?'

They drank to the idea, clinking glasses, then upending them. The drink didn't do much good. Both men sat staring at the phone, waiting for the call to come from Stockholm and across the water via Helsinki.

Hornberg picked up Tweed in his Volvo from the Grand Hotel at eleven o'clock. They drove through southern Stockholm, an area Tweed had never seen before, and he gazed at the solid-looking buildings with interest.

They continued due south and then swung east towards the sea. Hornberg drove just inside the speed limit, saying little as they proceeded through open country. Then he checked his watch.

'This island of Örnö is rather strange,' he remarked. 'Most of it is owned by a Count Stenbock. He has an apartment in the city but spends most of the year with his wife on the island. He also owns the car ferry from Dalarö to Hässelmara. That in itself is unusual – most of the ferries to the archipelago are public property.'

'I see it is practically on the edge of the Baltic,' Tweed commented as he studied the marine chart Hornberg had handed him.

'It is also in the middle of the area where the Soviet mini-subs are operating,' the Swede observed. 'It is not so far from Muskö, another big island and one of our naval bases. I have been thinking about what you said about those subs. You really think they could be a huge bluff?'

'They could be waiting to take Procane to Russia is what I said. And now we have three candidates in Stockholm for the role of Procane – Stilmar, his wife and Cord Dillon.'

'Four candidates,' Hornberg corrected.

'What do you mean?'

'Since early this morning. General Paul Dexter has arrived for secret consultations. He brought with him two of their top anti-submarine experts. Whether they will be able to tell us anything new is another matter.'

'Just a flying visit, I assume? Dexter's.' Tweed queried.

'Not entirely,' Hornberg commented and Tweed glanced at him. The SAPO chief sounded worried. 'It's a little crazy, but the oddest people do surprising things.'

'And what *is* Dexter doing?'

'You won't believe this – he is now walking the streets of Stockholm.'

'No!' Tweed's tone expressed sheer astonishment. 'He must be mad. And you permitted this madness?'

'The decision was never in my hands.' Hornberg shrugged his broad shoulders. 'I will say Dexter is well organized. The American Embassy had his size in clothes. They sent a complete outfit of Swedish civilian clothes – including shoes – to the air base where he landed. He is wearing a blue woollen hat bought from NK and a pair of large tinted glasses.'

'But why? Why is he taking this risk?'

'Apparently there is a saying about him in the States, a saying he often uses. "I like to see the geography of the target zone for myself." So, he is walking all over our city studying the layout. Likely areas for the landing of Soviet helicopters laden with troops – that sort of thing would be my guess.'

'And your Defence Minister allowed this?'

'It is those mini-subs – and that overflight of our air space by the MIG fighter which chased the Swedish charter plane. For the moment, they are very worried about Russia's intentions. I will say one thing for General Paul Dexter – his sense of timing is impeccable . . .'

'But the fact remains we now have, as you said, a fourth candidate for the role of Procane.'

'As you say, my friend. And now we are entering Dalarö.' He pronounced the town's name in the sing-song cadence so typical of the Swedish language. 'The

ferry leaves at noon. Coming back from Hässelmara
we have a choice of two ferries – four o'clock or five-
thirty. And while we are driving round Ornö maybe
you will tell me what so interests you about this
island.'

As it had been for so many days, the weather was
overcast with a second sea of grey clouds overhead
when they drove onto Count Stenbock's ferry. The
Swedes had had a bad summer and reckoned it was
the fault of the British who had enjoyed a heatwave
through the whole of July and August.

'You have stolen our summer,' more than one
Swede had said to Tweed humorously.

The ferry is long and narrow with vertical sides
which makes it impossible to see where you are going.
It carries a maximum of about twenty cars – but on
the day Tweed and Hornberg crossed less than a
dozen vehicles were aboard.

'It is Wednesday,' Hornberg whispered. 'At the
weekends it is packed with people coming to their
summer cottages. And while we are on the ferry
maybe you would not speak any English if anyone is
within hearing.'

Tweed nodded, wondering at the reason for this
request. He was also looking in the wing mirror on
his side of the car. The ferry was open at both ends
where the ramps were elevated at only a slight angle.
Hornberg had stopped the Volvo in a position amid-

ships. Tweed only realized they had left the mainland when he saw the view change at the bows of the vessel. The sea was smooth and calm as the proverbial millpond and a fine drizzle began drifting down. Hornberg took hold of the handle of the door on his side.

'Maybe you would like to stretch your legs? Take a look at the view from the bows? You are in the middle of the archipelago now.'

They wandered past the few other cars ahead of the Volvo and stopped just behind the elevated ramp. Tweed took in a deep breath of the Baltic air and stared fascinated at the panorama unfolding.

The ferry was sailing due east and then turned south as it began to thread its way through a maze of islands. It passed along a channel between two islands so narrow it seemed they must scrape the shore on one side or the other. It was at this point that the Swede made his observation.

'I doubt if you are aware of the fact, but we just may have been followed all the way to Dalarö.'

'The green Saab with the woman driver behind your Volvo.'

'That's the one. I think I'll go and have a word with her. Enjoy yourself. We have plenty of time – the crossing to Hässelmara takes twenty-five minutes.'

Tweed was careful not to look back as Hornberg left him alone. He looked forward and to each side instead, studying the incredible variety of islands. Some were large and shrouded with trees with, here and there, one of the summer cottages built of timber Hornberg had mentioned. Others were little more than rounded, brown-coloured boulders projecting above the oily surface. A paradise for lurking mini-subs.

He stood with both hands in his raincoat pockets, studying the islands closely. Yes, there was the occasional clearing amid the fuzz of dense green foliage behind the misty haze. Clearings large enough for a helicopter to land in.

'I talked with the lady in the Saab,' Hornberg said over his right shoulder.

'Blonde hair, cut very short and close to her head – like a golden helmet,' observed Tweed. 'Sits quite relaxed, her hands resting on the wheel.'

'Very good. She comes from south Stockholm – so she is a real Stockholmer, as we say. She is considering buying a cottage on the island but is uncertain. This second trip is so she can explore the island itself and make up her mind.'

'False alarm?'

'It explains why she followed the same route as we did. And we are going to a nice cottage on Ornö – a friend of mine owns the place and has loaned me the key. Also, his wife has packed lunch for us. Sandwiches in a cool box. We have a picnic in the cottage.'

'How very kind of her.'

'Maybe we eat it outside – like a couple of schoolboys.' He sounded pleased at the prospect. 'For a few hours we get away from all the problems of life – and horrible people who murder a man with some kind of stiletto.'

Inside the green Saab Magda Rupescu took her moist hands off the wheel and wiped them below windscreen level with a handkerchief. The conversation with that SAPO man had been unnerving.

Earlier she had parked her car in a slot outside the Grand and walked to the nearest phone booth. She had dialled the hotel and asked for Mr Tweed, mentioning the room number she had been given during her first visit days before.

As soon as Tweed answered the phone she broke the connection. The incident had occurred only minutes before Ingrid had knocked on Tweed's door, hoping they could have breakfast together. Rupescu had then returned to wait in her car.

She had been careful not to remain seated there too long. At intervals she had wandered inside the hotel. She had even sat down in the entrance hall, ordered coffee, and paid the bill as soon as she was served.

Her blonde hair was dyed from its natural red colour. She was well aware that Interpol held her detailed description inside its computer. The GRU had used Western 'hackers' to tap into that computer and knew all its secrets.

The flaming red hair she always wore in the presence of Oleg Poluchkin was a wig – skilfully constructed by the best hair stylist in the Soviet Union.

Rupescu watched the landing at Hässelmara approach as Hornberg and Tweed returned to their Volvo. She waited until three other cars had started their motors and then turned her own ignition key.

'What was that business about not speaking English while we were on the ferry?' Tweed enquired as Hornberg moved off over the ramp on to Ornö.

Hornberg drove up a narrow, tarred road which curves up a small hillside and is hemmed in on both sides by granite boulders and rocky outcrops. Even the first few metres on the island is wild and forbidding.

'Because,' the Swede replied, 'they are nervous here – due to the presence of the Soviet mini-subs. It was just possible they might question any foreigner – and I did not want to have to reveal my identity to vouch for you.'

'People are nervous,' Tweed agreed. 'On two occasions while I was having breakfast at the hotel I heard Swedish businessmen talking to Americans about the subject.'

'Now,' Hornberg explained as they moved on to the level above the sea and turned south along another narrow road lined with forest, 'we are heading for a place called Bodal, which is near another place called Brevik – on the coast south of Hässelmara.'

'I've got it,' said Tweed as he checked the larger-scale map of Ornö which Hornberg had produced from the glove compartment. It was titled *Ornökartan* in the top left hand corner and showed clearly the course the car ferry had followed through a splatter of islands which looked as though they had been cast haphazardly into the sea by a giant's hand.

'I think that green Saab is still with us,' Tweed added after glancing in the wing mirror.

'Probably the woman I spoke to is afraid of getting lost. In the middle of the week this place is pretty lonely.'

The road twisted and turned through the deserted forest. Here and there a ghost of a track led off to a cottage buried in the trees. The Swedes certainly liked their privacy, Tweed thought.

Alongside the winding road at regular intervals thin poles were planted on either side, poles painted orange and white. At more distant intervals taller, thicker poles reared up and these carried telephone wires with an electric cable for power slung underneath.

'Those small, striped poles – ' Tweed began.

'For the winter. Heavy snow hides the road. The only way you know where the damned thing is, is by driving between those poles. And here we are. My friend's cottage.'

Hornberg pulled over on to the verge off the road. Beyond, the ground sloped away to the sea, only a hundred or two metres away. Tweed looked around him curiously as he stood at the top of a flight of wide steps cut into the hillside. The green Saab drove past and the blonde-haired woman driver waved to Hornberg, who waved back.

The large cottage, built of timber, lay below the level of the road. While Hornberg collected the cool box from the rear of the Volvo, Tweed stood listening. The engine noise of the Saab faded and a heavy silence descended on the forest where a pale sea mist hovered among the trees, a silence he could hear and feel.

They walked down the earthen steps and Hornberg fiddled with the front-door key while Tweed wandered round the outside. He was struck by the sensation of being hundreds of kilometres from any kind of civilization – even though Hornberg had told him it was no more than fifty kilometres from the centre of Stockholm to the ferry point at Dalarö. The Swede gestured for him to come inside.

'The place has been shut for a while,' he said as they entered. 'With the recent weather it will be a bit cold – and that,' he pointed towards a window, 'is the Baltic.'

Hornberg went round turning on electric wall heaters. Tweed looked about with interest. Beyond the front door was a small lobby. To his left was the kitchen, to his right the spacious living room which he followed the Swede into.

The furniture was expensive and comfortable – low tables and easy chairs and couches. Big picture windows looked out from the end of the cottage and at the back where there was a splendid view down the hill slope to the water's edge.

Tweed peered through the window. The cottage was perched on a spit of land projecting into the sea. Beyond a film of pale green birch-tree foliage and the darker green of pines, he gazed at a whole string of small islands, some covered with fir trees. The peace of the place appealed to him until Hornberg disturbed it with his remark.

'While we are eating lunch maybe we can amuse ourselves watching the Soviet mini-subs cruising by.'

Tweed swung round and the SAPO chief was unpacking an incredible quantity of sandwiches protected inside a material that looked like Clingfilm. He had fetched plates from the kitchen and piled enough food on them to last them for a week. Bottles of beer were perched on place mats.

'We shouldn't starve,' Hornberg observed. 'Smoked salmon, ham, salad – '

'My mouth is watering,' Tweed replied as he settled himself on one of the couches facing the view of sea and islands.

'The wife of the man who owns this place will give me hell,' the Swede continued. 'Don't forget to get out the nice china was her last instruction.'

'We're camping out,' Tweed replied and bit into one of the sandwiches as Hornberg poured beer into glasses.

'And now, my friend, maybe you will tell me why you wanted to come to Ornö?'

'Because I think this is the route Procane will use to cross to Finland. I studied the map of Scandinavia and was struck by how your archipelago stretches out into the Gulf of Bothnia towards the Abo – or Turku, as the Finns call it – archipelago. A fast power-boat would do the job in a matter of hours. Then there are these mini-subs lurking about.'

'You may well be right. Why Ornö?'

'I can't tell you. It would reveal a source.' Tweed hurried on, away from the topic. 'Also I'm more convinced now we have arrived – it took us less than an hour to reach Dalarö from the middle of Stockholm. Procane could be here before we realized he had gone missing.'

'It is logical.' Hornberg munched another sandwich. 'I will put men here to watch the ferry points.'

'Going back to General Dexter. Is he really walking round the streets of Stockholm alone?'

'Of course not.' Hornberg smiled bleakly. 'He doesn't realize it, but three of my best men are following him. I will let you know what they report.'

To counter the chill and to air the cottage Hornberg had lit a fire of birch logs in a brick fireplace in the corner of the room, a fireplace which had a large copper hood which took the smoke away. They sat eating their excellent food and consuming their beer while Hornberg chatted about professional experiences.

Tweed listened, feeling content and away from it all, enjoying the crackling sound of the burning logs. Again he thought this was such a peaceful place and he envied the owner of the cottage. Peace, perfect peace . . .

Chapter Thirty

Magda Rupescu wore a camouflage windcheater and trousers tucked inside knee-length rubber-soled boots. She approached the cottage like a hunter stalking game, a pair of binoculars slung from her neck, a Luger pistol thrust inside her belt. The Saab was concealed on a side track, facing the tarred road.

Raising the glasses to her eyes, she scanned the whole area. She noted the Volvo parked off the road at the top of the steps leading down to the cottage. She saw the column of pale smoke rising vertically into the windless air from the chimney. Both men must still be inside the cottage.

She started moving closer and dead twigs crackled beneath her boots. She stood stock still and waited for any sign of movement. It was only her assumption that *both* men were inside the cottage. And she remembered vividly that afternoon in Germany with the BND – Federal counter-espionage.

The moment when Tweed had entered the room without speaking. The unnerving way he had – oh, so slowly – walked round her. His pause when he was directly behind her. A clever bastard. That was when she heard the squeak of the front door being opened down at the Bodal cottage . . .

'I think I'll stretch my legs, wander about a bit on my own. If you don't mind,' Tweed suggested.

'Thanks for helping to clear up. Go for a walk and I'll check things like the heaters,' Hornberg agreed. 'Then I'll drive you round the island. We must call in here on the way back to the ferry so I can make sure the fire is out.'

Tweed ignored the steps and trudged up the steep slope, picking up a short branch like a club. The ground was littered with half-submerged boulders covered with pale green lichen and he was careful where he put his feet.

His hearing was acute and he was sure he had heard something Hornberg had not appeared to notice. The sound of a car's engine revving as it bumped over difficult ground. Tweed had observed on the drive from Hässelmara that the side tracks off the tarred road were rutted and uneven. The sound had been like that of a car driving down one of these tracks not so far away from the cottage.

He picked his way amid the birches and firs and the scatter of half-submerged boulders underfoot, avoiding clumps of heather which reminded him of treks over Dartmoor. He moved noiselessly, walking round dead wood.

Then he heard it. The crunch of dead wood he had

evaded – followed by more of the same sounds. He veered quickly up on to the tarred road and walked rapidly south, away from Hässelmara.

He was staring in the direction the sounds had come from, his short legs moving with surprising speed as he covered ground rapidly. Behind a distant screen of trees he caught a glimpse of movement. He kept walking.

The next development was the sound of a car's engine being revved up. The first sound which had alerted him inside the cottage was repeated. Violent revving as a car moved along a rutted track. He was almost running when he came to a bend in the road.

He saw a flash of green vanishing round the next bend and stopped. The sound of the car's engine faded. He turned and began walking back to the cottage. His expression was a curious smile Monica back at Park Crescent would have recognized. The only thing he hadn't worked out was the blonde hair. Not yet.

Behind the wheel of her Saab Magda Rupescu's expression was grim and unpleasant as she drove at speed away from the cottage. Tweed, Tweed, always bloody Tweed! And the swine had damned near caught up with her as she ran for her car, crunching old branches underfoot and making far too much noise. Her frustration and fury were increased by the fact that she had no idea how the bastard had spotted her. And from inside the cottage!

She would give anything to obtain an order to kill Tweed. It would give her an almost sexual satisfaction to carry out the instruction. She drove like a madwoman, skidding round corners, braking at the last moment.

She calmed down as she drove on. This changed everything. She knew what she had to do next. Warn Tallinn. Return to Stockholm as soon as possible to send the message. Yes, this tiny episode had changed everything. And she would have to phrase her warning so no blame for the disaster was attached to her.

'Enjoy your walk?' Hornberg enquired as they climbed inside the Volvo.

Despite their large and satisfying lunch, he had had to dump a third of the sandwiches beside the metal garbage bin by the roadside at the top of the steps. He drove south – along the same route over which Tweed had walked.

'It was good exercise, yes,' Tweed replied. 'Incidentally, what time does the next ferry leave for Dalarö?'

'Four o'clock,' Hornberg said after checking his watch.

'Can we catch that ferry?'

'Certainly. It's your day.'

They drove over a large part of the island. It was a

wilderness with the road winding through the forest for mile after mile. At one point Tweed stretched himself as though stiff and suggested a brief pause for another spot of exercise. Hornberg drove on a short distance and turned down a lonely track.

'I think we are close to the sea. Let me listen.'

He stopped the car, turned off the engine, climbed out and stood quite still. Tweed followed him and his closing of the door was like a pistol shot. Amid the trees the sea mist was dripping and moisture formed on Tweed's glasses.

The same heavy, brooding silence descended on them. They were deep in the wilderness, but faintly in the distance there was a sound, a swishing surge of water meeting a coastline. Hornberg pointed with his right hand.

'You hear that? The Baltic is over there. Come on!'

He began walking, taking immense strides with his long legs. Tweed made no attempt to keep up as they threaded their way between the trees shrouded in pallid grey vapour. He was examining the ground as he strolled after the Swede.

He stopped at infrequent intervals and stamped his feet on the surface. Hard as a rock. And there were more rocks sunk into the earth, rocks covered with bright green lichen. Ten minutes later he saw Hornberg perched in the open on top of a platform of boulders, gesturing for him to hurry up.

'The Baltic – '

Hornberg pointed at the smooth water twenty

metres below, the sea rising and falling gently at the base of the rocks. Tweed turned up his raincoat collar – the atmosphere was damp and cold. More islands stretched away into the distance as the two men surveyed the view.

'Why were you stamping your feet back there?' Hornberg asked.

'Testing the ground – a helicopter could land anywhere with the greatest of ease.'

'You think they might use a chopper to take off Procane?'

'Can we get back to Hässelmara in good time for the ferry at four o'clock? I would like to wander along the waterfront – fishermen always fascinate me,' Tweed replied, ignoring the question.

'Certainly. We had better get moving . . .'

They drove back in silence, each man preoccupied with his own thoughts. At Hässelmara Tweed left Hornberg with the car and was away for fifteen minutes before he returned. Cars were already queuing for the ferry and Tweed settled himself inside the Volvo in the front passenger seat.

'I noticed you talking to that man with the big power cruiser,' Hornberg observed.

'He was the only one who spoke English. He hires it out to tourists during summer. He told me a lot about the fishermen – there are only a few left but those men know a lot about the archipelago. And I see your girl-friend with the Saab is also crossing with us.'

Ahead of them, at the beginning of the queue, the green Saab with the blonde-haired driver was parked. Hornberg nodded and said he had already noticed her.

'I may get out and have another chat with her while we are on the ferry,' he remarked.

'Incidentally, Gunnar, don't waste your time posting men at the ferry points here,' Tweed advised.

'Why not, may I ask?'

'Because they won't be using the archipelago route to take Procane across. Not now . . .'

Two hours later the phone rang on Colonel Karlov's desk in Tallinn. He broke off talking to Rebet in mid-sentence and grabbed the receiver. The operator inside the Soviet Embassy in Helsinki reported a call for him. It was Rupescu, using her Swedish pseudonym of Elsa Sandell. Her voice was brusque and urgent.

'Cancel the archipelago route for the expected consignment. Under no circumstances use that route. You understand?'

'May I ask why?' Karlov enquired, glancing across at Rebet who was listening in on the extension phone.

'Tweed. I must go now. *Not* the archipelago route,' she repeated in a rasping tone and then she broke the connection.

*

Hornberg drove from southern Stockholm into the centre of the city across the bridge via Gamla Stan. There was heavy commuter traffic going home but the flow was mostly in the opposite direction. He made the remark as he proceeded along the eastern bank of the Old City, passing the Hotel Reisen. Tweed could see the Grand Hotel, an imposing building across the far side of the water.

'I think I will check out that woman in the green Saab – she told me on the ferry coming back she had decided Ornö was not for her. Too lonely. But there was something about her – '

'Here is the registration number.'

Tweed pulled a crumpled piece of paper from his pocket and handed it to the Swede. Hornberg took it and crammed it inside his breast pocket.

'Thank you. I did memorize the number, but something written down is always safer. She really stepped on the gas when we hit the main highway into town. Streaked away from me – exceeding the speed limit. She must have arrived here some time ago.'

'Could you call me at the Grand after you have checked her?'

'Of course. Within the hour.'

He dropped Tweed outside the hotel and Tweed went straight up to his room. He found Ingrid sitting in the lobby when he left the elevator on the sixth floor. She was wearing a white windcheater, zipped up to the neck and a white, pleated skirt.

She was reading a magazine and glanced up, staring at him through a pair of tinted glasses. Placing a finger over her lips, she pointed towards Helene Stilmar's room and accompanied him inside his bedroom. While he locked the door and put on the chain she skipped round the twin beds and turned on the radio.

'What has happened?' Tweed asked.

'After breakfast, the Stilmar woman took a taxi. I followed her all round Stockholm. She changed taxis three times – one after the other. Then she had lunch in the Café de la Paix on Gamla Stan. After that she walked all the way up Drottninggatan – Queen Street – looking in shop windows. On the Hamngatan near NK she disappeared. I found her a few minutes later coming out of a public call box. She then took another taxi back here and went inside her room. She made the phone call – it would be I would guess about half an hour ago – while I was searching for her. I am sorry I lost her.'

'You have done very well,' Tweed reached across to where she sat on the bed and squeezed her arm. 'But shouldn't you now go back outside in case she goes out again?'

'She called room service a few minutes after she got back. I saw the waiter arrive with a snack on a tray and some coffee. When she opened the door she was in her dressing-gown. I am sure she is resting for some time.'

'Stay with me for a bit. You must be tired. How about some sandwiches and coffee for you?'

He was reaching for the phone when it began to ring. It was Hornberg and he sounded frustrated. He spoke tersely.

'I checked that number – her car registration. Computers do work sometimes. It was a hired car. From a place midway between the middle of Stockholm and Solna. I phoned them and they vaguely recall a woman. No real description – she wore a head scarf. Gave the name of Yvonne Westerlund. The computers come up with zero on that name. Investigation is like this. So many false leads.'

'Forget her,' Tweed advised. 'And from now on, call off the dogs. Don't attempt to stop any American going to Finland.'

'Anything you say – don't bother to tell *me* why. Actually it will be my pleasure – to drop this thing in Mauno Sarin's lap. One more development. You know that American I spoke of who was walking the Stockholm streets?'

'Yes.'

'The three idiots escorting him lost the gentleman for about fifteen minutes.'

'Whereabouts did this happen?' Tweed asked sharply.

'He walked into the NK department store. Wandered around the ground floor for some time. Suddenly he runs down into the basement area. There's another exit leading into the underground complex near Sergels Torg – a maze of tunnels. They lose him. Fifteen minutes later they find him again – standing in the square below street level, gazing up at the column.'

'How long ago?'

'Over half an hour ago. One of my men just phoned in. Of course, it might have been accidental – '

'I don't believe in accidents,' Tweed replied.

The second call to Tallinn had come through soon after they received the warning message from Magda Rupescu. Rebet was out of the room, visiting the lavatory, when the phone rang again. Karlov picked up the instrument and then pressed it close to his ear. Halfway through the brief conversation Rebet returned and the colonel gestured towards the extension phone.

'This is Adam Procane – Procane. You are expecting me?'

'Yes. Where are you now?' Karlov asked.

'Stockholm. I will make my own way to Helsinki – '

'When are you coming? We can help – '

'Within the next six days. I need no help.'

'When you reach Helsinki contact Tehtaankatu. Do you understand me?'

'Perfectly. Goodbye.'

Karlov had his mouth open to say more when the

connection was broken. He replaced the receiver and looked at Rebet, who was putting down the extension.

'That was quick,' Rebet commented. 'The action of a pro – but the voice was strange.'

'An American accent,' Karlov replied.

'Yes, but the voice was strange,' Rebet insisted. 'Blurred. And it sounded a trace effeminate.'

'I thought that, too.' Karlov stood up and started walking round the room, very like Lysenko. 'But the main thing is he is coming. Procane is coming!'

Chapter Thirty-One

It was the day after Tweed returned from Ornö when Mauno Sarin knocked on Newman's bedroom door at the Hesperia. He had to wait a short time before the Englishman opened the door, wearing a bathrobe. Newman gestured for him to enter and closed the door without greeting his visitor, his expression grim.

'I have some urgent news,' Mauno said. 'When you are dressed could we take a walk? I feel like a little exercise.'

He made a sweeping movement round the room with his right hand, indicating it might not be safe to talk indoors. Newman nodded and lit a cigarette before replying. Mauno noticed the ashtray was full of stubs. The Englishman was clearly under stress.

'I've just taken a bath,' Newman commented as he towelled his hair. 'Helps you to limber up.'

'You should try a sauna.'

'Too drastic. OK for you Finns – you're used to it.'

He dressed quickly in casual clothes; a pair of slacks and a sports jacket. Mauno sat in a chair and watched him light a fresh cigarette. He foresaw a difficult conversation and was glad it would take place outside. Tension was more likely to dissipate in the fresh air – when you were walking the body relaxed.

It was raining when they started down the Manner-heimintie in the direction of the city, a short, sharp shower. Hatless, both men ignored it as they walked side by side and Newman remained silent, staring ahead.

'I have had news from Tallinn,' Mauno began. 'We can go there together tomorrow – but although I have a written safe conduct for you it could still be danger-ous – '

'I'm coming,' Newman interjected. 'It's the *Georg Ots*?'

'Yes. But it is still not too late to change your mind.'

'The ship sails at 10.30? From the Silja Dock?'

'Yes. I could still tell them you have decided not to write the article. Please be very sure. It is Russia you are going to. OK for me, but for you – '

'Mauno, I am going to Estonia one way or the other. Either with you or by myself – that bestseller book I wrote made me a lot of money. Somewhere there is a Finnish fisherman who – for enough money – will land me on the Estonian coast at night.'

'Then you had better come with me.'

A tram rumbled past them down the street. The rain had stopped again and suddenly the dark clouds vanished. Overhead the sky was blue and the sun shone down on the two men as they approached the strange monument to President Kekkonen, two separate vertical slabs which bore no resemblance to a human being. Maybe it represented strength, Newman thought; not that he cared either way. He walked like a robot, his face bleak. As they passed the old bulk of a stone-built museum on their right he asked the questions.

'What is the schedule? Can I go where I like or have they laid down conditions?'

'Anywhere in Tallinn is the arrangement. You will meet Colonel Andrei Karlov – '

'Who will accompany us everywhere? So the locals will be very careful what they say to me?'

'No. We shall walk alone – just as we are walking now through Helsinki. I hope you don't mind my coming with you? That is the arrangement I made with Tallinn – I feel it is my responsibility to protect you.' Mauno grinned wrily. 'After all, I am chief of the Protection Police.'

'That's all right,' Newman said shortly. 'Do we follow a prescribed route?'

'Anywhere in Tallinn is the agreement. Down side streets. We can go where we wish – where you wish. They are very anxious you should see how things are there – so that your article will carry conviction . . .'

'How long will we be there?'

'The *Georg Ots* sails at 10.30, as you know. It reaches Tallinn at 15.00 hours. It then leaves Tallinn at 19.30 hours and arrives back here at 22.30.'

'A little over four hours ashore. That's not much.'

'You are an experienced foreign correspondent. You must have collected material for a story in less than that before now. If you could come to my office tomorrow at 9.30, please.'

'You allow plenty of time,' Newman commented. 'Ratakatu isn't far from the Silja Dock.'

'You agreed to submit to a body search,' Mauno reminded him. 'No hidden cameras, no weapons. That is also part of the agreement with Karlov. Or have you changed your mind?'

'No.' Newman paused on the pavement. 'I can catch a tram back to the Hesperia from here. Thank you for fixing up this trip.'

'My pleasure. And I am confident nothing will go wrong.'

Karlov was away from his office, inspecting a GRU unit in the countryside. Lysenko sat in his subordinate's chair, leant his elbows on the desk with his hands crossed and stared at Rebet.

'Tomorrow that English reporter, Newman, comes across the water with Mauno Sarin. You have made all the preparations I instructed you to make?'

'Yes, Comrade. Every available man – in civilian clothes as you ordered – will be in position all over Tallinn – '

'No communications problems?'

'They will all carry walkie-talkies – carefully concealed – so we will know exactly where Newman and Sarin are at any given moment. The transceiver is ready in that cupboard over there.'

'That is very important. I will supervise the tracking operation myself. We have to remember Newman's dead wife, Alexis Bouvet.'

Rebet looked worried, paused while Lysenko watched him, then he decided to speak. 'I am still not sure this is a good idea. The computer report on Newman records he is shrewd. Supposing that he does find out his wife was executed here? I do not see how he could – but just supposing that did happen?'

'Why do you think I am having him watched every second he is here?' Lysenko asked quietly.

'I do not understand you . . .'

'That is why I am a General and you hold the rank you do. If Newman finds out anything he will not leave Estonia alive.'

'That would be madness!' Rebet's expression was appalled. 'It would be a second monumental blunder – '

'And which was the first, may I enquire?'

Lysenko was no longer staring at Rebet. Picking up a pencil he began to doodle pictures on a notepad, his head bent over the desk.

'The killing of Newman's wife,' Rebet burst out. 'Even in Moscow they have had second thoughts.'

'At that time the hard line was strong. Ancient history,' Lysenko waved a dismissive hand. 'But this policy has been approved by Moscow. It is a calculated risk – an article by a reporter like Newman cleaning our slate here would neutralize all the Western reports of unrest in Estonia. On the other hand, if Newman becomes a threat he will disappear off the face of the earth. In Finland – '

'In Finland? How on earth are you going to manage that?' Rebet asked.

'By good organization.' Lysenko was still doodling on the notepad, had still not looked again at Rebet. 'A man of Newman's build and height – wearing Newman's clothes – will disembark from the *Georg Ots* and climb into the rear of a waiting car which will immediately be driven away by its chauffeur – '

'Mauno Sarin may have the car stopped and searched.'

'A car carrying diplomatic plates? I hardly think so, my dear Rebet.'

'Where will the car drive to? The Embassy?'

'Of course not. Remember, it will be night when the *Georg Ots* docks. The dummy Newman will pass for the real man. As to the car, that will be driven to a prearranged spot well north of Helsinki. The occupants – the chauffeur and the man acting as Newman – will leave the car and then push it into a remote swamp. A second car will be waiting to pick them up and return them to the Embassy. The following morning they return to Tallinn.'

'Sarin may have the car followed – even with diplomatic plates – and may even have it stopped on some pretext,' Rebet persisted.

'I have foreseen that possibility. That is why a second car will follow the first one. The task of that second car will be to stop any vehicle Sarin uses to try and follow the first one. An accident will be staged.'

'You seem to have thought of everything – except one point.'

'And that is, Comrade?' Lysenko drew a fresh doodle.

'Mauno Sarin. The arrangement is that he will accompany Newman all the time he is here.'

'And you really think it will be impossible to separate the two men? To persuade Sarin that Newman – in typical reporter fashion – has gone off on his own somewhere? That will be the least of our problems.'

'I still don't like it.'

'I do not recall anyone asking you whether you like it or not. Should an emergency arise, should Newman by chance find out how or where his wife died – should he take too great an interest in Toompea, then he will disappear forever. And the world will think he disappeared in Finland.'

Chapter Thirty-Two

Tweed made his decision the next day close to lunchtime as he sat in his armchair in his bedroom at the Grand.

'Please let me have a list of daily flights to Helsinki – and from now on I need a reservation to board at any hour.'

'I already have the list – here it is,' Ingrid replied and handed him a sheet of paper with departure and arrival times. 'And we need *two* seat reservations,' she remarked while Tweed studied the list. 'I shall be coming with you. I know Finland.'

'I don't know about that.'

She jumped off the edge of the bed and stood looking down at him. Her tone was vehement. She spoke with intensity.

'Have I not helped you all I could? If nothing else, I am practical. I know Scandinavia – you don't! You can never know it as I do. I was born here. I know how people think – I can see things you would never notice. I want to come with you, Tweed. I *am* coming with you!'

'If you say so. Better go and make those Finnair

reservations at the SAS desk in the lobby. Butler has taken over the watch on Helene Stilmar for the moment from you?'

'Yes. She is in her room down the corridor. Butler is outside, sitting by the elevators. Nield is watching Stilmar and Fergusson is following Cord Dillon.'

'So, we have them all marked.' Tweed gazed up at her through his glasses. Something in his expression alarmed Ingrid. She had the feeling he had grown younger, fiercer – as though he faced a major emergency.

'Is there a problem?' she asked.

'Call it intuition, if you like – but I have an overpowering sensation we are close to crisis point.'

'Crisis point?'

'Yes. That means the whole Procane business could blow up in our faces. Someone is going to make a move – maybe even today. A move to reach Finland. Stilmar, his wife, Cord Dillon, General Dexter. One of them. I – we – may have to fly to Helsinki today. And I'm still worried about Bob Newman – the man who might do anything. Still, better get down and make those reservations. For two, as you suggested.'

Tweed sat quite still in his chair after she had gone. He was bothered about his relationship with Ingrid. With all his experience he couldn't fathom what was in the girl's mind. And he wasn't sure what was inside his own mind.

*

In the lobby outside facing the elevators on the sixth floor Ingrid was surprised to see Butler sitting next to Nield. She ignored both men, pressed the button and left them behind as she descended to the entrance hall.

'She'll wonder what I was doing here,' Nield remarked, fingering his neat moustache as the elevator doors closed. 'She doesn't know Stilmar is visiting his wife. Odd – that they've got two separate rooms on different floors.'

'It happens,' Butler replied, keeping his voice low as he continued watching the closed door of Helene Stilmar's room. 'Maybe things are not going too well between them. Politicians have private lives, private problems – just like the rest of us.'

'What really worries me,' Nield commented, 'is that security is so lousy – our security. Does Tweed usually run things on so slack a rein?'

'No.'

'Christ Almighty! He is staying at the most prominent hotel in Stockholm – practically advertising his presence. Then he uses the phone in his room for all sorts of calls. He can't have forgotten all those calls go through the hotel switchboard. Or has he lost his grip – been too long out of the field? Tell me, Harry, do you understand it?'

'No.'

'Could it be that Swedish girl, Ingrid? Is he besotted with her? And that's another thing – he lets her hear everything. She's not a pro. I know you told me he's used her before – but she's not one of us. More lousy security. Lousy? Bloody non-existent! And what about that Finnish girl, Laila, he's using to try and keep tabs on Newman? How much does she know?'

'I haven't a clue.'

'Look, Harry. You've got far more experience in the field than me. I've raised God knows how many loose ends and you've just sat there – making no attempt to reassure me. That has to mean you're as worried as I am. Are you?'

'I've known Tweed quite a while,' Butler said. 'I can tell you he's the best we've got – '

'Working from behind his desk in London. But out here? Are you still saying he's the best we've got? I don't mind telling you I'm getting scared.'

'I'm waiting for something to happen.'

'Waiting for what?' Nield demanded.

'The old Tweed to show himself . . .'

'I have made the Finnair reservations,' Ingrid told Tweed as she perched on the bed, crossed her legs and folded her arms. 'Flight AY784. It departs Arlanda 15.10, arrives Vantaa – that's the airport for Helsinki – 17.00. It is only a short flight. Fifty minutes. Finland is one hour ahead of us – '

'I know.' Tweed checked his watch. '12.15. We still have plenty of time to catch it if there are developments.'

'You are expecting a – development?'

432

'Possibly.'

Tweed glanced across to the other bed, the one he slept in. His case was packed ready, the lid left open to avoid crushing the contents. He sensed from the expression on Ingrid's face that she had something more to say. He was getting to know – to be able to read – her expressions well.

'I don't understand it,' Ingrid began. 'Butler is outside which I do understand because he is watching Helene. What I do not understand is why Nield is with him. He is the man watching Stilmar – '

'Which means Stilmar is visiting his wife in her room down the corridor,' Tweed replied automatically. 'Perhaps the development I am waiting for is imminent.'

'It was Helene I wanted to talk about. I followed her again this morning as you asked.'

'Tell me what happened.'

'She takes more taxis round Stockholm after breakfast – like yesterday. Then she gets out at NK and wanders round inside.' Ingrid cocked her head to one side and stared at the wall, seeing the events she recalled. 'She bought nothing – although she is an American visitor – '

'You think she has spotted you?'

'That I do not know. She left NK and walked down Queen Street. Again like yesterday – but this time from Sergels Torg. She has an early lunch at Le Café – a very modern place. After coffee she makes a phone call from the restaurant. She spoke in Swedish. It was a short conversation. She said, "Do not worry. I have thought it over and can see you are right. I will come with you."'

'That sounds like Cord Dillon she was talking to,' Tweed interjected. 'The wording is significant. Please go on.'

'She leaves Le Café and takes a taxi to south Stockholm. The taxi drives slowly past the dock where the boat leaves for Helsinki.'

'At 18.00 hours, sailing up the Baltic overnight and arriving at Helsinki at 9.30 the following morning. A Viking Line ship. If I recall all the details correctly from that folder you obtained for me from the Tourist Office.'

'You have a good memory, Tweed,' she told him in a joking tone. 'The taxi then drives her back here and she goes up to her room.'

Tweed stood up, went over to his suitcase and burrowed under the carefully packed clothes. His hand emerged holding a slim file, the file on Helene Stilmar. He sat down again in the armchair and flipped over the sheets to a page which he re-read attentively. He was near the end of the page when someone rapped on the door, an irregular tattoo. He nodded to Ingrid, who slid off the bed and opened the door.

Harry Butler hurried inside as Ingrid closed the door. He stopped as he saw the open file in Tweed's lap. Only by an effort of will was he able to avoid glancing at Ingrid. Jesus! Nield was right. The security was non-existent – Tweed was examining a top security file with the girl in the room.

'I've got to get back outside,' he said quickly. 'I thought you should know that Stilmar is visiting his wife now in her room.'

'Thank you, Harry. Keep on watching them. Things are getting a bit tense – '

'So long as you know. I'd better get back outside.'

Ingrid waited until they were alone before she made her comment. Sitting in the same position, she waited while Tweed worked at his suitcase. Extracting the slim files, he lifted his executive case onto the bed, the case he would take with him aboard the plane.

Using a nail file, he eased up the bottom of the case, exposing the hidden compartment. Very carefully he fitted the files inside the compartment, replaced the false bottom and then piled in newspapers, insurance company magazines and a file of insurance papers. He closed and locked the case and returned to his chair.

'Butler is an unhappy man,' she observed.

'I know.'

'Why is he unhappy?'

'The pressure is telling. He is very stressed. No one can be sure at this stage what is going to happen. The uncertainty plays on people's nerves. Uncertainty is hard to handle.'

'But you look very calm, very relaxed. And you are the boss. You should be very stressed.'

'I should be,' Tweed admitted, taking off his glasses and rubbing the lenses with his handkerchief. 'The whole business has turned into a frightful muddle. But this can happen. And they all depend on me. So I go as cold as ice – '

He broke off as someone knocked on the door, an urgent sound which bore no relationship to the agreed tattoo. Tweed stood up and motioned to Ingrid to hide in the bathroom. She jumped off the bed, straightened the cover where she had been sitting, grabbed her handbag, glanced round the room to make sure there were no other traces of her presence and disappeared inside the bathroom, almost closing the door.

Tweed glanced at himself in the mirror, ran one hand through his hair and opened the door. The man standing outside was Stilmar, a very agitated-looking Stilmar.

Stilmar swallowed the glass of Scotch Tweed had poured for him in two gulps. Tweed selected a bottle of mineral water from the fridge and poured himself a glass, giving the Scotch time to take effect. He sat down in his own chair and looked at the American who occupied the other chair.

'I've just had one bloody hell of a row with my wife,' Stilmar burst out. 'I accused her of having an affair with Cord Dillon and she denied it. She was raving and shouting at me.'

'A normal reaction – under the circumstances,' Tweed remarked.

'I think she was hiding someone in the bathroom. I couldn't bring myself to see who it was – '

'Perhaps you ought to check my bathroom?'

'Oh, for Christ's sake! Can you imagine the scandal if that leaked out? If she is Procane? She was livid with fury.'

'As I mentioned before, a normal reaction. Supposing she had accused you of the same thing?'

'You're right. I'd have blown my top, I suppose. The trouble is, I have to leave secretly for Helsinki shortly. An unofficial meeting with – well, you can guess.'

'Our friends in Moscow are starting to hedge their bets – they are beginning to think Reagan must win. I have been waiting for this development.'

'It could be a bluff,' Stilmar protested. 'Something to divert our attention – to cover Adam Procane if he's about to cross over. Have you thought of that? And at a moment like this my wife has to play mothers and fathers with that bastard, Dillon.'

'You are quite sure you are right?' Tweed enquired gently. 'I take it you have positive proof?'

'Well, no. Strong suspicion, yes. By accident they were seen entering the same house together in Washington by a friend of mine. Why else would they do that?'

'What is the present position between the two of you – yourself and Helene?'

'We've had a major confrontation. She doesn't want to see me for a few days. She said she needs time to think it over, then we can talk again. I don't feel like waiting a few days. I'm going off to Helsinki – I'd like to know where I stand before I make that trip.'

'Let it alone for a few days,' Tweed advised. 'Go to Helsinki, do your job, then see her when you get back. By the way,' he added casually, 'does she know you're going to Finland?'

'Of course not.' Stilmar looked surprised at the question. 'The mission is highly confidential.' He paused. 'You may wonder why I've come to you to talk about this.'

'Because you can't talk to any of your own people.'

'That's it.' Again Stilmar looked surprised. 'I sensed you are a man who can keep his trap shut.' He pulled at the lapels of his suit and stood up. 'I have to go now. Normally I deal with my own problems myself – but sometimes the pressure gets a bit tight. Don't get up – I'll let myself out.'

Tweed sat quite still until he had gone, until Ingrid emerged from the bathroom and fastened the chain on the door.

'Poor man. I feel so sorry for him – ' she began.

'Unless he is a consummate – very clever – actor. Not a man to underestimate.'

'What do you mean?'

'It could be genuine. Marriage is a more difficult undertaking than most people realize. But it could be something very different.'

'I still do not understand,' she repeated.

'This incident with his wife he described gave him a perfect opportunity for informing me he is going to Finland. If he is Procane, it would be a brilliant manoeuvre for him to tell me openly he is on his way there – and why. And we are dealing with a brilliant man. He will suspect he is being watched – so he allays suspicion by informing me of his movements.'

'You do not trust anyone.'

'I can't afford to.'

Tweed stood up and went over to his suitcase. Closing the lid, he snapped the catches shut and locked them. He straightened up and looked at Ingrid.

'Be ready to leave at a second's notice.'

'I'm already packed.' Ingrid hesitated, then asked him the question. 'You looked at Helene's file. Did you find anything?'

'Helene has a Swedish sister who lives in Stockholm. But the file gives only brief details of Helene's background. The full details are back in London . . .' He returned to his chair and checked his watch. It was the only outward sign of the tension building up inside him.

'The next task,' he informed her, 'is to change our reservations to the last flight this evening. The last flight is SK708, leaving at 19.05 hours. And while you are doing that you should book three more seats for Butler, Nield and Fergusson – but in these names – '

He took the scratch pad off the coffee table and scribbled three names at random. P. Joseph. D.

Carson. A. Underwood. He tore off the sheet and handed it to her.

'But I booked your seat in your own name,' she said.

'Leave it in my name.'

'You think we shall be aboard that flight?'

'It is beginning to look very like it the way things are turning out. What I hope is that I get to Helsinki before Newman does something dangerous . . .'

Two hours later the phone rang and Tweed wondered whether he was becoming psychic. The call was from Laila in Helsinki. Her voice was controlled but under the surface Tweed detected alarm.

'Is something wrong?' he enquired.

'Newman has disappeared again. I am calling from my flat – '

'Disappeared? What do you mean, Laila? Just tell me.'

'I called at the Hesperia for him and he had checked out. He paid his bill and was carrying his suitcase. Tweed, can you come to Helsinki today? As soon as possible. Oh, *please*.'

'He left you no message?'

'No, but he may have left one for you.'

'*May?* Don't you know?'

'The receptionist at the Hesperia asked me my name. Then he handed me an envelope addressed to me. Inside I found another envelope – addressed to you. It feels as though it has a small key inside it – '

'Open it. Now. I'll wait.'

He waited with his hand over the mouthpiece. Ingrid, seeing his expression, came close to him.

'Is it the bad news?' she asked.

'Another problem. The trouble with an insurance investigation is you can't control the timing. I've had this before everything suddenly happens at once.'

He broke off and removed his hand as Laila came back on the line. She sounded both puzzled and worried at the same time.

'Tweed, it *is* a key. And a note from Bob to you – '

'Read it. Quickly. If I tell you to stop, do so at once.'

'It reads "Tweed. Left luggage locker at main railway station. Alexis's last letter." That is all he says. Should I go to the station?'

'No. Try and find him. Check all the main hotels. Intercontinental, Marski, and so on. You can do that today. Then be back in your flat this evening. I have the number. I'll get there as soon as I can.'

'Please hurry. I am so worried.'

'Check those hotels. You are a reporter – you know what to do. He may have used a different name. Check for someone who booked in today.'

'I'll start now. Please hurry here.'

'As soon as I can.'

He put down the phone and pushed the bridge of his spectacles further up his nose. Ingrid spotted the small gesture and knew he was worried. She sat on the bed and waited.

'Newman has again gone missing – disappeared,' Tweed told her eventually. 'He's slipped my rein – Laila – and he's running loose.' He frowned. 'Damn! I forgot to warn her. Newman is clever – he was staying at the Hesperia. He may have checked out, then come back an hour later and told them some story when he booked in again. A different room, a different name.'

'I do not understand.'

'He may have told them a woman called Laila Sarin was pestering him. He'd give them a note to hand to her and tell them not to let her know he was back. Plus a large tip. I'd better call her back.'

He dialled the number from memory. All he got was the ringing tone. Laila had already left her flat for the day.

Fergusson reported in at lunchtime. Tweed was eating a meal with Ingrid ordered from room service so he could stay by the phone. Fergusson phrased his report carefully, aware that his call was passing through the hotel switchboard.

'Cord is still inside the Karlavägen place. He's holed up there since last night.'

'Any visitors? For the conference, I mean,' Tweed asked.

'Not yet. He's on his own – probably working on

the minutes. The meeting may have been put back an hour or so – to give them all time to get here.'

'Please keep me informed of progress. I need to know of any important decisions they take at the conference.'

Tweed replaced the receiver. He buried his teeth into his fourth ham sandwich. Unless you have to, never endure the waiting on an empty stomach. That was what got to you – the waiting, the uncertainty.

'I am so full.' Ingrid rubbed her hand across her own stomach. 'How are things going? Should I not be helping?'

'Fergusson is watching Cord Dillon. Harry Butler is watching Helene Stilmar who, I suspect, like myself, is having her meal in her room. Pete Nield is watching Stilmar – and is the only one who hasn't reported yet. Give him time – '

He broke off as the phone rang again, as it always seemed to when he was explaining something. He expected Nield and instead it was Hornberg. Like Fergusson, he worded what he had to say carefully.

'Tweed, I thought you might be interested to know our friend who took a walk through the city has flown back to Denmark. I will make this call short, if you don't mind – I am spending a lot of energy searching for the people who played a dirty trick on Peter Persson.'

'Any progress?'

'So far, none. I will keep in touch.'

So, Tweed ruminated as he went on eating. General Dexter had returned to NATO territory. Probably en route for Washington. He waited until Ingrid had finished her tea before making his suggestion.

'Butler has been outside a long time watching Helene. When you're ready, fetch your case from your room. Take his place. If Helene goes out, take your case with you to the Volvo. Pay your bill for tonight and tomorrow before you take over from Butler. Your suitcase will make you look different while you wait outside – and you will have it with you if we have to make a dash for Arlanda. Everyone has their air tickets?'

'Except Fergusson.'

'You can hand him his at the airport.'

'This also will make me look different.'

She stood in front of the dressing-table mirror and tied a pale grey and green light woollen scarf over her head, concealing her hair. At Tweed's earlier suggestion, she had also changed into her powder blue pant suit. She gave him a little wave as she left the room.

Tweed wandered into the alcove and peered out of the dormer window huddled in the roof. For a change, it was a gloriously sunny day. Below him several of the white passenger boats were moored prow on to the waterfront.

Early that morning at a quarter to eight he had watched while one of the boats arrived and discharged passengers who hurried to work. It is one of the strange and fascinating aspects of Stockholm that people commute morning and evening from and to islands in the archipelago where they live.

The clear northern sunlight shone on the stately buildings which make Stockholm one of the most attractive cities in the world. The light reflected off the ochre stone, creating a golden glow he found entrancing. He could not imagine a more peaceful scene.

'What is the situation now?' Lysenko demanded as he prowled round Karlov's office. He kept picking up objects, staring at them as though he'd never seen them before, putting them down again, peering out of the window down into Pikk Street. His restlessness infected Karlov sitting behind his desk and Rebet seated opposite him.

'Rupescu has made her dispositions well,' Karlov reported. 'Poluchkin is in a car at the terminal where the ships leave for Helsinki. She has brought in three men from the airport. One is watching the apartment on Karlavägen where Cord Dillon has stayed all day. Remember, Poluchkin saw him buy two tickets for the boat to Finland – '

'I remember everything anyone ever tells me,' Lysenko snapped. 'Go on talking.'

'The other two men brought in from Arlanda are stationed outside the Grand Hotel. Both Tweed and Stilmar are still inside the hotel.'

'And what about Arlanda? You haven't left that wide open?'

'Of course not. Three men are still at the airport. That covers the six extra men we sent into Sweden.'

'And Bromma? That small airport in the city.'

'We can't cover everywhere.'

'Yes we can – and we will. Call Rupescu at once. Tell her to take one more man from Arlanda and send him to Bromma. I have to check everything myself – always I find some loophole that has been missed.'

'I will call Rupescu.'

'Where is she now?'

'At the apartment in Solna. That is the nerve centre they all report to – then Rupescu can keep me up to date. What I am really waiting for is one new development –'

'What development?' Lysenko rasped.

'The movement of Tweed from Stockholm to Helsinki. Then I will know Procane has arrived in Finland . . .'

Chapter Thirty-Three

Ingrid sat in an arm chair in the sixth-floor lobby facing the elevators. Her suitcase – prominently on view – stood by her chair. She had been sitting there forever, so it seemed.

She heard the door open and close down the corridor and bent her head over her magazine. Helene Stilmar walked past her and pressed the button for the elevator. Her chestnut hair glistened and she lifted one hand to pat a curl into place.

The elevator doors opened, Helene stepped inside, the doors closed. Ingrid grabbed her case and ran. She pushed open the door and ran down the steps, holding onto the rail to keep her balance as she danced down the stairs.

She reached the large entrance hall just after Stilmar walked out and headed for the exit. Ingrid followed her, frowning.

Ingrid walked more slowly, concentrating on Stilmar's feet, the way she placed them on the floor, the movement of her legs. Tweed's reading from the Helene file came back to her. *Helene has a Swedish sister*

*who lives in Stockholm . . . the file gives only brief details
. . . The full details are back in London . . .*

She paused at the top of the steps leading to the
outside world, watching Stilmar walk the last few
paces before she spoke to the doorman. She would be
ordering a taxi.

This was not the same woman, not the real Helene.
Ingrid had no doubt. This was the sister. She turned
round, retraced her steps and took the elevator back
to the sixth floor. She was going against Tweed's
positive instructions but she knew she was right. She
sat down again in the armchair and waited, dumping
her bag on the floor.

Poluchkin sat behind the wheel of his hired Audi
close to the dock where the ships leave for Helsinki. It
was five in the afternoon – probably just about the
same time when Ingrid took her decision to return to
the sixth floor at the Grand.

He had a good view of the Viking liner which was
due to depart for Finland at six o'clock. The hull of
the ship was a bright red – almost carmine – and
above it loomed the huge white superstructure. Twin
funnels, also red, reared up into the afternoon sky, set
well apart with wisps of smoke drifting into the air.

Poluchkin's gaze was fixed on the gangway slanted
at an angle where passengers would board the vessel.
Through the open window of his Audi he could smell

the usual mixture of aromas associated with docks. Tar. Oil. Resin.

On Rupescu's instructions he was dressed very differently from his normal garb. He wore *lederhosen* and perched on his head was a trilby with a coloured feather protruding from the hatband. He had the outward appearance of an Austrian – or German – tourist.

He checked his watch again. Five minutes after five. Soon the passengers would start arriving. He was watching for one particular passenger. And his new costume was worn for a specific purpose.

'Tonight,' Rupescu had said, 'I am sure you will be flying to Finland.'

Tweed stood alone inside the alcove, staring across the water towards where the Viking Line vessel berthed at the dock beyond a bend in the river. The ship, arriving from Helsinki at nine in the morning, would soon be homeward bound, heading back to Helsinki.

This evening he was convinced a certain passenger would board the ship. That single act would trigger off a whole series of events. The Procane business was moving rapidly towards a climax. He felt it in his nerve ends. He stood quite motionless, hands clasped behind his back, his head stooped.

There was an odd expression on his face, an

expression Monica, back in London, would have recognized. The 'old Tweed' Butler had waited for – with increasing anxiety – had surfaced.

Outside in the lobby, only a few walking paces from Tweed's room, Ingrid sat in her armchair with her magazine. Over and over again she asked herself the same question. *Have I taken the right decision?*

How many times – in different situations – had people asked themselves the same question? She dared not go to Tweed's room to tell him what she had done. She had to trust her own judgement. That was what Tweed expected of people – to think for themselves.

She heard the door open further down the corridor. She sat very still. She heard the door close again. Footsteps came closer. A woman's footsteps. Helene Stilmar walked past her and pressed the button for the elevator, carrying a suitcase in her right hand.

As the doors closed Ingrid repeated her earlier action. She grabbed her own suitcase, rushed for the doors to the staircase and flew down the steps. She entered the hall as Helene reached the flight of steps leading down to the exit.

Ingrid walked slowly past the American woman who was waiting while the doorman summoned a taxi. Unlocking the hired Volvo, she slipped behind the wheel, pushing her case onto the seat beside her.

She started the engine as Helene climbed inside a taxi. The doorman slammed the door and the taxi drove up to red lights and stopped. Ingrid backed out her car and crawled to take up a position with one vehicle between herself and the taxi.

The taxi moved off, drove past the Handelsbanken on the right, proceeded straight forward and then swung left across the bridge on to Gamla Stan. Ingrid had a brief period of triumph. She had been right! Then she was concentrating on not losing the taxi.

It continued along the east bank of the island, past the Hotel Reisen, then over the bridge to south Stockholm. Ingrid had a moment of anxiety. Was it driving on into the southern part of the city? No! It turned left again and headed for the Vikingterminalen.

Ingrid slowed down and switched part of her attention to the blue Audi parked near the dock. She had a brief glimpse of a man wearing a Tyrolean-type hat. Some German tourist waiting to see the ship depart.

She drove on past the taxi which had stopped opposite the gangway where passengers were already boarding the vessel and a procession of cars and taxis arrived and departed. Parking near the bows of the massive ship, she turned in her seat and watched through the rear window.

Helene Stilmar was walking up the gangway, carrying her suitcase. This time her walk was as Ingrid remembered it from her earlier observations. She watched until the American woman had disappeared inside the ship, looked through her windscreen and nearly jumped.

Behind the wheel of his hired Ford, Fergusson was watching her from his parked car. Their eyes met and Ingrid looked away. Christ! What was the Scot doing here? She turned her Volvo and drove back to the Grand, choosing a route twisting through Gamla Stan to avoid heavy traffic. As she left the ship behind she noticed Tyrolean Hat in the Audi had disappeared.

'You did well,' Tweed told her as Ingrid completed her report. He turned to Harry Butler with a wry smile. 'Don't you agree?'

'Like a pro,' Butler agreed.

'Helene has a sister – a twin sister, I suspect,' Tweed went on. 'I'll check that in the file when I get back to London. The sister was supposed to lead us out of the way – if she was being followed – to give Helene the chance to slip aboard the ship unnoticed. My guess is the two sisters shared the same bedroom for days . . .'

He broke off as, once more, the ringing of the phone interrupted what he was saying. It was Fergusson, speaking from a public call box. The Scot's report was terse and to the point.

'Cord left Karlavägen in a taxi half an hour ago with a suitcase. The conference was a success. He is now aboard the ship leaving Helsinki in a few minutes.'

'I expect he'll send me the details of the conference by air. You proceed at once to Arlanda. You know when the flight leaves. Dump the car at the airport. Hurry.'

He put down the phone and walked round the room, hands clasped behind his back. Butler watched him with a sense of enormous relief. He had noticed the change of tone in which Tweed had spoken. Crisp, decisive. All signs of drift and irresolution had vanished.

'That was Fergusson,' Tweed looked at Ingrid. 'You had best start now for Arlanda. Leave the Volvo there and find Fergusson. Give him his ticket and then travel alone. We can join up again at Vantaa when we reached Finland.'

He waited until he was alone with Butler and then started talking again.

'Fergusson saw Cord Dillon board the same ship for Helsinki which Helene Stilmar is travelling on . . .'

'Which confuses things a bit. It confuses me.'

'You mean which one is Procane?'

'There could be a simpler explanation,' Butler suggested. 'If they are having an affair it would be tricky to keep meeting in Washington. But far away in Helsinki they could do what they liked.'

'It's happened before,' Tweed agreed. 'There is another explanation. One is pretending to have an affair with the other. What better cover to make the crossing to Finland? Maybe one is tricking the other.'

'But which one?'

'It is still a mystery. The solution lies in Helsinki. And we haven't much time left to catch the last plane today. Your bag is packed, as I instructed?'

'Ready to depart in eighty seconds.'

'I have one more phone call to make. Meet you downstairs in the lobby. Then – Arlanda.'

Tweed waited until he was alone. Sitting in the armchair he dialled Hornberg's number. After giving his name, he was put straight through to the SAPO chief.

'You know who this is, Gunnar. I can now tell you I suspect you will find the killer of Peter Persson in that apartment block out at Solna – the one where you ran a check through Vehicle Registration on a certain car.'

'Bredkilsbacken,' Hornberg said promptly.

'The killer is probably a woman, a pro. Tell your men to proceed with extreme caution.'

'Thank you. We'll check at once . . .'

'Also, Gunnar, you will be relieved to hear I am leaving now for Helsinki. Your people at Arlanda will see me – but I preferred to tell you myself. Thank you for your help.'

'My pleasure,' Hornberg paused. 'May I also suggest that you proceed with great caution.'

*

Inside Karlov's office there was an atmosphere of high tension. It affected the three occupants in different ways. Karlov sat behind his desk, the bones of his face very prominent, but otherwise he appeared relaxed, leaning back with hands clasped in his lap.

Lysenko sat straddled across a chair, his powerful body hunched, his arms resting on the chair back. His eyes never left Karlov's. Rebet sat in another chair, his legs crossed, turning a pencil endlessly between his fingers, a mannerism which irked Lysenko.

'Stop fiddling with that bloody pencil.'

The phone rang and it was a loud noise in the silent room. Karlov reached for it, listened and then asked the caller to hold on for a moment. He masked the mouthpiece with his free hand und looked at Lysenko.

'Poluchkin. At the dock where the ship leaves for Helsinki. A nearby public phone box. Cord Dillon boarded the vessel a few minutes ago. Shortly afterwards Helene Stilmar also went aboard. The ship sails at six, Swedish time. Fifteen minutes from now.'

'That's it,' Lysenko decided. 'Tell them to get out – to Finland. Fast. By the agreed route. Tell Poluchkin, then call Rupescu.'

'But there is no report of Tweed leaving Stockholm,' Karlov protested. 'That is the signal I'm waiting for – '

'Tell Poluchkin. Now! They're to report to Tehtaankatu,' he said. 'They stay in Helsinki pending developments. Get on with it. Bugger Tweed – he's missed the boat. Literally.' He looked round at Rebet. 'Bad joke, eh?'

Karlov instructed Poluchkin, then broke the connection and called Rupescu. He put down the phone without speaking after a few minutes.

'Her number is engaged. She's probably speaking to one of our people at Arlanda. I'll call her again . . .'

Gunnar Hornberg sat beside the driver of the car speeding into Solna. Behind the vehicle followed two other patrol cars. Hornberg had taken Tweed's warning seriously. All his men were heavily armed, some with machine pistols.

There were no sirens blaring. It was a silent approach. As they came close to the Bredkilsbacken apartment block the cars stopped. Doors were thrown open and men debouched, some in uniform, some in plain clothes.

Hornberg led the way to the main entrance, climbing the hill. In his right hand he held his SAPO card. He was close to the entrance, one uniformed man by his side, when the door opened and Magda Rupescu walked out, carrying a case in her left hand.

She had just received the call from Tallinn and was on her way to Bromma Airport. She headed for her parked car and saw Hornberg and the uniformed policemen. She dropped her case.

'SAPO. Police,' Hornberg called out. 'Could I please have a word with – '

Rupescu was wearing a white dress and a white coat, open at the front. She reached inside her handbag. The hand came out holding a Walther automatic. She aimed it point blank at Hornberg.

'Don't!' Hornberg shouted.

She fired. The bullet grazed his shoulder as he ducked and fell flat to the ground. There was a shattering rattle of machine pistol fire from a man behind the SAPO chief. Rupescu was thrown back – thrown as though pushed by a giant hand. She fell and lay still in an unnatural posture. The front of her white dress was stained red, a growing stain which spread rapidly. She was dead when Hornberg reached her. He picked up her handbag and emptied the contents onto the ground. One of them was a slim dark tube. He pressed the button at one end and a steel needle jumped out. He knew he was looking at the killer of Peter Persson. *Thank you, Tweed*, he said to himself.

Part Three

HELSINKI

No Man's Land

Chapter Thirty-Four

Bob Newman had spent the day in the last place in the world Tweed would have thought of looking for him. In Stockholm.

He had caught an early morning flight to the Swedish capital. Equipped with his suitcase, he had taken a taxi into the city, dumped his bag in a locker in the main railway station, then walked the rest of the way to Sergels Torg.

In many cities there are known places where you can buy a gun – or drugs. In London it is Leicester Square. The local police are only too well aware of what is going on. Instead of saturating the area with their men and driving out the traders, they feel it wiser to maintain a low profile.

The reason is logical. They prefer to know where the transactions are taking place. Any attempt to clean it up would drive the arms dealers and drug peddlers underground, making them more difficult to watch.

In Stockholm the centre of these activities is Sergels Torg, the strange square where a large part is below street level but open to the sky. This lower level is reached by a flight of steps leading down from the surrounding streets. And from it you can walk inside the maze of tunnels leading to other exits one of them being the entrance to the basement area of the department store, NK.

As a foreign correspondent Newman knew exactly what went on here. He also knew how difficult it was to purchase a gun in Finland. It had taken him one hour to make the necessary contact. Without bargaining, he offered four thousand kronor for a hand-gun in excellent condition, plus ammunition.

He returned to the station with the .38 Smith & Wesson concealed inside his belt under his raincoat. Collecting his suitcase, he locked himself inside the end cubicle of the public lavatory. Dismantling the weapon, he packed it inside foam rubber he had purchased in Helsinki and secreted the various parts among his clothes inside the case.

He had lunch at the station restaurant, keeping an eye on the time, then caught another taxi back to distant Arlanda. He caught Flight SK706 for the fifty-minute journey back to Helsinki – by chance the flight before the one Tweed was hoping to board for the same destination.

Newman took off from Arlanda at 17.05 hours and arrived back at Vantaa Airport at 19.00, Finnish time. He waited at the carousel for his suitcase, picked it off the moving belt and walked unhurriedly through the 'Nothing to Declare' green exit. The following day he would travel to Tallinn with Mauno Sarin aboard the *Georg Ots*.

At Bromma Airport Poluchkin, travelling with false papers in the name of Reinhard Noack, waited for Rupescu, sitting inside the chartered jet.

He waited until the agreed hour, seven o'clock. He checked his watch frequently. Rupescu had plenty of time to drive from the Solna apartment to Bromma. It was really no distance at all. His instructions from Rupescu had been very clear.

'If I do not arrive by seven, you take off by yourself.'

He waited until five past seven. Not because he liked the woman. They had synchronized watches each day but if she arrived as the jet took off he knew who would take the flak. At five past seven he told the pilot to leave.

The pilot checked with the control tower. They were airborne within another five minutes, climbing steeply above the panorama of creeks and streets spread out below. Then the pilot headed due east for Helsinki.

Tweed had a shock when he boarded Flight SK708 alone – the rest of his team, including Ingrid, were occupying separate seats as though they didn't even know each other.

He moved slowly along the aisle towards the front of the aircraft. His face remained expressionless as he noticed the back of the head of a seated passenger next to a window. He moved closer and the passenger was Stilmar.

Tweed paused, then returned to a free seat further back. As he passed Fergusson, sitting in an aisle seat, he fiddled with his glasses and dropped them. Fergusson stooped and picked them up.

'Thank you so much. No, they are not broken,' he lowered his voice. 'Follow Stilmar. Ahead of you on the port side – he's wearing horn-rims . . .'

He settled himself in a vacant aisle seat and reached for a magazine tucked inside the netted compartment at the rear of the seat in front of him. This was a possibility he had overlooked – that Stilmar would be travelling aboard the same aircraft.

The American had taken simple precautions which effectively changed his appearance. Substituting horn-rimmed glasses for his normal rimless spectacles made him a different person. A precaution he might well take if he were meeting the Russians secretly in Helsinki. But there might be a more sinister explanation.

The aircraft began moving, cruised to take-off point, the engine pitch climbed and they were speeding down the runway. Tweed felt the elevation change, the absence of wheels bumping along concrete, and they were airborne.

In mid-flight the woman sitting next to Tweed asked him if he would mind changing seats – she found she didn't like being next to the window. Tweed obliged, so as they descended he peered out of the window with interest. It was some time since he had last visited Finland. He wondered whether its old fascination would still grip him.

It was dark, but the sky was clear and there was moonlight. Coming in to land, he had glimpses of islands of dark, dense forest. Other islands – small lakes – gleamed in the ghostly light. Here and there he caught sight of the lights of a house, hemmed in by the forest. The lakes were scattered everywhere. And he saw all this through a thin veil of broken mist. There was a dreamlike quality in the view. A magic land . . .

A bump jerked him out of his trance. They had landed. The machine, moving at speed, slowed as the flaps were lowered. Tweed sat quite still as the plane stopped and passengers stirred. Fergusson slipped past him as Stilmar made his way to the exit.

Tweed glanced back and saw Butler and Nield collecting their hand luggage from the overhead compartments. Ingrid was already walking down the aisle, staring straight ahead. Tweed stood up, hauled his executive case and coat out of his compartment and followed the others.

'Procane is definitely on his way to Finland.' Karlov put down the phone as he made his announcement to Lysenko. 'That call was from Galkin at Arlanda. Tweed boarded Flight SK708 for Helsinki, departing at 19.05 hours. That means only one thing to me – as I've said all along. The moment Tweed heads for Helsinki, then Procane is either there or on his way.'

'What time does that flight reach Helsinki?' Lysenko asked.

'21.00 hours.'

'And when do Poluchkin and Rupescu arrive there from Bromma?'

'Just about the same time, I would calculate,' Karlov told him. 'He might arrive a little ahead of Tweed – if you're thinking of Poluchkin – '

'I am. Borisov is our best man in the Finnish capital. Instruct him to meet Poluchkin in a hired car. It must be hired. No, just a minute – get someone else to accompany Borisov in another hired car. If Poluchkin arrives in time, Borisov is to tell him to follow Tweed – and again Poluchkin must be accompanied by Borisov in the other car. They follow Tweed to whatever hotel he is staying at – '

'He could make for the British Embassy,' interjected Rebet who had listened so far.

'No!' Lysenko was emphatic. 'Tweed will go nowhere near his Embassy. They won't even know he is coming. I want to know what Tweed is doing. When they arrive at Tweed's hotel Poluchkin can switch to Borisov's car – that way Tweed won't spot he is being followed. Tweed must be watched from now on for every move he makes in Helsinki.'

*

They left the aircraft by mobile staircase and a crocodile of passengers trailed the short distance to the main building. A sign above it read *HELSINKI – VANTAA*. The night air was chilly and invigorating. It was very silent and Tweed was conscious of the encircling forest which seemed to close in on the airport.

He took a taxi for the twenty-minute drive into Helsinki. He was thinking of Newman as the vehicle proceeded along the four-lane highway bordered with patches of fir forest and huge outcrops of rock.

Worrying about Newman, he arrived outside the Hotel Hesperia almost without realizing he was inside the city. He paid the driver, and registered in his own name.

Tweed had arranged for every member of his team to stay at the Hesperia, registering separately so it was not apparent that any of them knew each other. At this stage, concentration of his forces was essential.

Ingrid had been waiting for him in the large lobby, looking at the goods displayed in a shop. As he left the reception counter she wandered over to the elevators and stepped in behind him just before the doors closed.

'I am in Room 1401. The others are here – except Fergusson. Their room numbers are on this.'

She handed him a slip of paper. He tucked it inside his wallet, told her he would be in touch and walked out of the elevator. 'Tell them to have dinner,' he remarked. 'And you have dinner, too.'

'Can I help?'

'Yes. Later. I'll call you. Some time after dinner.'

The moment he was inside his room he dropped his case and dialled Laila Sarin's number. She answered immediately – so quickly he had the impression she had been sitting by the telephone.

'Tweed here. I'm at the Hesperia.'

'Oh, thank God.'

'Calm down. I'm in Room 1410. Can you come over now?'

'I'll be there in ten minutes.'

'Don't rush. And please bring that envelope Newman left for me. I repeat, take your time. I'm eating my dinner,' he lied.

Tweed had eaten nothing since lunchtime but he seemed tireless. His next call was to Mauno Sarin at Ratakatu. The operator asked him to wait a minute. He waited. Fifteen seconds. He timed it by his watch.

'I am sorry,' the operator informed him, 'but Mr Sarin is not in the building. Is there any message?'

'No message,' Tweed said and broke the connection.

The time span had been too short. He remembered Ratakatu. He remembered Mauno's habit of working all hours, his habit of walking frequently from office to office to see what was going on.

In case he was wrong, he dialled Mauno's home number – again from memory. Tweed had a phenomenal memory for numbers. This time Sarin's wife answered. She was very cordial and welcoming. She liked Tweed and Tweed liked her. Such a cheerful woman.

'I'm afraid he is not here,' she said. 'I am not expecting him for hours yet. Why not call him at his place of work?'

'Thank you. I'll do that. I thought I'd try him at home first.'

'You must come to dinner while you're here. I'll cook your speciality. You'll put on weight.'

'God forbid. And thank you for the invitation. If I have the time you won't be able to keep me away.'

'Fix it up with Mauno.'

'I'll do that. Goodnight.'

Tweed sat contemplating the phone. Mauno was avoiding him. Why? The idea disturbed him. It was quite out of character. He heard a gentle tapping on his door. It was Laila Sarin and her face was flushed. She must have run all the way from her flat. In her left hand she held an envelope she had just extracted from her handbag.

Dear Bob, In one hell of a hurry to catch the boat –
it leaves at 10.30. Adam Procane has to be stopped
Archipelago is my best bet. Am leaving now. Will
post this on my way to the harbour.
Alexis.

Tweed held the letter in his hand. Full circle. His mind went back to where it had all started. A postman attacked in London for Newman's mail. But Newman had collected his mail before the attack.

Tweed had no doubt he was looking at the last letter Alexis had sent to her husband. He was standing inside Helsinki's main railway station with Laila by his side, by the left luggage locker which the key Newman had left with the receptionist at the Hesperia fitted.

At that hour the large station was mostly deserted. There is nothing more depressing than a lonely station late in the evening. Few people were about in the cavernous hall. He read the letter again although already he could have recited its contents blindfold.

'This reference to a boat leaving at 10.30,' he remarked. 'Which harbour?'

'South Harbour,' she said promptly.

'And do you know which boat leaves South Harbour at 10.30?'

'The *Georg Ots*.'

'Where does it go to, Laila?'

'Tallinn.'

'My God! We've got to stop him – unless he went there this morning.'

'He couldn't have done that – I saw him pass me in a taxi and it was 11.30 – an hour after the *Georg Ots* sails – '

'From which dock?'

'The Silja. I know where it is.'

'Then,' Tweed said, calm once more, 'we have to

stop him tomorrow. We must be at the Silja very early.'

They began walking towards the exit. Tweed glanced quickly at the few people still in the station, checking to see whether anyone was taking an interest in them. Laila seemed to read his mind.

'That green Saab you spotted following us from Vantaa is nowhere about. I went outside to look as you asked me while you were opening the locker. The only car parked outside is a black Saab – a different make. There is a factory here which produces what we call a Finnish Saab – but really it is Swedish. They bring in the pieces and make them up into complete cars in Finland.'

'The letter mentions the word archipelago. Was Newman interested in that?'

'Yes, he was. I told him about both archipelagos – the big Turku archipelago and the smaller Swedish one.'

'Did he mention Adam Procane?'

'Not a single word.'

'And you couldn't find a trace of him after you found he had checked out of the Hesperia?'

'No. I tried every hotel. No Englishman who sounded like Newman had booked in anywhere. Where the hell can he have gone?'

'He's hiding somewhere. I think he wants to stay out of sight until he catches that boat tomorrow. He could be anywhere.'

They came out into the night through the main exit. It was a clear night and above them the moonlit sky was studded with stars which seemed to Tweed brighter and larger than any he had ever seen in Britain.

He glanced to his left and saw the black Saab Laila had told him about. Parked with its lights on, the engine was running.

As they stepped off the kerb Poluchkin drove forward. His instructions were to watch Tweed but the Russian was ambitious and headstrong – using a similar technique to the time he had killed Alexis Bouvet, he planned for Tweed to have a final accident. That should earn him commendation – promotion – in Moscow. Everyone in Tallinn was worried about Tweed. This was Finland, but if the Englishman was killed in an apparent accident how could there be trouble with the Finnish authorities? Just another hit-and-run driver . . .

The headlights of the oncoming vehicle were enormous. Like the eyes of some giant trundling forward. Tweed's first thought was for Laila. He swept out his right arm and pushed her back onto the pavement. He was stepping back himself when the car struck him a glancing blow on the forehead. The station fell on him.

Daylight flooded in through a window as Tweed opened his eyes. He blinked. Someone handed him his glasses. He put them on and blinked again. A white-coated man was staring down at him with a speculative expression.

He was lying in bed. His head was propped on a pillow. By the side of the white-coated man stood Laila, her expression anxious and concerned. He stirred, lifted himself up and felt pain in his head.

He forced himself to sit upright. Laila bundled pillows behind him. The white-coated man moved forward, a stethoscope dangling from his neck. He was brown-haired and youngish. No more than thirty.

'Where the devil am I?' Tweed demanded.

'In a clinic,' Laila told him.

'What the devil for?'

'You were knocked down by a car,' the white-coated man replied. 'You have a case of mild concussion. Luckily you stepped back, I gather. The car was moving fast. Another few inches and you'd be in far worse condition – '

'What day is it?' Tweed sounded alarmed.

'It happened last night,' said Laila, understanding at once the reason for his question. 'You have been asleep since then.'

'The time – '

Tweed reached for his wrist watch on a side table. Christ! 10.00 a.m. The *Georg Ots* sailed in half an hour. He threw back the sheets and found he was still wearing his trousers and his shirt. He sat on the edge of the bed, stood up and forced himself to stay erect as his head swam.

'I am Dr Vartio,' the white-coated man said. 'You must stay in bed and rest for at least forty-eight hours.'

'Like so many Finns, your English is very good,' Tweed observed to distract his attention. He walked to a cupboard, opened it and found the rest of his clothes inside.

'I spent a couple of years at Guy's Hospital in London. I must ask you to remain here for observation –'

'Laila,' Tweed handed her his wallet. 'Pay the gentleman for his services, please. We have to hurry. We also need a taxi urgently. You know the destination.'

'This is madness,' Vartio protested while Tweed used a wall mirror to fix his tie. A shave would have to wait. And he had suddenly realized he was ferociously hungry. That, also, would have to wait.

Inside Mauno Sarin's office at Ratakatu, Newman also was dressing. They had just completed the body search. They had found nothing. Mauno watched him and was apologetic.

'It was necessary, Bob. As I told you, it was part of the agreement with Tallinn. And I rely on your common sense when we get back. Finland is a peaceful country. Unlike so many parts of the world, we have little crime. No organized gangs, no criminal syndicates. Of course we do have the occasional murder – but it is always domestic. A man and his wife, or a mistress. You don't shoot people in Finland – '

'I know,' replied Newman. 'When do we board the ship?'

'Just before it sails. Here is your visa. And I have a copy of your safe conduct in my pocket. The original is in my safe.' He fingered his beard. 'You are sure you want to come with me?'

'I thought we'd gone through all that before . . .'

The *Georg Ots* is a white four-decker with a single, squat, flat topped funnel. Five lifeboats are slung from davits on both the port and starboard sides. The name of the ship is inscribed in blue and in Cyrillic near the stern. From the Silja terminal you board the vessel by passing through a glass-walled entrance elevated on a platform.

The taxi containing Tweed and Laila stopped at the entrance to the terminal. There had been a brief shower but now the clouds had evaporated. The only traces were on the pavements and the roads where the recent rain was drying rapidly, leaving damp patches like stains. The sky was a clear blue, the air invigorating, and the sun shone brilliantly.

Tweed paid off the driver and the cab departed. He stood beside Laila who stared into the distance. She swallowed several times before she could speak.

'Oh, Lord. We are too late . . .'

The *Georgs Ots* had left the dock and Tweed watched its stern as it cruised slowly between the peninsula and a small island. It seemed there was hardly space for the ship to pass safely through but it sailed on, still at cruising speed, heading south for the Gulf of Finland and Tallinn.

'We do not know for sure he is on board,' Laila said with a hint of desperation in her voice.

'He's on board all right.'

'How do you know?'

'He left behind for me the last letter Alexis ever wrote him, the original, not a photocopy. When a man does that it suggests to me he thinks he may be making his final journey . . .'

Laila glanced quickly at Tweed but could read nothing from his expression. It had sounded as though he was recalling some personal experience.

Chapter Thirty-Five

'Helene Stilmar and Cord Dillon are staying at the Kalastajatorppa,' Butler told Tweed as they wandered along the network of paths which snake through and up the hills of Well Park at the top of the peninsula.

They had come there by taxi a couple of hours after Tweed had watched the *Georg Ots* sail. It is the quietest place in the city, a place where there is no danger of being overheard. Pine trees were scattered amid the grass and they had frequent views of the harbour where small craft plied and the water glittered in the sunlight.

Tweed had tightened security to the hilt. He had communicated with Butler at the hotel by sending Laila to his room with the message to meet him outside the museum near the President Kekkonen statue. They had hailed a taxi when Butler arrived which had dropped them at the entrance to Well Park.

'I thought they might be staying there,' Tweed commented.

'What made you think of that place?'

'It is just outside Helsinki. It is quiet. It is the place

both Alexis and, later, Bob Newman stayed at. You checked on the helicopter pad?'

'Yes, it's at the edge of the water – which looks more like a lake than a bay of the sea, but it's very beautiful.'

'Typical Finnish scenery.'

'The funny thing is,' Butler went on, 'I found Helene and Dillon are staying in separate rooms. Of course, that could be cover for their affair – '

'If any affair is taking place. Perhaps one is using the other to disguise the real purpose of their arrival in Helsinki. Was there a chopper on the pad?'

'No. I gather it isn't used much at this time of the year. A local firm has an office inside the hotel. They take people on local flights. The main thing is it looks suitable.'

'Suitable to airlift Procane out of Finland?'

'Ideal, I'd say,' Butler replied.

'And what about Stilmar himself? Any news from Fergusson? He kept track of him when he followed Stilmar off the aircraft?'

'Yes. He took a taxi straight to the American Embassy. He's stayed holed up there ever since. Nield is watching Dillon and Helene at the Kalastajatorppa. Everything is under control.'

'I wonder? Did Fergusson give you any comment on Stilmar?'

'He thought it fitted in with his explanation to you that he's here to meet the Russians secretly.' Butler hesitated before he went on. 'I get the feeling you're waiting for some specific development to take place.'

'I am.'

Inside his office on Pikk Street Colonel Andrei Karlov sat alone behind his desk. His lean face showed concentration as he covered a large sheet of his notepad with a series of calculations.

He was working on a series of mathematical formulae and equations and the sheet was crammed with figures written in his tiny handwriting. He was so absorbed that he didn't notice when General Lysenko entered, closed the door quietly and watched. Eventually Karlov wrote a final equation and threw down his pen.

'That's it,' he said aloud to himself.

'It is what?' Lysenko demanded, walking behind the desk to look over Karlov's shoulder.

'Just because I am no longer in Moscow does not mean I stop working – '

'Working at what?'

'Oh, you wouldn't understand any of it. This is my latest theory for how we can counter the so-called American Star Wars project. The Strategic Defence Initiative. Only the analysts back in Moscow would understand.'

'May I take that sheet?'

'I was going to shred it.'

Lysenko reached out his hand. Karlov tore off the

sheet and handed it to him. Lysenko folded it carefully and put it inside his tan calf wallet.

'The latest situation?' he enquired.

'Everything coming together at once. Too much, too quickly. It always happens with these operations. Newman and Mauno Sarin are approaching Tallinn aboard the *Georg Ots*. All our people are distributed inside the city waiting for them. Tweed, as you know, is in Helsinki at last. He is staying at the Hesperia Hotel. And at 9.30 this morning Cord Dillon and Helene Stilmar disembarked off the boat from Stockholm. They took a taxi to the Marski Hotel. Waited half an hour, then took another taxi to the Kalastaja-torppa. That worries me – '

'Why?'

'Dillon is a pro. It seemed a primitive way of concealing his real destination.'

'Perhaps he is in love,' Lysenko suggested ironically. 'Perhaps he is bringing his lover with him.'

'Perhaps.'

'As soon as Newman's visit has ended satisfactorily – one way or the other – I will stamp and sign your movement order. I want you in Helsinki to help Procane cross over. He said he'd contact our Embassy. I think he's waiting now – until Tweed's back is turned.'

'Tweed never turns his back.'

'All the more reason why you should be in Helsinki to take control.'

*

During the voyage of the *Georg Ots* across a calm sea to Tallinn Newman remained in the restaurant drinking coffee. Which surprised Mauno Sarin. He stayed with the Englishman but there was little conversation between the two men.

Newman, his expression detached, sat silent for a long time. Mauno smoked cheroots, drank strong black coffee, cup after cup, respecting this silence. As the passengers stirred, going up on the outer deck to see the view, Mauno spoke.

'Do you propose to take written notes in Estonia?'

'Reporters sometimes do. Why? Will they want to see everything I note down?'

'The question never arose – but they are rather sensitive.'

'But it was not part of the agreement?' Newman leaned across the table. 'Was it?'

'You're like a time bomb – that is what really worries me.'

'Which was the purpose of your question – to test my reaction. Look, Mauno, I've subjected myself to your bloody body search – something I've never done before. They've said that I can go where I like in Tallinn. If you're going to change the rules in midstream I'm not playing along. Is that quite clear?'

'I'm simply asking you to be diplomatic – '

'Which also wasn't part of the agreement. I'll ask them what the hell I like – whatever comes into my head. Is that also clear?'

'Perfectly. But I would ask you to remember that

I also am involved in this expedition into the unknown.'

'I'll bear it in mind,' Newman replied and drank the rest of his coffee as the ship's engines slowed and the *Georg Ots* prepared to dock in Soviet territory.

'I have an idea,' announced Lysenko. 'I want you to follow Tweed wherever he goes – even if he leaves Helsinki. God knows what happened to Rupescu, but we can't bother about her at this stage. Poluchkin can continue the job. With back-up, of course. He may be the first one to point the finger at Procane – to identify him for us. Send a signal at once.'

'I'll have to be quick. The car bringing Newman and Sarin here will arrive at any moment,' Karlov warned.

He suppressed a sigh. How typical of Lysenko to steal an idea and present it as his own. From the very beginning he'd told Lysenko that the arrival of Tweed would tell them Procane was in Finland. He picked up the phone to send the message.

Newman and Mauno were treated like VIPs from the moment they disembarked. They were ushered to a gleaming black Zil limousine of the type reserved for members of the Politburo in Moscow. Karlov's secretary, Raisa, an attractive brunette of thirty with a full figure and slim legs was introduced as their guide.

'Welcome to Estonia, Mr Newman,' she greeted him in perfect English. 'I am here to make your visit as comfortable as possible.'

Inside the rear of the long vehicle she perched herself on a flap seat facing him and eyed him frankly. He grinned as he relaxed and winked at her. Bloody honey-trap, he told himself. They are starting early. Her next words confirmed his opinion.

'If you wish to stay overnight and spend an extra day here it will be quite in order,' she assured him. 'And I am available,' she paused for a few seconds, 'for dinner,' she concluded.

He grinned amiably as the car moved off, the droll grin which women found so encouraging. Her well-shaped knees touched his. He made no attempt to break the contact.

'Let's see how it goes,' he suggested.

Mauno was taken aback at this sudden change of mood. He tried to catch Newman's eye to warn him, but the Englishman was staring back at Raisa. The girl clearly thought she already had him in the palm of her hand. But she was very attractive, Mauno admitted to himself.

As the car proceeded at a leisurely pace Newman peered out of the window up at a castle perched on a hill he estimated would be between a hundred and two hundred feet high. His expression remained

interested as he studied the weird and ancient structure which looms above Tallinn, the peculiar and
distinctive towers stationed at the corners where the
stone walls turned.

'That is Toompea,' Raisa explained. 'We call it the
Small Fortress. It was started by the Danes in the
thirteenth century and later renovated.'

'I'd like to visit that,' Newman told her cheerfully.

Raisa hesitated and Mauno, foreseeing a confrontation, stiffened. 'I'm sure that can be arranged, Mr
Newman,' the girl went on.

'It is part of Tallinn,' Newman pointed out. 'We're
already inside the city. And I was told I could go
anywhere.'

'It will be our pleasure for you to see Toompea.'
Raisa assured him again.

They drove the two men in through the best
preserved part of the Old Town along Laboratoorium
Street, which lies between Vaksali and Lai Streets. The
buildings on either side are two or three storeys high
with steeply gabled roofs. There is a Hans Andersen
touch to this section of Tallinn and Newman gazed
out of the window until the car turned a sharp corner
with a huge old round stone tower on their left. There
was something ugly and sinister about the edifice.

'That is called Fat Margaret's Tower,' Raisa said,
following his gaze. 'And we have just passed under
the Great Sea Gate. Now we are in Pikk Street where
Colonel Karlov is waiting for you.'

The Zil stopped. Raisa opened the door and hopped

out, holding it while Newman and Mauno alighted. The Englishman had a shut-in feeling, as though the buildings were closing in on him. The street was unnaturally quiet. Hardly any people and not a car in sight apart from the limousine.

Mauno led the way to the entrance where a tall, thin man in civilian clothes awaited them.

'This is Captain Rebet,' Mauno introduced. 'He does not speak English.'

Raisa looked over her shoulder, saw the two visitors disappear inside the building. She opened the front passenger door and slid into the seat. Opening a flap, she grabbed a microphone and spoke rapidly in Russian.

'They are coming up. Newman showed considerable interest in Toompea. He wants to go back to see the Fortress – '

'Understood.'

In the small room leading off Karlov's office, the room where Olaf Prii, skipper of the trawler *Saaremaa*, had reported to Karlov on his interview with Tweed at Harwich, Lysenko switched off the transceiver. *Toompea* . . .

'Colonel Karlov,' Mauno began in the next room, 'this is Mr Robert Newman. Bob, Colonel Andrei Karlov, who speaks excellent English. He has spent time in London.'

'Welcome to Tallinn, Mr Newman. You are our guest. Please sit down.'

'If you don't mind, Colonel, I'd like to get on with

looking round Tallinn. We only have two hours before the *Georg Ots* sails for Helsinki. On the other hand, Raisa suggested that it might be possible for me to stay overnight and have a good look at Tallinn. Perhaps I could travel back tomorrow?'

'We have a very tight schedule,' Mauno intervened, alarmed at the Englishman's suggestion. 'I don't know whether – '

'You are very welcome to do that.' Karlov was still standing after shaking hands with his guests. He was dressed in the full uniform of a GRU officer. 'Two hours is not long for you to see everything, I agree,' he continued. 'So, you sleep here tonight. I will make immediate arrangements. Meanwhile, if Mr Sarin and yourself would like to start touring the city? Please go where you like – Mr Sarin knows the place well.'

When they had left Lysenko unlocked the door between the interconnecting rooms and came in. He looked very serious but Karlov spoke first.

'They are staying a little longer. It was Newman's suggestion. They will be with us overnight and leave tomorrow.'

'I see,' Lysenko's tone was grim. 'Did you know that Newman has already expressed unusual interest in Toompea?'

'What do you call unusual interest?'

'Raisa warned me over the car radio. He specifically asked if he could see the Fortress when they drove past it.'

'Hardly surprising – it is the great feature of Tallinn.'

'I don't like two things which happened within only a few minutes of his arrival. Toompea – and his wish to stay on overnight.'

'Well, why don't we simply wait and see what happens?'

Karlov kept the thought to himself – but he realized that Lysenko's conscience was troubling him over the murder of Newman's wife. The General was in a suspicious mood – looking for tiny signs which might indicate Newman was going to find out too much.

'How are you progressing with your investigation into the killing of those GRU officers?' Lysenko demanded abruptly.

'As you know, when I have a problem I write down the facts on a piece of paper. That way the solution often stares me in the face. Two facts caught my attention. All the officers killed were senior to Poluchkin for promotion. Fact Two. The murders took place when Poluchkin was present in Tallinn. Since you sent him to Stockholm there have been no more murders.'

'Poluchkin? That is preposterous,' Lysenko spluttered.

'It would also be dangerous if we have an unbalanced man on the loose in Finland,' Karlov insisted. 'God knows what decisions he might take on his own – '

'I refuse to discuss this nonsense any more!'

Lysenko, his face very red, stormed back into the adjoining room to sit by his transceiver. Karlov heard the key turn in the lock after the door was closed. The colonel sat down behind his desk, very worried. Lysenko was in an explosive mood. If Newman made the wrong move the general would react violently.

Chapter Thirty-Six

Raisa was waiting for them when Newman and Mauno came out of the building into Pikk Street. She approached Newman with her welcoming smile. She wore a dark blue, two-piece costume, very form-fitting, and a white blouse with ruffles at the neck and cuff.

'You may wish to tour the city by yourselves,' she began. 'On the other hand, if I can be of service – ' she paused, staring directly at the Englishman ' – I am at your disposal.'

'Why don't you meet us at Toompea?' Newman suggested. 'We're walking through the Old City first.'

'I will go there now and wait for you.'

Mauno waited until the Russian girl had climbed inside the limousine and the chauffeur drove off. The Finn looked round carefully to make sure they were alone as they wandered towards Fat Margaret's Tower, following the route they had entered Tallinn by in reverse.

'What are you up to, for God's sake?' he hissed.

'I don't know what you're talking about,' Newman

489

replied in the same genial tone he had adopted since their arrival.

'First you alter the schedule – we were supposed to catch the boat back to Helsinki this evening. And you seem to have forgotten there is no ship returning tomorrow – we have to wait until the day afterwards.'

'I'm sure Colonel Karlov will lay on something for us to get us back tomorrow,' Newman said airily as he glanced down a side street. Little more than an alley, it looked as old as time.

'Then,' Mauno persisted, 'we were supposed to look at Tallinn by ourselves. No guides. You insisted on that. Now you ask that Raisa girl to meet us at Toompea. You're not thinking of going to bed with her, I trust? You know her real role – '

'Do stop worrying, Mauno. And I may need you as interpreter if I want to talk to someone. OK?'

'There is a myth – you read it in guidebooks – that the Finns and the Estonians speak the same language. Not true. They are *similar* – but it is easier for an Estonian to understand Finnish than the other way round. They have different words from us. I will do my best,' Mauno ended brusquely.

He could not understand Newman's change of mood. He was worried about the Englishman's potential relationship with Raisa. He didn't like Newman altering the agreed schedule. He was edgy and bad-tempered because he didn't understand.

They strolled along Pikk Street. Newman stopped for a moment to look at Fat Margaret's Tower. She was fat all right, her girth immense. She seemed to grow out of the ground.

'Must be a hundred feet high,' Newman observed.

'Eighty feet,' Mauno corrected. 'And, believe it or not, the walls are seventeen feet thick. It was built in the early fifteen hundreds as a defence tower.'

'A very durable old lady. Mauno, you see that man over there gazing into a shop window. Ask him something about Fat Margaret, the first thing that comes into your head.'

'If you say so.'

A short, stocky individual in his forties, brown-haired and with sallow complexion, he had both hands in his dark overcoat pockets as he continued staring inside the shop, a bakery. Newman moved closer as Mauno began talking.

He heard Mauno conversing in Russian. The Finn turned round to call out to Newman. The man returned to his examination of the goods inside the shop.

'Fat Margaret was built between 1510 and 1529.'

'Ask him his profession. Tell him my hobby is guessing the profession of people from their appearance.'

More conversation in Russian. This time the man glanced at Newman before he replied. Mauno turned round and found Newman at his elbow.

'He is a teacher at a local school.'

'Thank you . . .'

Newman wandered on and they passed under the

archway of the Great Sea Gate which curved over-head. Soon they were back in Laboratoorium Street, lined with ancient, steeply gabled roofs piercing the skyline above the mellow brick-built houses below. To their right the ground rose up a high hill. Mauno pointed to this.

'That is Rannavarava Hill.'

'Could you ask this young woman how she finds life here?'

The woman had emerged from one of the houses and carried a shopping basket. Among other items the basket contained a small woollen pullover. She stared at Newman curiously when Mauno spoke to her in Finnish. While they were talking Newman glanced up. A man in shirt-sleeves peered down into the street from the first floor window of a house which was lop-sided.

'She says life is hard but she is content,' Mauno said.

'Ask her if she has any children. If so, how many and also where they are.'

Newman could not get rid of the claustrophobic sensation. He felt the city was about to envelop him, which was odd because there were so few people about, which again was odd at that time of day.

'She says she has three children,' Mauno paused and he had a strange expression. 'She says they are all at school. She is on her way to collect the youngest.'

'You see,' Newman remarked amiably as they proceeded along the street towards Toompea.

'See what?'

492

'Oh, come off it! That man gazing into the bakery. You had to speak to him in Russian. I'll bet you tried Finnish first? You did – just as I thought. And he was caught off-guard when you asked him his profession. A school teacher? When the schools are still working? He was GRU in civilian clothes. We are being watched every step we take.'

'You are going to put that in your article?'

'Of course not. Someone is just making sure nothing happens to us while we're here. Aren't those the towers of Toompea in the distance?'

'Imatra! We are going to Imatra,' Ingrid exclaimed while she studied the map of Finland spread out on her knees as the train left the main Helsinki station. 'And Imatra is on the Russian border – '

'I know,' said Tweed, staring out of the window.

They had caught the 13.10 train and Tweed had bought the tickets without revealing their destination. Their overnight bags were perched in the racks above their heads.

'Why Imatra?' Ingrid asked.

'Because, as you've just pointed out, it is on the Soviet border. We shall be tired tonight. It is two hundred and fifty kilometres east of Helsinki. We arrive there at 16.48. I will leave you at the Valtion Hotel when we get there . . .'

'Why do you leave me? I can come with you.'

'Not to the frontier zone, you can't.'

'How do you get there from the hotel?'

'Take a cab. It's only about ten kilometres from the hotel to the border crossing.'

'You expect to meet someone there?'

'You ask too many questions. Look out of the window. Finland is a beautiful country. This way we shall see it at its best. Autumn is a lovely time of the year.'

'Sorry,' she said, and looked out of the window.

At the far end of the coach Poluchkin also pretended to gaze out of the window. The Russian was no longer dressed in his Tyrolean outfit. He was clad in a Finnish suit and lightly tinted glasses were perched on the bridge of his nose.

During the two-and-a-half-hour journey they passed through an infinite variety of Finnish landscape. There were fields of stubble in the cultivated areas. The land stretched away to the horizon, punctuated here and there by a splash of bright colour which was a lonely house. There were many colours – pale green, red, a bright rust-red, yellow ochre.

The houses were built of wooden slats and often had a steep central gable. Others were farmhouses, standing in isolation, large buildings with ramps leading to the first floors, the homes of the people who farmed the immense landscape in summer and lived there through the long dark winters.

Later the forests appeared, a dense and dark green

wall closing in on the railway line on both sides. Birches and pines mingled with the solid evergreen firs.

The birches dripped with the gold of late autumn, splotches of gold like coins suspended in midair. The train rushed on past the occasional shrub so red it was like a flaming torch. There are six stops before you reach Imatra and all the way Tweed said hardly a word.

'We're there,' he remarked as the train slowed down, standing up to reach down their bags.

'So close to Russia,' Ingrid whispered.

'About as close as you can get – without crossing over,' Tweed agreed.

The station at Imatra is a platform elevated high above the town and surrounding countryside. When they alighted Tweed was in no hurry to make for the exit. He wandered along the platform as the train left and proceeded east. Soon it would turn north, parallel to the border, heading for Joensuu, its final destination.

'What a lovely day,' Tweed remarked as he strolled along the platform. 'Do you see that sheet of water over there? Lake Saimaa. The largest lake in Finland – or so they say. There are so many of them.'

Poluchkin had disappeared inside the entrance hall and was making enquiries about train times at the ticket office. The warm sun beat down on Tweed and Ingrid out of a cloudless sky. He breathed in the fresh, invigorating air which was like champagne.

Another passenger was also lingering on the long platform after leaving the train, taking pictures of Lake Saimaa with a camera. A tall thin man in his early thirties, he approached Tweed with a cigarette in his mouth.

'Have you by chance a light?' he asked in English.

Inside the palm of his right hand, held close to his body, he showed Tweed a folder. Protection Police. Kari Eskola. Tweed reached inside his pocket for the Feudor lighter he always carried for other people. He took several attempts to make the lighter work.

'There are no trams in Imatra,' Eskola whispered.

'This young lady with me will be staying at the Valtion Hotel,' Tweed said quickly. 'If anything happens to me, ask Mauno to put her safely aboard a plane for Stockholm.'

'I am sure he would be glad to do that.'

Eskola moved away. He took another photograph, puffing at his cigarette. Then he disappeared through the exit via the neat, one-storey entrance hall building.

'What did he mean?' Ingrid asked. 'There are no trams in Imatra – '

'It was a warning. So close to the border . . .'

Chapter Thirty-Seven

The Valtion Hotel in Imatra is one of the strangest in the world. Originally a castle, it has been rebuilt and renovated three times over the ages.

Five or six storeys high – according to your viewing point – turrets sprout from it like branches from a tree. There are small turrets and large turrets, some with cone-shaped tops like witches' hats. The entrance porch is vast, a solid and square edifice reminiscent of Indian architecture.

Tweed had booked from Helsinki the only accommodation still available, a suite costing eight hundred markkaa. After registering – in his own name – the receptionist took them up in an ancient lift with grille doors on both sides.

The suite comprised a spacious living room, a large bedroom and a bathroom, the first two rooms leading off a lobby. Ingrid was delighted to find the living room was located inside a large turret with rounded walls and long, high, narrow windows.

'A suite?' she asked Tweed when they were alone. She gave him a sidelong look. 'We sleep here tonight?'

'No. We catch a late train back to Helsinki when I return from visiting the border.'

'I am coming with you.'

'I cannot allow that. Under any circumstances. While I am gone you wait here. You keep the door locked. You open it to no one. The only exception is if Kari Eskola phones you from reception downstairs. Kari Eskola,' he repeated. 'If he does, you go with him back to Helsinki. I will follow later – '

'That means you will never come back.'

'Don't be silly. I've brought a thriller in Swedish for you to read. I'm going now. Remember, you admit no one unless it is Eskola. Make him identify himself by asking him what he was doing at the station before he spoke to us.'

'I am scared.'

'Don't be silly,' he repeated. 'And don't give me any trouble. I had enough argument with Butler back in Helsinki before I left.'

'So he was scared for you, too.'

'I have to go now. Read your book . . .'

Tweed settled back in the rear of the taxi as it left the Valtion Hotel's compact grounds, a tiny park, turned on to the main street and very quickly turned again across a bridge spanning a deep gorge.

The gorge, deep and rocky, was famous in winter. Water from distant Lake Saimaa roared and churned down the narrow defile, creating a small maelstrom. Anyone who slipped into that had no hope of survival.

The taxi proceeded along a lonely road, starting as a two-lane highway with a grass verge down the centre. Later, as it approaches the frontier, the grass verge vanishes and the road narrows.

There was no other traffic in either direction. No sign of human life as the vehicle headed steadily east into a wilderness. Several times the driver had glanced in his rear-view mirror at his passenger. He was fat-faced, heavily-built and sported a red moustache.

'I am Arponen,' he said eventually. 'You wish to proceed to the border, wait a few minutes and then return to the hotel?'

His English was excellent, too excellent for Imatra. Tweed had waited some time for the taxi he had ordered from the receptionist. He suspected he was being driven by Kari Eskola's partner. On a job like theirs, the Protection Police travelled in pairs.

'No,' Tweed replied, 'that was not what I told the receptionist. We go to the border, yes. But we wait there until I ask you to go back. It may be a wait of some duration.'

'It is not a good place to wait too long,' Arponen replied, his dark eyes watching Tweed in the mirror.

'I'll be the judge of that,' Tweed told him sharply. 'And I am paying for the trip.'

The border point at Imatra is no Checkpoint Charlie. There is nothing dramatic about the place – only a feeling of loneliness and desolation. The taxi stopped.

Tweed got out to stretch his legs, to have a look around. A striped red and orange automatic barrier was lowered across the road. It was very quiet, a brooding silence you could hear. A single-storey white building stood beside the barrier and there was a large orange notice board perched on two metal stilts that gave instructions.

At the top of the board in the left-hand corner the silhouette of a black hand outstretched gave the message symbolically. Stop! In the right-hand top corner a crude picture of a camera was cancelled out with a diagonal red line. No photographs! Below the message was spelt out in five languages.

Finnish, Swedish, German, English and French. The English version was simple and direct. *FRONTIER ZONE. No entry without special permit.* Tweed was looking up at the board when a frontier guard in olive-grey uniform and a peaked cap, carrying a holstered automatic on his right hip, emerged and came over to the taxi driver.

They talked for several minutes and then the guard walked back and went inside the building. Through a window Tweed saw him using a telephone. He wandered back to the driver.

'What was all that about?'

'He wanted to know who you are – and why you are waiting here. I don't think he was satisfied with my replies. He is calling someone now. I think we should go – '

'This is Finnish soil I am standing on. I see no reason for anxiety.'

'I advise you to get inside this taxi at once.'

'Thank you – for your advice. But I shall be staying for some time. Which was the arrangement I made with the receptionist at the hotel who phoned you.'

Tweed turned his back on the driver to end the conversation and walked away. He knew the risk of waiting. It was highly unlikely that a car-load of Russians would suddenly drive over the hill where the road beyond the frontier post disappeared, that they would arrive and bundle him inside the car and take him over the border. Highly unlikely. But not impossible.

The blue sky had vanished. A sea of lowering clouds massed overhead. He was looking south-east where the forest was more dense than any he had seen so far. Nothing moved in the sullen landscape. The dark forest spread away into endless distance. He was looking straight into Soviet Russia.

He went back to the taxi, climbed into the rear seat, closed the door, and settled himself once again. He was thinking of Bob Newman, wondering whether he would ever see him again. Of Ingrid, waiting with growing anxiety back at the hotel.

He had only allowed her to come with him because he wanted to keep an eye on the girl. He had counted on Mauno Sarin having him followed wherever he went – and he had been right. If things went badly wrong Eskola would get her back to Helsinki.

'Can we go now?' Arponen asked in almost a pleading tone.

'No. We must wait . . .'

Chapter Thirty-Eight

Karlov heard the urgent rattle of the key unlocking the door leading to the next room. The sound prepared him for Lysenko's outburst as he rushed into the room.

'A call has just come in from Poluchkin via Helsinki. He has followed Tweed to Imatra. Imatra! Come and look at the map – '

'I know where Imatra is.'

But Lysenko had gone back into the other room. Karlov went after him, pulling down the bottom of his tunic. It was a mannerism he was prone to in time of crisis. Look your best.

On a wall of the adjoining room Lysenko had pinned up a map of Finland. As Karlov came in the general jabbed a stubby finger at Imatra. He was very agitated. It crossed Karlov's mind that they had the wrong man in the job. Lysenko would be first-rate leading a forward division into battle – but for this type of work the cool, clinical Rebet was far better suited.

'Imatra,' Lysenko said again. 'What the devil is Tweed doing there?'

'I have no idea. Didn't Poluchkin tell you?'

'Yes. Tweed went by train to the place. He left his
bag at a hotel and took a taxi right up to the border.
He is still there, waiting. Waiting for what?'

'It is a strange development,' Karlov agreed.

'Strange! It's bloody alarming! Have we got this
business all wrong? We expected Procane to contact
the Soviet Embassy in Helsinki. Supposing he has
bypassed the Embassy? He will be in a nervous state.
Is Procane also heading for Imatra – to cross over
there?'

'It is possible,' Karlov agreed again.

'This alters everything.' Lysenko began to pace
round the small room. 'You had better travel to
Helsinki tomorrow morning with Newman and Sarin.
We can use one of the big patrol-boats to get you
across. I will sign your movement order at once. You
take complete control of the search for Procane.'

'As you wish. How do I explain this to Newman?'

'That is easy. Tell him you are returning the courtesy of Mauno Sarin's visits here. Newman will think
it quite normal that we maintain close contact with
the Finns. If we have got this all wrong it could be a
disaster.'

Panic stations, Karlov thought to himself. The crisis
at long last has arrived.

'So this is Toompea,' Newman said to Raisa, who had
been waiting for them in Lossi Square which lies
under the shadow of the Small Fortress.

She had led them up the steep incline and they were standing under the hulk of one of the immense towers which loomed at the corners of the rectangular fortress. The north-west corner.

'This is Pilsticker Tower,' Raisa informed him.

Mauno Sarin stood beside Raisa in silence, a prey to his own anxious thoughts. He still couldn't work out the reason for Newman's extraordinary change of mood once they had arrived in Estonia. Newman peered over the wall and stared down at a park which spread away for some distance. A road ran alongside the park and it seemed familiar.

'What is the park?' he asked.

'That is Toom Park.'

'And that road bordering Toom Park?'

'That is Vaksali Street.'

'May I wander around a bit on my own?'

'Of course. Please go where you wish. If you walk that way – to the south-west corner – you will see Tall Hermann Tower. It is a hundred and fifty feet high, thirty feet in diameter, and the walls are nine feet thick . . .'

God, she sounds like an Intourist guide, Newman thought as he wandered away. Which she probably had once been. He walked slowly over the cobbles, his expression now bleak. This was the place, the bloody killing ground of Alexis.

He could see so clearly in his mind the horrific film Howard had screened for him back at Park Crescent in London. Alexis throwing up her hand as the car's headlights glared at her and came forward. The weird castle with the strange towers in the background. He was walking inside it. The Small Fortress.

And he was pretty sure he had located the spot where they had murdered her. Vaksali Street. Alongside Toom Park. The geography was right. He stopped and looked up at Tall Hermann. Another brute of a tower. He heard feminine footsteps coming up behind him and composed his expression. He swung round with a smile.

'Do you think we could go for a walk together after dinner?' he suggested.

'Of course,' replied Raisa. 'It would be my pleasure.'

'I'm interested in old castles. This place is marvellous. I'd love to see it from a distance. Don't you get a really good view from Vaksali Street?'

'Excellent.' Her eyes stared into his. 'And it will be a clear sky tonight. I heard the weather forecast. A little chilly. But the moon will be out. It should be nice –'

'I'd like to see that, too,' Mauno said over her shoulder. 'And I always take a walk after dinner . . .'

Raisa, her back to Mauno, pouted at Newman. *What a stupid man*, her eyes said, but she also managed a smile as she turned round and spoke to Mauno.

'You will be very welcome, Mr Sarin.'

'Maybe we could find our own way back to Pikk Street,' the Finn suggested.

'Of course. The car is still waiting. I will go back

with the chauffeur and meet you there. Tonight we all have dinner at the Olympia Hotel. You will like that.'

'What the hell are you playing at?' Mauno demanded when they were alone. 'That girl could be leading you into a trap.'

'I doubt that,' Newman replied amiably. 'She probably wants to make my memories of my stay in Tallinn pleasant.'

'I think you're crazy. And while we're on Estonian soil I'm sticking close to you every minute – whether you like it or not. I'm responsible for your safety and I have no intention of letting you balls it up – if that's the phrase – '

'That's the phrase,' Newman agreed as they began the descent into Lossi Square. As they passed the Church of Alexander Nevsky, neither man noticed the figure watching them from inside the almost-closed entrance doors. Captain Olaf Prii, skipper of the trawler, *Saaremaa*, watched them until they were out of sight.

'Karlov,' Lysenko said in an ominously quiet voice which made the colonel look up quickly from behind his desk, 'Raisa has just radioed in the news that Newman wants to go for a walk after dinner along Vaksali Street.'

'Could be a coincidence,' Karlov responded promptly.

'I don't believe in coincidences. Of all the streets in Tallinn, why that one? You know what happened there.'

'I knew what happened after the event. I have told you before, killing Alexis Bouvet was more than a crime, as Talleyrand said, it was a blunder.'

'What's done is done. Now I have to consider whether it is too dangerous to let Newman ever leave Estonia. I also have the problem of deciding whether Adam Procane is going to try and cross over through Imatra. You made those calls to Helsinki? What is the position across the water now?'

'A team of men has been flown from Leningrad to Imatra. I heard fifteen minutes ago from the Helsinki Embassy that Cord Dillon is still at the Hotel Kalasta-jatorppa with the Helene woman. Stilmar himself has not left the American Embassy. No one has made a move yet – '

'Except Tweed,' Lysenko reminded him. 'And with all this going on, I haven't phoned my wife. Have you called yours?'

'Not recently. I have been a little preoccupied.'

'How are things between you two?'

'Very good. Luckily, as you know, she has an important job as a biochemist to occupy her time.' Karlov looked at the general. 'It would be even better if I could be posted back to Moscow.'

'Your duties lie here for the moment.' Lysenko changed the subject. 'My immediate priority is

Newman. We shall have to see what he does tonight. Then I take my decision . . .'

Mauno Sarin arrived back with Newman at Pikk Street totally unprepared for the shock which awaited him. Raisa ushered them up the winding staircase to Karlov's office where the colonel was watering the Christmas cactus plant he kept on his desk. He carried the pot to the window and placed it on the narrow ledge.

'I think it needs more light. Welcome back. I trust you enjoyed your walk? Oh, Mauno, there was a call for you from your office. They asked you to phone back. Urgently. I'll leave you alone to make the call. Please use my chair.'

Newman wandered over to look at the cactus as Karlov left the room through the staircase door and Sarin sat down and dialled a number. The Finn knew the conversation would be monitored and tape-recorded by Karlov's technicians. Normal procedure. He carried out the same process when in Helsinki he received a call from the Russian. He was put through to his deputy, Karma.

'Sarin here. I gather you called me.'

'Yes. You asked me to keep you informed about that swindler who has disappeared,' Karma reported. 'We haven't found him yet – but we believe he is in Turku, Imatra or Vaasa.'

'If it's Vaasa he may be making for Sweden. Warn the coastguard – '

'I have already done that. There is no doubt he did photocopy the documents. We have checked the machine.'

'I am returning tomorrow instead of tonight. Let me know if there are further developments while I'm here.'

Mauno put down the phone and his expression was frozen. He was appalled. Marooned overnight in Tallinn and he had this news. The 'swindler' was Tweed, a code-name chosen by the Finn who had a dry sense of humour. And Tweed was in the second place Karma had mentioned. Imatra! On the bloody Soviet border! Had Tweed gone mad?

Now he had two major problems to keep him awake. Tweed in Imatra and Newman playing some strange game here in Tallinn. What the hell *was* going on? Newman walked away from the window.

'Bad news, Mauno?' he whispered.

'Just a setback in a complicated case I am handling. But it will sort itself out – these things have a way of doing just that. See if you can find Karlov and tell him we are ready for dinner at his convenience.'

Mauno sagged in the chair and stared into space. He had a nose for disaster. He was convinced now that he was in the middle of a major disaster area. In Finland. In Estonia . . .

Chapter Thirty-Nine

Tweed arrived back at the Valtion Hotel and hurried up the stairs, ignoring the creaking lift. He knocked on the door of the suite and Ingrid called out almost at once. She had been pacing up and down the lobby inside.

'Who is it?'

'Tweed. Let me in – ' he continued talking as soon as she closed the door. 'You haven't unpacked anything? Good. We are leaving immediately. The taxi is waiting.'

'Thank God! I was almost crazy with worry locked up inside that turret room.'

'We are flying back to Helsinki. We have just time to catch the last flight from Lappeenranta – that's the last stop on the train before Imatra. I've paid the bill. We must move now.'

Arponen, the same driver who had taken him to the frontier, broke the speed limit time and again, racing along superbly maintained and ruler-straight roads. On either side the forest rushed past in a dark green blur.

Tweed glanced back through the rear window

several times. The only vehicle on the otherwise deserted highway was a blue Saab which kept its distance but also kept up with them. He had no doubt the man behind the wheel was Eskola. *There are no trams in Imatra . . .*

Tweed took out his wallet and handed Ingrid a folded wad of banknotes. He told her when they arrived to book two one-way tickets to Helsinki. Then he glanced back again and frowned. He was gazing back along an exceptional distance of the highway.

Behind the car which he felt sure was Eskola's another vehicle had appeared. It was also moving at great speed. He shrugged and stared ahead. Ingrid pulled at the elbow of his coat.

'Is there something wrong?'

'Yes. We shall catch that plane by the skin of our teeth . . .'

At Lappeenranta Airport Tweed waited at the entrance while Ingrid bought their tickets. The blue Saab pulled into the kerb a few metres from where he stood. Tweed walked up to it and spoke as the driver got out of the car.

'Eskola, we're catching the flight back to Helsinki. You'd better run if you're going to get your ticket. Tickets – if Arponen is coming with you –'

He walked rapidly back inside the entrance hall before the Finn could reply. Five minutes later Flight AY445 was cruising down the runway, ready for take-off. Several rows behind Tweed and Ingrid the two Finns, Eskola and Arponen, occupied separate seats.

The last man to board the plane just before they closed the door was Poluchkin, who chose a seat at the rear of the aircraft.

During the thirty-minute flight to Helsinki Tweed's mind raced over the problems he faced, the positions of the various human pieces on the board. Newman and Sarin, he was convinced, were in Tallinn – unless they had returned by the late evening boat. He must check with Butler at the Hesperia as soon as he got back – check to locate Cord Dillon, Helene and Stilmar.

Above all he hoped that Monica in London had successfully despatched the signal he had alerted her to send over the phone before he had left for Imatra. That signal was very important.

Monica had called Welwyn, the chief cipher clerk at the Admiralty, as soon as she finished talking with Tweed. He had left the signal – a series of figures – with her before he had flown to Stockholm. Years ago, it seemed to Monica.

Welwyn had reacted immediately. The stream of figures had been radioed into the atmosphere, preceded by the call-sign. Aboard the trawler, *Saaremaa*, berthed in Tallinn harbour, the wireless operator, Olaf Prii's brother, crouched over his transceiver, had noted down the figures on a pad.

When the signal ended he wrapped the notepad in an oilskin wallet and tucked it away inside a locker under a pile of canvas. He had no fear that a Russian listening station would pick up the signal. If it did, there was no cipher expert in the whole Soviet Union who could have unlocked the meaning of those figures. The Russians were not the only ones to use one-time codes.

As soon as she had phoned Welwyn, Monica made another call – this time long-distance. Tweed had explained to her the two actions were interlinked – how, she hadn't a cat's idea in hell.

She called the SAS Hotel in Copenhagen which lies on the main road leading from the city to Kastrup Airport. Casey, the helicopter pilot, was lying on his bed reading *The Mystery of Edwin Drood* when the call came through. He loved Dickens. And he took turns with Wilson, his co-pilot, to wait by the phone.

'Casey speaking.'

'Monica here – nothing to do with Dickens.'

'Why the dickens not? He's a damned good writer.'

'The trip is cancelled,' she continued. Identities had been established according to the prearranged wording. 'You can take some leave. Not too many women, this time.'

'Why not? I like Dickens. I like women.'

Within an hour the large Alouette helicopter was cleared for take-off from Kastrup. Casey, a jokey man of thirty, was at the controls with Wilson, a more taciturn type, alongside him. He lifted the machine off the ground and headed east across the Öresund, the narrow stretch of water which separates Denmark from Sweden. As he flew the Alouette to a higher altitude he chewed gum. He had a long way to go.

His route lay across the broad toe of southern Sweden, then north-east to Arlanda where he would refuel. From Arlanda he would fly below radar level south to the island of Ornö in the Swedish archipelago.

He planned to land in a remote part of Ornö where he would wait for his final instructions. The Alouette was equipped with the latest and very powerful transceiver. Wilson was also an experienced radio operator. On Ornö they would receive the signal instructing them to proceed to their final destination. The helicopter pad at the edge of the sea next to the Hotel Kalastajatorppa.

While Newman and Sarin were dining with their hosts at the Olympia Hotel, Captain Olaf Prii was taking his evening stroll round Tallinn. Eventually he reached Pikk Street, which was deserted.

He strolled on, glancing up at the sky studded with stars, huge glittering lights in the black velvet night. The moon would rise shortly. He stopped when he came to Fat Margaret Tower, staring up at the huge edifice as Newman had earlier that day.

Turning left, he collected his bicycle from behind the Great Sea Gate. Prii's long sturdy legs cycled fast to the harbour. The moment he boarded the *Saaremaa* he went straight to the radio room. His brother looked up as he entered and closed the door.

'It's come,' he said.

Collecting the concealed notepad, he handed it to Olaf and locked the door. The captain extracted a tiny notebook from the secret pocket inside one of his sea-boots and settled down to work out the cipher. He worked slowly and carefully and it took him half an hour before he was satisfied.

The message was in German, the common language he had conversed in with Tweed during their meeting in the English port of Harwich. He read it through twice, took out a box of matches and burnt the piece of paper in a saucer. Then he set light to the sheet containing the original figures. He washed the charred remnants down the small corner sink. Only then did he look at his brother.

'We sail immediately,' he announced.

'Our destination?'

'Is the powered rubber dinghy in good working order?'

'I checked the engine only this afternoon,' his brother replied. 'It is in perfect condition. Our destination?'

'First the Finnish port of Turku west of Helsinki – '

'And then?'

'The island of Ornö in the Swedish archipelago.'

Chapter Forty

The Olympia Hotel is no asset to Old Tallinn. A modern slab of concrete, it rears many storeys into the sky. All the windows are alike. It resembles an ugly human beehive.

Newman, who had been hoping for some ancient tavern, disliked the place from the moment they entered it. Karlov was the host and led the way into the dining room. His guests were Newman, Sarin and Raisa, who sat next to the Englishman.

'I shall be accompanying you back to Helsinki tomorrow,' the colonel announced over the main course, a large helping of herring with vegetables. From somewhere they had produced a good Chablis and Newman sipped at his glass as Karlov explained. 'I am returning the many visits Mauno has made to Tallinn. And I like Helsinki.'

'Tell me, Colonel,' Newman requested. 'Who is in charge of security in Tallinn?'

'I am. Also for the whole of Estonia. What prompted you to ask that question?'

'The fact that the place seems so well-behaved. No drunks on the streets. It makes a pleasant change.'

517

'I don't know.' Karlov drank some of the Chablis. 'When I was in London I had the same impression.'

'Obviously you weren't about when they turn them out of the pubs.'

'That is late at night, is it not?' Raisa remarked. 'When we go for our walk you will be able to see what it is like at night here, too.'

At the end of the dinner Karlov excused himself. He had a lot of paper work to catch up on. They liked their rooms at the Olympia, he trusted? He bowed formally and left them.

After coffee they were driven from the Olympia back to the Old City and the limousine stopped at the entrance to Vaksali Street. There was a clear moon as Newman alighted with Raisa and Mauno trailed behind them. Raisa took Newman's arm as though it were the most natural thing in the world and for a moment her firm left breast touched him. They walked slowly alongside Toom Park and then Newman stopped. Turning round he looked back.

The Small Fortress threw long black shadows, a lonely hulk perched on its isolated eminence. Just about here, Newman was thinking. Just about here – where I'm standing – they killed her.

Vividly, he could recall in his mind's eye the background in the film of the murder. He was staring at an exact replica of that background. The weird castle with the strange towers. It gave him a strange feeling to know that he had at last found the place.

Who is in charge of security in Tallinn? I am ... Karlov

was the man who had killed Alexis. And Karlov was coming to Finland with them tomorrow. The coincidence was incredible. Newman went on staring at the castle, a dreamlike look on his face. But he was living a nightmare.

In his room at the Olympia Newman was ready for bed. They had provided everything needed for an overnight stay. A pair of pyjamas, a dressing-gown, shaving kit. He was getting into bed when he heard the light tapping on his door.

He got out again, slipped on his dressing-gown and made a lot of noise unlocking the door. Raisa stood outside. She wore a housecoat gaping open at the front. Underneath she wore a pair of skin-fitting pantyhose tights and a transparent nightdress. She was very much on view and her full lips parted in a half-smile.

The door behind her opened and Mauno stood in the entrance. Her eyes flickered and she closed the housecoat. She turned round and spoke briskly.

'I was coming to you next. I have just heard the patrol-boat which will be taking you back to Helsinki leaves at 8.30 in the morning. Or is that too early? You will be collected from here at eight o'clock.'

'That is very acceptable,' Mauno replied.

'And for you?' She turned to Newman and he thought he saw a hint of disappointment in her eyes. 'That will be all right?'

'Fine. Breakfast at seven? Then we don't have to rush.'

'As early as you like. Sleep well.'

Newman winked at Mauno before he closed his door. This was a rendezvous they had expected – Raisa coming to Newman's room. They had arranged that the Englishman would make a lot of noise opening his door to warn Mauno.

Inside his room Newman lit a cigarette. He was planning ahead. The gun he had bought in Sergels Torg was lying inside one of the lockers in the left luggage section at Helsinki main station. The key to that locker was concealed inside his wallet which now lay inside his pillow.

Lysenko was holding a midnight conference in Karlov's office. Rebet was also present and he listened in silence as the general reviewed the situation.

'Do we let Newman leave tomorrow, is the main item on the agenda. Raisa has reported that Newman showed great interest in Toompea – but as a tourist, she thought. What I do not like is that he walked along Vaksali Street. He even stood at almost the exact spot where his wife was executed by Poluchkin.'

'You get a good view of the Small Fortress from there,' Rebet pointed out. 'And has he said one word about the death of Alexis Bouvet since arriving? Not so far as I am aware.'

'That is true,' Lysenko admitted. He looked round

the table. 'We form a troika here. Let us vote on the decision. Those in favour of letting Newman return to Helsinki raise their fists, please.'

Rebet suppressed a sigh. The clenched fist. So out-of-date. So typical of the old Bolshevik. Would he never realize times had changed?

Karlov and Rebet lifted their fists. Lysenko stared at them in turn. He nodded his head without lifting his own. Now he had shifted the responsibility for releasing Newman to other shoulders – just in case later there was a kickback from Moscow.

'There is one more matter I think we must discuss, Comrade General,' Karlov said formally. 'You mentioned Poluchkin. I am in charge of investigating the murders of the GRU officers here in Tallinn. I told you Poluchkin was always in Tallinn when the murders took place, that all were senior to him, so their murders open the way to his promotion. And no more of these killings have taken place since he left for Stockholm. I decided to search his quarters.'

'You have found something?' Lysenko enquired.

'This.' Karlov unlocked a drawer, drew a glove over his right hand and lifted out an object which he placed on the desk. It was a loop of wire attached to two wooden handles. The wire was stained in places with dull patches and specks of some black substances dropped onto the desk.

'I found it up the chimney,' Karlov explained. 'The black muck is soot. And it looks very much to me as though the wire is stained with dried blood.

Comrades, I think we are looking at the murder weapon. The garrotte . . .'

'I had already decided – on the basis of the circum-stantial evidence – that when he returns from Finland, Poluchkin must face a military tribunal,' Lysenko announced. 'This clinches it. But at the moment I think we leave Poluchkin in Helsinki to complete his task. The paramount problem is still Adam Procane.'

'I see Procane as a very cautious man,' Karlov commented. 'During all the time I was in London I never had a clue as to his identity. I believe he will remain cautious to the end.'

'Until he has arrived safely in Moscow,' Lysenko concluded.

Part Four

HELSINKI

The Procane Crossing

Chapter Forty-One

Landing at Vantaa Airport, Tweed first took Ingrid by taxi to the Intercontinental Hotel next door to the Hesperia and booked her a room there.

'I will have your clothes brought over later,' he told her as they stood in the new bedroom. 'Or, if you prefer it, you can come over yourself to do the job. But don't come near me. I will phone you here or come over to see you.'

'Why, Tweed? I would sooner be with you –'

'Security. We are close to locating Procane. I need someone I can call on who appears to have nothing to do with me. It may be very important.'

The explanation appeared to satisfy her. Tweed left with a feeling of relief. He didn't want Laila to meet Ingrid. Any emotional problem at this critical stage was something he could do without. Walking across to the Hesperia, carrying his overnight bag, he made straight for Butler's room.

'How are things?' he asked when they were sat down together over a drink. 'Any changes while I was away?'

'Not really.' Butler sounded disappointed. 'Fergusson is still watching the American Embassy. Stilmar hasn't left the place since he arrived. I find it peculiar – '

'And Cord Dillon?'

'The same situation. He hasn't left the grounds of the Kalastajatorppa. He goes for walks with the Helene woman along the seashore in the little park where they have that helicopter pad. Nield keeps a close eye on that. He could so easily be airlifted out in a matter of minutes.' Butler drank some more of his Scotch. 'It's almost as though Procane – whoever he is – is waiting for someone to arrive to escort him into Russia—'

'An interesting observation,' Tweed replied. 'Keep up the watch. You relieve each man from time to time? Good. We shall soon know. Just a little more patience . . .'

Back in his own room, Tweed sat down and telephoned Monica. She answered quickly, which meant she was keeping up her vigil and staying by the phone.

'I sent the signal confirming insurance cover for the Shangri-La consignment,' she reported. 'They have now despatched it.'

'Good. What about the other consignment?'

'I also issued cover for Ruby Stone. That consignment is also on its way. Everyone seems happy with the way we've handled things.'

'Good. I expect you sent the Shangri-La confirmation by air express?'

'I did that personally. How are you?'

'Never felt better.'

Tweed put down the phone and hoped he hadn't sounded as tired as he felt. Shangri-La was the Alouette helicopter which by now should have landed secretly on the island of Ornö in the Swedish archipelago. His later reference to 'air express' informed Monica that the second signal should be sent from the Admiralty in London to Casey, the Alouette's pilot. *Proceed to the landing pad at the Hotel Kalastajatorppa at the agreed time.*

Ruby Stone was the *Saaremaa*, skippered by Olaf Prii. Monica's reference to it confirmed that Prii had sailed, was probably already lying off the Finnish port of Turku. At the worst he would be there by the following night.

Everyone seems happy was the most important part of their brief conversation. That told Tweed a signal had been received from the *Saaremaa* after the vessel had sailed from Tallinn.

He absorbed all this as he made his way down to the first-floor restaurant. Tweed was ravenous. The buffet laid out on a large table at the Hesperia was excellent. He helped himself to generous quantities of food and carried the plate to a table well away from the other diners. If he was right, tomorrow would see the success or complete flop of his difficult mission. As he ate he tried to push his growing doubts out of his mind.

*

The following morning the Soviet patrol-boat moved at high speed across the forty-odd miles which separate Tallinn from Helsinki. The large craft with a high bridge left behind a broad white wake on the calm and sunlit Gulf of Finland. The sea was as smooth and blue as the sky above it.

Inside the cabin Mauno Sarin was staring out of the porthole as Newman stood up. The Finn was in a mood of great anxiety. No more reports had come in from Karma and he was wondering what had happened during his absence from his home base.

'I think I'll go up and chat to Karlov on the bridge,' Newman remarked.

'You may not be allowed on the bridge,' Mauno warned. 'We are aboard one of their newest patrol-boats – look at the pace it's keeping up.'

'I won't know unless I try,' Newman replied.

There was no trouble as he mounted the steps to the bridge, holding on to the rail as the vessel changed course and heeled to starboard. Karlov opened the door himself and gestured for Newman to join him with the ship's commander.

'A beautiful day for me to visit Helsinki,' Karlov remarked as they reached a point about midway across.

'You expect to stay for several days?'

'God knows how long . . .'

'Colonel – ' Newman lowered his voice, uncertain whether the commander or the helmsman spoke English ' – I have certain information I'd like to talk over with you. I also have a deadline before I send my story about my visit to Reuters. Can we meet some-time late this evening? Somewhere we won't be seen?'

'I don't see why not. Have you any particular rendezvous in mind?'

'The Well Park – at the tip of the peninsula Helsinki stands on. Do you know the area? Good. Not far beyond the Silja Dock there is a lay-by – a place where cars park – '

'I know it.'

'Can we meet there?'

'What time?'

'Ten o'clock tonight. Then we won't be seen together. You'll come alone?'

'I don't need anyone to hold my hand. So, ten in the evening. The lay-by at Well Park.'

The Soviet patrol-boat stopped close to the Finnish Coastguard vessel and waited. Both ships were in mid-Gulf with no other craft in sight. The Coastguard lowered a small motorboat which sped towards the Russian ship. The three passengers – Newman, Karlov and Sarin – were transferred to the motorboat which returned to its mother ship.

The patrol-boat from Tallinn was already on its way back when the three men clambered aboard the Finnish ship. This way their arrival in Helsinki would excite no attention. The Coastguard vessel proceeded towards Helsinki.

'When we arrive,' Mauno explained to Newman

below deck, 'two cars will be waiting. I will take one, Karlov the other. We know you are at the Marski – Karma, my deputy, toured the hotels with a copy of your photograph. Do you mind going back there by taxi?'

'Suits me.'

'I will call you later when I have had time to catch up on the latest developments. If any – '

'Do that.'

'Has that medical congress started at the Kalastaja-torppa?' Tweed asked Butler as they ate late breakfast in his bedroom.

'Yes. I should have told you when you got back. They flew in yesterday – a whole flock of doctors from all over the continent. It makes Nield's job more difficult – watching those two with the place so crowded.'

'Not to worry. He'll cope. Have you any idea where Laila Sarin is?'

'She came to the reception desk when I happened to be there. I heard her enquiring about Newman so I said I might be able to help and she joined me for a cup of coffee. I told her I was a friend of Newman's and that I was trying to locate him. She said she was checking all the hotels and if she couldn't find him she was going down to the harbour.'

'She'll be lucky ever to see him again. We can't do

anything about that. Did you hire those cars as I asked? They must be fast – '

'Dealt with. A couple of Citroëns – both the same colour and model as you instructed. They're parked here and ready to go. But go where?'

Tweed seemed not to hear the question. He sipped at his coffee and spread butter and marmalade on a roll. After eating the roll he asked his next question.

'Nield is our best driver, wouldn't you say?'

'Drives like hell – when he gets the chance. He's fast – but skilful and safe.'

'And no change yet with our American friends?'

'None at all. Fergusson and Nield reported over the phone just before you asked me to join you for breakfast.' Butler yawned and covered his mouth with his hand. 'Sorry, I was up all night relieving them both for a few hours' kip.'

'Keep up the surveillance. And get some sleep when you can. You won't get much tonight.'

'Something is about to break?'

'Be prepared. The Boy Scouts' motto.'

Butler stared at Tweed who regarded him calmly through his glasses. He knew Tweed, knew him well. Tweed was rarely facetious – only at times of maximum stress. Without another word Butler got up from the table and left the room. Mauno Sarin phoned Tweed about an hour later.

*

Laila spotted Newman coming ashore by chance. Not entirely by chance – she had been driving round and round South Harbour for a long time. She saw him carrying his bag, climb into a taxi and followed him.

The taxi drove along the tree-lined Esplanade past the Akateeminen Bookshop where they had bought publications on Estonia. She expected it would then turn right along Mannerheimintie until it reached the Hesperia. It did turn in that direction. Then, to her surprise, it stopped outside the Hotel Marski.

She found a parking slot and slid into it as another car headed for the same slot. Feeding the meter, she ran inside the Marski just in time to see Newman walking into the elevator. She ran inside before the doors closed, wondering why he had not registered.

'Hello.' Newman said. 'And how are you?'

'Worried out of my bloody mind about you,' she raged. 'I do not know why I bother. I really do not know why I bother . . .'

She followed him inside the room he unlocked, went over to the window and folded her arms, facing him as he locked the door. Her face, normally a good colour, was flushed with fury. Newman remembered the remark she had made early during their acquaintance. *When a Finnish girl blows her top, Boom!* Something like that . . .

'I checked this hotel trying to find you,' she stormed. 'I checked every hotel in Helsinki. Where have you been? Why didn't you register when you arrived this time?'

'Because I had already registered earlier the other night. All right, maybe I owe you an explanation. I checked out of the Hesperia. By the way, did you give Tweed that envelope?'

'Yes.'

'Did he do anything about it?'

'Ask *him*! He is staying at the Hesperia – '

'As I was explaining,' Newman continued patiently, 'after I left the Hesperia I came here. I registered in the name of René Charbot. I speak fluent French so no one thought it funny.'

'I don't think it funny either. Where have you been?'

'Better you don't know.'

'But you know now who killed your wife?'

Astounded, Newman stared at her. She stared back, her arms still folded, her cheeks still flushed. He went to the coat cupboard and took out a bottle of wine room service had sent up before he left for Tallinn.

'Would you care for a glass of wine?' he enquired.

'I need one! I have been so worried about you.'

'Why did you make that remark about my wife?'

'Your expression. Your manner. All the tension has gone. You are in a very strange mood – like a man setting out on a long journey into nowhere.'

He handed her the wine. They drank without clinking the glasses. Newman sat down in a chair and Laila sat in another one close to him. She drank all her wine and he refilled her glass.

'Laila, we shall not be meeting again. And, for your

sake, we must never be seen in public again either. Not even for dinner . . .'

'Then we can use room service. I will be fixing myself in the bathroom when they bring it up – '

'Not a good idea.'

'Then I shall follow you. Everywhere you go. Which is it to be? Dinner together. In here? Or I follow you.'

'I'll call room service. Early this evening.'

The Alouette helicopter was perched in a remote clearing amid the trees on Ornö. Flying in from Arlanda it had settled gently on the firm rock-strewn ground. Casey had hovered over several possible areas before choosing this improvised pad. It fulfilled all the conditions he was seeking.

It was well away from the many summer cottages scattered over the island, well clear not only of a road but also of even one of the many tracks which criss-crossed the island. It was also very close to the Baltic coast.

'We fly in tomorrow,' Wilson had told him hours later after taking down the signal from Admiralty on his transceiver. The reception was faint but clear enough for him to receive the signal.

They ate the hard rations they had brought and drank mineral water. Through the chilly night they slept under the machine inside sleeping bags. The incredible silence of the island got on their nerves eventually. They played cards in the morning and were glad when the time came to depart. Casey marked on a chart their position before they departed, refolded the chart and put it inside his pocket.

If they had been discovered, Casey was ready with his story – engine trouble. He had even tampered with the machine to back up his story. Now it was in full working order. He checked his watch again and then started up the rotors.

'Thank God to be on the move,' Wilson said. 'It's waiting that tells on the nerves.'

'That's what Tweed always says.'

The machine rose above the treetops, hovered for a moment, and then flew east – east for the Gulf of Bothnia, Finland, and the landing pad at the Hotel Kalastajatorppa.

The trawler, *Saaremaa*, lay off the coast of Turku, its nets out. Inside his cabin Captain Olaf Prii checked the time once more. He peered out of the window. Soon it would be dark and he would be looking at his watch constantly.

Prii was not in the least nervous. He had lived a double life for too many years. Sometimes he thought he had become a very hard man. But that was the only way to survive working in an underground movement. He lit his pipe and went out on deck.

The sea was calm, the sky clear. Perfect conditions for what he had to do. God knew he was receiving frequent weather forecasts. His brother had not left the radio room since they had sailed from Tallinn. He, too, had become a hard man. Everyone paid a price for the life he – or she – lived. And like Casey, Olaf Prii looked forward to being on the move.

Chapter Forty-Two

'How many men have we at our disposal, Karma?'
Mauno asked.

'Normally forty – '

'But how many tonight is the question I asked.'

'Thirty-six. We are four short due to illness.'

'This is what I want you to do.' Mauno was pacing
round the floor of his office at Ratakatu. 'Send a dozen
to the Kalastajatorppa. With all those doctors there
they won't be noticed. Six more are to be in the
vicinity of the Soviet Embassy. Another six round the
American Embassy. That leaves twelve. Send six to
Vantaa Airport. The remaining six can stay here in
reserve.'

'I will issue the instructions at once. If I knew what
was going on – '

'I'd like to know that myself, Karma. You know
about all the rumours concerning some American
called Adam Procane who is on his way to Russia?
We don't want an international incident on our doorstep. Oh, from the reserve, send one man to watch the
Hesperia. Show him a picture of Tweed.'

'After that?'

'After that we can only wait. It is going to be a long night. Phone my wife to warn her. But only when you've carried out the instructions I've given you.'

The Alouette flew in at the same low level it had kept for the whole flight. The sun was close to the horizon as it hovered, then put down on the chopper pad next to the landing stage by the Kalastajatorppa.

The hotel building nearest the sea was a blaze of lights. The Round House restaurant was full of waiters preparing for the banquet laid out for the medical congress. On the landing stage stood the figure of a small man who had watched the helicopter coming in over the smooth sea.

Casey jumped out of the machine and handed the figure the folded chart from his pocket. No one inside the hotel saw the man hurry away through the trees, slip inside the hotel entrance and down the staircase to the underground passage leading across to the building on the opposite side of the road.

Tweed walked at a leisurely pace through the main entrance hall. Once outside he quickened his pace, turned right and climbed inside the parked Citroën where Butler waited behind the wheel.

'Move,' said Tweed. 'Back to the Hesperia – but keep within the speed limit.'

At the chopper pad three of Mauno's men had already arrived, alerted by the sound of the helicopter landing. A fourth man ran inside the hotel to phone Mauno. The chief of the Protection Police, seated behind the desk in his office answered at once.

'What is it, Karma?'

'A chopper has just landed at the Kalastajatorppa pad. A big Alouette.'

'Hold it until I get there.'

Mauno arrived within ten minutes. He found Casey standing by the helicopter, arguing with one of his men. The pilot was holding a sheet of paper in his hand. He showed the man his identity folder.

'Sarin, Protection Police. What is going on?'

'I'm Casey, pilot of this machine. Four doctors – British – are needed urgently back in Stockholm. An emergency case. The four men I have to pick up are consultants.'

'Really?' Mauno's tone was sarcastic. 'And what is the name of the patient back in Stockholm?'

'Someone very important. I'm not at liberty to reveal his identity. The four consultants urgently needed are believed to be attending this congress –'

'Really?' Mauno repeated. 'And are their names also confidential?'

'Of course not.' Casey handed him the sheet of paper. 'You have their names there. I'd appreciate your co-operation in locating them.'

Mauno passed the sheet with the four names to Karma and told him to check them against the list of visiting doctors. He called out to summon his men surrounding the helicopter.

'Search this machine from end to end. Go over every centimetre of it.'

'What are you looking for?' one man enquired.

'I'm not sure. Bring out anyone you find on board.'

'This is a British aircraft,' Casey protested.

'And you are on Finnish soil where I have total jurisdiction. Get on with the search,' he told his men.

Half an hour later Mauno was in a mood of total frustration. The list of all the doctors attending the conference had been checked and none of the four names on Casey's list were included.

The thorough search of the helicopter had produced nothing. It was stalemate. Some of the doctors had wandered out into the small park to see what was going on and were kept at a distance by a rope strung from poles erected by Karma. Night had fallen like a black curtain so characteristic of Finland. In the gloom men moved about holding torches like human glow worms.

'I don't understand any of this,' Mauno told Casey. 'Why are the doctors you were to collect not here?'

'I don't understand it either. If you'll excuse me, Mr Sarin, I have to radio the news back to Stockholm. Then I had better take off to fly back to Arlanda.'

'Tonight?'

'This machine is equipped with the most sophisticated navigational aids. Flying at night is easier than flying in the daylight – there is hardly any other air traffic in the sky at this time of the year.'

540

'You have enough fuel to fly all the way to Arlanda?'

'Of course not. I shall refuel at Turku. Permission to take off, please?'

'Go to hell.'

Mauno waited until he was sitting in the front passenger seat of his car with Karma behind the wheel. He sat thinking for a few minutes, listening to the Alouette's vibrating roar as it ascended, then the fading sound of the engine as it headed west across the bay.

'It's Tweed,' Mauno said eventually. 'I can sense his touch. But what the devil he is up to I'm damned if I know. Back to Ratakatu. And I want to get there yesterday.'

Newman drove the hired Saab he had paid for in advance, together with the cost of an ample supply of petrol, through the maze of streets at the head of the peninsula. He parked near a corner he had selected earlier, a corner where he had a good view of the Soviet Embassy at Tehtaankatu.

He had collected the .38 Smith & Wesson – now fully loaded – from the station locker. The weapon was tucked inside his belt. He put a cigarette in his mouth but refrained from lighting it. He checked his watch. Nine o'clock. He settled down to wait.

The large old building which houses the Embassy

was half-hidden behind the railed wall and the trees which stand behind it. All the curtains were drawn so the place appeared uninhabited. At 9.30 p.m. a familiar figure in civilian garb came out of the main entrance, climbed behind the wheel of a Volvo and drove out.

Newman started his engine and followed Colonel Andrei Karlov. He was going the wrong way to keep his rendezvous in Well Park, heading off the peninsula towards Mannerheimintie. Newman, who had once raced cars, speeded up and drew alongside the Volvo in a deserted street.

Accelerating, he cut in front of Karlov at an angle. He heard the screech of brakes as he stopped, threw open the door of his car and ran back. Opening the front passenger door of the Volvo, he slid inside, his gun pointed at the driver.

'We have an appointment, Karlov – or had you forgotten? Back this car, then get it moving to the lay-by down by Well Park. Make one clever move and I'll blow you away.'

'I was on my way to meet you.'

Karlov, seeing Newman's expression, backed the Volvo as he spoke and drove on. Newman had the gun in his lap, the muzzle pressed against the Russian's body.

'Of course you were,' he replied. 'By a roundabout way. A very long roundabout way.'

'I swear to you – '

542

'Just keep driving.'

A silver-coloured Citroën passed them going in the other direction. Every seat was occupied and Newman thought he recognized one of the two men in the back seat. He turned and stared briefly through the rear window.

'Lose that car,' he ordered.

'It was travelling away from us –'

'It may U-turn. Go left here, now left again. That's good. Now make for Well Park.'

'May I ask what all this is about?'

'You'll find out. Soon enough.'

Newman heard his own voice and it sounded strange. Hoarse with a deep timbre. His throat felt dry and he would have given anything for a drink. Mineral water. No emotion at all – and this surprised him.

It was quiet at that time of night along the waterfront by South Harbour. Ships lay berthed at different points without any sign of life. The street lights reflected in the water, a shimmering dazzle. Karlov pulled in to the remote lay-by and turned off the engine as instructed. Newman got out, slipped into the rear of the car and occupied the seat behind the Russian. He pressed the muzzle of the gun into the nape of his neck.

'Colonel, you did tell me you are in charge of security over in Estonia?'

'That is correct. I still don't understand –'

'You will. You murdered my wife, Alexis Bouvet, while she was in Tallinn. You killed her on Vaksali Street.'

'That is a bloody lie. I only heard about the crime after it had been committed.'

'At least you admit it was a crime. For your information I didn't like my wife any more. We were on the verge of a split. After only six months of marriage. But when a man's wife is murdered the husband is supposed to do something about it. I bet there's no way you can prove what you say.'

'But there is.' Karlov hesitated. The gun muzzle pressed deeper into his neck. 'She was killed by a psychopath – one of my men. He faces a military tribunal when he returns to Tallinn.'

'Who? And where is he now then?'

'A man called Poluchkin. He is here in Helsinki. I left him back at the Embassy not three kilometres from where we are now.'

'You said you could prove this crap.'

'I can. If you will let me take some photographs out of my wallet.'

'Be very careful, Colonel.'

He told Karlov to switch on the overhead light for a moment and studied the three photographs the Russian had obtained from Olaf Prii. Obviously taken by one of the latest infra-red cameras, the pictures were horribly clear. Newman stared at the face of the man behind the wheel of the car driving down Alexis.

544

The shots had been taken at the moment of the first impact. He began to feel sick.

'Why should I believe you didn't order this?' Newman asked. Ignoring the gun, Karlov turned round and stared straight at the Englishman. His dark eyes were steady and there was a hint of resignation in them.

'If you don't believe me, pull the trigger. Get it over with. Shoot the wrong man.'

'Does this Poluchkin speak English?' Newman asked.

'Yes. He's a mute.'

'A mute?'

'Our term for a man who pretends to speak only Russian but is also fluent in other languages. That way people sometimes talk indiscreetly in his presence.'

'That call box back there. You could phone him? Persuade him to come here at once? In English? Tell him it's for security reasons.'

'I could do that, yes. The man's a psychopath as I told you. I really don't care.'

Newman walked behind Poluchkin who moved forward uphill inside Well Park with a heavy plodding tread. The Russian looked back twice, and each time as they made their way along the twisting paths through the trees Newman was holding the gun pointing at him.

The moonlight threw shadows of the pine trees across the path at intervals and in the distance the lights of the harbour were specks like the stars above. It was very quiet. No other sound but the soft tread of two pairs of footsteps. They climbed higher and higher towards the summit, moving along the route Newman had walked over twice before. Once during the night when he had waited for the voyage to Tallinn the following day.

Ten minutes later Newman returned down the path alone. He was hardly aware of the chilly temperature. His feet followed the path downhill towards where he had let Karlov go. When he reached the road along the waterfront he looked carefully in both directions, then he crossed the road.

He threw the gun far out into the harbour and it disappeared. It was still loaded. It had not been fired. *You do not shoot people in Finland.*

Newman walked all the way back to where he had left his car before he had transferred to Karlov's Volvo. Sagging behind the wheel, he switched on the ignition and drove back to the Marski. He felt exhausted.

In the morning he would catch the flight to Paris via Brussels. He owed it to Alexis's sister, Marina, to let her know what had happened. Uncertainty could drive a woman – or a man – mad. And he had always liked Marina. Maybe he had married the wrong girl.

After Paris he would start wandering – wandering all over the world to visit those places he had always wanted to see. At least he had the money to do that – his book, *Kruger: The Computer That Failed*, had made him a fortune. But, oh God, he was tired.

He would always be haunted by that scene in Well Park. He had taken Poluchkin up to the summit at the very tip of the peninsula, a summit of rocks and a small smooth plateau standing high above the path seventy feet below. From the plateau the ground dropped as a sheer rock wall until it reached the path.

They had stood there, Poluchkin with his back to the drop as Newman faced him with the gun. Again the Russian, his face sullen and resentful – mingled with alarm – had protested in English.

'What the hell is all this about? I haven't done anything to you – '

'Only murdered my wife – Alexis Bouvet.'

'What are you talking about?'

Newman produced one of the photographs Karlov had given him. It was moonlit on the rocky bluff and, still pointing the gun, he took two paces forward so Poluchkin could see it clearly. The Russian gasped and stepped backward – over the edge. He threw up both arms as he fell into space. He screamed, a horrible sound. He plunged down seventy feet and the wailing scream ended abruptly. Newman could have sworn he heard the heavy thud of his body as it smashed onto the path.

He looked down the abyss and Poluchkin was a vague, shapeless shadow far below. Newman turned away and began the long walk back down through Well Park.

Chapter Forty-Three

'Stilmar is still inside the American Embassy,' Karma reported to Mauno who sat behind his desk. 'But there may have been a development. Half an hour ago a limousine delivered someone to that Embassy. One of the limousines the Russians use.'

'So, there is a secret meeting between the Russians and the Americans. What about Cord Dillon?'

'Another development – I was just coming to it. He and Helene Stilmar have moved late this evening to the Marski. They must have changed hotels at about the time you were questioning the pilot of that Alouette.'

'The Marski?' Mauno, hunched over the desk, straightened up. 'That is much closer to Tehtaankatu.'

'At least we think it was Cord Dillon,' Karma added. 'Our man positively identified Helene Stilmar – but he wasn't too sure of the identity of the man who travelled with her. He was muffled up in a hat with the collar of his coat turned up.'

'Anything else?'

'Yes,' Karma continued in his methodical way, reading from typed sheets on his own desk. 'Tweed has disappeared from the Hesperia.'

'What!' Mauno jumped up from his desk and went to stand at Karma's shoulder. 'When did this happen?'

'As far as we can tell, again about the time you were checking that chopper pilot.'

'That Alouette – ' Mauno started walking round the room, his head bowed in thought. 'You know I think that could be a cunning diversion. Tweed tactics. And the pilot said he had to refuel at Turku. Plus the fact that there is doubt as to where Cord Dillon is. Is there a car available? Good. I want to reach the Turku airport yesterday. So I will drive. You come with me. We may still be in time . . .'

The silver Citroën sped along the highway close to Turku. In the front Tweed sat beside the driver, Butler. Ingrid sat in the back beside the fourth passenger. On his knees Tweed had spread out the map of Turku Captain Olaf Prii had left with him when they met in the Customs Office at Harwich.

'You turn left soon now, I think,' he warned Butler. 'Slow down a bit so I can see the street signs.'

'Do you think Fergusson and Nield's dummy run will work?' Butler asked.

'They are in the same car as us – same make, same model. So let us hope so. It is a great mistake to underestimate our friend, Mauno. He gets intuitions.'

*

'We now know the type of car Tweed is travelling in,' Mauno said to Karma as he replaced the microphone of the radio car and took hold of the wheel with both hands – much to Karma's relief. 'A silver-coloured Citroën. Tweed was seen getting into the car by a garage attendant at the Hesperia. A pity he went off duty afterwards for a while for his coffee break . . .'

'At this speed,' Karma commented, 'we have to be in time.'

'Don't you like driving at night?' Mauno enquired with a dry smile.

'I don't mind – just so long as we stay on the road.'

'But you see,' Mauno explained, 'this is where my official position comes in useful. Tweed won't dare to exceed the speed limit.'

He accelerated even more and beside him Karma braced himself.

'We've got him!' said Mauno. 'Look in front – just going round that bend. Did you see the red tail-light?'

'Yes. Perhaps we could slow down a little?' Karma pleaded.

'It is the silver Citroën. Now we shall find out what Mr Tweed has been up to all this time.'

He raced round the bend and Karma leant his shoulder against the frame of the door. He didn't want to be thrown out while they were travelling at this speed. Mauno turned on the siren as they came

551

up behind the Citroën, swung out past it and reduced speed as the Citroën slowed, then stopped.

Mauno jumped out of the car and walked rapidly back to the parked vehicle. He held his identity folder in his hand and he heard Karma, who had taken over the wheel, backing behind him to lock in the Citroën.

'Protection Police – '

Mauno stopped in mid-sentence and stared as Nield lowered the window and looked up at him, fingering his moustache. Alongside him Fergusson turned off the radio. Nield played it cool, saying nothing while Mauno peered at the empty seats at the back.

'You know a Mr Tweed?' Mauno demanded.

'Last saw him at the Hesperia back in Helsinki.'

'I see. And where are you proceeding to?'

'Turku. For a short holiday – '

'You're on the road to the airport.'

'Must have taken the wrong turning. Can we go now? Or have we committed some offence?'

'Not as far as I know.'

Mauno told Karma he would take over the wheel. As he slipped inside the car he watched the Citroën in his wing mirror. It was performing a U-turn. He waited until it disappeared round the bend the way it had come.

'I was right,' he said. 'It's the airport. It's that damn Alouette. We'll find it waiting there.'

A kilometre or two in the opposite direction Nield heaved a sigh of relief. He turned west on to the road to Turku and rammed his foot down.

'Now we'll join Tweed,' he remarked. 'Get out that copy of his map he drew for us.'

The large rubber dinghy propelled by a powerful outboard engine and guided by one of Olaf Prii's crew left the shore near Turku and proceeded towards the *Saaremaa*. It was chilly on the water and Ingrid, sitting next to Tweed with the others behind them, pulled up the collar of her coat.

Tweed sat quite still, motionless as a statue. The sea was fairly calm but the craft bobbed over the waves. He was very prone to seasickness and already felt queasy. Popping a Dramamine into his mouth, he swallowed and grimly faced the next half-hour before the tablet took effect.

As instructed, Captain Prii remained in his cabin while the passengers came aboard and went down to their quarters. The moment the dinghy was hauled over the side he gave the order to sail. Tweed then came to see him in his cabin.

'I'd like to know when we're clear of Finnish territorial waters.'

'Any moment now,' Prii replied in the same language Tweed had used, German. 'We should make landfall early tomorrow morning.'

'Then I'm going to bed. I need a little sleep. Only wake me in case of a major emergency.'

*

'Your Alouette refuelled and took off again over two hours ago,' the Turku airport controller informed Mauno.

'I see. And it is not *my* Alouette. What destination?'

'Arlanda.'

'Thank you.' Mauno said nothing until they had returned to their car and he was sitting alongside Karma. 'Thank God for that.'

'I thought the idea was to catch them,' Karma commented.

'The main thing is they are clear of Finland. Should there be any enquiry we can at least say we tried. I repeat,' he said as he started the car, 'they are out of Finland. Perhaps we can now look forward to a period of peace. And we'd better get back – my wife will think I have deserted her . . .'

They were aboard the rubber dinghy again, moving in close to the island of Ornö. The crewman from the *Saaremaa* seemed unsure of his bearings and Ingrid had borrowed the chart from him – the chart Casey had handed to Tweed outside the Kalastajatorppa.

'What do you know about charts?' Nield asked.

'Maybe more than you do. I had a boy-friend once who was crazy about sailing. He often brought me out into the archipelago. I recognize that rock . . .'

She pointed to a huge round mass of smooth rock protruding from the water, its top covered with stringy heather. Staring at it, Nield's expression was one of total disbelief.

'They all look alike.'

'No, they don't. That one had a pool of water inside it – a pool shaped like a seashell.' She gripped the crewman's arm and pointed to an inlet with a small beach, gesturing for him to make for it.

'I don't believe it,' Nield replied, looking round the sea at a score or more of tiny islands and rocks of various sizes. 'I simply don't believe it.' He glanced at Tweed who sat very stiffly. 'Are you all right?'

'I suggest we land there whether it's the right place or not.'

Casey walked down through the trees to the water's edge with a pair of binoculars looped round his neck. He helped drag the dinghy close in and spoke as the passengers alighted.

'I've been watching you for half an hour. How the hell you found this godforsaken spot I'll never know.'

'Ingrid found it,' Tweed told him and glanced at Butler who had been so suspicious about her earlier. 'Now, get us to Arlanda. I don't want to miss our flight.'

They avoided drawing too much attention at Arlanda by a simple stratagem thought up by Tweed. Fergusson and Nield left the helicopter and, carrying their bags, made their way to the taxi rank and told the driver to take them to the Grand Hotel.

'Nield and Fergusson will catch a flight back tomorrow,' Tweed told Butler. 'You two go to the gents' lavatory and change your appearance. And here is the passport. I want to have a quiet word with Ingrid.'

He took the Swedish girl into the buffet where they collected coffee and sat down at an isolated table. He passed to her a long fat envelope.

'That is your fee. I am very grateful. You were enormously helpful.'

'Tweed, why can I not come to London and work with you?'

'Because you are not a girl to sit behind a desk all day, going through dull insurance files. And I have a small outfit. There is no vacancy.'

'So we shall not see each other again?' she pressed.

'When I am next in Scandinavia we shall.'

'And when will that be?'

'I have no idea,' he admitted. 'But we can keep in touch.'

'Maybe.'

'No maybe about it.' He checked his watch. 'I'm going to miss my flight if I don't leave now. Thank you again.'

She watched him go but he didn't look back. Nothing showed in Tweed's expression revealing his mixed emotions. Time to go, he told himself.

As Flight SK525 bound for London soared into the air Ingrid watched the aircraft until it disappeared. Then she walked slowly, carrying her bag, to the taxi rank. It was 9.20 a.m.

A little over an hour earlier Newman took off aboard Flight AY873 for Paris. He was driven to Vantaa Airport by Mauno, who had picked him up at the Marski.

'A dead Russian called Poluchkin was found at the foot of some rocks in Well Park,' he remarked to Newman as they were approaching the airport. 'You know Well Park?'

'I have wandered through it, yes.'

'The interesting thing is Tallinn is not too worried about the accident. This Poluchkin apparently faced a military tribunal when he returned to Estonia. Something to do with corruption, I expect. Perhaps he knew and walked off the summit of Well Park last night.'

'So you have no problem?' Newman suggested as the Finn pulled up at the entrance to Vantaa.

'Oh, I always have problems. But that is life. I think that you are wise to leave Finland for a while. You will be publishing your article?'

'It's already on the way. And I wish I could have stayed here a little longer.'

Before he boarded the aircraft he caught sight of the Finnair symbol – a tilted letter 'F' with a line speeding from its base. For Newman it summed up his experience. He had been in Finland for some time – but that time seemed to have passed in a flash.

As the aircraft took off he stared out of the window. In the morning sunlight the lake and forest and rocks spread out below. One day he would return.

Chapter Forty-Four

'Let me introduce you to Adam Procane,' Tweed said to Cord Dillon.

The American had flown back direct from Helsinki to London the following day. Helene Stilmar had flown with him but she had travelled separately. A car had waited at Heathrow and Dillon had been driven to the old town of Wisbech in East Anglia.

The world left Wisbech behind long ago. The old warehouses which line the river, several storeys high and with a lifting-hook projecting from the highest storey, are due for renovation as they moulder at the edge of the river.

Tweed made his remark to Dillon as he escorted him through a back entrance inside one of these apparently abandoned old edifices. There was a musty smell in the cavernous ground floor, an atmosphere of desolation and age. The floor was strewn with beaten down straw where many footsteps had trod and Tweed led the way up a shaky wooden staircase.

At the top he walked down a long timbered corridor and the only sound was the thud of their footsteps on the wood. He knocked on a door, an irregular tattoo, and the door was opened inwards by Butler who stood holding an automatic pistol aimed at Tweed.

'Come on, Cord.'

'What is this place?'

'If you follow me you'll see.'

Dillon went inside and Butler locked the door again and slid two well-oiled bolts into position. The room was unfurnished and looked as though it hadn't been inhabited for ages. More straw littered the floor. Butler led them to a side door which he unlocked, standing aside for them to enter.

'Cord, meet Adam Procane.'

The room was different and Dillon realized it was at the front of the warehouse, overlooking the muddy river. It was furnished with wall-to-wall Wilton carpet, a pale grey colour. In the middle of the room stood a modern black-topped table with chrome tubular legs. Six chairs in the same modern style were placed round the table. On top of the table was a tape-recorder. The windows were so covered with grime they were opaque. The light was dim and eerie.

One man sat on a chair behind the table, facing them. He stood as the three men entered and looked out of place in his sports jacket and navy blue slacks. Tweed turned round and gestured to Dillon.

'Cord, meet Adam Procane,' he repeated.

'I am pleased to meet you, Mr Dillon,' said Colonel Andrei Karlov.

*

'It was the most tricky and nerve-racking task I have undertaken so far,' said Tweed as he stood in his office at Park Crescent, hands clasped behind his back.

'I still don't understand,' Monica replied.

'Karlov sent me a radio signal by a roundabout route telling me he wanted to come to the West permanently. He is a prize catch – Russia's most brilliant authority on the so-called Star Wars counter-measures planned by the Kremlin. He was based in Estonia. No one can leave that place without a move-ment order signed by a GRU general. I had to think of some convincing reason for Lysenko to send him to Finland.'

'So you could escort Karlov from there to the West?'

'Exactly. I thought up the fictitious Adam Procane – who already existed as a name.'

'Name? Explain, please.'

'While Karlov was in London, attached to the Soviet Embassy, he decided he liked the West. Also, on a personal level, he detested his wife. He fed me information through intermediaries. To protect him I supplied *him* with data supposedly coming from a mysterious American, Adam Procane. I gave him information we knew the Russians would soon obtain anyway. Then he changed his mind when Moscow recalled him with the promise of promotion to high rank.'

'He sounds unstable.'

'He's a Russian. They always have a nostalgia for the motherland – until they get back and find out they

don't like it. My first task was to spread rumours that
Adam Procane was crossing over to the East. Hence
my trips to Lisa Brandt in Frankfurt, to André Moutet
in Paris, Alain Charvet in Geneva and Julius Ravenstein in Brussels. They all spread the rumour that
Adam Procane wanted to reach Moscow.'

'They knew what you were really doing?'

'Of course not! I told them I had heard Procane was
on his way and to find out who he was, when he was
coming. Inevitably, the grapevine did its work. The
rumours reached London, Washington – and, most
important of all, Moscow.'

'The stage was set for them to look for him?'

'Exactly. The timing was fortunate. With the
American Presidential elections in November, the
Kremlin saw a last-ditch chance to stop Reagan getting a second term. If a high-ranking Washington
official crossed over to Moscow, the scandal would
destroy Reagan. That was the bait I felt they had to
bite on.'

'The Americans knew what you were up to?'

'No! Only three people in the world knew the truth
– the P.M., the American President and myself. I
couldn't afford a leak. That was what worried me – I
had to fool so many old friends – but it was the only
way to get Karlov moved to Finland. As I hoped,
Lysenko put him in charge of the Procane project – in
case it blew up in Lysenko's face –'

'Then Karlov would carry the can?'

'Lysenko has always worked like that.'

'It all went according to plan then?'

'No, it didn't. It never does,' Tweed said with feeling. 'Newman nearly mucked up everything at the last minute when he grabbed Karlov. I actually passed them in my car on the way to pick up Karlov outside the Soviet Embassy. Luckily, for reasons I'm not talking about, Newman released him.'

'Karlov must have played it clever,' Monica commented.

'Yes. He even left behind with Lysenko some phoney calculations about how to counter the American Strategic Defence Initiative. With a bit of luck the Soviet analysts will be led up the garden path for a few months.'

'But why did you go to the Soviet border at Imatra?'

'To divert Lysenko's attention away from Helsinki. Funny when you come to think of it – everything hinged on a cactus plant Karlov placed in his office window. That told the man who got us out to head for a certain rendezvous, plus the signal which you sent. But that man hated Karlov – so I had to deceive him, too. He never met the secret passenger he was bringing out.'

'As I see it, everything depended on Karlov being permitted to go to Finland?'

'Exactly,' Tweed agreed. 'To convince Moscow Procane was on the way, we had to have several Americans travelling to Scandinavia. The President ordered

Cord Dillon and Stilmar to go to Europe to track down Procane – without telling them Procane didn't really exist.'

'The affair Cord Dillon was carrying on with Helene Stilmar must have upset your calculations.'

'On the contrary,' Tweed interjected, 'there was no affair. The President added a twist of his own. Worried about Dillon, he instructed a woman he totally trusted, Helene, to keep close to Dillon. The only way she could do that was to pretend to be having an affair with him.'

'I still don't see how you could be sure Dillon would take a boat to Helsinki. And Butler told me – for God's sake don't repeat this – that your security in Stockholm was terribly slack. Everyone staying at a top hotel, phone calls through the switchboard, talking about everything in front of Ingrid.'

Tweed looked exasperated. 'Don't you see? That was deliberate. I wanted the Russians to know where I was. If they did hear what I said on the phone it was further confirmation that Adam Procane was on his way to Russia.'

'But what about Dillon taking the boat to Finland?'

'The President had instructed Dillon before he left Washington to take his orders from me. Cord came to me late one night at the Grand as arranged. He didn't know why, but I told him to board that ship. And before he left he phoned Karlov pretending to be Procane, telling them he was coming – and disguising his voice so it could have been a man or a woman. Helene going with him was a complication I didn't understand.'

'So once Dillon and Stilmar were in Helsinki – and you turned up – Lysenko thought Procane must have arrived.'

'And despatched Andrei Karlov to Finland to take charge as I had hoped. And Karlov has been clever – he kept sending reports to Moscow casting doubts on Procane, so the last thing they'd ever think of was that Karlov himself could be Procane. And I took with me a passport in the name of Partridge with Karlov's photo in it – which he gave me in London in case he decided to come back. He walked past Passport Control at Arlanda as an Englishman.'

'As you said, it must have been nerve-racking.'

'It was. Put simply, everything hung on making Lysenko think that Procane was in Finland, so Karlov was sent to escort him to Moscow. The whole Procane cover was to bring Karlov on to neutral territory so I could spirit him away.'

'And now we have built up a terrific credibility in Washington.'

'The P.M. knows what she is doing,' Tweed replied cryptically.

'You do need a new suit,' Monica said as she brushed Tweed who stood rather self-consciously. 'You must look your best for your interview with the P.M. And I thought of something else to ask. What happened to Bob Newman?'

'God knows, poor chap. When Fergusson got back today from Stockholm he told me Laila had phoned the Grand, trying to get hold of me. She saw Mauno saying goodbye to him at Vantaa Airport. They seemed to be on good terms. And she'd heard a funny rumour about a dead Russian found at the foot of some rocks in Well Park. I have no idea what it all means '

'You think we'll ever see him again – Newman?'

'I hope so – but that's up to him.'

'It must have been difficult for you.' She stood back to survey him. 'You'll do.'

'Yes, it was difficult – fitting all the pieces of the jigsaw together.'

'Jigsaw describes it rather well.'

'The trouble was some of the pieces started walking in their own direction. I suppose I'd better get moving,' he said with no enthusiasm.

'She's going to offer you the top job. Howard is on his way out.'

'If I accepted . . .'

'Oh, my God! You're not thinking of refusing the post?'

'Look at it this way. Deceiving the opposition is one thing. I've had to fool all my friends – Hornberg, Sarin, Charvet, Moutet, Lisa Brandt and Ravenstein. To say nothing of my own staff – Butler, Nield and Fergusson. And you.'

'They'll never know. You told me the President is keeping it all quiet. Cord Dillon had to know because he's sharing the debriefing of Karlov. And afterwards Karlov isn't even going to the States. You're giving him a new identity. No one will ever know,' she repeated.

'I know,' he said, and walked away.

Colin Forbes
The Heights of Zervos
Pan Books

'. . . THE GERMANS HAVE GOT TO BE STOPPED FROM TAKING ZERVOS.'

April 1941. The monastery on the heights of Zervos dominates the sole escape route for the small British expeditionary force. A mighty German army is invading Greece.

Ian Macomber, professional saboteur, together with Grapos, Greek patriot, and Lieutenant Prentice and Sergeant Ford, are the only four men who stand in the way of the oncoming Nazis heading for Zervos.

The action begins at sea and continues non-stop on Greek soil in a bitter winter. The race to reach the monastery starts – with the *Alpenkorps* close behind the four men – in a murderous mind-killing ascent up the icebound mountain. How can the tiny Allied team destroy the élite German force? The climax at the summit is thunderous . . .

COLIN FORBES
'has no equal' SUNDAY MIRROR

Colin Forbes
Year of the Golden Ape
Pan Books

'THE WHOLE OF THE WEST MUST SUFFER AS WE ARE
 SUFFERING IN PALESTINE. . . '

The extremists have taken over. Against the weapon is oil.
Masterminding the plan to destroy Israel, Sheik Gamal Tafak has
hired professional terrorists – including LeCat, the French killer,
and Winter, the enigmatic Englishman.

The action races from Cairo to Hamburg, Paris, London and
California. The worldwide conspiracy unfolds. Russia and the west
are stunned.

A super-tanker bound for San Francisco is hijacked, armed with
a nuclear bomb. The extremists sail for the Golden Gate Bridge,
threatening to annihilate America's most beautiful city. Only two
people can turn the tide – Winter, professional adventurer, and
Betty Cordell, expert marksmarkswoman.

COLIN FORBES
'has no equal' SUNDAY MIRROR

Colin Forbes
The Stone Leopard
Pan Books

'AT CERTAIN MOMENTS IN HISTORY IT IS A SINGLE INCIDENT
WHICH TRIGGERS OFF A WHOLE SERIES OF EVENTS . . .'

An assassination attempt on the President of the Republic; rumours
circulating of an impending coup d'état and a dying man whispering a codename – 'The Leopard'. Prefect of the Paris police, Marc
Grelle, guesses there's a connection – a connection that could tear
France apart.

Records show 'The Leopard', a former resistance hero, is dead.
But Grelle discovers he is very much alive, one of the most
powerful politicians in France and a top enemy agent.
Meanwhile a vicious gang of the killers are intent on bringing
death to the few witnesses who can verify 'The Leopard's'
identity. Grelle must act to save them – and his country.

'Hard, bitter and compulsive'
DAILY MIRROR

COLIN FORBES
'has no equal' SUNDAY MIRROR